PRAISE FOR JONATHAN SHAW'S

NARCISA

"Finally, after twenty-plus years of coaxing, cajoling, pleading, and basic needling on my part, my ol' scallywag brother, Jonathan Shaw, has put his pen to paper, dragging and drudging up virulent and violent hallucinations from his not-so-cute brainscape. Been waiting too long for this. So have you, whoever you are, believe me.

"If you don't yet know him, you will. If you didn't want to, too bad. Once he's in, he's in. Jonathan Shaw's words, work, life, lives, deaths, rants, rage, hilarity, and taste rank with the best of 'em.

"If Hubert Selby Jr., Charles Bukowski, Ernest Hemingway, Jack Kerouac, William Burroughs, Neil Cassidy, Dr. Hunter S. Thompson, the Marquis de Sade, Antonio Carlos Jobim, Joao Gilberto, Edward Teach, Charlie Parker, Iggy Pop, Louis-Ferdinand Céline, R. Crumb, Robert Williams, Joe Coleman, Dashiell Hammett, E. M. Cioran, and all of the Three Stooges had all been involved in some greasy, shameful whorehouse orgy, Jonathan Shaw would surely be its diabolical, reprobate spawn."

—*Johnny Depp*

"Jonathan Shaw has had his passport stamped in hell so many times he could get his mail there. Vile as junkie-cum, beautiful as a dead drunk's bible, this story will keep you clawing at the pages, wondering how one man can wreak so much havoc, suffer so much for Art, and still have enough brains left to put a sentence together, let alone the heart to create this unique, riveting, hyper-colorful adventure. Written in blood, Jonathan Shaw's writing takes us places most people never come back from. This is gonna hurt, motherfucker, but the author is living proof that whatever doesn't kill you can get you laid. What are we, in the end, but the sum of our scars?"

—*Jerry Stahl*

"Jonathan Shaw is a shameless evildoer, a decorated veteran of the drug war whose deviance is only exceeded by his clever ability to weave his own sickness into a true classic of American literature. He is Oscar Wilde and Charlie Manson tattooing a portrait of Dorian Gray on the white underbelly of a society desperately in need of this type of fearless storytelling."

—*Marilyn Manson*

"Jonathan Shaw's writing is one hell of a wild ride through the bizarre netherworld of his own damaged consciousness. His experiences are real, and his language and insights kinetic and brutal. This is what the French would call *littérature maudite*, and Shaw's writing certifies him as a subversive and criminal inhabitantof the world of human expression."

—*Jim Jamusch*

"Jonathan Shaw is the great nightmare anti-hero of the new age."

—*Iggy Pop*

"Jonathan Shaw's passionate descriptions of the surreal, paranoid jungle he inhabits capture the haunting poetry of his soul."

—*Hubert Selby Jr.*

"Is he bitter? Oh, just a tad."

—*R. Crumb*

OUR LADY
of ASHES

infinitum

nihil

HARPER ● PERENNIAL

NEW YORK ● LONDON ● TORONTO ● SYDNEY ● NEW DELHI ● AUCKLAND

CSA

JONATHAN SHAW

FOR DORIS, TALITA, ALESSANDRA AND JULIA

HARPER ● PERENNIAL

HarperCollins books may be purchased for educational, business, or sales promotional use. For information, please e-mail the Special Markets Department at SPsales@harper collins.com.

Previously published with slightly different text by Heartworm Press.

FIRST EDITION

Designed by Michael Correy

Library of Congress Cataloging-in-Publication Data has been applied for.

ISBN 978-0-06-235499-0

15 16 17 18 19 OV/RRD 10 9 8 7 6 5 4 3 2 1

"Because the only people for me are the mad ones, the ones who are mad to live, mad to talk, mad to be saved, desirous of everything at the same time, the ones who never yawn or say a commonplace thing, but burn, burn, burn like fabulous yellow roman candles exploding like spiders across the stars and in the middle you see the blue center light pop and everybody goes 'Awww!'"

— *Jack Kerouac*

INTRODUCTION

You can't save anyone from themselves. You will lose everything by attempting to play savior. You will never heal the wounded. You cannot repair the damage already done by selfish parents, vicious ex-lovers, child molesters, tyrants, poverty, depression or simple chemical imbalance.

You can't undo psychic wounds, bandage old scars, kiss away ancient bruises. You can't make the pain go away. You can't shout down the voices in other people's heads. You can't make anyone feel special. They will never feel beautiful enough, no matter how beautiful they are to you. They will never feel loved enough, no matter how much you adore them.

You will never be able to save the battered from battling back at a world they've grown to hate. They will always find a way to pick up where the bullies have left off. They will in turn become bullies. They will turn you into the enemy. They will always find a new method in which to punish themselves, thereby punishing you.

No matter how much you've convinced yourself that you have done absolutely everything in your power to prove your undying devotion, unfaltering commitment and unending encouragement, you will never be able to save a miserable bastard from their self.

The wounded will always find a way to spread their pain over a vast terrain, like an emotional tsunami that devastates the surrounding landscape; an ever-expanding firewall that will singe everything and everyone in its wake. The longer you love a damaged person, the more it will hurt you.

They will mock your generosity, abuse your kindness, expect your forgiveness, try your patience, sap your energy and eventually murder your soul. They will not be happy until you are as miserable as they are. Then their incredible self-loathing will be justified by the perpetuation of a cycle from which there is little recourse.

Once you enter their free fall, it will be virtually impossible to turn your back on them. You will be racked with guilt, frustrated by your own impotence and made furious for ever buying into their shit in the first place. Of course the more damaged, the more charismatic, the more brilliant. The more sexually intoxicating. The more dangerous to your own mental health.

Love is a battlefield, a land mine, a slaughterhouse, a refugee camp, a whorehouse, an insane asylum, a prison; a purgatory of abusive repetition rippling off into infinity; a twisted funhouse mirror that mimics Dante's Nine Circles of Hell. A place where the lonely souls of the eternally damned dance a wicked dervish steeped in the desperation of those determined to throw themselves deep into the pit of a flaming volcano, seeking a baptism of fire, in search of paradise, nirvana, heaven, a return to the Garden from which they have and always will be banished.

Jonathan Shaw's *Narcisa: Our Lady of Ashes* is a heartbreaking tome of diseased lust that oozes a tortured poetry of bloody sweat and sperm; a grotesquely beautiful love song steeped in the perpetual twilight horror of an unbearable trauma bond. An Odyssey in which the twin Furies of Addiction and Codependency bitch-slap you with a big dick whose own insatiable hunger attempts to feast again and again. And in return it feeds back to the victim-turned-victimizer a mad love, an overwhelming sex-magick magnet to the darkest forces of our own primordial essence.

Narcisa is mandatory reading for anyone who has ever been fucked-up, fucked over or fucked with to their very core in a fit of possession; anyone who's been blindsided by love and lust and shackled by passion to a lowlife scum-sucking junkie vampire whose devastating beauty and raw animal magnetism painted them as Dark Angel and Ancient Mystic—a purifying fire-breathing, flesh-eating demon, whose warpath and wrath against the world and everything in it, by some twisted kink in our own psyche, became the tortured path we willingly spiraled into, in search of our own redemption, in the desperate hope of saving our mirrored reflection from the bottomless pit of love's eternal negation.

Lydia Lunch
Barcelona, 2010

PROLOGUE

In Tibetan myth, the Dakini embodies the spirit of female wrath and fury.

She has been known over millennia by many descriptions and names, such as *She who traverses the sky* or *She who moves in space*. Sometimes, she is called simply *Sky Dancer*. Her archetype is of an angry, savage she-devil, dancing across the heavens in a wild frenzy, hell-bent on destruction, chaos and violent upheaval. Naked, but for a necklace of human skulls, in one hand she holds a dagger; in the other, a skull filled with blood, which she drinks.

The Dakini is usually depicted dancing on a man's corpse.

Great energy, determination and pain are needed to achieve spiritual growth. The Dakini's violent imagery seems to represent the fervor required to vanquish our inner demons. Only to our lower nature is the Dakini focused on annihilation—never on random destruction for its own sake. As St. George slays the dragon in Christian iconography, so the Dakini cuts off the heads of entities that represent our own personal curses.

Journal entry: Rio de Janeiro, 13 April, 2010—It hasn't rained for over sixty days. Sterile, dumb, cloudless skies; cold and barren as lunar dreamscapes.

Two months into this cosmic indignity, I sit by sad shores of moonless night again, scratching old mosquito scars on my tired, forlorn feet, smoking a cigarette, tasting the bitter chemical burn on my tongue from kissing Narcisa.

Narcisa, my wounded love, her childish pink lips sucking on the crack pipe all day and all fucking night.

She's off on another mission. Four days running now, sitting up in the attic of that old abandoned house in Lapa, smoking crack in the dark; surrounded by ghosts and spiders and rats and bats, and things that move so fast in the shadows of her disturbed, nightmare vision they have no name or definition—even in her own surreal, supernatural vocabulary.

She came breezing in here last night, belching and farting like a truck driver.

She stripped off her clothes and laid her perfect teenage ass on my worn old leather sofa, snarling like an angry Rottweiler.

"Let's go, Cigano, let's fock! C'mon, bro, let's go, go go!"

I was already hard, working myself deep into that special, ineffable darkness of her, the only place I've ever really wanted to be, grabbing that hard, goose-bumpy, candy-apple ass in my hands; clutching her wiry young carcass to me like a life preserver, feeling complete and whole as her long arms and legs wrapped around me, enveloping my soul, like the wings of a giant praying mantis, taking me down, down, down, into realms of peace and comfort and death.

Narcisa. Dakini. The Bitch of a Thousand Whores!

The one I love. The one I hate.

*Half an hour later, she was up on her feet again, getting dressed, a soldier suiting up for battle. She stormed across the room, snatching my cash off the dresser like a bird of prey as she flew off into the hot, murky night, yelling over her shoulder in that crooked, singsong acid-chant: "**Thank you come again!**"*

I fell back into a fitful sleep, wondering if that supersonic, screaming fuck was a dream or a nightmare, or some terrible karmic debt I must pay over and over again.

Soon she'll have to crash, and then I can get some sleep at last—without being awakened every couple of hours to fill her hole with sperm and her hands with cash and coins and candy and bubble gum and trinkets and cigarettes, and a handful of ashes from under my sad old tired gypsy balls.

1. PRODIGAL SON

Rio de Janeiro, March 2006—I came to, bleary-eyed, sitting in the cab of the rusty, faded blue truck I hitched the last ride in, all the way from the south of Bahia. Journey's end, emerging through the cracked lens of a bouncing, vibrating, dusty, cracked windshield.

Coming home again, at last. After so many years away, I wonder if this might all be just a long, weird dream.

RIO DE JANEIRO—15 KILOMETROS

A sour, nostalgic stench of sewage invades my senses, and I'm wide awake now, squinting into an animated morning dreamworld.

The road signs here ought to say: **ABANDON ALL HOPE**.

Columns of black smoke rise like witches' spindly fingers, beckoning across acres of miserable tin-roofed hovels.

The devil's backyard; faceless, soot-blackened, ramshackle brick buildings and shacks; smoke clouds billowing up from crooked gray smokestacks, against a flat blue sky of circling vultures; desolate fragments of factories sinking into the barren red mud like broken teeth in an undernourished corpse's gaping mouth; infernal wastelands, sprawling out forever.

This is not the Rio de Janeiro of my youth's frivolous memory: a wistful city of verdant mountain vistas and smiling, sensuous, Samba-dancing mulatto girls' dreams. Nowhere to be seen are the sparkling blue waters of those sun-drenched tropical days and humid, blinking whorehouse nights.

No. This is not the place I once knew. This poverty-infested horror show is a depraved massacre of the soul. Black-smoke garbage fires burning alongside a dusty road to hell, like belching farts from a thousand dying assholes. Shirtless skeletons of what used to be men, anthill spirits of the damned, stand hoisting impossible burdens onto defeated, leathery backs from a line of smoke-spewing, idling trucks; scrawny mutts slashing savage red fangs at each other in vicious little circles in the tortured, infertile urban sod.

Hell. I'm thinking of the terrible Inferno of Dante as I look out over the infinity of drab, shit-colored hollow brick dwellings, wondering if I might have died in the malarial, buzzing jungle wastelands, somewhere between Mexico City and here.

Could this really be hell?

Am I a ghost now?

Well, if I've finally made it to the Bottomless Pit, God and the devil both know there's a place here for Ignácio Valência Lobos.

God and the devil know I've got a whole gang of friends on the Other Side.

In waves of creeping dread, I look around as we're sucked into a grinding whirlpool of early-morning traffic, the scenery converted into an eternal rattling swarm of horn-blaring, jittery jalopies, all different hues of speckled rust and dust and decay, darting between rumbling, lumbering trucks and buses packed with dull-faced masses of doomed, eternally damned sinners.

I choke on the acrid hell stench of sulfur and brimstone; poisonous black fumes spurting in clouds of jagged, mufflerless flatulence; a perfect doomsday vision of hell, enveloped in a greasy, toxic gray drizzly mist.

What have they done to my home?

Where the fuck is Rio de Janeiro?

Hell's early morning; a shitty swamp of drab, oppressive foreboding, trouble and strife, somewhere on the ill-starred, forgotten outskirts of Babylon: Rio de Janeiro, City of God, in the Year of Our Lord, 2006.

2. FIRST LIGHT

Rio de Janeiro, March 2006—The ancient red-light district by the port shrugs off another hangover, like a lazy old mulatto whore. I'm trudging up steep, winding streets of broken-down colonial buildings, making my crooked way to the flat where my elderly aunt Silvia lived and died and left me in her will.

The walk is defined by Rio's teeming favelas—the ever-present, pounding, throbbing shantytown ghettos. Walking sideways like a crab scuttling along these slippery cobblestone paths, I merge with frenzied hawkers of desperate street commerce, as I march through a lunatic flow of human traffic. My bloodshot morning eyes stumble across labyrinthine alleys, winding like hieroglyphics, up, up, up, into the bursting hillside slums, taking it all into my senses again.

Back in Rio de Janeiro after all these years, I pass a decaying Portuguese building, its ornate colonial façade fallen into poverty and weathered decay. Row upon tangled row of clotheslines crisscross a once-stately courtyard, home now to hordes of naked shit-brown children. Weeds growing into small trees jut out of a crumbling brick wall. A marble statue of a pigeon-shit-encrusted angel looks down from its rooftop perch with lifeless yellowed eyes of timeless stone apathy.

I move on, inhaling glimpses of scattered, sun-bleached fish bones lying in the dust; straw hat and parrot-feather detail; smoking meats on grills; scent of garlic and roasting sardines, spilled beer, sweat, piss and exhaust fumes, all stewing together in the pregnant, pounding pre-Lenten tropical air.

Whole families crowd together in the shadows of fading wooden doorways, packed in like dummies, watching me with eyes dull as lead rivets. I look back as I pass, trudging, stumbling over the swarming half-remembered sidewalks of my youth, limping along among zigzagging hot shadows of kamikaze motorcycle boys; horns blasting, engines screaming, drilling into my ears in a cacophony of drumbeats, firecrackers and shouts. Unseen voices from jukeboxes spitting out random scraps of James Brown and nostalgic old Roberto Carlos songs. Radios blaring hysterical soccer games amid the dull electrical hum of traffic, music and rawboned, noisy life. People everywhere.

My people. Cariocas. My lost bastard tribe of Rio de Janeiro.

I drift by neighborhood stores, shabby corner botecos, paderias and lurking alleys full of dark-skinned, gun-toting bandido boys, who smirk and squint and wink and blink into the magical maze of crazy equatorial patterns; lights and shadows and rhythms of a new day's familiar and baffling old Carioca character.

Marching the dusty ghetto streets of this expired dream, I pass the Macumba candles burning beside plates of oferendas. Bottles of cheap cachaça rum, tobacco and matches laid out on the ground at a crossroads; ubiquitous offerings to those ever-present spirits of the dead—unearthly entities I've never seen with my eyes, but who I know in my heart are there, always, moving in silence all around us.

Maybe I could feel them whispering to me from afar, traveling across wormholes and gulfs of time and space and other dimensions; phantom voices calling out to me over the years of my absence from a tangled underworld web of throbbing powers and devices; moving, dancing, laughing, playing, mocking us all, driving men's mad desires through these sprawling, septic favelas, rolling hills, cracked industrial wastelands, slums, buildings, beaches and barrooms. A shadowy blanket of life; a subtle parallel existence, a World Unknown. Always present. Always there, awaiting my eventual return to the dark, uncharted depths of myself.

I can feel it all again now as I wander these long-forgotten streets—the steady, vital Presence of an obscure, arcane energy field. Something unseen and alive, vibrating behind smiles and laughter, showering the people, my people, with a special grace; that industrial-strength, ironclad Carioca humor, charity and style, twisting mortal flesh into a bulletproof armor of courage and fortitude as they run through their lives here, robbing and killing, fucking and loving, cheating and lying, living and dying, dancing forever in this unforgettable human ballet of hideous beauty, decadent opulence and crawling rat-shit squalor, stench and crazy, hungry, raw, passionate life; Cariocas—this perverse and enigmatic race of people to whom I, Ignácio Valência Lobos, shall now once again belong.

My weathered little Mexican leather traveling bag weighs heavy across my shoulder as I pass a short, stout paraíba sweeping at the sidewalk **sssskkk ssssskkkk** outside a shadowy little hole-in-the-wall boteco.

Skinny, barefooted mulatto kids kick a dull, deflated rubber ball around a weedy, abandoned dirt lot. A sudden staccato popcorn **pow pow pow** of gun-fire. Two bulky gray-uniformed thugs pushing, shoving, dashing, flashing around a corner behind a darting brown shadow; a bare-chested Negro teenager running ahead, two guns held aloft **pow pow pow,** just like in a movie.

Nothing's changed.

This isn't a movie. It's just Rio de Janeiro, City of God, in the Year of Our Lord, 2006, and Ignácio Valência Lobos is finally returning home.

Home. Shit. Twenty years gone by like a yellowed old newspaper dream and now I'm back. A no-name stranger returning to a strange old homeless home of rootless gypsy memories. Clean and sober, many years older, a tiny bit wiser even, perhaps. And just for today, this little lost idiot ghost called Ignácio is ready as he'll ever be to face whatever the fuck comes next.

3. SCATTERED PIECES

"LIFE'S A VOYAGE THAT'S HOMEWARD BOUND."
—*Herman Melville*

I settled in to the simple studio apartment fast; the top floor of a weathered, prewar, five-story walk-up in the old working-class neighborhood of Catete.

Moving in consisted of unpacking the meager contents of one small travel bag. I'm used to traveling light. The only thing I've ever managed to get right.

After three whole years clean and sober, the time has come to greet the past. Plenty of time tomorrow to shop for whatever items that odd proposition might entail . . . *What's it been, how long now since I've seen this place? Twenty-five years?*

Vague memories, fragile as cobwebs in a stranger's crypt, closed in around me as I turned a corner and plodded up the street. Approaching the building where my Tia Silvia had lived and died all alone, I thought of my long-estranged spinster aunt. Maybe the shadow of solitude that covered her like a moldy blanket in life was what gave her the dubious distinction of being the only one of my people who'd managed to sidestep the Curse and die of old age.

A white-haired *porteiro* shuffled over to greet me at the building's entrance. Addressing me with the absurd formal title of *"Seu Doutor Ignácio,"* he graced me with an ancient mulatto smile; that singular, playful Carioca smile putting me right at ease as he handed me the keys to Aunt Silvia's flat, five floors up.

I stood before the stairway, looking up. No elevator . . . *Good . . . Need all the exercise I can get now . . . Been out of shape ever since I got out of prison* . . . Then, a step at a time, I climbed the uneven wooden stairs, all the way to the top floor, thinking, remembering, one step at a time, up, up, up to the hoary old *conjugado* where my aunt had read the cards and *buzios*, and told the questionable fortunes of lonely, superstitious old Carioca whores.

Even after being expelled from the *kumpania*, cut adrift from her gypsy roots, she'd always fancied herself a traditional Romani healer, a *partragri* from the old country. Much to my surprise, Tia Silvia had named me in her will, bequeathing me the one-room studio flat, with its sunny view of downtown, and the crooked green jumble of trees framing a partial view of the bay. She'd even left me a little money; just enough to get settled. That's what some *gadjo* lawyer said in an email.

I'd won out by default, of course, being her only blood relative still above the ground here. The rest of the clan were long eating grass by the roots before I'd hopped on a rusty Panamanian freighter and left this oddball half-a-home behind, running like the damned, trying to get away from the Curse that plagued the Valência Lobos. Valência Lobos, the name of my people. My name. My blood.

And what blood! Suicides. Murders. Overdoses. Bad livers. Bad lives. Bad half-breed, half-*gadjo*, half-Romani gypsy blood. Blood of the Curse, and all that went with it: Jailhouses. Nuthouses. Whorehouses. Crackhouses. Disappointment. Disillusionment. Destruction. Death. A world of sudden, violent death.

I never knew or gave two shits who my father was. My mother did the best she could, for an aging, outcast gypsy whore with a bad name and that bad, bad blood. My whole bloodline laid to waste.

All dead from the Curse; brothers, sister, cousins, aunts, uncles. Most gone before I was old enough to know I was alive—all but my mother, Dolores Valência Lobos, and her older sister, Silvia.

My mother had hung in there for a while, but chronic alcoholism is a rabid bitch from the lower realms; and then she was gone too. Dead by the time I was five . . . *So much blood . . . Bad blood, bad, bad blood . . .* Aunt Silvia was the only family left after my mother went in the hole. Old Silvia tried her best to take care of the kid. But little Ignácio was already broken beyond repair. Tainted. *Mahrime.*

Tainted by the Curse, he took it in stride, and took to the streets around the age of ten. And he did whatever he had to do to survive. Shoemaker's glue. I can still smell that shit now. Some memories are there to stay, I guess, in the blood, along with the rest of the mess. The glue did the trick, though, all through my adolescence, till I stumbled onto a bigger, better world of backstreet barrooms and *cachaça* and cocaine, opening the way to a lackluster career of petty teenage crimes and punishments.

Yeah, I was lucky to survive, I suppose. But I'd always been a survivor, right? Sure, a hardened little gypsy warrior. *Cigano guerreiro*, that's me. That's what the urban street gypsies of Copacabana, who took me in and fed me from time to time, used to call me. And somehow, unlike the rest of my people, I managed to survive all the liquor, and even the hardest of drugs. At least till many years later, working for the syndicate in Mexico, running *chiva* between Sinaloa and Baja California.

That's when the goddamn Curse caught up with me again. There were so many "agains" over the years. But that time had been my last. That hell-sent *chiva* had brought me to my knees for good. *Chiva*: the Goat. Pure Mexican black tar heroin. The devil's drooling maw. I'd thought I was riding high there, till I got knocked down, set up to take a fall for some big shot *politico*. Busted. Prison. Stopped.

I'd crashed and burned and died a thousand deaths in there. And then I was done. Finished. The End. When I got out of jail, I moved into a humble little room in a working-class colonia of Mexico, D.F. I took a shitty factory job and became a worker among workers, a friend among friends. That's where I finally got sober. And then, one gut-wrenching day at a time, I did whatever I had to do to stay that way. I stayed that way. Over the next few years, I changed a lot.

So, that's my fucking story in a nutshell. And here I am now, back again. Right back where the whole gruesome little nightmare began, a long time ago.

Ignácio Valência Lobos. *Cigano guerreiro.* Wide awake now. Picking up the shattered pieces of a faded, fuzzy little jigsaw puzzle nightmare called Home.

4. SHADOWS OF THE PAST

"Do not dwell in the past, do not dream of the future,
concentrate the mind on the present moment."
—*Buddha*

At the top of the stairs, I stopped to wipe the sweat from my face and adjust my funny new glasses . . . *Still can't get used to wearing these things! Can't get used to being over forty . . . When did that happen? Where did my whole fucking life go?*

Thinking, remembering, I walked along the dark, empty corridor up to the old apartment. I put the key into the lock. It fit. Squinting, I stepped inside to a sweet, nostalgic smell of mildew. Standing there in the musty shadows, I was hit with putrid scents of a putrid past. Shuddering, despite the stagnant greenhouse heat, I pulled a string to a 40-watt attached to the dusty old wooden ceiling fan.

I looked around the hot little space. High ceiling. A few framed pictures on rough plaster walls. Faces. Landscapes. Getting my bearings, slowly merging into a place of forbidden memories. Bits and scraps of furniture. Same comfortable old leather sofa. Same pair of frayed wicker chairs. The same wobbly mosaic table where she used to do her *consultas* with the cards.

Recognizing pieces of a past life, putting together abstract memories, my eyes made sluggish contact with other little details, strewn about like frozen ghosts; the tiny kitchen, a small, modern-looking fridge. At the top of a short wooden ladder, a masculine, no-frills loft bed with fluffy feather pillows.

No television . . . *Good . . . No time to waste watching TV . . . Time to live, like it's my last fucking day on earth . . . Yeah, time to outlive the goddamn Curse now.*

I ambled over and stood leafing through a pile of old, yellowed books on a dusty shelf, examining them, one by one. Occult Spiritist literature. The Book of Spirits. The Gospel According to Spirits. Allan Kardec. Years since I've read anything in Portuguese. After the half-remembered Romani gypsy dialect of my people, Portuguese was always my native tongue. But, save a few random encounters with the odd Brazilian here and there in my travels, over the last twenty years, I've only spoken it in nightmares.

Fascinated, I leafed through the old, familiar texts, time-traveling, reaching out for more memories, like flowers in some forbidden garden.

Shit, there it is . . . How could I ever forget this one?

Turning it over, I stared at the back cover: **NOSSO LAR: FRANCISCO C. XAVIER'S CLASSIC PARANORMAL SAGA. AN ACCOUNT OF A SPIRIT'S EXPERIENCES IN THE AFTERLIFE.** I remembered how I'd once devoured those books, so many years ago, in a foggy, long-forgotten quest for knowledge. As an adolescent, I'd pursued the Spiritist Doctrine and the Umbanda. Seems I'd always been seeking some illusive esoteric relief from the *Maldicâo*. The Curse.

I could hear a bitter little guffaw emerge from my throat like a ghost as a new wave of vague, uncomfortable recollections crawled up my spine. Maybe I'd pursued all that shit too far for my own good. And now, here I was again, after all these years.

You can run, but you can't hide, little Ignácio . . . It all comes back around.

I closed the book and wandered into the bathroom. I pissed long and hard, the way a man pisses after a long, demanding trip. As I flushed the toilet, sluggish brown water filled the bowl. I jiggled the handle to jump-start the long-neglected plumbing, remembering the place had sat empty, unused for years. I watched as the bowl filled with clean, clear water. Grinning, I tested the faucet on the yellowing sea-foam-green porcelain bathtub.

Waiting for the rusty sludge to run its course, I went over to stare out a large window in the main room, peering down at the scruffy green plaza below.

Feeling a sudden gasp of claustrophobia, I threw the shutters open wide. Humid tropical air enveloped me like a giant mouth as I stood listening to the city's lumbering machinery, pounding and humming and buzzing below.

Ship's horns. Motors. Sirens. Roosters. Dogs barking. People coughing, spitting, shouting, laughing, singing, living, dying . . . *And I'm still alive!*

Poking around, not much in the way of personal items. Maybe some other lost gypsy ghost had already cleaned the place out of valuables.

Guess that's what happens when you die.

Whatever. I don't give a shit. Why should I? I never cared much for televisions or valuables or personal effects anyway.

Who needs all that crap to worry about? What does a man really need? A few good books. Some spending cash. Maybe a girl to pass the time. A pen and paper. Change of underwear, whatever . . . I oughta get a motorcycle, though, as soon as I get a hold of that cash.

Yeah! First thing! Mobility.

Vida Cigana. O lungo drom. The long road to nowhere. Gypsy Life. Freedom. Yeah. That's all I ever needed.

Feeling a giddy wave of anticipation, I stride across the little apartment and crack open a rain-spotted wood and glass door. Stepping out onto a tiny, dirt-coated Portuguese-tiled balcony, I stand there awhile, looking around, thinking, taking in the sunny green view. A comfortable view. A blank canvas.

Yeah, just get a cleaning woman to come and mop up a little and it'll all be okay . . . Yeah. Okay. This is good . . . I can do this now.

The hot, fetid stench of afternoon reminds me that nothing good can be accomplished during the day; that rot, decay and death are the only games in town. Ah, but at night, Rio's shadows fill with that lazy perfumed lure . . . *Saudade* . . . I can feel it calling as I close up the apartment and pocket the keys.

I descend the creaky wooden staircase, and then I'm out in the late-afternoon shadows again, traversing the familiar paths of my old home. Walking along, I reminisce, wondering who's still around, what random ghosts I'll unearth as I begin this weird archeological dig into the murky back rooms of my life.

The mad, alien chant of the *cigarras* hisses from a massive ancient mango tree in the plaza as I wander among dim phantom whispers of a long, dragging pre-Carnaval afternoon. Nearing the throbbing downtown sprawl, stumbling through crooked, humming electric memory-gardens of dusk, the muggy air feels tinted with a patina of the past . . . *Saudade* . . . I move along in a spell, stepping over scattered pieces of time's broken artifacts, breathing in a magical world of details; crowded shouts rising from dusky restaurants and *botiquims*; people everywhere, talking of soccer scores and lazy late-afternoon topics of little consequence.

Ragged beggars shuffle shirtless among the outdoor tables of smiling men in thin, crisp business suits, holding gleaming glasses of cold *chopp* beer aloft, gesturing hands dancing with those well-manicured fingers, tanned on sunny weekend beaches. All the details of Rio are tattooing themselves across my brain again in heart-stabbing, sensual waves of shaking hips; a gay avalanche of lovely female faces, ivory teeth and erotic pink bubble-gum lips, smiling in frozen snapshots of wild expectation and excitement, laughing, yelling, spilling their careless, drawling Carioca chatter out to the sweaty rush-hour winds.

Weary, defeated office warriors and working-class commuters move past under the enormous building shadows, like lost herds of cattle, lumbering along in quiet submission to their poverty. Looking around, I know I'm really, finally home.

Smiling to myself, I stride over to a bus stop, where the big buses marked **COPACABANA** fly past. A clamoring red and yellow *lotacão* rolls up to the curb, hissing like a conveyer-belt time machine.

I pull some coins from my pocket and climb on.

5. PRINCESS OF THE SEA

"BENEATH ALL STORIES OF THE WORLD, IS A STORY ABOUT LOVE."
—*Nick Wong*

A ship's horn booms long and deep and low across the water as I stand looking across the half-moon stretch of white white sand and tall whitewashed buildings.

I wonder like a child at the first lights of dusk, twinkling like a spectacular jeweled necklace on Her Majesty, Copacabana Beach, Princess of the Sea.

My eyes follow the great glowing primal form of a cruise ship, creeping out from behind the granite mass of mountain; an enormous silent phantom, backlit by a purple-red setting sun reflected on dreaming clouds. As it emerges, plodding and surreal, it feels so close, as if I could reach out like Godzilla and snatch up the heady little dream shape. A haze of bottled-up tears clouds my vision; all cabins are alight, glittering like a thousand fairy torches as it lumbers across the water. The warm waves roll in and out, gentle as baby lambs murmuring at my feet.

Like a character in some old black-and-white movie, I'm sitting at a wobbly wooden table by the waves, drinking coconut water from a straw.

Taking in my first night home, the sights and sounds shuttle me back in time, and I envision myself sitting here in this same place, laughing and drinking with friends and lovers, long ago, in another lifetime, another dream.

After prowling the lonesome planet for decades like a crazed ghost, I'm really back. And it feels as if I never left, like an old, potent drug covering me in a rushing wave of invisible water, filling my nose, ears, eyes and skin, as a warm sea breeze blows through me, like a timeless song I have always and forever known.

I watch as a ragged group of mulattos with *cavaquinhos* and *padeiros* approach in the early evening shadows, singing to some tourists. Gringos, drinking strong, sweet rum caipirinhas, standing around, getting hammered, grinning like retarded children, laughing at nothing. I close my eyes and listen to the voices and rhythms. I have the old song's lyrics memorized again by the time the *garotos* push empty tambourines into pudgy pink gringo faces. I look on as they extort their cash, then weave among the tables like cats in search of a new batch of mice.

As they drift off down the beach, they pass me right by, as if I'm invisible. They sense from my devilish goatee, crooked gold teeth and jailhouse tattoos that I'm negligible, an unprofitable equation, a phantom. A gypsy. Invisible.

I call the guy over, pay for the coconut, then walk on; a scarred, downbeat old ghost shadow, moving along past clusters of healthy, bare-chested young men playing soccer in the cooling evening sands. My eyes scan the lively beachside kiosks, where the living still sit at tables beneath swaying palms, drinking in the pastel summer sunset; lovers and friends sharing idle words at the sea's edge at day's end; sounds and shapes and spirit whispers working their dark, healing magic in my bad old gypsy ghost blood.

I'm home again, and, like a ghost, I'm nowhere, at ease in the comfortable cloak of my own invisibility. Details light up like tiny pinball machine bulbs in my road-weary, dusty old brain, carving themselves into the expanding collage of the evening; a tiny blue and white fishing boat rolling by beyond the wave-line, dusky black boatman standing at the helm like an afterlife spirit guide across River Styx. Final remnants of sunset burn across rolling breakers, like distant funeral pyres, waning, surrendering to the salty spell of tropical night. Huge dancing seabirds dip drunkenly over the water, white as sailors' dreams.

Drawn to a sound of familiar music under a cluster of chattering palms, I stop again, thinking, remembering . . . Déjà vu . . . The sounds float soft on a gentle wind as nostalgia envelops me like an old lover's embrace. A group of elderly men with battered instruments stand in a circle by the crashing waves, constructing gentle bossa nova prayers to the sea.

Taking a seat by the kiosk, I watch the humble couples dancing unashamed beside the sand; rough, working-class people, clinging to each other like timid children, lest the force of emotions carry them right off the solid ground beneath their sailing feet.

My gaze fixes on a stout, full-faced young Negress, crazed eyes laughing with mystic African exuberance as she gyrates around a wrinkled, weather-beaten old fisherman a full head shorter than she. Seems I've been sitting, observing the world like this forever. Waiting. I know I look like an outsider. Not a tourist or a foreigner. Just . . . different. Untouchable. Apart. Marginal. That's how they always saw me here, if anyone ever saw me at all; a predatory shadow. Crooked, swindly, antisocial, unapproachable; dangerous.

I never meant to scare people off; it was just this thing I had. As a kid, I wanted to fit in, and I tried to in awkward little ways. But they could always see right through me. Like a ghost. When I tried to smile, people would check their wallets. Today, I know it's better like that. Keeps the rats away.

I sit back, watching the timeless parade of Copacabana whores parading past in giddy, giggling droves. The running of the *putas*, there they go, holding those proud, round asses out in that special Carioca way, like sharpened cats in heat. I wonder how they manage to move in three directions at once and still walk straight.

I sit for a long while like that, taking in the night, breathing in the humid seaside air, watching and waiting, scribbling random thoughts into the beat-up little pocket journal that hasn't left my side since the day I got out of prison.

Suddenly, the image of her face comes flashing like lightning across eons of time, blasting straight into my awareness; a short-circuit electric-chair explosion of childlike joy-fire-passion, freezing my blood to cement in my veins.

And the world screeches to a halt.

6. THE DAKINI

"WE ALWAYS RECOGNIZE THE PEOPLE WHO WILL CHANGE
OUR LIVES. AS THOUGH WE'RE KEEPING APPOINTMENTS MADE
BEFORE WE WERE BORN, OR IN FORGOTTEN DREAMS."
—*Justin R. Smith*

Her crooked Mona Lisa grin lights up the night like a flashing straight razor, and it's on. Our eyes meet, and I know I'm fucked. Hooked. Done for.

Trapped like a bug in those eyes, my stomach turns to ice.

For a millisecond, I picture Luciana with her blazing teenage eyes of mischief and boundless, untamable life. But twenty-something years have gone by, and Luciana is old now, over forty, like me.

I know in the core of me that I *know* this one, somehow. No one else could ever look like the feral young creature hovering before me. Insane, brilliant eyes of supernatural liquid crystal vision, popping like an acid-dream cocaine overdose, a burning hellfire infinity of bottomless want; the excruciating, longing vision of a haunted, abandoned child; a hungry ghost, staring me down from an exquisite cracked porcelain ivory-white face. Long, brown hair, thin, delicate arms and endless legs, impossibly high cheekbones, and big, bulging brown alien eyes.

She stands there, dressed to kill, to wound, maim, rape and destroy, facing me down like an old-time gunslinger pirate; sizing me up, melting my brain with flamethrower eyes of rapid-fire doom and redemption. Eyes that could knock the fucking planet off its axis! *And she's looking straight at me! Oh shit! I know her!*

In a flash, I take in the whole picture; a long-boned, gangly juvenile delinquent stance. High buckskin boots. An aura of savage elegance and danger; boyish frame wrapped in a handmade patchwork denim gypsy skirt hanging low on slender hips with unearthly perfection. Delicate shoulders curved in a lazy, defiant slouch under a thin purple shawl. Translucent white skin; deep blue veins running like ice-cold subterranean rivers in forbidden lands of extraterrestrial dreams.

At once, I know it in my heart, without words to explain it to my mind. *She's a vision, some kind of crazy man-eating angel!*

She turns and wanders away.

I stand and follow, staggering like a zombie around the musicians.

"Com licença, senhorita . . ." I hear my voice croak in the long-lost Portuguese of a misspent whorehouse youth.

She spins around and fixes me with a stun gun of eyes, cocked like twin shotgun barrels.

"Where *you* from, hein?" She looks me up and down, scanning me, turning me inside out, paralyzing my soul with shameless laser precision.

I know that look . . . *Danger.*

I swallow hard. *"Eh, sou cigano . . .* Gypsy . . ." I stammer with a gold-toothed rigor mortis grin. " . . . *Sabe* . . . Anywhere's home, y'know . . ."

"Cigano? Gyp-say?" She smirks back with undisguised predatory interest. "You one of de gyp-say peoples? *Na moral?"*

"Uh-huh . . . Buy ya a drink?" I gesture toward the table.

"I don' like drink no alco-ol, mano . . ."

"Um água de côco então?"

She shrugs. We sit. The *caboclo* brings over a pair of *côcos*. He opens them with two deft machete strokes, reminding me of the flashing twin swords of my heavenly protector, Ogum. I notice he's wearing a medallion of São Jorge too, just like mine. Saint George. Ogum. Another Son of Ogum. *Um filho de Umbanda*, like me.

The shiny green coconut descends into my hand like a prize. He hands us a pair of straws and we drink. She sits studying me across the table with those intense, lively eyes; sizing me up, reading my body computer, right down to my DNA.

In a sudden gesture of surrender, she speaks. *"Se for o diabo, cara, pode qualquer parada comigo, tá ligado.* If you de devil, man, you can do whatever you wan' with me, only don' hurt nobody else I know, cuz they got nothing to do with it, only me alone, got it?"

I don't get it, but I nod. Whatever. *Devil?* I'm used to crazy chicks who don't make much sense. Truth be told, they've always been my specialty.

Our straws gurgle in unison as we finish our *côcos.*

She grins, showing her crooked teeth, like a baby cat. "Okey, *pronto,* Cigano, next? Let's walk, move de leg, *anda logo, vai vai,* go!"

I get up. We walk off down the beach path together.

Her name is Narcisa. As we stroll along, the sound of the breaking waves lends a dreamlike percussion to her weird, melodic speech. She talks on and on, waxing soft and eloquent, and incomprehensible. Out of nowhere, she begins talking about Sacred Geometry and weird paranormal visions; and something enigmatic about mysterious hybrid human-extraterrestrial royal bloodlines or something.

"Is many thing I see in these world, Cigano," she whispers. "But is de kinda thing what only I know about. Nobody else ever can get it . . ."

I nod. I like her; like that she calls me "Cigano." Gypsy. The same casual nickname they gave me on the streets here, back when I was a wayward, abandoned runaway, bastard kid. Cigano. A stranger. An outsider. A homeless, rootless, no-name nobody, haunting the beaches and zigzaggy roads of Rio de Janeiro, a million years ago.

I watch Narcisa as she talks. She reminds me of the kid I once was. Sharp and fast, just like me. I've only known her fifteen minutes and she's already given me a nickname. My old *apelido*! How does she know so much?

As she chatters on in her hypnotic, slang-laden, singsong chant, I feel that funny sense of déjà vu again, as if I've always known her.

" . . . *Oiii, Cigano* . . ." Her voice crashes into my musings with a strange, random question. " . . . You ever been inside there, hein?"

"Huh? Where?" I look at her, puzzled.

"Pay attention, bro!" She frowns and the world turns dark. "In de Academia Brasileira de Letras. You ever go inside de building there, hein?"

I shrug, shaking my head, fascinated, bewildered.

The Brazilian Academy of Letters building downtown? Why's she talking about that place? I passed right by it today . . . How would she know I'm writing a book? Coincidence? Did she see me scribbling in my notebook back there?

I get that wave of déjà vu again; some odd telepathic subtext underlying her speech. It turns weirder as we move along the shore, her lilting, childlike chatter floating in the air like a strand of the night's gentle winds, weaving a spell.

"Futuristic archeology!" says Narcisa. "Check it out, Cigano, de inscription outside de Academia building! It e'say, '*Ad Immortalita Tem.*' That's Latin, brother, got it? You know de meaning of it, hein, Cigano?"

I shrug again, waiting for her to tell me.

Without telling me, she giggles and goes on. " . . . An' de Loja de Maçonaria. You know it? *Porra, cara!* I gone inside these place one time . . ."

"Huh? The Masonic lodge? *E daí?* What about it?"

"I break inside in de night, Cigano, got it?" Her voice drops an octave, confiding her special secrets in a frenetic, childlike whisper. "*Caralho!* I discover too many thing about de Freemason e'society. Hah! I e'study de secret Rosacrucz book I steal from there, an' I read all about it!" She pauses for a moment, as if unsure of something.

She looks around, then goes on. "I think may be they don' wan' de young girl know all de secret thing, so I gotta make e'special care 'bout who I e'say all these kinda business. These peoples no just de normal human being, you know. De *antropologia secreta* e'say about how them breed together with de lizard peoples, e'star peoples, long, long times ago, before de Babylonia civilization times, got it?"

I don't quite get it, but my head nods, needing to hear more.

7. FUTURISTIC ARCHEOLOGY

"SHE'S MAD BUT SHE'S MAGIC. THERE'S NO LIE IN HER FIRE."
—*Bukowski*

S he grins and goes on. "Lissen, Cigano. Is like these: all de e'same mestizo bloodline peoples is de president an' king an' queen an' princess an' bank master an' corporation boss, all de big power peoples on de earth his-tory, from beginning to modern times, got it? Is too much crazy e'sheets going on in de world what de peoples don' see!"

She stops and fixes me again with those big, intense lazer beam eyes. "I can e'say it to you all about de secret earth his-tory, mano. But is just one thing is *really* secret. You wanna know it, hein, Cigano?"

I shrug and smile.

She smirks and goes on. "De secret, de real big *segredo* is there is *no-oo* secrets, got it?"

I get it. Sort of.

As we shuffle along, the weird maze of Narcisa's thought-world seems way beyond my means to navigate or comprehend. But I go with it. She takes my arm and we walk on, moving along in perfect sync, as if we'd been traveling that same beach path together for eons. I can't believe my good fortune. I've fallen right into the orbit of some oddball kindred soul, and on my first night back; a fascinating, vibrant young beauty; a wayward, lusty spark of genius.

"*Ei, Cigano!!*" She's tugging at my arm like an impatient child. "Let's go an' do something real crazy now! Right now, *cara*, go, go!"

I say nothing, waiting to hear her idea, waiting for the adventure to unfold.

" . . . You like it de young pretty geer-ool, hein, Cigano?"

I nod.

"Okey! *Perfect, Max!* So you an' me we gonna go now an' meet some other young pretty girl, an' then we gonna make it, how do you e'say it, de party! You know someplace we can go an' hang out tonight, bro, hein?"

"I'm staying over in Catete."

"*Perfect, Max!* Hah! When we go you place, I gonna show you all my poetry an' drawing, an' some other crazy thing I discover in my researches!"

When I ask her to elaborate on her mysterious "research," she starts talking about Russian poetry, of all things . . . *What? Another coincidence? How could she know my people came to Brazil from Russia?*

" . . . You wan' me e'say to you all about de Russian *poesia*, hein? You e'speak these language, de *russo*, hein, Cigano?"

"Uh, not really . . ." I stammer. "It's Romani, not Russian . . ."

"How many you gyp-say peoples they got in de Russia, hein?" She asks questions, not waiting for an answer. "You look e'same like de *russo* peoples, so maybe you come from there, I thinking, hein? I wan' go there too. So lissen, bro, you gonna take me with you next time you going over there, okey, hein?"

I smile to myself as she rambles on, jumping from one random topic to another, like a crazy acid-eating grasshopper. I get the distinct impression that this strange, charismatic girl is putting on some kind of act; showing off her eclectic cultural repertoire, as if she desperately needs to let someone, anyone, into her hallucinatory, solitary little world; wanting to be a part of something, anything.

"I can tell you more! All bout de *arquitetura*, an' de secret sacred *estrutura* of de buildings, Cigano! Everything in de world is about de *numero*, see? Is all about de equation, formulas, *numeração secreta*, got it?"

I don't get it. I look at her, a standing question mark.

"*Crowwwn crowwwn crowwwn, ha ha!*" Narcisa cackles. "De Masonic peoples know all de secret *numerologia*, an' they design all de thing same way in all de building. They build everything to confuse de peoples, for make them think they sit inside one box, an' really they go an' sit in de other box, got it?"

I don't get it. Narcisa keeps going, oblivious, giggling at her own odd words.

"You know, I travel all round these whole country, hein, Cigano, an' every different city an' all de town, e'same e'system I see, always. Hah! I just come today from de mountain. Visconde de Mauá, know it?"

"What were you doing there?"

"They got de secret portal there for travel to de other dimension." She grins. "My father, he come from there, I think. He was de e'smuggler by de Bolivia border in de Mato Grosso, know it? Or maybe was my uncle, I donno, some guy who e'stay with my mother when I was little geer-ool. Whatever. Don' matter about de dead peoples. *Thank you come again!* Hah! From my most early memory, I all de time go travel with these guy. I see it where they grow all de *cocaina*, got it? Hah! My father, de guy he gone to prison there. I think maybe they kill him or something. Whatever. Maybe he know too much bout de peoples' secret business."

For some reason, I ask her to tell me about her mother.

"*Minha mãe!?*" She spits on the ground. "*Porra! Essa porra é doida, mano!* Hah! She complete crazy! She take me all around de country. She was de young hippie girl when I borned, got it? Maybe thirteen year old, whatever, an' she carry me round like de little hippie doll, de little pet monkey! Hah!"

"So where'd ya grow up, Narcisa?"

Even as the words leave my mouth, I already know it's a stupid question.

She laughs. "Grow up? Hah! I grow up on de long-distance bus, bro! These e'stupid retard woman, she got in a big fight with some e'stupid boyfriend an' he try kill her. An' then, no more travel, she just go away an' live in de e'stupid military city, Resende. Know it? After then, she e'start talk all de day with de Je-sooz! Hah! I e'say fock these e'sheet, mano. Fock you, Je-sooz! Fock you, e'stupid military brainwashing place, an' I go! Get de fock out from there, got it? Go! Hah! *Next?*"

"Where'd ya go after that?"

"Nowhere, bro. I just go an' e'stay in de mountain, together with de nature. Bird an' bee. River an' tree. Ever'thing good. But I don' never encounter too much intelligent life in de country, an' so I e'say, *bor-ing!* *Next?* Then I come de Rio."

"So where do ya live here?"

She just laughs as she tightens her grip on my arm and points to the ground.

"De only place to live is right *here*, mano. Right here an' now, got it? You know, Cigano, I don' got de e'same *cultura* like all de peoples here, you know, with de home, de family, de job, de routine an' all these kinda thing, got it? *Bor-ing!*"

"So whaddya do for money? Ya work?"

"Work?" She spits the word out like a curse. "Hah! My only job like de house pet for de rich peoples, you know? Like a little poodle dog, or maybe de cat, play with de mouses, whatever, ha ha . . . But I am a pretty good little animal, so long de peoples nice to me an' don' talk alotta e'sheet in my head an' make all de rule an' regulation for me. I don' like all these kinda e'sheet, no no no! Peoples make too much pressure on me, brother, I gotta *go!* Got it? *Thank you come again! Next?*"

I watch her closely, feeling that weird sense of kinship growing.

" . . . I just like to go out in de e'street, you know, for meet some interesting new peoples sometime. I don' like think bout nothing too much, just go. Go wherever, follow de wind, walk round in de e'star light, e'same like de night! That's me, Cigano. Whatever happen next, that's de plan, got it?"

I get it. But when I try to ask her what part of town she's staying at in Rio, I realize it's another stupid question.

"Hah! Whatever place I e'stay, always de right place for me, got it? Better if is maybe some kinda little corner for me lay down inside an' e'sleep when I feel tire, you know, maybe got some good food, some interesting peoples for talk to. But I don' care much bout these kinda thing, really, you know. I just like to learn de new thing an' keep move around, got it?"

I get it. I nod. She stops and looks at me, as if debating saying more.

Then she winks. "I like de travel between de different dimension too, bro, whenever I got it de right kinda e'substance. Is very good for my e'study, I think."

"Whaddya study, Narcisa?"

"I like e'study . . . you know, de Earth peoples . . ."

With a deadpan look, Narcisa informs me she doesn't really belong on planet Earth; that she's stranded here—just visiting, from the constellation of Alpha Centauri.

That would eventually explain many things about Narcisa.

She begins telling me of her interactions with psychedelic-plant-based spirit cults and the Umbanda, UFOlogists and students of Christian mysticism, the Intergalactic Ashtar Command, and the ancient esoteric teachings of the Kabbalah.

My head is swimming as she goes on. "All de knowledge an' de most secret e'science, Cigano, is always got to do with de *numero*, got it? De universe is all de big mathematics equation, got it? E'same like de computer! You know something bout de Matrix? Well I do! Hah! I take it de little Red Pill too many time, ha ha! Or maybe is de Blue Pill, can't remember, whatever. *Doiiiiing! Delete! Next? Hah!* When I go an' e'stay with de mountain peoples, all de time we go de Santo Daime ceremony for drink de ayahuasca tea. Then I see it *all*, bro!"

"See what, like visions?"

"Hah! Forget it! Is too *complexo* for try e'splain with de human languages, mano. I think I maybe e'stay too much time on these e'stupid planet now, you know, an' she finally make me crazy. De peoples on de mountain e'say to me all de time I gotta e'study Kabbalah. *Porra, cara!* When I go an' e'start research these e'sheets, it make me really confuse! *Crowwn crowwwn crowwwwn*, ha ha! You know de Kabbalah, Cigano? Fock, mano, I know *too-oo* much about these crazy e'sheets!"

Narcisa talks on. Like some enigmatic idiot savant, the words flow from her perfect baby-doll lips in frantic, perplexing torrents. I can't shake the persistent sense of déjà vu, a weird, lingering impression that I've known this captivating sixteen-year-old prodigy before; somewhere, sometime, a long time ago.

Silent lightning flashes out over the ocean as an approaching wall of rain moves in across a suddenly choppy sea, conjuring memories of the explosive summer lightning storms of my youth.

As if on cue, Narcisa begins singing a strange, haunting chant in a deep, husky growl. *"We gonna run run run to de city of de future . . ."*

I look over at her and smile. With her haunting beauty, natural charisma and off-the-charts IQ, Narcisa is clearly homeless only by choice; and she seems to have no care for money. She's open to any new adventure. A nomad. Street-wise. Not a prostitute, though, I'm certain. Nothing like any whore I've ever met. She just wants some interesting company, maybe a roof over her head for a long, stormy night.

She winks at me, sealing the deal.

Then, without a word, she takes me by my arm again. My kind of people. We move toward the bus stop. She's just right. Spontaneous, uninhibited, wild; Narcisa is a true gypsy spirit, someone who lives only for the day she's in, and knows the score—which she shows me as soon as we get to my new apartment.

Taking off her clothes, she stands admiring herself in the dresser mirror with undisguised narcissistic fascination.

I watch in grateful admiration as she makes herself at home, occupying the comfortable, worn leather sofa as if she owns the place.

Maybe she does.

Narcisa. Naked. Perfect and unashamed as a blinking white Siamese cat.

8. SAVAGE GRACE

"ALL CHARMING PEOPLE ARE SPOILED. IT IS
THE SECRET OF THEIR ATTRACTION."
—*Oscar Wilde*

For the next couple of years, Narcisa darted in and out of my life like a deranged seagull. Over time, she began to exhibit a weird sort of mean streak, a vicious wild animal nature.

As she dropped her ashes on my floor one day, I tried to hand her an ashtray.

She glared at me, then swatted the thing to the floor.

"De world is my ashtray, bro!" She spit at my feet. **"Got it?"**

I got it. Whenever Narcisa didn't get her way, she would pout and sulk, or shout and whine, cranky as a spoiled, autistic brat crossed with a bitter old cunt.

But then, out of the blue, she could also be sweet; charming and kindhearted, ingratiating, large of spirit and generous in that odd, reckless way that only children and wild animals, and maybe Lucifer, can be.

Narcisa just loved to argue. That was her weakness. It was as if she couldn't help herself. She would spend hours on end debating with anybody about any silly little thing at all. She even spoke of putting her talents to work and becoming a lawyer someday. And she criticized everything she saw, machine-gunning crazed insults at random strangers on the streets of Rio. She was especially brutal with the people closest to her. As time went by, I realized there weren't any people close to Narcisa.

Nobody but me. Somehow, though, I didn't mind.

Narcisa was obsessed with the color purple; the mystical color of redemption and spiritual rebirth. Everything she owned or wore had to be purple. When she couldn't find the things she wanted in purple, she would settle for pink.

Even her food had to be purple or pink, and Narcisa ate heaps of beets, devouring big, overflowing plates of beet salad at the cheap downtown eateries we went to together—maybe in hopes of shitting purple, just for good measure.

Narcisa craved attention. A lot of attention, often the negative kind. Didn't seem to matter one way or the other, as long as she got attention. She talked loud and cursed a lot to get it, too. And she dressed eccentrically. Sometimes she would even wear her bra and panties outside her clothes—then hurl venomous curses and insults at people on the streets when they stopped and gawked.

Narcisa was an enigma to me, with her many weird, eclectic, contradictory tastes; everything from the writings of Nietzsche, Sartre and Descartes, to corny Brazilian soap operas and asinine old American sitcoms dubbed with preposterous, outdated TV Portuguese. Soon after she came around, she nagged me to buy her a little portable television. She loved watching the children's shows and cartoons. She would spend whole days with her eyes glued to the screen, while devouring pizza and chocolate, and drinking Coca-Cola—always with lots of ice cubes. She liked to make a lot of noise chewing up the ice. Some Brazilians say it's a sign of sexual frustration when a woman chews on her ice cubes. As more would be revealed about Narcisa's personal history, that quaint bit of folklore would begin to make sense—especially given her surreal background of childhood sexual abuse.

She liked to eat messy snacks in bed; even sitting on the toilet, or in the shower. She would eat and chew on her ice cubes while I fucked her.

Sometimes she liked to sing during sex, usually when she was high.

Narcisa consumed great quantities of pink bubble gum, and stuck it to the walls and furniture all over my place, like some neurotic little devil dog pissing on things to mark its turf.

One day, early on in our bizarre friendship, she bitched me out mercilessly for ten minutes straight, standing on a busy downtown street corner. All because I'd bought her some blue bubble gum. The wrong color for Narcisa.

"Porra! These e'sheet is blue, Cigano! Blue! Argghh!" she screeched, throwing a wadded up ball of gum at me, bouncing it off my head as passersby stopped on the sidewalk to watch. *"De blue color is de color for de boy, Cigano, don' you know it? Maybe you don' notice I am de gee-rool, hein?"*

I stood there, shocked, frozen in horror as she pulled her pants down and flashed her shaved pussy at me accusingly, like some undernourished house pet I'd neglected to feed. A crowd gathered and stood around, watching, gawking, commenting, spectating as Narcisa railed on. *"Geer-ool! Girl is pink, you see? Got it now, hein?"* She spun around and stood flashing the bewildered crowd.

Some of the men leered and made lecherous comments as I cringed with embarrassment. *"Bu-ceta! Buceta bo-oa! Go-od pussy!"* A toothless old bum cackled to the delight of one and all. I wanted to rip his lungs out with my bare hands, but Narcisa's crazed scandal held my attention like a straitjacket.

" . . . So de next time you wanna buy de Chiclet for me, bro, you better remember is only de pink Chiclet for de Narcisa, got it? Hah! Now you got it!"

She turned to the crowd again, throwing the remaining bits of bubble gum at the shocked spectators, still yelling as she hiked up her pants. *"Okey, de e'streep teaser show finish for all you e'stu-pid little monkey face peoples. That's all folks! Hah! Now we gotta go, gotta go go go! Next? Thank you come again! 'Bora, Cigano!"*

Then she grabbed my arm, leading me off, like a dog on a leash, as if nothing had happened. Just like a long-forgotten little boy named Ignácio, being dragged along those same crowded downtown streets, behind a rough-handed, scandalous, drunken gypsy whore, back in another lifetime, a long time ago.

One afternoon, I was out walking when I spotted a group of local gypsies gathered on a busy downtown corner. I recognized some of the older ones from back in the day. Like my family of origin, they belonged to a scattered network of city-dwelling Roma; humble underground traders who'd long ago swapped the old nomadic life-style of horses, mules and caravans for cars, motorcycles and cramped little backstreet flats. Still, they were Roms to the bone; outsiders and natural-born hustlers.

Like my Tia Silvia, the colorful *ciganas* would take to the streets in their traditional long, flowing skirts, bead necklaces and exotic gold jewelry. They spent their days reading palms in the busy downtown *praças*, while their men stood in nearby clusters, wheeling and dealing, buying, selling and trading whatever they could acquire for cheap and dispose of for a quick profit—mostly used vehicles.

As I passed, a man's voice rang out, calling my name above the rumble of traffic.

I turned. A face emerged from the crowd like a memory, grinning gold teeth under a wide-brimmed black fedora. *"Mixztô, mer'mão!"*

I did a double-take and stopped. It was my old friend, Luca.

"God has sent you, Ignácio!" He rushed over and kissed me on the cheek.

After exchanging warm backslaps and pleasantries in the familiar Portuguese-laced Romani of our youth, he led me around a corner to show me his latest treasure: a slightly battered black Yamaha XT-600. Just the motorcycle I'd always dreamed of owning someday. Luca's asking price was affordable, and the engine was sound. Best of all, having known me all my life, he offered to sign it over for a small cash payment, then trust me for the rest over time.

Once again, I was in the right place at the right time.

I handed him a few hundred reais as he put the keys and papers in my hand.

I rode off, beaming with pride and smiling like a fox.

"Das dab ka i roata le neve vurdoneski, mer'mão!" Luca waved behind me, wishing a fellow gypsy "steady wheels for the new wagon."

That fortuitous acquisition would mark the real beginning of a new life for me in the city of my youth. For the first time in years, I had something of my own and nobody else's.

It was a good feeling.

9. ALL ABOUT NARCISA

> "ONE MAY UNDERSTAND THE COSMOS, BUT NEVER THE
> EGO; THE SELF IS MORE DISTANT THAN ANY STAR."
> —*G. K. Chesterton*

Narcisa liked the mountains, but she couldn't take the solitude.

Narcisa, I would come to learn, didn't like to be alone. Ever. She liked the rain; didn't even care about getting soaked in an apocalyptic tropical downpour—which happened more than once as we flew through the nights on my new motorbike. Maybe she didn't mind because it gave her something to complain about.

Narcisa loved to complain.

When not complaining, Narcisa enjoyed classical music, old Brazilian rock and roll, bubble baths, bubble gum, and anything to do with smoke and fire.

She always said she'd smoke anything; literally, anything at all. To prove it, whenever she was around, she would chain-smoke all my cigarettes, then dig through the overflowing ashtrays searching for butts.

She consumed copious quantities of weed. She even puffed on tobacco pipes and cigars. Narcisa didn't care. She would smoke any damn thing that came her way, including PCP, DMT and crack cocaine; and, speaking of smoking, she wanted to be cremated, not buried, not under any circumstances, when she died—which she hoped would be real soon. To that end, she'd leave lighted cigarettes burning on the furniture in random spots around my place—maybe in hopes of fulfilling her death wish by starting a fire and smoking *herself* as a swan song.

Narcisa was well named.

Obsessed with mirrors, she could stand before one for hours on end, lost, hypnotized, looking at herself, studying, preening, flirting, admiring her own marvelous, sensuous, ghostly image in the looking glass.

As I got to know her better, I realized she was quite opinionated. There were so many people, places and things she disliked, the litany of her pet peeves was hard to keep up with.

Narcisa hated anyone in a uniform, particularly waiters, police and the military; fat people, Argentines; Forró and Caipira music were a constant source of annoyance to her, as well as all religious art, newspapers and newscasts. She also despised poor people. But, as an equal-opportunity hater, she disliked rich people just as much. Basically, Narcisa loathed the whole human race.

Sports (soccer in particular, Brazil's national passion), popular fashion trends, sunshine and the beach were all high on Narcisa's shit list; airplanes and air traffic irritated her to no end too. Above all else, she hated old people. And Narcisa absolutely detested "stupid" people—especially the ones in her long-estranged family of origin.

Despite an almost pathological narcissistic fascination with herself, Narcisa had a special dislike of her physical body—her "space suit" as she referred to it—and she punished it without pity, every chance she got, often provoking street fights with strangers, just for the hell of it, thereby getting them to do the job. Narcisa was covered in battle scars and stitches, bruises, cuts and messed-up homemade tattoos. She also liked to cut herself with sharp objects.

As an extension of the perfect adolescent body she despised, Narcisa hated her bodily functions. She had no patience with going to the bathroom, producing waste, shitting; "defecating," she called it, not even caring to verbalize the word *shit* for its intended usage.

Narcisa abhorred her period, her pussy, her tits, and she spoke of having them cut off her someday—tiny as they were—if she ever got enough money to pay for plastic surgery.

She often lamented having been born a female, and she didn't care for women much, as a whole. Still, she was always oddly tolerant of other teenage girls like herself—especially when she wanted something from them. Usually sex.

Yes, Narcisa also hated men, at least that's what she claimed—a fact that would make my intimate dealings with her a challenge.

Despite her many antisocial, abrasive ways, Narcisa was also witty, engaging and convincing—even charming, in a surreal manner. And Narcisa always got whatever she wanted. The only problem was that what she tended to want was mostly chaos, confusion and conflict.

Narcisa professed to be expert in all sorts of shadowy mind-control techniques, things she'd picked up at a young age, supposedly, from reading stolen books on Satanism, occult Freemasonry and black magic. She even claimed to have participated as a child in ritualistic pacts with the devil.

Oh, and Narcisa hated any words printed on clothing, too.

She would cut all the words and labels off her clothes, even the expensive designer stuff she always mysteriously acquired. One day, she showed up at my door, covered from head to toe in catsup and mustard. She refused to discuss how she'd come to be a walking hot dog. I let it go. As I ran a bath for her, I went into my stockpile of bootleg swag and handed her a brand-new fake Calvin Klein T-shirt to wear. Right away, she took a scissors from my drawer and cut the name off the front, leaving her own hated breasts exposed to the world as a trade-off.

"Out! Out!! E'stupid gringo bool-e'sheet!" She cackled as she "customized" the shirt. *"Que merda!* Who de fock these focking Calvin for me, hein? Focking e'stupid reptile! If de Narcisa ever gotta walk around like a focking circus clown with some e'stupid gringo name on front of me, they better give it to me plenty focking gringo dollar an' pay me for advertise, got it? Hah! *Next?"*

I got it. Anything would be better for Narcisa than to be a walking billboard for some unknown gringo *parasita*.

Narcisa also detested machines. I was obliged to hide my cell phone whenever she was around, just to keep it from flying out the window.

She was fond of destroying all sorts of other costly, imported gringo appliances, like cameras, radios, blenders and toaster ovens.

Speaking of blenders and toaster ovens, Narcisa abhorred the boring earthly concept of food. In her baffling extraterrestrial philosophy, eating was just a crude necessity, at best. She said she wished she could dehydrate food and smoke it in a big spliff, thereby bypassing the unpleasant chore of taking nourishment altogether.

She claimed she would soon invent a scientifically sound method to do just that, then become obscenely wealthy from selling her smokable meals to all the other unfortunates like herself stranded on this stupid, backward planet.

Only problem was, there wasn't anybody else like her.

She scoured the Internet for weeks on my little laptop, searching for a global market for her grand idea—until one day the terrible reality of it all sank in. Then she sulked and pouted for days on end; a very rough time for poor Narcisa.

"Everything's going to be all right, princesa." I tried to console her.

"Is never gonna be all right! Nunca!" She howled like a dying coyote.

And for just that moment, I almost believed her.

Contrary to the malevolent, badass image she projected to the world, though, Narcisa was essentially good. And it was that native goodness, more than anything else, that made her life a raging battlefield.

Narcisa was a walking, talking, living, breathing mystery to me; one that, as time went on, I became more and more obsessed with solving.

One day, she explained what she'd meant the night we'd first met, when she'd said, *"If you de devil or something, you can do whatever you wan' with me, but don' hurt nobody else I know, cuz they no got nothing to do with all these."*

Turned out she'd been tripping on acid. Seeing my gold teeth and dark goatee, she'd come to the logical conclusion that I must have been Satan himself, the Dark Angel she'd once made some stoned-out "pact" with.

When she told me she'd thought I was the devil, come to take his due at last, I didn't know whether to feel insulted, flattered or afraid. When Narcisa was high, she was generally creepy, if not more or less criminally insane.

When she wasn't high, though, she was often even worse. And she seemed to know it. Drugs were important to Narcisa, so she did anything in her power to never be without them. Including selling her body.

One time, after hours of sweaty, marathon sex, during which she suffered the humiliating indignity of having multiple orgasms, I made the mistake of asking her if she liked me . . . Maybe just a little?

Narcisa glowered at me with the coldest, most jaded look of disdain she could produce and snorted like a haughty Thoroughbred.

"Hah! Only de *queer* like de mans! I like de mo-ney, bro. Got some for me?"

Although she could never quite openly admit to being a straight-up whore—even to herself—at that moment, the penny finally dropped for me.

Of course! That's where all the money comes from!

Knowing Narcisa, it made sense.

After all, how else would someone like her get the cash to pay for all those drugs and the endless, shape-shifting array of expensive designer clothing she always wore, then threw out or gave away as soon she grew bored?

Yes. Narcisa turned tricks.

10. DICKLESS TRICK

*"THERE ARE SOME SOLITARY WRETCHES WHO SEEM
TO HAVE LEFT THE REST OF MANKIND, ONLY, AS EVE
LEFT ADAM, TO MEET THE DEVIL IN PRIVATE."*
—*Alexander Pope*

I hadn't seen Narcisa in about a week when I spied her standing on the sidewalk on the Rua do Catete, talking to this weird old nerdy-looking fellow.

I'd been having lunch in a little *boteco* across the way. As I watched from the counter, she appeared to be bitching the guy out about something I didn't quite get.

Curious, I stepped outside and called her name. Narcisa's face lit up like she was surprised to see me. She halted her harangue and left her victim standing alone as she came running over.

"*Oí, Narcisa, tudo bem?* Who's the old guy?"

"Oh, is only de Doc, Cigano."

I raised my left eyebrow. "Doc?"

She laughed. "Yeh, brother! D-O-C. Hah! It mean 'Dickless Old Cushion'!"

I raised my other eyebrow.

"Is de *apelido* I give it to him, de nicknames, got it?" She gave me an evil wink. "Lookit de guy, Cigano! Don' he look just like de *almofada*?"

I glanced over to where the pear-shaped little man was standing. He did look kind of like a pillow. I shrugged, waiting to hear more.

Narcisa grinned with pride. "Hah! These guy, Doc, he is my *zumbí*, got it?"

I didn't get it. "Your *zombie?*"

I looked over at the odd little fellow again. His thick black hair had a skunklike white streak at his balding forehead, which gave him an overall Bride of Frankenstein look. Creepy.

"Ya-ah, is like my e'slave, Cigano, got it? *Um zumbí.* He always do whatever little thing I wan' for me! An' whenever he got some mo-ney, then I make him give it to me. Hah! *Thank you come again!*"

"You're fuckin' that old creeper?"

Narcisa burst out cackling like a mad crow. "Hah! No way! *Porra, cara!* How I e'suppose to fock some guy like that? *Como?* He is *gay*, or whatever, don' got no focking dick, e'stupid old e'sheet! *Crowwn crowwn crowwwwwn, ha ha!!*"

"Well ya must be doin' something for him." I scratched my head.

Narcisa glared at me, hands on her hips. ***"Nada! Porra nenhuma! I never even kiss he ugly face! Nunca! Fala serio! I never would fock such a guy, no focking way! No even in he ass-hole with you dick, Cigano! Forget it! Eu hein!"***

I watched the pudgy, pallid little pillow-man shuffle off down the street.

Narcisa told me she was famished, so I brought her into the bar and got her a plate of beans and rice with spicy *rabada* stew. I watched her eat as she told me more about this mysterious Doc character.

"These guy, *mmmh*," she mumbled, attacking her plate like a starved pit bull, "I meet him first time, I donno, *mmh, nhmm*, was long time ago, when I first time come de Rio. Maybe I thirteen, fourteen year old then, I donno, whatever. One time I help him out with, *mmmh, nyamm*, ah, some little thing, got it?"

I didn't get it. "Helped him out?"

"Never mind about all these, Cigano. Don' interrupting me! Is irrelevant these e'sheet. Just shut de fock up an' lissen, *porra*!"

She babbled on breathlessly, spitting scraps of rice across the counter as she shoveled food into her machinelike mouth. Her bright, stoned-out eyes flashed like tumbling neon dice as she told me all about her weird, mutually parasitic relationship with her old "zombie slave."

"From first time I know these Doc, *mmh, nhmmm*, de guy always e'saying he wanna adopt de Narcisa, like de daughter, got it? Hah! But I don' wan' nothing with him! He don' got enough mo-ney for do nothing for me! *Crowwn crowwn crowwwwn, ha ha!! Next?*"

"So what were ya yelling at him about just now?"

"*Agghh!* Only sometime I need some little thing, so then I call him, got it? An' when he e'saying me he don' got de mo-ney, then sometime I gotta get, how do you e'say it, heavy! Hah! He just de dickless old cushion for de Narcisa."

From what she told me, this poor old do-gooder seemed to fancy himself Narcisa's Personal Savior. And he'd maintained a strictly "platonic" relationship with her the whole time, too, spending a small fortune over the years, bailing her out of every sort of self-inflicted crisis and drama—all the while claiming to be "in love with her mind rather than her body."

She, in turn, returned his fanatical devotion by gleefully nicknaming him Dickless Old Cushion. This Doc was pussy-whipped by little Narcisa, apparently. Well, just whipped. No pussy. I didn't get the whole "platonic" bit. At least I had an excuse for putting up with her crap. This poor soul just lapped it up for giggles.

"So, what's th' guy's angle?" I looked at her, wondering how she did it.

"Donno, bro, *mmh, nhmm* . . . I guess he think he my daddy or some kinda e'stupid e'sheet, an' so he wanna save de Narcisa from all de bad thing in these bad bad world. Hah!"

"How'd ya meet him?" I prodded.

He was just some lonesome old loser, she shrugged, who'd appointed himself her benefactor, right from the time she'd first hit town. For his troubles, she'd worked the silly bastard to death over the years. She bragged about calling on him for all sorts of unneeded assistance, pretending, whenever it suited her purposes, to give a shit whether he lived or died.

This fool was on a holy mission, apparently, to get Narcisa to go straight. As she talked on, I could see it was a real give-and-take relationship she had with her obsessive, dickless zombie. He gave, and she took . . . *Thank you come again!*

The dickless cushion fancied himself some kind of brilliant mind, she snickered, laughing him off as an "Intellectual," a lover of "European Classical Culture" and "the Arts." From what I gleaned from her derisive depictions, he was some kind of wannabe bohemian, an aging closet hippie, waxing nostalgic for the sixties. A nine-to-five drone of polite society, old Doc seemed a bored, solitary little weekend warrior; a dabbler on the wild side of life—other people's lives.

His biggest thrill, she scoffed, was living vicariously through all the drama, mayhem and confusion created by her and a few other not-so-beautiful losers who dubbed themselves "anarchists" and "nihilist punks"—inhabitants of the Casa Verde, an infamous local squatters' refuge. Doc was endlessly fascinated with that whole crew of career fuckups, unwashed underground reprobates who seemed to always orbit around Narcisa like bits of toxic space debris.

As time went on, whenever I got fed up with her shit and put the boot to Narcisa's perky ass, this Doc would always seem to be right there, somehow; forever lurking around like some lovestruck old cartoon buzzard, waiting to take her in and pick up the pieces.

A very bizarre cat.

O ne day, a few weeks later, I met old Doc in person.

He was escorting Narcisa down the street, his hand on her elbow, as if he were taking a prized toy poodle for a stroll; corralling her along with a proud, dainty, self-important stride. With his jaunty, slightly effeminate gait, he came across like a pudgy, homosexual clown, all pimped out in white cotton socks, a pair of shiny brown open-toed sandals, plaid Bermuda shorts, and a starched white shirt; a bow tie completed the whole surreal picture.

They were on their way to a classical cello concert or some pompous horseshit event; whatever the latest wholesome "cultural activity" this fine, upstanding fellow had cooked up to stimulate Narcisa's brilliant young mind.

Unfortunately, her pillowy, pear-shaped escort was blissfully unaware that she'd already made other plans with me. As they approached the corner where I waited on my motorcycle, Narcisa broke away from her puffed-up little chaperone.

She ran over to where I sat lurking like the Angel of Death's bastard spawn. Jumping on the bike behind me, she squeezed me so hard I thought I'd puke.

"'Bora daqui, Cigano! Let's go! Go, go, go, go, go-ooo!"

Narcisa was wearing this fancy new purple denim jacket I knew she'd been wanting, and a brand-new shiny pair of expensive-looking pink sneakers. I gathered she'd already gotten whatever cash and goodies she could squeeze out of her victim. She was ready to move on now, tossing him aside like a used-up snot rag, without so much as "bye."

I fired up the motor and started to pull away.

That's when Doc lost it.

He ran up, sputtering, hollering his tonsils out. *"That's it, Narcisa! Puta! After all I've done for you, you're still nothing but a dirty, degenerate little slut!"*

I couldn't believe my ears. The poor old chump was so pissed-off and poisoned with the bitter disillusionment of years of self-imposed, thankless sacrifice and martyrdom, he couldn't restrain himself. Even in front of me—a six-foot-three, 240-pound tattooed gypsy thug, who looked like he was late to a knife fight, but would be glad to take a minute to slice off your face.

"Puta-aa! Vagabunda-aa! Piranha! You were born to be a whore, Narcisa!"

As he ranted on, he was turning so red with rage I worried he might try a grab for my little chicken. ***"Your mother's a dirty, diseased whore, and you're a whore, and you'll always be a filthy little whore! Puta-aa! Ordinaria-aa!"***

Narcisa rolled her eyes and nudged me in the ribs.

I shrugged . . . *Shit . . . Guess I gotta go do the right thing.*

I cut the motor, got off the bike and stomped over to where Doc stood spewing. He ranted on, as if in a trance, oblivious to my presence. He seemed possessed, so obsessed with Narcisa and wound up in his own raging, self-righteous indignation, he didn't even see me. He really reminded me of an angry pillow. I could feel Narcisa's eyes boring into the back of my skull, egging me on.

Like a well-trained guard dog, I bared my gold-toothed fangs and growled.

"Eí, maluco! Segura aí, mermão! Porra! Que merda é essa, hein?"

The blustering, pissed-off pillow-man stopped, as if suddenly seeing me for the first time. His sputtering tongue froze like a woodchuck in the path of an oncoming truck as he stood there, regarding me in mute shock.

I put my battle-scarred mug an inch from his smooth, beet-red, double-chinned face, sneering. "Easy there, tough guy! Or ya need me to teach ya some fuggin' manners?"

His eyes trembled with fear. "Wh-who, who are you? What do you want?"

"Ya shouldn't be talking all that kinda rude shit to my lady friend," I hissed, "cuz you're being disrespectful to me, too, got it?"

He got it. He started whining an apology. *"Ahhh, me perdoe, senhor!"*

Weak-kneed, whiney, whore-bullying bitch! I glared at him, taking a step forward, ready to knock him on his ass.

"I, I didn't know . . ." He backed away, mumbling. "I mean, I, I was only—"

"Chega! Just can all that noise, man! Even if it *is* true! All right?" I gave the old stuffed shirt a playful shove and a sharky devil's wink, then turned away.

Sauntering back to where Narcisa sat watching the show, I grinned at her, my gentlemanly duty fulfilled.

As I blasted off into the sweaty afternoon traffic, with his prize prodigy smirking from the back, I had this funny feeling that she was sticking her tongue out at him.

Doc just stood there, rubbing his lonesome, mad, balding head.

11. WILL TO POWER

"THE LUST FOR POWER IS NOT ROOTED IN STRENGTH, BUT IN WEAKNESS."
—*Erich Fromm*

Later, back in my place, Narcisa reached into her ever-present purple Coleman knapsack. I watched her in wonder, scratching my head . . . *Where the fuck does she get all this expensive imported shit? Did this Doc buy that thing for her too? Whatever . . . Probably just a souvenir from some unlucky gringo trick.*

Grinning like a fox, she produced a big can of shoemaker's glue from her magical bag of tricks. The chemical stench was overpowering as she popped the lid with a long, deadly-looking screwdriver she also just happened to have in her possession. She proceeded to huff the horrid, eye-watering paste from a plastic bag. Within seconds, she was high as a satellite orbiting Alpha Centauri. Then, she began rambling about her mysterious little weirdo again.

"These e'stupid old *almofada*," she yelped, "he *so-oo* ignorant, Cigano!"

I stood staring at her, shaking my head.

"*Na moral, cara*, he really got de big obsession in his retard brain."

"Why's he so hung up on you, Narcisa? I mean, ya told me you never even had sex with the guy, so what's his deal?"

"Donno, mano. He believe de Narcisa got some kinda e'special lucky magic powers. An' he e'say he get it all de time de telepathic communications from me in de night when he no can e'sleep. He e'say he need me e'stay all de time around him for give it to him my occult powers!"

I lifted an eyebrow.

She laughed. "Is *truth*, Cigano! *Porra, cara!* From de first time he e'say it to me these e'sheet, I know de guy *maluco!* But maybe he no so crazy he gonna eat de dog e'sheet or burn all his mo-ney, so I e'start think, *hmmm*, an' I e'say to him, *'Okey, Doc, you gotta go an' bring it to me de jin-jin, got it? An' now you gotta do whatever little thing I e'say, got it? An' if you don' obey to me, then I gonna make de big curse on you, an' you really get fock up ba-aad, got it?'"*

I got it. Narisa was an emotional terrorist.

I stared at her in awe . . . *How does she get away with this shit?*

"*Papo serio, cara!* An' now de Narcisa got it de own personal *zumbí*, see? Hah! Is pretty good job for me, hein, Cigano? *Perfect, Max! Next?*"

Suddenly, she changed the subject. "*Oiii, Cigano!* You got some cigarette paper here? I wanna roll a big *basiado!* '*Peraí.* Maybe is better you make it de joint for me . . ."

"Ya can't do it yourself?"

"Hah! I too fock up to see good."

I kept gawking at her.

"De altered perception don' affect de human emotion an' feeling, Cigano, but is better when you got de physical help! *Crown crowwn, haha!*"

Her stoned eyes seemed to roll in different directions at once, like a shaken doll.

"Huh? Whaddya talking about?"

"De explanation only exist to confuse, bro, got it?"

Got it. Narcisa philosophy. Nietzsche on bad acid.

I cocked my head and sat watching, fascinated, as she dropped a handful of dirt-brown marijuana—stems, seeds, dirt, pocket lint and all—into a crumpled-up paper bar napkin she pulled from her jacket pocket. Then she proceeded to roll up the most crooked, fucked-up joint I'd ever seen. When she was done, the thing looked like a cross between a Fidel Castro cigar and a dried-out dog turd.

As she reached for my lighter, I wondered if she might set herself ablaze from the volatile glue fumes oozing from every pore, like a suicide bomber going to paradise in a flaming flash of glory. Narcisa lit up and smoked, then started coughing and choking like a tubercular old geezer. The stench of the burning weed filled the room like a diseased elephant's fart.

I ran over and opened the window.

After catching her breath, Narcisa rambled on about her dickless zombie. "One time, Cigano, these e'stupid *almofadinha*, he take one big acid trip. He don' never know it, bro, but I put de *micro-ponta*, de gringo LSD in his hamburger!"

"You dosed the guy with acid?" I laughed.

"Yeh, mano! But I never e'say nothing to him." She smirked.

"What th' fuck did you do that for?"

"Donno, bro, I just wan' make de researching onto his retard brain, for see how he gonna reacted, got it? An' then he e'start sing an' dance an' bark like de dog. Hah! But then he go on de real ba-ad trip, an' my e'sperimentation she blow up, *bum! Crowwn crowwwn crowwwwn, hah!*"

"So what happened?"

"Fock, Cigano! He e'start get all *paranoided*, an' he attack me an' try hit me, so I smash him *bum!* in his face an' I run away, go! Hah! *Crowwn crowwwn crowwwwn, ha ha! Next?* E'stupid old e'sheet!"

As she babbled on, I learned that, like everybody who gravitated into Narcisa's weird orbit, Doc was an odd bird in his own right; an odd bird who harbored dark secrets in his crooked little nest— despite the fact that, for all the world, he appeared a harmless little desk monkey with too much time on his hands.

According to Narcisa, he'd often bragged to her about murdering his alcoholic mother for her money. He'd supposedly held a home-made electric-chair-style headpiece fashioned from a frying pan and a toaster-oven to the old lady's head, zapping her with a fatal high-voltage jolt as she'd sat boozing it up in the bathtub.

I stared at her in disbelief.

"Yah, brother!" Her big eyes grew wider. "Is *truth*, these e'sheet! De Doc he tell me an' my friend Pluto at de Casa Verde all about how he done it! An' after he' kill de mother, he e'suppose to take de money an' send me to *europa* for de e'spensive gringo e'school!!"

"So what happened? Where'd all th' money go?"

She sneered. "Good focking question, bro. He was gonna e'spend it with me, but then he wanna celebrate, an' he go e'spend it for de e'stupid parties with his rich playboy friends! *Porra!* Every day he buy de e'spensive import whisky an' cigar an' fireworks. He even rent de circus clown an' dancing chimpanzee! He gone crazy an' use up all de money fast! *Fock!*"

She flashed an evil grin. "But then de big fancy playboy party all gone to e'sheet, cuz he e'start feel de guilt for kill de mother, an' he go even more crazy. He e'say she come back in de night for molest him, an' he can' go e'sleep no more! *Crowwwn crowwwwn crowwwwwn, ha ha!* He e'start cry all de day, an' he e'say I am de e'spirit channel to de dead mother! *Porra, cara!* He e'say to ever'body at de Casa Verde she come back from de hell inside de Narcisa for make de big revengence on him!"

"*Fala serio!*" I gawked at her. "Are you fuckin' kidding?"

"*Pois é, cara!*" Narcisa looked at me, wide-eyed. "Now I know is better I don' give him no more these focking *acido*, or maybe he gonna flip up an' kill me too! *Puta que o pariu! Porra! Que merda!*"

As I sat looking into her bulging, glue-addled, tripped-out eyes, I half suspected this Doc had made up the whole sordid story. Maybe, wanting to impress Narcisa and the other burnouts at the Casa Verde,

he was just trying to fit in there by offering up his own special nasti-
ness . . . *"Bet ya can't top this one, kids!"*

The more I thought of it, I could see someone like that weaving
such morbid tall tales, just to create some dark mystique to his life of
quiet desperation.

But who really knew?

Anything was possible, I figured, when Narcisa was involved.

12. NUMBING DOWN

"Don't talk, don't trust, don't feel."
—*Claudia Black*

One morning, after one of her regular mysterious weeklong disappearances, Narcisa showed up at my door, grinning like a hungry dog.

She proceeded to move right in on me, like it was the most natural thing in the world. I suppose, for us, it sort of was. I never asked her where she'd been as she strode in and started unpacking her knapsack. I didn't care.

By then, I sensed I might have been falling in love with her, but I was cautious to never slip up and show it—even to myself.

It was weird. Between us, there always seemed to exist some deeper identification, born of a deep, unspoken bond; an underlying sense of kinship. It was as if loving Narcisa were like loving some wayward, feral strand of myself; a distorted funhouse mirror image of my own brutalized, mangled, forgotten inner child, restructured into rude juvenile delinquent female form, with a crooked, charismatic smile of mischief at the end of her fuzzy pink tongue.

Even though I never told her, I always felt she was like some kind of a psychic Siamese twin; a wayward soul mate, floating free and aimless as a cryptic, psychedelic message in a bottle, forever bobbing out there, somewhere over the deep, turbulent seas of my world.

Now that she was back, I guess I'd assumed we'd just pick up where we'd left off the last time she'd been around—cruising the night for girls, on the prowl for new adventures.

But this time, things were different.

For one thing, there wasn't going to be any sex anymore—with or without the other girls. Once again, Narcisa had sworn off drugs . . . "*forever.*"

Whenever Narcisa abstained, she became especially cranky, taciturn and maladjusted. Now, true to form, she'd gone as frigid as the ungodly ration of milk shakes she consumed daily to chase down a mountain of chocolate bars, potato chips, pizza and other edible garbage she stuffed into her foul-mouthed little mug, bitching and complaining all the while. It was murder.

Over the years, I'd tried taking her to some of the AA meetings I went to—mostly when she was depressed and suicidal, consumed with self-pity and fed up with her miserable lot in life; moaning and groaning that she was done getting high. But she'd always fallen right off the wagon again, after only a few days.

It became a familiar pattern. As soon as she'd begin to feel a little better about things, she'd go get loaded again, and flush it all down the toilet—every single time. Eventually, she stopped asking me to take her to those meetings, preferring to rely on her own dubious "willpower" to stay clean; going it alone, white-knuckle style—until her next inevitable relapse.

She'd been on this latest "clean and sober" kick for days already by the time she showed up. She'd given up drugs "forever," she insisted. And of course, she'd become the usual grumpy, disgruntled little pain in the ass.

But this time was worse than ever before. She'd even gone fullblown Born Again Hare Krishna Vegetarian now, strutting around my apartment, parroting random phrases from the Bhagavad Gita, like some crazed evangelical television preacher, rummaging through my icebox and throwing out all the meat and cold cuts, even the expensive salami she used to love.

I had to beg her not to toss all my pots and pans out the window, which she claimed were infested with the tortured karma of "assassinated animals."

Narcisa was really on a mission. She wouldn't even let me smoke a cigarette around her anymore. All she wanted to do, it seemed, was bitch and moan and groan as she sat around on her lazy, disgruntled ass, whining and criticizing everything in sight, while she stuffed her angry little pie-hole with food.

The only time she calmed down for a moment was when she was staring bug-eyed into the little television I'd bought her after being nagged and ragged half to death about how "boring" everything was in Rio.

As I watched her sitting there, glued to the TV, I scratched my head, baffled, wondering how anyone could be "bored" when, for me, there never seemed to be enough hours in the day to do half the things I wanted.

Still, I sympathized. I knew Narcisa was sick.

Jittery and irritable without her drugs, she was suffering an edginess I knew well. It was a familiar symptom of the same mental Curse I'd struggled with all my life. And I knew she really needed help. Serious help. The kind of help an alcoholic or addict requires in order to live without their deadly medicine—at least if that's what she really wanted, as she kept insisting.

But I also knew there's no forcing anyone into recovery. People afflicted with addictions need to find some humility for themselves in order to recover, usually through pain, humiliation and utter desperation. So I just hung out, watching her struggle through the torments of the damned, battling on the volatile, solitary minefield of her own pissed-off, unsatisfied mind.

I knew it was just a matter of time before she'd blow her pretty little top again, then dive back into another stoned-out, anything-goes orgy of mindless debauchery. And I knew at least I'd get laid when that happened.

Maybe, at the end of her next run, just maybe then, I mused, she'd finally be beat-up enough to come back to the meetings and get some help . . . *Maybe next time* . . . After all, I knew from experience that all the drugs Narcisa took were just her way of self-medicating for a much deeper malady. The Curse.

Meanwhile, I sat around like a patient old alligator, watching, waiting through the long, stifling, frustrating, sexless vigil.

Somewhere around the fourth day, after the umpteenth cold-shoulder brush-off as she paraded around in only her panties, finally, I couldn't take it anymore.

"Lissen, princesa." I sat down beside her on the sofa. "If ya can't stand the idea of sex anymore unless yer high, y'know, I guess I gotta get used to it . . ."

She crossed her arms over her perfect little milky white tits and glowered at me, as if I'd just said something incredibly offensive.

"Look, I'm just sayin', Narcisa . . ." I shifted in my seat. " . . . I don't wanna be th' one to push ya into an early grave or anything, and I'm glad yer tryin' to stay clean and all, but . . . Lissen, princesa, I know ya didn't like the people at those AA meetings I took ya to before, but maybe if ya tried some different ones . . . I dunno, maybe you'd like the Narcotics Anonymous groups better. They got a good one over in Ipanema we could go t—"

"Menos, porra! I don' need it all you e'stupid self-helping e'sheet, Cigano! Shut de fock up an' stop all you e'stupid talk about de droga all de time! Just lemme look de television an' I gonna be fine, got it? Go get de Coca Cola, go!"

"Okay, whatever . . . Look, I'm really happy yer tryin' again, princesa, y'know, believe me . . ." I sighed, handing her a glass of Coke with ice.

She looked up at me like I was a bug she was thinking about killing.

"Look, I'm *glad* you're clean and all, even if it's not . . . *arrgghhh*, whatever. It's great yer stayin' straight, Narcisa. I'm proud of ya. The way you did drugs, it was totally killin' ya . . . But, shit, man, I got feelings too, y'know . . ."

Silence.

I stood there, shifting from foot to foot as Narcisa guzzled her soda and chewed up the ice cubes, glaring at me with that cold, empty look of contempt.

Shit! Numb as a fucking potato.

13. POISON IVY

"FAIR PLAY IS PRIMARILY NOT BLAMING OTHERS
FOR ANYTHING THAT IS WRONG WITH US."
—*Eric Hoffer*

After a long, awkward pause, I cleared my throat. "Uh, so . . . um . . ."
Narcisa stared into the television, ignoring me.

" . . . I guess I'm sorta . . . I dunno, I guess I'm kinda getting hung
up on you," I mumbled, feeling like a guilty little schoolboy caught
jerking off in the bathroom.

She just sat staring at the TV in frozen silence . . . *Cold as a stone
. . . Shit!*

I took another deep breath before stumbling ahead. " . . . And, I
whatever, that just makes all this kinda . . . weird for me, y'know . . . ?"

Silence. I shifted back and forth on my feet, watching her, waiting.
Nothing. She kept staring into the television.

"Look, princesa . . ." I went over and turned the volume down.
" . . . If ya don't feel like havin' sex with me anymore, y'know, without
all the drugs, I get it, it's cool, okay? I mean, look, I know yer pro'lly
all confused right now, and I get that, y'know . . . I know how hard it
is to stay clean, believe me . . ."

Silence. I waited. Finally, she looked up at me, tapping her foot and
scowling.

Whatever I was trying to say wasn't coming easy, and her cold, belligerent glare wasn't helping. I swallowed hard and stumbled forward.

" . . . But look, I gotta think about my own feelings too, baby . . . And this platonic shit isn't gonna work fer me, y'know? Not with ya staying here . . . Y'know . . . ?"

More empty staring. More uncomfortable silence.

Fuck this shit! Now or never . . . Just say it, man . . . Whadaya got to lose?

I took a deep breath, then I dropped the bomb.

" . . . Uh, so maybe it's time to just go our separate ways for a while . . ."

Nothing. She reached over and turned up the volume on her television.

" . . . As friends . . ." I added. " . . . Y'know . . . ?"

After another awkward silence, I turned the TV down again.

That did it.

After long days and restless nights of angry, sexless, affectionless tedium, all the coiled-up, angry springs she'd been sitting on, stuffing them down with food and TV, came flying up in my face like a plague of snapping rattlesnakes.

She leapt up from the sofa, spitting, hissing like a cornered wildcat. ***"Porra! Que merda!"*** She began storming around the room, snatching her clothes, stuffing them into her knapsack, yelling, cursing. ***"Is always e'same focking thing, porra, ever'where I go! Que saco! You just like ever'body else, Cigano! I no gonna sit here an' listen all these retard e'sheet about de love! You e'same like all de focking mans! Mesma merda de sempre! Arrrggghhh!!"***

I stood frozen in horror as she ranted on.

"You all e'say to me you e'stupid booll-e'sheets about de love an' you e'stupid feeling, an' then you go an' kick me out! An' now you e'say we gonna be friend! Que amigo, hein?! You nobody friend, Cigano! You don' care about de peoples, got it? Just cuz I don' wan' do whatever you wan',

then you e'say get out you focking house, an' you wan' be my focking friend? Arrrggghhh!"

"I *am* yer friend, Narcisa! And I always have been. But that don't make me yer fuckin' doormat! *Porra, cara!* I'm only human! Just cuz I don't kiss yer ass and tell ya whatever ya wanna hear like that old zombie Doc, it don't make me yer fuckin' enemy! I'll always be yer friend, princesa, no matter what, but . . ."

"What focking friend, Cigano? What is doormat, hein? Porra! You wan' throw me out on de e'street like de garbage, just cuz I don' wan' make de puteria with you all de time! Fock you! I never gonna do what you wan'! I prefer go e'stay with de focking Doc. At least he don' wan' only using me for de sexo! I prefer go e'sleep in de focking bushes or on de park bench or de beach then e'stay with you any-more! So fock you! You can fock you own self now, cuz these is de only fock you ever gonna get, e'stupid e'sheet!"

She was stomping around the apartment, screeching, knocking things over, breaking my stuff as she searched for some random misplaced item.

Her hairbrush! Jesus God!

Accusing me of stealing it, and using her hair to make some kind of black magic "gypsy love spell," Narcisa kept going, her voice trembling on the edge of violence.

"Why you teef my escova, hein!? Is no fair! Give it back my brush, Cigano! I wan' it right now, or I gonna break ever'thing in you precious home where I can' e'stay no more cuz you so egoista! Cadé? Give it to me, porra!"

She was possessed, screaming, insulting, calling me an evil gypsy spell-caster, throwing things onto the floor, raging, insane.

"Whoa! Take it easy, Narcisa." I stepped up to her.

"Vai tomar no cu com sua macumba de cigano de merda, viado velho!"

"Just calm down. I'll help ya look for yer goddamn brush . . ."

"Arrrggghhh!! Va se fo-der!! Porr-rrraaa!!" She howled, raking a stack of books off the shelf onto the floor.

That did it. I grabbed her by the shoulders and shook her hard, trying to contain her rage. *"Chega, porra!* Stop! Just calm th' fuck down, Narcisa!"

"Nao me toque, porra! Get you dirty hand from me, seu viado!" She jerked away, bearing her teeth, spitting like a poisonous viper. *"Don' you never focking touch me, e'stupid old pervert e'shee-eet!"*

I let her go like a burning log.

She stomped across the room and snatched my wallet off the table. In a flash, she was standing by the window, glaring at me, holding my billfold out over the street below.

"Hah! How much it gonna cost to you if I throw these e'sheet down now, hein?! All you e'stupid documentos, hein?"

My heart jumped into my mouth.

"Whaddya doing, Narcisa? Gimme my fuggin' wallet, man!"

She stood her ground, looking at me with a taunting little grin. *"Ahhh,* so now you wan' it back, hein? Well, you teef my thing, bro, so now I got you thing too, got it? Eye for eye! Hah! Okey! *Now* you got it! So now we gonna make de little negotiations, got it?"

I got it. Narcisa had the upper hand. I watched her and waited.

She let out a cruel little snicker. "I wan' fifty bucks . . ."

I just stared back, dumbfounded.

Her eyes blazed. *"You better give it to me de money, you e'stupid e'sheet!"*

"I can't believe this shit, Narcisa! I have no fuckin' idea what th' fuck ya did with yer fuckin' hairbrush, man! I swear to God!"

"Fock de God! An' fock you too, Cigano! Now you gonna

give it to me one hundred buck, got it? Or is bye bye to you focking carteira!"

Glaring at me, she held the wallet farther out the window, dangling it between two fingers as my brain cringed.

Fuck! It won't last two seconds down on the street! My motorcycle papers, my identity card, driver's license, phone numbers, documents, everything!

Jesus! Checkmate! She wins! Fuck it . . . I reached in my pocket, pulled out a hundred note and held it out, the way you feed a scrap of meat to a strange pit bull.

A gleeful smirk lit up Narcisa's face as she snatched the money and stuffed it into her jeans. But instead of handing back my wallet, she hurled it right out the window, singing, ***"Thank you come again!"***

Fu-uck! No-ooo! I felt my heart sink as I watched the wallet flutter in the air like a dying sparrow, before plummeting straight down.

Narcisa brushed past me and grabbed her knapsack, heading for the door.

As she reached for the doorknob, I grabbed her and spun her around.

Furious, I slapped her face.

Swaa-aaackkk!

She said nothing, but from her look of pure hate, I knew it hurt. It hurt us both.

She kicked her beloved television off the table with her big, heavy steel-toed combat boot. A sad little plume of smoke rose from the murdered squawk box as she stormed out the door and out of my life.

That was the last I saw of Narcisa. Something told me that this time, she wouldn't be back. Even consumed with regret, I realized right then that, even for all our uncanny complicity and deep, soulful identification, I was still nothing but a means to an end for her; a necessary evil. A man: a walking, talking penis, attached to a piggy bank.

And Narcisa could never respect any man.

By a stroke of luck, the watchful *porteiro* returned my wallet intact—minus the cash. But that was the least of my worries.

Regret was my constant companion in the days and weeks to come.

Narcisa's absence would become far worse for me than the depressing little tantrum that sent her running back out in into the bottomless night of another flaming circus adventure in her long, dangerous tightrope walk of the soul. Because one day she'd been there, overrunning my world like a wild invasion of squawking green parrots, filling my world with lust, obsession, sex, desire, passion, hunger, frustration, noise, and frenetic, urgent drama, eating me alive with her fiery, savage grace.

And then, in one sudden, violent flash, Narcisa was gone.

14. DANCING WITH MYSELF

"TO DARE TO LIVE ALONE IS THE RAREST COURAGE; SINCE THERE
ARE MANY WHO HAD RATHER MEET THEIR BITTEREST ENEMY
IN THE FIELD, THAN THEIR OWN HEARTS IN THEIR CLOSET."
—*Charles Caleb Colton*

When she ran off that day, Narcisa forgot to take her journals with her.

All those notebooks filled with mad, visionary poetry, pages and pages of her inspired, mystifying writings were still sitting on my shelf.

As the weeks passed without word from her, it hit me that she was really gone for good this time. Feeling increasingly guilty and confused, I started reading through her stuff, searching for some clue to her possible whereabouts.

I found nothing. One particular passage, though, would stick with me:

. . . ONE POSSESSES A SURE AND INDOMITABLE INTELLIGENCE, A SAVAGE LOGIC, A POINT OF VIEW THAT CANNOT BE SHAKEN. TRY TO BE EMPTY AND FILL YOUR BRAIN CELLS WITH A PETTY HAPPINESS. ALWAYS DESTROY WHAT YOU HAVE IN YOU. ON RANDOM WALKS. THEN YOU WILL BE ABLE TO UNDERSTAND MANY THINGS . . .

As time went on, those enigmatic words would come to represent for me the unencumbered essence of Narcisa, lingering on the hazy fringes of my memory, the night I'd first stumbled across her; two marginal shadows merging on a random walk in Copacabana. Or was it really so random? I wondered.

Since sobering up and embarking on a haphazard spiritual quest, I'd slowly come to trust in an essential intelligent order to all things, seen and unseen. The concept of casual, random occurrences was no longer a part of my reasoning.

From time to time, I would take out that notebook and read the mysterious phrase again, as if it might somehow sum up Narcisa's existence, bringing me some small degree of comfort in her absence. But it didn't. I missed her, the way you miss a pain that goes away, and with it, your whole concept of life.

Every other girl I went with after Narcisa would be little more than a weak, futile attempt to relive the furious magic and frantic, reckless fuck-the-world passion she'd brought me.

As time crawled by, I would come to fully understand that Narcisa had been a gift—a deadly, sweet-smelling poison that had blessed and cursed me with each day we'd spent together. And then, one day she was gone, like a wild, translucent, wandering phantom. A dream. Just like that. Gone. Like a ghost.

Bit by bit, I began to accept it, as one comes to accept a sudden, tragic death in the family.

About a week after she left, I shrugged off the sadness and began busying myself with the unfinished task of reconnecting with my lost, tangled roots.

I woke up alone and showered off the sweaty musk of the last night's hooker. I got dressed and puttered around the apartment. Then, around noon, I went out to continue rebuilding a relationship with the shadowy old city of my youth.

I walked the crowded downtown pedestrian alleys for hours that day, making small talk with strangers, street vendors, hawkers, merchants, beggars, gypsy fortune-tellers and whores. Sitting on park benches, people-watching, reading a newspaper, I was getting familiar with the world again; Ignácio Van Winkle, waking up from a long, lonesome heroin nod.

I'd always loved the teeming wholesale districts of the Centro, and its bustling shopping mecca, known as "Sahara" for its Syrian-Lebanese immigrants and the exotic wares they sold in tiny stores lining the cramped alleyways. Across the thundering Avenida Presidente Vargas was the big lofty old Central do Brasil train station, always swarming with frenzied human activity.

My heart rejoiced as I revisited all those spots. As a kid, I'd always been entranced by the lopsided little zigzag paths off the Rua Uruguaiana and the hoary old Praça Tiradentes, with its looming colonial statues and lazy Portuguese mosaic sidewalks. Those bustling urban labyrinths had once been my playground and school and family and home. Now I was back, experiencing it again; exploring all the enticing, obscure nooks and crannies of long-forgotten childhood memory.

Standing on a corner by the *praça*, staring at the ancient pool hall across the street, I marveled that it was still there after all these years; just as I remembered it—those shady back rooms, still frequented by thin Negro *malandro* hustlers in their old-time straw hats and suspenders; living photographs from another era.

Fascinated, I wandered over and peered inside, watching them moving around in shadows behind old-time patterned green glass windows; ghosts of Madame Satá and his/her murderous turn-of-the-century gang of transvestite bandidos. All the legendary crimes and passions of underworld daring and old-school *malandragem* were written in the dusty molecules of that enticing little time warp, floating in the musty air within, taunting me to decipher their haunting folklore language, whispering ephemeral tales of my own deepest roots.

The spirits were all around me now, letting me know I was really, finally home again, walking old, familiar streets, lost in the sights and sounds and smells of the surreal metropolitan funhouse of Rio de Janeiro.

For weeks, I spent my afternoons like that, trudging through those fertile memory gardens, plodding from *rua* to *rua*, store to store; taking long, solitary lunches at the little hole-in-the-wall working-class eateries downtown, bathing my senses in a nostalgic world of spicy garlic-swaddled beans-and-rice meals, strong dark coffee and cheap black-tobacco cigars.

After lunch, it was back to exploring my old haunts. I was that curious ten-year-old gypsy kid again; little Ignácio, out on his own little dreamlike quest, slowly awakening, desperate for any small scrap of a lost, abandoned youth he'd never quite gotten to live. Anxious to make up for it now, I was falling in love again; a strange, exotic new love affair with a city of fuzzy, forgotten dreams, searching for any little missing scrap of myself in the alluring rubble of people, places and things rediscovered on those magical urban walkabouts.

Soon I found myself even shopping for things, the sort of things I'd never dreamt of owning; little odds and ends and decorations for my pad. A picture to hang on the wall here. An extra pillowcase there. Some new towels. A frying pan.

For the last couple of years, I'd just been more or less camped out there; a rootless nomad, always ready to pack his bag and hit the road at a moment's notice. A restless, reluctant visitor; someone just passing through. Now, though, with Narcisa gone, I began claiming the place as a permanent residence.

At first, it felt a bit awkward, buying possessions for an apartment; my first real settle-down home ever—at least my first time living alone. I'd been married and shacked up, over the years, with an assortment of girls in the many places I'd lived since leaving Rio. For most of my adult life, I'd been what they call a serial monogamist— going from one steady affair to another, like a lovesick, hungry lost soul; but always repeating the same habitual codependent patterns, over and over again—forever expecting some new outcome with the next romance.

In truth, I'd really just been trying to dominate some other poor, misguided soul—either that or depending on the Other like a grabby little brat clinging to his mommy. In the end, they'd all turned out to be the same unholy alliance; one sweet, needy companion after the other; different names and faces—some lasting for years, even—but always marked by the same repetitive lifelong habits; the emotional equivalent of hijacking a revolving door.

Thinking about it, I recalled a phrase I'd heard at an AA meeting in Mexico City one day, early on in my recovery. *"Alcoholics don't form relationships; we take hostages."* That was me, all right. Einstein had defined that sort of behavior as insanity—doing the same thing over and over, expecting different results. Since getting sober, I'd had to face some unpleasant truths about my old ingrained attitudes. Now, for the first time ever, I was making a living attempt to really change; a conscious effort to grow up and learn to care for myself, physically and emotionally, like an autonomous, self-reliant adult—one of the prerequisites to any lasting respite from the self-destructive, mind-powered scourge that had plagued me all my life. After all the pain, loss and misery I'd been through with the Curse, I'd finally come to take the whole concept of psychic change as a matter of life or death. "Change or die." That's what they had said at those early AA meetings.

That compelling admonition had continued to evolve in my consciousness, until I'd come to accept it as my highest priority. And there I was now, trying to change and grow, living all alone, for the first time ever. Dancing with myself. Just me and little Ignácio. Just me and my shadow. Me and my ghosts. No more liquor, no more drugs, no more girlfriends or shack jobs to lean on or boss around or live

in constant daily combat with; no more "significant others" to pull
the focus away from myself and my search for psychic healing. No
more Narcisa. Nobody. No distractions; nothing to divert me from
my daily meditations, reading, writing and solitary reflections, my
new friendships and new sober life; my confused, slowly mending
heart and mind.

I was finally all alone; wide awake and stone-cold sober, back in
Rio, the very place where little Ignácio had grown up too fast, and
never drawn a sober breath.

At first, it all felt sort of overwhelming, all that unfamiliar solitude, while trying to live a straight, crime-free life—especially in a
place so haunted with brutal old phantoms. But Providence provides.
When I'd first got out of prison in Mexico, I'd been obliged to do some
honest manual labor for the first time in my life. That had equipped
me with a little stash of money. Those humble savings, together with
my meager inheritance from Tia Silvia, were just enough to keep me
going; a nest egg, buying me time to pursue my writing, and even
keeping me honest—at least if I lived modestly. For the most part, I
did.

I didn't require much, really; just some food, and a little company
from the many cheerful hookers packing the street corners of the city
at night like chattering packs of coked-up spider monkeys. Those girls
really took the edge off all that self-imposed introspection and solitude; that and the lazy, sun-drenched afternoons at the beach, bumping into old and new friends and acquaintances in that bright, sandy
democracy where rich and poor and black and white are all a big,
animated human stew under the blazing Carioca sun.

For a few blessed hours every day, I would lose myself in that
sprawling brotherhood of half-naked strangers, diving into the crashing waves, like a giant washing machine for the soul. It was essential. Those life-affirming swims in the sparkling summer sea were the

highlight of my days, before going over to sit on a rock by the waves, in quiet contemplation; writing in my journals, composing short stories and even beginning a long-projected novel.

For the first time ever, creative juices were really flowing for me, as I sat at my regular spot near the fisherman's shack in Copacabana—the same place I'd met Narcisa two years before. Now I had plenty of time to spend at my lovely outdoor *escritorio*, with its magnificent view of the ocean and the rolling waves below, alternately diving in and out of the rushing summer breakers, and scribbling into a notebook. Later, I'd go home and sit at my table by the window, often working till way past dawn, editing and transcribing all the day's work into the laptop I'd saved up and bought myself as a three-year-sober anniversary present.

I began spending time with my few surviving childhood friends too. With Narcisa out of the picture and plenty of time on my hands, I'd finally gotten in touch with Luciana. A recovering addict herself now, she became my new best friend and an angel of mercy. She and her sister Veronica and I began hanging out a lot. With their easy laughter and warm, unconditional love, sharing a fond complicity of communal memories, we became the kind of close-knit little tribe I'd always longed for as a kid, but had never known. I was home at last.

A couple of times a week, Veronica would have us over for dinner, sometimes with a few other friends—artists and writers and musicians. Luciana and I would usually wind up the evenings sitting by the waves at one of the beachside kiosks we both loved over in Copacabana, drinking coconut water and talking about philosophy, recovery, art and travel, gossiping and laughing about the past, sometimes till long after midnight.

Out of nowhere, I'd acquired a pair of delightful sisters. Suddenly, I was a happy bachelor; a single man, self-sufficient and autonomous.

I even started to cook in my little kitchen, in order to save money. All in all, I was doing all right.

Yet there was still something missing. Like an itch on an amputated limb, always begging to be scratched; something invisible kept nagging, tugging at my heart like an impatient, hungry child; an elusive, diminutive shadow, darting around corners in the busy downtown crowds, troubling my sleep, as the cars and buses of morning whined and rumbled and tumbled and raced their frantic paths to nowhere outside my shuttered windows.

Narcisa. Yes. I still missed her. There were days when I thought of her and couldn't stop thinking, until it was almost unbearable. Even in the best of times, those were the worst times too—the deep, dark, cold and lonesome moments, feeling the stinging longing of wanting to talk to her again, to apologize, to hold her, to smell her, to hear my sweet little friend's crazy, lilting singsong laughter, her endless childish stream of mad, poetic, apocalyptic nonsense. I wanted to go out and look for her, to find her somehow and bring her back into my life.

But, alas, Narcisa was gone.

15. WAKE-UP CALL

Longing for news of Narcisa, as the weeks dragged by, I fell into the habit of sleeping with my cell phone on—just in case she ever called.

Early one morning, a week short of two months after her disappearance, the phone began ringing. As it buzzed in my ear like some evil overgrown insect, I regretted having left that horrible ringer on . . . *Narcisa! Shit! After all this time, of course she decides to call right when I'm fast asleep! Goddammit! Typical . . .*

Groggy, I fumbled for the accursed instrument and pushed the green button.

"*Pronto!*" I croaked into the phone, glancing at my watch.

Jesus! Nine o'clock . . . And I just got to sleep an hour ago!

An efficient man's voice, crisp and abrasive, jolted me out of my stupor.

"*Alô, ahhh, bom dia. Isto é o . . . Cigano?*"

I instantly hated him.

"*Eu!*" I grunted.

"*Ahh . . . Bom dia, senhor!*" The irritating voice grated against my eardrum.

I was about ready to curse him to hell . . . *Fucking telemarketing shit-flies buzzing in my ear! Bastards!* But something held my tongue . . . *Wait!*

No one calls me "Cigano"! That's what Narcisa calls me . . . Everybody else calls me Ignácio . . .

I said nothing. I just lay there, fuzzily assessing the odd little early-morning mystery.

"Ahhh . . . Alô? Bom dia?" The hateful disembodied voice insisted.

"Que bom dia, porra?!" I spat into the phone, exasperated. "What's so fuggin' good about it, man? Jesus! I'm sleeping! Whaddya want? Who is this?"

"It's Doc, Narcisa's . . ."

Doc! Narcisa's . . . what?

" . . . Narcisa's guardian."

Guardian? Who is this fucking freak? And why's he calling me now? How'd he even get my number? What does the little shitbird want with me?

Wait! Maybe he knows about Narcisa! Maybe she told him to call!

I sat up, wide awake. "Oh, yeah . . . Right . . . *Oi."*

"So sorry to have, ahhh, awakened you . . . ?"

"Uh, yeah, uh, sorry . . . Sleeping . . . So, uh, I guess you're looking for Narcisa?" I mumbled, hoping maybe he'd take the hint and tell me something.

"Ahhh, well, no, not really, Cigano . . . I was just calling to say hello . . ."

Hello? To me? At nine in the fucking morning? Goodbye's more like it!

"Oh, well, uh . . . Lissen, uh, Doc. I haven't seen Narcisa for a while now." I was already fluffing up my pillows, getting ready to hang up and sink back into dreamland. "I'll tell her ya called though, uh, if I see her around sometime, okay?"

"Well, ahhh, actually, I was hoping to speak with you, Cigano."

"Eu?"

"Yes. Just to chat, you know. But I'd prefer to meet up and talk in person."

I was dumbfounded.

Meet up to chat . . . in person? I don't fucking think so!

" . . . Narcisa has always spoken very highly of you, and I'd really love to meet with you! Do you think we might get together for lunch this afternoon?"

Meet with me? Get together for lunch? What is this shit? Narcisa spoke "highly" of me to this little prick? She sure never spoke too highly of him!

After establishing that he hadn't been in touch with Narcisa, I blew Doc off, telling him I'd call him later. Then I went back to sleep.

Somehow, "later" never came.

I didn't give it another thought. The next day, though, he called again. I recognized the number this time and didn't pick up.

As the day went on, I forgot about it. I didn't have time to be curious. I was keeping busy with sweaty, hectic mornings on the downtown streets, running around town, hustling for cash—followed by those long, hot summer afternoons, sitting alone by the seaside, writing, reading and swimming, usually till after dark. Later, I'd go visit the dingy, piss-reeking old whorehouse alleys of Vila Mimosa, the ramshackle old red-light district down by the port. After years in jail, I relished every lusty minute of it, rocking the saggy, cheap hotel beds with lively, athletic chicks young enough to be daughters of the whores I'd once laid up with there, decades before, in another fuzzy, faded dream.

I rarely made it home before dawn those days. By late afternoon, I'd be back at the beach, sitting up on the rock, reading, writing, bodysurfing and staring out over the breathtaking ocean view; then home for a cool shower, a nap, a cheap bowl of *mocoto* stew in the nearby favela, before going out to a movie; maybe a meeting or coffee with Luciana or some other acquaintance, and then I'd be out on another midnight prowl, like a leather-clad vampire bat.

I was enjoying a simple bohemian bachelor routine, at last. But without the hard liquor and drugs this time; without all the fights, brawls, beatings, arrests, cops and jails. Without the bone-chilling, debilitating hangovers. Without the bleeding misery and torturous bouts of suicidal despair.

A new life.

Those early days back in Rio were good times. Times to cherish forever—a living apology to the shabby little ghost of that poor, sad, dirty-faced street kid, Ignácio. A day at a time, I was learning that it's never too late to have a happy childhood; a new history made of long, productive days, and fun-filled nights of easygoing, unrestrained passions—a living amends to the long-lost kid inside me for all the failures and fuckups of a turbulent, unhappy past. I was enjoying a second chance at life; a new incarnation I would remember fondly this time around—even if my little nest egg was steadily evaporating. But I didn't worry about even that. I just kept staying active, doing odd little hustles here and there for extra cash.

The closest I ever got to my old life of professional larceny was practicing a few simple, harmless scams, like buying cheap fake designer watches from the wholesale Arabs downtown to sell to the *gadjos* and gringo tourists by the beach.

All in all, things were all right. The wolf wasn't at the door yet—even if I sensed he was lurking around the neighborhood; but I'd cross that bridge when I got to it. I still had enough money to get by for a while. And I didn't want for much. So, day by day, I just kept going, maintaining a positive mind-set and keeping happily and usefully occupied with my new sober existence.

When Doc called again the next day, I blew him off again.

After that, he began calling every day—two or three times a day sometimes.

I couldn't figure what his angle was, but as the phone kept ringing at odd, inconvenient hours, he was starting to get on my nerves.

Jesus! This guy's as pushy as a Vila Mimosa whore! What does he want?

One day, after I had forgotten to turn the ringer off, he awakened me again; this time from an early afternoon nap—right after a vivid dream of Narcisa.

This time, I picked up and spoke to him.

In a half-dream state of nostalgia, longing for a Narcisa who only existed in dreams anymore, I was hoping the repugnant little creep might be able to offer me some insight to her whereabouts.

With some reluctance, I took him up on his invitation to meet for lunch.

16. INSECT TALK

"I WONDER WHETHER IT IS POSSIBLE FOR AN INDIVIDUAL WHO
HAS NEVER HAD A PROBLEM—IF THERE ARE ANY INDIVIDUALS
LIKE THAT—TO HAVE ANY SIGNIFICANT INSIGHT INTO THE
PROBLEMS OF INDIVIDUALS WHO DO HAVE SERIOUS PROBLEMS."
—*Wendell Johnson*

As I pulled up to the curb in front of the cheap local self-service cafeteria Doc had suggested, I spotted him strutting toward me from a shabby little plaza to my left. His uneasy, slightly arrogant gait gave him the overall bearing of a nervous, self-important chicken. He seemed to have been standing there, lurking, waiting for me, like an anxious stalker, even though I was a few minutes early.

Greeting me with an overbearing, obnoxious air that was a bit too friendly for my liking, Doc stood before me, looking me over from dark, crafty eyes that barely concealed a ratlike glint of mad obsession. His short, rapid breathing and skittish hands were not those of a wholesome person. My gut impression was of some slithery closet pederast or chronic masturbator; an unctuous, unhealthy being who had never in his miserable, lonesome life engaged in sexual intercourse . . . *Narcisa sure nailed it when she named this guy Dickless* . . . Just looking at him gave me the creeps.

Against my better judgment, I shook his trembling outstretched hand. His pallid left-handed grasp was unusually firm, but clammy as an eel.

"*Ahhh*, it is so good to finally meet you personally, Cigano!"

He leered, bearing down on me like some soul-sucking nightmare creature, eating me alive with those ugly, hollow bughouse eyes. Even hearing him call me "Cigano" made my nutsack shiver. This Doc reminded me of a giant mosquito; and he seemed to have no recollection of our previous unpleasant encounter.

I didn't bother reminding him. "Have ya seen Narcisa?" I blurted.

He made a big fuss of studying a shiny fake Rolex on his wrist, as if he was trying impress the world as a busy impresario or something. "*Por favor!* Let's sit down and eat, *meu amigo!*" He took my arm with a grand gesture, expertly shifting the focus. "And please, do have *anything* you'd like! Your meal shall be my treat!"

Shrugging off his grip, I looked over the cheap, ratty little feeding hole he'd chosen for our big encounter and restrained myself from spitting on the floor. The way he made a point of calling me "my friend" and playing the big shot made my bullshit detector tremble . . . *Danger* . . . It was clear this guy had some kind of agenda, a need to butter me up or impress me for some reason. But as I sized him up, I realized it was probably nothing quite so sinister. Just another sad little people-pleaser, a weak-minded, natural-born ass-kisser, trying too hard to be liked.

I knew the type. Looking at Doc, I flashed back to when I was a kid, remembering how my mother used to have this one old *gadjo* trick she'd always bring home. Sometimes, he paid the rent when things got tight—which was often toward the end of her crazed, unhappy life.

Leonardo. A real asshole. That old sucker had become a regular fixture in our dysfunctional little excuse for a home, always slithering around like a sneaky old rat, acting all fatherly, calling me *moleque* and *filhinho*, forever trying to bribe me for details of the old lady's erratic comings and goings. He'd never gotten far with me, though. I hated old Leonardo, and avoided him like the police when he was around.

After the old lady checked out, he'd shown his true colors. When he came and tried to take back all the cheap trinkets he'd bought her, Tia Silvia jumped on him like a wildcat. She almost threw the bastard down the stairs head-first. That was the last I ever saw of him, but it was the beginning of my lifelong distrust of two-faced, passive-aggressive do-gooders like the one standing before me.

Struggling to ignore my distaste for Doc, I tried to stay focused. I still needed to keep him talking long enough to squeeze some information out of him.

We went and got our food from the cafeteria line, then sat down at a corner table, away from one of the ubiquitous blaring restaurant televisions that Narcisa always sat right in front of whenever we went out to eat together.

"So, how do you know my daughter, *senhor*?" Doc smiled like a jackal, almost causing me to choke on a mouthful of cauliflower.

"*Daughter?* I had no idea you were related to Narcisa!" I stared into his shifty eyes. "I mean, she told me she met you on the street in Lapa a few years ago, said she hardly even knew ya . . ."

He waved his hand dismissively. "My goodness! Well, it is really more of a spiritual paternal bond that I have with our dear Narcisa . . ." Doc chortled in a phony, condescending "confidential" tone. "We actually do communicate quite profoundly, and a very great deal at that . . . But on a purely *paranormal* basis, a special sort of mental telepathy . . . So I suppose you might say she's really more of an *adopted* daughter. My *spiritual* ward, you see?"

I didn't see. Narcisa had told me she'd met the little freak one day when he was reciting corny poetry and bumming change on the street; that he had inspired her pity with some sentimental sob story. And she, feeling sorry for such an obvious loser, had tried to help him by giving him leftover meal scraps from time to time, and even paying for a cheap rooming house once so he could get cleaned up to go look for a job.

That's where his obsession with her had apparently begun.

He squirmed with a sigh when I queried him on the topic. "Well . . . *ahhhh*, when I first met Narcisa-ahhh, I was indeed suffering from a deep, prolonged depression. A profound and terribly complex existential crisis. I was quite low in funds as well, I'm afraid, practically destitute, actually, and I was so discouraged, I just didn't care if I lived or died anymore. *Ahhh*, well, my friend, Narcisa was the only person who treated me with dignity! She has always had a good heart, you know, Cigano, despite the terrible hardships she's had to endure, poor dear . . ."

I put my fork down and planted my elbows on the table, looking into those swirling, unwholesome insect eyes as he continued with another deep, world-weary sigh. "*Ahhhhh* . . . You must know, of course, that her mother is an alcoholic, and a common prostitute, no?"

I shrugged.

" . . . Yes! A terribly low-class, ignorant woman! An illiterate peasant!" He flashed a haughty, yellow-toothed sneer. "She claims to be some sort of evangelical Christian today. *Hurrumph!* Well sir, she was only thirteen years of age when she gave birth to Narcisa, and, well, poor Narcisa observed that filthy, immoral creature doing things I'd rather not speak of with hundreds of men, right from the time she was born. A terrible role model for a young girl, I'll tell you that! *Ahhhhh.* Why, when Narcisa was only six years old, an angry client attacked her mother with a knife. He stabbed the dreadful woman ten times in the chest, almost killing her right in front of little Narcisa! A terrible incident for a mere child to have witnessed! Narcisa was actually the one who had to call for help to save the wicked creature's life! Did she ever tell you about all that?"

I gave a slight nod, not wanting to divulge much. I was there to listen.

Narcisa had indeed dropped hints about an unstable, ultraviolent childhood, not unlike my own. But, like me, she played it cool when talking about her past. That, and the fact that she could lie as artfully as any full-blooded gypsy, had kept me from pressing her for details. Silence had always been my code too.

Doc, on the other hand, was a real talker. He sighed and prattled on with pompous authority, his voice trembling with pent-up emotions. "*Ahhh,* you know a child can simply never recover from such terrible, traumatic experiences, Cigano!"

I kept quiet and nodded again, feeling like a nuthouse head doctor.

" . . . But there's more, Cigano. Much more!" He waved his hands around with the frantic air of a self-righteous, indignant reformer. "*Ahhhh!* The men who raped Narcisa and took her virginity when she was only twelve were acquaintances of her mother's! *Ahhhhh!* They also introduced her to cocaine for the first time! So you can clearly see that Narcisa's unfortunate upbringing was solely responsible for warping her values. She's just another innocent victim of this morally corrupt, lawless modern society, Cigano!"

I winced with distaste at his words. I didn't buy the innocent-victim pitch. Even with all my own shitty childhood baggage, I didn't consider myself a victim of life. I alone was responsible for my actions and attitudes today. People like Narcisa and I may have once been victims of extreme abuse and trauma as children, sure, but there was no place in my philosophy now for shedding such maudlin pity on anyone—including myself. I knew the tired-out old victim story is the surest road to hell for an addict. I'd played that pathetic card for most of my life, and it had almost killed me. An addict with an excuse is like a monkey with a machine gun. This Doc, however, seemed light years from that concept.

Curiosity outweighing my growing urge to walk out and leave him sitting there talking to himself, I dummied up and nodded as he rattled on.

" . . . Well, after that sordid little affair, my friend, Narcisa quickly rebelled against everything, and then she fled home for good. Of course, she soon became a prostitute herself. It's quite fascinating how the fruit always seems to fall so close to the tree, *amigo*, is it not?"

I cringed at the way he called me "friend." Between sighs and unpleasant, fastidious grunts as he savored his crappy food, Doc powered on in an obsessive litany of detailed accounts, spilling a rancid cornucopia of minutiae onto the table.

As I examined the strange, bitter fruit, it all fell into place with random bits and scraps that had slipped out in Narcisa's stoned-out ramblings over the years.

In a sickening flush of identification and compassion, the mystery of Narcisa all began to make perfect sense to me.

17. BORN TOO LOOSE

"THE FACTS ARE TO BLAME, MY FRIEND. WE ARE ALL
IMPRISONED BY FACTS: I WAS BORN, I EXIST."
—*Luigi Pirandello*

As Doc's monotonous mosquito voice droned on in my ear, it seemed to be infecting my soul, like some unwholesome, insidious virus. And still, I listened, clinging to each word falling from his vile, sluggish lips like an old witch's curses.

When Narcisa was just a little girl, he sighed, her grandfather used to give her and her sister cheap, sugary *paçoca* candies in exchange for French kisses, while he pulled his withered old pud and stuck a wrinkled finger into their bald little pies—just as he'd done years before with Narcisa's mother. Later, Grandpa would teach the girls other little "tricks" for candy treats, bubble gum and coins—tattooing onto Narcisa's impressionable young Alpha Centaurian mental matrix the earthly concept of sexual favors in exchange for material gain as the established norm for intimate human interactions.

Doc let out another deep, irritating sigh. "*Ahhhhh* . . . When I first met our young friend, I instinctively knew that she was in desperate need of a benefactor, a protector, and I simply made it my business to see that nothing like that would ever happen to the poor child again."

When I queried him as to how he'd gone from such noble aspirations to being the recipient of Narcisa's financial charity, he began to squirm.

Between annoying melodramatic pauses, he stammered a vague explanation. "Well, *ahhhhh*, I was . . . I found myself rather lost at the time, Cigano . . . Practically homeless, actually, it is true, yes, but . . . *ahhhhh*, well, I'm terribly ashamed to make mention of all that now . . . It's simply appalling to think that I could have ever fallen so low . . . *Ahhhh*, it's an awfully long and complex story! Perhaps I'll tell you more about my own life sometime . . ."

What, and brag about how you killed your own fucking mother, you malignant little pustule? Just get on with it, fucker!

I could feel sweat gathering under my shirt. I looked around the hot, stuffy little eatery, shifting my aching butt in the hard metal chair, suddenly longing to be riding along the beach on the motorcycle, with a cool ocean wind in my face.

"Anyway, Cigano, Narcisa was only thirteen when I first found her. She was already sleeping with many wealthy foreigners in Copacabana, and earning quite good money at it. Far too much for a foolhardy child like that to possibly know what to do with! Well, sir, I gave her good advice on how to invest her ill-gotten gains, but she just squandered it all away on drugs, spending a small fortune on those filthy 'punk anarchist' delinquents she associates with! *Harrumph!*"

The sputtering air-conditioning unit above the door conked out and died, once and for all. My brain was melting as Doc droned on.

" . . . One of her clients, I recall distinctly, was a European tourist. Italian, I think. The fellow had gone back home and left behind a whole suitcase filled with expensive clothes. That's what Narcisa told me, anyway, when she gave me all those beautiful imported designer suits one day. Or perhaps she just stole them from someone. Who could possibly tell? Our dear Narcisa has always been quite larcenous, you know. I'm certain you've been exposed to that side of her character . . . ?"

Declining the invitation to get into it, I shrugged.

Doc sighed and went on. "Well, *ahhhh*, the point is, she gave me a treasure chest, Cigano! She even paid for a room for me, gave me money to eat, and then she presented me with all those wonderful suits and shirts! After that, I was able to rejoin the workforce and find myself a dignified job, the same steady employment I have to this very day. Narcisa's kindness frankly changed my life, Cigano. The kindness of an innocent child who has literally been through hell, who by all rights should be dead from all the terrible abuse and degradation she's suffered!"

The walls were closing in. Still, I listened on, hypnotized in horror, as that droning nasal voice led me down into a dark, humid well of nightmarish images, piecing together the unhappy jigsaw puzzle of Narcisa's past.

Like myself, Narcisa was a bastard child; something she'd never known, according to Doc, until the fateful morning she'd slunk home at dawn, cowering in postcocaine jitters, after being used like a rubber fuck doll all night long by her mother's drug-peddling cronies. That same day, Doc informed me, the man Narcisa had grown up calling "Daddy" had disowned her for the crime of being born. In the midst of a heated argument, he had revealed that she wasn't his "real" daughter, but just an accident of birth; the result of some drunken infidelity. Narcisa was only alive, the stepfather shouted, because her mother couldn't afford an abortion.

As her stepfather dismantled all remaining scraps of her fragile self-worth that day, Narcisa's mother had stood by in stony, cow-faced silence. That's when Narcisa officially went Bad Seed. She took to the road with a burning rage in her heart, running like a singed cat from her backward provincial hometown, never to look back.

Again, I found myself relating to her . . . *Poor kid! Raped and betrayed by her own fucking people, then tossed out like a used rubber!*

I recalled how she had spoken of spending her early teenage years raising hell in the drab interior city of Resende, ransacking cemeteries and conducting satanic rituals with dug-up human skulls and the blood of small animals.

I thought back to her tales of breaking into crypts and Masonic temples. I'd always related to Narcisa's hilarious juvenile delinquent exploits, having been there and done all that as a homeless, runaway, throwaway street kid myself. Now Doc was giving me the details, filling in all the blanks. After leaving home, she'd gone to look up her biological father and found out a few other things she'd have been better off never knowing. Among them, she'd learned that her real father was dead. Her paternal seed had been an alcoholic; a barfly, a criminal and third-rate drug smuggler, a notorious local cokehead; a stoned-out, womanizing lowlife who'd died in prison, leaving Narcisa without even a proper surname. And he'd known about his daughter all along, but just couldn't be bothered to contact her before going to hell.

Shit! Poor baby! She was even abandoned by a ghost! Her late father's relatives treated her like the unwanted bastard she was. As Doc talked on, I could picture some ignorant small-town family shooing my poor little friend away like a stray cat in the garbage, as her mother tried to rein her back in with fire-and-brimstone pie-in-the-sky demands that she accept the Lord Jesus and repent . . . *What a mess!*

Narcisa, of course, wanted no part of any "family" anymore, Doc sighed. Rather than submit to a life of creeping provincial boredom and mediocrity, she'd stuck her thumb out on the highway and sold her leggy adolescent body to truck drivers for the few coins needed to eat and survive on her way to the hard-knock dogfight streets of Rio. Any world she could find must have looked better to Narcisa than the hell she came from. I could relate.

Drugs were a regular staple of the hippie ghettos and anarchist punk squats dotting the long, hard road to perdition like errant gypsy camps. Sex, drugs and rock and roll. Violence. Rape. Abuse . . . *Perfect, Max! Just like home sweet home!*

By fifteen, after crisscrossing the countryside for years, often alone, sometimes in the company of other teenage runaways, she'd eventually covered as much ground as the seasoned truckers and traveling salesmen she met up with along the road. But the only thing Narcisa had for sale was her gangly-limbed, fresh-faced innocence—or whatever was left of it.

Doc looked across the table, rolling his mad eyes. "Unfortunately, Cigano, by the time I found her, Narcisa was already a hardened, streetwise adolescent prostitute in Copacabana. In many ways, it was simply too late by the time I made her acquaintance . . . *Ahhhhh!* I must say, though, she was always far more attractive and popular than those other ignorant streetwalkers. Infinitely more intelligent, resourceful and well-informed, as well . . . *Ahhhhh*, well, as you can imagine, she inspired a good deal of envy from those dreadful trollops! She simply refused to conform, even in that sordid, low-class criminal subculture! Narcisa, you know, has always been unable to get along with others, even with the other prostitutes, mostly poor, ignorant, illiterate mixed breeds and Negros, all the inferior races . . ."

He stopped and looked at me with pride, as if waiting for me to shake his hand as a fellow member of the Aryan Brotherhood or some shit.

I remembered Narcisa telling me of this guy's dark, ugly Nazi leanings, of how he'd always declared himself a big admirer of "real leaders" like Hitler, Mussolini and Pinochet. Still, I said nothing, waiting for the whack-job to go on.

Taking my stone-faced silence for tacit complicity, Doc grinned like a mule, then picked up his demented musings. "Perhaps," he speculated, playing cafeteria psychoanalyst, "she simply hated those low-class whores because they unconsciously awakened traumatic memories of her own prostitute mother."

With her light-skinned, sassy good looks, youthful health, native zeal and charisma, Narcisa soon gravitated up the ladder of high-priced *garotas de programa*, granting her access to a more discerning world of prettier, younger, whiter, top-shelf call girls; a better grade of whores, catering mostly to well-heeled gringo tourists at the luxury beachfront hotels of Copacabana and Ipanema.

That was around the time she first met this Doc and "changed his life." And that's when he'd decided Narcisa should become the purebred psychic progeny he'd never had. Whether she wanted to be or not.

He stared across the table at me with the eyes of a rabid puppy, scrunching up his face like he was taking it in the ass. "*Ahhhhh* . . . I've done everything I could possibly think of to get that unfortunate youngster away from that disgusting life of crime, vice and homosexual perversion. I've really *tried* to convert her into a decent human being, Cigano . . . *Ahhhhh* . . ."

I wondered if he was even aware he was implying his beloved "daughter" was less than a "decent human being," for being a whore. I had a sudden urge to pick up my uneaten plate and give it to him right in his smug, effeminate, Nazi-loving kisser . . . *Knock this puritanical, gay-bashing, haughty old Boy Scout right off his fucking high horse!* But as he whined on, something stopped me.

As I watched him, I thought he was going to start crying. He looked crazy; a full-time victim, a well-intentioned bleeding martyr, buckling under the weight of Narcisa's heavy cross. I couldn't help almost feeling sorry for the poor, misguided little bastard as he sighed again, shaking his head like a broken-down old horse shrugging off flies. Then he continued, telling me so many things about Narcisa that soon my own head was reeling in a confusing, unpleasant sentimental stew.

Finally, I couldn't take it anymore. "Lissen, Doc," I blurted out, swallowing my distaste for everything about him. "I'm really worried about Narcisa! We had this stupid fight a coupla months ago, then she just split. I haven't heard from her ever since. She's disappeared . . ."

As I talked on, he stared at me with a weird, longing expression.

" . . . Look, man, it's been tough for me not knowing what's become of her. I haven't heard from her for months now . . . You seem to know Narcisa better than anybody. Where do ya think I might be able to find her? I really gotta talk to her, man. Have you got any idea where she mighta gone . . . ?"

Silence.

After a long, suspenseful pause, he rubbed his womanish double chin and spoke. "You mean you didn't *know*, Cigano? You don't know what's happened?"

Happened?!?

My gut went cold.

18. ALL THAT GLITTERS

"ALL SINS HAVE THEIR ORIGIN IN A SENSE OF
INFERIORITY, OTHERWISE CALLED AMBITION."
—*Cesare Pavese*

My blood froze in my veins. "Know *what*, man?" I croaked.

Narcisa! Please God, no! Please don't tell me she's dead! No-oo!

Silence exploded in my ears.

"Where is she? Tell me! Please . . ."

Doc's beady eyes bored into my face for a painful, mute eternity, as if he was trying to assess whether I was serious. I watched him in silence, waiting.

Finally, I spoke again. "*Por favor . . .*"

Time stopped. He stared back at me across the table.

Then, like a crooked old tomb, his mouth creaked open in hellish slow motion.

"*Ahhhh . . .* Well, Cigano, Narcisa's in New York."

"New York? *What?*" I almost shouted, feeling my stomach going weird.

"She married a foreigner, the banker, that John Gold fellow, you know."

I didn't know. I dropped my fork onto my plate and pushed it aside. "*Como?* Whaddya talking about, man? What foreigner? How? When?"

"But . . . Well, I just assumed you already *knew* about the banker, Cigano. You and Narcisa always seemed to be so close . . ."

"Seemed" close . . . Past tense . . . And with just so subtle an air of conde-scending, resentful spite . . . Bastard! Doc was feeding on my pain from the bomb he'd just dropped on my heart. I stopped breathing and glared at him with twin daggers in my eyes.

Silence.

I could feel my guts trembling with frustration, anger, confusion, panic. I had a sudden mad urge to jump up and punch him in the face.

"*Ahhhhh* . . . Well, I just assumed she must have told you, Cigano. After all, she *has* been involved with this fellow for years now, of course, and, well, *ahhhhh* . . . she finally married him, and then they left Brazil together . . ."

I stared at him.

"You mean to say you really didn't know, Cigano?"

"I knew nothing about it, man. *Nada!*"

He looked at me with a mixture of feigned pity and thinly dis-guised triumph, letting out another long, melodramatic sigh. "Well, *ahhhhh*, I'm terribly *sorry* to be the one to be telling you all this, Cigano . . . But I suppose you really *should* know . . ."

I wanted to scream . . . *Stop calling me Cigano, you shit-fed little parasite!*

I knew he wasn't the least bit sorry to be telling me any of it as he launched into a smug, spiteful new accounting of events and details that shattered my heart like a beer bottle dropped on a dirty, cold whorehouse floor.

When Narcisa was sixteen, right around the time I'd met her, somewhere during those first ribald days and weeks we'd spent together—and unbeknownst to me—Narcisa had met a man. Well, a boy, actually.

Doc smirked, rubbing it in. "He appeared to be a nice enough young fellow, Cigano. An investment banker from Israel. He'd been living and attending graduate school in New York City. Very intelligent, well-mannered young fellow, you know, despite his obvious . . . *err* . . . ethnic shortcomings."

"You *met* this guy . . . ?"

"Oh yes!" Doc beamed as I fought to keep from spitting up my half-eaten meal in his face. "Narcisa brought him around to the office where I work. It was just after they started dating. She introduced me to him as her father!"

What? Dating? His obscene words nailed my soul to the cross . . . *Her father?*

"I was happy to meet him, actually." Doc smiled. "After all, I suppose one really can't be entirely to blame for being born a, a . . . *Jew.*" He scrunched up his nose at the word, as if pronouncing some incurable disease. "*Ahhhh*, yes, well, I even took the two of them out to lunch. After all, I knew that, realistically, well, let's just say that a girl in Narcisa's position can't exactly afford to be terribly picky, you know. And, well, I wanted to show my, my . . . solidarity. Very nice, well-bred young fellow, in his early twenties, I'd say. A college student with a promising future, you know, upstanding family, all that. He'd come to Rio on his spring vacation, and then he met Narcisa at the beach in Copacabana . . ."

The beach?!? She's always hated the beach! We used to fight like convicts whenever I tried to drag her to the beach! Must've been the Copacabana ho-stroll . . . That's about as close to the water as she'd ever get.

They rarely had sex, Doc implied, prattling on about a "platonic love." But apparently, Narcisa had hooked her victim up with some of her nubile young colleagues, trapping him in a soul-numbing mind-control bubble.

Doc shook his balding, skunk-striped head with theatrical distaste. "She even boasted to me how she actually encouraged her new boyfriend to have sexual relations with those disgusting strumpets while she *observed*, Cigano!"

Everything he was saying made sense. I knew Narcisa hated sex, at least with men, but sometimes she liked to watch. That's what drugs and other young Copacabana whores were for to her, to make it all tolerable. I sat listening with morbid fascination as Doc's monotonous drone plowed through an exploding minefield of details.

According to him, Narcisa had herself convinced she loved this gringo.

No way! How? She couldn't! She's not just gonna fall in love with some guy . . . Narcisa doesn't have those skills in her bag of tricks! Forget it!

Shifting in my chair, I listened as Doc rattled on like a clamorous funeral procession, plodding toward the moldy old tomb of Betrayal.

Even as I dreaded what he would tell me next, I found myself leaning forward at the table, staring into the hell-pits of his eyes, needing to know more.

19. MAGIC TRICK

"The first impossibility required of the adept in
Black Magic is that he should love God before he
bewitches his neighbor; that he should put all his
hopes in God before he makes a pact with Satan; that,
in a word, he should be good in order to do evil."
—*The Book of Ceremonial Magic*

Apparently, their courtship had lasted for two whole years. As Doc told the story, I sat listening in shocked, befuddled silence, thinking back over the years of my relationship with Narcisa . . . *The whole time she was reeling him in, she was in and out of my life, and my bed! And I never even suspected . . . Shit!*

During each of her regular ninja-like disappearances, I'd always figured she was just running around town as usual, peddling her sweet ass, or seducing other young chicks. That was just Narcisa. Why would I give it a minute's thought? She always came back to me, eventually, so what did I care? I'd never dreamt of her having some kind of weird secret love life. And certainly not with some guy.

But now, sitting across a table from her Dickless Old Cushion, with a New York blizzard raging in my stomach, it all started to make sense. As Doc talked on, I recalled something Narcisa had said to me the last time we'd been together. I'd thought nothing of it at the time. Now I realized it had been significant. A clue, whizzing right past me.

We'd been hanging out for days on end that final week. I'd needed to go out one afternoon to take care of business, some little money-making scheme.

When I'd told her I had to run out for a few hours, Narcisa had pitched a violent tantrum. She'd started yelling, threatening, screaming that if I didn't blow off everything to take her shopping, I could forget ever seeing her again.

I was shocked. At the time, I'd already been trying to justify all the time and money I was murdering with her frigid little ass as she bombarded me with absurd demands for full-time attention. Narcisa had begun turning into some sort of soul-sucking energy vampire; testing me, teasing me, slurping away my lifeblood. As Doc rambled on, I replayed the whole scene in vivid detail—the words I'd said to her that day, pleading for compassion from the criminally insane.

"Whaddya want from me, Narcisa? Jesus! All you ever wanna do is sit around and watch television and stuff your face all day. I just gotta run out and take care of some stuff! What's the big deal? I been with ya every day and night for a week! I can't just keep you company all the time! I feel like a babysitter! Anyway, how am I supposed to take ya shopping if I'm broke? I gotta go out and make a little money, ya know? I can't be two places at once!"

Narcisa's wild-eyed reply seemed especially significant now.

"Forget about de two place, Cigano! I wanna man who gonna take care of me! All de time! I don' care about money! I don' care if I gotta go live under de focking bridge with somebody! I just don' wan' e'stay alone! Nunca! Got it?"

I hadn't got it. Not then. But now, looking into Doc's ugly, leering face, the sound of Narcisa's angry words rang in my ears like a revelation. That kind of neediness coming from someone as headstrong and self-reliant as her had seemed cryptic at the time. Now I realized she'd been giving me that bitch-beating just to see how far she could push me.

She'd been testing me!

All at once, the penny dropped. It wasn't that Narcisa didn't want to depend on anybody. She just didn't want to have to reciprocate. Ever.

Of course! She was trying to turn me into a slave! A mind-control zombie, another Doc! Narcisa! The living, breathing epitome of infantile, self-centered egotism! I must've failed the test, and then some dumb-ass, clueless little gringo comes along! Bingo! A new, improved, clueless, wealthy doormat! Perfect, Max!

As Doc rambled on about Narcisa's elopement with the mysterious young foreign banker, I thought back to another time, way back in the beginning, when, in the middle of the night, her cell phone had started ringing; someone calling from a weird long-distance number.

Narcisa had reached over the bed and grabbed the phone out of my hand, then started bitching out some guy in English for "leaving her all alone"; she told him she'd found "somebody else" to "take care of her," and that she never wanted to see him again. Then she'd hung up, turned the phone off and gone right back to sleep.

At the time, I'd figured it was just some little hooker-gringo-mind-fuck game. The usual ho-stroll drama routine. I'd never given it another thought. Until now.

Now I realized the call must have been from him. Her Magic Gringo, this John Gold the banker! *She musta been raking the poor guy over the hot coals all along, even back then. She was slowly cooking, tenderizing, preparing her victim's tender pink gringo heart, getting ready for the Big Feast. Poor bastard!*

"I wanna man to take de care of me. All de time!" Sure she did! That's all she ever wanted! A Knight in Shining Armor! Santa Claus! Daddy! A husband! A high dollar, full-time trick! "I don' wan' e'stay alone! Nunca! Got it?"

Suddenly, I got it. Narcisa's unquenchable need for attention had the power of a hardy tropical weed breaking through a brick wall.

"One thing I'll tell you, Cigano . . ." Doc interrupted my unhappy musings. "Like most goddamned Jews, that Israeli boy must have been extremely well-off! My goodness, the way he flew back and forth to Rio every month just to see her, and always staying at the most expensive hotels in Copacabana, always at Narcisa's beck and call. My God, how do these dirty Hebrews manage to control so much of the world's capital?"

Doc continued ranting about "dirty, money-grubbing Jews." I said nothing as he painted a sickening picture of long-distance phone calls, emails and weeklong visits; days and nights of merciless emotional blackmail, mental torture, drama, fistfights, infidelity, breakups, death threats, drunken, stoned-out partying and cruel, frigid, sexless mind-control power plays.

" . . . *Ahhhh*, I had to go to the *delegacia* in the middle of the night more than once to negotiate with the police and get them both out of jail after she destroyed the Jew's five-star hotel rooms in Copacabana!" He beamed at me, as if expecting me to hand him a medal or something. "And there were some *terrible* incidents, believe you me! One time, at the Copacabana Palace, of all places, she actually threw a television out the window, right into a swimming pool full of people! My goodness! Can you imagine such a thing? She could have maimed someone! Well, sir, there was *quite* a fuss over that little incident, I'll tell you . . ."

As Doc prattled on, I had to stifle a grin, despite a growing knot in my gut.

" . . . The poor fellow couldn't speak a word of Portuguese, of course, didn't have the slightest idea how to make an 'arrangement' with our police here. But he always paid in the end. All the same, I was the one who had to get out of bed in the middle of the night to go and sort things out for them. They always called on me, every single time there was trouble. And there was always plenty of trouble, believe you me, whenever that silly Jew came to visit. And do you think either one of them ever thanked me or offered me a centavo for my troubles?"

Assuming it was a rhetorical question, I shrugged.

"*Pooh . . .*" Doc snorted like an old woman. "After he went away, Narcisa would stop by my office several times a day, begging to use the computer to read all his silly emails. You know one can never say no to her, of course! That word's simply not in her vocabulary. Well, sir, sometimes there would be more than twenty emails. The Jew was really taken with Narcisa! I'm sure *you* know how charming she can be, at least whenever she *wants* something! Ha!"

I had to look away as he poked at me with his mad eyes, like a spiteful old queen.

" . . . She never wrote him back, though, of course. She would just use the office phone to call him collect when she wanted money sent. And never so much as a 'thank you' to me, naturally, much less any sort of gratuity! Ha! Well, sir, eventually, my employer put an end to the calls because of all her shouting and vulgar language. I'm certain you must know what a foul mouth that one has. Narcisa was absolutely brutal to her young suitor!"

After another portentous pause where I had to avert my eyes again from his foul gaze, Doc sighed. "*Ahhhhh.* I honestly can't imagine how even a *Jew* could ever put up with that sort of treatment long enough to actually marry the little trollop! My God! Aren't there any girls in New York? Seriously! I couldn't believe how he kept coming back to visit her like that. He must have spent a fortune in airfare alone! Not to mention all the other money he threw away here, all the expensive presents, always dining out at the finest restaurants, hotels, excursions, rental cars and all the rest! Never once invited me to join them, of course . . ."

Doc scrunched up his nose, describing the frequent brief visits from Narcisa's well-heeled Prince Charming. She would always be left alone again, though, he said, at the end of another weeklong honeymoon whirl, reliving those same old stinging childhood wounds.

I could see a pattern. Narcisa, left all alone, abandoned, again and again, flaunting all the expensive trinkets the gringo bought her under the noses of every jealous hooker in Copacabana, generating more envy and resentment, before trading them off, one by one, for drugs.

As soon as she turned eighteen, Doc said, they were married in a simple civil ceremony. She got an expensive emergency passport issued at the airport, then packed off with her fancy new husband, off to gringo-land.

Everything I was hearing suddenly explained all those mysterious weeklong disappearances . . . *Of course! Narcisa must have been with her mark! She just couldn't wait for her big chance! How not? Marriage would be her magic-carpet ride out of here! The gringo was a living, breathing, walking, talking escape hatch from the dirty old pista. From Rio. From her past. Her life. Her ghosts and demons. Herself.*

Following a whirlwind monthlong honeymoon in Tel Aviv with her new husband's respectable family, it was off to the Land of the Free: America.

After that, Doc had lost contact with her.

Having found out all I could, for better or worse, I made up an excuse to bid the Dickless Old Cushion farewell. I stood up and got out of that nasty little roach-hole in a hurry.

That was the last I would see of Doc for quite some time.

O ver the months to come, the mystery of Narcisa began falling into some kind of linear order in my consciousness. Like they were broken artifacts in a ghostly archeological dig, I pieced the clues together into a perfect jigsaw puzzle timeline of fuzzy, half-forgotten events. Again and again, I kept going back to our last week together, remembering how nervous and antsy Narcisa had been in the days before she'd flipped her lid and split. It all began to add up as I thought about what had been happening all along, right under my nose . . . *And all this time I was so sure she'd just taken off on the road with some other young chick or something!*

Sweet Narcisa! My prodigal, bug-eyed Alpha Centaurian Space Goddess, run from an impoverished provincial backwater to Copacabana, seeking a shiny new path along her long, hard road of earthly exile. And now she'd done it at last, manifested it all.

A banker named John Gold.

John, as in Trick. Gold, as in All That Glitters.

Only Narcisa could pull off such a perfect poetic sting! Yes. When it came to the hustle, she was never just a mere garden-variety hooker.

Narcisa was Art Personified!

20. CAPTAIN SAVE-A-HO

"HE THAT WOULD EAT OF LOVE MUST EAT IT WHERE IT HANGS."
—*Edna St. Vincent Millay*

After that day, I didn't hear from old Doc again.

Narcisa was a ghost, haunting the shadows of my memory. When she didn't return to Rio, over time, like a ghost, the image of her started to fade. I began to forget her. Finally, I accepted the loss of Narcisa and let her go. I got on with my life.

If I ever thought about her at all anymore, I just pictured her destroying her fairy-tale marriage, then limping off to die somewhere out in the world, without a trace.

I couldn't see it going any other way for someone like her.

I mourned Narcisa's passing, and then I moved on. But, in some illusive, forgotten little corner of my soul, I always lingered behind with my fuzzy, faded memories of her, visiting them, from time to time, in an improbable little dreamworld where we'd once shared a few half-forgotten hallucinations. At times, I tried to reconjure the image of my long-lost, lovely little friend; mostly when I wandered the dirty old streets of the Prado Júnior red-light district, down at the ass end of Copacabana, late on hazy pre-Carnaval nights.

It was well past midnight on such a long, foggy summer evening when I stumbled across Narcisa again; almost a full two years after my fateful lunch with Doc, and more than three years since I'd first met her a lifetime ago.

I'd been out on the prowl, rambling through the familiar prostitution jungle of Copacabana's furtive underbelly. The *zona*. The hostroll; whores out looking for trade, and lonesome, wandering men out looking for company. Clusters of snappy-eyed teenage *garotas* standing in shabby yellow streetlight shadows. An army of horny, fugitive ghosts, occupying the lazy late night air, lounging on corners of narrow streets leading up the hill to the other world. The hidden world. The world behind the surface: the world of the favelas, where cocaine is king, and skinny, gun-toting slum boys with thick gold ropes hanging against bony brown chests stand leering at an angry moon; shadowy figures covered in rude tattoos, ruling the deadly ghetto alleys behind the tall white buildings of the Avenida Atlantica, while the other city sleeps.

Watching the cars creep by in the tired, muggy, late-night heat, I edged the old Yamaha to the curb. I got off and walked along, smoking a cigarette, passing the outdoor tables crowded with gringos and whores; bars little Ignácio used to cruise like a hungry young wolf, skimming tips from saucers, a tiny, fleet-footed shadow, scanning the chairs for a dangling purse to dash off into the night with. Up the darkened side streets, drunken gringos stumbling out of short-time hotel doorways, feeling warm and fuzzy after an hour with a bright-eyed mulatto hooker, were always easy to pluck as groggy chickens.

Reveling in a humid stew of memories, I lingered awhile in front of the old Holiday Bar. I was chatting with a cute little whore with fiery black eyes and a razor-sharp red-light grin, when, over her shoulder, I spied a familiar shadow.

I did a quick double take.

Narcisa!

She stood out through the humid mist like a blurry white icon.

It sure looks like Narcisa . . . Fuck! It is! It's her! It's gotta be!

There she was. Standing all alone, huddled in a ratty, torn purple bomber jacket. Leaning on a parked car on the greasy old sidewalk in front of the whorehouse. She was shaking, and seemed to have been crying.

I couldn't believe my eyes . . . *Holy shit! It's really her!*

As I wandered over to where she stood like a statue of Pride with its head hung low, I realized she didn't even recognize me.

She didn't seem to notice much of anything going on around her. Edging closer, I could see she looked all strung-out; dirty and disheveled, shivering there in her own dark little world, mumbling to herself, demented and emaciated; defeated, humiliated by life.

As my eyes met hers, I could see that the girl I'd known before was gone. This one was different. Older. Crazier. Down-and-out. Almost four years after first meeting her, Narcisa was finally shattered. Lost, abandoned and burnt-out.

But she's alive! Thank God!

I stepped up, smiling. "Narcisa! What are you doing here?"

Silence.

Blank-faced, she stared back for a fuzzy eternity. Finally, she let out a long, weary sigh. "What it look to you like I do in these place, hein?"

I stood before her, grinning like a farmer.

As her answer registered, she spoke again in a meek little tone.

"*Oi, Cigano.* Is good to see you, bro."

"You too, baby. Ya look great!" I lied.

She rolled her eyes with a crooked little smile, but said nothing more.

"Well then," I leered, "I guess if you're, uh, straight up selling it out on the *pista* here, I'm gonna get to be your next lucky customer."

"I can' charge you for de *programa*, Cigano . . . You my friend . . ."

I laughed. "Well, if yer giving it away, wrap it up and I'll take it, *amiga.*"

"You know better, Cigano! I gotta get de *grana* tonight. Narcisa need money. I got, how do you e'say, de e'spenses. Real high de e'spenses for me now . . ."

I nodded. Having smoked plenty of crack myself over the years, and having seen it take so many others for the long, hard ride to hell, I knew all about Narcisa's "expenses." One look at the pemature wrinkles and dark bags under her sunken eyes told me the whole sad tale. Still, I wasn't going to let her go.

I heard myself speak again. "All right then. *Bora nessa!*"

"How much you gonna give me, hein, Cigano?"

"Whatever it takes to keep you around for the night, Narcisa. We got some catching up to do, *né?*"

She nodded and hugged me shyly, gratefully, melting lopsided into my arms as we staggered over to the motorcycle together.

I didn't know it then, but that was going to be "It"—one of those larger-than-life, destiny-defining moments that hit you and your world can never be the same.

I was just happy to have found her . . . and sad for Narcisa at the same time. As we got to the bike, I stopped. Turning around, I looked into her eyes and told her she was still pretty.

She cocked a skeptical eyebrow at me. "You e'same like de *abutre mãe*, Cigano, you know it?"

"Whaddya mean, baby?"

She shot me a shy little Mona Lisa grin. "For de mama vulture, her own baby always de most beautiful one of all de bird, got it?"

I got it. I felt blessed and flattered by the sudden casual acknowledgment; an offhanded nod to our oddball spiritual kinship.

So she knows it too, even after all these years . . . Fuck! I guess love really is blind . . . Deaf and dumb too . . . Yep . . . Good old Captain Save-a-Ho . . . That's me.

I had no choice but to take Narcisa in that night.

As if following the dictates of a predestined script in some eternal cosmic drama, an unavoidable little play whose outcome was written on some vaguely familiar, faraway star, Narcisa had no choice either; no other option but to follow me home like a hungry stray mutt.

21. FATEFUL REUNION

After a long, passionate fuck, we kicked back on my sofa together. Just like old times. But the whole thing felt different now. Narcisa was different.

I studied her face in the shadows of the room, like someone trying to decipher the secrets of the universe . . . *She's changed, poor baby . . . Totally wrecked!*

Somehow, though, Narcisa was even more attractive to me than ever before. She looked almost angelic now, in some deep, untouchable, soulful way.

I couldn't bring myself to press her for any account of the last two years of her life, and none was forthcoming. I just sat there beside her, caressing her knee in the dark, musky, after-sex languor of the moment.

The lazy sound of the overhead fan stirring the air, Narcisa settled back against my chest, as if it was the only safe place left in the world. I ran my fingers through her long, greasy brown hair, petting her like a big, beautiful, feral cat.

Finally, I broke the spell. "It's been a long time, baby."

Silence.

"*Na moral, meu. Puta saudade,*" I murmured. "I missed ya, y'know . . ."

We sat in silence for a long time more. Then, finally, Narcisa began to tell me about the events that had brought her back to Rio—back into my arms.

"I miss you too, Cigano . . . I miss Brazil . . . I miss de Rio . . ."

"When'd ya get back?"

"To Brazil, maybe one or two month . . . I think . . ." She gave a confused little look, then went on in a husky, childish tone, almost a whisper. " . . . Maybe is three or four month, whatever . . . I donno . . ."

I could see she was lost in time and space, struggling to find herself. I'd been there. I said nothing. She sat beside me, just breathing. It was a moment that could last forever. I was in no hurry.

After a while, I invaded the silence again. "Why didn't ya call?"

Narcisa shrugged, as if only just then daring to ask herself why she hadn't been in touch. "I wanna call you, Cigano . . ." She sighed.

I felt her firm white skin trembling, twitching like a street cat with fleas.

" . . . I only come back de Rio for couple days now, you know . . ."

I played dumb. "Where were ya?"

"For long time, I e'stay de Nova York . . . An' then I was in São Paulo for couple month after. But I don' got you phone number. Don' got nothing. I loose it all my possession, first day I come back, loose ever'thing in de street in São Paulo, an' then I don' got no mo-ney or even de *documento, pasaporte*, nothing no more! *Nada!* I just e'stay homeless on de street long time there, like de beggar . . ." She trailed off.

Silence.

"*Fock!*" She cried out, as if suddenly remembering what had transpired. "***They teef me!*** First focking day I get to de e'stupid São Paulo! ***Filhos da puta!***"

"What were ya doing in São Paulo?" I asked, bringing her back

"I fly to there from de New York City, Cigano . . ." Her tone sounded pained, as if recounting the details of a nightmare.

Narcisa stopped talking again and reached over to light a cigarette. Silence. I watched her, saying nothing, waiting.

Finally, with a sad little moan, she inhaled, then sighed out a long cloud of smoke. "*Porra, cara,* I still got it de new cell phone an' de money, American dollar, all de pretty clothes from New York. I go out for drink de wine with some punks an' then I pass out on de e'street, an' when I got up, *bum,* they teef it all my thing! *Que merda!* An' then I gotta e'stay in these focking e'sheet place! *Porra!* An' I e'stay an' e'stay an' I e'stay there, bro . . ."

She contemplated her cigarette, as if debating if it was safe to say more.

"So what happened then?" I prodded.

"*Nada.*" She pursed her lips, shaking her head. "I just get tire of de São Paulo, so I e'say fock these place, an' then I come back to de Rio, go. *Next?*"

"How'd ya make it all the way up here from São Paulo?"

"Hitchhike . . . *Porra, que azar . . .*"

She fell silent again, brooding, smoking her cigarette down to the filter.

Finally, she stubbed the butt out in an empty cup on my coffee table and went on. "After I loose all my money an' thing in São Paulo, bro, I just get suck down inside de big cement dragon there, an' then I spit out on de e'street again. *Porra!*"

Her sad little singsong tone droned on, her words blending with the lazy, hypnotic *whooooosh* of the ceiling fan, the silent music of the moment. As Narcisa unburdened herself, I filled in the blanks. Confused, too impatient to deal with a simple airline connection to Rio, what else would she do but go out and get drunk with a bunch of local street kids? She'd lost all her stuff, then dove straight into the cold, gritty, heartless streets of São Paulo, a dark compulsion moving her frantic little steps like a broken marionette.

" . . . When I wake up an' no got more nothing, I just e'say fock it! I go right to de Santa Ifigênia, near to de Antiga Rodoviaria, you know it these place, Cigano?"

Santa Ifigênia . . . Shit!

I stared at Narcisa, rubbing my eyes, as if I could stop the visions in my head. Sure I knew the place. Knew it all too fucking well. Crakolândia.

Crack Town.

22. CRACK TOWN

"São Paulo. That's where evolution has really been pushed to its limits. It's not even a city anymore, it's a sort of urban territory that extends as far as the eye can see, with its favelas, its huge office blocks, its luxury housing surrounded by guards armed to the teeth. It has a population of more than twenty million, most of whom were born, live, and die without ever stepping outside the limits of its terrain. The streets are dangerous: even in a car, you could easily be held up at gunpoint at a traffic light, or you might wind up being tailed by a gang. The most advanced gangs have machine guns and rocket launchers. Businessmen and rich people use helicopters to get around almost all the time, and there are helipads pretty much everywhere, on the roofs of banks and apartment buildings. At ground level, the streets are left to the poor—and the gangs."
—*Michel Houellebecq*

Narcisa talked late into the night, telling me of her time in São Paulo; long, lost months trudging the tragic depths of that throbbing apocalyptic megalopolis, scrounging around in the shadows of the infamous skid-row Crack Town, down by the old, abandoned bus terminal.

I sat listening in silence, shaking my head. My poor little friend had clearly paid a dear and painful penance for the sins of her failed flirtation with the American Dream.

"Porra!" She spat on the floor, then went on, as if describing some terrible movie she'd been subjected to. "São Paulo, these de only place in de whole world where I ever e'smoke so much focking crack I don' even wanna e'smoke it no more! Crazy place, de Crakolândia, Cigano! So many different drug dealer there, one hundred *traficantes* in every street, an' always de big Chevrolet Blazer full up with de cops, all de rifles pointing out de window, all de night they just sitting at every corner, watching, but don' do nothing. *Fock!* What de fock they even doing in there?"

"Maybe just waiting around, y'know, for getting payoffs from people?"

"Hah! *What* focking peoples, hein? No focking *peoples* in there, bro! Only de Crack Monster. Hah! Nobody know even nobody else focking *name* in these focking place, got it? In de Crakolândia, they know about only one thing, de *dado*, de big e'square-shape crack rock, e'same like a big dice, *cara*! One big *dado*, always e'same quantity, e'same size, *bem servido, ta ligado* . . . In de Crakolândia, for fifty reais you get de real big dice, like these, so, sooo much!" She held up her big sooty thumb and forefinger, indicating a massive crack rock.

I whistled. "Fuck! That's enough to kill a fuckin' rhino!"

Narcisa's latest fall from grace had really taken her down this time; all the way down into the dull, soul-swallowing dungeon of Crakolândia.

As she rambled on about São Paulo, it all played out on the screen of my mind. My poor, wild-eyed little friend, stuck in that monsterous drug-slum, crawling like a crippled white lab rat through the dismal, death-blackened, dead-end crack alleys of Santa Ifigênia.

Santa Ifigênia. The same merciless hell-pit I'd once been stuck in. A place of total darkness, the only light provided by cruising police meat wagons, trolling the night for cadavers.

Crakolândia.

As Narcisa talked, I conjured up the shady figures of dark, dingy urban despair, moving in the blighted shadows of my memory, like crippled phantom tree sloths; haunted, lost souls of the damned, firing up cheap, formaldehyde-laced crack rocks in sooty alleyways, trudging along in a dull, endless procession through the Valley of the Shadow of Death. In a flash, I was there again, reliving my own tortured fall, down, down into that stinking psychic purgatory—seeing it all again in the frantic, flashing light in Narcisa's eyes. Filthy concrete mazes of narrow, greasy, dead-end alleyways; a world of creeping shadows, the darkness punctuated only by the sad little flickers of cheap plastic lighters.

As she spoke on, my mind's eyes watched the whole vivid replay of hellish images; the befuddled, huddled, subhuman mummies of Crakolândia, lurking in a long, senseless nightmare of perpetual concrete night, wrestling with the specter of doom in ratty makeshift tents of tattered newspaper and shit-encrusted plastic garbage bags. Dregs of humanity, unwashed and demented, amputated from society, cut off from life like abscesses from the pallid arms of dead junkies' shambling, rambling, wandering ghosts.

"*Porra, cara!* I never get so low down in de life before till I go these focking place, Cigano! Only thing I listen inside my head de whole time de e'same e'stupid song, over an' over. De Doors, '*This is de enn', my only frien' de enn'...*'"

I pictured Narcisa there, shuffling through a cold, dark season in hell, just as I had done decades before; back in another lifetime, another nightmare.

Choking back tears, I looked at her. "Why'd ya stay there so long, Narcisa? I mean, what did you do every day?"

Even as the words left my mouth, I knew it was a stupid question.

It didn't matter. Narcisa needed to talk. "Whatever, bro. Nothing to *do* in there, Cigano! *Porra!* Time don' exist in these focking place, got it? You do only e'same e'sheet all de day. Just go de one corner, get de rock, then run run, go de other corner, e'smoke e'smoke, run run, go. Then back de next corner, e'same thing, like de focking rat! '*This is de ennn'...'*"

I watched her face in ghostly silhouette as she mumbled the eerie song lyrics. Then she fell silent. For a long while, the only sound was the soft, steady hum of the overhead fan.

Finally, she spoke again. "De whole time I e'stay there, I know it gonna be over soon, bro, cuz I know I gonna dead in these e'stupid rat e'sheet place. An' I don' even care no more, don' give e'sheet for nothing, got it? Just e'smoke! *Nada mas!* Only e'smoke an' wait for de end come. *Porra, que merda!*"

I could feel the soul-numbing futility she experienced there. Narcisa, tormented by loneliness, self-loathing, guilt, regret. Her big, triumphant return from the great American Dream, all reduced now to a long, lost weekend in hell. Months of new traumas piling up on top of old ones... *Poor baby!* I couldn't stop the visions marching across my brain as I pictured my sad-faced, lonely little friend limping along the grimy gray pavements of São Paulo's cold, dull neon forests, like a deranged, depressive little meat puppet, sinking down, down into the shadows of that faceless, teeming slaughterhouse of souls.

As she narrated the horror movie playing in my head, I didn't ask how she paid for her monster crack habit. I didn't have to ask. I could see it all reflected in her eyes, like some rancid delirium dream; Narcisa selling her emaciated, crack-ravaged carcass to cabdrivers and lonely old men for the cost of the next cheap hit.

She let out a painful little groan. "So that's it, Cigano. An' then I just e'stay there like that . . . I donno how long de time. Forget about de time, bro! Time e'stop. Forget de New York, forget de Rio! Forget ever'thing else. No more past, no more future, just be in de Crakolândia, like de dirty old ghost. De *zumbí*, got it?"

I got it. I nodded. I knew.

" . . . Sometime, de taxi driver, they give it to me whole ten for de quick *boquete* in de car, an' then I got enough to e'smoke . . ." She trailed off again. Silence. Narcisa was thinking, remembering, putting the pieces back together.

When she went on, she spoke more softly, as if describing something that happened to someone else. " . . . An' you know, Cigano, I never even got rape. No even one time . . . Cuz in these Crakolândia, de thing work different, got it?"

I didn't get it. I knew Narcisa was no stranger to rape, but her casual mention of it in such a surreal context seemed especially odd. I just looked at her.

She seemed to sense my next question. "Nobody in these focking place wanna know about de sex. *Não importa o sexo!* Only wan' de crack, *mermão*, de *droga*, got it? Ever'thing is a case of violence if de crack she no good. Only de *droga* mean anything in there. When de drug she good, is all peaceful. When you got some mo-ney, you can get de good drug, an' then you just rent de little cubicle in de building for only five buck for a couple hour, an' then you can get out from de e'street an' go e'smoke you stash all alone. E'smoke till you ear she e'start ring like de police siren! Hah! But when you no got de mo-ney, bro, *fock*, then you gotta go e'smoke on de street with all de Crack Monster peoples!"

I asked her if she'd had any trouble with the cops, remembering my own ultraviolent days in Crakolândia and its sinister, brutal netherworld of beatings, muggings, stabbings, shootings and lootings; the professional thugs armed with heavy, long wooden clubs, coming down the sidewalk every morning to clear the crack zombies out when the local shops raised their noisy metal shutters, opening for business.

Narcisa seemed to be thinking for a moment, remembering. Then, her eyes darkened. "One time I get de big *problema* in there, Cigano, when one e'stupid guy try an' sell it to me de bad drug, he gimme de focking mothball for e'smoke, an' then I choke up an' almost dead . . ."

"Ya smoked a chunk of fuckin' mothball? *Fala serio!*" I grimaced, wondering how much punishment one person could take.

"Yeh, bro. Make me *so-oo* sick. *Afff!* Then I get piss off an' go to de focking guy what sell it to me these e'sheet. Hah! I cut up de focker face with de broken bottle! An' then all de *policia* come from nowhere, *whooooooop!* An' all de Crack Monster peoples run away fast, go, go, an' only they catch up on me alone! *Fock!*"

"What happened?"

"*Nada*, mano. Just de usual terror. They make me take off my shoe an' all de clothes in de street, an' then de one real ugly fat cop, he put de *pistola* in my mouth an' e'say I gotta give it to him de *boquete*, de blow job to de gun, an' they all laugh laugh laugh. They e'say they no wanna see me again, if I don' e'stay away, they gonna throw my cadaver in de river!"

I winced at the image of my poor little friend being stripped and taunted like an animal, humiliated and bullied by a gang of hard-faced, beefy street cops, all armed to the tits, standing around mocking her, threatening her unhappy little life.

" . . . These São Paulo cop, he don' give e'sheet for take de mo-oney for let you go either, Cigano, cuz he got it already too much cash from all de drug dealer. Nobody wan' no trouble in these place! Daytime, all de Crack Monster peoples gotta e'stay off de e'street an' wait like de *vampiro* for de night. *Porra!*"

I remembered it all from my own miserable, strung-out days there. She was telling me nothing new, just reminding me of a dark, sinister netherworld I knew too well. Narcisa's present was my past. A living hell. I said nothing more. I wanted to let her keep talking it off, like bleeding an infected wound.

"De next time de cop see me there, almost they kill me! They beat me up bad an' take away my mo-ney an' all my *droga*. They e'say these de final warning. Next time, de Narcisa gonna be dog food . . ." Her big, soulful eyes grew round as saucers as she drew her finger slowly across her throat. "These when I e'say, okey, fock these e'stupid place, an' then I hitchhike back to Rio. *Crown crowwwwn! The End. Thank you come again! Hah! Next?*"

She shrugged with a weak little grin.

Behind her poor little attempt at humorous bravado, I could hear it, feel it—the dark undertone of pain in her voice, a bitter tone of disappointment, resignation, humiliation, failure, defeat. Maybe she sensed the pain I felt listening to her stories. I don't know. But for some reason, Narcisa opened up her heart to me that night, and I fell in like a trapped beast.

"*Serio*, Cigano . . ." She looked away and sighed. "You know it, before even all these e'sheet happening to me there, already I got so much trouble, I just get so tire with de life, then I only wanna dead an' finish forever!"

She fell silent again. I could see her face lit in eerie profile as she squirmed around on the sofa, trying to make herself more comfortable in a world of everlasting pain and discomfort. Then she settled back against me again. Not wanting to disturb whatever unburdening process she was going through, I stayed quiet, like someone listening to a confession, gently stroking the back of her neck, waiting for more.

She shifted around, then went on. "*Na moral, cara!* I wan' only to dead anymore, Cigano, for just get de fock out these e'stupid Crakolândia an' go back my home in de Alpha Centauri, go! So then I decide to make de *suicidio* . . ."

Suicide? I couldn't imagine Narcisa taking her own life. I winced at the thought. After a while, curiosity outweighed my horror and I asked. "So, what happened? Why didn't you do it?"

Silence.

Narcisa just shook her head and smiled.

Finally, she nodded and told me she'd tried.

I felt a lump forming in my throat.

"How?"

23. THE END

"AND THE SMOKE OF THEIR TORMENT ASCENDETH UP
FOR EVER AND EVER; AND THEY HAVE NO REST DAY NOR
NIGHT, WHO WORSHIP THE BEAST AND HIS IMAGE, AND
WHOSOEVER RECEIVETH THE MARK OF HIS NAME."
—*Revelation 14:11*

I sat beside Narcisa on the sofa, choking back tears, fondling her pale, knobby knee as she talked on, describing her suicide attempt. One cold, drizzly, strung-out gray afternoon, she hiked out to the middle of a crowded pedestrian bridge, the expansive old Viaduto do Chá, the busy São Paulo landmark, looming high over the throbbing downtown streets.

"When I go walk on de center of these *viaduto*, Cigano, all de peoples walking there, walking, go go, on de way to work, e'school, dentist, whatever. So many peoples walking around like de insect robot, all walking, but nobody look, nobody e'stop, nobody see nothing, nobody think, only walk an' walk, go go go. *Fock . . .*"

She stopped talking and lit a cigarette. She took a deep drag and exhaled. "I go all de way out to de highest part an' then I e'stop. Nobody never e'stop on these place, you know? An' I thinking, *'Why I e'stop here now, hein?'* An' then I can hear a voice e'say, *''Cuz now you really gonna be nobody here'* . . . No more no *body*, got it?"

Her big eyes darted around like skittish fish in a cloudy aquarium. "An' so I just e'stand like e'statue, Cigano, no thinking. I look down de

big *precipicio*, an' I e'say, *'Goodbye, e'sheet place, fock off, e'stupid world,'* an'
I climb up on de railing an' I look around. Just when I gonna jump, I
look down an' I see my tennis e'shoe! *Porra!* De original purple Nike
shoe, Cigano, only thing I e'still got from de whole time in New York!
An' then I thinking, *'Porra! Que merda! De last focking thing I gonna see
in these world gonna be some e'stupid gringo shoe!'* An' I hear it whole time
e'same music in my head. *'This is de ennn' . . .'* an' I e'say, *'Okey, now or
never! Go!'* An' I let go de rail an' I hold out my arms for fly away, free
now, go . . ."

The End. I closed my eyes and envisioned Narcisa standing there,
my only friend, arms spread wide like a tall white stork, like Christ
the Redeemer.

Tears flowed down my face as she recounted how, at the last
moment, a pair of powerful hands reached out of the crowded pedestrian stream and plucked her from the air.

"I donno who it was e'save me, Cigano! *Porra!* Some e'strong guy,
maybe de Angel from God, de Je-sooz, whatever! I just feel de big hands
hold on to me, an' then he take me down an' put me on de ground. De
guy look me an' e'say, *'Think about it!'* Then he walk away, an' *boo!* He
gone! *Porra!* I e'say, *'Okey, fock it! Desisti!'* I go an' walk back through all
these e'stupid insect peoples, all de way back to de Crakolândia. *Porra!
Que merda!"* She stubbed an angry cigarette out in a glass.

I sat there beside her, shaking my head. Poor Narcisa. Thwarted
again. Whoever saved her life, she never even knew him. Abandoned
again, even by her Random Angel of Salvation.

It was right then, she told me, that she'd made a bitter decision.
From that day on, the only way she would end her life, she swore,
would be from a massive overdose of crack cocaine; that or go crazy
trying.

After another long, brooding silence, she looked up at me with a
pained expression. "All my focking life, Cigano, all de e'stupid peoples

always e'say me how I e'suppose to live, an' they try an' force it all de e'stupid human rule on me! *Porra!* All de life I been lock up, tie up, beat down, rape, confine, drugged, restrain, use for de *sexo*, molest, abuse, abandon an' left all alone for dead."

Then she riveted my brain to the moment with the full force of those big, urgent, tormented eyes, sucking me down into a terrible whirlpool of anguish.

"Do you ever got rape, Cigano?"

I shook my head, feeling sort of guilty.

"Hah! Me, I get rape so many focking time I can' even remember it, *cara!* I e'stop count from when I twelve year old, got it? Never even got it my own way with these e'stupid body I e'stay de prison here with you focking earth peoples, never got it de *privilegio* for do nothing I wan' about no focking thing in these e'sheet life on you e'stupid e'sheet planet!"

I could feel stinging tears streaming down my face like acid rain.

She spat on the floor. "Hah! An' even de one time I try an' fly out from here for go back to de home planet, I get e'stop *again* by some e'stupid focking man! ***Filho da puta!*** So now I just wan' control one little thing in de world, got it? An' with these thing, only I decide! So de crack gonna be de way Narcisa gonna get de fock out from these e'sheet place. De way to dead gotta be de authentic way, ***my*** own way, got it? Nobody else way no more now, got it?"

I got it. I took a deep breath and wiped the tears from my face as she reached for another smoke and went on. Narcisa spent her next months in São Paulo on the run, dodging the roving midnight death squads, running, *go go go,* fast and frantic as a red-eyed burning demon in hell. Until she ran out of fuel and gave up with a sad little whimper.

Then, one cold, lonely night, she quietly slithered back to Rio; back to the Copacabana ho-stroll; right back where she'd started. Back to the shitty old *pista*. Patrolling the familiar, greasy old streets of Co-pacabana, living off the charity of Doc and nameless, faceless gringo tricks; depending, like some wayward Tennessee Williams character, on the random kindness of strangers.

Yes. Narcisa was back from her big New York City adventure at last. Back with her old tribe of glue-sniffing punk rat squatters at the Casa Verde. Back home to the losers and down-and-out nihilist anarchist addicts, winos, lunatics, beggars, murderers and whores of her dark, unhappy past.

Back home to herself.

Her Curse.

24. FALLING

"The landscape is littered with damaged souls. And damage
is a kind of love. Because what's more seductive than
destruction, whether it's one's own or someone else's?"
—*Jerry Stahl*

As the night merged with the hot, cloudy daybreak sneaking through my window, I could see in the morning light just how tired, beat down and vanquished Narcisa really was.

Right before my eyes, she turned into a cave woman. She sat down on the kitchen floor in her sooty, threadbare dress, like a mangy dog, devouring cold leftovers from my fridge, clutching the food in her filthy, ash-blackened hands.

After she'd eaten, I took her into the bathroom to get her cleaned up. Apparently, it was her first real shower in a long time. The soapy water ran black off her septic, bruised, beaten carcass. Trembling like a wet kitten with mad, malnourished, sleep-deprived crack jitters, Narcisa set to the long-neglected task of shaving her crotch like someone attacking a dreaded, gruesome chore. Golden-brown hairs flew off her like sparks from a blacksmith's grinder as she hacked away at her poor, battered cunt. As she hurried to get it over with, blood ran down her legs like feathers falling from a beaten bird.

I watched in horror. "Jesus, slow down, Narcisa. Yer not butchering a fucking pig here!"

We began giggling like a pair of idiot children as she looked up at me, pale and wet, shivering, cupping her hands over her tiny, boyish nipples like an embarrassed crane on public display at the zoo for the first time.

That did it. I grabbed her and pulled her hard, naked white body close to me. She tightened up for a moment, fidgeting, pushing me away weakly, but I held on tight, forcing the hard cock right up against her. Then, as if remembering why she'd come home with me, she began to soften, giving in. We lumbered back over to the sofa together, like some mythical two-headed beast from hell. She knew she was in for it again, and with a deep sigh she opened her long, skinny legs, a tired old codger shrugging defeat.

Like a surgeon making a decisive incision, I stuck it deep up inside her warm, weeping wet hole, plugging us in again, *pow!* and we were swallowed up again in that crucial, deadly electricity we both hated and loved.

Like two drowning sailors clinging to a stinking little life preserver, our sex was hungry and frantic and raw. At the end, we tumbled away from each other, rolling across the floor like vanquished combatants; sweating, exhausted, murdered; gasping like moribund fish for one last crucial breath of life.

I had no choice but to take Narcisa in off the merciless old streets that had broken her poor, vanquished heart at the ripe old age of nineteen; no choice but to fall in love with her all over again too.

But, it wasn't the kind of "falling in love" you see in the movies.
Not at all.

Right from the start, this mad new love was more like some dark, unholy tandem enslavement; a sweet and compelling torture, rubbing rock salt into the deepest wounds of ancient pains and traumas we both harbored in our flayed, skewered hearts, then feeding it back and forth between us, in a noxious, agonizing tango of self-perpetuating torture and mutual addictions.

With Narcisa, I found out what it means to "fall" in love—what they mean by *falling*; like the feeling you must get after jumping off a very tall building, wishing, halfway down, that you could stop, as it dawns on you that you're powerless.

I think I'd always known my association with Narcisa was going to hurt someday. I'd sensed it the moment I'd first laid eyes on her, years before.

She even tried to warn me off this time. The next evening, out on the *pista*, she seemed surprised to see me coming back for more.

She looked at me with an air of pleading sincerity I'd never seen before. *"Lissen, Cigano, you don' wanna get involve with me. I am de Crack Monster now! De real crack addict, got it? One time you go up these road with me, bro, you can' never go back no more. I can really fock it up de life to you, cara, belief me! I tell it to you these thing now as you friend . . . Don' get you self no more closer to de Narcisa world now, got it?"*

I got it. She knew what she was up against. And so did I—at least in theory. If I'd really had any idea what I was really signing up for, though, I'd have bolted like a scorched antelope. I will always remember the words that left my mouth that night as I took her by the arm and walked her over to my bike again.

"Ya can't scare me with that shit, baby." I'd laughed. *"I'm in already, into you right up to my eyeballs! Já que vou pro inferno, não custa apertar a mão do diabo! Long as I'm goin' to hell, I might as well shake hands with the devil."*

"Whatever, Cigano . . ." Narcisa rolled her eyes and came along.

I brought her home seven nights in a row that week, feeding her from my little icebox like an undernourished kitten, always giving her just enough cash to keep her with me overnight.

I was going broke fast, but it seemed important. And unavoidable.

We would fall asleep together after hours of long, hard, unforgettable sex, then have another desperate, sweaty go at it when we awoke
the next day. Afterward, I'd give her a few cigarettes and a shower,
hand over the money, then give her a ride back to Copacabana.

The favela where she copped clung to the hillside, a frozen, tangled brown avalanche of poverty, just blocks from the sparkling blue
waters of the fabled tourist beach. I always dropped her off in front of
the same narrow alleyway leading up into the crowded, smelly slum.
I'd cut the motor and sit on the bike, watching her disappear up the
long, grimy old cement path.

Sometimes I'd hang around at the bottom of the hill, waiting for
her to finish smoking and come down again. When she emerged, we
would walk across the street to this busy little local *paderia* for a quick
cafe de manhá.

Sitting together at the cracked marble countertop, Narcisa always
got the same thing: a glass of fresh squeezed orange juice and a
Danone yogurt. A cup of hot milk with tongue-numbing heaps of
sugar, and just a drop of sweet black coffee on top. Warm French
bread with lots of butter. Two fried eggs, sunny side up, which she'd
dip the bread into, tearing off frenetic little chunks, sopping up the
gooey orange yolk and leaving the white.

Usually, I'd have the same. Over the weeks, that became our little
daily routine. Somehow, sharing that late-afternoon breakfast ritual
made me feel closer to her. Narcisa and I were bonding—like a pair
of symbiotic mutant organisms.

As we were finishing our breakfast one afternoon, a chubby, unattractive, whorish-looking mulatto woman came in, dragging a
screaming child by the arm.

The kid, a beautiful little girl, was bawling her eyes out. The mother
yanked and yelled and pushed and prodded and shouted. When the

sad little doll refused to stop crying and struggling, the furious woman started spanking her on the behind, hard. The little one just bawled louder and louder.

Narcisa winced in disgust.

Then, she flipped. *"Porra!"* she yelped.

Before I could stop her, she leapt up from the counter and stood glaring at the ugly, dull-faced mother, with balled-up fists, spitting like a wildcat. *"These a very good way for teach you childrens to be de good citizen, hein!? Focking e'stupid old e'sheet monster whoo-oore!"*

I knew she was about to jump on the unlucky creature. I grabbed her by the arm and led her out onto the sidewalk before she could take a shot. I'd seen her turn violent on strangers so many times over the years, I wasn't taking a chance. Poor Narcisa had enough trouble.

As I hustled her away down the street, she raged and cursed like a drunken, bloodthirsty pirate, hurling insults in all directions, as pedestrians stopped to stare.

Finally, nearing the beach, I stopped and faced her. "Lissen, baby, just take a deep breath and try to calm down."

"I am very much calm down, Cigano!" Flecks of spittle flew like shrapnel from her pinched up, hate-contorted mouth. *"I ha-ate it all de fat e'stupid ugly old womans! Focking Baby Maker!"* She spat in the road as we crossed the Avenida Atlantica. *"You know what? Soon as de young girl e'start make de babies, she finish! Now she just one big fat e'stupid old man-woman thing with de big black poo-sy hole like de tunnel to hell! Fat ugly old e'sheet-monster cow! Chicken head with two fat-ass elephant bottom! E'same like my e'stupid retard mother, mano! Focking fat old angry pig peoples! Porra! Beat de childrens, is only way they know . . ."*

After a while, Narcisa grew quiet. I breathed in the fresh ocean air as we plodded along beside the crashing waves. She began speaking, more softly. "Hah! I remember when I was a little girl, I use to hide under de bed from my mother. These ridiculous woman, she all de time go an' get de metal clothes hanger an' put it to de fire from de wood oven, make it red hot for beat us! *Porra, que merda . . .*" She trailed off.

As we reached the shore, she started cursing again. ***"Filha da puta! My sister got so many e'scar all over de body! Porra, que merda!"***

I didn't know what to say. We walked along in silence.

After a long while, Narcisa looked at me and grinned. "When I was twelve year old, one time, I smell so much de focking *cocaina* my whole face go numb. *Fock!* I don' go e'sleep for de whole week an' don' eat nothing too. Hah! These e'stupid old who-ore, you know what she do, Cigano? She take me away to de crazy hospital for get me lock up! Hah! She try e'say to them I *maluca!*"

"Yeah? So what happened?"

She shrugged and started to laugh. "*Nada!* Hah! I just go inside an' talk to de doctor. We go an' talk for long long time. An' then he come out an' e'say to my mother *she* de one who most crazy! Hah! He e'say she need listen more to what I e'say cuz I de only one who sane an' rational there. So then I get out, go. *Crowwwnn crowwwnn! Hah! Thank you come again!* No more crazy hospital for de Narcisa, got it?"

I got it.

Like most addicts, Narcisa's troubles had very deep roots.

25. INTO THE WOUND

"WE COULD IMPROVE WORLDWIDE MENTAL HEALTH IF WE
ACKNOWLEDGED THAT PARENTS CAN MAKE YOU CRAZY."
—*Frank Zappa*

Looking down the long white expanse of sand, drinking in the sounds and smell of the sea, I wished I could show her how beautiful life could be.

But Narcisa was lost on an angry, lonesome battlefield of memory.

Overflowing with ancient resentments, she growled and snorted. "I save these e'stupid old bitch life one time, after she drink too much *cachaça*, an' she go crazy an' try to run under a truck, I pull her out from de road! Fock! An' then I gotta save her focking life another time when she take de big cocaine overdose. Come home from de e'school an' she all flipping around on de floor like a big ugly fish, de big e'stupid crazy eye popping out from her ugly face, all foamy mouth like sick dog. *Porra!* I run an' call de neighbor come, an' they take her to hospital. E'stupid! I shoulda run away an' leave her e'stay dead, e'stupid cow. But I only a little geer-ool then, maybe seven year old, an' I don' wan' e'stay all alone. Hah! Woulda be better for me! But what de fock I know about all these e'sheet then?"

I looked at her, shaking my head. "How could some ignorant whore like that give birth to someone like you? You're a a poet, a philosopher, a warrior. I don't get it, Narcisa. How'd ya turn out so different from th' rest?"

She got so quiet, I wondered if she'd even heard my question. I left it alone. We strode along the long mosaic boardwalk, the same beachside path we'd walked together that first night, so many years and trials and adventures ago. The sound of the crashing waves seemed to have calmed her, soothing her angry thoughts.

Finally, she spoke again. "You think I learn to read de books *how*, hein? *Como*, Cigano? You think de peoples teach it to me? *Nada!* My e'stupid mother, she don' even know how to read. I was little baby an' I go look de symbol on all de thing in de kitchen. An' then I ask de woman tell it to me, '*What thing is this, what is that?*' An' she e'say me, '*These is de soap, an' these one is call sugar,*' an' then I e'say de first word an' *boo*! I know how to read! *Pronto!*"

I scratched my head. Could she have really said her first words and learned to read at the same time? With Narcisa, I knew, anything was possible.

"*Simbologia*, Cigano!" Her raspy little voice blended with the sounds of the sea and the steady hum of passing traffic. Then she began to laugh again.

"Hah! I learn it just from lookit de symbol, a, b, c, an' all that. Symbols are word. Word are symbols, Cigano, got it? De word they so *importante!* They got so much power! These why you must never use de word casually like all de e'stupid clones peoples, for argument, debate, insult, criticize, whatever . . ."

I thought how ironic it was that Narcisa, for all her intuitive wisdom and knowledge of metaphysical law, could never seem to practice what she spoke of.

She sighed. "You know, Cigano, I was borned right in de middle of all de machines an' noise, bro, nothing but de chaos an' confusion ever'where! Motor an' drill an' electric saw! *Fock!* After I leave de home, I go an' live all alone in de mountain with de nature, only de waterfall, wind in de tree an' de rain, bird singing . . ."

As we trudged along the sand, she kept talking, sharing her bizarre life's journey with me, detail by detail—all the exotic, multicolored happenings Narcisa remembered with her uncanny photographic memory, describing each thing in a glittering cascade of surreal poetic minutiae. I marveled, once again, at what a mutant, paranormal genius Narcisa could be, if only she hadn't spent half her life attempting to erase all the trauma attached to her memories; trying to murder as many brain cells as she could.

"Who was it my *genitora*, hein, Cigano?" She began musing out loud. "Who de fock it is these ugly old man-woman thing they call de mother?"

I realized she hadn't forgotten my original question, reminding me of the reason for my immense respect for Narcisa, my fascination with the power of her beautiful, terrible mind.

"What these e'stupid woman ever *know*, hein? What thing she ever really know about? Only de thing what got impose on to her in these e'sheet life. Only what got brainwash inside de woman baby mosquito brain by all de humans e'society she gotta live with! Fock!"

She took a deep breath, then began shouting again, waving her hands in the air, as if her hated parent were standing right in front of her.

"E'stupid cow! She don' know about nothing! Nada! She nothing but de mind control robot for de big sinister one who she serve, an' she don' even know what de fock she serving! De Je-sooz Church? Hah! De e'stupid preacher e'say to all de peoples, 'Hey, never mind an' don' ask no question! Just go talk to Je-sooz an' ever'thing gonna be okey, qua qua qua!' Hah! They all gonna go to heaven inside de big plastic box marked 'E'STUPID'!"

I laughed, feeling a sudden urge to stop and write down everything she said. But there was no time for that as Narcisa marched forward,

like a furious soldier on an exploding minefield of recurring griev-
ances.

*"What de fock these e' ignorant woman ever know about
de architecture or de science, de culture, de mathematic,
philosophy, de art an' music or de physics, hein? Only she
know what de church leader e'say, de authority peoples of
these e'stupid clones peoples world she gotta live in! Fock!
What do she even know how to e'say, hein? 'Oh, hello. Good
morning, good afternoon, Merry Christmas, Happy New
Year, whatever. What do you do? What kind de food do you
like? Do you e'study? What kind e'subject do you e'study?
What kind de e'sport you like? What is it you futbol team?
Where you go de e'school?' Hah! Porra! What she ever really
KNOW, hein? Nada! Porra nenhuma!"*

She stopped and stood in the sand, glaring at me with blazing hate
in her eyes. I knew it wasn't for me as she turned and stomped off. I
shrugged along behind as Narcisa screeched on beside the waves.

*"Hah! De woman just a thirteen-year-old ignorant geer-
ool, pregnant like dog with de puppies, an' now how she
gonna raise them? How to survive, hein? What she can
teach to de childrens, hein? She gotta go prostitute her fat
ass to de ugly old mans for even buy any food for de childrens, an' then she go e'spend it all on de clothes an' e'shoe
an' drugs, an' de childrens gotta e'stay hungry! Fock!"*

Like a windup doll running out of power, she grew quiet. Her expression and body language changed, as if she were time-traveling,
shape-shifting back into a child. Then she began speaking again, in a
soft, whimsical little singsong tone, slipping away into another chamber of memory.

"When I was little, Cigano, my mother was a very very pretty girl!
Really she was! She was like de muse for me. She was so-oo beautiful,

so pretty young geer-ool, Cigano, even more e'skinny long leg an' more prettier even than de Narcisa! An' I use to got it so much de excitement, you know, when I look on her an' go close to her. De e'smell of her, *ahhhh . . .*"

She fell silent again, lost in thought. Then, her face grew hard as a machete blade.

She kicked at some imaginary obstacle in the sand and wailed. ***"Then she go an' get e'stab by de e'stupid focking trick! Filho da puta! An' then she get de big depression, just e'stay in bed all de day an' take de crazy medicine! Now she nothing but a big fat old e'stupid e'sheet cow Baby Maker monster! Only e'sleep an' go talk with de e'stupid Je-sooz! Vaca inútil! E'stupid cow! I hate her! I wanna choke her neck like a big fat focking chicken!"***

She stopped yelling. We walked along in silence some more. I felt so bad for Narcisa. She was struggling with her past, drowning in a poisonous whirlpool of her own hate, lost in a dark, unhappy dungeon of memory; trauma, betrayal, disappointment.

She turned and asked the question again. "What it is these thing they call '*mother*,' Cigano, hein?"

I didn't answer. I had my own dark ideas about the concept of motherhood.

She spat in the sand and stormed off down the beach, screaming. ***"Is de big focking galinha! Hah! Big e'stupid old chicken! Coo coo coo! What de focking mother ever do, hein? She only exist for hatch de focking egg! All she e'stupid little eggs! An' then she gotta sit on de egg! Sit. Sit all de day! Bo-ring!"***

I followed along, a silent witness to her battle with sullen old ghosts.

"Confuse an' e'stupid an' ignorant! Angry! Violent! Crazy! What de fock do she ever know, hein? What do a cow

know about her own existence, hein? Moooo! Do she ever look up to de e'star an' e'say, 'Is that my place, de place of my origin? Where do I come from? Where I am going? Why I am here in these place? Who all these peoples who wanna eat me, eat my little egg that I sit on for so long? For what? Who I am eating, hein? Why?'"

She stopped and threw her hands up in frustration. "*Porra, Cigano!* Nobody deserve these kinda focking mother! Why me?"

I shrugged and said nothing.

Her face took on a confused, anguished expression. "You know, I e'still remember it, de first time I come these place, Cigano, de day when I was borned, an' I see her face looking me, an' I already thinking, '*Fock! I never shoulda gone out from my daddy dick!*'"

I looked at her and burst out laughing.

"*Poisé, mermão,* I better off to just e'stay up inside there so I never gotta end up in de ridiculous uterus of these ridiculous e'stupid cow woman! *Serio, mano!* An' you know, when I borned, I can remember it, bro, very first thing I look up an' see these earth woman ugly face, she ridiculous cow eye looking on me. *Porra!* I know it right then that I make, how do you e'say it, I make de wrong turn, an' go de wrong place, an' I really gonna get focked here!"

"You remember your birth, Narcisa? *Como?* Nobody remembers that!"

"These why I remember all, Cigano! Cuz I am *Nobody* here, got it? Really Nobody! I remember I e'start cry so loud when I come these e'stupid planet, cuz I wan' only go back up inside my daddy dick, safe an' warm so I no gotta exist here. Just wanna go back to de Alpha Centauri! Got it?"

I got it. I could relate to Narcisa's anger, her sense of betrayal; the rage and indignation of an abandoned, neglected, abused throwaway child.

I knew.

Even with her difficulty communicating with the world from the barren terrain of her mind's brutal landscape, Narcisa often coughed up these odd, bitter little scraps of venom, coming from some deep, primal need to simply exist—despite her avowed aversion to the whole concept of existence.

As she was sucked deeper into the swirling haze of her addiction, coughing and spitting would become Narcisa's only voice. And I would be left struggling to translate her escalating weirdness into words.

26. JINGLE DAYS

"WE DON'T LOVE QUALITIES, WE LOVE PERSONS; SOMETIMES BY
REASON OF THEIR DEFECTS AS WELL AS OF THEIR QUALITIES."
—*Jaques Maritain*

The weeks rattled by like a long, surreal funeral procession.

With the cash I gave her in my well-intentioned efforts to keep her off the dirty old *pista*, Narcisa unleashed a full-blown Crack Monster. The self-destruction derby was on full blast now; a blazing, white-knuckle marathon race to hell.

After each brain-battering new run, Narcisa came back looking like a once-superfine fashion model who'd been dead for days. Her long, elegant fingers were blackened witch claws of burned, ashy filth, crowned with cracked, yellowed nails. Her crystal-clear, haunting brown eyes were bloodshot and blurry, bulging out of her head like a pair of putrid grapes, framed with puffy, sunken bags of sleep-deprived dementia, giving her the overall appearance of a distempered ferret.

Narcisa was a mess in a dress. Her face was covered in ugly purple malnutrition blemishes, those regal, high cheekbones riddled with pimples and leprous-looking blotches from digging her septic claws at infected crack sores, trying to pick out the hidden "microchips" the "Shadow People" had implanted in her flesh.

Her sweet baby-doll mouth and pouty pink lips were chapped and cracked and burnt from sucking on a blazing stem all day; her teeth turned a ghastly yellow-brown, glazed with a sickly patina worthy of a decaying sea lion's skull.

One night, I watched in horror as she sucked so hard on a burned-out crack pipe, she inhaled its red-hot molten metal filter, vacuuming a blazing lava orb straight into her lung. That little mishap sent her into a bug-eyed state of shock, almost killing her dead as a roach. It was really something to see!

Narcisa was about as hopeless an addict as I'd ever known; and I'd known plenty over the years—including myself. But back in the days of my own drug addiction, for the most part I'd been a junkie; a simple, garden-variety heroin addict. That had been my high for years. Decades. Of course, I'd consumed plenty of liquor and cocaine over the course of my career too, and I loved shooting speedballs into my veins—a deadly thrill-ride mixture of heroin and cocaine. Like any well-rounded addict, I'd smoked my share of crack too. But my first love had always been the opiates; Sister Morphine and Queen Heroin were my favorites—until I'd kissed the gutter and thrown in the towel for good.

I'd thought I knew all about addiction. Firsthand. What I didn't fully get still was that a heroin addict is like a sedated, punch-drunk old tree sloth, compared to a hyperactive ring-tailed monkey of a su-personic crackhead like Narcisa.

Junkies can go on circling the drain for years. Not so with crack-heads. Crackheads, man, you just got to just take the poor devils out and shoot them!

Even before teaming up with Narcisa, I knew that smoking crack is like taking the express lane on the road to hell. But seeing it first-hand, living with it up close and personal, that was something else. My heart went out to her. She loved that song by Lenny Kravitz, "Fly Away," and would sing it out loud while we fucked, or flew through the humid tropical nights on my motorcycle, her voice breathing the familiar lyrics into my ear . . . "*I wan' ta get away, I wan—na flyyyy a—wayyy, yaaahhh yaaahhh yaaahhhhhhh!*"

Those were the only times poor Narcisa ever seemed happy; briefly released from the constant screaming torture chamber of her own unfortunate existence.

For the most part, though, she was just miserable; disgruntled and crabby—pissed-off because she couldn't find a way home from this stifling, stupid hell-planet she'd somehow ended up on. Narcisa really wanted out. I could relate.

As our haphazard union picked up momentum, Narcisa and I jumped right into each other's battered old souls, without a care; without a backward glance. We became inseparable, following each other around town like a pair of alley cats; and, like cats, wherever we went, we just belonged. We trudged the crowded city streets together, like a pair of shell-shocked soldiers in some desperate, undeclared subterranean war, observing the dramas of the metropolis unfolding, like our own personal television *novelas*.

Jingle days. One long, hazy afternoon, we stopped to watch a battalion of hard-faced gray-clad military police thugs pushing a crowd of bearded Fidel Castro clones against a wall plastered with communist slogans. We laughed as their thin paper fliers floated through the air like huge albino butterflies.

Around another corner, a gang of ragged street kids descended from the sweaty shadows like a flock of angry bats. They tripped up a sluggish, white-haired businessman carrying a briefcase, then plucked him like a chicken. The old guy just lay there on the dirty sidewalk, yelling, flailing around helplessly, as he lost wallet, watch, money, hope, dignity. Then, as quickly as they'd appeared, the tiny goon squad scattered off into the lumbering cattle crowds of indifferent downtown shoppers.

"Hah! Look look lookit, Cigano!" Narcisa cackled. *"Caralho!* They take even de guy *e'shoes*! *Hah! Ha ha! Perfect, Max! Thank you come again! Next?"*

And so we moved through the throbbing human herd, observing the world like a pair of invisible visitors from outer space. Magical times. Those long, hazy, lazy, crazy days and nights with Narcisa all blended together in a consuming, kaleidoscopic collage of indelible, dreamlike visions of my prodigal return to the steamy tropical homeland of my youth. One at a time, new déjà vu moments were being tattooed onto my soul in a slow, surreal cascade of details.

Details: A colorful Candomblé shrine in a cramped, dusty old shop window. The musky scent of ritual incense. Sights and smells, dark, antique wooden hues of long, aimless afternoons out on the prowl together, drifting like spirit wanderers through a twisted, mystical maze of shared hallucinations.

Jingle days.

Narcisa and I wandering through a deserted cemetery; dusty acres of dingy graves and murmuring phantom sensations; trudging through the quiet, empty old monument gardens, searching for a spot to fuck. Narcisa smoking the last of her stash behind a crumbling, moss-covered tombstone.

Details: Plodding along in lengthening afternoon shadows, inhaling clouds of tiny corpse-feeding insects hovering in the heavy air. Sickly-sweet-smelling flowers for the deceased wilting by gravesides, rotting away in gloopy little piles under the pounding South American sun. A blackened mass of melting candles burning like a funeral pyre at the rusty, ancient ironwork gates as we emerged from the rambling metropolis of the dead, bickering like a pair of angry ghosts.

Narcisa and I fought often, right from the start. Sometimes we argued violently, trading insults, slaps, curses, blows, howls and kicks;

often in public—because that's the way we lived now, like a pair of feral street urchins. But the storms would always pass as quickly as they flared up. And then the sun would emerge again, steam rising from the sizzling asphalt of our passionate, wrathful, lightning-bolt outbursts.

Sometimes the force of our combined rage drew other troubled souls into our ceaseless battles, like magnetic shavings attracted to a dark, unwholesome nucleus.

Late one foggy night, we ended up in a rock-throwing fight with some drunken businessmen on an empty downtown street.

Crazy, jingle-jangle summer days and long, steamy Carioca nights.

Narcisa and I running from the cops together, merging into humid nighttime shadows, hand in hand, laughing through it all.

Jingle days.

Times to remember forever.

27. THE DIRTY GREEN HATE MACHINE

"He that is not jealous is not in love."
—*St. Augustine*

Time passed. Life went on. Things got weirder.

One night, a couple of months after her return, Narcisa was sitting on my sofa, cracked out of her skull, seeing things only she could see. Then, out of nowhere, she started bombarding me with an insane barrage of bitter verbal abuse.

At first, I couldn't believe my ears as she railed away without pity or respite, spitting and cursing at me for hours on end, calling me "old" and "fat" and "ugly," again and again, insisting that I needed to "lose weight."

Assuming she was just pissed-off because I'd dared to suggest she give the crack pipe a rest, maybe even eat something before her eyes popped out of her fucking skull, I just laughed and told her she should try to get some sleep.

That did it. Narcisa blew her top.

"Porra! Que sono? What focking e'sleep, hein?! Fala serio! Better for me to e'smoke more crack! I don' wan' sleep an' eat an' get all retard an' obese like you e'stupid fat ass focking clones peoples! Nunca!"

I gawked at her, speechless, as she railed on.

"You so-oo focking fat, Cigano! Obeso! Why you look me so, hein? Better you watch you own self, mano! Lookit you

big old ugly fat self! Ugghh! Pigman! You hurt my focking eyes, got it? You think I e'stay here together with you 'cause I like you, Cigano? Hah! Forget it! You too ugly an' fat an' old!"

Ugly? Fat? Old? What the fuck?

Clearly, Narcisa was hallucinating again. I'd never been called "old" or "fat" or "ugly" by a girl before. I stared at her in shock.

"Why you e'study me these way, like e'stupid old pig, Cigano, hein? I don' like de mans! Only one man I ever attract to my husband! Because he de beautiful, innocent young boy, got it?"

I got it. My guts went cold with the bitter green sting of jealousy.

Sensing she'd touched a nerve, Narcisa went right in for the kill, rubbing my nose in it hard. "An' you know, Cigano, I really miss him so-oo much! I use to got ever'thing I ever wan' with him! *Porra!* We got de good good life together in de New York . . ."

As I stared at her, Narcisa's expression changed. "Fock! Then I gotta go to throw it all away, *porra!* Just for go get addict to these e'stupid *droga!*"

I smiled. "Well, it doesn't gotta be a death sentence, y'know. You don't have to keep smoking that shit forever. An addict can get clean, Narcisa."

Oblivious to my words, she started talking to herself, seething with angry remorse, as if arguing with some invisible accuser. "*Não importa!* Soon, very soon now, my husband gonna come an' look for me an' he gonna carry me back there . . ."

Then, leveling her eyes at me like a pair of flaming daggers, Narcisa focused all her spite and regret on me again. " . . . ***An' then I gonna get out from these e'sheet life an' you finish forever, Cigano, got it? I e'stay here only cuz you de most convenient trick, got it?"***

I got it. Like a knife in my chest. I stared at her, baffled and hurt.

She spit on the floor and glared back. *"Is truth, porra! Is only cuz I too much tire now for go out an' make it de real trick on de Copacabana! Is all you fault, e'stupid fat old fock monkey! Cuz I too tire from listen you always criticize an' e'say how I gotta e'stop e'smoke, an' eat an' e'sleep an' all you e'stupid talk!"*

"Fuck, man, I was just tryin' to tell ya—"

"Well, fock all you e'stupid clones peoples' conspir'cy! I don' wan' nothing with you, Cigano! Nada! No way! You old an' ugly an' e'stupid an' fat! Soon as I get better, I gonna go away, back de New York with my husband, an' forget you!"

"That's not a very nice thing to say, Narcisa." I sighed, fighting to remind myself that it wasn't her talking, but the Crack Monster. Still, her words had the power to hurt me, to make me feel insecure, worried, jealous.

I looked at her, scratching my head. "Jesus! We used to be friends, Narcisa! What th' fuck happened to you, huh? You know ya don't mean that shit . . ."

"Hah! If de truth she hurt you, Cigano, is no my problem, got it? All you e'stupid peoples so hypocrite! No me! Narcisa is authentic! These why you all hate me for e'say you de truth! But I am honest, got it? An' you fat an' old an' you ugly! These is truth! You don' like it, then you can go sue me, got it?"

I got it. She was losing her fucking mind, and there was nothing I could do.

She got a greedy, spiteful, faraway look in her eye. "My husband take so good care of me! In New York, I got de who-ole big walk-inside closet, just for all my e'shoe only. My husband mother, she *really* hate de Narcisa, cuz she jealous. Hah! She know he e'spend more mo-ney on me than de mommy an' daddy all time e'spend with him for whole two year de NYU business e'school an' apartment rent an' ever'thing! *Hah! Perfect, Max! Thank you come again! Next?*"

I looked at Narcisa in disgust as she beamed, shamelessly bragging of her perverse accomplishment in New York; how much destruction and devastation she could inflict on one unfortunate family in so short a time.

To hear her tell the story, it was a matter of honor.

Like winning a big shit-throwing contest or something.

For Narcisa, it seemed, the more unhappiness she could spread to others, the more she loved to revel in the results.

28. THE AMERICAN DREAM

"WHAT SHALL IT PROFIT A MAN, IF HE SHALL GAIN
THE WHOLE WORLD, AND LOSE HIS OWN SOUL?"
—*Mark 8:36*

The next night, after seriously considering giving Narcisa a break for a while, in the end, I caved in to desire. Like a man in a trance, I rode over to Copacabana. Snatching her up off the *pista*, I brought her home.

After another long, crazy fuck, she settled herself on my sofa, like a queen ascending the throne. Then she got out her stash, leaned forward and took a hit.

Silence.

I watched her eyes bug out as she held the lethal smoke in. The lazy ceiling fan stirred the smoky, dark, demon-choked air.

After a long while, she exhaled, then started in on another mad, torrential stream-of-consciousness rant, as if she were continuing a long-standing dialogue, picking up some weird conversation with someone else.

Narcisa was talking to herself, rambling on and on about her adventures in New York and Israel. As her bizarre pipe-dream discourse unfolded under the spell of the drug, I listened, fascinated, trying to decipher the intricate alien code behind her words. And all the while, it seemed she was still trying to inflict pain on me somehow, striving to break me under a stinging lash of jealousy. For reasons only the Crack Monster could know, she kept insisting how much she missed her wonderful life back with her long-gone Golden John.

As she waxed nostalgic for her delusional days of glory, I realized Narcisa was so far gone she remembered little of her time in Israel, recounting only a hazy whirlwind of dancing and partying at round-the-clock electronic music raves.

"All de night they got de big psychedelic trance raver partys over there! Only de *young* peoples, *beautiful* peoples an' so many pretty *geer-ool*. Ever'thing *so-oo* cool! *Perfect, Max!*"

As she crowed on, I shook my head and grinned at the surreal image of Narcisa, stoned out of her skull in the Holy Land, stumbling along the same ancient paths where Jesus Christ once tread the Way of the Cross.

Her eyes lit up like a pinball arcade. "I *love* it de Israel, bro! Is de *best* place in de whole world! Ever'thing modern an' clean an' technological over there, no like these e'stupid e'sheet third-world place! Me an my husband was completely in love, an' ever'thing was perfect . . ."

She took another hit and her face darkened. " . . . But it all change after we go away to de e'stupid New York!"

"What happened there, Narcisa? I mean, if you were so fuggin' happy with yer gringo, why'd ya leave him to come back here?"

She spat. ***"Fock de New York! Focking e'sheet place! I hate it de americano! E'stupid gringo cow peoples! Mooo-ooo!! Mooo-ooo!!"***

As she ranted on about why all fat-assed Americans should be ground up and made into McDonald's burgers and fed to the poor people of the world, her words began to reveal the true source of her festering grudge against New York City.

" . . . Is these focking place where I e'start first time e'smoke de good crack!"

I shrugged and asked her how such a self-induced misfortune as crack addiction could be blamed on a whole city.

"Is all happen because I get so much *bore* in de e'stupid place! My husband, he no got no more time for take care of me, an' he don' give no more attention to me. Only work! Work all de day, only de *work*! E'stupid focking place! All these e'stupid *americano* peoples just wanna work all de time. No fun! E'stupid country! *Capitalista de merda!!* He become de focking Robot Man over there!"

She sighed with a sad, confused little look. " . . . Was ever'thing so e'strange . . . Before I go away with him, I think I really know these guy . . . But de peoples very different, I guess, when they on de vacation, you know?"

I knew. Her Golden Gringo John wasn't on his fun-filled Copacabana adventure anymore. The party was over for poor, needy Narcisa. As she talked on, I pictured it all going straight to hell for her, the minute the honeymoon ended and her Magic Savior had to go back to work at the firm. Back to a boring nine-to-five schedule at the bank.

She told me how, for the first months, she'd played along, spending her days holed up in an apartment on Manhattan's plush Upper East Side, smoking the endless supply of weed that Mr. Gold bought for his pretty little Brazilian pet.

" . . . But then de guy family they e'start worry an' e'say to him I too much *disocupada* from e'stay all de day alone in de *apartmento*, an' I need to go an' find some other thing for be doing all de day, you know?"

"So, what did ya do then?"

"Well, first, I go to de art e'school."

"You went to school in New York? Really? How was that?"

"*Fock! Bor-ring!* After these e'sheet, I get *really* bore, an' I e'say fock it. I go back in de apartment an' e'stay inside, an' don' come out no more. I get ever'thing delivery by phone. I don' go for months outside, got it?"

I got it. Narcisa felt abandoned. I could picture her perverse, self-centered mental process slowly poisoning her fairy-tale marriage.

Her husband had committed a crime so foul, in Narcisa's trauma-warped perception, as to be punishable by slow, insidious torture. Ample justification for the dreadful Curse she was about to unleash on his unsuspecting gringo ass.

29. GIRLS JUST WANNA HAVE FUN

"Heaven has no rage like love to hatred turned,
Nor hell a fury like a woman scorned."
—*William Congreve*

As Narcisa detailed her stint in New York playing *hausfrau* to the up-and-coming young banker, I could picture it all. Under the spell of her fast, crooked nihilist-anarchist double-talk and superficial knowledge of Kabbalah, he must have hoped it would all pay off—even if she wasn't the Nice Jewish Girl his family had hoped for. She *was* smart and pretty and fun, in a quirky, exotic way.

"Hah! I donno what de fock these guy thinking 'bout when he wanna get marry to me! He think I gonna conform an' be de 'happy camper' like de e'stupid bourgeois geer-ool? *Hah! Fala serio!* I am raised by de *anarcista* punks, bro! Destroy! I don' give a fock 'bout no e'stupid focking e'stock market!"

She rambled on in a puzzled little contemplative tone, lamenting to herself, as if I weren't there. "*Caralho!* Was ever'thing so e'strange to me! Sometime I don' know what de fock I doing in these place. Was like de big crazy acid trip. My husband he got de one little cousin, de Jewish *americana* geer-ool, Long Island *geer-ool.* Focking sixteen year old an' she got de new BMW car an' de Lady Rolex watch an' big diamond necklace, all these e'sheets from de daddy! *Fock!* She got even de plastic surgery nose! *Putinha babaca!* Just de sixteen years old e'stupid little who-ore, mano, an' she got it all these focking e'spensive thing like de rich *madame*, an' I thinking, whoa, what de fock going on here, hein?"

Narcisa shook her head with a sad little guffaw, then stared off into space. "Hah! All kinda crazy thing I see in America! I never see nothing like these kinda e'sheets before, mano. *Porra!* Me, I come from de country, got it? Ignorant peoples, poor peoples. In my town, de family don' even know how to talk, only growl an' bark like animal. Only thing they wan' do is get drunk, an' then go break up their own thing, e'stupid poor people thing, television, radio, whatever, an' then they even more focking poor. Hah! E'stupid animal peoples. *Affff!*"

Narcisa stopped talking and concentrated on her next hit. Then she looked up again, shaking her head, grinning. "After I leave de home, Cigano, when I first come to Rio, I go e'stay de Casa Verde, you know? An' there was even worst de focking peoples, hah! In de Casa Verde, they only know to e'say, '*Destroy destroy!*' There, I listen only de urban sound, de broken bottle, police siren, shooting guns, *bum bum bum!* *Musica urbana*, got it? My *familia* here always been de e'squatter peoples, de punks, de whore an' criminal. Was only these thing I know ever, got it? An' then, *bum!* I go de New York City, living in de big luxury building in Upper East Side Manhattan! *Fo-ock*, bro! Gotta go visit all de *museo*, Natural History, Modern Art, Guggenheim, whatever, go all de fancy party! Was e'strange for me, you know? De peoples really try to be nice, but I know I never gonna belong . . ."

Narcisa grew silent again, studying her empty crack pipe.

"I donno, bro . . ." She shrugged with a sad little smile, "I e'start to feel kinda, kinda sad . . . *confusa*, you know? Fock, I really *try* to fit in, Cigano, but I never see nothing like all these thing before! An' then I just e'start freak out . . ." Her eyes grew sadder. "Lissen these e'sheet. One time, I gone together with my husband an' his mother, go de Modern Art Museum, an' I see a guy there, a gringo, de old-time trick from Copacabana, you know? An' he come over an' e'say, '*Hullo,*

Narcisa! What you doing here in New York?' My husband mother, she look me an' e'say, *'Where you know it from these man, dear?'* Fock, Cigano! What I gonna e'say to these woman, hein? That I know all de mans only from de *puteiro*, hein? So after these I just go inside an' e'stay in de house. An' my husband he gotta go out every day, go de work all de day an' I just e'stay inside all alone, got it?"

I got it. Culture shock. Intimidated and overwhelmed by the Big Apple, ashamed of her crude whorehouse roots, Narcisa lost her game. Like a cat in a thunderstorm, she ran for cover, stuck her head in the closet and shut the world out for good.

Narcisa became a couch potato. She told me how she'd spent months like that, ensconced in a dark flat with the blinds pulled shut. She passed her long, idle days there smoking weed, playing video games and looking at naked little girls on her husband's fancy new Apple computer, infecting it with every creepy porno virus. She was keeping herself busy, though, as best she could, just waiting for her husband to come home for dinner.

"Dinner?" I looked at her, surprised. "You cooked?"

"Fala serio! What *cook*, Cigano, hein? Of course I don' cooking. What you think? You know I hate de focking food, mano!"

That made sense. Narcisa wouldn't know a fucking pot from a pan. And I knew she wouldn't want to get her hands dirty to dish out supper for any Man named John with enough Gold to take her to the finest eateries in New York City.

She scrunched up her nose with a look of profound disgust. "Only time I ever go out from these place anymore only for go eat! Eat eat eat! *Afff!* All de time he wanna go de e'spensive restaurant with de daddy credit card! *'Gotta go eat!'* Hah! Fock! Every day de guy e'spend so much on de food, *porra*, more money than a whole year my mother make for clean up people house, de guy he e'spend it for one focking dinner! An' de food still taste like e'sheet! Gringo don' know how to cook, mano. I e'say de e'stupid waiter, '*Hey you, garcom! Take these e'sheet back in de kitchen an' tell you e'stupid cozinheiro learn how to cook de focking steak, mermão, go! These e'sheet is raw! I look like de dog? Woo woo! No? Okey, pronto! I no gonna eat it de raw meats then, got it?*'"

I chuckled, picturing her genteel gringo husband cringing in horror as she raised hell at his trendy watering holes. What an image! Narcisa in New York! An earthly nightmare of confusion for the poor, enigmatic country girl with trembling acid visions and shadow demons flashing behind those crazed, bulging eyeballs.

Eventually, she grew restless again. Bored with the lazy pot-head housewife routine, consumed with cabin fever and desperate for action, one fine day Narcisa summoned the courage to venture beyond the corner deli. She took the subway all the way downtown to meet her husband after work.

She got sidetracked, though, and never showed up on Wall Street.

Narcisa grinned, her eyes glowing like a Bowery bum's trash fire. "I take de wrong exit, bro, an' I get out from the metro on de Union Square e'station. Fock! In these *praça*, I meet all de Rasta peoples, an' they give me de good strong *maconha*, Jamaica-style ganja. Hah! *Perfect, Max!* After then I go back ever'day an' e'smoke with all de freak peoples. Better than sit all de day inside de empty apartment. Better than e'stupid museum an' de boring art school, got it?"

I got it. Water always finds its own level. Even in the gutter.

Narcisa had stumbled into a Brave New Underworld, peopled with punks, poets, dreamers, schemers, lowbrow scammers, sidewalk screamers, druggies and winos, street people, junkies, runaways, hustlers, whores and lost, jittery, pissed-off malcontents, just like herself . . . *Just like Home Sweet Hovel at the Casa Verde!*

Perfect, Max!

After that, she was never waiting on the sofa anymore when Mr. Gold got home from the bank.

"What de fock he e'spect, if he gonna left me all alone in de e'stupid apartment all de day, hein? Fock that! I am de young girl, Cigano! Wild girl, crazy geer-ool, got it? I no gonna sit around all de life an' wait some focking guy come home, an' then he wan' only go eat an' tell me all about de boring day in de e'stupid bank! *Porra! Bor-ing! Fock these e'sheet, got it?*"

I got it. Girls just wanna have fun.

30. UP IN SMOKE

"To pursue the American Dream is not only
futile but self-destructive, because ultimately
it destroys everything and everyone."
—*Hubert Selby Jr.*

Narcisa kept talking, spitting out her mad, crucial accounts. Like a prolonged ritualistic, lucid anxiety attack, her voice rose and fell with dramatic cadence late into the night.

Running amok in the streets of New York, Narcisa would go missing for days on end. At his wit's end, her hapless husband finally used the family's "Secret Jew Connections" to get her a job; something to keep her busy and out of mischief while he was off at work, struggling to bring home the bagels.

A friend of the Gold family, another Israeli, owned a chic SoHo tanning salon, where Narcisa became gainfully employed as an "Airbrush Girl."

As night blurred into another misty morning, I sat, spellbound, listening to her breathless, delirious tales. Between fucks, smoking crack and weed, Narcisa chattered away in a surreal torrent of imagery. Ensconced in the dark bunker of my little apartment, she was an actress in a starring role, wowing her adoring audience of one from the stage of my sofa.

Narcisa's big New York work adventure consisted of "tanning" teenage fashion models' perfect bodies with an airbrush. High as a satellite orbiting Alpha Centauri, she described her "erotic" new career in wide-eyed, blow-by-blow detail.

"Hah! They really love de Narcisa on that place, Cigano! Is because I am de real *artista*, got it? I make all de peoples look beautiful, e'same like de Narcisa! An' they all de time calling to me come to an' work de extra hour!"

Obsessed with her new art-form, Narcisa shot to the top of the pecking order of airbrush girls.

Crowing, smirking, she went on. "I always choose it de *cliente*, bro! Hah! I only make de paint to de most pretty girl! Young girl, top fashion model geer-ool! Always I pick de client to work on. Nobody get de airbrush job from de Narcisa if I don' like de way you look, got it? Hah! *Perfect, Max! Next?*"

Even under such ideal, ego-feeding circumstances, it was hard to imagine Narcisa showing up at a job every day, having to keep regular hours and maintain a normal work schedule. But according to her, she did. And she did so well at it, soon she was making thousands of dollars a week in fast-folding cash.

"Sometime de fancy gringo lady give it to me de whole hundred-dollar tips, Cigano! Hah! These focking peoples got too much mo-ney! So many time I make de paint for de big famous peoples, an' I don' know who is it, don' give a fock! All de other airbrush-girl come an' e'say me, *'Hey, Narcisa! You know who is these gee-rool you just make de paint to? These one so an' so, de famous movie star, or top model cover geer-ool, de Kate Moss, de Christy Whatever, bla bla.'* But me, I never give e'sheet, got it? To me is only one more perfect body. These de only thing I give a e'sheet for, no de name or de title, got it? Only de pretty young geer-ool body, an' then just gimme de money, bro! Hah! *Thank you come again! Next?*"

To hear Narcisa tell it, she'd become some kind of superstar airbrush artist by the time she finally grew bored with the daily grind.

"Fock, I donno what even to do with so much money, got it? One day I just get de fock out an' don' go back no more! Out! Go!"

With all that cash burning a hole in her hot little hand, Narcisa was right back out on the downtown scene; a scene that would lead her straight into the wonderful world of crack cocaine.

As she began the grim metamorphosis from Mrs. Gold to Mrs. Crack Monster, her unsuspecting husband became the first casualty. Narcisa hauled out the big guns from her native arsenal of seduction, emotional blackmail, manipulation, flawless debate, maudlin self-pity and expert mind control. There were bogus and even real suicide attempts, followed by death threats and extortion.

Beaming with pride, Narcisa described how, in a matter of weeks, she bled him of all available funds, before plucking their happy home clean of all valuables while he was off at work, struggling to keep their floundering American Dream Cruise afloat.

Narcisa would come home at all hours of the night, demanding money from her sleepy, overworked, browbeaten victim. It was a losing battle as she punished the gringo with increasing savagery. Finally, he realized that the faster he bailed water from the sinking Love Boat, the quicker it poured in through gaping new holes popping up everywhere. Ever-larger amounts of cash were needed to feed the hungry gang of demonic entities growing and multiplying behind the harsh Nazi Death Camp searchlights of her crack-addled, bugged-out eyeballs.

Oh shit! Look out! Here it comes! Hitler Youth on Crack!

It was a mini-Holocaust. Without the slightest remorse, Narcisa giggled, bragging of how she'd disappear for days, running wild in the vermin-infested low-income housing projects of Brooklyn, Queens and Spanish Harlem—one time even turning up dazed and confused, tripping her eyes out on some bad ghetto acid in Las Vegas, where a high-rolling Puerto Rican drug dealer had grown tired of her shit and left her stranded in the middle of a sprawling, glittering casino.

"What did ya do then?" I chuckled, picturing Narcisa in Las Vegas, lost in a psychedelic reptilian feeding frenzy; a whirling, flashing pinball machine vortex of apocalyptic Fear and Loathing.

She told me she'd just called Mr. Gold collect, demanding passage home. He'd sent her a one-way ticket—which she cashed in and converted to Las Vegas crack, eventually hitchhiking back through a swirling whirlwind of wild new On the Road misadventures . . . *Perfect, Max!*

Back in the Big Apple, Narcisa dove right down into its rotten core again, running the gritty streets and blighted ghetto housing projects of Harlem and the Bronx, till she ended up in the crack-ravaged black ghetto of Bedford-Stuyvesant.

"*Porra!* I was de only white peoples in these whole focking place! Only de *criolo* there, Cigano, an' all them all de time e'saying, '*What de fock you doing here, Brazil?*' These what ever'body call me there, just 'Brazil' cuz nobody can even pronounce my name, e'stupid gringo! An' all de time they e'say to me, '*Hey you, Brazil! You better get back outa here, focking white gee-rool!*' *Porra!* White, black, what de focking difference, hein? These why I hate de *americano*, Cigano! These e'stupid peoples all big focking *racista*. So I e'say, '*Fock you, I don' gotta do what you tell me, e'stupid!*' An' I e'stay in de Bed-Stuy ever'day an' e'smoke de best, most e'strongest crack there, got it?"

I got it. Narcisa had disappeared into the shadows of the concrete forest for good, only going home now to awaken Mr. Gold in the middle of the night, shaking him down for cash with desperate, wild-eyed pleading rants, emotional blackmail and threats . . . If he didn't give her what she needed right now, it would be on his head that she had to go out and spread her legs for fat ugly old niggas who took better care of her than his cheap Jewish ass. But she really loved him, *sob sob*, and she really didn't want to have to do all those terrible, nasty, degrading things, and she was really going to quit! *I swear, I promise! Tomorrow.*

Narcisa squealed with delight as she described her reign of biblical vengeance on the Jewish banker. I could picture her with those big, teary E.T. puppy dog eyes, pleading, sobbing crocodile tears, expertly guilt-tripping the unfortunate gringo with cynical, heartless command performances. Justifying her foulest terror tactics, she accused him of turning her into the Crack Monster. And there it was again, Narcisa, the eternal victim.

Of course! All her fanatical crack attacks were someone else's fault! His evil doing, his wrong for being too busy to give her all the love and attention and care she needed! It was all his just reward for the heinous crime of neglecting poor Narcisa in a big hard, mean-spirited capitalist land, just a poor innocent waif, seduced away from her humble country roots, abandoned in that cruel, sterile alien culture! She had no choice but to raise hell! Of course! It was all just a stifled little cry for help! Got it? She just needed More Love and More Compassion, More Understanding . . . More More More . . . "More twenty dollar, just these one last time, por favor, I swear to God . . . Please please, if you really, really love me . . ."

I knew Narcisa could be as coldhearted as any Waffen-SS officer; and at the same time, the neediest person who ever lived; clinging, clutching, demanding constant attention, energy, care, feeding, companionship, love and compassion, twenty-four eye-bleeding hours a day. And God pity the poor bastard who didn't give in to all her irrational, infantile demands!

She told me how she was finally arrested for breaking in to ransack the apartment at the end of another weeklong crack mission. After Mr. Gold filed for a restraining order and had the locks changed, Narcisa had come slinking home again, while he was away at work. When her key didn't fit, she'd lost her shit, and in a crack-fueled burst of supernatural Crack Monster strength, she'd put her shoulder to the door, knocking it right off its hinges. Then, she laughed, she'd gotten into a "little argument" with a neighbor lady.

When I prodded her for details, I learned she'd actually beaten the poor woman bloody when she threatened to call the cops. After ransacking the apartment, Narcisa flew off into the night like a blood-thirsty vampire bat.

They caught up to her wandering the street in front of a Jamaican Chicken Spot on 125th and Lexington at three in the morning—demented, raving, violent and foaming at the mouth.

According to her, it had taken a half dozen of New York's Finest to restrain the ninety-five-pound screaming, hissing, biting Crack Monster.

She'd then been sentenced to a course of court-ordered psychiatric care and mandatory compliance with a state-approved drug-abuse outpatient program, as a condition of her probation on charges of breaking and entry, burglary, aggravated assault, and drug possession.

"Drug possession? *Caralho!*" I howled with laughter. "Sounds like ya shoulda been charged with *demonic* possession, man!"

To worsen Narcisa's dilemma, she whined, there was pressure from her husband's family that she check in for long-term treatment at some fancy Long Island rehab they'd found. I could imagine how well that must have gone over with her. Rather than suffer the indignity of some "boring" recovery clinic, when the whole problem was "all his focking fault" to begin with, Narcisa decided it was time to do what she did best; time to burn another bridge.

She burglarized their not-so-happy home one last time, scraping together enough swag and cash for one last mother crack mission, and a one-way ticket back to Brazil. Then she split—a fugitive from justice in the Red White and Blue. An Undesirable Alien from Alpha Centauri . . . *Thank you come again!*

And thus ended Narcisa's fairy tale American Dream marriage to her fabled Prince Charming Gringo . . . *The End. Next?*

Even all those months later, she remained blind to the real-life implications of her self-inflicted exile from the big Air-Conditioned Nightmare. Narcisa was still clinging to the delusion that her victim would soon come running back to Brazil to rescue her from herself again.

She was so convinced of that persistent pipe-dream, she even had me half believing it. And she used that threat as a constant bludgeon to inflict jealousy, insecurity and anguish on the Crack Monster's latest willing hostage: me.

31. PETS

No matter how brutal Narcisa ever was to me during those first long months after her return, whenever the dust cleared, we always made up. Sex was a last, grasping hope of salvation for us in an irate universe of pounding mutual confusion.

After each new raging battle, we would end up fucking like a pair of delirious weasels, cannibalizing each other alive with all the frantic desperation of two lost souls clinging to one last fading scrap of goodness. Sex was that one tiny blossom of hope, sprung up like a mutant flower, leaping like a bullfrog from the stinking sewage of our common agony.

Aside from the Venus flytrap between her legs, Narcisa had other subtle ways of atoning for her many mad transgressions. One way or another, she always reeled me right back into her hypnotic web of drama, trauma and high-tension adventure.

One afternoon, after threatening to have me murdered, she called a few hours later, begging me to meet her by the beach in Copacabana. When I got there, she was waiting on the corner, wearing this red plastic strap-on clown nose she'd ripped off from one of her squatter friends at the Casa Verde. My heart melted as she ran up to greet me with a wry little smile.

How could I ever hold a grudge?

Before I could say hello, Narcisa reached in her pocket and handed me this weird exotic-looking tropical flower. It looked like an alien spore sitting in a big brown seed husk, like a heart-shaped walnut shell. It was a heartwarming gesture, a quiet little declaration of love.

Then she took me by the hand and led me to a crowded little eatery. "Lookit what I get, Cigano!" She winked, flashing a horse-choking wad of cash. "Where'd ya get that?" I stared, dumbfounded, not really expecting the truth. "I *liberate* it from a gringo!"

I raised my eyebrows. "*Fala serio!*"

"*Na moral!*" She giggled. "I teef these e'sheet! Hah! Listen how: de trick wan' me get him some *cocaína*, so I e'say, '*Okey then, you gotta give it to me two hundred reais, an' then I gonna be right back with de bagulho!*'"

I sat back and listened to Narcisa describing her latest *golpe*.

"Then he insist he wanna come up with me. *Fock!* Why de gringo always so, how do you e'say it, *par'noided*, hein? An'way we go up de *morro*, an' he looking real nervous when he see all de guns! Hah! I e'say, '*Hey you! Is danger for you come up in here, maybe de guy gonna wan' teef you an' kee-eel you, got it?*' So he e'say, '*Okey, okey!*' Hah! An' he give me all de money an' then I run in de alley an' get the fock out! *Thank you come again!*"

I sat across the table, staring at her in awed admiration. Narcisa had more balls than any full-blooded gypsy horse thief I'd ever met.

She smirked, gracing me with another wicked wink. "These e'stupid gringo pro'lly e'still wait up there now for de Narcisa come back, too e'scare for move! *Crowwn crowwwn!* Hah! Perfect, Max! E'stupid trick! *Ahhhh!! Hahahaha!*"

Narcisa cackled with glee as I dug into her delicious stolen meal.

A week later, following another hysterical blowout where she'd threatened to torch my place with me in it, Narcisa appeared at my door a couple of hours later, sporting that old crooked grin, as if nothing had happened. Before I could speak, she presented me with a huge bouquet of colorful bird-of-paradise blossoms. I was so overwhelmed with the quiet poetry of the gesture, I didn't even ask whose garden she'd just laid to waste. That wasn't the point.

Something else was happening.

Suddenly, Narcisa had become more than just a friend; more than a regular fuck partner. Even more than another sick, suffering addict I hoped to help someday. Narcisa was morphing into something resembling a girlfriend.

Whenever she came knocking at my door to wake me from a fitful slumber, she always seemed to be holding out some weird little peace offering: flowers, scraps of trash, and other singular found objects she would convert into mini-sculptures to present me with as she stood waiting to be let in from the wars.

As we grew closer, Narcisa started acting oddly domestic.

One day, she announced that she wanted a pet—a unusual ambition, on the face of it, since I knew she was incapable of caring for another living being. But I had a feeling it wasn't so much about the animal for her, as the idea, the *image* of "having a pet." For Narcisa, it would be a handy little prop, connecting her with the "real" world; a safe, predictable fantasy realm beyond the nightmare hellscape of her own haunted mind. She instinctively craved something cute, cuddly and furry to love now; something to identify her with all the wholesome, normal things that so-called normal people supposedly did.

After she pestered and nagged me for days, how could I refuse?

First, there was the Fish.

She begged me to go out and get it for her, since she never seemed to have the time to pick one out herself. After all, Narcisa only wanted to *look* normal—not actually act normal.

"Narcisa too much busy now, Cigano!" She pleaded and whined. "I wan' you go buy it de surprise fee-eesh for me, go!"

I took a deep breath. "Well, what kinda fish you want me to get, Narcisa?"

"You *know* it what kinda feeshes! I donno what de *title*, bro. Just de little feesh who sit in de bowl an' e'swim around, whatever. Go an' give it to me, go!"

I asked her to at least tell me what color this thing ought to be.

There, Narcisa was more specific. "He gotta be *super-colorido!* De *crazy* color! Multi-*psychedelic* color, mano, got it?"

I got it. The next day, while she was off smoking crack somewhere, I stopped by the little pet store in Lapa, the one where they sold barbecue grills right out front. I never quite got that . . . *What are the grills for? Filet Meow? Only in Rio!*

I went in and picked out a healthy-looking, shiny little indigo-blue Siamese fighting fish called Betta. The clerk told me of its homicidal nature when I tried to purchase another one to keep it company. It was a solitary, narcissistic creature, he warned me, who despised the company of its own kind.

The perfect mascot for Narcisa.

I smiled to myself as I paid for her new pet, its food, a bowl and the little bottle of drops you put in the water—the whole deal.

The Fish occupied a shelf my bathroom, swimming around in a little glass jar above the toilet. It spent its lonesome, watery days there, doing battle with its own hated image in the little hand mirror Narcisa placed beside it.

She was thrilled with her new aquatic companion. For about a minute. Of course, I always had to feed it and change the water when it got so cloudy you couldn't even see it. She rationalized not wanting to feed her fish, claiming she didn't want it to get "fat."

Then, one scorching hot afternoon, feeling sorry for the thing, she dropped some ice cubes from her Coke into the fishbowl—killing it dead as rust.

Narcisa woke me from a sound sleep as she tapped at the bowl with a furious toothbrush—*pling pling pling pling pling!*—yelling at the floating Betta. *"Oi!"*—*pling pling pling pling!*—*"Alô! Alô!"*—*pling pling!*—*"Oiii-iii! Hey you in there! Fee-eesh! Wake up!!"*—*pling pling!*—*"Moo-oove, e'stupid!"*

I rose up with a groan, then went over and dumped the Fish into the toilet, its final resting place . . . *Thank you come again! Next?*

32. THE KITTEN

"THE TROUBLE WITH A KITTEN IS THAT
EVENTUALLY IT BECOMES A CAT."
—*Ogden Nash*

After the Fish, there was the Kitten.

We were riding down the hill from the favela one day, when, all of a sudden, Narcisa started slapping me on the back like some demented midget race horse jockey.

"Pare aqui! E'stop, Cigano!! E'sto-op!!"

Before I could pull the bike over, she hurtled off the back and ran across the street, almost getting herself flattened by a passing taxi.

A moment later, she swaggered back, smiling that lopsided, toothy grin, holding a tiny, mewing gray-striped furball—the cutest little kitten.

Narcisa was in love. A heart-warming moment.

That all lasted a couple of days. But the Kitten wanted far too much attention.

One evening, Narcisa's pride and joy started playing with her boot strings while she was taking a hit of crack. The honeymoon was over. She punted it across the room like a football, and I said, "That's it! One more stunt like that . . ."

The next day, the unfortunate kitty was perched over the toilet bowl, lapping up water. A sweet, idyllic picture of furry innocence.

"Look, princesa! C'mere and see. Look how cute!" I fawned.

She crept over to watch the magical Kodak moment as I turned away to get my little camera. Suddenly, *splash!* The kitten screeched like it was being dismembered by hyenas.

What the fuck? I turned around and ran over.

Narcisa had pushed it into the toilet! *Shit!* The unfortunate creature came scrambling out, looking like a drowned rat. Shoving Narcisa out of the way, I felt like murdering her on the spot. For a second. Then I remembered what they'd done to her when she was little.

I glared at her as I wrapped the shaking kitten up in a towel, like a burrito. "*Why!?!* What th' fuck is *wrong* with you, Narcisa!? How could ya do some fucked-up shit like that to an innocent little kitten, man?"

"I do these only for help de *gato*, Cigano."

"All right." I stood looking at her, holding the trembling bundle in my arms. "So tell me now, just exactly how does pushing a cat into a toilet help it, huh?"

"Is because she too much trusting de human being, bro. She gotta wise up! From now, she never gonna let her ass expose to de peoples no more got it? Is best for de cats these way. De next time, she gonna be e'smarter, got it?"

I got it . . . *Next time? Ain't gonna be no next time!*

I took Narcisa's kitten and gave it to an elderly neighbor down the hall. The woman was happy with it. It grew to be a big, beautiful, healthy mouser. I liked to stop and pet it when I saw it prowling the hallway. It always came right up to me, arching its back to rub up against my leg and purr. Nice cat.

It always kept its distance from Narcisa, though . . . *Guess she really taught it . . .* She would even get jealous when I'd bend down and stroke it, telling me that was the only pussy I'd get anymore if I didn't hurry up . . . *go go go!*

But who needed a pet? Having Narcisa around was already just like having a cat—a big, exotic, dangerous feline; her funny little peace offerings dropped like dead mice at my feet.

Being with Narcisa was like keeping a wild young tiger for a pet. You never quite knew when it might turn feral and rip your bleeding lungs out in one playful moment of savage instinct run amok. And I was her big old shaggy dog. That's what she called me. And whenever she called, I came—again, and again. A dog comes running, wagging its tail when you call it. It's loyal, faithful and obedient.

Narcisa was none of those things. She just came when she wanted, then left when she was done . . . *Thank you come again!*

But when she was around, sometimes she'd sit on my lap and purr, tolerating a bit of love and kindness and affection—until she'd had enough, and it was time to get up and stretch her beautiful, long legs. Then she would hop off and slink out into the night again, like a magnificent, silent predator, out on the prowl for a victim.

Sadly, Narcisa's victim was usually herself.

She would always come back, though; whenever she was cold and hungry, fed up with the wild life, the brutish struggles of the concrete forest and its murderous faces and poisoned booby traps. Then she'd come limping inside to lap up some milk from a saucer and purr.

She'd curl up on the sofa to rest for a while, maybe even play with some string, all cute and cuddly, and I'd go *oooh* and *aahhh* and call her Cream Puff and Princess, fawning over her stunning, untamable elegance, all goo-goo eyed in her electric, feral presence.

I knew I could never be a part of her unstable, deadly world out there, though. Those days were done for me. The best I could hope for was to admire her from afar, while basking in the rare privilege of getting to feed her and fondle her from time to time—before holding the door open to let her go off again, slinking back out into the restless, angry city night, all alone.

And still, Narcisa always returned—often a lot worse for the wear—all cut up and hurt, bleeding and ruffled up; half an ear chewed off, chunks of fur torn away. And then she would sit on my lap and purr again, for a while. She would lick her wounds and recover, getting ready for her next wild, death-defying adventure.

33. CAT WOMAN

One afternoon, I woke up alone in the loft bed, startled by some noisy commotion going on down below.

Curious, I peered down from my pillowy perch.

The apartment was covered in tiny white Styrofoam balls, all flying around like snowflakes in the wind of the ceiling fan.

Still half asleep, I rubbed my eyes, dumbfounded.

The whole place was awash with jumping, dancing, giddy little balls.

What the fuck? Was I dreaming?

Narcisa was chasing around below with a broom, trying to curb the weird synthetic flurry, wearing nothing but my red cotton underwear and a pair of socks she'd pulled up to her pale, knobby knees.

"What's all this, ya little maniac?" I mumbled, climbing down the ladder.

She looked up with a startled expression as I stood staring at her.

"Don' be anger to me, Cigano!" Her big, expressive eyes darted around like a crazed little jungle cat.

It was impossible to be mad at the cute kitten who'd licked up all the butter. With a sigh, I plunked down on the sofa, smiling at her in fuzzy bewilderment.

"I just open it up these e'stupid thing . . ." She pointed to my leather beanbag chair. "I only wanna look it an' see what inside there! I open these zip, an' *boo!* De millions little e'sheets fly up on my face an' then, *boo!* Is e'snowing in you house!"

"Snowing, huh?" I sighed.

Her eyes widened. "Is no my fault, Cigano! How I suppose to know bout all these e'stupid little e'sheets inside, hein?"

Rolling my eyes, I shrugged and smiled.

"E'stupid!" She kicked the beanbag like a pissed-off five year old, and a new avalanche of dancing balls exploded into the whirlwind.

"Hah! Lookit . . . *Poxa!* Is e'snow in de Rio, Cigano!" She squealed in delight as I scrambled over to zip the thing shut.

I stumbled into the bathroom and threw some water on my face. As I stood brushing my teeth at the sink, she slid up beside me, like a horny ghost.

In the mirror, I could see Narcisa was suddenly all dressed for business, in her denim miniskirt and a skimpy tube top. A pair of big round purple shades completed the surreal vision. Lolita Meets Burning Man on acid.

She rubbed up against me like an alley cat in heat. "I am de *goo-od gee-rool*, Cigano."

Her hot breath tickled my ear . . . *Meow. Meow* . . . Staring into space, I could see the little balls dancing around behind her, like shattered thought balloons from her crazed, crack-toasted brain.

Narcisa glided back into the room, silent as a cat. Sitting down on the edge of the sofa, she raised her impossibly long leg, like a freak show contortionist, peeling the stocking off her big white foot, giving me a dick-tingling peek at the oversized red underwear loosely covering her bald, smiling crotch.

Then she started biting at her toenail like a big retarded child.

I watched her going about her demented business. Then, like a zombie, I moved in for the timeless, screaming fuck-feast. I fit it right in where it belonged, holding on to her like a log going over a waterfall. Time stopped, and then I was coming forever into her mad, magnetic essence, with a high-voltage electric jolt that left me twitching and panting, screaming and yearning for more . . . *Fuck! Fuck! More more more!* I could taste the blood pumping into my heart, my dick, my nose, my mouth . . . *Eyes popping . . . Ready to explode . . . Fuck fuck fuck . . .* as we both came, screaming like flaming, howling fireworks tigers, again and again . . . *Fuck fuck fuck fuck . . . More more more!*

It was powerful, plentiful, crucial sex with Narcisa. Sex for crack money. A force of nature. Need! Want! Desperation! That passionate, hungry, savage animal lust was a drug. Amazing! Compelling! Addictive! Raw! Nothing like ever before.

This was sex with the Crack Monster.

Afterward, we sat back, lounging naked on the sofa together, glowing in the aftermath of that mad thrill ride that seemed to have taken us both by surprise.

Narcisa pulled her long, elegant fingers through her dirty brown hair. Preening, like a cat cleaning its claws after torturing and eating a small animal.

Classy. A hundred thousand years of practice.

Finally, she looked over, regarding my vanquished member like a fish on a market slab. "Now, *these* e'sheet de real *dick*, brother! No too much e'skinny, an' no too fat . . . An' is *big*, you dick, Cigano. Long too. But no too much long. No de Kidney-Killer Dick of Death. Is *perfect*, Max! Congratulation! They give it to you de good one when they distribute de dicks."

I raised my eyebrows and looked at her. I could swear she was purring.

She gave it a playful nudge. "An' you know how to *operate* these e'sheet too, bro, de good way, e'start out nice an' e'slow an' easy, an' then go go go hard when you e'suppose to go hard. Good feeling you got, *amigo*! De intuition, these e'sheet important. For de geer-ool is very much important." She blinked like a cat. "You know how to fock, Cigano! These almost never happen, belief me, is de very rare thing. I know."

I looked at her in fascination as the Crack Monster weaved its crooked spell.

"I oughta know it, hein? You know, I always understand what I talking bout! Before I was fourteen year old, Cigano, I already been inside every big hotel in Copacabana, together with de trick from all over de world. Every country, bro. Hah! Even one time I go with a guy from de Transylvania. I thinking maybe he some kinda *vampiro*, hein? Hah! *Crowwn crowwwn crowwwwn, ha ha!*"

Narcisa chattered on with gay abandon, grinning, bearing her pointy little teeth at me like a baby wildcat. "All de mans always e'same e'sheet. *Bum! Finish! Thank you come again! Next?* But you different, Cigano. Hah! An' is first time ever I really can enjoy it de *sexo* with any mans, got it?"

I got it. Sort of. I half suspected she was just feeding my ego. Stroking me. Setting me up for a fall. She was doing it so expertly, though, so sincerely, I didn't care. Who knows? Maybe she even meant it, at least for that one little moment as she sat spinning her web of seduction, reeling me in.

Then she surprised me again.

"If de mans can all fock de e'same like you, Cigano, maybe then de Narcisa don' wan' be *lesbica*, maybe just, how do you e'say it, part-time, hein?" She blinked again. "An' you wanna know something more, Cigano?" She reached over and lit a cigarette. "De young mans, they don' got it e'same *energia* like you. What I gonna do with some e'stupid young guy, hein? No mo-ney, no e'sperience. Useless! Hah! *Next?* Fock like de little rabbit, *bum bum bum*! Stick it in de poo'sy an' *bum, finish*! *Thank you come again!* Is big focking crime! But no with you! *Porra!* You can go for hours, bro. I tire out even before you finish! An' you so sick, you always wan' go again! *Porra, cara!* I got more time fock with you in only de few week together than de whole two year I e'stay marry with de gringo!"

I looked at her, speechless.

Narcisa reached over and shook my hand. "Is *truth! Papo serio!* Congratulation, mano! You gonna make de pretty young girl de very happy gee-rool one day."

"What about you, Narcisa?" I was falling in the trap, caught like a mouse in that alien starlight shining in her lunatic feline eyes. "Couldn't I make you happy?"

She laughed. A bitter little guffaw. I'd said something absurd.

"*Eu? Hah! Sem chance, mermão!* For me is *finish* these e'stupid life, brother! Too late for de Narcisa! I am already, how do you e'say it, de damage good. You don' wanna get youself involve with nobody like me, mano, no focking way! I am de crazy Crack Monster who-oore. Big problem. Bad brains. Hah! Forget about me, *amigo*, belief me."

But it was too late, I knew.

Deep inside, we both knew it.

Around midnight, Narcisa started for the door, cash in hand, on her way out on another mission. Then, without a word, she halted in the doorway, turned around and gave me a heart-wrenching, hopeless look.

I went over and hugged her to me, hard. She tried to pull away, as if she was afraid of losing her own sense of worthlessness. Love and compassion seemed to hurt her somehow. Giving Narcisa a hug was like throwing water on the Wicked Witch.

That's when I really got it.

It wasn't just the drugs that were killing Narcisa. It went far deeper; it was the Curse; the Demon Seed; that invisible pith of self-loathing;

something hateful, planted deep in her core inner matrix. Like a dark offering on an altar of doom; a monstrous, insidious booby-trap; a remote-control killer, preprogrammed to self-destruct on command from sinister forces way beyond her control.

Tears welled up in my eyes as she stood by the door, looking at me with that compelling air of sorrow. All the abuse and trauma she'd ever heaped on me just melted away.

I pulled her toward me and hugged her again. This time she let me. Burying my face in her dirty brown hair, I breathed deep of her smell, luxuriating in her mad, feral essence. I could have stayed like that forever.

Narcisa began to fidget, like a cat you hold too long.

I let her go.

She hung her poor, tragic head in shame and slinked toward the door again, mumbling. "I gonna be better, Cigano . . . I promise."

"Not as long as ya keep smoking that shit, princesa." I shook my head.

She shrugged and turned away, muttering to herself.

I stood in the doorway, watching her mope off down the hall, like a sorry old condemned man trudging the final mile. As she vanished into the stairwell, I shut the door, limped over to the window and looked down at the damp, steamy streets below.

Tears clouded my vision. Nothing moved out there in the dismal depths of foggy night. Only the Crack Monster and its shivering minions.

A minute later, I saw the frail, solitary, feline figure of Narcisa emerging from the building. I watched her dart across the street; a stealthy, furtive little shadow puppet disappearing around a corner and fading into the bowels of darkness. A frightened, lonesome old alley cat.

After what seemed like a very long time, I turned away from the window and fell onto the sofa. Laying my head down on the little pillow, still reeking of our desperate, compulsive sex, I passed out.

After a couple of hours of troubled sleep, I heard Narcisa scratching at my door, like a cat begging to be let in from a driving rain.

I got up and held the door open for her.

Without a word, she breezed right past me, shaking her poor, troubled head in mute, listless despair, an injured stray cat's ghost.

She collapsed onto the floor in the corner by the bathroom door and sat there, staring off into a dark, forlorn space I was unable to decipher.

I just stood there, looking at her, feeling powerless and sad, watching poor Narcisa sinking down into the deep, dark ash-gray sea of her own private hell.

No one spoke.

34. TV HONEYMOON

"LOVE IS THE INFINITE PLACED WITHIN THE REACH OF POODLES."
—*Louis-Ferdinand Céline*

The weeks slithered by like a surreal, humid, prehistoric fever-dream. The world took on a dreamlike quality. Reality became obsessive, single-minded, defined only by random explosions of pristine, savage lust. Narcisa and I were too shell-shocked to even talk anymore; sex had become our only common language.

Whenever she stumbled through my door, I'd take Narcisa in and feed her. I'd clean her up, then take her into my arms and get to work, trying to breathe some life back into her bone-clacking, emaciated death-camp skeleton.

I fucked her like a day laborer, fucking her long and hard and good; fucking her so she'd *stay* fucked. I sweated over her like a bricklayer in the sun, a sweating, laboring peon, working like the damned to make her come, to make her pant and cry and groan and feel; pumping the numbness out of her, willing her to live . . . *Live, goddammit . . . Live . . . C'mon, baby, just one more day . . . Another hour!*

Forcing Narcisa back to life through those screaming, primal animal jolts, I slapped her awake, again and again, in crazed, furious, passionate sexual first-aid infusions of life. Dirty, sweaty, bloody, greasy, gritty, critical life.

And, like me, Narcisa had nothing to lose. Nothing to do but follow another wayward soldier shadow with nowhere else to go. And I followed her too, wherever the road of our common desperation led. Because I had finally found between Narcisa's legs that crucial Something that makes men quit their jobs and go running out into the night, naked, screaming, insane. We were bound together in a perfect limbo of haunting new experiences, sensations and addictions; a freakish, unholy, overwhelming life force that neither of us understood or wanted—or had the slightest power to avoid. And in that lusty, hungry swirl of strange days and nights, I was freed at last of all cares, constraints and social obligations to the rest of humanity; liberated from the bondage of self, oblivious to the gluey stares of curious neighbors, glassy-eyed television-watchers and cops.

There was nothing but me and Narcisa, running hand in hand through sweaty doomsday streets of careless desires, propelled like ghosts over rain-slick pavements where the spindly fingers of trees beckoned like lopsided phantoms. And in that frenzied, fevered whirlpool of passions, we ran and ran and ran together, running from death and despair, running, running; damnation, devastation and ruin always waiting around the next trembling corner.

Times to remember. Long, crazy, jingle-jangle days and nights of lusty delirium. I didn't care about anything else. Only Narcisa. Because she was the time of my life, her pulsing, magic crab-claw cunt the only home my corrupted old soul had ever known.

I've been sleeping . . . The window is closed, shut tight, a thin barricade against another burning sunny day outside.

Late afternoon . . . Hot summer Sunday . . . Been up all night again . . . Too beat to face the sun-damaged, heat-maddened, beer-drunk crowds of a cut-rate Dante's Inferno at the beach, I've locked myself in here, resting like a vampire, waiting for the night, sleeping away another long, blazing hot day in the dark, musty shelter of my room, hibernating under the fan's steady, monotonous hum.

Narcisa? Disappeared again, off on another long, lost weekend in hell . . . Three days off the radar . . . Missing in action on another mission.

Dead? Jail? Nuthouse? Ran off with another gringo? Who knows? Tired of worrying, too distraught to pray anymore, I console my latest loss with others . . . But it's like trying to embrace a shadow . . . The whore I was with all night just left . . . I can still smell her sickly-sweet perfume on the pillow . . . Can't sleep . . . Shit.

Drifting in and out of a foggy stupor, floating between sleep and fuzzy-tongued, blurry-eyed dementia, the shutters pulled tight against the murderous tropical sunlight outside, I am safe, sheltered from the pounding terror machine of another stupid, senseless Sunday.

Wait! What's that? A frantic little knocking at the door . . . **tap tap tap** *. . . like a child . . . Who's out there? . . .* **tap tap tap** *. . . Soft and insistent . . .* **tap tap tap** *. . .*

God, I hope the chick didn't forget an earring or some shit! How many earrings are wedged between the mattress and the wall here? My bed's a fucking earring cemetery, haunted by the slippery ghosts of every whore in town . . . . **tap tap tap** *. . . What's going on?*

I stumble down from the loft in my striped briefs . . . Same cheap underpants I bought downtown the other day with Narcisa . . . All cotton . . . Six for a fiver . . . Narcisa disappeared with most of 'em . . . God knows where they ended up . . . Whatever . . . These are the last ones . . . I don't care . . . I like that she's the only bitch around here who's got the balls to wear boy's underwear . . . I long for the perfection of her wonderful, hard white ass, in my underwear or anything else.

The tapping grows in intensity . . . **tap tap tap taptaptaptaptap** *. . . Like a rat scrambling around in a cage . . . Fuck! I move toward the door in a dreamlike trance, thinking of Narcisa's perky young tail, wondering what's going on.*

Taptaptaptaptap taptaptaptaptap taptaptaptaptap

I pull the door open and . . . **poof!** *The Genie in the Bottle. Narcisa!*

There she was, standing in the hall, grinning, bug-eyed, shouting, holding a television set in her arms! Like some fucked-up overgrown robotic Cyclops baby she was about to tell me was mine . . . *What's going on?*

"Hurry up! Go-oo! Porra, cara, anda logo, vaiii-iiiii! Help me with it, porra! Take it these e'stupid thing, go! Take it, Cigano, go go!"

"What's this, princesa?" I stood there, looking at her with a groggy smile.

She dropped the heavy plastic box into my arms, rolling her eyes like a pair of crooked dice. **"Is tel'vision, seu idiota! For us! To look it! Plug it in! Go!"**

Pushing in past me, a child dodging around an annoying obstacle, she tore into the kitchen and started rooting around in my refrigerator like a giant foraging white rodent. I stood there in awe, holding the television, watching as scraps of food fell to the floor, a present for the mice and roaches. An invitation to tell their friends.

Fuck it! Who cares? She's back! Thank God! Narcisa, making her path of blessed destruction through my life again!

She rattled on nonstop, battling through a mouthful of leftovers, chewing, mumbling, grunting like a deranged monkey, chattering in a mad flurry of excitement. " . . . An' then, *mmmh, mmh,* I go to these e'stupid rich guy big penthouse in Ipanema, hein?"

"Where'd ya get th' TV?" I stared at her in wonder.

"Wha' you think? I go, how do you e'say it, *mmmh,* I making de tricks . . ."

I winced, feeling my stomach drop . . . *Turning a trick . . . Whatever . . . How you gonna be jealous of a fucking whore, man? Thank God she's alive!*

" . . . De e'stupid guy finish, *mmmh,* an' then he go to e'sleep an' he forget to pay me! *Babaca!* Maybe he think I gonna e'stay there an' e'sleep together with him all de focking night. Hah! Maybe I e'suppose to wake up an' go eat de strawberry an' cream together with some focking trick in de morning now, hein? Hah! *Fala serio!* E'stupid old fock-monkey! *Mmmmh, yum nyum, nyamm . . ."*

Munching away like some mad, infernal eating machine, Narcisa shoved food into her gullet, swallowing without chewing. *" . . . Mmmh, mmyh . . .* So now I thinking 'bout how I gonna get my cash an' get de fock out from these e'stupid place without wake de guy up an' gotta see he e'stupid playboy monkey face again . . . *mmmh, mmh nyamm . . ."*

I reached over and handed her a towel. She dropped it on the floor with a handful of crumbs and kept eating. *" . . .* An' so I go look outside de window, bro, an' I see de doorman e'sneak out an' walk away from de building, you know, walk down de e'street for meet these girl, *mmmh . . .* I look them go in to de park. Hah! *Perfect, Max!* De *porteiro* abandon his *posto* for go with de girl! I know he won' e'stay away too long, *mmmh, mmmh, ynum, yumm . . .* but these geer-ool, she pretty, very pretty girl, you know?" She winked like an evil circus clown.

I gawked at her with mute admiration as she rambled on, a rampaging babbling, rushing stream of Narcisa. *" . . .* But he gonna e'stay away enough time, I know, *mmmh,* an' these e'stupid trick e'sleep, an' now no *porteiro,* nobody for watch de building door, got it? An' then I e'say, *'Now or never, Narcisa! Go!'* An' so I carry it right out de door de focking guy tel'vision! ***Crowwwwnnn crowwwwnnn crowwww-wnnnn!! Ha-ah!! I teef it de tel'vision, Cigano!! Hah!! I teef it!! The tel!! vision!! Fock!! So-oo perfect, Max!! Aahhh hah haahaha!!"***

Narcisa was shouting and singing, jumping, laughing, chattering, chirping like a branch of gleeful monkeys.

Crash!

Shit! There goes my last fucking plate!

"Droga puta merda caralho! Son of a who-oore e'sheet! Mother fock! Po-orra!" She cussed like a bloodthirsty pirate, crumbs flying from her mouth like wood chips from a churning buzz saw. *"You e'stupid kitchen, she too focking e'small, Cigano!! No place for put nothing! Bring de broom, cara, go, clean it up these e'sheet now! Go! Go go go go go!"*

Blasting past me, she leapt up onto the sofa and began attacking a big bowl of crackers, sliced pineapples, stale pizza, olives and gooey sweet *doce de leite*, all mixed together in a nauseating, overflowing heap. Narcisa was an obscene, infernal, furious machine. The way she shoveled that food into her pie-hole, it was as if she hadn't eaten in a week. She probably hadn't.

I stared at her in lovestruck wonder. "You're a fuckin' animal, Narcisa!"

She kept shouting and gesturing, talking, big chunky wet crumbs flying from her mouth, shooting like bullets across the sofa, landing on my arm.

I was most impressed. I could feel my heart swelling like an overworked vacuum cleaner bag about to pop as I started laughing. "Careful, ya little beast. Ya might actually swallow some of that shit before ya spray th' whole fuckin' room with it!"

"Shut de fock up, e'stupid, go! Mmmhh, mmmhh, nyamm . . . Oí! Oí! Go an' give it to me de Coca Cola! Thirsty! Drink! Go!"

"Hey, Narcisa!" I grinned. "I got an idea!"

Her blazing eyes peered up at me over the mountain of food, like a raccoon peeping its snout out of a garbage can.

"Next time ya could steal us a fuckin' blender!" I cackled. "Then you could mix up all that food and just hold yer nose and swallow it. Yer always in such a big hurry, just think of all th' time you'd save not havin' to chew and all, y'know, more time to sleep and watch yer new television, when yer not toasting yer brains out on that fuckin' crack . . ."

"I get it this tee-vee for *you*, Cigano!" She frowned, pouting. "You don' remember de time when you broken de other one?"

"The *other* one?" I almost choked. "That was like three years ago! And *you* kicked th' fuckin' thing over and busted it!" I howled. "What th' fuck?"

"Menos! Nevermind these e'sheet! Is irrelevante! Shut de fock up! Mee-noos! Go plug it in an' e'stop all you e'stupid talk, Cigano! Maybe you just e'say, 'Thank you for de new tee-vee, Narcisa' . . . Eí-íí, where it is my Coca-Cola, hein? Go! Now! Go! Go! Thirsty! Go go go!"

Still chuckling, shaking my head, I handed her a glass of soda. Then I saw her eyes fix on the bulge in my underwear. It was on. I peeled the stolen cotton briefs down over those long, beautiful legs. Narcisa twisted around, raising her butt off the sofa, looking at me, playing with her perfect shaved hardwood clam.

Just as I was about to mount her, she pointed to the television.

"Peraí, cara! Plug these e'sheet in, Cigano! Go! Naa-ooow! Go-ooo!"

I stared at her, drooling like a lovestruck hamster.

"Go, Cigano! Vaiiii! Go! Then we can look it while you focking me!"

Now she had my full attention . . . *Of course! Watch TV while we fuck! Business and pleasure! Two birds, one stone! The best idea ever!*

Preferring to read and write when I was home alone, I'd never bothered replacing the little television she'd smashed. There was just my plastic portable radio. Narcisa would sing along with the popular songs while I shagged her, hypnotized, lost in her brittle, cracked-up voice. I couldn't get enough of her singing. I loved Narcisa's voice as much as I loved everything else about her; that rough, sandpapery rasp, like the ghostly wails of horny alley cats in heat in the plaza below my window on sultry summer nights; a husky edge of danger and primal violence. And all I wanted to do anymore was fuck.

I would screw Narcisa all day long when she'd let me. Somedays that's all we'd do. Eat and fuck and sleep, falling in and out of each other, rolling around in a comfortable tangle of arms and legs, in and out of the Land of Sleep and the Land of Fuck, while she snored or sang with the radio songs, or rattled away with that manic, childlike, singsong growl of hers, unleashing dazzling torrents of stupefying alien poetry and wild, surreal stream-of-consciousness rants.

And now it was a television, a new addition to our funny little nuthouse honeymoon; like a new baby, or a puppy. *Perfect, Max!* I grinned at her like a kid at Christmas.

"Put it on, Cigano, go go! Naa-ooow!"

I got up, went over and plugged the thing into the wall. Standing there with a throbbing hard-on in my hand, I watched as the TV sprang to life, like some mad scientist's laboratory monster. An old black-and-white western movie; two rugged-looking gringos in cowboy hats sitting on horses in front of a Wild West saloon, talking in badly dubbed, outdated television Portuguese.

"*Ye-eah! Mmmmh, yumm, yum, mymmh . . .*" Narcisa shoved another moldy slice of pizza into her mouth. **"Leave it on these e'show! Don' touch it, Cigano!"** She sprayed a new flurry of soggy crumbs across the floor.

I watched her like a cat as she stared at the television. Her crazed, crack-maddened eyeballs were bugging out, riveted to the flickering screen with the intense, unblinking focus of a late-show-movie zombie. Her brain sucked up like an albino moth into the little gray box vibrating away in the dark corner, Narcisa was gone, mesmerized, lost in TV land. Under that haunting blue electronic spell, she didn't even seem to notice as I slid down like a cat burglar on the sofa behind her, lifted her long, pale leg up and worked myself into her from behind.

It was on. The perfect TV honeymoon.

We stayed like that for hours, for days; coupled together, grinding our careless sex away in the shadows, before that eerie, glowing, all-seeing, all-knowing television eye. We slept like that and woke up in the same befuddled televised trance, the sofa groaning and sagging under the weight of our churning, machinelike sex; through movies and *novelas* and comedies, westerns and game shows, soccer matches, newscasts and boring agricultural programming, late-night test patterns and commercials; nights and days, all merging together in a steamy limbo fuck-stupor stew; sailing the airwaves together, dick and pussy melded into one solid, unified unit, we fucked and fucked, an unstoppable, mindless hump machine, only disengaging from time to time to eat snacks or go to the bathroom, before resuming the idyllic fantasy-ride fuck-dream life had become.

35. THE HOUSE OF LOVE

"I AM 'THE FACE OF RIO' . . . THE PEOPLE OF THE UNDERGROUND
ADORE ME! I AM THE QUEEN OF THE UNDERGROUND!"
—*Narcisa Tamborindeguy*

When not smoking, fucking, watching television or sleeping off a mission, Narcisa began spending her time in this ratty little rented room downtown.

The Crack Monster's new headquarters was a run-down transient rooming house in the dark, greasy backstreets of Lapa. The place was called Love House. Love House Hotel.

When Narcisa was on a run, I just had to put some distance between us sometimes. A matter of psychic survival. And the Love House's rates were cheap. There was one drawback, though. The place was infested with roving herds of frightful-looking, over-the-hill transvestites and their shifty-looking tricks.

The Love House "girls" were strange, tragic-faced creatures. I shuddered at the sight of them, stumbling around the narrow mazes of darkened hallways in their ratty, cum-stained lingerie, like potbellied old truck drivers in clown makeup.

Too destitute to think of getting real breast implants, the dilapidated drag queens there would inject themselves with industrial truck tire silicone from the nearby flat-repair joints—or so Narcisa's breathless stories went.

Lapa, the Love House's neighborhood, was Rio's traditional old bohemian quarter. Situated on the run-down edge of the Centro, its ancient cobblestone backstreets and alleys had long been a refuge for threadbare local artists, poets, musicians and old-school *malandro* street hustlers. In recent times, the once-folkloric district had degenerated into a filthy, crime-infested labyrinth of crumbling tenements, cheap hole-in-the-wall bars and humble working-class eateries. After nightfall, the streets of Lapa morphed into a chaotic, booze-soaked netherworld, where Cariocas and foreign *turistas* went slumming to bask in its rotting air of nostalgia and local color. They spent the sweaty nights there singing, dancing and drinking till they puked. On the long summer weekends around Carnaval, Lapa was like an open portal to hell.

Outside Narcisa's window at the Love House, a steep *escadaria*, hundreds of steps long, climbed into the winding hillside *ruas* of Santa Teresa, a vintage tangle of timeworn colonial mansions, surrounded on all sides by a cancerous sprawl of deadly shantytown favelas. The landmark stairway—the neighborhood's only real saving grace—had been converted from a former piss-soaked, pestilent eyesore into a multicolored mosaic-tiled work of art by a visionary painter named Selarón.

When not painting, the globe-trotting Chilean immigrant had spent his years in Lapa productively. Lovingly, patiently, the eccentric poor man's Gaudí had singlehandedly transformed a filthy, crime-ridden, abandoned concrete blemish into a living masterpiece. A neighborhood fixture, old Selarón was always to be seen out on his *escadaria*, wearing his trademark floppy red hat, chatting through his bushy handlebar mustache with neighbors and visitors. For over a decade, a day at a time, he had worked his dream into a reality with a single-minded obsession, proudly maintaining and adding new tiles to the ever-evolving project.

Eking out a meager living to support his ambitious urban monument by peddling unique, soulful paintings to locals and foreign tourists, Selarón was the heart and soul of Lapa; a true old-school bohemian *artista*. On nearby brick walls festooned with his distinctive candy-colored glazed ceramic tile paintings, Selarón had added effusive sections of vibrant poetry to the glittering collage, dedicating his enchanting walk-through sculpture garden to the people of his adopted homeland:

"Brazil, I love you," one read. Another colorful panel declared: *"I will only end this mad and singular dream on the final day of my life."*

Ironically, he would be found murdered on his beloved stairway early one morning; doused with a can of his own paint thinner, then set ablaze by one of the subhuman, glue-addled bottom-feeders of Lapa, who had converted his magnum opus into a noisome spawning ground for drug dealing, petty larceny and strong-arm muggings of curious visitors attracted to the artwork there.

Selarón's mad dream would eventually be destined to rats and ruin; a living testament to the ugly undercurrent of Rio's infamous melting-pot neighborhood, Lapa. Within days of his death, the legendary Escadaria Selarón was appropriated by the greedy, blood-sucking pimps of Rio's corrupt, draconian Prefeitura—always eager to take an official bow for works of popular artistry whose penniless creators they neither sponsored nor encouraged in life.

To add insult to Selarón's final betrayal by the city he loved, the police blatantly covered up his murder, loath to delve into a crime that might leave an unsightly bloodstain on the lucrative tourism racket. His savage extermination was deemed an official "suicide"—though everyone in Lapa knew better.

To me, it was hardly a surprise. Poverty and decadence, greed, corruption, envy and malice had always been a way of life in the

passive-aggressive social landscape of the city of my youth. No wonder
Narcisa chose to blot it all out in a swirling maelstrom of deadly crack
befuddlement.

Across from the Love House sat a grungy, low-rent open-air bar.
That dreadful roach pit was the definitive unofficial borderline between the asphalt world of the "real" city and the lawless underworld
"other" city within a city at the top of Selarón's steep mosaic stairway—a world of teeming, crime-infested hilltop favelas, where all
the usual urban street codes and social norms were automatically
reversed, replaced with unwritten, inflexible, merciless ghetto-world
codes—strange, random laws enforced by roving packs of gun-toting
teenage bandidos, minions of the shadowy *donos*, the drug bosses.

Organized crime was the only de facto government up in those
lawless shantytown slums, sprawling like a ragged human cancer of
poverty across the once-verdant hills of Rio de Janeiro. Prophetically,
Selarón himself had included a haunting little admonition in his
jinxed crazy quilt collage: *"Living in a favela is an art. Nobody robs. Nobody
hears. Nothing is lost. Those who are wise obey those who give orders."*

Like the favelas from which many of its patrons hailed, the shabby
boteco below Narcisa's window was a distribution point for drugs. All
kinds of unsavory characters would gather around the open-air pool
tables and rickety wooden stools out front at all hours of the day and
night, drinking, bickering, smoking weed, dancing and sniffing cocaine in paranoid little clusters at the end of the bar. Samba and Forro
blasted from a pair of big, weather-damaged speakers in a pounding,
distorted cacophony; an obnoxious soundtrack for the ceaseless loud
arguments raging in that marginal netherworld of petty crime and
sleepless vice.

In the predawn hours, the boisterous barroom debates would escalate, rising in crescendo like some mad doomsday symphony. Trouble
would break open like a burst of billiard balls there, the festivities

often ending in a staccato rattle of gunshots ripping through the greasy night air, bottles falling off tables, breaking like crashing cymbals as the bar's ragged denizens scrambled like rats for cover.

The backstreets of Lapa were host to a splendidly dysfunctional little society.

Narcisa had spent the last two days there at the Love House, tweaking her brains out in her airless cubbyhole, while I did some laundry and tried to recover from her last visit.

As soon as she came up for air, she called me, and off I went.

When I pulled up half an hour later, Narcisa wasn't waiting outside, as planned. I looked up and down the street, then up on the crowded mosaic stairway.

No Narcisa.

Sitting back on the bike, I waited, sucking down a sweaty soda from the bottle, then another. Lighting a cigarette, I waited some more, observing the freak parade: winos, pickpockets, skinny preteen thugs, degenerate gamblers, aging transvestites, saggy old alcoholic whores and dog-faced losers. Squinting through a humid, sickly-sweet cloud of marijuana smoke hovering over the motly crowd occupying the stairway, time was an endless loop of tedium. Bored and edgy, I began scribbling impressions of the night into my little pocket journal, while fending off the constant stream of freeloaders, hustlers and bums as they came over to hit me up for change and smokes. Finally, I got off the bike, marched up under Narcisa's window and yelled for her to come down.

Nothing. I must have taken too long after her call; she'd already been out to do whatever she had to do. She was holed up in there now, smoking alone in the dark.

I waited some more, but I knew it was useless. She wouldn't come down. Not till she'd smoked the last fucking crumb. Not till she was done searching every crevice of the rotting wooden floor in her coffinlike cubicle. I winced as I pictured her up there, crawling around like an overgrown Kafka cockroach, foraging for imaginary coke flakes no self-respecting crackhead would drop. By the time the sun comes up and the birds are singing, I knew Narcisa would smoke Margaret Thatcher's old yellow toenail clippings without a second thought.

Swallowing a bitter little groan, I went back to the bike and sat again. Leaning back on the seat, I glared at the sordid procession of petty crooks, coming and going from the bar to the stairs, like forlorn legions of the damned.

"*Porra, que merda!*" I cursed under my breath, feeling like a strung-out chump. My eyes wandered over to a creepy-looking geezer with a brutal flat face, sitting at an outdoor table littered with empties. The guy's whole head was deformed, as if he'd been dropped on the ground at birth, or clobbered with an iron skillet or something. A nasty-looking specimen. He lurked across from another drunk passed out at the table. As I watched, Flat-Face started going through the other guy's pockets. Casting furtive rodent looks around, like a vulture feeding on a corpse, he glowered at me, sneering, baring his rotten, ratlike underbite in my direction.

I felt a sudden mad urge to march over and smack him right across his evil, subhuman mug with my Coke bottle. *Pow!* But something stopped me.

I remembered that Narcisa knew every one of those crummy barflies and smelly lost souls by name . . . *Don't make trouble here . . . She's got enough trouble!*

I swallowed the frustration and hate of my progressive addiction to her. Plastering a blank look on my face, I averted my eyes. Still, my fucking blood boiled to think that she'd gladly spread her long, elegant white angel legs for any one of those dirty, degenerate creeps, for the price of a few lousy crumbs of rock.

To add to my mounting jealousy and stress, Carnaval was approaching like a cackling demon train from hell. The drums had been pounding all over town for weeks now.

I looked around, taking it all in, hating everything.

The whole fucking city's already swarming with pink-faced gringo sex tourists with their bulging gringo wallets . . . Fuck! They're coming in from the four corners of hell now . . . It'll be a fucking heyday for Narcisa this week, if she even survives it! Carnaval! Shit! Five full days of demented, mindless, directionless, godless, piss-guzzling Roman debauchery!

If I don't get her off the streets soon, she's a goner!

Right then, it hit me. I was going to have to make sure Narcisa never ran out of crack again. I was caught like a fly in her greasy sex web. Sitting there, I could hear her voice echoing in my brain, whining, pleading, cajoling, threatening.

"Cigano, I need mo-ore mo-ney. Why you so focking cheap, cara? I gotta go e'spend de whole night with some e'stupid fat old gringo trick again. An' is all you fault, 'cause you don' wanna take care of me! How these make you fee-el, hein? What kinda man make his geer-ool-frien' go out an' suffer all de day these kinda e'sheet life, hein?"

It was a losing battle. Sick with love-lust for Narcisa, Cupid was a greedy, blackhearted cosmic pimp, having his strong-arm way with my soul.

36. DARK CARNAVAL

"LOVE DEMANDS ALL, AND HAS A RIGHT TO ALL."
—*Ludwig von Beethoven*

Journal entry: Carnaval—Monday—The streets were littered with mobs of somnambulant jaywalkers tonight. Fucking zombies. I don't know if they were just drunk or so burnt-out they'd been drained of all will to live. After four days of nonstop partying, they wandered around like stray chickens, staggering right into the road. Everyday people, letting their demons out to play, their shuffling, stupefied demeanor said it all: "Just kill us, g'wan, we don't care. We just wanna lie down somewhere, anywhere. The gutter, the hospital, the morgue, whatever."

I looked up and down the street, hating the whole distasteful mess.

Carnaval. Shit. Strange deal, this shit-brained, monkey-fart of a holiday. I guess people just aren't meant to have a whole straight week of nonstop license, with nothing to do but jerk off and party and drink themselves stupid. Idle masses, as far as the eye can see, hovering, milling around, drinking, shuffling back and forth, to and fro, bleating like diseased sheep, jumping up and down like worn-out, raggedy old circus chimps and sick, mangy dancing bears, twirling around and around in befuddled little circles of shit.

My eyes wandered to the bar. Up on the TV screen, another Carnaval; a distant fantasy parade of perfect coffee-skinned dervishes, gyrating away under twenty-foot statues of naked African warriors, shaking supernatural television hips to the breaking point atop gigantic trembling floats, paid for with drug-dealing mafia blood money. Everything looked so perfect onscreen, pulsing to an unnatural rhythm of glittery, sweaty TV life, a shimmery kaleidoscope of sequined, flashing

color, motion and music; a swirling parallel dimension of toothy smiles and spar-
kly eyes, cheery televised faces, laughing amid explosions of pounding, apocalyptic
drumbeats and color; singing, dancing, waving hands in the air. Familiar faces of
mailmen and maids, the hardworking wage slaves of my city, peeking like cartoon
mice through little cracks in a clammy blanket of crappy mundane concerns, not
thinking, just for that one sweaty, beer-soaked little moment, about all their bills
and infirmities, their miserable lives of slavery, violence, poverty and decay.

Looking back at the real Carnaval on the street, I shuddered with revulsion as
a foul epiphany struck me in the heart: these fuckers really **need** *to be caged up*
in factories and offices. Take that away for five whole days, and they degenerate
into these unruly destructive savages, slithering through the gutter like demented,
deranged reptilian vomit-monsters. The horror! Left to their own devices, people
will just dive straight into the toilet every time, like deviant, overfed, masturbating
monkeys, wallowing in the sequined, drunken, glittery glory of their own filth!

I paced the streets, mingling with the delirious hordes, watching the revelers
staggering, scrambling, stumbling around, babbling, stuttering, stammering in a
dull-witted, incoherent language of the damned, like packs of giant rats crawling
around an overturned trash can.

People. Pathetic shit-eating vermin! Rats!

Then it hit me. No! That's an insult to rats! Rats don't neglect and abuse and
torture and abandon their offspring. They just eat them when there's too many to
feed. People keep making babies and throwing 'em away. Cranking out their sad
little meat puppets and throwing 'em away. Popping out the Meat. And the streets
are teeming with the Meat tonight. Rotting meat. Reeking of futility. Idle hands.
Idle minds. And now they're all partied-out, wasted, bored to stupidity. Shit.

*C**arnaval—Late Monday night. Fat Tuesday morning. Last day of this long,*
demented shit-fest. Thank Christ it's almost over now. Two hours to sun-
rise, and the boozy night air is still humming with these stupid, drunken, degen-
erate cockroach crowds. Insect-people, stumbling around like stunned mosquitoes,
gorged with booze and debauchery. Dizzy, lazy, intoxicated, burnt-out. They're

just about ready to drop. I can feel it. And my tragic, mad-eyed crack baby's still holed up in there, locked away in her musty little tomb. God help us!

Restless and edgy, finally, I couldn't take anymore. I stomped into the shabby little hotel lobby. In a hazy corner, a fat man with holes in his socks sat slumped in a chair, sleeping, with a newspaper over his face. My eyes pleaded with the weary-looking old Arab lady at the desk as I asked her to go up and please tell Narcisa I was there, still waiting. She gave me a wry look, then shrugged off down the hall.

A few minutes later, Narcisa appeared, looking gray and disheveled.

"Whassup, Narcisa? You pissed-off at me or something?"

"Of course I no pe-eess off! Why you e'say it to me these thing, Cigano?"

"Well, I came by twice today, and you never came down . . ."

"*Arrhhhh,* well . . . you know." That precious shifty little-girl grin.

She's been up there smoking all day again . . . Musta hooked another gringo to get the cash for all that crack . . . Carnaval . . . Shit . . . They're still swarming all over the place out there . . . Fucking gringos . . . Fucking Carnaval . . . Shit.

"So what's the plan, baby?" I looked in her eyes. "Whaddya wanna do?"

"I wan' it, you know, some *mo-ney* . . . for some more little thing to e'smoke . . ."

The little girl who ate all the cookies . . . I nodded. At least I had some cash again. One good thing about drunken *gadjis* and gringos in a big, milling, stupefied crowd. And little Ignácio still had his old pocket-fishing skills . . . *Perfect, Max!*

"Okay." I stared at her, lost in her eyes, her smell, the need to hold her, to fuck her. "I'll take ya up to cop . . . But first, well, you know what I want."

She smiled back.

"*Porra*, Narcisa!" I took hold of her arm as we stepped out onto the street. "I'm really hooked on you. It's getting bad, just like a drug."

"I am de only drug, ya-ass." She nodded. "I am de e'same thing you feel when you take de first drink, bro, when you e'smell it first time de *cocaina*."

I took a deep breath. "Let's go then?"

She nodded again with that guilty, crooked little-girl grin as I started the bike. She jumped on behind me and held on tight as we blasted off through the stupid mob of aimless, milling, bleating revelers. Swept away.

Riding along the dark streets, I ran my free hand up and down her leg, in awe at the force of my own obsession. "Fuck! I'm strung out on you, princesa. Just like you on that crack."

"Narcisa de only *droga* for you now, Cigano, hein?" She gave the roaming hand a meaningful little squeeze. She knew.

I smiled . . . *Fuck the world* . . . *Twin Flames* . . . *Burning fast* . . . *Go go go!*

After another long, crucial workout in Cupid's Gymnasium, I dropped her off at the Love House. I watched in awed admiration as she vaulted off the back of the bike and trotted away, like a healthy young mountain goat.

I called out behind her. "Hey, Narcisa, ya forgot something!"

She stopped.

"Come back here and kiss yer man goodbye, ya rude little cunt!"

With an expression of tragicomic sorrow, she turned around and looked me in the eyes. Right then, that heartbreaking look weaved itself into the fabric of my soul. Beaming with love, I stared at her beautiful, evil, porcelain baby-doll face.

She drifted up and I hugged her close. I could feel her heart beating against my chest like a dying monkey. I was choking on some deep, twisted tangle of errant emotions; feelings I didn't care to know or remember or understand.

I heard myself whispering. "I love you, Narcisa."

"Don' give up on me, Cigano . . ."

"I'll never give up, *amor* . . . But I gotta go now. Just be careful. *Por favor.*"

I knew she had a date with a deadly, soul-sucking, parasitic entity.

The Crack Monster was far more powerful and persuasive than even our twisted, mangled, unbreakable bond. And I couldn't stick around for that scene.

At least I still thought not.

The next night, though, I was back, standing outside her window again, waiting, longing, wanting. The smell of Narcisa haunted my thoughts. I could almost hear the sound of her ghostly moans as we fucked and fucked, rocking back and forth, like some insane, malevolent rocking horse, digging a plodding hole to hell.

I stared up at her darkened window, wondering, watching, thinking; as if the sordid little drama going on behind those crooked old wooden shutters might somehow reveal the secret to life. Maybe it would, at least for me in my own little corner of the Abyss.

I hung around until way past midnight, wondering if she'd survive these final hours of Carnaval, or if this would be the night when her heart would finally freeze up and stop like a rusty old broken-down lawn mower.

God help us, help me . . . Meu Pai Ogum, me ajuda, por favor! I need your help!

As I prayed, Narcisa's last words to me rang in my ear, echoing and zinging like the overpowering, debilitating buzz of a good, strong hit of crack.

"Don' give up on me, Cigano . . . Don' give up . . . Don' give up . . ."

I knew right then I wouldn't give up.

Not then. Not ever.

I realized I'd do anything now to get her off those goddamned slobbering streets.

I got on the bike and tore off into the night, looking for cash.

This time, I knew just where to get it.

37. THE PUSSY ARCADE

"SEDUCING A WOMAN YOU DON'T KNOW, FUCKING HER, HAS BECOME
A SOURCE OF IRRITATIONS AND PROBLEMS, [. . .] ALL THE TEDIOUS
CONVERSATIONS [. . .] TO GET A CHICK INTO THE SACK, ONLY TO
FIND OUT [. . .] SHE'S A SECOND-RATE FUCK WHO BORES THE SHIT
OUT OF YOU WITH HER PROBLEMS AND TRIVIAL OPINIONS, LIKES
AND DISLIKES [. . .] IT'S EASY TO SEE WHY MEN MIGHT PREFER
TO SAVE THEMSELVES THE TROUBLE BY PAYING A SMALL FEE."
—Michel Houellebecq

Journal entry: Carnaval. Fat Tuesday. After Midnight. Looks like they've yanked open the gates of hell down by the Prado Júnior. The Pussy Arcade. Coked-up gangs of funny-faced whores, all standing ready to face the ashy dawn, like grim, determined warrior ants of the apocalypse. They're all out for the last night of Carnaval, huddled together in protective little whore-gaggles, waiting for the next car to roll up, the next boring exchange of futile ho-stroll banalities.

Gringo tourists, businessmen, the odd lonesome neighborhood playboy, a few henpecked husbands hopping the conjugal fence for one last boozy night out. The usual, predictable, end-of-season ho-stroll lineup.

A hot wind blows in across the water from Mother Africa, the full moon lighting up my mind like a pinball machine, and it's on.

I cruise up and park, taking it all in like an old, familiar dreamscape. Same old dejected faces of eternal disappointment, and that odd little glimmer of innocent, heroic optimism. All eyes alive, flashing like searchlights, look-

ing for the big, last-minute Carnaval score: the legendary Hundred-Dollar Gringo Trick.

The competition is thick as pissed-in pizza dough here, ten or twenty young whores for every swinging dick, and plenty more where they come from, packed like showroom dummies into cramped little one-room Copacabana backstreet flats reeking of transvestite piss and garlic, stale beer and weed smoke; howling babies, funk music, angry shouts and the occasional small-caliber gunshot from down the hall.

The lucky ones emerge from the disco bar, hand in hand with their gringos; sleek, muscular, well-tanned Italian boys in tight designer jeans and crisply pressed, colorful shirts, or the typical balding, sloppy, sunburned americanos. As they step out onto the sidewalk, they're bombarded by an army of beggars and pushers, hollow-faced flower peddlers, strong-arm taxi drivers, pimps, killers, hustlers, shakedown cops, bandidos and glassy-eyed, glue-sniffing eight-year-old wallet-snatchers.

I kick back on the bike, light a cigarette and sit watching the action.

The Pussy Arcade.

Got a ringside seat for the grim festivities from my crow's nest perch.

Watching the freak show flesh-parade of lost souls, an idea pops into my brain, like a cartoon lightbulb.

I fire up the motor and roll off down the twinkling yellow Avenida Atlantica, stopping in front of the Holiday Bar, the old whorehouse where I finally found Narcisa again.

Now it all seems like another lifetime.

I park and get off, already feeling disgusted with the tired-out scene; same stale old loveless mating rituals. Gringos and whores. Whores and gringos. American and European sex tourists. Lonesome, horny refugees from the frigid puritan wastelands of the North, where sex is a virtual video game played by solitary, middle-aged white men on glowing computer screens—a pathetic perversion of the real world. But this is another kind of perversion. Little Ignácio's real world. In living color, sight, sound, smell, touch, memory.

Gringos, cabdrivers, cops and muggers, pimps, pushers and whores. Dozens of whores, with their worn-out plastic heels, shitty tattoos and saggy-flapjack-baby-sucked breasts, the same old nondescript, misshapen creatures clustering around in the late-night shadows, like gangs of hungry rats, milling around in ravenous, giggling rodent droves. Faceless, graceless, loud-mouthed, razor-sharp hustle-bitches, straight out of the teeming, dirt-poor whore-factories, the dusty, godforsaken slums of the Baixada. Cold-hearted, predatory pussy, eyeing the nervous little clumps of gringos, like slobbering jackals circling a henhouse.

The tricks are all tricked out in their crisp white linen suit jackets, Panama hats, and gringo party wear, ready for their big Copacabana Carnaval Adventure. The same stupid, faceless foreigners who kept little Ignácio in food and clothing, drugs, lodging and whores, back in another time, another life, another dream.

Easy enough to spot the cokeheads in this crowd. Always was. The punters stand out like donkeys at a horse race down here. Shit, I should've been a shakedown cop. Just keep an eye on the men's room and watch for the gringo coming out rubbing his nose with that guilty little "just did a bump" look on his pasty pink gringo mug.

Easy pickings down here, as usual.

Same old whores. Same old gringos. Same old hustle. Same old shit.

Some things never change.

I spotted Fernanda standing on the far edge of the ho-stroll.

Dressed for business in a denim miniskirt and knee-high brown leather fuck boots, my little friend was looking pretty good, as always.

Her face lit up in fond recognition as she slid up beside me like a shaggy cartoon ghost, greeting me with a quick hug and a humid little peck on each cheek.

Fernanda knew the score, and was always down for whatever. And she knew how to dress. I always liked that. The attractive, aging, hard-drinking *paulistana* was a talkative, anorexic little lifer with a mouthful of razor-sharp doomsday humor, a good-natured, seasoned *veterana*. We'd had some fun times together when Narcisa was away. Long, easygoing bullshit sessions sitting out on the predawn *pista* on slow winter nights; nothing to do but talk shit and wait for the dawn. I'd hang out on the corner with her, buying her shots of *cachaça* and feeding her cigarettes while she leaned on my bike, entertaining me with local whorehouse escapades in her hilarious, world-weary *paulista* drawl.

Fernanda had a few regular gringos, and she always kept her ear to the ground as she drank away the long, steamy summer nights at her regular street corner post, forever waiting for the big payoff, which never seemed to come for her.

Not being big on the *brizola*, whenever a john wanted to score some blow, she'd toss the business to the roving coke-running cabbies patrolling the night like sharks; a tip to the friendly drivers who set her up with high-rolling gringos at the expensive beachfront hotels.

She stayed at this cheap little rooming house over in my neighborhood. Sometimes I'd give her a ride home at the end of the night if she didn't score a trick. More often than not, she'd reach over and give my crotch an affectionate grope halfway there. I'd take her back to my place and she'd stay over for a few drinks and some company, rather than limping home all alone in defeat.

Fernanda liked my little crib. She called it "the doll's house."

She liked me, and I liked her, but that's as far as it went. We were friends. And she knew all about my hopeless love for an apocalyptic phantom named Narcisa.

Taking her by the arm, I led her over to a street corner booze vendor and bought her a double shot of *pinga*. She powered it down in one quick, professional gulp, flashing me a grateful smile that lit up the night.

I grinned back, putting my hand on her delicate shoulder. "Lissen, 'Nanda." I leaned in, whispering in her ear. "I gotta start making some quick cash around here . . . Ya know any gringos who wanna score some blow?"

She cocked a weary eyebrow. *"Já 'tá nessa, Ignácio?* You running de *brizola?* Wha' happen to de clean-an'-sober thing, *gato?* You falled off de wagon now?"

"No way, kid. *Nada disso.* I just need a little hustle is all. Strictly business."

"'Tá bom, gatinho . . . Pagando uma de avião agora, hein? Tst tst . . ." She clicked her tongue with mock reproach. "You always surprising me, Ignácio!"

After a little pause, I gave her the punch line. "Narcisa's back. Got it?"

She got it. *"Pobre gatinho!"* She frowned. Reaching a long, elegant hand out, she gestured for a cell phone. *"Tá legal, gato. Me presta seu celular."*

I reached in my pocket, handed her the battered old Nokia and watched as she dialed, then pushed the speaker button so I could listen in.

"Copacabana Palace Hotel, boa noite . . ." A melodic little voice crackled. *"Boa noite."*

"Por gentileza, o senhor John Johnson, por favor."

"John Johnson? *Fala serio!"* I laughed. "Ya gotta be shittin' me, 'Nanda."

She smirked and winked, holding a warning finger to her lips, as another voice with a distinctly American accent came on the line.

"Hullo?"

"Hall-oo, John-ee! Eees Fernanda, bay-bee!"

"Hey there, Fer-naaan-duh."

"Eii, John-eee . . ." She smiled, cooing sweetly in the most adorable English. "Lissen, *ném,* you remember de little t'ing we was talkin' 'bout de night befo' . . . ? *Sim, iss-sso . . . Poisé, ném . . .* Ye-aah . . . Well, I got somebody over here I like for you to know . . ."

38. WAR ZONE

"Poverty is the parent of revolution and crime."
—*Aristotle*

A familiar pungent sewage stench invaded my senses. Almost there. I gunned the motor harder, scrambling up the hill, up, up, over the slick, dark cobblestone path, up, up into the rambling hillside favela.

Little fruit bats flittered in the looming shadows of a giant ancient mango tree, dancing around my head as I rode past, reminding me at the last minute to pull off my helmet and cut the light as I neared the slum's entrance, headed for the *boca*.

The *boca*. The Mouth. The Drug Spot.

It was a tense, well-guarded place nowadays, with many strict new rules; best to show your face when approaching the fortified ghetto drug markets these days, if you wanted to keep from getting ripped to shreds by a burst of automatic weapon fire from some shell-shocked, coked-up, trigger-happy teenage lookout.

Entering the *comunidade*, I reminded myself I was heading into a war zone. This place was no longer the familiar, easygoing hillside shantytown I used to come and go from as an innocent adolescent coke-runner.

That was a million years ago. Things were very different now.

I rolled along the dark, garbage-strewn path, reminiscing about my old life there with my ragtag teenage gang, forever waiting for the next score in our myopic little world of bohemian *malandragem* and petty crime. Yeah, things were all different up in the hills of Rio today. Desperate. Hard-edged. Deadly.

I cut the motor and coasted in silence down a bumpy, mottled alley, past the ever-present graffitied letters, ***CV***, spray-painted on walls—a constant reminder of just where I was going . . . ***CV****. Commando Vermelho.* ***CV****. Red Command turf.*

Rattling along through rows of sleeping shacks, down into the dark, deserted favela plaza, I eased the bike to a quiet halt beside an idling yellow taxi. Setting the kickstand down, I sat there, looking around.

Easy does it, man. Don't wanna come tearing up beside someone and give 'em call for suspicion, paranoia, a sudden violent reaction. Quiet, gentle, slow, easy.

I shot a casual glance at the guy behind the wheel . . . *Looks cool . . . But you never know up in here* . . . I knew it could easily be Death sitting in that car. Could be anything, anyone, any time of the day or night up there on the hill. I gave the driver a quick nod and a casual thumbs-up, then looked the other way, getting my bearings, waiting for someone to come out of the tangled maze of alleyways ahead, so I'd know which way to go next.

Sitting on the bike, I reached in my pocket and pulled out my smokes. I could feel the gringo's cash rolled up in the pack . . . *Two hundred and fifty . . . Plenty to work with here . . . I'll just give him fifty's worth and keep the rest for Narcisa.*

I lit up and sat there watching a skeletal little tiger cat, tipping across the dark clearing in the shadows. All of a sudden, a bright red dot from a high-powered assault rifle's laser sight appeared beside her.

The cat stopped, still as the night, watching the shiny little light like a bug. Then she pounced. The red spot moved a few inches. She cocked back her haunches and pounced again. I smiled. I like cats. I hoped the kid on the other end of the gun liked cats too.

Spooked by footsteps, the tough little creature scurried off to live the next of its nine lives. Just then, the taxi's passenger emerged from the dim, narrow *beco* ahead, walking fast with that furtive, jerky, "just copped" body language.

I watched as he got into the taxi. He said something to the driver and they pulled away . . . *Perfect, Max!*

Now it was all going to be easy. Simple. All I had to do was go down the same alley, then follow the trail of rifle-toting teenage thugs to the spot.

I got off the bike. Glancing around, I put my boot down on the last of my cigarette, then strode down toward the *boca*.

Back in Lapa. I parked under the trembling flicker of the battered old neon sign. As I stepped into the lobby, an elderly Arab man gave me a weary nod.

Above his head, an ancient wall clock said it was 4 a.m.

Taking the shabby wooden stairs two at a time, I grinned, playing the tape over in my mind. A dozen skinny, bare-chested teenage bandidos standing around the *boca*, laughing, funk-dancing, flirting with local whores, shouldering big assault rifles that weighed half as much as them. Favela life. A naked brown baby sitting on a trash-strewn dirt path, crying all alone, howling into the smoky night—neglected, unattended, abandoned like a dead man's sneaker.

Walking down the hall to Narcisa's room, I could still feel the warm ocean wind on my face. I savored the details, replaying the satisfied look on the gringo's face as we'd sat up in his luxury hotel suite overlooking the dark rolling sea; Mr. John Johnson, slowly, methodically cutting out lines with his platinum credit card on a spotless green glass tabletop; his look of mild surprise when I declined his imported whiskey on the rocks. The huge bump he cut out for me sitting neglected on the table. His big friendly gringo smile as he handed me five more crisp blue hundred notes and portioned me off a taste. *"One fer th' road, ol' buddy.*" That soft, warm gringo handshake as he told me he'd be staying in Rio for another week. And me thinking to myself, *Yeah, and there's a thousand more just like you where you came from, ya grinning gringo prick!*

I knew right then that I'd be able to keep going with Narcisa now; that I'd stay on this mad, demented, fever-dream destruction derby ride to hell till the fucking wheels melted.

39. BUSINESS AS USUAL

"It is impossible to understand addiction without asking what relief the addict finds, or hopes to find, in the drug or the addictive behavior."
—*Gabor Maté*

knocked on the door and Narcisa opened up fast.

She was ready for me this time . . . *Crack pipe in hand . . . Check . . . Seductive grin on face . . . Check . . . Ready . . . Set . . . Go! Go! Go!*

Like telepathy, like magic, she knew she really had me at last. And she was ready to really work it now, standing in the doorway in her skimpy denim miniskirt. Miles of long, gangly white legs and knobby Lolita knees; a glowing, ethereal neon fairy. She'd even donned her good old whorehouse heels.

Narcisa's flat, bare alabaster belly rubbed against me like a cat in heat. I put my arm around her waist. Kicking the door shut behind me, I led her over to the window. As her crack-furnace breath tickled my neck, I was already hard as steel.

We stood looking down at the drunken hordes of Carnaval's last gasp. Holding her close, I could see them all down there, scrambling around like rats in an overturned garbage can.

At the back of my mind, I had a hazy plan to help her out of her self-made hell . . . *There's still a chance, if I can just outlast that fucking Crack Monster . . . Just gotta keep her alive now, long enough for her to burn out and cry for help.*

I held out a big, waxy yellow crack rock. Her eyes lit up like a short-circuited slot machine. Slipping it back in my pocket, my hand wandered down her spine and latched like a talon on to her firm, perfect ass.

"*Fock!*" Narcisa breathed with a sheepish grin. "You gonna keep give it to me these kinda *presente*, Cigano, I gonna be in love with you . . ."

Without a word, I pulled her underwear down, leaned her over the window ledge and slid it inside. *Pow! Bang!*

A paralyzing electric shock therapy jolt to the soul, and I'm hard as a diamond, breathing in the musky fragrance of her scalp, pulling her long, greasy brown hair, pushing it deep inside her, drooling, slobbering like a horny cartoon wolf, grabbing that hard Garden of Eden Apple ass, and we're hanging over the window, fucking like the damned, dancing in a raging sea of lust, like electrocuted puppets on the devil's high-voltage high-wire, fucking up and down, all around the room, knocking things assunder, and it's raining mad, hungry spirits of debauchery and mayhem, and I don't care, don't care, don't give a fucking shit anymore, all ashes, ashes, ashes, raining down down down down down!

I spun her around and clutched her to me hard, running my hand up and down the velvet highway of thigh, kissing her with a burning desperation, inhaling her hot, musky breath like a strong hit of crack . . . *Breathing her in, eating her alive, fucking her hard, harder, bouncing her perfect white ass up and down on the dirty ledge for all the world of drunken slobbering slobs down there to see and eat their dirty black rat-shit hearts out, because I am with Narcisa, and I am blessed, holy, alive, bathing in eternal pounding waterfall mists of motion sex sound energy, crazy electric spirits dancing us away away into the ashy dawn of never forever, forever.*

Journal entry: Ash Wednesday—7 a.m. *The world of day is coming to life at daybreak. Riding up to the top of the hill, up, up, into the favela again, nothing more to do now but sit and watch the sun coming up over* *the city. Sweaty skin still tingling from a short-circuit glow of lust-drunk passion. All is dreamlike and magical up here. Nothing but sleeping shacks and nature, and a devastating ocean view of a fairy-tale world spreading out below, pastel-gray sea shimmering into eternity, a silent, blinking crystal vision. An alien nirvana. Dawn over Alpha Centauri.*

A small yellow bird lands on a branch. A loud cheeep, a tiny crunch of claws grasping at wood, then whooooosh overhead. Hundreds of wild black ducks moving past in a crooked formation. Twenty seconds later and they're gone again, just a blurry, wobbly little line, moving away over the mute ghost town below, fading into distant mountains and jungles, across murky visions of Guanabara Bay.

Watching, waiting for the first orange pinprick of sun poking through gray morning mists; another loud, piercing birdcall, another row of ducks, a crooked, trembling shadow approaching, and I hear a windy rush of another two hundred powerful beating black wings, and then they're gone again.

Pale purple and blue hues of new day appearing, overtaking the tiny lights twinkling across the water, distant buildings and factories, crippled gray worker-ant wastelands emerging across the glassy mirror of water.

After sunup, I rode back down the hill, buzzing past graffiti-scarred brick walls, through my humble working-class neighborhood. Skirting past the ornate ironwork fence around the Gothic stone grounds of the old Hospital Português, I could see the White Ambulances of Death, still coming and going, screaming like bloodthirsty harpies in the early-morning haze, hauling load after load of Carnaval's expired casualties, like delivery goods to a macabre meat market.

Carnaval. A crippled slaughterhouse of stabbings and shootings, car wrecks, overdoses and quick, undignified death. People dead and dying at the party's whimpering finale, drunken victims of themselves. Another long, dark, ugly circus of mayhem and murder and mindless, godless debauchery. Idle hands, forever still.

I rode on, past run-down colonial buildings, crowded street corners and open-air *botecos*. People still milling around in wilted, sweat-soaked costumes from the night before; still drinking, laughing, dancing, staggering along the *ruas* of the ramshackle, run-down old bairro, tops of graying Negro heads crowned with withered headdresses, bobbing down the dirty cement battlefield of Carnaval's last pathetic tweet; dying feathery explosions of expired exuberance and hope.

Ash Wednesday. The sheeple were going back into their pens at last, just as poor and lost and ignorant and exploited as before their big, happy-go-lucky piss-fest. Just as fucked. I could hear Narcisa's words echoing in the wind. *"E'stupid e'sheets!"*

Riding along like a stealthy black vampire bat beating leathery wings to close the coffin, it dawned on me that, for all their jovial, artificial joy and drunken, shouting Carnaval abandon, nobody had a fucking thing on me now. Because I was in love! And isn't love the greatest power a man can ever know?

So what if my love was for a psychotic, violent, abusive, foul-mouthed, unsanitary crack whore with a hell-bent rage and an insatiable appetite for destruction? So fucking what?

As I parked, the nostalgic words of an old bossa nova tune popped into my head. Humming like a man in love, I strode across the dark, quiet lobby . . . *Tristeza não tem fim, felicidade sim . . . A felicidade é como a pluma, que o vento vai levando pelo ar, voa tão leve, mas tem a vida breve, precisa que haja vento sem parar . . . e tudo se acabar na quarta-feira . . . tristeza não tem fim, felicidade sim . . .*

A happy sort of sadness without beginning or end occupied my heart like a plea, merging with the haunting, melancholy lyrics echoing in my brain.

Climbing the creaky wooden stairs, I thought of the past week, playing it all over in my head. Five flights of stairs. Five days of Carnaval. Five days into the gates of hell . . . *Tristeza não tem fim, felicidade sim . . . Porra! Que merda!*

And now, Ash Wednesday had dawned at last, closing the musty old tomb on another absurd human carnival of rats and ants and ashes and ruin.

And the whole world's a cold, old, smoldering empire of ashes.

40. MANIC MODE

"The sick woman especially: no one surpasses her in refinements for ruling, oppressing, tyrannizing."
—*Nietzsche*

Carnaval was over. Weeks crawled by.

The city was getting back to a prosaic workaday pace. Winter was just around the corner. My life with Narcisa was its own Dark Carnaval; a surreal, thundering cavalcade of escalating weirdness.

Since I had fallen into her mad trajectory, three months had passed in a swirling haze of passion and drama; a relentless flurry of days and nights of love and terror; danger, drama, excitement, lust, addiction, and impending mental collapse.

Between her grueling, soul-shattering, weeklong crack runs, I'd still try to take Narcisa to a movie, a beach walk at night; something safe and stable and normal, like a quiet *água de côco* beside a palm tree by the gentle waves. Things were getting worse, though, and she wanted to do that sort of thing less and less.

I was getting worse too.

I couldn't deny it as I watched my own compulsions running amok. Like some distant, impartial observer, I could see the madness unfolding, but I was powerless to stop my fall into a dark, dangerous vortex of petty crime, self-doubt and trouble—all in my desperate efforts to keep her voracious habit sated.

I feared for my sanity. But never once did I feel the urge to pick up a drug. Narcisa was all the drug I needed. And I tended to her like a flickering, dying flame; still trying to pretend, all the while, that everything was fine, that it would somehow turn out all right in the end. We both knew it wouldn't be all right. But when all that's left is the power to pretend, you take what you can get and do the best you can with it.

As the weeks slithered by, Narcisa began slipping into this crazed, frenetic manic-mode, whenever she was high. She would morph into an insane alien deity, dancing a savage, sensual, militant, extraterrestrial goddess dance; rattling on for backbending hours on end, jumping and writhing, gyrating around my cramped apartment with the music blasting away at top volume.

Musica! Musica! Go! Go!

I loved it and I hated it, all at once, like everything else about Narcisa when she jumped into that wild, compulsive go-go mode. And, like everything else about her, I knew I couldn't change it, even if I'd wanted to.

I didn't want to.

I was standing alone on my balcony late one hot, misty afternoon, looking out over the city. Another long, manic day with Narcisa. I stared out at the breathtaking visions of Rio de Janeiro; daydreaming, thinking, my weary, sleep-deprived eyes searching the view, scanning the horizon with a deep sense of longing, seeking some fleeting glimpse of normality. A cooling ocean breeze blew in off the expansive blue bay, caressing my tired flesh; a vanquished mortal shell, beat and worn, pained and spent after fucking Narcisa long and hard into the murky dawn.

Sex with Narcisa had become like smoking crack for me. Powerful, compelling, ecstatic, debilitating, raw, obsessive, addictive, deadly. The more I got, the more I had to have.

More more! Want want! Go go!

After going at it all night long, I stood there in a trance, replaying the fuzzy visions of our wild, unstoppable sex excursions.

Narcisa was still going, smoking inside the darkened apartment, frying her brains out, all alone . . . *Jesus! She can't stop!*

I ventured back inside. Exhausted, I crawled up to the loft bed and collapsed.

Minutes later, I was jolted awake by the Crack Monster and its endless, hyperactive noise machine, going, going, going . . . *Go go go go go go go!*

Bang!! Boom!! Crash!!

Fuck! She just broke something else down there . . . Pretty soon there'll be nothing left to break in this fucking place!

I didn't move. I just lay there, listening, beat, destroyed. Narcisa hadn't slept at all; and after three days up, without food or water or rest, she still wasn't tired.

Finally, I got up and stumbled back out onto the balcony. Groggy, I stood there, scratching my ass, staring off into space. A parrot flew by, squawking away into the distance. Dogs barked. Roosters crowed. A soft summer breeze rustled through the palm trees down below. A ship blew a deep, mournful horn, heading out to sea. I watched it out on the horizon, moving across the sparkling blue carpet of water, thinking of my own long-ago days as a sailor, my first few days at sea, feeling glad to be back in Rio.

Taking in the sleepy sights and sounds, I thought of how nice it would be now to lie down in the raw cotton comfort of my hammock and spend the rest of the day just lounging on the balcony. I could sleep out there, unperturbed, while she clanged and banged around inside, battling the invisible demons.

Then I remembered. There was no hammock anymore. Narcisa

had pulled it down and used it to cover the window, to block out the sun, the sea, the beautiful green view. Then she'd set the fucking thing on fire.

Fatigue was overcoming me like a shadowy shroud. I limped back inside, climbed up to the loft bed and closed my eyes again. But I couldn't sleep.

She was still down there, dancing all alone, her taut, wiry body gyrating around like some deranged spring-wound marionette . . . *Go go go!*

I looked down. Narcisa was wearing nothing but the pink polka-dot bikini she hadn't taken off for days now, except to fuck. I watched her as she twisted and turned, writhing and shimmying across my dirty, scuffed-up floor, hurtling through time and space . . . *go go go* . . . dancing to the earsplitting monkey chatter from the boom box I'd bought her after she traded off my radio for crack. The noise assaulted my ears, torturing my nerves, making me want to kill. I wondered if she knew or cared that I wanted to kill her.

Finally, she turned the music off and there was silence . . . *Sweet, blessed silence* . . . I tried to fall back into the pillows and rest. But it wasn't a peaceful silence. This new silence was haunted by the creepy Crack Monster and its desperate, manic demands for attention, movement, action . . . *Go go go go go!*

I listened to the sounds of her crashing and banging around down there. She was going mad, right below my head, dragging the remnants of my wrecked, soot-blackened furniture across the floor like a paranoid, psychotic wrecking crew; scuffing, breaking, dismantling, destroying my home, building her crooked little barricades to hide from the Shadow People.

The clumsy, frantic noises seemed to be rattling outward from the hellish core of her mind—punctuated by the sound of her little red

Cricket lighter, flicking, flicking, flicking in the dark . . . ***Ssskkk.***
Ssskkk.

Too creeped out to move, I just lay there, listening.

Ssskkk. Ssskkk.

Silence.

"Cigano . . ."

"Yeah?"

Silence.

"Cigano . . ."

"What?"

Silence.

"Cigano!"

I didn't answer . . . *She's tweaking . . . Spun . . . Crazed! Shit! Please stop!*

"Cig-aa-noo!!!"

"What!?!"

"Where are you?"

"I'm right here."

"Where?"

"Up in the loft, Narcisa. Where I've been the whole time. What th' fuck?"

Silence.

Crash!

Great! Breaking my stuff again! Fuck! She's gone completely nuts!

Silence.

Flick. Flick. Ssskkk ssskkk.

Her lighter . . . Smoking another hit. Shit!

Silence.

"Cigano."

Silence.

"Cigano."

Silence.

"Cig-aa-nooo!!"

"Shut th' fuck up, Narcisa!!"

Like a grotesque jack-in-the-box, her startled face appeared at the top of the loft ladder. Her eyes were darting around like maddened houseflies, her features frozen in a cold gray mask of terror . . . *Crack paranoia . . . Great! Now what?*

I sighed in disgust as she crawled across the bed like a crippled spider.

Without a word, she began examining my tattoos carefully, one by one, checking to see if I was an impostor. I groaned, rolling my bloodshot, sleepy eyes.

She thinks I'm a fucking "clone" again . . . I've seen all this before . . . Shit!

Narcisa picked up on my disdain. Sitting down beside me, she lowered her head like a sick parakeet.

"You are tire of me now, Cigano. I know."

"What makes ya say that, baby?" I ran my hand through her hair.

41. THE GHOST

"There are more things in heaven and earth, Horatio,
than are dreamt of in your philosophy."
—*Shakespeare*

Before I could grab Narcisa in another horny embrace, the room started spinning, slowly at first, then faster, faster. I was going cross-eyed, dizzy, my vision blurry.

Surrendering to fatigue with a sad little grunt, I fell back on the mattress and passed out. I slept for a while. Maybe a whole hour. Or maybe it was only minutes. Time had turned sideways. The world was a dreamlike, fuzzy smudge.

It was the middle of the night, just before dawn, when she poked me on the arm, waking me with a start.

My eyes jumped open. "Wha' . . . wassup?"

Narcisa was sitting on the bed beside me, looking at me with a dazed expression. "Come down an' watch me dance, Cigano."

"*Por favor*, baby, I just gotta rest a little more, just a few more minutes, okay?"

Without a word, she slithered back down the ladder. Just as I was losing consciousness again, her pallid, ash-blackened hand appeared beside my head.

The long, spindly white crack-claw grabbed and tugged at the corner of my blanket, slowly, strategically snatching it from atop my defeated carcass.

I couldn't move. I just lay there, wondering what time, what day it was.

It was cold and damp and uncomfortable on the dirty, bare mattress . . . *Whatever happened to all the sheets here?* There was no time to do laundry anymore; no time for anything but tending to Narcisa like a sick, retarded child.

I knew she was down there, sitting like a mangy dog on the cold, dirty floor, studying her ash-gray, raccoon-faced image in a sliver of broken mirror . . . *Using my blanket as a floor pillow for her lazy, self-centered ass while she smokes herself stupid . . . Shit!*

I stuck my head over the ledge, like a shy turtle peering out of its shell, looking down at a depressing, self-absorbed display of unrestrained narcissism running amok.

Finally, my vision dimmed and I fell back again.

Just as I was fading out, I felt another urgent little tapping at my shoulder.

Startled awake, I sat up . . . *There she is again! That fucking hand! Bored with lighting the goddamn crack pipe! Waking me up again, for a fuck, a touch of human companionship, warmth, company, money, cigarettes, an argument, something, anything to lift her up out of whatever deadly pit she's smoked herself into, sucking on that filthy little funnel to hell . . . What now?*

Coming to, I looked around in the clammy predawn stillness.

Silence. Dimness. Nothingness.

It wasn't Narcisa in the bed with me.

It was *something*. But it wasn't her!

What the fuck?

Baffled and disoriented, I leaned over the loft and looked down.

There she was. Still sitting in the same place, transfixed before her little mirror scrap, staring at herself, obsessed, lost in her own private hell.

Then, I felt it again! ***"Arrrggh!"*** I let out a stifled yelp.

Fuck! Some ghostly hand, touching me! Ugh!

Wide awake, I could feel the goose bumps covering my body in a crashing wave of panic as I scrambled down the ladder. Narcisa barely glanced up as I threw on my clothes and stumbled for the door . . . *Gotta get outa here, go for a cup of coffee, anything . . . Gotta get away from this madness . . . Gotta breathe!*

Just as I was about to close the door behind me, I turned and looked at her.

That's when I saw it. I saw it in her face.

The same creepy *something* that had just awakened me out of a sound sleep with a scream and a chill . . . *Jesus! She's really done it now! She's finally managed to open some horrible portal to hell and conjured up an ugly spirit of self-obsession. She's unleashed some heartless, inhuman, hateful phantom, unleashed a demon into herself, into the room, into the world! Shit!*

Narcisa was still sitting on the floor, staring at herself in the mirror as I picked up my case of heebie-jeebies and bolted out the door, without looking back.

I ran downstairs, got on the bike and sped off to the corner *paderia*.

Sitting down at the counter, instantly I felt better, surrounded by busy normal people having their normal morning coffee there, on their way to work. Comfort. A normal world of normal things. Old Roberto Carlos music playing on the radio. Buses and taxis rumbling down the street. The sun emerging into a cloudy 6 a.m. sky.

Sipping my coffee, I lit a cigarette and stared into space, fretting, trying to muster the courage to go back and rescue Narcisa from the Crack Monster.

I knew I had to try to save her. But how?

I called for another *cafezinho*. I smoked another cigarette. I worried. I prayed. I stared off into space some more, thinking.

I'd known right from the start what I'd signed on for with her.

Didn't I? I'd been warned . . . Why the fuck didn't I just listen to her then?

I could still hear the pleading sincerity of Narcisa's words.

"You don' wanna get involve with me, Cigano. I am de Crack Monster gee-rool now! I can really fock it up de life to you, brother, got it?"

I'd gotten it. I thought.

But I'd always had plenty of her overpowering Love Drug in steady supply, blinding me, seducing me, overpowering my reason.

Now, I realized I'd only *thought* I was ready for whatever came with it.

I remembered my own words that night, as I'd laughed off her shy little warning . . . *"Long as I'm going to hell, baby, I may as well try to beat the devil . . ."*

Now, I knew the sinister occult forces were really closing in.

42. EXTREME NARCISSISM

"THE EDGE. THERE IS NO HONEST WAY TO EXPLAIN IT, BECAUSE THE
ONLY ONES WHO REALLY KNOW WHERE IT IS HAVE GONE OVER IT."
—H. S. Thompson

After three cups of sweet black coffee and half a dozen cigarettes, I got on the bike and rode back. Climbing the creaking wooden stairs up to my flat, I could have sworn I saw a fuzzy, indistinct shadow darting around in the darkened hallway. Spooked, heart pounding, I held my breath and opened the door. There Narcisa sat. Right where I'd left her an hour ago.

Still sitting in front of the same broken mirror . . . Playing around with that fucking crack pipe . . . Opening the gates to hell again and again . . . Jesus!

I stood in the middle of the room and glared at her. She looked up. Somehow, she seemed a bit more human in the soft morning light.

"What's up, Narcisa?"

"Last hit . . ." She loaded up the pipe.

"Great . . . *Fucking hell* . . ." I scowled and turned away, muttering.

I limped out onto the balcony. Brooding miserably, I avoided saying what was on my mind. I lingered there, thinking, worrying, watching the bright red sun of another sleepless morning emerging in the murky sky, like a cigarette point burning through a sickbed sheet. I could hear squawking parrots and the distant rumble of the awakening urban machine.

After a while, I peeked back inside.

Narcisa sat in her ash-strewn corner, mumbling strange, incoherent words, babbling, conjuring up dark spirits.

I stood there in silence, shaking my head, watching her slap at the invisible phantoms nipping at her flesh. She was coming undone, a demented, demon rag doll.

With a heavy sigh, I limped back inside.

I plopped down on the sofa, holding my head in my hands.

After an eternity, I looked up and said it. I begged it. "Baby, please! Just go up to bed and lie down for a while. *Por favor!* You just gotta try to get some sleep now . . ."

"I don' gotta do nothing you e'say!" She snarled at me. **"You only wan' for me to go e'sleep so they can kill me, an' then you got you revengence!"**

My mouth fell open. "*What?!*"

"Hah! You think I so e'stupid, hein?" She recoiled, moving across the floor like a shell-shocked crab. **"I know all about it you conspiriation together with them for finish me! Well, fock you an' go to e'sheet, seu velho otário! I never gonna go e'sleep around you focking Shadow Peoples! Nunca!! Got it!?"**

"*What* Shadow People? It's just me here, man. This isn't even you talking, Narcisa. It's the demons, the crack. It's all in yer mind! If ya just try to sleep and get some rest they'll go away. I promise! Just try it, *por favor* . . ."

"Menos! Shut de fock up an' e'stop make all these focking pressure on me! I don' wan' no e'sleep! E'sleep is for de old peoples, e'stupid peoples, retard peoples, got it? I no got de time, Cigano! Too much e'speriment an' research for do . . . An' don' try an' make no more you sabatoge on me! I know what you up to, cara!"

"I'm not up to anything, Narcisa! Jesus, just look at yerself, man. You're a fuggin' mess! Maybe ya oughta think about getting some help and putting that shit down, before ya end up goin' nuts and kill-ing yerself . . ."

"Hah! I wish I can kill myself, Cigano!" Her big, anguished eyes blazed.

I sighed. There was a long, uncomfortable silence.

Finally, she broke it with a dark whisper. "Narcisa know you work-ing together with *them*!" She fixed me with a hateful look that froze my soul.

I could feel gooseflesh on my arms. I knew that look. The same look that poor, mad drunk woman used to give a frightened little boy named Ignácio.

"Arrrggghhh!! You think I so e'stupid, hein? Tá bom! Just e'say it to me! Which one of them send you to kill me, hein? E'say it to me, porra! Don' be so focking covarde! Got de balls to look me on de face an' do it when I awaked!"

What the fuck? Oh, God, please help her!

She fell silent again as I prayed . . . *Help us, God! Por favor!*

Then, with a tone of iron-fisted authority, she barked like a seal. **"Food! Fome! Foo-oood! Na-oow, Cigano, hungry hungry, go go go!"**

As I fixed her a sandwich, Narcisa ranted on about the Plot, a big, sinister Satanic Plan. Slipping into a greasy bog of panic and despair, I stood there in the little kitchen, hiding, worrying, contemplating my situation.

Is this my fucking life now? Am I a slave to the Crack Monster, like her?

I knew she wanted nothing to do with my suggestions to get help. How many times had I begged her to let me take her to treatment, or to an NA meeting? Somewhere. Something. Anything. It was no use. Narcisa always rationalized her delusional behavior by insisting it was all a part of some big Satanic Mind Control plan.

I'd thought my feet were planted in a solid bedrock of my own recovery. I'd told myself I was grounded enough to reach into the pit when the time came and pull Narcisa out.

But now I was losing my footing, getting sucked down with her.

Now the Curse was taking a bitter toll.

My life was reduced to a sordid little comedy. Four-hour shifts of worried solitude and prayer, punctuated by two-hour stints spent together, fucking like angry baboons.

Or fighting. As if anything we fought about mattered anymore.

43. CRASH DAY

In a world of untold uncertainty, one thing was always certain. When Narcisa didn't sleep, nobody slept. The Crack Monster unfailingly saw to that.

According to her bulletproof armor of irrational rationalization, all her insane behavior was just part of some big, elaborate Pact she claimed to have made with Lucifer. And now, she announced, Satan had brought me to her at last, like a cat dropping a crippled mouse at the feet of the one who serves it.

According to Narcisa, I was her new mind-control slave. Her *zumbí*.

Handing her the sandwich, I wondered.

As I watched her devour the food like a hungry dog, I thought back to when we'd first met, how she'd been fixated on the idea that I was the Dark One himself, come to collect for delivering the goods with her Golden Banker. Since the husband was history now, maybe I *was* the next sacrificial lamb. Still, I knew that the sandwich and all the mad, delusional ranting that went before it were a prelude to imminent relief; a sign that her mission was about to expire. Narcisa was coming in for a blessed crash landing. I knew it the minute she asked for food.

As she babbled on, I bit my tongue, waiting for her to run out of fuel.

I prayed as she whirled around the room, spitting out curses, knocking things asunder. I was waiting the demons out till they would suck away her last frantic burst of energy; waiting for the Crash. I lived for the Crash.

Watching as Narcisa began to go glassy-eyed. I sighed with relief as her knees grew wobbly. Then she crumpled to the floor like a dropped puppet, the half-eaten sandwich dangling in her hand and a cigarette burning at her fingers.

She stayed in a comatose state for the next twenty-four hours.

After moving her to the sofa and lying down beside her, I began to relax. As a hot summer rain droned outside the window, I lay there, half awake, savoring the moment like some exotic new drug. It was the first real rest for me in a long time too. But, tired as I was, just lying there beside Narcisa, inhaling her wild, intoxicating essence with every sleepy breath, it was too much to bear.

Stealthy as a cat burglar, I pulled her panties down over her legs. Then I worked myself slowly, gently, up into her sleeping wet cunt.

I stayed like that, fucking her for hours as she snored gently.

Shagging Narcisa while she slept was a new, tremendous kind of thrill; like playing with a doped-up Bengal tiger, listening to its thunderous, feral heartbeat, running my fingers across the ferocious man-eating teeth.

Taming the sleeping Crack Monster was something special, enticing. And compulsive.

After I'd finished, I got up and washed off in the sink. Tiptoeing back into the room, I glanced down at her amazing, ethereal beauty sprawled out there like a fallen angel. Freshly fucked and dead to the world, Narcisa seemed so peaceful, serene and innocent; harmless as a raging hurricane seen from outer space.

Soon I was rock-hard again.

I fucked Narcisa again and again, at least half a dozen times, as she snored the afternoon away on the sofa. Soft, melodic classical music massaged my weary brain from the box as the steady rhythm of the ceiling fan blended with the steady rainfall at the window, lulling my sex-crazed senses into a soporific zone of peace and comfort, like a deep, sensuous heroin nod.

Sated at last, feeling like a blood-glutted vampire climbing into its coffin, I crawled up to the loft and slept, while Narcisa stayed passed out on the couch.

She slept like a corpse, well into the next day, interrupted only by short waking bouts to stuff herself with food while watching her favorite chattering television cartoons. The blaring noise from the TV awakened me again and again, but I didn't succumb to the Crack Monster's wicked enticements to make me murder her. I just covered my head with the pillow, waiting for her to pass out again, so I could go back to sleep too. Eventually, I did.

Somehow, it all worked out.

Having Narcisa on my hands had become like living with a new-born infant . . . *You gotta sleep when the baby sleeps . . . Cuz when that goddamn Crack Monster's awake, it's all go go go . . . But Crash Day . . . Ah, Crash Day!*

I lived for those blessed moments of peace, whenever they came around.

Even Narcisa's pet fish would conk off in the darkened chamber of my room on Crash Day, lying sideways at the bottom of its cloudy bowl, motionless and lopsided, like a cockeyed Lapa wino; drunk on the overripe, sensual musk of slumber in the cool, shadowy air. On Crash Day, we all hibernated like a pack of sleeping vampires, secure and safe, shuttered away from the blazing tropical daylight world outside.

When Narcisa came to at last, she bellowed like a wounded water buffalo, calling for food. I didn't mind. With pleasure, I tended to her every need.

We even watched a movie on the TV, cuddling on the sofa together for hours, as she fell in and out of consciousness. By the end of the film, she'd disappeared back down the ladder of dreams into a deep delta slumber.

I got up and swept the floor, cleaning away the debris of her ravenous waking moments.

Still exhausted, the moment I lay down with her again, my hand fell right to that firm, irresistible ass. And then it was on again.

Again, again, more, more, more! Twin Flames! Twin addictions!

Passing out beside her, blurrily contemplating the days ahead, I didn't know whose addiction would generate more devastation for us in the long run: hers to the crack, or my addiction to her.

As sleep engulfed my throbbing, battered brain again, I didn't care.

44. SHIPWRECKED SAILORS

The next day, Narcisa arose to greet the world, spitting and cursing, as usual.

I handed her a few bucks to get rid of her before it could escalate into trouble, and off she went to cop . . . *Thank you come again! Freak!*

A day at a time, I was learning to deal with the madness.

I went out for a quick snack at the *paderia*. By the time I returned, she was already back at my place, sitting on the sofa, waiting.

Somehow Narcisa always seemed to know when I'd be home. It was weird; like this uncanny tweaker radar. Even not having a key to my apartment, she always managed to gain entry somehow.

I stood in the doorway, staring at her.

How did she get in here this time? Picked the lock? Scaled the side of the building like the fucking Spider-Man?

I didn't bother asking. Nothing Narcisa did could surprise me anymore.

As I closed the door behind me, she ran over and jumped up onto me like a crazy child, her long, wiry arms and legs wrapping around my torso.

Still breathing hard from scaling the stairs, I grabbed her firm, bony ass cheeks with both hands, like a pair of fuzzy new peaches.

I couldn't have let go if I'd wanted to.

I didn't want to let go. This was where my hands lived now. When they weren't clutching that ass, they were nothing but a pair of useless appendages. Crippled beggars. Homeless, shivering derelicts.

I heard myself speaking. "I'm a lost soul without my hands on this ass, princesa."

Narcisa cracked that evil clown grin and jumped down, hitting the dusty floor like a cat. I watched in awe as she sashayed across the room to examine herself in the mirror. She stood there, turning around and around, checking out her strange, spectral image from every angle, like a naughty schoolgirl seeing herself as a full-fledged Whore Goddess for the very first time.

"You're spectacular, baby!" I whistled, blowing her a kiss.

"Hah! You crazy! *Fala serio!* You don' see it, hein? I already e'start to get old, Cigano. Old an' ugly an' *flacida* . . ." She turned around again, studying herself with a sad, doubtful look. "Old . . . Definite!" She frowned. "I don' got it no more *tchans* . . . *Fock!* I don' even *exist* no more. Only de old e'solitary ghost. That's me . . ."

"You're not old! Shit, man, yer only nineteen." I laughed. "Ya do exist, Narcisa! And yer not ugly. To me, you're the most beautiful girl in the world . . ."

She turned, hands on her hips. "Hah! I dunno if you only liar or you complete insane too! Or maybe you go blind, hein, Cigano? Whatever. Can't never trust whatever thing you focking gyp-say peoples e'saying."

"Whaddya mean? Whaddya know about my people, huh?"

"More than you thinking, *mermão!*" She chuckled. "When I was a little girl, de gyp-say peoples always come on de horses an' build de camp outside my town. I know all de *cigano* ways. Hah! You focking peoples all teef, an' cheater an' liar too . . ."

"Well, that may be true, Narcisa." I grinned back, unbuckling my belt and stepping out of my jeans. " . . . But the truth is still true, even when a lying gypsy says it. And this shit don't lie . . . C'mere."

She came over and stood before me, obedient as a schoolgirl.

"Take off yer shorts," I said, and she did.

As her underwear hit the floor, I grabbed her ass, lifted her up and fit it right into her, like a missing jigsaw piece. I pushed her up against the wall and moaned as she stroked my hair, her hot, dry teeth resting on my shoulder.

I could feel her breath burning like a furnace on my neck as I got harder, harder, hard as rock. Hard as steel. Hard as a diamond. Superman hard! Then she pinched my dick, twitching, contracting that insane, lethal Supersonic Extraterrestrial Paranormal Pussy Muscle, driving me crazy.

Drooling like a happy old sea dog, I moaned and rocked her back and forth as we fell into a soft, easy rhythm, like a boat taking to the waves, headed out to sea; and like a happy, drunken sailor, Narcisa started to sing, crooning a moody, raspy little dirge with such a deep, soulful passion, I began to cry.

I held my mouth close to her chapped, dry lips as they moved, feeling her feral, crack-toasted breath burning on mine. Watching her calloused pink tongue flickering in her mouth, I was a hungry cat stalking a lizard. Total focus.

We stayed like that, fucking, lost at sea, bobbing up and down, sailing the horizon, as she went through her lazy repertoire of melancholy song lyrics, like ancient pirate shanties; we were two starving, shipwrecked sailors, gorging on a spontaneous feast of timeless lust.

An hour of lovemaking with Narcisa, feeling her hard, childlike body clutching at me, grinding away under the ever-present shadow of impending loss, it was always worth the most freakish mental torments she'd ever subjected me to.

All her spiteful, infantile rants and rages, violent cursing tantrums and broken glasses; the dirty dishes, the unflushed toilets and angry cigarette butts stubbed out on my clean floor, or in my face; all the bites and scratches, the torn shirts and mangled hopes and bloodied, beaten, broken, abandoned dreams; it all just went away.

And then there was nothing but comfort.

Until the next storm.

Always looming out over the horizon.

45. APOCALYPTIC SMOKE HOLE

"LIVING WITH INSANE WOMEN IS GOOD FOR THE BACKBONE."
—*Charles Bukowski*

By the tail end of her latest run, I'd fucked Narcisa again and again, for days on end. My dick was soft and sore. My eyelids were salty little sandbags, dragging me down into a world of fuzzy, sex-numbed incoherence.

Narcisa sat on the sofa beside me, cranking out maniacal, mystical, torrential streaks of delirious, paranormal crack-chatter. I listened and watched, transfixed, as explosions of alien poetry raged from her apocalyptic smoke-hole, an open gateway to some higher, weirder dimension.

I was captivated, trapped, spellbound. But I was coming to that point of delirious sleeplessness where I just had to shut my eyes, or drop off the edge of sanity. Or die. That's how it always felt. Like impending death.

Narcisa always had the most demonic timing, totally out of sync with all mundane, terrestrial affairs; it wasn't surprising that this would be the precise moment for her to wax eloquent. And surreal: Cosmic Mysticism, Secret Science, Satanic Ritual, Quantum Mechanics, Sacred Geometry, Occult Politics, Crop Circles, Vampirism, Necrophilia, Futuristic Archeology, Alpha Centurion Philosophy. Epic supernatural revelations, bubbling from her mouth in wild, manic torrents.

She took a big hit, then exhaled, barking through the smoke. ***"Capitalismo selvagem! Hah! All de capitalist savage, do they***

know how to choose de quality things that is necessary but no obligatory for de benefit of de existence, hein?"

"Huh?" I looked at her, rubbing my chin. "Whaddya mean, princesa?"

"*'What you mean? What you do?'*" She mimicked me, speaking to an idiot. "*Afffff!* All de time e'same e'stupid questions! *'What you do?'* Hah! E'same like de peoples in de e'stupid Je-sooz church do? Or maybe de peoples at de work e'say you gotta do, hein? E'school? *Hah!* E'stupid question all de time! *Porra!*"

I stared at her in awe, fighting to keep my eyes open as she ranted on.

"Is so many thing ever'body gotta buy an' aquire an' consume! Why, hein? *'Because these de normal way to do it,'* they all e'say. De common peoples e'say, *'Oh what a big e'sheet, de government, de country, my familia, baa ba ba!'* Is maybe a good beginning, to ask all these question, cuz maybe they wanna know now what is it that exist beyond de hole that exist in all de thing they wanna possess. But really is no good! *Hah!* Try again! *Next?*"

Her voice shifted to a squeaking sarcastic tone. "*Ooh! Lookit!* Here he come now, de famous *doutor de fisica*, de big genius *cientista* come from de far away place, *oooh*, an' he come make de *visita* to our little land! *Ooh, aahh! Fantastico!*"

"Huh? What physics doctor, Narcisa? Whaddya talkin' about?"

"*Pay attention, Cigano!* Look it these e'stupid old e'science guy, what de name, hein? E'Stephen Hawking. *What e'sheet!* All de peoples e'say he de big e'scientifical genius. An' he sitting on a focking *wheelchair! Afffff!* How de e'stupid little cripple gringo gonna teach any thing to de earth peoples about de physics, an' he can' even clean his own physical *asshole, hein? Hah! Ridiculo!*"

I laughed. "What does one thing got to do with the other?"

"Is too much *complexo* for me e'splain it to you, Cigano. An' here it come again, *more* e'stupid question! *'What it gotta do with de other thing?' 'What you mean?' 'What do you e'study?' 'Home e'school? Baa baa baa!'*"

"What questions, Narcisa? What th' fuck are you going on about?"

"De *question*, Cigano! Like they make in de *escola*! Fock!"

"School?" I looked at her. "What about it?"

"You know, I always *hate* it de e'stupid e'school, Cigano, I hate it *so-oo* much! Hah! One day I e'say, '*fock these e'sheets*,' an' then I go an' walk outside to de bush an' I put my hand inside de bee-hive . . ."

"What!?" I winced. "What th' fuck did ya do that for?"

"I do it so I can e'say now I am cripple too, e'same like these e'Stephen Hawking. *O grande genio!* Hah! I think if I get myself cripple, then I gonna be de big e'science genius too, an' then I don' gotta go de e'stupid e'school no more."

I laughed out loud. "Great. How'd that work out for ya?"

"No so good, bro." She started to giggle. "They e'say I am de 'problem *e'studante*,' an' they go, '*Home e'school for these geer-ool!*' Well, I e'say, '*Fock you!*' Hah! An' then I go! *Out! Next?* Get de fock out. No more home, no more e'stupid home e'school. *Logico*, hein? Simple like that, got it?"

I got it. The act of studying and learning, all those irritating, boring, ugly gray rows of words and numbers scratching at her brain, demanding her attention, were a deep offense to the alien poetry of Narcisa's soul. It wasn't just that she was unfit for everything. It was that she truly wasn't of this world.

"*Matematica! Numero!* These is de only real e'science, mano, got it? So I e'say, '*Fock you e'stupid home e'school!*' Narcisa go to de e'street! Better de street e'school for me, got it? Hah! *Perfect, Max! Next?*"

She stopped, fired up another rock, then went on. "When I was in de e'stupid *escola*, de *professor de matematica*, she wan' try an' teach 'bout de Pythagoras, but she don' know nothing! *Nada! Porra nenhuma!* I ask to her what do she really know about it, de Pythagorian *teoria* an' de number system, hein? When I was only fourteen year old, you know, I already de most youngest *kabalista* in de world!"

I raised my eyebrows at her latest bombastic claim.

"Is *truth*, Cigano! An' then these e'stupid mathematic teacher she sock me on de face! Just because her equation *wrong*, an' I e'say to her, '*These is e'sheet!*' Right there in de class! *Crowwn crowwwn crowwwwn!* Hah!"

"Yer teacher punched ya in th' face? What th' fuck?"

"*Poisé, mermão!* De focking e'science professor too, he wan' teach it to me all de wrong e'sheets! An' de history professor? Hah! Forget it! These one don' know *nothing* 'bout no focking human history. *Nada!* Lissen, Cigano. I e'say him, '*What are you, hein? Are you de focking artista? Cuz you make it up, invent it all these bool-e'sheets for teach it to me who know already more about de human history than you?*' An' he e'say to me, '*Get out my class room!*' An' *boo!* I go, an' I never go back. Then is de e'street e'school only for de Narcisa! You think for me is a punishment? Hah! No way! *Next?* They make de big favor for me!"

"Howzat, baby?"

"Because in de e'street I meet de peoples who gonna teach it to me all de thing I need learn about! *Geometria. Fisica. Musica. Matematica.* An' de philosophy. Nietzsche, Cigano! You know him? I think like Nietzsche, cuz I see all de thing a different way, Cigano. '*Fock you, I don' do what you tell me,*' got it?"

I nodded. I got it.

"I never got no interest to be involve with nobody in de human e'society, no past an' no *futuro*, only live for these day today, got it? These why I involve only with my own self now, Cigano, cuz I am Nobody here, got it? I no accustom for de life on these *planeta*, all de e'stupid human society, I don' know how they wan' do all these focking thing. Hah! I don' care about no public recognition, de follower, de e'stage, de fame, de diploma, de money, de plan, de goal. Hah! Fock all these e'sheets. E'spontaneity! That's me. Next? I never gonna respect nothing just because they e'say I gotta respect, but only if I feel like it, got it?"

I stared at her in awe, wondering if I would ever fully get Narcisa.

46. HIGHER EDUCATION

I was seeing double with fatigue. But Narcisa was just getting started.

She hopped along, from subject to subject, like a cocaine-crazed, hyperactive little fairy, flittering between realms of thought I could barely fathom.

I forced my eyes open. What else could I do? I needed to know all about her paranormal genius mindscape; to understand why Narcisa was the way she was.

As if reading my thoughts, she went on, telling all.

"I no come from de city, Cigano. I know 'bout only de country thing, de plant an' de water an' de weather patterns, an' I know de little animal habitat, an' all they habit. I know where to get de food an' de water an' de real psychedelic mushroom, an' how to make de ayahuasca tea, an' how to talk to de plant e'spirit peoples too. I know all 'bout these kinda thing. But de human e'society, forget it! Is like one big alien program for de Narcisa. *Afffff!* '*My e'shoelace, my e'shoes!*' *Argghhh*, I don' like it de e'shoe an' de clothes, all these e'stupid technological e'sheets, is only for de caution an' de organization! *Fock!* No good for me! What de e'stupid human society wan' for me to do, hein? I don' wan' all de e'stupid peoples asking to me all de day, '*Hey, hey you, Narcisa, what you mean? What do you do? What thing you e'study? Where you work?*' ***Arrggghhh! Shut de fock up! Porra!***"

I stared at her in mute fascination as she powered on.

"Lissen, Cigano. When I first time come to de city, I go live with de most worse tribe of de *anarcista*. Destruction punks, got it? An' they e'say it all de day, '*Lixo, lixo! Trash trash! Destroy!*' In de city, nothing but noise! ***Arggghh!*** De whole focking zoological garden can e'scream in their animal language to me now, cuz I don' care! But I am here living in these e'stupid earth, so now I gotta just accept it. What else I can do, hein?"

She stared at me, waiting for an answer.

Bewildered, I shrugged.

Just then, an airplane passed overhead. She ran over and slammed the window shut, holding her fingers to her ears with a pained look.

"Tecnologia! Arggghhhhh! I got enough of these focking noises an' I don' wan' it no more! If Santos Dumont come up out from de grave today, I gonna take a big e'sheet on his head for all de e'stupid airplane traffic that make me crazy, got it? What de fock I doing here, Cigano, hein? Why I gotta e'stay on these e'stupid planeta? What it can be my mission with de earth peoples? Is no my tribe! No way I ever gonna believe I got de e'same DNA like these focking race of machine builder an' telemarketer! No no no!"

Her voice changed again, into a haunting little robotic drone.

"'*Din din! Hello? good afternoon! My name is Maria, Joanna, Talita, Sofia, Julia, Alessandra, whatever. Din din! We got it de e'special promotion for you, can you buy it? Din din! You got de credit card? I wanna sell to you so I can get more money, so I can buy it on installment plano too. Din din! My name Maria, Talita, Julia, Whatever, bla bla bla . . .*' ***Fock! E'stupid! Porra! Que merda! Affff . . .***"

I watched as she loaded another huge rock into the pipe, fired it up and took a deep, long hit. When she exhaled, there was no smoke.

What th'. . . ? Where'd all that smoke go to? Narcisa! Strange alien physics!

"I don' wanna participate in any of these e'stupid e'sheet, got it?" She sat up, yelping, her eyes blazing, interrupting my drowsy musings. **"Get me de fock out from here, mano! Out!! Arrrg-gghhh!!"**

I cocked my head like a curious dog as she ranted on.

"All de human systems only exist for disguise it de true nature of de existence! Is only by de anarchy system where peoples ever gonna know them-self! De human being is de beast, de killer, de savage, de who-ore! I don't even wanna take a e'sheet on you consumer world an' all de human waste production machine! An' I don' wanna make no waste or influence nobody! No focking way! I don' wanna do no-thing on these e'stupid earth! Nada! Porra! Frustra-tion! Arrghh!"

Struggling to follow Narcisa's mad discourse, I felt like I was inter-viewing an elusive extraterrestrial visitor who was on a tight sched-ule. Maybe I was. Transfixed, I got out my little notebook and began scribbling away like a nuthouse scribe.

"Arrrggghhh! Din din din din! Hahahaha! Everywhere I go on these e'stupid planeta, de focking earth peoples all de time come an' ask to me e'say all what I know! Arrgh! Fock, Cigano! Why me? I don' wan' it! Don' wan' know 'bout noth-ing! What I gonna do with so much informations, hein? If I live five thousand more year here, I can' e'say all de thing I already know 'bout! Affff! Why?"

I shrugged and kept writing down everything she was saying.

"Is good!" She smiled, gesturing at my note-taking. "Cuz I always gonna be these way, Cigano, you know, so I wan' only for you keep going an' write it down all these e'sheet. I give it all to you, all of who I am, for you to do whatever you wanna do with all these informations. Hah! Maybe *you* can figure these e'sheet out. I only e'say it to you these one thing: Narcisa can be de beginning an' de end of all de thing, de Alpha an' de Omega. But they *never* gonna put me in de middle of de road here, got it? *Nunca! Ne-ver!*"

Her face seemed bathed in a strange, majestic, angelic glow. "*Porra!* I can think of a million thing to do, *mermão.* Whatever thing any human being can do, I can do it better. So that's it. *E agora?* What now, hein? What I e'suppose to do? My mind? Hah! Completely without ambition! *Afffff!* Only I wan' exist anymore for teach it all to you now, Cigano, got it?"

I got it. I nodded and kept writing, scribbling, scrambling to get it all down.

" . . . But I don' understand it all de peoples who wanna be de animal doctor, de *veterenario*, Cigano. Why? They wan' be e'specificly doctor to de dog? Or only for horse. For de poodle, or maybe de pony, hein? Or maybe de *pato*, de duck! *Qua qua qua quaaaa! Pato-logia?* Hah!! What about de insect? How come they no got de doctors, Cigano, hein? They got it de cats doctor, de donkey doctor, even de rat doctor, but no got it de insect doctor! Why? *Injusto! Porra! Discrimination! Why, hein? Meow meow! Woof woof! Qua qua quaaa quaaaaa!* An' what about it all these e'specialist doctor? De foots doctor, hein? Do insect got de foots? Wear de little e'shoe? What is it de size, hein? Where do this subject e'start? What it is de relevance, hein? An' then they e'say is me gotta be lock up in de crazy house? Where they get such e'stupid idea, hein?"

I looked up from my writing, holding back laughter.

"I really wan' try an' believe it there some kinda force fields or de metaphysical e'sheets like that, or some very big Somebody who responsible for all these focking question. *Serio!* Is better for me if there gonna be some kinda gods or something, got it? Cuz, fock, mano, what if I gotta be in charge of so much e'sheet only by my self, hein? *Arrrggghhhh! Fock!* Nothing can fill it, de void of de existence, got it?"

I was fading fast, but I got it. Sort of. The bottomless pit ain't got no bottom.

"An' what about these e'stupid E'Stephen Hawking guy, hein?"

"Huh?" I looked up again. The room shifted in and out of focus. My brain was shutting down, melting. Everything was going fuzzy and weird.

"Oi Cigano!" She nudged me on the arm, snapping me back to attention. *"What is it de ambition of all these cripple deficient peoples, hein?"*

I shook my head and shrugged.

"Conspiracy! They wanting to teef it what can' never be teef or be for sale or purchase or find it or give or even inherited, but only can be acquire, Cigano, only by de intellectual naturality of de biological sanity, de e'shielded e'spirit body, perfect, unaffectable, infinito! An' then they only wanna use it all they knowledge an' understanding, for go an' destroy ever'thing! Destroy destroy! Why? Arggghhh! E'stupid human race! Clone peoples! E'stupid focking military machine! Heroic champions of destruction! Chaos! Ridiculous competition! Porra! Why, Cigano, hein? Para que?!?"

I shrugged again and again as Narcisa ranted on, her big, mad eyes bulging out of her head like a pair of rocket ships about to shoot off into space.

"Better they got de focking pope in de Holy Vaticano than all these e'stupid politico e'sheets in charge of de earth now! War! Hah! Fock! Was better here when you got it only de priest and sacerdotes to rule you e'stupid planeta! Better I

go an' look inside my own focking poo-sy an' ask inside my *ass-hole, 'Hey, where is de God? Anybody home?'"*

That did it.

I began to chuckle out loud. I laughed and laughed, until I was crying; the irrational, cackling, delirious laughter of the insane.

I looked at Narcisa through a haze of humid, sweaty tears.

Her face was fading in and out of focus.

Like a ghost.

47. TOSS UP

"WHO WILL PITY A SNAKE CHARMER BITTEN BY A
SERPENT, OR ANY WHO GO NEAR WILD BEASTS?"
—*Ecclesiasticus 12:13*

My brain was burnt toast.

I stopped laughing, feeling dizzy and faint. Cold sweat. Delirium.

Sleep! Please, God, I gotta get some fucking sleep!

I put down the notebook and squinted at Narcisa, trying to focus. I was fading away, and she was still going strong, traveling at a speed of thought way beyond my ability to keep up.

"Pay attention, Cigano!" She stabbed me on the arm with my discarded pen, nagging like a cackling crow. **"De imposed earth disease can' never kill it de immortality of de chronic intellectualism! E'stubborn! Hard! Persistent! Inflexible! Water-resistant! Bulletproof! Hah! What to do? Look around an' wait for de inspiration?! Fala serio! Ashamed for de imposed want of de irrefutable changing mental attitude, hein? Para que, Cigano, hein?"**

What the fuck? Sleep . . . Gotta sleep . . . I sat there, shrugging like a drooling idiot child. I was done in, down for the count . . . *Gotta go lie down.*

"Nothing is de secret of de sensorial existence of de earthly physical matter in all de material e'states! Nada! Got it? Solid, liquid, gaseous, elasticity, indivisibility

beyond all de human measurement! Hah! An' what about my little decadent reality, hein? To accelerate de aging process? De bruise an' de contusion, 'Crack Monster,' hein? Aggghhhh! What to do, hein? Fight? Yell? Insult? Fart? Spit? Vomit? Yawn? Burp? Sneeze? E'say, 'God bless you'? Jump? Dance? Push? Pull? Fall down? Get up? Fly? What? Hein? What de fo-ock!? Arrrggghhh!! Need something to relax! Por favor! Confused! Turbulent phases of de thought process, so much focking informations! Too much talk! It only serve to complicate de afflicted consciousness! Porra! Fock! Aggghhhh!"

"Huh?" Half delirious, hallucinating from fatigue, I rubbed my eyes.

"Ei, wake up, Cigano!" She pinched my arm, hard. *"Where is it my lighter, hein? Give it to me! Where is it my little white Bic lighter, hein? I gotta e'smoke some more now, bro! Bic Bic Bic! Hah! Pick! Pick! Crowwn crowwwn crowwwwn, ha ha! Din din din! Thank you come again . . . doiiingg . . ."*

Sleep . . . Oh God, I need rest . . . I was feeling overwhelmed, confused, disoriented, lost, like little Ignácio watching his mother as she toppled over, again and again, in the fuzzy barrooms of my warped, mangled memory banks . . . *A crazy woman . . . Drunk, raging, raving, shouting wild, incoherent, incomprehensible words . . . words . . . words . . .*

Narcisa ranted on and on about mad, fantastical things that were way too strange and much too big for my baffled little mind to comprehend anymore. My brain was throbbing like a sore, beaten, bloody nose. I rose to my feet. As she raved on, oblivious, I crawled up to the loft bed, fell back, and closed my eyes. Drifting in and out of consciousness, I could hear her storming around below. Then, just as I began to fade, she jolted me awake again, singing, screeching at the top of her lungs.

"Arrrggghhh!! From hee-ee-rrrrrre to eee-terrrr-nit-yyyyy!!" Again and again. Over and over. *"From herrrrrre to eeeterrrrnityyyyy!! Arrrggghhh!!"*

It was as if she was doing it on purpose, trying to drive me mad.

But I knew better. Even with all her grandiose talk of a big Satanic Master Plan, I knew she was just being Narcisa . . . *Just doing her thing, wrecking shit, making noise, singing, screaming, freaking out, go go go, nothing personal, got it?*

She called out. *"Eiii, Cigano . . . Cigano! Cig-ah-noo! Oiiii!"*

I groaned. "Huh? Wha' . . . whassup?"

"Wanna play a game of chess?"

What?!? Chess?!? Shit!

I rolled my eyes and grunted. "Uh, I'm just gonna rest my eyes up her for a minute, princesa, I'll come down and play with you in a bit, okay? Promise . . ."

I settled back into the pillows . . . *Sleep, sweet sleep!* Soon, I was dreaming my way down, down, into a deep sea of slumber.

I don't know how long I was out. Everything that happened next was a blur. Awakened with a jolt, I felt that creepy death house chill, like when the weird phantom shadow tapped me on the shoulder. I cracked my eyes open in that foggy state where you don't know what day it is or if it's day or night . . . *Coming to . . . Some weird noise . . . What's going on?*

I looked up and saw Narcisa's face, hovering over me on the bed like a bad acid hallucination. I blinked, rubbed my puffy eyes and looked again. It was really her this time . . . But there was something about her look. Something strange.

Her eyes . . . What the fuck? It gave me a chill right down to my core. She just sat there on the edge of the bed, staring at me with this goofy, distant look on her face, making these constipated little choking sounds.

A sudden wave of panic froze my gut . . . *What the fucking fuck? Oh, shit! No! She's having an overdose! Shit! Oh, God! No! She's finally done it! Any second now, she'll be foaming at the mouth, bleeding from those big bugged-out eyes, flipping around on my fucking bed like a hooked trout! Oh God! No! Shit!*

With a short gasp, I sat up and shook her by the shoulders.

"Baby, what's wrong, Narcisa? Talk to me . . . Narcisa! Say something!"

She said nothing. She just sat there making those odd little *hhuaa hhuaa* noises, like a cat choking on a hairball.

Edging toward me, she put her face over my chest, as if she was trying to tell me something important . . . *Oh God, please make her be all right! Please, God!*

Praying, I moved closer so as not to miss her dying last words.

Suddenly—**huuunnhghhh!** A gushing geyser flew out of her mouth, bathing me in vomit! A steaming shower of beans and rice, chocolate, Coca-Cola and half-digested pizza . . . *Fuck! Chocolate-colored puke, spewing all over me like a fucking shower! Jesus! No-oo!*

Paralyzed with shock, I watched in mute, creeping horror as she cocked back that gaping, toxic blowhole. I saw the gates of hell creaking open, then she let it fly again . . . **Huunnngghha! Splash!**

What the fuck? Where does such a skinny little thing keep so much food and liquid waste!?! Holy shit! A round little green pea rolled down a slimy vomit trail into my belly button . . . *Jesus, look at this shit . . . A pea! And it's intact! There's another one! Fuck! And here's a baby carrot! Christ on a shish kebab! This batty bitch swallows small legumes whole! Oh God! Fuck, what the fucking fuck?!?*

There were bits of white rice everywhere. Suddenly, I thought of maggots . . . *What the fuck is this shit!?! Oh God . . . What if she's infested with internal larvae!? Shit! Please, God! No . . . No, it's rice! It's gotta be rice! Fuck! What next!?*

Slowly, Narcisa turned and rose up from the bed. She slithered back down the ladder and slapped across the room as if nothing had

happened, dripping a slimy trail of puke—*fwap fwap fwap*—
across the floor behind her.

"Are you fucking insane!?!" I bellowed like a stabbed gorilla.

Wide awake now, realizing the full horror of it all, I lifted myself
from the bed. Vomit slid down my torso—*fwap*—onto the floor as I
climbed down and searched for a towel, cursing her under my breath.

Narcisa just looked right through me, as if I weren't even there.

I lost it. *"The bathroom's over there, Narcisa!"* I stood
pointing my finger at the door. *"The bathroom! The toilet! The
fucking sink! Bathroom, bathroom! O banheiro, porra!
Ya know, the place where ya spend half yer miserable life
smoking crack and staring at yerself in th' fuckin' mirror?
Bath—room!"*

She continued to stare off into space.

*"Why, Narcisa? Just tell me, okay? Why do I deserve this
shit? Why?"*

She faced me with a glazed expression. "I will clean it, Cigano."

"Yeah, right!" I began cleaning up, mumbling muffled curses as I
mopped away at the slimy wreckage. *"Fucking crazy bitch . . . Shit . . ."*

Feeling better now, lighter, all cheerful and perky after her nice,
healthy purge, Narcisa sauntered over and turned up her boom box,
full blast. Then she started dancing, gliding across the floor, moving
her feet around—spreading the stinking trail of puke far and wide as
I tried to wipe it up.

It was a losing battle. I stopped and stood watching her in disbelief,
aghast.

"What th' fuck are you doing, ya fuggin' psychopath?!"

"I am dancing, Cigano."

She's talking to a simpleton, an idiot! I dropped the towel and kicked
her boom box across the room with my barf-coated foot, bouncing

it against the wall, breaking it, silencing the accursed torture device forever.

"Wha' happen to you now, hein, Cigano? You de one who e'say always how much you love to watching me dance!"

Oh, Jesus! Really?

It was true, of course. When Narcisa danced, it was pure electricity; spellbinding, kinetic alien poetry. But this was different.

"Not like THIS, ya fuggin' freak! You're dancin' around in yer own fuggin' vomit, fer fuck's sake! Who th' fuck DOES that?!? You're completely insane!"

Narcisa continued dancing around, without any music now, struggling to keep her dying crack buzz going.

I leveled an angry finger at her. *"In-sane!"* I repeated, as if I had just discovered some Great Truth.

She shot me a bitter, condescending look. She stopped and sat down in her ash-strewn corner, talking to herself, muttering.

"Is no fair!" she whined, accusing me with those big, sad eyes that made me want to cry for her—or just kill her and put an end to her terminal madness.

I turned my back on her and kept mopping.

That did it. She jumped up, glaring at me, shouting, crying, wailing.

"You so focking hipocrita, Cigano! All de time you e'say to me how much you love when I dance, e'say me I dancing like de angel! An' then I go make de nice dance for you, an' you yell at me, e'say I am insane an' criticize me! Why?"

I stopped cleaning and stared at her in horror.

". . . Is alway e'same e'sheet with all de mans! When I do bad thing an' I treat you bad, then you love me an' wanna eat de e'sheet from my asshole like candy! An' then I feel

e'sorry an' I try make it better, an' I dance for you to make
you happy, but then you hate me an' e'say to me all these
insulto! An' you think is me who insane? Hah! Is you! All
you mean, jealous peoples de one who insane!"

She stopped yelling and stood there, scowling at me with her hands
on her hips, like a bewildered, offended child.

The effect was immediate. I was consumed with shame . . . *Shit!*
Poor Narcisa . . . What have I done? I was a heel, an ingrate, a selfish,
self-centered shit.

I questioned my own sanity.

"Okay, okay. Lissen, lissen, I'm sorry, baby. I love you! I was just . . .
Look, I'll get ya a new radio, I promise. I didn't mean it, okay? But it's
just not, not normal to throw up on somebody when they're sleeping,
and then dance around in vomit while they're trying to clean it . . . *ya*
know . . . ?"

I looked at her, hoping she might grasp the logic in my plea.

It drew a blank. Her sour look of disdain told me my call to reason
was just another waste of spit. I may as well have been singing "Happy
Birthday" to a prune.

48. SHOWDOWN

"To knock a thing down, especially if it is cocked at an
arrogant angle, is a deep delight to the blood."
—*George Santayana*

Guilt was mounting me like a jailhouse rapist as Narcisa put shovel
to dirt and began digging my grave.

She stood before me, bellowing, bawling, hands on her hips, anguished tears running down her face. ***"I am e'sick of you, Cigano!"***

I felt a deep sense of shame and regret. I was a monster. I'd lost my
temper and made poor Narcisa cry. And all she wanted was to please
me in her own fucked-up way.

Shit! I could see where it was all going. Narcisa was boarding the
Self-Pity Express. Next stop, Righteous Indignation . . . *All aboard!*
As the Hell Train picked up speed, I knew that soon there'd be no
stopping it. I just stood there, watching it all unfold, like an old horror
movie I already knew the ending to.

***"Whatever I do, you always wanna criticize! No-thing
ever right! I am de insane girl, de Crack Monster, de crazy
whoore, hein? No hope for me, hein?"***

"But . . ."

***"No! You deserve some better girl, Cigano! I try to make
you happy, but ever'thing I do is only wrong! I am no good!
Defect machine! Delete, hein!? Next?"***

"No, princesa! It's not like that at all. I was just . . ."

"Okey! I got it!" She powered on, waves of dramatic, teary-eyed shrieks washing over my weak protests like a vomit-flavored tsunami. ***"I understand all now! Now you tire of play with de defect toy, hein? Okey! So now I gonna go away an' die an' save you de problema that I am! Delete! Next!"***

"But—"

"No! I warning you in de beginning, don' get youself involve with these defect Crack Monster girl, Cigano! But no-oo, you don' wanna lissen, não-oo! No, you gotta come back an' look for me every night! An' now you sorry, hein?"

"No, baby, please . . ."

"Hah! Well, is gonna be ever'thing all better for you now!" She was rummaging through her stinking pile of moldy, tattered rags. ***"Don' worry no more, cuz now you never gonna see de insane girl again, never again, got it?"***

My heart sank like a stone as she began stuffing her clothes into a bag.

"Please!" I pled, falling into her trap. "I love you, princesa! I'm sorry! Don't go . . ." I reached over and took her things from her hands. "*Por favor*, Narcisa! Everything's gonna be okay, baby. I'm sorry I yelled. I was just groggy. Please . . ."

Now I was crying too. Narcisa had me, and she knew it.

She glared at me like a bug. "I got it, okey! I understand ever'thing perfect, Cigano!" She snatched her clothes back, her icy, reptilian eyes flaring at my weakness. She was a deadly, coldhearted predator, moving in for the kill.

I am nothing! Worthless! I cry like a sissy! I am weak!

Then it hit me . . . *Wait a minute! Now **I'm** the fucking bad guy here?*

She stood there, sneering, growling. ***"You wan' just de rubber doll with de poo'sy an' no de real authentic geer-ool, Cigano!***

You e'say you love me, but this is no love! You only wan' con-
trol me! But you can' never control me! Nunca! Know why?
Hah! Because I am insane! Complete insane, Cigano, got it?"

I got it. Narcisa was trying out for the fucking bug-farm.

She screeched on, her puke-laced spittle flying into my face. Her
crazed, bulging, bughouse eyes were popping out of her skull like a
vein-twitching horror show psycho. My stomach ached as I stood
there, feeling sick, pumping my fists, struggling to keep from clob-
bering her. She kept taunting me, peppering me with abuse, like one
of those Mexican *picadors* throwing darts at the bull, tormenting and
teasing the big animal, poisoning it with its own fear and rage and
frustration; weakening it, just before they come in for the final death-
blow. An ugly, depressing spectacle.

My grave was dug. Now I just needed to hop inside.

I pulled my coffin shut as Narcisa drove the nails in. One word at
a time.

"You never gonna see me again! Hah! You don' love me,
Cigano! You don' love nobody! Ninguém! Nada! You don'
even know what is it de love! I hate you an' I never wanna
see you no more, never again, got it? Nunca!!"

Driving the last nail home like a spike through my heart, she poked
my chest with her big, sooty finger.

That did it. I snapped out of her spell, feeling screwed, betrayed, raped.

My heart went cold as a lizard's dick. *"That's fine with me, ya*
fuggin' bitch! G'wan! Beat it! Get th' fuck outa here and go
find a new sucker to put up with this shit!"

I turned away, ignoring her as I went back to mopping up the mess.

I just wanted her gone.

No dice.

She advanced like a hissing cobra, pointing her finger in my eye,
taunting, tormenting, pushing, prodding, poking as she jabbed that

filthy black crack-claw right in my nose. A stench of death invaded my
nostrils. The battle was on!

All of a sudden, some invisible little fuse blew, somewhere way back
in my brain. ***Pop!*** I felt my hand shoot up, slapping her face with a
resounding ***smack***.

The stinging blow was so forceful, it knocked Narcisa sideways.
Her head shot back and ricochetted off the wall with a sickening
thunk. She jumped up and stood glaring at me in mute indignation.

"Get out, ya little shit!" I heard my voice thundering, as if
from very far away. ***"G'wan! Rala peito, sua merdinha! Beat
it, before I break every bone in yer fuckin' body!"***

Narcisa tore out the door, her shrill, fiendish curses echoing away
down the hallway again, for all my neighbors to enjoy.

49. THE LOVE TRAP

"LOVE MAKES USE OF THE WORST TRAPS.
THE LEAST NOBLE. THE RAREST."
—*Jean Genet*

We were caught in a trap; like two wild animals locked together in mortal combat, when the trap catches one, it catches both.

The trap was Love, and I knew it would be a hard one to get out of.

Love was my worst crime against Narcisa. Because I loved her so completely and unconditionally that, no matter how hard the Crack Monster ever tried to drive me away or turn me against her, I'd always forgive her. I would take her right back in again; every time, the minute she came slithering home.

I had become like one of those inflatable life-size Punch-Me dolls that spring back up after being knocked over. And now, my whole life was a raging battlefield of Love. Living with Narcisa was like being in the army—always being rudely awakened at odd, unexpected hours, dragged out of a sound sleep and forced to march for agonizing miles over desolate, rugged terrain, struggling along with burning blisters, a furious tyrant barking orders into trembling eardrums. Random orders, cruel, senseless, angry insults; capricious whims and demands.

"*Cigano, go get me de Coca Cola with lot of ice, go go!*"

"*Cigano, where's my focking hairbrush, hein?*"

"*Cigano, get the fock outa my way, porra! I wanna watch de tel'vision! Moo-ove, e'stupid! Go go goo-oo!*"

"Cigano, you gotta gimme more mo-ney! You so focking Jewish, you cheap old gyp-say e'sheet! I gonna go back to Copacabana an' find a rich gringo who more younger than you, an' he gonna take good care of me all de time, an' you never gonna see me again! Hah! Last chance, e'stupid, got it?"

At times, the endless barrage of senseless harassment and verbal abuse got to be too much for me. Feeling all of my instincts under attack at once, at a loss for words, reduced to a primal animal level, I'd just glare at her and growl like a pissed-off Doberman.

But I'd never smacked her hard like that before!

Shit! What's happening to me? Now I'd even crossed that line . . . *Another line crossed . . . Dear God! Where will it end?* And once again, Narcisa was out the door and running the streets in another deadly, self-destructive rampage.

As I paced the floor, I began to ponder my dilemma. I realized I had two basic options. I made frantic mental calculations. One choice would be to just beat her to death with my bare fists and finally be done with her shit, once and for all.

But that would entail having to dispose of a body. Her body. *Shit!*

I knew I could never bring myself to actually murder poor Narcisa—even knowing I'd probably be doing her a huge favor by putting her out of her misery.

Could I? I'd just be helping her. A charitable act, like putting down a rabid dog.

I began to fantasize about how the grim task might be accomplished.

I could hit her on the head with a hammer, then chop her up in the bathtub . . . Flush the meat and entrails down the toilet, till there's nothing left but bones.

Yes, butchering Narcisa like a pig would be the most efficient method, I decided—thinking about it at all, of course, only in anticipation of an eventual overdose; a likely scenario, I told myself, if things kept up the way they were going.

But what about her bones? How to get rid of a whole human skeleton? I hadn't figured that part out yet . . . *Maybe I could break them up with a hammer or something, then grind 'em into sawdust and scatter the powder around town . . . Yeah!*

That's it! Sure! The ho-stroll. The favelas. The cop spots. Lapa. Copacabana!

Wait! Maybe I could drop all the bone dust into my gas tank and blow her ashes out the exhaust. Ye-aah! Narcisa, up in smoke in one last joy ride! Perfect! She'd love that!

But wait a minute . . . What about her cunt? I could never bring myself to flush that thing down the toilet! Uh-uh! No way!

Wait! Maybe I could make it into a wallet or something . . . Ye-ah! That's it! A nice little sentimental Narcisa wallet! Sure! I could stitch a zipper in there and use it to hold all the cash I'd be saving not having that fucking Crack Monster to support anymore!

As the morbid images danced around in my head, finally, I came to the conclusion that it was all just too much work.

Murdering Narcisa was out.

My other option was plenty of work too.

Yeah, but it's good work . . . Wholesome, honest work! A man's job! Something he can be proud of at the end of a long, hard day's labor!

So far, I'd always chosen that option . . . *Just yank her panties off before she can speak, climb on top of her like a shark attack, overwhelming her, don't give her a second to bitch or complain or argue or fight, sticking it right up into that quivering raw pussy, covering her protesting motor-mouth with mine, pulling her hair, clutching that hard, peachy ass, working it in deep, deeper, in and out in and out, her stifled protests melting into wild savage cries of pain and pleasure as I sweat, toiling like a day laborer, a beast of burden, slamming, banging, fucking, hitting it, till a warm pool of piss surrounds the plundering dick and we just keep going, fucking, go go go, harder, harder, till we're climaxing, screaming, collapsing in a puddle of sperm and sweat, piss, blood, exhaustion, panting like dying dogs, rolling away from each other across the floor like a pair of injured prize fighters, rolling over clothes and cigarette butts, empty bottles and pizza crusts, rolling, rolling our flayed, beaten, broken carcasses collapsing in a humid slaughterhouse of sex and love and passion and desire and pain, living and dying under the eternal, miserable, ecstatic death sentence of Love.*

50. SYMPATHY FOR THE DEVIL

Like the bell in a prize fight, the phone rang, interrupting my delirious, sleep-deprived sex fantasies. With a weary sigh, I picked up, wondering if Narcisa had listened to my shameful, guilt-ridden snuff-thoughts via telepathy, and was calling to damn me to hell, once and for all.

"*Pronto?*"

"*Oi, Cigano . . .*"

"*Oi, Narcisa . . .*"

Silence.

I waited for the shrieking recriminations to commence.

They didn't. She spoke again in a meek little tone. "*You wanna see me?*"

Silence. I was too surprised to respond.

"Lissen to me, please, Cigano. I am very e'sleepy. I wan' come back you place now, only for e'sleep. No *problema* no more. *Juro!* I promise! *Por favor!* Come an' get me. Casa Verde, okey? Come now, amor, go go . . ."

Truce. The battle was over. Just like that.

Of course, I'd never forget it. And I knew Narcisa would now have a whole new folder in her bulging filing cabinet of emotional blackmail ammunition.

I hung up the phone, picked up my keys and bolted out the door.

Pulling up to the Casa Verde, I cut the motor and waited on the bike. When she appeared on the sidewalk, Narcisa looked like she was ready to keel over and die . . . *Worn-out, torn up. Beat. Beaten . . . By me this time! Shit! Poor thing!*

She staggered over like a broken doll. I gave her a hug and kissed her on the forehead. In silence, she climbed on. As we rode away, she held on to me like she would never let go. Without a word, I took her straight home.

Back in my apartment, she climbed up into the loft and collapsed onto the mattress. Within minutes, she was snoring. Too tired to even think about sex, I lay down beside her for another long, blessed crash.

Neither of us stirred for the next twelve hours.

The minute Narcisa's eyes popped the next morning, though, it was the same old song, blasting into my sleeping ears. ***"Puta que o pariu! Porra, que merda, que saco! Son of a focking bitch bastard who-ore motherfock! Sheet, fock, sheet focking e'sheet! Focking fock! Porr-rraaa!"*** She roared on and on.

Narcisa had never been what you'd call a "morning person." But, times like that, she was like a monstrous demon from the depths of hell, transformed by daylight into a hateful, screeching, spitting monstrosity; a toxic, spiky, spindly devil-thing, consumed in raging flames; a furious, hateful harpy.

I turned in the bed and put a gentle hand on her arm, trying to soothe her unnamable existential anguish, whispering. "What's the matter, my angel?"

"Pfffffffff! Sheet sheet sheet!" She jerked away, blowing pissed-off air through pursed lips, like a haggard, cynical old Frenchman at war with the world.

"Que foi, meu amor?" I asked again.

"E'shee-eet! Fock fock fock fock fock!! Porra! Pfffffffff!"

But I already knew what was wrong . . . *Everything, that's what's wrong . . . Fuck!* I was only half awake, still hoping it might just be another one of her passing nightmares. I lay back in the bed, praying she would roll over and sink back into her jerky, troubled slumber. But no. Narcisa groaned and began kicking the blanket off herself with that familiar frantic urgency . . . *That's it . . . Shit! She's awake . . . Here we go again!* The trauma was about to begin.

"What's the matter, princesa?"

"*Pffffffff!* Fock! I don' ***know*** . . ."

But I knew. Narcisa was awake, conscious again, after another twelve hours in a comatose stupor. Awake to the goddamned life she hated. And now, everything was wrong. Existence. The world and everybody in it was her problem.

Life. Smell. Sight. Sound. Touch. Taste. Unbearable!

Such was the terrible nature of her plight. Narcisa was up, and life sucked.

Groggy, I climbed down from the loft as she scurried behind me. She plunked down on the sofa and sat glaring at me with poison darts in her eyes.

I listened in dread as she started in with her habitual litany of complaints. Huffing and puffing, bitching and moaning, sulking, pouting and groaning, Narcisa sat in a simmering, fuming rage, insulting me without mercy or respite.

The torture would go on and on like that for the rest of the day.

It was murder. As she bombarded my tired, beleaguered ears with foul curses, Narcisa seemed the most unfortunate, miserable, unhappy soul I'd ever known; totally unsatisfied and utterly, completely discontent with the whole of existence.

I knew that blaming me for all her problems was madness. Still, I said nothing. I knew there was no way to win with Narcisa—not when she was in the throes of the Curse. The best I could do was pray to weather the storm and get through another one of her seething, psychotic tirades with both of us intact.

It wasn't easy. As the cowardly barbs flew from her toxic trap, the only thing that kept me from slaughtering the poor thing was that persistent mix of curiosity, compassion and identification with her unbearable psychic plight.

All along, I'd sensed there was more to our bizarre relationship than met the eye.

Lately, I'd begun to consider that Narcisa might even be a blessing in disguise. A trial—a series of blazing, white-hot, brutal, ego-puncturing purifications for my own shattered soul's crooked spiritual evolution; some kind of terrible karmic debt that must be paid now, once and for all, no matter what the cost.

51. SHATTERED VESSELS

"You are seeking to resolve something and make something whole within yourself. To show yourself how unwhole you are, you have created a situation of tremendous separation that appears to be outside of yourself. It looks as if your drama has to do with a powerful man against a powerful woman. Which one is going to be the victim? Who is right and who is wrong? What is this internal drama actually saying? What is this outside mirror that images what is going on inside of you."
—*Barbara Marciniak*

Narcisa's violent mood swings were the price I paid for living with her unearthly beauty, spectacular charisma and bottomless suffering.

Perhaps because of my willingness to hang in and grow from the experience, something like empathy was creeping into my own cold, numb heart. Identification, unconditional love and concern; sympathy for another's pain.

That was all new for me.

As she raged on that day, I remembered listening to a guy at an AA meeting in Mexico City. It had been years ago, back when I'd first stumbled onto the rocky road of recovery. As I crept into the cramped little church basement and took a seat, another ex-con had been talking about how radically he'd changed.

"It took me a long time to wake up, and I'm still working on it today, one day at a time. I'm no saint either, believe me. But I have gotten better, 'cause I've been willing to change. For me, love and service to other sick, suffering drunks have been the key to my own recovery. And thanks to the program, I've finally learned to care about other people. For a selfish old drunken bum like me, that's a miracle in itself."

Those words had rung true and clear as a temple bell. A lifetime of addiction had swept me into the gutter. I'd spent years in prison contemplating the consequences of the selfish attitudes and actions that had ended me up there.

After getting out, those meetings had been my last chance to salvage my life. Like Narcisa, I'd been a real stubborn, prideful case, stumbling blindly down a road of slow, steady, drug-induced self-annihilation for decades. I was almost dead by the time I finally threw in the towel. Like her, I'd always been too proud to ask anyone else for help. Me, I'd had to taste complete defeat before getting willing to humble myself and recover.

The only difference between me and Narcisa now was that I was just a bit less proud than she. That kind of stubborn, irrational bravado had been beaten out of me by the Curse. I didn't walk on water, I knew, but I *was* getting better; slowly recovering from the mad, egocentric commands of my own trauma-warped brain.

If some benevolent Higher Power had changed me from a pathetic, pissed-off, lying, thieving shitbag, why would it drop me on my ass now? No. It didn't make sense to live in that kind of doubt anymore. Faith was my key to sanity today.

Even as Narcisa backed me to the wall like a cornered rat, again and again, I always came out unharmed somehow—even strengthened, by the harsh, painful experiences. One sober day at a time, my soul was being fortified, along with my unshakable belief in a hopeless addict's ability to change and grow and recover.

Even against all odds, I knew Narcisa could make it too. I just didn't know how. Staring into the blazing, tormented pits of her eyes that day, I wondered what it would take to carve a chink in the Crack Monster's ironclad armor. I prayed it would be enough for the light to shine through, before she ended up dead, like all the others.

"You wanna take a focking foto? Why de fock you just stand there e'studying me, hein, e'stupid?" She kept taunting me, daring me to react.

I rolled my eyes and sighed, but I didn't take the bait. I just watched her, groaning under my breath. "Jesus! Where does this shit ever end?"

"What de fock you talking about de Jees-ooz now, hein? What happen to you, e'stupid old e'sheet, hein? Too focking retard to know you alive . . ."

I bit my tongue again, reminding myself how soul-sick she was. No matter how bad she ever treated me, I had to keep standing beside Narcisa, like a shipwrecked sailor, watching the horizon for any little glimmer of hope, a message in a bottle, anything. I could never forget that time she'd looked at me with that heartbreaking expression of helpless, pleading despair. Every time I found myself starting to hate her, I would see the hazy image of her standing in front of the Love House the night she'd uttered those fateful words: *"Don' give up on me, Cigano . . ."*

Right then, my soul had heard her soul's stifled little plea, and responded with a deep, unspoken commitment to never give up on her—no matter what. And I never had. I'd never lost hope that Narcisa could make it; that she could change.

Well, she hadn't changed a bit, I realized. But I had.

Somehow, over the months, I had found an unusual degree of patience, tolerance and compassion. Just by virtue of my being willing to try to help her, *I'd* been changed in some deep, essential way. And through it all, I'd maintained my own daily reprieve from drug addiction. As Narcisa raged on and on that endless, horrible afternoon, I realized I'd never been tempted, even in the most dreadful moments of terror and desperation, to just grab the fucking crack pipe out of her hand and join her on that enticing old thrill ride to hell.

It never even crossed my mind. Not once.

The same strung-out loser who couldn't get through a day without massive amounts of hard liquor and drugs wasn't the least bit interested in them now! That alone was miraculous. I simply wasn't prepared to run away from trouble anymore, no matter how bad things ever got. For the first time in my life, I was determined to stand up and face whatever was happening, head-on, like a man.

I may have never been able to save Narcisa, or even help her to rescue herself—not if she didn't want it. But, somehow, she was helping *me*. Just wanting to help her was forcing me to change and grow and evolve.

But there was more. As a recovering addict myself, well familiar with all the occult mechanisms and insidious subterfuges of the Curse, I could always see right through the smoke screen of her vicious maladjustments.

To me, Narcisa was like the Wizard of Oz: A lot of blustering, empty sound and fury, ultimately signifying nothing. All her posturing and angry huffing and puffing were just an elaborate show of thunder and lightning, designed to keep people away. I could see it. Narcisa could put on a terrifying performance, all right, but I knew it was all just a show. A front. Behind that ironclad mask of defiance, I sensed she was seeking a bond with another human being—the one healing force that could save her from the solitary Curse of herself. Why else would she keep coming back? Why would she want to be with someone who understood what she was going through, unless it was a muffled little cry for help?

Still, the time would always come when I had to give her the boot; and then off she'd go again, back out onto the shitty, gritty coldhearted old streets that were her world and her only other interaction with humanity. Narcisa would wander those harsh, dark, dangerous paths of night again, incurring all the sufferings, punishments and consequences of her crappy crackhead attitude, until there was nowhere left to go. Then, she'd come slithering back, complaining, cursing, whining and lamenting, oozing self-pity, rage and resentment from every stinking, unwashed pore, blaming me and everyone else for all her self-inflicted woes.

It was a painful thing to witness.

As she bitched and moaned, late into the long, hazy afternoon that day, I contemplated how pain seems to be the only real path to growth for most people. Ironically, that was exactly what her favorite philosopher had said.

Exasperated with her irritating tirades, I got out a book and found the familiar passage where her beloved Nietzsche had made that very declaration:

I began to read out loud. "The discipline of suffering, of great suffering, do you not know that only this discipline has created all enhancements of man so far?"

"Menos!" She jumped up and knocked the book from my hand, barking like an angry Chihuahua. **"You so focking ignorant, Cigano! You don' know nothing! Nada! You ugly an' old! E'stupid old hypocrite loo-oser! Just shut de fock up an' don' e'say nothing to me about Nietzsche, cuz you too e'stupid to get it!"**

I laughed. All the abuse she sprayed me with just rolled off me now, like jizz dripping down the face of a molested child. After hours of listening to her bitch and rant and rave and complain, lamenting about her unjust lot in life, hurling her poisoned darts at me, I started laughing, like a battered kid retreating into his own funny little fantasy world. Shutting down, I could feel myself growing numb.

Finally, I stopped giggling and smiled at her. "Are you done yet, Narcisa?"

My indifference only fueled her rage. The Crack Monster was moving her lips like a demented hand puppet, demanding violent retribution from me, insulting, yelling, twisting the knife with each new insult, digging it in deeper and deeper.

"You too focking old, Cigano!"

Nothing.

"You too fat, Cigano!"

Nothing.

"You ugly an' e'stupid like a retard old fock-monkey, Cigano!"

Bitch! I'll ring your fucking neck, you miserable little shit!

Stop! She's getting to you! Keep cool! Don't do it! Just let her spew.

Narcisa's beautiful, savage voice had been usurped by an evil possessing entity, converted into a hoarse, hellish, demented croak. By the time that long, trembling afternoon oozed into the murky shadows of night, I was so consumed with stifled hatred, I was ready to pull out my knife and gut her like a fish.

If she doesn't shut up, I swear to God, I'm gonna stab her right in her dirty black crackhead heart! Anything to not have to look at that nasty ratlike sneer anymore!

And still, she rattled on. *"Covardee-ee! You too coward to make it with de real womans, so you gotta be with a focking who-ore, hein? Well, you never gonna control me, Cigano! Hah! First I gonna kee-eel you, got it?"*

I got it. Narcisa was really cruising for another beating.

Rage grabbed at my bowels like nuthouse sheets clutched in a madman's fist. I wanted to slaughter her like a diseased goat. But with the memory of recent violence still nagging at my conscience, I was determined not to snap.

Somehow I managed to stay calm, reminding myself that, deep inside, Narcisa was just a garden-variety addict. For such unfortunate souls, everything's just wrong all the time. Even as her curses bounced off the walls like maddened wasps, I couldn't help but sympathize with her plight. How not? Hadn't I been there myself?

In the end, my patience paid off. After another excruciating hour of abuse, finally, I gave in and threw her a ten-spot to go cop. That did the trick.

She struggled into her filthy denim jacket. With a final *"Fock you!"* she spat on my floor, then stormed off into the night, slamming the door behind her.

I listened to her footsteps clomping away down the hall, the echo of her angry voice squawking down the stairwell, like a blackhearted demon crow flapping off to hell.

Thank Christ! She's gone! Taking a long, deep breath, I limped over and stood at the window. I watched her emerge onto the street below, then trudge across the plaza, her shadow dissolving into the dark summer haze.

A garbage truck stopped on the street, blocking my view for a moment, and when it moved on, Narcisa was gone, swallowed up in the septic humid mist, like a ghost.

Gone, like a fart in the wind! Thank you come again, ya miserable bitch!

I fell back on the sofa and sighed with relief. Despite all the abuse I'd just swallowed, I was happy. Because, once again, I had manifested a Miracle; all throughout her latest raging tantrum, I had miraculously kept the big switchblade knife in my pocket—and out of poor Narcisa's crumbling, devastated, broken heart.

Turning sideways, I fell into a long, deep, dreamless slumber.

52. ENDS JUSTIFY MEANS

"SEX IS KICKING DEATH IN THE ASS WHILE SINGING."
—*Charles Bukowski*

Morning came, and Narcisa was back from the wars.

She jumped in bed with me, as though she hadn't just spent the previous afternoon trying to drive me to drink, murder and destruction. Silent as a cat, she got astride me.

Still half asleep, I tried to say something, anything. Something conventional, casual, mundane. Something stupid, like "good morning, baby . . ."

She held her hand over my mouth, silencing me with those big, piercing, popping eyes, while her other hand worked me up into her—deep inside, right where I belonged.

Then, from deep in the crazed, alien, primal core of her, Narcisa gripped me with that amazing, pulsating, supersonic, paranormal, extraterrestrial pussy-muscle that only she had, tickling, stimulating, driving me mad all at once.

When I was so hard I thought it would break off inside her, she began to fuck me like she meant it, slamming her wiry body against me hard, a ferocious, silent predator feeding on a dying animal. My hands locked on to her relentless, pounding buttocks, holding on for dear life.

Then I felt it.

In a flash, I was a little girl, being ravaged by a big, brutal centaur as she clung to me with a bloodthirsty desperation, a madness so intense, I started to cry. By some weird sexual telepathy, I was experiencing the roots of Narcisa's own deepest trauma.

Rape.

For that one little moment, I *was* her!

We fucked and fucked, a thundering, unstoppable, infernal fuck-machine, as if the erect penis holding us together was a pulsing, thick, iron-hard umbilical cord. It was hers, while that swirling ocean of pussy was mine, being raped and ravaged and plundered and possessed, again and again. We were one energy, one being. I could feel the juices flowing, and they were ours as one, as she came all over me in delirious spasms.

Then, with a deep, weary sigh, she went limp in my arms, like a sleeping child. Our dying sex twitched and pulsed all around us, a living, breathing mist.

All of a sudden, with a ghostly scream that wasn't my own, I could feel the marrow of my core, my very soul, being extracted from me . . . *Oh, God! Coming coming coming!* ***"Arrggghhh!"*** I lay there, shaking all over, screaming, gasping, dying, again and again and again. ***"Fuck fuck fuck fuck!"***

I held Narcisa close, feeling our two frantic heartbeats drumming away like a pair of spastic lab rats. Then, I passed out.

When I awakened, it was late afternoon and she was gone. Gone with my cigarettes, my lighter, and the fifty I'd left sitting on the dresser the night before . . . *Shit!* I was broke again.

I didn't care. Even if it was my last money, my last hope of a meal, a liter of gasoline, a pack of cheap bootleg Paraguayan cigarettes. I knew I'd just have to go out and hustle up some more cash . . . *What else can I do? Fuck it! It's worth it . . . Worth anything . . . Worth dying for!*

Desperate for the means to support our long, ecstatic rides, I spent the rest of the day wandering around the busy downtown plazas of Cinelândia, thinking, scheming, worrying, looking for a score.

Then I saw them.

Bingo! Tourists! Plastic surgery faces! Those perfectly tended tanning salon, yoga-toned bodies! Expensive watches . . . Designer jeans . . . Gucci loafers . . . Well-dressed, rich, clueless cash cows . . . Easy pickings . . . Perfect, Max!

I strolled over to the well-heeled, middle-aged gringo couple and pretended to ask for directions. Starting up a casual conversation in English, I baffled the guy with a practiced line of bullshit. With casual ease, I began reeling him in, just like old times for little Ignácio.

Within minutes, we were old pals . . . *Some kinda fancy-pants entertainment lawyer from Miami . . . Says he works for Madonna . . . Must have plenty of cash.*

I'd spent enough time running drugs into Miami back in the eighties to talk all the Miami Beach *gadjo* talk with him. I knew just what to say to put the guy at ease. Sure enough, he invited me to join him and his woman for lunch at the big, swarming Amarelinho café.

Perfect, Max!

We took a sidewalk table and sat making idle conversation about the wonders of Rio's beaches, the Samba, Carnaval, and then—*bang!* I had his bulging alligator-skin wallet in my pocket. A minute later, I slipped his lady friend's expensive designer purse from an empty chair beside me and stuffed it under my jacket.

The gringo was still smiling like a big, self-satisfied kid when I got up to go to the bathroom. I ducked out the side door and took off down the street, adrenaline pumping in my chest . . . *Go go go go go! Thank you come again! Next?*

Grinning like a wolf, I disappeared down a teeming pedestrian alley. I got to my motorcycle and took off.

Did I feel guilty for being the black eye on some idiot gringo's exotic Rio de Janeiro holiday? Not at all . . . *Hardly! Fuck 'em!*

On the ride home, I thought back to what one of my old gang had told me once, back in the day. My childhood friend, Mateus—also known as "Smiley"—had been an infamous professional bank robber in Rio. That guy had been a big influence on my thinking. The newspapers had dubbed old Mateus "the Smiling Bandido" for his trademark impeccable manners and friendly, ingratiating grin while plying his chosen trade. A classy career criminal, Mateus had taught me a lot about class. And crime. And criminal rationalization.

Riding along, I could hear his words echoing down the halls of my memory.

"When de teef he teef from de other teef, Ignácio, God, he only laugh!"

To me, all gringos were basically thieves, just by virtue of being gringos. Like those corrupt, thieving banksters Mateus had cheerfully robbed with his notorious winning smile, gringos were like some evil race of jet-setting vampires, traveling the world, sucking the planet's resources dry for the benefit of their own disproportionate luxury and decadent, self-centered comforts. Out of necessity, or simply by habit, most Brazilians were natural-born thieves, too. But the biggest, most shameless, greediest bandits had always been the richest, most powerful of my countrymen. They'd been taught well by their masters; those cowardly, warlike bullies to the north, the hated *americanos*, who made the rules the rest of the world was forced to play by, or go hungry.

I parked the bike and nodded to a fourteen-year-old mulatto shouldering a big black assault rifle. He grinned back, giving me the familiar thumbs-up okay to proceed. Swaggering down the shadowy path, I was still thinking of Madonna's lawyer . . . *And fuck that stupid old cunt Madonna too! Silly cow! Fuck 'em all!*

Yeah, I was proud of my latest sting. My bad old gypsy blood was pumping hard with the sweet aftertaste of another successful score as I approached the spot.

It was all for a good cause.

I was betting with our lives now; wagering everything in the hope that if I could just manage to keep Narcisa in drugs long enough to still be there by the time she hit bottom and cried out for help; then maybe, just maybe I'd finally get a chance to haul her up out of the dark, solitary, lethal pit she'd smoked herself into.

As I haggled over my pilfered goods with the bandidos in the *boca*, I played it all out in my mind . . . *Yeah, those stupid rich gringos can always go out and buy themselves another fucking camera, a new set of credit cards, a new iPod, another cell phone, more money, more property, luxury and prestige . . . Fuck 'em! What do they care? What do I care?*

I knew my latest victims would survive and continue to thrive, as rich gringos always did. They'd be fine . . . *But not Narcisa . . . My poor little friend is dying . . . And she's counting on me not to give up on her! And I'll keep that fucking promise, or die, or go back to prison trying! What do I got to lose?*

I told myself I was still strong enough to deal with the devil, that I could afford to compromise the integrity of my tattered old soul, just one more little time.

Just for today, the ends still justified the means.

They always would, for me, when it came to loving Narcisa.

53. STRANGE PHYSICS

"THERE IS NO PAIN COMPARED TO THAT OF LOVING A
WOMAN WHO MAKES HER BODY ACCESSIBLE TO ONE AND
YET WHO IS INCAPABLE OF DELIVERING HER TRUE SELF—
BECAUSE SHE DOES NOT KNOW WHERE TO FIND IT."
—*Lawrence Durrell*

Later that evening, Narcisa was back at my door again, knocking like a timid ghost. When I opened up, she breezed in past me like a wave, then plopped her long, glowing white electric eel body down on the couch.

She looked up at me, grinning. "So what's de *plano*, Cigano?"

I knew what the plan was . . . *Fuck fuck fuck! Money money money! Smoke smoke smoke! More more more! Go go go! Perfect, Max!*

Her big feet dangled over the sofa's edge. She kicked off a scuffed old pair of plastic shoes I hadn't seen before. Picking one up, I stood examining it, like a work-weary archeologist holding a petrified dinosaur turd.

"You like it these *sapato*, Cigano? I just today find them again!"

"Found 'em where?" I asked, turning it over in my hands.

She smirked with pride. "These de old e'shoe I leave at de Casa Verde before I gone away to New York. I use to love these one. My husband he buy it to me in Ipanema. They was de very e'spensive import high heel fashion e'shoe, you know?"

I looked at the shoe again. There was no heel, just five centimeters of worn-out rounded plastic at the back . . . *What's this little maniac going on about now?*

"I am de footwear engineer, got it? Now they de original, authentic Narcisa design e'shoe! Hah! I modify it these e'sheet from de high heel e'shoe myself!"

"How?" I mumbled, without interest. My mind was on other things as I sat down and fondled her firm white leg . . . *Sex sex sex . . . Go go go . . . More more more!*

"From de mathematical walking, bro! What other way to do it, hein?"

"Mathematical walking?"

"Lissen, Cigano . . ." She sighed, like someone trying to explain algebra to a German shepherd. "One night I go walk from one end of Copacabana to de other side, got it? An' then, *boo*! No more high heel! She all wear out! Hah! But is *so-oo* much more *comfort-able* now! An' check it out! You wanna see what e'strange?"

I nodded as she took the shoe from me and hefted it in her hand.

"Lookit, mano, see de way de left-e'side heel, she wear off double more faster than de right-side one! Is de very e'strange mathematic, hein, unusual physics, hein, Cigano?"

She handed it back for my inspection.

I examined the shoe more closely, as if it might somehow contain the answer to some deeper mystery of Narcisa's soul.

"How it can be these kinda thing, hein?" She grabbed the shoe out of my hand again and held it aloft like a trophy. "I no cripple geer-ool, mano, never go walking sideway like de crab, hein? De pressure on de e'shoe e'suppose to be e'same for left or for right foots, no?"

She fell silent as I moved closer, drinking in her mad presence like a vampire, waiting for her to speak again. I was a hungry dog watching its master, salivating, waiting to be fed . . . *More more more!*

"Is de working of de Shadow Peoples, got it?"

"Shadow People? Whaddya mean, baby?"

"I *see* it, bro! These focking *vultos* can do anything! They change de direction of de *materia*, de *fisica*, got it? Is de very e'strange physic."

I raised a curious eyebrow.

"Lissen! All de time, is de very e'strange thing with all my e'speriments, Cigano! But I can' never e'say too much about these to de other peoples, or they gonna e'say I *maluca*. One time they even go lock me up in de crazy house!"

"What? When?"

"Yeh, mano! When I first come back from America, Cigano! Was *horrível!* Was these e'stupid Doc's fault, bro! *Fock!* He make de plot for deceive me, e'say to me he gonna take me e'shopping, an' then he give it de e'secret note to de taxi driver an' e'say him take me to de crazy house! Is *horrível* these place, Cigano! De *medico* even more *maluco* than de crazy peoples! They gimme de crazy medicine, an' I just e'stay there in a big white room, drooling like de focking *zumbi! Fock!* An' de guys who work in there, they molest me while I knock out from all de crazy drug. But they never can keep me inside there! Hah! No way! Know why?"

I stared at her, waiting for her to go on.

"I make it de ex-cape, these why! Hah! Out de focking window, *go*! Get de fock out! *Thank you come again! Next? Crowwwn crowwn! So-oo* e'stupid these focking Doc! An' who de fock these e'stupid *medico*, hein? These peoples so focking ignorant they keep de window open in de crazy house! E'stupid! Hah!"

Narcisa fell silent, remembering.

Finally, she spoke again. "After these time, I don' never e'say no more nothing to any peoples about no focking thing no more. *Nunca!* No more never again Narcisa talk about my e'speriment to nobody! You de only one, Cigano. De only one what understand Narcisa, who ever wanna lissen me. So I e'say it to you now these thing cuz is too many de e'strange happening what I seen, belief me . . ."

I looked at her, curious, fondling her knee, listening as her voice dropped to a whisper. She looked around the room as if Doc might be sitting in a corner listening to her deranged secrets, holding a tape recorder, gathering evidence to put her back in the bug-farm.

"When I e'stay de Love House, inside de room, Cigano, when I go an' e'smoke de crack in there, all de time I can e'smell it . . ."

"Huh? What smell, baby?"

"De odor of de *enxôfre*. How do you e'say it, de *sulfur!* An' I listen to de voices too, e'screaming with *agonia*. I can hear it all de hell peoples e'scream an' cry inside de *inferno! Arrrggghhh! Horrível!*"

I remembered those haunting sounds. Typical crack-induced audio hallucinations. As she talked on, I could feel myself getting hard. The scent of Narcisa floated in the air like a command. I watched her lips moving as my hand drifted to her thigh. Drooling with lust, I wanted to fuck the demons away, wanted to fuck her back to sanity.

"Whaddya think happens, Narcisa?"

"I *know* wha' happen, Cigano! These what I try an' tell you! *Porra!* Pay attention, *cara!* All de time I see it these big focking shadow!"

"A shadow . . . ?"

"Yeh, mano! I see it when she go an' move de thing around, you know?"

I knew. Shadow People. Sleep deprivation. Crack psychosis.

I kept quiet as she rambled on. Listening absently, nodding. Stroking her rock-hard stomach with one hand as I caressed her long brown hair with the other, and then I was gone. It didn't matter what she was saying. She may as well have been talking about the Paraguayan economy; marketing strategies for plastic birdcage liners; the history of the Burmese teakettle.

Whatever.

I sat there mesmerized, watching her lips moving. I was lost, drunk, sucked away into her insane magnetic field, trapped under the weight of a mad, compulsive passion and desire . . . *Those amazing, babble gummy pink lips . . . Her yellowed ivory teeth, moving, talking . . . The texture of her perfect milky white skin . . . That wild animal female stench . . . Fuck!*

"Hah! Someday, Cigano, I gonna go an' catch it!" She whispered on as I lifted her skirt and pulled off her panties. "Never mind!" She moaned, raising her butt up from the sofa. "Someday soon I gonna discover all about these e'strange physics! An' then I gonna catch them up, these focking Shadow Peoples!"

"How ya gonna do that, baby?" I mumbled, working myself into her.

"Simple, bro! I just gotta keep e'smoke these e'sheet! Hah! These way I gonna be able see more faster, e'same speed like these focking *fantasmas.* An' after I found out all de secret of these crazy physic, then I gonna be finish with my e'sperimentation, got it? An' then I can e'stop e'moke de e'stupid crack forever. *Thank you come again! Next?"*

Stroking in and out, drooling like a happy old dog, I held her tight, feeling her taut, warm skin . . . *Playing her ribs like an accordion, my hand behind her, moving all over, up and down her spine, her buttocks, cupping that perfect hard-apple ass-cheek in my palm, smelling her dirty, musky brown hair, breathing her in, her consuming feral essence, the texture and color and smell and taste of endless need and want, inhaling Narcisa like a big, long hit of crack, holding her deep in the core of my soul, all lit up like a fucking casino, coming, coming! Fu-uck!*

"*Finish now, Cigano! Finish, anda logo, cara, finish finish, go go go go . . ."*

What? Narcisa was talking in that wild, frenetic singsong growl.

"*Go!* Hurry up an' finish, fast, Cigano! *Go go, fast fast, Cigano go go go!"*

Fuck! Fuck! Fuck!

"Finish it, go, *mermão,* you taking too long time now, go go go! Finish up, go, hurry up, fast, fast, faster, you gotta finish *up* now, *go!*

You gonna give it to me de mo-ney now, *okey*, Cigano? Yes? *Hein?* Okey? *Hein?*"

Yes yes yes!

"*Sim?* Okey! An' you gonna take me up to de *boca* now, yes? Gonna give it to me de *moto* ride to de favela up in Santa Teresa now, *sim?* An' then you gonna get it for me de very most very best crack for e'smoke tonight, yes? Okey? Hein?"

Yes yes yes! Fuck! Fuck! I'm nodding, agreeing, complying, conceding, relin-quishing, surrendering, dying, selling my fucking soul for her sex, her essence, her need, her want . . . Yes yes yes, anything! I'll take you to hell! Purgatory! The nut-house! The crackhouse! The zoo! Whatever! Wherever! Anywhere! Everywhere!

Fuck! Fuck! Fuck! Fuck! Fuck! Fuck! Fuck!

"**Ebaaah! Yaa-aasss!**" She howled with delight. "**Let's go now, Cigano, go go go, hurry up now go, go, finish now, an' then I gonna go do it my es'perimentation! Finish now! Go go go go go!**"

Fuck! Fuck! Fuck! Fuck! Fuck! Fuck! Fuck! Fuck! Fuck! Fuck!

"**Arrrrggghh!! Fuck! Fuck! Fuck!**" I rolled off her with a primal scream exploding up from deep in my churning lungs.

Narcisa was already up on her feet again, getting dressed as I lay there, screaming, climaxing, dying. "**Arrrrggghh . . . Fuck! Fuck! Fuck! Fuck! Fuck . . .**"

I fell back, panting, staring up at the ceiling like a drunken fish at the bottom of a cloudy aquarium . . . *Fuck fuck fuck fuck fuck fuck fuck!*

As my breath began to slow down, I could hear the mellow, le-thargic chant of night birds. Their songs faded, little by little, giving way to a new, truculent morning song of day birds. It was like an invisible aviary changing-of-the-guard, as the first light peeked through the shutters, glowing like a giant oven warming up outside my window.

Narcisa stood there, fully dressed, staring at me, watching, waiting for me to take her up to the deadly war-zone favela. Her voice was charged with excitement as she chattered away about this fantastic new spot she'd found, where they had the very best crack in Rio.

I stood up.

Like an obedient soldier setting off to battle, I suited up and followed that perfect, bouncing, happy ass as it marched out the door.

54. IN THE GHETTO

"I CAME INTO A PLACE VOID OF ALL LIGHT, WHICH BELLOWS LIKE
THE SEA IN TEMPEST, WHEN IT IS COMBATED BY WARRING WINDS."
—*Dante*

A flaming red sunrise loomed over the bay. The scent of night rain and garlic invaded my nose, waking my soul to a new morning's magic.

A short, olive-skinned *paraíba* was sweeping at the sidewalk as we emerged onto the street. Squinting into the copper-toned dawn, I started the bike and we rode off into the crisp morning air, sprung like caged pigeons into the world of day,

Riding along, I grinned into the early-morning scenery, a swirling alphabet soup of alien poetry, passion, lust and surreal zombie movement. The world was fine and pristine, unfamiliar and new; a spinning, mad collage of indelible details and impressions, as we sped, tumbling through the neighborhood, flashing past lazy wooden doorways framed by lush green vegetation; crooked little trees growing from the crumbling, ancient stone walls. Lights and shadows of insect-buzzing daybreak; humid, septic smells of another long, hot, sleepless summer day, a rapid-fire jumble of crazy freeze-frame life.

Flying up the steep cobblestone road, up, up, into the topsy-turvy heights of the antique colonial *bairro* of Santa Teresa, we buzzed past an abandoned, bullet-ridden police cabin and a little corner *paderia*. The smells of fresh-baked bread and coffee followed us into impossible hairpin curves, bouncing over the twisting, bumpy roadway as we blasted around a pair of wobbly old yellow wooden streetcars rattling along their rusty, uneven iron tracks.

Narcisa pointed the way as we approached the entrance to the favela, shouting directions in my ear. We turned into a sudden half-hidden turnoff, then cut between a pair of decaying old Portuguese mansions, emerging onto a narrow, dusty dirt path, leading down into the slums.

Everything changed as we followed the claustrophobic maze of steep blind alleys. Down, down we went, into a purulent stew of teetering hillside shanties and undignified, sweaty, piss-reeking, garbage-strewn lives; teeming, dark ghetto rat-paths of vile humanity, crawling with gun-toting bandidos—anonymous teenage soldiers of endless undeclared wars between the populous prisoner communities of thriving drug trade commerce, a shadowy, sprawling underworld limbo of seething vice, random violence and sudden, ignoble death.

No turning back.

Everywhere I looked, the pitted, unpaved road was crowded with scrawny, bare-chested little slum-monkeys, swaggering teenage sol-diers of the war zone, all armed to the eyebrows. Their whistling eyes followed us along like creeping cats as we squealed rubber downhill into another long, precarious series of slanting, winding depths of vi-brating shantytown dwellings.

I steered onward, surrounded on all sides now by an infinite jumble of raw humanity; it was another world, another reality, a sinister, throb-bing, hallucinogenic netherworld of sewage and garbage and dirt. Pov-erty and crime flared all around us like the smoking flames of Hades, a crooked urban nightmare, piled up in chaotic rows of miserable shacks; haphazard, ramshackle structures, all stacked atop one another like tipsy phantoms, towering up to the heavens, blotting out the sky, ob-scuring every trace of the other city we were just in, only minutes before.

Everything looked distorted, crooked, bent, broken beyond any hope of repair or redemption. Crooked people. Crooked houses, crooked dogs, cats, babies. Hungry, crooked bovine eyes, following, watching. Cold, inscrutable looks, like insect machinery, all bearing down, staring at us, silently judging, measuring, weighing, calculating, summing us up for value and vulnerability . . . *Waiting for one fucking wrong move, and life could end right here, right now. Just like that. The End. Game Over, right here on a litter-strewn dirt path by an open sewer.*

Another motorbike whizzed past with a fat teenage girl on the back holding a dull black 9 mm pistol. The rider slowed down before us, just long enough for his passenger to pass the heavy gun to a very small child standing in the dirt.

As we lurched forward behind them, I felt a queasy wave of paranoia and dread spreading across my brain like a slow, fetid sewer flood. I glanced around, feeling anxious and out of place, like a gringo, a foreigner, a stranger in my own city. Breaking out in a sticky sweat, I battled with a dark premonition that, at any moment now, every living soul in that reeking, unhappy underworld would run out of their hovels, armed with machetes and dull, rusty knives, to slaughter us like pigs.

I was succumbing again to the usual sleep-deprived morning hallucinations. Gruesome images of imminent death invaded my brain like a nervous swarm of hornets.

One wrong step here, and it's all over!

Underfed, mangy mutts were barking all around us. I took a long, deep breath and swallowed hard as Narcisa rose up on the seat behind me, her hands resting on my shoulders, steering me along through another roughhewn brick and dirt network of cramped, sweaty garbage-strewn alleyways. Her skinny finger pointed left and I turned left, piloting up another steep, narrow path, where hollow-eyed children no larger than dolls sat on the ground, staring at nothing. As we passed, they just sat there, blinking in listless bewilderment, as if wondering why they'd ever been born into such a hopeless, miserable shithole.

Another wave of irrational fear hit me.

These favelas are all different today. This is a bad place! We don't belong in here!

Then, I reminded myself it was cool. As I rode on, getting my bearings, breathing in and out, acclimating, I remembered everything was all just as it should be there. We were just there to buy drugs. Legitimate business. I felt my neck muscles relax.

"Pare aqui! E'stop, e'stop, turn in these beco, Cigano!" Like a drunken pirate barking orders from a crow's nest above my head, she directed me into another tangle of dark, serpentine alleyways.

I hit the brakes at a curve, burning rubber, then gunned the throttle into another twisting, narrow *bequinho.* Her spindly finger waved in front of me, pointing like a tattered Jolly Roger flying in the smoky, humid mist. *"No! Don' e'stop in here! E'stay de way you going! Aqui! Aqui, cara! Go! Turn up these way now, Cigano, go go! Pare aqui! No no, no here, keep go on, go go!"* Twisting around behind me, she piloted me along like a horse. *"Cuidado, mermão! De policia, they can see us from de e'street above, got it?"*

I got it as Narcisa's voice sounded in my ear like an air raid siren, a soundtrack of doom. *"Fica ligado, Cigano! Cuidado! Go! Go! Anda logo porra, vai, vaiii-iii!"*

I could feel a poisonous taste of rancid adrenaline invading my mouth again. I knew the ghetto was off-limits to the cops; as long as we were in there, we were safe from the law. But, sooner or later, we would have to ride back out.

For now, though, it was cool. The only purpose cops served in the crowded, crime-ridden shantytowns was as target practice for local bandidos. As authority figures, the police in my city had always ranked about as high as garbagemen. In the favelas, even that dubious status was reduced to the level of weak, insignificant annoyances—rats, pest, insignificant vermin to be shot on sight.

The cops would keep their distance, I knew, clustered around the entrance up on the street, standing safe by their vehicles, guns ready, watching and waiting for the occasional payoff from people like us. Addicts coming out, holding drugs.

That was what worried me.

The uniformed scavengers were up there right now, I remembered, looking down through their binoculars, watching everything, lurking, waiting, like a murderous pack of unseen predators.

55. HOLY ARMED HARMONY

"YOU WANT TO SAY YOU'RE THE COUNTRY OF THE FUTURE? YOU WANT
TO BE THE COUNTRY OF PROGRESS? THEN HAVE IT SO KIDS HAVE A
CHOICE BETWEEN A BROOM AND A GUN, SO PEOPLE DON'T HAVE TO PICK
THROUGH GARBAGE TO EAT, THEN COME TALK TO ME ABOUT BRAZIL."
—*Nick Wong*

After a bumpy, sweating, nervous eternity, we came to a little dirt clearing. I slowed the bike and looked around. Legions of poor people were trudging past in the dusty path, on their way to work in the giant asphalt labyrinth below. Men and women dressed in crisp, clean work clothes. Uniforms of janitors and doormen, bus drivers and servants, cooks, gardeners and maids. Children in identical, crisp blue-and-white school uniforms.

I sucked my teeth and spit in the dirt, muttering under my breath. "Who th' fuck says they ever abolished slavery in Brazil, eh?"

On one end of the little plaza was a simple one-story brick building, painted a dirty off-white color, a bit more tidy than the other ratty hollow-brick dwellings.

I glanced up at the neat, hand-painted sign above the door:
IGREJA EVANGELICA MUNDIAL DE JESUS CRISTO SENHOR

Across the road from the evangelist church sat a weather-beaten card table, where a rawboned mulatto youth manned a makeshift open-air office, leaning back in a rusty old metal folding chair. As we approached, Narcisa leapt off the back of the still-moving bike like a cartoon ninja superhero, landing on her feet before a group of amused-looking teenaged bandidos. They seemed to know her face.

On the table sat a large green plastic supermarket sack, filled with glassine bags and little foil bundles. From the motorcycle, I could read the stamps on the crude homemade labels. Colorful packages of weed. Cocaine. Rock. Crack. Cheap little bags of brand-name Death . . . *"Hulk"* . . . *"Poderoso"* . . . *"Pancadão"* . . . *"Boladão."*

Sitting beside the product was a notebook, and the other usual items. A compact Uzi machine gun. A battered black semi-automatic pistol. Taurus .40. Military police issue . . . *Cop killers . . . And those fucking pigs are up there right now, watching us through their fucking binoculars, waiting to pluck us like chickens the minute we ride out of this fucking dump! Great!*

Raising one knee and slapping it twice in some weird ghetto code, Narcisa grinned at the boy at the table. He reached into his bag and handed her a couple of bundles of the rock. She tossed my last fifty down on the table. The kid snatched up the cash and wrote the transaction down in his little ledger. Business as usual.

Still thinking of the cops lying in wait up on the street, I contemplated an alternative route out of the ghetto drug market . . . *Another Great Escape with Narcisa . . . Fuck! Escape or payoff now . . . And no money for a bribe anymore either . . . Straight to fucking jail for me this time . . . Shit!* I pictured myself back in the *cadeia*, fighting for space in a vermin-infested jail cell the size of my apartment, crammed in with a hundred other stinking caged animals, ankle-deep in human excrement.

My mouth was dry. I could feel the paranoia creeping in again, poisoning my guts.

Sitting on the bike, I snuck guilty little glances around. The fear was on me good now. I swallowed another mouthful of bitter spit, trying to act cool. But I was wearing panic like a sweaty straitjacket. I hoped it didn't show.

Another scrawny, cracked-out kid with pasty mulatto skin and burned-out, jaundiced eyes leaned on a nearby brick wall, smoking a fat *basiado*. He wore a red and black knit cap and was holding a tarnished 12-gauge shotgun. A battered AK-47 was slung over his bony shoulder.

Both the lanky bandidos wore flip-flops, colorful Bermuda shorts and stylish, sporty tank tops, just like the rich playboys at the beach in Ipanema. But I knew those swaggering, skinny teens didn't play. They were working for the *dono*, the Operator, the Owner, the Boss of their *morro*—which was surrounded by a huge, tangled complex of other favelas. Each *comunidade* was separated from the other sprawling shantytowns all around it, only by the rival *donos* in charge of the drug turf, and the ragtag gangs of scraggly gun-jockeys who ran their retail sales.

A fragile ecosystem of loosely organized crime.

All the bosses and teenage soldiers were at constant war now; at war with each other, and at war with the cops; all for control of their respective territories. I knew that all the different police factions were at war with each other there too, over who sold the guns and protection and strategic information to the many opposing factions and their high-rolling ghetto-superstar bosses. The younger lookouts and other wannabe bandidos up there were all at war with each other, as well, fighting for lucrative position, status and rank. Every one of those shirtless little slum rats dreamed of being a *dono* someday.

Most wouldn't live to take a legal drink, of course. It's a complicated place. Culture shock for the average middle-class Carioca.

For a majority of Rio's citizens, though, the shadowy netherworld of the favelas is the only home they'll ever know. The real culture shock for them is down in streets of the big, heartless metropolis down below; that familiar "other" world. The asphalt jungle. *O Asfalto*. The Concrete. The City. Rio de Janeiro.

As soon as you come up into the hillside slums from the city proper, you can feel this weird, subtle shift; the immediacy of a constant, unspoken, life-and-death tension. Paranoia crackles in the air like a dark, deadly electrical current. I could smell it in the hot, fetid wind as I sat there on the bike, waiting.

On one side of the dusty plaza, a thriving open-air drug market. Across the way, the Gospel Church. The evangelical Churches, like most cultural abominations in Brazil, were imported from North America—straight out of the white-trash Bible Belt of that other degenerate, modern-day Babylon, a direct bull's-eye strike into the latter-day slave colonies of third-world South America.

Small churches are big business up in the ghettos, always open at night, when people come straggling home from work, tired, worn-out, beaten, broken, humiliated, spent. At day's end, *favela-dos* have always had limited options for entertainment, after toiling all day at the ass end of the soul-grinding asphalt machine of the city. Most go home and switch on the television *novela* to numb their minds down to face another day in the murderous capitalist matrix below.

Others occupy themselves in the raucous open-air *botecos* owned by the drug bosses. There they can drink cheap cane rum *cachaça* and snort, smoke and gamble their many cares away, carousing late into the long, sweaty summer nights. Many turn up late for work down in the concrete slaughterhouse the next morning, jittery, hung-over, stunned and baffled, with even shittier prospects than the day before—but just as powerless, just as fucked.

Looking around that smelly ghetto dirt pile, it made sense to me that so many younger *favelados* would gladly give up on the rat race to join the swelling ranks of bandidos, with dreams of taking the things they wanted at gunpoint. Ambition doesn't always die in the ghetto; it just takes on surreal, desperate proportions.

Most of those kids wind up cold and stiff as a dead dog, of course, lying in a muddy ditch with a mouthful of roaches; often, within their first year living by the gun. Others who don't make the grade end up in one of the notorious favela "microwaves," a macabre drug trade practice used to weed out the rats and cowards by stuffing them alive into stacks of old truck tires, then dousing them with gasoline and lighting a match.

Retribution, I knew, had always been swift and unforgiving up in the hills.

Living in the shadows of such brutal realities, an ever-popular option for mindless distraction was for sale at a bargain price, right there at the little Gospel Church—a welcoming refuge for honest, hardworking, gullible slum dwellers. A place where they could donate 10 percent of their meager slave-wages to some fast-talking, foaming-mouthed, false-prophet preacher, the self-appointed rep-resentative of a pissed-off, Made-in-America, fundamentalist doomsday McDeity.

The church was doing a thriving business there too, peddling its noxious concoction of spiritual pride, social intolerance and stifling puritanical "morality," Satan and Evil and Sin. The concept of Evil was something people could surely relate to, of course, in that fear-fueled nightmare stew of soul-stifling poverty, violence and crime. How not, living at the shit end of the Mass-Market Consumer Dream Culture? Such is the day-to-day reality in this Brave New Rio de Ja-neiro, City of God, in the Year of Our Lord, 2010.

Just like the drug bosses, the favela preachers had a lucrative racket going for themselves. All that and a big old Made-in-America Day-Glo plastic Jesus on their side too. And they wouldn't want to mess it all up by pissing off the guys with the big guns, doing business right across the road from their little white church. So everybody just lived and let live—or let die, depending on the time of day—in a tenuous symbiotic coexistence, each gang pushing its own brand of dope or salvation to the masses, and not making waves.

God-Blessed, Government-Sponsored Holy Armed Harmony had always served the social order well in the land of my birth. A perfect tool for keeping the sheeple in line, and not making trouble for the real Bosses. The Big Boys. The Top Gangsters, those corrupt, reptilian *politicos* sitting in their clean, air-conditioned offices, sucking the lifeblood of the people, while fixing the larger issues of the republic to suit their own exclusive gangs; selling a nation's future to the gringo banks, and spending all the money on themselves . . . *Living in obscene luxury, while the rest of us gotta limp around in circles in these dirty, ass-reeking slums, like a bunch of broken windup toys . . . Fuck! No wonder Narcisa wants no part of this fucking world!*

As Narcisa completed her transaction, neither of the young drug dealers even glanced in my direction. They knew I was there, of course. Hard to miss a long-haired, gold-toothed gypsy, covered in prison tattoos, sitting right beside you on a motorbike. Still, nobody looked.

It didn't surprise me. In that place, a simple look could kill.

To them, I could've been anybody sitting there, armed with grenades and a gun, maybe sent by the cops or the rival *donos* across the way to start another lucrative turf war. Those boys knew, all too well, that my face could be the last one they'd ever see; and they just preferred not to look. I didn't blame them. I got it. I didn't look at them much either. It's always better that way, up in the hills.

Her business concluded, Narcisa jumped back on the bike.

As I rode off, she started slapping my back like a horse again, shouting orders, breathing hot licks of flame into my ear . . . *go go go!* I gunned the motor as she chattered away nonstop, a crack-maddened radio announcer of doom and obsession, speaking in a language we both knew well. Addiction.

"Go, Cigano, go, that way down there, turn left, go, go! We gonna go out de other side, go! No policia there now, got it?"

I got it. The bandidos had tipped her off, thank Christ, to an alternate route out. I grinned, feeling a happy wave of relief as I turned and coasted straight down the hill, safe and sound, away from the cops.

"Take me to Love House now, Cigano, fast, go go, vai logo, anda, cara, vai-aii! I gotta make de important e'speriment right now, go go go . . ."

I obeyed with pleasure. Her wish was my command. Narcisa was a benevolent dictator that day, and I was willing to do whatever I had to in order to keep her happy.

The thought of her going back to Copacabana to spread her long white angel legs for pink-faced gringos in dark hotel rooms by the sea had become intolerable to me, a constant threat to my fragile peace of mind.

I knew I would do whatever I must now, in order to keep her close, while continuing to hope and pray for our redemption.

56. VILLAGE OF THE DAMNED

"IF MISERY LOVES COMPANY, MISERY HAS COMPANY ENOUGH."
—*Thoreau*

Then, one day, Narcisa disappeared again.

I'd spent the previous week catering to her every bizarre whim and demand, running her back and forth to the favela at all hours of the day and night, trying to keep up with her mad, crack-fueled metaphysical "experiments."

Finally, one evening, my brain twisted into a spiky tangle of sleeplessness, I threw in the towel and let her out of my sight. I simply had to get some rest, so I handed her a few bucks to go out and cop on her own, then I crashed.

That was the last I saw of her for days.

Then came the searing mental agony of not knowing if she was dead or alive. More sleepless nights, sitting up worrying, imagining her getting fucked in the eyes by gangs of rabid, drooling gringo sex tourists, and worse. Worried sick, I went out looking for her. I searched all the usual spots. Narcisa was nowhere.

As a last resort, I decided to take a ride over to Vila Mimosa.

Could she have sunk so low? I wondered. Could Narcisa really be so desperate and depraved now to have ended up at that infamous lowlife sex ghetto? It was a long shot, I knew, but in her present state, I figured anything was possible.

It had been ages since I'd been there, but I would've known the way blindfolded as I rode through the sleeping downtown streets, past the shadowy dockyards of Praça Mauá and the dark, deserted Praça da Bandeira.

Making the familiar turn onto the old Rua Ceará, there it was, dead ahead. Vila Mimosa. The end of the line for legions of Carioca whores; the beginning of a new life of debauchery and degradation for emerging generations of bright-eyed young favela girls. An apprenticeship. A brutal, rough-and-tumble initiation into the fascinating, compelling, profitable world of dick.

Most of the *garotas* there hailed from the poverty-blighted wastelands of the Baixada, where life is cheap and short for all but those born under a lucky star. The poor in Rio grow such calloused souls that even sex must be fast-paced, clumsy and heavy-handed, like a barroom brawl. Like heat-crazed tropical insects that only live for a day, those girls know they won't have much time to spread their wings and fly. They have to get their kicks and their dick while they can, how they can, wherever they can. And in Vila Mimosa, there's always plenty of dick. All sizes, shapes, ages and colors. From the misshapen, throbbing purple bananas attached to sweaty, hardworking garbagemen and construction grunts, to the sleek golden-brown members of well-toned Ipanema playboys, Vila Mimosa is a true democracy of the dick: the land of the fifteen-minute, fifteen-buck, short-time fuck. I rolled along past the darkened little hole-in-the-wall bars on the outskirts, where gangs of outlaw bikers sat like laconic alligators at crooked wooden bar tables, plotting mayhem and glory, drinking beer in the greasy yellow shadows.

Parking the bike near the entrance to the *zona*, I strolled on, past the late-night meatpacking warehouses, where sleeping delivery trucks lined the piss-slick cobblestones, waiting for dawn to transport their deathly red cargo to the city's hungry mouths. And then, there it was, another parallel meat market, a slaughterhouse of cheap, easy, short-time sex. Prostitution's Heart of Darkness.

Approaching the chaotic jumble of winking, blinking, trembling, run-down two- and three-story whorehouse dwellings, the pounding cacophony of a hundred competing jukeboxes grew louder and more consuming with each step.

By the time I reached the middle of the action, it was a polluted wave of hellish noise, a distorted doomsday symphony of chaos. The narrow alleys branching off like diseased arteries from the main road were where the action was. As I turned into the first little *beco* and made my way through that pulsating, demented sperm derby, the giant loudspeakers assaulted my ears from every angle, like a traffic jam on the road to hell. Brushing against sweaty crowds of scrawny, shirtless favela boys, I navigated the lusty human sewer like a nervous ghost.

On either side of the reeking corridors were cramped doorways, cluttered with flabby, drunk, coked-up, naked meat puppets; misshapen, dark-skinned women and girls, all gyrating to the earsplitting rhythms, like tortured ghosts trapped in unbearable skin bags.

Here and there, a bold, shadowy hand reached out of the dark human muddle to grope at my crotch, like a greedy monkey grabbing at a banana. Swatting the intrusive claws away like insects, I moved on, deeper into the humid, urine-reeking mist, feeling around like a sleepwalker searching for something that's gone.

That's when I realized I was looking for something more than Narcisa there. Something elemental. Something essential. The past. My youth. These poor, pathetic, sad-faced bitches' youth. Whatever. I was longing for something. Anything. But there wasn't anything anymore. Nothing. It was all gone now.

Good times gone . . . And here I am, a lonely old loser, lost in a freaky, obsolete House of Mirrors . . . A living horror gallery of flaccid, naked, tortured

human meat with the look and texture of moldy fruit rotting in the pissy tropical
air, waiting for the flies, the ants, the cockroach feast to begin . . . Shit.

I shuddered as I passed another lineup of dilapidated aging hookers. Dull-eyed, crabby old fish-faced legions of the damned, standing around in broken doorways, teetering on sad, cheap plastic heels,
dancing their tired-out, sordid gyrations into the dung-colored night.
I cringed at the sudden realization that, like Narcisa, perhaps I'd finally managed to corrupt my rusty old soul to the breaking point,
that there was really no turning back anymore.

This is it. The End. End of the line. And I'm still here. Broken. Damaged.
Wrecked beyond repair or redemption. A pathetic old sex junkie looking for a fix!

I trudged on through that deathly, dark circus of broken souls. Finally, giving up on finding Narcisa, I spotted one who looked half
alive. I made the approach, and off we went through a dim little bar
and up a wobbly metal spiral staircase.

After a lackluster ten-minute fuck, I zipped up my jeans and beat
it out of the dank, greasy little cubicle, longing for air . . . *Thank you*
come again!

Wiping the sweat from my face, I wandered over to an open-air
food stand. The old mulatto gave me a knowing grin as he handed me
a stale sandwich that smelled of rotten eggs and rotten sex. I limped
over to a sidewalk table and sat, watching the worn-out, slimy old
sex parade slithering by; saggy, tragic-faced whores and confused-
looking insect droves of hungry men. Wage slaves. Worker ants out on
the town, searching for a quick, cheap grunt.

All of a sudden, a booming, crabby voice, like a giant spider talking
to a fleet of flies, came bashing through the shadows. Some beer-
drunk moron had turned up the bar TV to watch the political debates
for the upcoming presidential elections.

I winced at the candidates' faces as they spoke, spewing their incoherent political double-talk into the night. They reminded me of a

bunch of lousy actors, reading bad dialogue from a boring old soap opera script.

What the fuck are these shit-breathing, sanctimonious ass-clowns talking about?

I couldn't for the life of me understand a word they were saying.

Taxes. Sewers. Education. Inflation. Labor laws. Infrastructure. Child prostitution. Health care. Swine flu. Shit-eating. Rat-fucking. Public safety. Order. Progress. Jobs. Drugs. Culture. War. Peace. Change. Hope.

Bullshit. Horseshit. Catshit. Dogshit. Ratshit. Batshit. Flyshit.

Death was all I could see and hear. I gawked at the woman candidate's angry reptilian face and I shuddered in revulsion. The smug, pugnacious, short-haired old crab who would soon become Brazil's first female president looked as dreadful as the most decrepit old whore staggering by on the sidewalk.

I looked out over the stumbling legions of worn-out, drunken floozies, tottering around on their battered whorehouse heels. It was all the same shit. Shit-talking, shit-eating, lies, betrayal and death. That's all there was to look forward to.

I got up and crept into another whorehouse. A snaggletoothed guy with a decent selection of stolen cell phones was working his game at the bar counter in there. I sat down in a dark corner, looking over the purloined devices, waiting for him to finish snorting his next line of coke, hoping to hurry up and pay him off so I could have a cheap phone to give Narcisa, if I ever found her again.

It would be nice to stay in touch with her somehow, I mused, ignoring the concept that a cell phone, like anything else, wouldn't last a fucking night with the Crack Monster. Finally, Snaggletooth slid up beside me at the bar, chewing on his words like some furious, hellbound, nocturnal rodent. I handed him a ten spot and pocketed a shiny pink Motorola with a glittery plastic heart sticker on the back.

Some unfortunate whore would be incommunicado now. Oh well.

Out on the street, two young hookers stumbled along in shiny new high heels and skimpy, tipsy rags of glittery nothing. Holding hands, shrieking in drunken delight, they skipped across a puddle of bum-vomit in the greasy cobblestone road, like a pair of schoolgirls playing hopscotch. In their wake, an obese mulatto whore waddled past like a hideous, crippled human garbage truck. Tired-out fuck music blared from a pair of weather-damaged speakers beside me; an earsplitting avalanche of hellish, nonsensical monkey-spew.

I was done.

I knew Narcisa would rather die than end up in this place. Time to go.

I walked off down the road, jumped on my bike and headed out the way I came.

Riding away from the decrepit old fuck-jungle, past the sullen clusters of undernourished killers and thugs who patrol its shadowy outskirts like gangs of toothless barracudas, I wondered again where on earth Narcisa could be.

57. BROKEN PICKERS

"WE ARE ALL BORN MAD. SOME REMAIN SO."
—*Samuel Beckett*

As the days oozed by, I worried about Narcisa; but on another level, I knew it was a blessing for me that she was gone; a rare chance to rejoin the world for a moment.

It had been months since I'd seen any of my friends. The next day, I called Luciana. She asked me if I'd been away traveling again. Over the phone, I gave her a brief rundown. She got it. That's why it's good to have friends. They get it. Friends are like God's way of making up for the fucked-up families people like Narcisa and I got. I was grateful for the few I had. And I really missed Luciana.

She told me to meet her at the late-afternoon AA meeting we used to go to over in Copacabana. It turned out to be a fine idea. When I arrived, she greeted me with a warm hug. We sat in our regular corner. The coffee and homemade snacks were good, and the meeting was inspiring. Some guy was talking about the misadventures of his active addiction. His ribald war stories made me chuckle. I laughed long and hard, despite a dull, lingering heartache.

It felt good. I hadn't laughed in quite some time, I realized. It was liberating. The laughter of identification—the best kind. Laughing at yourself is like strapping on a clown nose and thumbing it at the Curse.

As I sat there giggling, Luciana grinned at me.

I leaned over and nudged her, whispering. "When ya can't make fun of yourself, it's kinda like inviting the whole world to do it for you, huh?"

Even as I said the words, I knew I was still thinking about Narcisa.

After the meeting, we wandered over to the beach. We sat at a table by one of the little shacks by the waves. It was a warm late-summer afternoon and people were out strolling on the sand. We got a couple of *côcos* and sat looking out over the ocean, talking and laughing, sipping our coconut water. I wished Narcisa was there to enjoy the evening too. I wished that talking and laughing, or anything at all, could ever come easy with Narcisa.

Luciana ordered a plate of fried fish. When she offered me a bite, I realized I still had no appetite, despite not having eaten much for days.

Worried sick about Narcisa again, I fell silent, brooding.

Luciana got it. "She has you going pretty bad, hey, Ignácio?"

I shrugged. "It's that obvious, Lu?"

She pursed her lips and grinned. "Takes one to know one, baby."

I laughed. "Oh yeah, I almost forgot. What was his name? Santiago, right?"

"Ha! You got a pretty good memory for an old dope-head . . . *Aiii, Santiago, meu amor!*" She giggled, poking fun at herself.

That cracked me up. Luciana's last "true love" had been a dog-eyed, homeless alcoholic scam artist, a comical, tragic little derelict from the favela where she lived. He'd pretty much run her life into the dirt, I remembered, before ending up in a ditch.

She stifled another sad little grin, shaking her head. "We sure do know how to pick some winners, hey, Ignácio?"

"Yeah, well, they say people like us got broken pickers. But it's strange . . ."

She shot me an inquisitive look.

I sighed. "This girl, Narcisa, I dunno . . . She's different, Lu."

She guffawed. "They all are, man! But even with your broken picker, I can't wait to meet her. Sounds like my kinda people."

After an hour, we parted ways. I went back home.

No Narcisa.

I knew I couldn't afford to think about it. But I did. I reminded myself that worrying is like praying for bad shit to happen. In an effort to keep my mind off all the bad shit, I tried to write for a while, but I couldn't concentrate.

Exhausted, finally, I passed out on the sofa.

A couple of hours later, just before nightfall, I woke up in a cold sweat. My fuzzy thoughts zeroed right in on Narcisa again, wondering where the hell she could be. I tried to go back to sleep, but I couldn't. I sat up. I tried to pray. I puttered. I paced. I wrote in my journal again for a while, but I couldn't focus.

Just when I thought I'd crawl out of my fucking skin, the phone rang. I jumped up and looked at the screen. . . . *Collect call. Thank God! Narcisa!*

Her raspy, crack-ravaged voice was a song of angels . . . *Oh, thank Christ! She's alive! Salve Ogum!!* She told me to come and meet her at Arpoador, the big granite rock overlooking the surf at the end of Ipanema Beach.

I threw on my boots, picked up my keys and hurried out the door.

Twenty minutes later, I was rolling along the shore. I slowed down and cruised out to the end of the little cobblestone road, looking over the long golden expanse of sand. I could see the giant green hills of São Conrado off in the distance, twinkling across the water. The lights were just coming on in the sprawling hillside shantytowns of Vidigal and its sister community, Chácara do Céu, the favela where Luciana lived in a humble hut with a spectacular view of the ocean. Searching for Narcisa, my eyes scanned the area like a pair of searchlights.

I stopped and stared at the rocky cove with its giant mounds of granite jutting out into the crashing waves. Swimmers and surfers dotted the water's surface. Families were sitting around on *kangas*, talking and laughing at day's end, drinking cold sodas, beers and fresh lemonade, eating greasy homemade snacks peddled by the ever-present troops of leather-skinned roving beach vendors.

I started the bike again and rolled along some more, cruising slowly, breathing it all in. Clusters of palm trees rustled in the warm, salt air by the little seaside kiosks selling beer, green coconuts and fried fish. Working-class families were out strolling. Dusky Negro children and teenagers from the neighboring favelas rolled around on the sand. The odd tourist wandering around, looking lost. Local couples out for a walk after work. Distant figures down by the shore, silhouetted against the sparkling waves in the setting sun's orange reflection.

No sign of Narcisa anywhere. Just as I was about to ride off, she jumped out from behind a clump of palm trees like a deranged monkey.

"*Perdeu! Surprise attack, Cigano! You dead! Hah! Perdeu! Give it to me de moto, go go, give it to me all you mo-ney, you life, go! Ha-ah!*"

I gawked as she stood before me, waving her arms around like a mad, animated scarecrow. Shocked at her sudden appearance, I was even more taken aback at the state she was in . . . *Jesus! Fuck! She looks like a fucking train wreck! Shit!*

Narcisa was a demented human rag doll . . . *Poor baby!* Her face looked like a melting Carnaval mask of the Grim Reaper. Her tall, wiry body contorted in mad, jittery puppet movements as she rattled out a litany of incoherent, ranting, apocalyptic gibberish.

Her eyes popped. Spittle flew in spasms of soul-shivering crack madness as she grabbed my shoulder, hoisting herself up onto the bike behind me like a wild chattering demon.

"Ha-ah! I wanna destroy! I am de goddess of Chaos! I am de devil! I gonna destroy these focking place an' all these e'stupid peoples! Look out, you fockers! I got de neuron detonator inside my brain!" She dug her fingernail into the side of her head. *"If I go, ever'body go! These whole e'stupid world finish now, got it?!"*

I held my breath, speechless.

"Hey, eííí, oííí, Cigano! I wanna get a hamburger, de big fat burger, an' a giant size milk shake too, go! Go! 'Bora daqui, mano! Anda, vai vaii-ííí!"

"You got it, princesa!" I exhaled, feeling a sudden gnawing bite of hunger.

58. TAINTED

"IF THERE'S A HARDER WAY OF DOING
SOMETHING, SOMEONE WILL FIND IT."
—*Ralph E. Ross*

Feeling as if I'd been locked away in a dark sensory-deprivation chamber for days, weeks, months, a great longing swept through me as I looked out over the beach, remembering how much I missed being outdoors.

Contemplating the tranquil surroundings, I turned to Narcisa and gave it a shot. "I was just thinking, baby, I kinda wanna go for a quick swim here first . . . . Okay?"

Even on such a long, hot, muggy afternoon—perfect for a dip in the sparkling blue summer waves—I knew it was a risky proposition. I didn't really expect it to be okay. It was rarely okay with Narcisa if she didn't get her way immediately and without question.

To my surprise, her eyes lit up.

"Sim sim!! Ti-bum! Ti-bum! Ya-asss, I wanna go for de e'swimming, Cigano! Yeh! Perfect, Max! E'swim e'swim! Ti-bum! Ti-bum! Now! Go! Go!"

Gratitude filled my heart as I maneuvered the bike over by the edge of the big rock. I got off, stripped down to my underwear and headed toward the water, as she threw her filthy jeans to the ground beside the motorcycle. Thankfully, she was still wearing the bottom of her pink polka-dot bikini.

Narcisa charged out onto the sand, flinging her shirt at me as she passed, her perfect little tits bouncing like bare 100-watt lightbulbs in the setting sun.

"Wha' de fock you looking, hein, e'slaves?" She flew past me, scowling at a gang of suntanned adolescents sitting under an umbrella, staring at the weird topless spectacle. *"Why don' you take a focking foto, hein? You too focking e'stupid for know you even alive! Hah! Focking clones! Arrrggghhh!"*

As she ranted off down the beach, curious onlookers gawked at her weird, ghostly white visage. Pretending not to know her, I followed behind at a distance, prepared to step up and defend her if anybody got bold.

They didn't, of course.

Somehow, nobody ever messed with Narcisa. Something just told them she was insane; deranged, off-limits. Tainted. It was uncanny how, for the most part, even the craziest, most fucked-up, most dangerous people always seemed to just stay clear of her. It was as if she were invisible or something.

Just the week before, I remembered, she'd talked me into giving her a ride in the middle of the night to go cop at the Complexo do Alemão, an unfamiliar, ultraviolent favela deep in the sprawling, dusty backwaters of the Baixada.

The area had a deadly reputation. But there had been a shoot-out going on at her regular spot. Rather than wait for things to calm down closer to home, she'd insisted on risking her life to score elsewhere. Located somewhere south of hell, the place was a godforsaken, volatile no-man's-land, which even the most desperate addicts shunned.

Not Narcisa. She didn't give a shit . . . *go go go*!

After a long, hair-raising ride down the ass end of Avenida Brasil, I could smell the filthy, gargantuan, impoverished hell-pit, even before I saw it. As we entered the notorious complex of tangled favelas, the stench was unbelievable, as if every living soul living there had shit their pants all at once.

Turing off into the chaotic, septic, raw-brick morass, I steered down into the heavily fortified *boca*. It was the ugliest slum I'd ever seen. As I cut the motor and coasted forward, I could hear a prolonged flurry of gunshots up ahead, all different calibers, popping away like firecrackers in the dark ghetto sprawl.

I knew we were in the kind of place where people just disappeared, where your cheap plastic wristwatch is worth more than your fucking life. Concerned for Narcisa's safety going in there alone, I'd offered to walk with her to the spot and watch her back.

She gave me a look like a dog sucking on a mango.

"Y'know . . . just in case . . ." I shrugged.

She grabbed my shoulders, fixing me with those crazed, blazing eyes, her hot, feral breath licking at my face like hellfire serpent tongues of doom.

"In case what? There no kinda cases here, bro! Lissen, Cigano, I don' need you protect me or watching my back in here, got it? You know why? Because ever'body know I don' got no-thing for loose, okey? Only one thing I got to loose now is you, got it? So now you e'stay here an' take care for you own self, cuz any bad thing ever happen to you, mano, de Narcisa finish forever, got it? Just you sit an' wait me here and I gonna be back right now. Go!"

Before I could utter another word, she snatched the money from my hand and took off running like a rat in a maze, disappearing into a dark, musty, garbage-strewn alley of memory.

With a sigh, I followed as Narcisa dashed across the sand like a ragged comet, shooting straight into the water with a blood-curdling **whoo-oop.**

Splash!

Right away it started.

"Ooohhh, e'sheet! Fock! Brrrrrrrrrr! Fock fock fock! Porra! Is too much focking cold in here, cold! Arrrggghhhh, e'sheet sheet sheet! Brrrrrrrrrrr! I am fro-zing to death, come here fast, fast, Cigano! Come here now an' hold me, go! Go go go!"

Wading into the shallow, lukewarm cove where she floundered like a drowning porcupine, I wrapped my arms around her pale, scrawny frame.

She pushed me away, screeching like she'd been stabbed with an icicle.

"Na-ooo! Left me go, no, no, don' touch me, get away! You all over wet! Is too focking wet here, Cigano! Oohh! Brr-rrrrrr! Arrrggghh! Fo-ock!"

"It's the fucking ocean, baby." I laughed. "Of course it's wet, what th' fuck do ya think? You just told me to come and hold you!"

"Never mind it whatever thing I e'say, go! Pay no atten-tion at me! I am de crazy bitch, remember? Crazy, in-sane! Gotta go now, go, go! We gotta go-oo, Cigano! Right now, hurry, go go go! Please Cigano, go! Por favor! Bora!"

Still yelling, she stomped out of the water and stormed across the beach, looking nervous, miserable as a drenched kitten.

I ran up behind her, dripping wet. "Whaddya wanna do now?"

"Arrrggghhh! Some other place now, go, go! Naa-oow! Por favor!"

She spun around and around like a mad, disheveled, drunken der-vish. Still laughing, shaking my head, I sprinted back to the bike. Catching up to her a ways down the beach. I yelled her name, but she didn't seem to hear. That's when I noticed her staring at something, with a fixed, fearful look of panic slashed across her face. I gunned the motor to get her attention. She snapped out of it and came running over, a nervous, waterlogged little ghost.

She jumped on behind me and we took off.

Right away, she began to fidget, shifting around on the back of the bike, shaking all over, twisting and turning, talking with unseen spirits of the dead in the hot rushing afternoon air.

It was turning out to be a rough run for her.

Narcisa had been up for way too long this time. Her mind was plummeting south fast. Soon, she'd be ready for the fucking rubber room.

Shit!

Riding away from the shore, I worried about getting her home in one piece.

59. OFF WITH THEIR HEADS!

"IF THE INFANTILE PSYCHE PERSISTS INTO ADULT LIFE,
HOW WILL ITS PRESENCE BE MANIFESTED?"
—Harry M. Tiebout, M.D.

As we rode along, Narcisa kept wobbling around behind me, jabbering, chattering like a mad chimpanzee. As I picked up speed and turned off into the crowded streets of Copacabana, she was barely hanging on.

Ignoring my pleas to keep still, she continued jerking, shifting her weight back and forth, bouncing up and down on the seat, nearly making me lose control and fly into oncoming traffic . . . *Jesus fuck! At this rate we'll both be dead before I get this freak home . . . If there's one thing that really burns my ass, it's a cunt who can't hold still on the back of a fucking bike!*

After a second close call, I was done.

I pulled over to the side of the avenida, skidding to a halt right in front of the old Holiday Bar—the place where I'd found Narcisa standing in the fog after her inglorious return from New York. I cut the motor and sat there in silence, fuming.

"What de fock you doing here, Cigano? No-oo! I don' wan' you e'stop at these e'stupid place now, go, go! Anda, porra, vaii-iii! Go go, go . . ."

Turning around, I put my pissed-off face up hers and shouted back. **"I don't give a shit what you want, Narcisa! Shut th' fuck up!"**

Sparks of rage crackled in high-voltage oscillating flames between us, like two snarling Rottweilers straining at their leashes.

"I wanna go now! Go, porra! Go! Go! Go!"

I spat back, mimicking her. " *'I want, I want! Go go go!' That's all you ever wanna do, Narcisa! Go go go! Nothing's good enough, no place is ever right! The beach? Too much sand! Water's too fuckin' wet! Always hassling me, bitching, pissing, moaning! Go go go! Wanna go here, wanna go there. Well fuck that shit! Now I'm stopping, cuz ya can't even sit still on the back of a fuggin' motorcycle goin' eighty kilometers an hour, ya daffy cow! Fuck you, Narcisa! Ya got a death wish, no problem, but you ain't taking me with ya, tá ligada! No fuckin' way, got it? Got it now? Understand?"*

She glared back at me for a second. Then, in a lightning flash, she was off the bike, standing at the curb, screaming, bellowing, eyes bugging, foaming at the mouth, spittle flying.

"You focking fock, you e'sheet e'stupid fock, I ha-ate you, Cigano! You have destroy my life an' make me crazy!! I hate you, hate hate ha-ate you, e'stupid dick!! You never gonna see me again, never gonna touch me again, you gonna go an' jack off forever now! Go an' find de fat ugly old nigger whoo-oore! You can go fock you e'self, cuz I never gonna fock you again! Nunca!!"

She pointed at the whorehouse and raged on. *"I gonna go back to these focking puteiro! An' then I gonna fock everybody, but never more with you! Va se foder! I gonna fock de midget! I gonna fock de clown!! I gonna make de sexo with de army, de navy, de two hundred midget an' clown an' beggar mans, and cripple mans too, but never with you, never more again, Cigano, nunca!! Vá pro inferno!! You gonna go fock you self forever, you focking e'stupid e'sheet!!!"*

Somehow I managed to keep my cool. I crossed my arms, saying nothing.

Not getting the kind of reaction she was trying for, Narcisa lost it completely. She started hitting me about the head and shoulders, childish blows that didn't hurt much, but I could feel all her hurt, frustration and psychic pain, the delirious rage of a broken heart, a deranged, drug-addled brain, a shattered soul.

People stopped and stared, gawking at the angry little sidewalk freak show. As I tried to fend off her furious fists, she began whaling on me harder. I felt like some kind of plastic punching bag toy as she flailed away at my face, drawing blood from my upper lip.

I grabbed her wrists and held them together tight. Then she started kicking me in the shins, trying to knee me in the balls, biting my hands like a rabid badger.

I let her go and stepped away, dodging her kicks like a matador.

One of the passersby laughed and made a humorous comment.

Narcisa heard it and turned. Her mouth flew open like a raging sewer, focusing her rage on him. *"Tá olhando o que, sua merda!? What de fock you looking, hein? E'stupid old e'sheet-face monkey clone loo-ooser!"* She spit out the words like popping gunfire, raving, raging, vomiting hatred and violent intent. *"Suas mumias, babacas! You focking e'sheet peoples are all dead, got it!? Too e'stupid to live! Zombies! Fat, ugly old cow dead mummy peoples, you old an' e'stupid an' boring!! So e'stupid you gotta e'stop you e'sheet little life for lookit de crazy drug addict whoore!? E'stupid mummies!"*

As her screams got louder, the crowd of spectators seemed to grow and gather, swelling like storm clouds on a volatile horizon.

"You are all e'sheet! Clones!!" Her curses boomed in the air like rolling thunder. *"I prefer to be dead than gotta live like all you e'sheet little cow peoples! Mummies! E'slaves! E'stay*

an' watch all de day you e'sheet e'stupid focking tel'vision,
an e'shake you e'stupid boring old zombie head like de cow,
an' e'say all you e'stupid e'sheet monkey-face thing about
de crazy who-oore!! Hah! Is because you too much boring
dead peoples for make de comment on you own e'sheet life!!
E'slave, puppet, mummy, robot!! Clones!"

As Narcisa raged on, I knew I'd have to get her out of there fast, before she got herself lynched by an angry mob.

She was really trying this time.

60. ROLLING THUNDER

"PEOPLE IN RAGE STRIKE THOSE THAT WISH THEM BEST."
—*Shakespeare*

As the crowd grew, I looked around and fretted.

Fuck! She's fucking insane! You can't just stand around insulting strangers on the streets of Rio like this. There's too many other fucked-up dead-end losers with nothing to lose by just murdering you. And God knows they got some strange gadjikano laws here, like if you get beat to death by a crowd of more than ten, it's not even a crime.

One, two, three . . .

Making mental calculations, I counted the heads of the gathering lynch mob as Narcisa spit and cursed at the people like a screaming demon from hell.

. . . nine . . . ten . . . eleven . . . twelve . . . Fuck!

Shit! Gotta get this crazy kamikaze cunt outa here!

I swallowed my anger and pride like a dose of bitter elixir . . . *This is all my fucking fault . . . Why why why the fuck did I have to stop here, of all fucking places? Right in front of this shitty old whorehouse . . . And right at the height of rush hour, with all these fuckers out on the street milling around, bored, gawking . . . Why?*

Feeling helpless and guilty, I put a gentle hand on Narcisa's arm, trying to distract her from her victims. "Lissen, baby, I'm *sorry*. It's all my fault. I'm really sorry! Please, forgive me. Please, please just take it easy and come with me now, *por favor*! Just lemme get ya outa here before ya get yerself killed . . ."

"Hah! I wish I can get kee-eel, Cigano!" She yanked her arm away, hissing, spitting poison. *"No-body got de balls for finish me! Nobody, no even you! Ninguem! I am indestructible! Narcisa swim with de focking sharks! I gonna bury all you focking e'sheet peoples, got it?"*

I got it. I had to get her out of there now, right away, fast.

"I'm sorry, Narcisa. Let's just go home now. Please, baby. I love you . . ."

"Hah! Liar! What kinda love it is when I e'saying go an' then you e'stop here, hein!? You only e'stop these place for make de e'stupid cow mummy face clones peoples come look on me like de focking who-ore animal in de who-ore zoo! These is no de love, it is hate! You do it to me on pur- pose! Cuz you hate me, e'same like all de e'stupid clones peoples!"

"No baby, I didn't mean it. I swear! I just had to stop before we had an accident. Fuck, man, you were twisting all around and you were gonna make me wreck the bi—"

"Hah! Liar! You e'stop these place only for try an' humil- iating me! You wan' kill me! But you can' never do nothing to me, got it? Cuz I dead already! Already dead all de years! I am borned already dead, Cigano, got it? Abortion girl! Crazy geer-ool! In-sane whoo-oore!!"

"Please, Narcisa." I gestured at the people. *"Por favor!* Let's just go now . . . Please?"

"Why you so worry 'bout de focking e'stupid clones peoples, hein? I no e'scare for nobody, Cigano! I hope some- body gonna kill me right now! It is do me de big big focking favor, belief me . . ."

She spewed out some more feeble insults, first at me, then at the crowd, but Narcisa's tirade was running out of momentum, winding down. As her voice lost its edge, I could tell she was growing tired under the looming shadow of the Crash. Still, I knew she couldn't afford to lose face in front of all those strangers. Not now. In her frazzled, agonized state, her pathetic little show of bravado was all that was left of poor Narcisa's soul.

I looked between her and those blank, miserable faces, standing around watching, like a row of stop signs. I knew she'd have rather had red-hot daggers shoved under her fingernails than ever admit it, but I could tell Narcisa wanted to go. I could see it in her eyes.

I leaned in and whispered in her ear. "Fuck 'em, princesa. *Mumias!* You're right. These stupid insects don't deserve to breathe th' same air as you. Don't waste yer spit on 'em anymore; they're not worthy of yer attention. C'mon, baby, I'm sorry. Forgive me. Please, let's just go home now." I nodded toward the bike. "Please, Narcisa, 'bora, *por favor . . .*"

"Okey, Cigano. *Menos!* I gonna go with you. But only on condition you don' e'say nothing! I don' wan' hear you focking voice talking in my head no more, got it?"

"I got it, baby." I breathed a heavy sigh of relief.

I got onto the motorcycle and she climbed on behind me, slowly, deliberately, like a queen ascending her royal throne.

Fuck! Her Majesty, the Queen of Hell!

"Now we can go, Cigano. **Go!** Take me home *now*, go!"

I exhaled. "You got it!" I let the clutch out and eased into the heavy traffic.

Suddenly, Narcisa twisted sideways in the seat again, shouting. ***"Bye-bye, all de e'stupid little chicken peoples!!"*** She raised her middle finger in the air like a conquering sword, glaring at the blank-faced onlookers. ***"Lookit all de little chicklets face, de e'stupid little ignorant monkey peoples! Hah! Go back*** *inside you little chickie home an' lay you e'stupid little egg now! Go! Make it de big chickie omelette for de Narcisa breakfast! Hah!"*

I said nothing. Concentrating on the road, listening to her ranting nightmare monologues behind me, I rode along in worried silence, praying for the Crash.

Please, God, just let her wear herself out soon!

Back at my place, Narcisa still bitched and complained, but more quietly now, like a tired, bitter old codger muttering about the state of the world, mumbling weird, muffled curses, talking to the unseen spirits.

Poor thing! Please, dear Christ, just make her give it up and go to sleep!

Then, all of a sudden, she stopped.

What now?

She turned and stared at me for a moment. Then she began to whisper, her eyes growing wide, flashing with a look of panic-stricken terror.

"Cigano! Lissen, mano! I see him *again* today . . . When I go into de water!"

"Huh? Wha' . . . ?"

"At de beach, *cara*! I know he following me ever'where! He wanna make it to me de electronic shock *sabotagem*! He trying to kee-eel me!"

I looked at her, baffled. "Who, princesa? Who's following you?"

"*Doc!*" she hissed. "He all de time watching me!"

"Watching you?"

"Yeah, mano! He e'stay there at de beach de whole focking day today! Day before too, he follow me all round de city! He even come up in de favela when I gone there, an' then I see him another time when I go back down de hill! He following me ever'where I go to now!"

I scratched my head . . . *Now people are following her . . . Fuck . . . More lunatic crack delusions . . . Where does this madness ever end?*

I must have looked pretty skeptical.

She grabbed my arm and stared right into my eyes, breathing fast, frantic. *"Is truth, Cigano!"* She shook me, digging her fingernails into my flesh. *"Belief me! Narcisa may be crazy, but I no de idiota! He de one who maluco! An' now he wanna kee-eel me with de electricity shock, e'same way he kill de mother! I can feel it when I go in de water today! Ai aiiiiii! I feel it all around me now, de electricity shocks he e'sending all over my body! Ai aiiiiii, ai aiiiiii!"*

Doc? Why all this talk about that shitheel all of a sudden? Electric shocks? What the fuck? I'd never seen such terror in Narcisa's eyes before. She was really scared . . . *Jesus! She's panting like a fucking dog! Fuck! Hyperventilating with fear! Poor baby!*

Then, without another word, she began to fade. Her eyes rolled back in her head, and then, just like that, she was out, snoring softly, a cigarette burning in her hand. I covered her sleeping form with the blanket, then puttered around the pad for a while, still wondering about the source of her latest paranoid tirade.

Doc? Why's she all freaked-out about this guy now? I hadn't seen the old pillow-man since our encounter at the cafeteria . . . *And that was like two years ago . . . What the fuck? Who is this guy to her? Agh! Whatever. Just another haunted phantom of her guilty conscience.*

I shrugged Narcisa's Dickless Old Cushion out of my mind. The vision of his prim, prudish red face slunk from my consciousness like a dog who'd crapped on the rug.

It was over. I didn't care anymore. All her crazed delusions were just another nightmare memory now. As long as she was safe at home and sleeping, that was all that mattered.

Looking down at Narcisa's snoring carcass littering my sofa, I lit a cigarette and breathed out a long, deep, smoky sigh of relief.

61. OTHER BEINGS

If it still wasn't painfully clear to me yet just how fucked-up things were getting, I would be reminded again, just a few days later.

After hours of sex, we'd been sitting on the sofa, basking in the eerie, hypnotic, shifting blue light of the TV, when, all of a sudden, Narcisa settled into this odd, Zen-like state of peace. I sat watching as she reached over, grabbed her crack pipe from the table and smoked a big rock.

Then she drifted right off into outer space.

I stared at her in wonder. *Fuck! She's gone! Right out of her body! Pffffttt! Just like that! Gone!* Right then, I sensed a new level of weirdness.

When she looked back at me, I could see from the glazed, other-worldly look in her eyes that this new Narcisa was nothing like the frenzied, hyperactive antagonist I'd always known.

She appeared to be in a state of Grace. Serenity.

That's when it hit me. This was exactly the kind of zoned-out, drug-induced nirvana she'd been seeking all along; a nice little psychic vacation from the brutal dungeons of her mind. Ironically, though, it seemed she wasn't even *there* anymore to enjoy her long-awaited moment of release. Narcisa was gone. Only her body remained, looking at me, talking to me . . . *But it's not her! This isn't Narcisa speaking . . .*

She's just a shell now, a poor, dilapidated little vehicle for some creepy phantom visitors . . . Other beings! What the fuck is this shit?

I sat across from her on the sofa, watching in dread, my nerves tingling with a weird occult chill as she rambled on in this calm little fairylike voice.

"Is true what you thinking, little Ignácio, is no de Narcisa what e'say these thing to you now, so you better listen an' pay good attention, cuz now is de other e'spirit inside de Narcisa physical body." She blinked once, then her face went blank.

As I sat staring at her in shocked silence, she rolled her eyes back, then started screeching. ***"Arrgghhh! Shut de fock up! Is too much memory in these focking head! Fock! Time to e'smoke de crack pipe again an' push de delete button, Doioioiiin-nggg! Computer program! Radio wave! Tape recorder! Do-ioioiiinng! Delete! Delete! Delete! Porr-rraaa! Arrggghhh! Doioioiiinggg!"***

I listened with a sense of impending horror as the mad voice raved on. Then it switched to another weird inflection, a tone that was definitely *not* Narcisa's.

"Maybe I am only de recording device now, hein?"

"What? Recording device?" I rubbed my chin.

"Sure. Why no, hein? You know de Narcisa use to make de big pot of tea from all de cassette tape she find in de garbage, an' then she drink it! Hah! Maybe is too much information got record onto de Narcisa DNA from these e'sperimentations, an' so she try to get rid of all de data now! Hah! Composition an' decomposition of de organic matters . . . E'speculation . . ."

Her lips were moving like a demented puppet's, hammering those chilling words into the depths of my soul. Then the voice began to speak of happenings from my own past, things I knew Narcisa had no way of knowing about.

" . . . You think maybe you mother, these Dolores *programa*, she make it all de craziness just for fock up you mind, hein, little Ignácio?"

Speechless, I gawked at her. I couldn't believe my ears.

"Forget it! Is no true, Ignácio! Don' you never trust these fock up programing! *Delete!! Doioioiiinnggg!* She only do it all for teach it to you about de human reality so you can survive in de e'stupid earth *programa*, got it?"

What the fuck? Dolores! My mother's name! Am I hallucinating? No! I just heard her say it! But how the fuck did she just say my mother's name? How could she know? I've never talked about my . . . Where's all this crazy shit coming from?

" . . . An' what's about these other lady, you auntie, de Tia Silvia, *cigana cartomante*, hein, de one who can e'say de future, who give it to you these *apartamento*? Why you think is it de purpose for these thing, hein? Maybe is just de big *coincidencia*, hein? Hah! Or maybe is for make some kinda new e'sperimentations, de *laboratorio* for de big e'speculation, de esoteric crack e'smoke debate? Hah! *Wrong again! Delete! Next? Doioioiiinnggg!*"

What? Tia Silvia? Cigana cartomante . . . gypsy fortune-teller . . . I heard it . . . She just said that! How? Shit! What the fuck?

I sat in horrified fascination, watching her lips move, thinking, wondering.

How the hell did she know my mother's name? And Tia Silvia? How? And Narcisa never called me Ignácio before! How did she even know my name? I never told her! What the fuck's going on here? Maybe Doc was right! Maybe she really does channel spirits of the dead!

She kept going. "Better you run away from de Narcisa an' save you own self soon! Go to de road home, hein? *Lungo drom! Hah! Next?* After you go, Narcisa finish with all de focking earth peoples. What kinda work she gonna do here, hein, Ignácio? Research de future of e'stupid humanity, hein? Research, research an' make more de e'speculations?

Forget it! She really don' wan' nothing more in these planet! *Nada! Gotta go. Thank you come again!*"

As I sat staring at her, I could feel the presence of the occult closing in around us in sinister shadows of doom. Gooseflesh spread across my back in a cold wave of apprehension as she droned on in that eerie little childlike voice.

" . . . We would really *like* it if they can convince de Narcisa to find de practice or profession, whatever, something to use for de life in these place. But here in these earth we never encounter it yet de one individual who got de sufficient *intelligencia* for show de Narcisa how de creative act in you material reality can be relevant in our philosophy. *Nothing* is de only thing what make any sense for de Narcisa, Ignácio, got it? *Nada!* An' so de Narcisa she like to do it only de most intolerable an' repugnant thing! You know why? Is for e'stimulate only de *hate* in de other peoples, so maybe they can feel it their own true nature as de *beast*, Ignácio! So now she finish her job here! *Pronto!* Okey? She can go home now? Work finish? Okey! Gotta go! *Delete? Thank you come again! Next? Delete! Doioioiiinngggg!*"

I'd been thinking about Doc all week, ever since Narcisa's paranoid fit over having supposedly seen him at the beach. Even though she'd claimed no recollection of it later, I'd been haunted lately by his claims that Narcisa was a psychic channel for weird otherworldly beings.

Suddenly it all seemed plausible . . . *Jesus! Maybe the old clown was right about her!*

"Don' worry, Ignácio." The entity interrupted my musings, digging Narcisa's fingernail into her forehead till it bled. "Narcisa, she only de *crianca*! Only just a child. So now we gonna have a good little *bate-boca* here, an' we gonna talk just us two together, without she here for make no more interferences . . ."

Saying nothing, I sat watching Narcisa's face, like some horrible slow-motion disaster unfolding. Whoever, whatever it was kept talking,

telling me strange, oddly familiar things. Things from the World Unknown. Spine-shivering, esoteric, enigmatic things I couldn't understand, but only feel, a deep sensation of *knowing* in the pit of my gut . . .
Jesus Christ! There's really some kinda alien spirits with us here!

As if reading my mind, she smiled and went on. " . . . Wha' happen
to you? You think is only you an' de Narcisa all alone in these little
earth play drama, hein, Ignácio? No-oo focking *way*! Is *many* de other
ones together with you all de time here!"

My eyes widened. Whatever was talking through Narcisa noticed.

"You feel frighten of these other ones? *Por que?* Is no necessary you
got de fear, Ignácio. Just think! It would be so lonely here, so boring
without all these e'spirit company together with you. You can even
die from so much bore! *Que tedio, hahaha!* But is really no so much de
bad thing, mano, is only de true nature of these little earth game you
playing here. E'same like de chess game, got it? So now is you turn to
move, Ignácio!"

Narcisa continued talking. And the whole time she rattled on, I
found myself shifting in and out of this surreal, hypnotic, trancelike
state. All of a sudden, I had the most powerful sense of déjà vu in
my life; like in a dream, but much more real—as if that weird inner
knowing was reminding me that I'd already been here and lived this
whole experience before. It was like a movie I'd already seen and
knew the ending to, but had somehow forgotten, the way you mis-
place a set of keys.

Maybe it's just the sleep deprivation . . . I wondered.

Narcisa's finger pointed at me as the entity fixed me with that faraway look, grinning. "Hah! You de pretty tough little gypsy warrior,
hein, little Ignácio? *Um ciganinho guerreiro,* hein? Yeh! You really de
goo-ood adversary, *hahahahaa!!*"

It kept staring at me. Caught in that dark alien gaze, I felt my blood
freezing over again.

Then, all of a sudden, Narcisa was back. She stood up and began spinning around the room like a frantic, lopsided human top, singing this odd little song she seemed to be receiving as she went along, composing, grabbing the words from the air.

A sorrowful little lament of her earthly exile, homesick for Alpha Centauri.

"Da da da . . . Can you show me—where de exit—on these e'sheet world—cuz I tire tire tire—of de human being . . ."

After a while, she began slowing down again, running out of gas. Then she collapsed in the corner like a fallen puppet. Leaving her lying there, I crawled up to the loft bed and passed out.

What else could I do? Weirdness was in the air.

62. THE WHORE OF BABYLON

"AND I SAW THE WOMAN DRUNKEN WITH THE BLOOD OF THE
SAINTS, AND WITH THE BLOOD OF THE MARTYRS OF JESUS: AND
WHEN I SAW HER, I WONDERED WITH GREAT ADMIRATION."
—*Revelation 17:6*

At the tail end of the next weeklong mission without food or sleep, Narcisa finally crashed. After only a couple of hours, though, she rose up again, wild-eyed and furious.

I was still fast asleep as she sprang to life, bleating like a goat.

"Pizza!"

"Wha . . . ?" I jerked into consciousness, unsure if I'd dreamed the word.

"Coca-Cola!"

Shaking the veil of slumber from my shoulders like a thick layer of dust, I attempted to take it in stride.

"Good morning, baby . . ." I called out from the loft.

"Shut de fock up, Cigano! Pizza! Coca-Cola! Chocolate!"

I rolled over in bed, putting a pillow over my head, a weak shield against the coming avalanche of whining demands.

"Pizza, coca cola, chocolate! I wan' chocolate, Cigano!! Go go go . . ."

I groaned and buried my face in the pillows, but her voice was a

bleating goat tone, vibrating like a hammer gong in my eardrums . . .
Go! Go! Go!!

The more I tried to ignore her, the louder the awful spew of rapacious orders rose in volume, a relentless buzz saw cutting through the fuzzy mist of my sleepy brain; a greedy, godless mantra of bottomless Want.

Go go go go go go go go!!
Pizza-Coca-Cola-chocolate-pizza-Coca-Cola-chocolate-pizza!!

"*Shit . . .*" Muttering under my breath, stumbled down from the loft.

Fumbling around in the dark kitchen, I searched for something to feed her, anything to shut her up. Before I knew it, I was running back and forth like a harried waiter at lunch hour . . . *No other way to shut up this bleating Goat of Mendes! Lucifer! Mephistopheles! Satan! No way out! Addiction! Want! Need! I must serve all of its insane needs and demands!*

Finally, I staggered over and sat beside her on the sofa, holding my head in my hands like a rotting cantaloupe, listening to the sounds of munching, crunching and slurping as she tore through leftovers; a plague of hungry termites, undermining the weak foundation of my sanity.

Nychata nychata nychata nychata . . .

Suddenly, the monotonous noises were punctuated by breaking glass.

Clang-caarasssh!

"***Oops! Porra!***" she yelped, startling me out of my stupor.

Wide awake again, I hurried back into the kitchen for a towel to throw onto the creeping black lagoon of Coca-Cola spreading across the floor like a toxic oil slick . . . *Back and forth. Go! Floor. Go! Sink. Go! Water. Drip drip drip . . . Crunch crunch, slurp, smack smack, slurp.*

Nychata nychata nychata nychata.

I am so so fucking tired!

Plopping down beside her again, I fell over sideways, lying across the sofa at a cramped, crooked, awkward angle, trying to rest somehow. Uncomfortable and weary, I began thinking of ways to get rid of her, wondering if I would ever sleep again. After a while, I began to doze. Just as I was losing consciousness, I felt a shadow creeping across my face, like some dark, ancient Curse. Opening my eyes, I saw Narcisa there, hovering over me, lurking like a black flapping vulture.

Oh God! What now?

"Wake up, Cigano!"

"Huh? Wha? Whassup?"

"I am . . . how do you e'say it, I am . . . horny."

"What!?!"

"I am horny, bro. *Horny!* Get up an' give it to me, Cigano, go go!"

Her eyes were drilling into my soul, bugging out like a crazed wild lemur. With Herculean effort, I raised my eyelids like a pair of rusty little umbrellas creaking open.

Narcisa's face bored down on me with those 100-watt bulging bughouse eyes of doom, breathing in my face. "I mean it . . ."

"You just want some money to go cop, Narcisa."

"No! I mean, yes, I wan' de mo-ney, always I wan' money. But I feeling like I wan' it de fock now too. *Serio*, Cigano, I wan' it, go! I wan' these crazy gyp-say dick! Wan' it now, give it to me, *go, go!*"

"Well . . ." I sat up, smiling. "I guess I oughta make th' most of it while yer in th' mood or whatever . . ."

"*Sim sim*, Cigano, I got it de *mood!* An' now you gonna get it for free today, no charge now, only for these one e'special time. Hah! Is better you take it when you got it for free, *yeaa-asss!* These is de rare occasion . . ."

And so it was. In more ways than one. Because, for once, I didn't even want sex.

Shit! There it is again! Narcisa's perfect timing.

I didn't want anything; nothing more than to roll over on the sofa and go back to sleep. But I sensed this was like one of those lightning-bolt One-Time-Only Clearance Sales.

Everything must go! Go go go! Even if you didn't want anything, need anything, you just gotta buy it anyway! Because if you don't get it right now, you just might regret not having bought that cheap pair of pliers, that Garden Weasel, or that big package of tube socks. Fuck!

Sleep deprivation was taking its toll.

I looked at Narcisa again.

Then I saw it. A startling vision: The Goat of Mendes, standing like an old-time carnival barker beside a gigantic pink gate of throbbing vaginal flesh.

A big, bloody red banner fluttered above its head:

LIQUIDAÇÃO!! OFERTA ESPECIAL!! GOING OUT DE BUSINESS!! HALF PRICE POO'SY CLEARANCE SALE!! BUY IT NOW, PAY IT LATER! GO GO GO!!

What the fuck? Hallucinating again! Oh God!

Still, I couldn't refuse.

"*Arggh*, why not? Jesus! What a fucking racket!" I muttered as I grabbed that perky young ass and jumped inside.

It started up again while I was fucking her.

Narcisa began speaking slowly, deliberately, at first. Then, as the fuck-thrusts picked up speed, so did her bizarre, hallucinatory alien dialogue.

As was common practice when having sex, she was talking about one of her favorite topics again. Young girls.

"You gotta enjoy de pretty little flowers when is e'still blooming, bro . . ." She winked and yawned at the same time.

Narcisa always had her own odd way of seeing things—and she

was the only person I'd ever known who could actually *swagger* while lying down, even with a rock-hard cock pumping like a steam engine piston between her legs.

" . . . Cuz is too much very soon de young geer-ool gonna be old an' dry up an' wilted, an' then she go all soft, like de old flower, soft an' wither out, got it? *Fock!* These de way de focking God create it de woman race, hein, Cigano? *Putz!* Only for, how do you e'say it, for be de *vaso*, de vessel for de new life? Only for e'stupid baby making? *Afffff!* Is too bad luck for de female *especie*, hein? These e'sheet a terrible karma for de human e'spirit!"

I finished up and pulled out. Getting comfortable, I lay back beside her on the sofa, panting like a happy old dog, listening as she ranted away, oblivious to my presence.

I watched her in wonder, as her beautiful, innocent-looking, baby-faced lips moved like some weird extraterrestrial butterfly, flittering between expressions of soulful anguish and a bitter disdain beyond her short years of earthly hardship.

"How de fock can de womans ever be *contente*, hein?"

I looked at her and shrugged.

She spat on the floor. "How to be authentic when you gotta live de life these way, with big e'stupid e'smile like focking cow, hein?"

I shrugged again, waiting for her to go on.

Narcisa grew quiet. She sat across the sofa from me, staring off into space.

Silence.

Then, without warning, she raised her head and brayed like an imperious donkey.

"I am de Whoore of Babylon!"

Hello! I gawked at her as if she'd just sprouted another head.

She spat again, hissing like a cobra snake. **"Ya-asss! I am de 'hedonista,' de 'lesbian,' de 'pedophile,' an' I am proud for** *be these way! Hah! Is my little desperation cry to de pas-sion! My big fock-you fart in de face of these e'stupid polit-ico society of mans! These sociedade hipocricia. I e'say fock you mother to all e'stupid man law an' social rule, got it?"*

I got it. Sort of. I raised my eyebrows and stared at her as her fran-tic words began picking up speed, like a barrage of incoming missiles.

"You know I like it de very young girl! These what I like, Cigano! *E porque não, hein?* Narcisa just de e'same like de mans these way, hein? Only one thing different: I would never hurt any geer-ool! *Nunca!* No like de mans! Hah! These pervert society law, she got nothing to do with de nature law, de God law, got it? Is so, *so-oo* e'stupid! Hah! *Ri-diculo!* Listen to me, Cigano! If these Macho Man God he wan' for de womans only make de *sexo* on e'stupid 'legal'-age eighteen-year-old, why it is you think he create de womans for make de baby from age twelve an' thirteen year old, hein? Too young? Why? You think maybe these Macho Man God make de mistake? Some little miscal-ulations? *'Oops! Sorry, try again,'* hein? Hah! So *e'stupid*, so anti-nature these hypocrite rules de e'stupid mans make up! E'stupid monkey face ignorant mind-control clone peoples regulation!"

I blinked as her voice rattled on like some crazed, unstoppable hell-train.

"Maybe you can e'splain it for me, please, Mister e'stupid Man-lawmaker *politico*, what it is de young pretty pink gee-rol with she new fresh menstruation power poo'sy suppose to do with it, these beautiful young thing now, hein? Maybe she suppose only to sit on these holy bloody power *sexo* de God give to her, hein? Only sit on de young poo'sy for next five or six year time, an' wait till these she come to be 'legal age'? How to do, hein? *Why, hein?*"

I looked on as her face turned red with screaming rage.

"Okey, I gonna e'say it to you why, Cigano! Is only for create de focking frustration! Conspir'cy to castrate an' kee-eel de

e'sacred sex power! Aaarrrggghh! Gotta wait! Fear! Ashame! Frustration! Guilty feeling! Fock! All de peoples gotta wait an' wait until de e'stupid cow-peoples e'society e'say, 'Okey, now is acceptable for de young geer-ool holy social position!' What de focking position, hein? Doggie e'style? Wooo wooooo! Hah! Leg open! Marry woman! De legal whoore! Open leg dog fock social position, hah! Porra! De man law e'say only she suppose to e'stay sitting an' wait wait wait for de pederastical ass-fock homosexual pervert Je-sooz church preacher to e'say her, 'Okey, now is okey for you make de sign of de Cross on de holy piss water Je-sooz church altar! Poo'sy approval! Legal whoore!' Haa-aah! An' only then she can open it up de leg for de first time an' give it up she holy Christianical poo'sy! But is gotta be for only de one man! De sanctify legal husband man! Hah! E'stupid! Bo-oring! Fock that, Cigano! Is no good for me these e'sheet life, no for even one day for de Narcisa! No-oo way! Nunca! Fock you! I never gonna do what they telling me! Fock that! Never, got it? Ne-ver! First I gonna dead, got it!?"

I guessed I sort of got it. Death Before Dishes. Something like that.

Finally, Narcisa began to slow down again, like a windup doll running out of momentum. She lowered her voice to an intense little whisper and kept staring at me with those big, intense, bulging eyes.

"Now I gonna e'say it to you de real secret thing, Cigano, but is for you never e'say it to no one else, got it?"

She stopped. I kept quiet and waited. After a long, suspenseful pause, she took a deep breath and exhaled.

"Okey, so you listen careful now, bro. The thing like these: you got de real peoples on these planet who are de real human being. These are de one who eat only when hungry an' go to e'sleep when they tire. But most de one they call de 'human' here no so e'smart! That is de clones peoples, Cigano! They all gotta eat de lunch at midday cuz these de '*lunchtime*.' An' they go an' brush de tooths an' go to work all de e'same time too, got it? But is no cuz they *wan'* do it these way, but cuz of de *programa*, what de Shadow Peoples e'say they gotta do. Is for de training . . . Brainwash program, got it, Cigano?"

She looked at me and shrugged. "What de fock, bro! De Narcisa don' got it de e'same kinda sentiment or morality as these e'stupid robot peoples, Cigano! So I never can make no participation to these human e'society of clones peoples here! Forget it!"

She fell quiet again, lost in contemplation.

After a while, she went on in a sad, confused little tone that broke my heart. " . . . But you know, Cigano, I feel it sometime like I really wanna participate in *something* . . . I just don' know what *is* it . . . you know?"

I knew . . . *Poor Narcisa.* I said nothing. I just sat shaking my head as she burbled on in a weak, trickling stream of garbled crack-babble, till she was drooling like a sick animal . . . *Shit!*

Narcisa was nearing the point of no return. Meltdown was imminent.

The Whore of Babylon was in urgent need of rest.

63. PAVING THE ROAD TO HELL

"IN FORMER DAYS, WHEN IT WAS PROPOSED TO BURN ATHEISTS,
CHARITABLE PEOPLE USED TO SUGGEST PUTTING THEM IN THE
MADHOUSE INSTEAD [. . .], NOT WITHOUT A SILENT SATISFACTION
AT THEIR HAVING THEREBY OBTAINED THEIR DESERTS."
—*John Stuart Mill*

Her lips were dry as cardboard. Finally, she began croaking like a parched tree frog.

"Liquid! Thirsty, Cigano! Liquido! Juice, water, go!"

A lightbulb lit up in my brain.

With Narcisa's whiny pleas for refreshment ringing in my ear, I got up and went into the kitchen. Desperate for a break, I crushed up some downers, mixed them into some mango juice with ice and went back to where she sat.

Snatching the glass from my hand, Narcisa powered down the sweet, sticky liquid in one long, greedy gulp, then sat chewing up the ice cubes.

Yes! Perfect, Max! I grinned to myself and waited.

I'd been thinking about dosing her for some time. Now I wished I'd done it sooner. It was the most natural thing in the world. At that point, there seemed no other way.

As I sat waiting for the drug to take hold, she spun around the room, ranting, breaking things, banging into the furniture like a panicked bird flying against a windowpane.

Finally, the stuff kicked in. She slumped down on the sofa. Her hoarse, raspy curses merged into gentle snores, and that was that.

Lights out in Babylon.

I laid her out on the sofa and had my way with her sleeping carcass, then got up and washed her sex grease off in the bathroom sink.

I put a blanket over her, and kissed her on the forehead.

The Whore of Babylon was in dreamland.

Smiling, I climbed up the ladder and fell into my long-abandoned bed.

Just as I began to doze off, the phone rang.

Picking up, I glanced at my watch . . .

Midnight . . . Who the fuck would be calling now . . . ?

"*Por gentileza.* May I speak with Narcissss-ssa please?"

I recognized that frigid, creepy, too-polite reptilian hiss. Even after years. "She's sleeping right now. Can I help ya with something, uh, Doc?"

"Well, *ahhhh*, I must tell you, frankly, Cigano, I'm quite concerned about our dear Narcisa. She's barely spoken with me since her return from New York, you know, which I find extremely distressing, I might add!"

I said nothing, waiting for him to go on.

"I've been seeing her around the neighborhood a great deal lately, but she never even stops to speak with me anymore. My goodness! She ignores me as if I were a complete stranger! Most disturbing, I must say! Why, I saw her on the street just this very afternoon, in fact, coming from the direction of your apartment . . ."

I held my breath, staying quiet, waiting for more.

After a portentous little pause, he went on. " . . . I'm aware, of course, that she has been in constant contact with *you* . . ."

How the fuck does this guy always "know" so much?

And now he knows where I live? Como? How did that happen? What the fuck?

" . . . And she really doesn't look well at all to me, my friend, not at all . . ." His irritating nasal voice took on a subtle accusatory edge.

I could sense a vague threat lingering between his words . . . *What does this freaky little shit want? What's his angle? Maybe Narcisa was right about him stalking her.*

" . . . When I tried to confront her to tell her she needs to stop taking all those awful drugs, Cigano, she became most aggressive with me! She actually picked up a bottle and smashed it on the pavement, threatening to cut my face with it!"

Doc sighed. After another melodramatic pause, he began laying his cards on the table.

" . . . I've been in constant contact with her mother, you know, and we both agree vehemently that Narcisa really must be committed to the state mental institution immediately. Her internment needs to be organized as soon as humanly possible, before it's too late!"

"What!?!" I burst out. "Now ya wanna throw Narcisa in th' fuckin' nutbin again? Why? Just because she doesn't wanna stop and chat with you when ya follow her around and hassle her on the street? Are you fuckin' serious?"

"It's for her own good, *senhor!*" he snapped. "And if you have the slightest regard for her welfare, you must help us! I need you to bring her to the Rio Sul shopping mall tomorrow at noon. It's just down the street from the Pinel Mental Hospital. I'm sure you can convince her to go with you if you tell her you're going to buy her a new pair of shoes. My goodness, the shoes she was wearing today! Disgusting! How can you let her walk around like that? She looked like a homeless beggar. And her hair—"

"Whoa!" I cut him off. "Lemme get this straight. You want me to betray Narcisa's trust and trick her so you and her mother can get her locked up and pumped full of dope? *Como?* So she can sit in a room with bars on the window staring out at a fuckin' tree? You think that's gonna help her?"

"It is for her own good, sir! Narcisa is clearly out of control! Even someone like you should be able to see that!"

I lost it. ***"Outa control!? Whose fuckin' control? You and her stupid mother's? What about her free will? What about her rights as a human being, huh? Narcisa's an adult, over eighteen! Who th' fuck are you to decide what's right for her? Ya can count me out!"***

"But she's become a degenerate criminal, a hopeless drug addict, Cigano! A menace to herself and to society!"

"Lissen, man, I'm a recovered addict myself, and I been tryin' to get her to wake up and ask for help! But that's the only way it works. An addict's gotta ask fer help, got it? They gotta want it! That strong-arm shit of yers don't get it. That just turns people like her away. Then she'll never wanna get better. She's gotta be willing, and it don't just happen when ya snap yer dainty little fingers cuz ya got snubbed by her on the street. So, until Narcisa asks me for help with her problem herself, there's no way I'm getting involved with some sneaky, backhanded scheme to trick her into th' nuthouse. *Sem chance!* No fuckin' way!"

"But, Cigano. I have it all worked out! Everything's already been arranged! You must listen to me. We—"

"No, Dickless! You lissen to me! Ya wanna stick yer nose in other people's business and ream my ear out about Narcisa's problems, then you fucking lissen! I'm the only person she trusts even a little. In time, she may wanna get help, but that's gotta be her call! Not mine and not yours, and sure as fuck not her stupid pill-poppin' whore of a mother! Where was that dumb cunt when Narcisa needed a mother? And who th' fuck are you to go around getting people locked up? Whaddya trying to kill her, like ya killed yer own mo—?"

Before I could finish, he butted in. "Well, I'm sorry you feel that way, my friend. But I think it's quite likely the *policia* would have quite a different view of the matter! Especially if they knew that a convicted criminal was holding Narcisa captive! One who supplies her with drugs in order to keep her in sexual slavery and bondage! I've done a bit of my own private research into your checkered history, senhor Ignácio Valência Lobos—aka Cigan—"

"You fucking sick son of a whore!" I hung up.

A bitter taste invaded my mouth . . . *Bastard!* Unable to think of sleep, I paced the room, seething, fuming . . . *Dirty son of a bitch!* My head pounded with an unrelenting, churning fury. My guts were stewing in adrenaline as I thought about different ways to murder Doc. Then a familiar phrase began repeating in my inner ear . . . *The spiritual life is not a theory. It has to be lived* . . . I doubled over with a pounding headache. Tears of hate and frustration flooded my eyes . . . *The spiritual life is not a theory . . . It has to be lived . . . The spiritual life is not a theory . . . It has to be lived . . . Okay! All right! I got it! Stop! Shit!*

Killing Doc was out.

As Narcisa snored away on the sofa. I swallowed a handful of aspirin. I sat down and turned on the television. Flipping through the channels, trying to keep my mind off murderous thoughts, I landed on the news . . . *The World Today. Shit! War. Poverty. Politics. Lies. Mass stupidity. Institutionalized insanity. A world worthy of Narcisa's worst nightmares! No wonder she wants no part of it! When will the fucking human race ever learn? Maybe we're all better off dead!*

Just as I was getting drowsy, the phone rang again. I ignored it this time. The answering machine clicked on. A woman's voice . . . *Narcisa's mother!*

What the fuck? How did this demented cow get my number?

I'd spoken to the mother a couple of times over the years. Just the odd casual hello when Narcisa had handed me the phone, fed up with listening to her praising Jesus.

The woman's voice sounded different now. Aggressive, demanding, hysterical. *"Alô! Alô! Somebody say something! Aggghhh! Answer me! Say something! Argghhh! Alô! Alo!"*

I was halfway across the room to pick up when I heard her tone darken. Then the fireworks began. *"Answer me, you filthy bastards, in the name of Jesus! Agghh!! Listen to God's holy word, you dirty godless gypsy pimps!"*

I stood frozen by the phone, listening in horror as the anguished voice screeched on.

"Alô!! Alô! I know what you doing to my poor, innocent little daughter, feeding those horrible drugs to my poor baby girl to satisfy your perverse sinful sex pleasures! You won't get away with your crimes! Argh! Repent your evildoing, you dirty heathen faggot scum!!"

I couldn't believe my ears as the insane ranting rattled in the air.

"Aggghhh!! Release my daughter from your filthy gypsy clutch or you will regret it for all eternity!! Aggghhh!! God will punish you. You're going to burn in everlasting hellfire!! Doc was sent to me by Jesus!"

Doc! That sick ratfucker's behind this! Two-faced, evil little prick gave her the number, led her to us right by the nose . . . Bastards! I looked down at Narcisa, snoring peacefully on the sofa as her mother's mad metallic bleating rose in furious pitch, screeching in my ear like some deranged, Bible-spewing parrot . . . *Aggghhh! Jesus! Jesus! Aggghhh . . . Jesus! Hellfire! Fuck!*

Tiptoeing to the phone like a disturbed rattlesnake, I pulled the wire from the wall . . . *Goodbye and Amen, Jesus, Joseph and Mary! Thank you come again!*

Seeing double, I crawled up to the loft and fell into a deep, nightmarish slumber.

64. FOWL PLAY

"HE WHO DOESN'T KNOW ANGER DOESN'T KNOW
ANYTHING. HE DOESN'T KNOW THE IMMEDIATE."
—*Henri Michaux*

The next day, I was awakened by a hellish racket.

***Crrrraaasssh!* "*Fock!*"**

Narcisa was clattering around in my kitchen again, breaking dishes, scattering food across the floor, wreaking havoc. The usual.

Too tired to protest, I lay back in the bed, holding my breath, listening to the sounds of destruction, followed by another stream of angry curses.

"*Sheet, sheet, focking e'shee-eet! Is nothing to eat here, Cigano! Que odio, porra, puta merda! Never got no focking food in these place!*"

I groaned, climbing down the ladder. "Whaddya wanna eat, Narcisa?"

"*Go, go, call de boteco, mano, get it de roast chicken deliver! Now! Go, now! Hungry, hungry! Go go go go go go go!*"

With a weary sigh, I picked up the phone and called. Too impatient to wait, Narcisa plopped down on the sofa, stuffing leftovers in her mouth, scraps falling to the floor. Then she slumped over sideways and passed out. As she snored away, I kneeled beside her, cleaning up the wreckage, like an obedient pilgrim paying homage to a savage, bloodthirsty goddess.

A few minutes later, the guy was knocking at my door with her chicken. Grinning, I brought it into the kitchen and covered the clear plastic container with a towel, like a fevered alien baby sitting in an incubator.

I climbed back up to the bed and fell asleep.

A few minutes later, she was up again, shouting. ***"Chicken! Chicken! Where de focking chicken, hein? Hungry, Cigano! Fome!! Give it to me, go!"***

I rose, stumbled back into the kitchen and prepared her a plate with bread, cheese, olives and the chicken. As I set the food down on the coffee table before her, without looking up, Narcisa began savaging the steaming bird like a famished jackal. Ripping a dripping hunk off with her dirty hands, she shoved it into her mouth and swallowed. Then she reached over and grabbed my freshly laundered comforter to use as a napkin.

No-oo! Shit! I just washed that goddamn thing! Stop!

"Please, baby!" I pled. "You're gonna get that greasy shit all over our nice clean quilt! Wait, Narcisa, just use the plate on the table in front of you! *Por favor!* Here, hold on a second and I'll get a towel. Plea—"

"Menos!! Shut de fock up, Cigano! Leave me be, porra! Go!"

I tried to hand her the cloth. She slapped it to the floor.

"Fock off, old Dona Maria! You so pessemista, e'same like e'stupid old bitch!"

"Whaddya mean I'm pessimistic? Take it easy, man! I'm just giving you a fucking towel to clean yer hands with so ya don't dirty up the clean blanket, Narcisa! What the fu—"

"E'stupid!! Don' you know it? Ever'time you think an' talk about some focking bad thing, then you make it happen!"

To demonstrate her profound metaphysical discourse, Narcisa wiped chicken grease from her face with the comforter, as a half-chewed drumstick fell into her lap.

Bitch! That does it! I tried to grab the quilt. She clutched it with her greasy, grubby mitts. It was a nuthouse tug-o'-war! Exasperated, I yanked it away from her, hard.

Narcisa glared at me with a look of hatred. Then, quick as a bunny, she grabbed the whole chicken in both hands, and hurled it at my face! ***SPLAFT!***

The steaming, fleshy projectile exploded into a thousand greasy splinters, coating me and my apartment with mangled carnage! *Fu-uck!* Then she was up on her feet, raging, pulling books off the shelves and throwing them at me, one by one. I cringed as she hurled the fluttering missiles across the room, bellowing.

"Pronto! Now you e'satisfy, hein, old Dona Maria? Is all you fault! You create de violence! You predict it an' make it happen! You wanna see more, hein? Okey! Now I gonna go up to de favela an' pay de bandido to come here an' kill you, Cigano! You better get de fock out of Rio fast, e'stupid, cuz these time I gonna finish you!"

I looked around at the gruesome slaughter she'd just wreaked on my clean, orderly little pad. The home I'd taken her into. My blood was boiling. Looking at her smug, sneering face, I snapped. I leapt on her like a tiger and grabbed her by the neck. *"Bitch!"* I threw her onto the sofa and shoved my knee into her throat, pinning her.

Even squashed down like a bug, immobilized, Narcisa screeched on.

"Hah! Bravo-oo! Congratulation, Cigano, now you gonna beat me, hein? Hah! Is good, very good! Bravo!! Now you de

big man, big tough macho man, de bruto! Well, you better enjoy it now, you big ugly e'sheet, cuz these gonna be de last day of de focking life for you, I promise!!"

I didn't believe a word of her blustering, delusional threats. Still, I wanted to skin her alive . . . *Dirty lowlife bottom-feeding bitch!*

Furious, I spat in her face. *"Look what ya done, ya stupid twat! I let you come and stay here after you got kicked outa everyplace else ya ever show yer ugly crackhead face—"*

She glowered back with a hateful smirk. *"Hah! Only you de ugly face in here! Old an' ugly an' e'stupid! That's you! Old Dona Mari—"*

"Shaddup, bitch!" I lowered my weight down on her. *"I'm still talking here, cuntface! I just spent th' last two days feeding you, taking care of ya like a sick brat! Spent my last cash to buy you a fuggin' chicken! And then ya go and turn my home into a trash can! Fuck you, ya filthy, degenerate whore!"*

An evil grin spread across her face. *"Hah! You never gonna see de dirty whoo-ore again! I am leaving forever these time! Hah! An' you can have you nice clean apartment back. You can sit all alone an' masturbate all de day in here while you thinking about me an' all de young handsome mans I gonna making love to while you wait for my amigos come an' kill you, hahaha!"*

"Amigos!?!" I screamed back. *"Amigos!?! You're fucking insane! You got no friends, Narcisa! Nobody can stand you! Wise up! Ya can't even stand yerself, ya evil little shit! I'm the last fuggin' friend you have, and look what ya do to me! Look at this fuggin' mess!"* I gestured at the grusome poultry shrapnel covering every surface.

"Ever'body love me, Cigano!" Her glassy, lifeless eyes stared out at me like a pair of spiders from the depths of a cave. ***"Them all hate you an' wanna kee-eel you! Doc gonna kill you! Hah! I gonna tell him how you beat me up, an' he gonna come an' kill you good! Hah!"***

Doc!? What the fuck? Bitch!

I was ready to slaughter her. I pushed my knee down on her throat. She squeaked like a rubber toy. Her face began to change colors. Even as I choked the life out of her, nothing could contain Narcisa's arrogance. She just grimaced back with that smug, defiant smirk.

Then, in her silent, twitching battle, she kicked the coffee table over, spilling passion fruit juice all over the whole disgusting mess. I wanted to drive a bloody spike through her heart.

Enraged, I slapped her twice in the face . . . ***Swak! Swak!***

"Bitch! Bitch!"

She yelped as if she'd been speared with a harpoon.

Then, all of a sudden, I snapped out of it. Disgusted with the whole affair, I let her go.

Standing up, I glared at her, pointing to the door.

"Out!!"

65. THE GREEN HOUSE

"THIS MISERABLE STATE IS BORNE BY THE WRETCHED SOULS OF
THOSE WHO LIVED WITHOUT DISGRACE AND WITHOUT PRAISE."
—*Dante*

Narcisa jumped up. Snatching my money off the table, she stormed out into the hall, screaming, threatening, raging. I listened to her footsteps, thundering off down the stairs like a pair of cannonballs racing each other to hell. I didn't move.

I didn't give a shit if I ever saw her again. I didn't care about the mess, or the cash she'd taken, nothing, as long as it got her out of my sight. Muttering under my breath, I got busy with a towel, a broom and a mop. It was easier than I'd thought. Finished, I took a long, cold shower. When I came out of the bathroom, I started picking up my books. One of them was laying open on the floor. Lawrence Durrell's *Justine*. For some reason, I felt compelled to stop and look at the page it was flung open to. I sat down on the floor in my underwear and began to read:

WHAT WAS I TO DO? JUSTINE WAS TOO STRONG FOR ME IN TOO MANY WAYS. I COULD ONLY OUT-LOVE HER—THAT WAS MY LONG SUIT. I WENT AHEAD OF HER—I ANTICIPATED EVERY LAPSE; SHE FOUND ME ALREADY THERE, AT EVERY POINT WHERE SHE FELL DOWN, READY TO HELP HER TO HER FEET AND SHOW THAT IT DID NOT MATTER.

By the time I came to the end of the page, I was crying; weeping uncontrollably. I closed the book, gathered up all the others and placed them all back on the shelf, leaving that particular one sitting at the feet of my colorful plaster statue of Ogum, my heavenly spirit guide and protector. Choking back tears, I lit a candle and placed it on the little altar. Then I mouthed a short, simple Umbanda prayer for Narcisa.

"*Cobre ela com a Sua proteicão, por favor! Patacori Ogunyé! Saravá, meu Pai!*"

I climbed back up to the loft and fell asleep to troubled dreams; skulls and screeching demons, Doc strapping Narcisa into an electric chair—the usual stuff. But I slept. Mercifully, she didn't come back.

S haken awake the next morning by the sound of a shrieking, jittering telephone, I stumbled down and grabbed the receiver.

Collect call. I accepted . . . *Here we go again.*

Her voice. That prideful, raspy growl.

"*Tudo bem, Cigano?*" Narcisa chirped, as if nothing had happened.

"*Tudo bem, Narcisa.*" I smiled, as if I hadn't almost murdered her.

Narcisa sounded happy. I was happy too. I'd survived the nightmares again. It was a new day, and I was armored with a full night's sleep.

"Well, you gonna invite me for lunch, hein, Cigano? *Hungry!!*"

I glanced at my watch. Noon.

"Where are ya, princesa?"

"Casa Verde . . ."

"*Ehhh?* Whaddya doing there?"

" . . . *Não viaja, cara. Relaxa.* I only come here for e'sleep, bro, just wake up now. *Hungry!* Come now, Cigano! *Fome! Fome! Go go go . . .*"

"Whoa, wait a minute. I just paid a whole week at the Love House so ya wouldn't have to go back th—"

"They kick me out from de e'stupid Love House!"

"*What?!?*" *Kicked out?* I was shocked. How could even Narcisa manage to get kicked out of that lowlife rat-hole?

"Is no my *fault*, Cigano!" she cried. "Is only because all de e'stupid bar owner on de e'street go complain about me to de Arabian peoples at Love House! *Porra!* Is big *conspiration* against Narcisa in de whole Lapa now!"

"Hold on! Back up! What th' fuck are ya talking about?"

"All these e'sheet happen because I go walk pass de birdcage in de *boteco* on de Love House e'street, an' I go an' free all de bird!"

"What?"

"*Pois é*, Cigano. An' all de e'stupid clones peoples there, they e'say to de Arabian they gotta put de lock on de birds cages now, because de Narcisa e'stay there, an' they wan' de Love House peoples pay for all de bird I liberate. An' now ever'body anger to me there! Hah! All cuz I make these e'stupid peoples to loose de hostage animal!"

"Why'd ya go and open up th' cages?"

"Because I can understand it all de bird languages, Cigano, got it? So I know when de peoples lissen to de bird singing, really they all de time e'saying, '*Fock you, e'stupid peoples! Lemme de fock outa here, you fockers!*' So I just go an' do it, got it?"

I got it. I was speechless.

"An' you wanna know de most crazy thing, Cigano? All these bird don' even wanna go out for fly no more! E'stupid animal! Fock! I go an' open up de cage an' e'say, '*Okey, go, go, get out, ever'body free now, let's go!*' An' they just sit in de focking cage an' look back at me! E'stupid e'sheets! *Arrrgghh! Hungry, Cigano! Fome! Come get me! Casa Verde, go, let's go!*"

"See ya in a minnit, princesa." I grinned, grabbing my pants.

T he Casa Verde. The Green House. The infamous punk-anarchist flophouse resembled a crumbling, crooked, moss-encrusted tombstone.

Sitting at the end of a winding cobblestone alley in Santa Teresa, the overgrown hillside maze of decrepit colonial mansions and teeming favelas looming above Lapa, the abandoned old structure leaned to the left like a lopsided, hollow-eyed drunk, threatening imminent collapse.

Home to a noxious, shape-shifting squatters' community of drunken artists, trash-scavenging sculptors, clumsy acrobats, illiterate poets, uncoordinated jugglers and not-so-funny street corner clowns, the Casa Verde was a breeding ground for glue-sniffing bums and bottom-feeding derelicts—a crash-landing strip for Lapa's wandering legions of winos, beggars, petty criminals, panhandlers, murderers and all-purpose creeps.

Before moving in on me, the Casa Verde was where Narcisa had holed up on her marathon crack missions, consorting with her "tribe" of babbling, drug-addled anarchists, satanists, and so-called nihilists.

The place was a putrid, vile nest of lost souls; shit-eating, subhuman degenerates and garbage-picking parasites, with faces the color of mold, as if they'd all been dredged up from the bottom of a stagnant sewer.

Since most of the career losers there were too lazy to work and too cowardly to rob, they dubbed themselves "conceptual artists"—art, in this case, being the last refuge of scoundrels.

Once upon a time, as local legend had it, the motley bottom-dwellers of the Casa Verde had put their greasy paws to the Rock of Culture, grandly christening the place a *"centro cultural."* A ragged assortment of "abstract" sculptors and painters—egged on by none other than that stalwart patron of the arts, Doc—had even ventured downtown to the Prefeitura, demanding a grant to fix up the diseased, rat-infested hovel. They claimed they intended to turn it into a community art center, ostensibly to spread the heady blessings of Culture far and wide among residents of the poor, illiterate neighborhood.

They never pulled that scam off, of course—though the boldness of the very attempt was an impressive testament to the overall persistence and crablike tenacity of the Casa Verde's delusional tenants and supporters.

And, speaking of crabs, the whole place was infested with head lice. Everyone who ever landed there was instantly converted into a walking, talking parasite farm. Once in a while, someone would shoplift a bottle of delousing shampoo, which they'd all pass around like a flask of cheap wine, rubbing it into their communal natty dreads for relief. Of course, the cure never worked, since they all kept going back there to crash, instantly reinfesting themselves. From time to time, in a collective fit of desperation to curb the plague of tiny vermin, they'd all bleach their hair en masse, so when you went in there, it was like entering some terrible, bleak netherworld of demented white-haired ghosts.

Rats, spiders, roaches and the antennae of giant albino centipedes would brush against the ankles of anyone desperate enough to venture into that damp, unwholesome pit. The Casa Verde wasn't even so much a *place*, to my way of thinking, as a gaping portal to hellish realms of perpetual chaos; an open vortex to hell. A loathsome heart of darkness, where moribund nuthouse refugees gravitated in a frenzy of common agony and failure. Its unfortunate residents seemed to have been sucked into a fetid whirlpool of chaotic psychic sewage there; a godforsaken, phlegm-colored purgatory, from which there seemed no possible escape.

And now Narcisa was back again, holed up at the Casa Verde with her pet Crack Monster . . . *Shit! What a mess!* What the fuck was wrong with me? I wondered as I ran off to her rescue again. Approaching the squat, my stomach began to twitch like a cat with fleas . . . *This cannot be good . . . When will I ever fucking learn?*

Waiting for Narcisa out front, I got to talking to a familiar Casa Verde denizen named Pluto, a hollow-cheeked mulatto anarchist kid—Narcisa's androgynous male doppelganger on the streets.

From him, I got the real story behind Narcisa's expulsion from the Love House. It didn't surprise me to learn it was more significant than her grand saga about captive birds.

According to Pluto, Narcisa had heard noises in the middle of her last night there. Certain it was the Shadow People coming to get her, she'd panicked. Running out of her room, she tore butt-naked through the hallways, screaming about "*vultos*" and ghosts appearing at her window, together with Doc, trying to murder her with "electromagnetic shocks."

Her latest meltdown had done it for the Love House management, once and for all, hardening even their bulletproof hearts to Narcisa's legendary antics. When she got back from copping the next morning, she'd found all her junk sitting out on the sidewalk. From there, it was back to the Casa Verde.

Even before Pluto finished talking, I'd had my suspicions. As confirmation, he told me Doc had indeed been stalking Narcisa over there for days.

I sucked my teeth in disgust. It all made sense . . . *Fuck! He musta been lurking out there all night, trying to get in through the window! Bastard!*

I was on to the old kook now. Still, not wanting to add more fuel to her paranoia, I decided not to mention it to Narcisa. Judging from the complaints of Pluto and some of the other shaggy stoners loitering out front, Doc had been showing up at the Casa Verde a lot too lately, consumed by a fanatical fervor to reform all the squatters. I figured it was probably just an excuse for stalking Narcisa. But when he couldn't find her there, he would indeed focus his attentions on the other resident head cases. There was hardly a freak in the joint who hadn't been sent to the loony ward, at one time or another, because of Doc.

When the persistent old mommy-whacker was on the prowl for her, I knew Narcisa would avoid the Casa Verde like a Narcotics Anonymous meeting—unless she was on the outs with me. Then she would hit Doc up for whatever cash she could get. Narcisa would always gladly pawn a chunk of her tattered soul for a few coins. But she was always as slick as a gypsy pickpocket. Even when bargaining with the devil himself, Narcisa drove a hard one; as soon as she'd gotten what she wanted from her dickless old zombie, she'd beat it, leaving him all the more pissed-off and frustrated.

Pluto told me he'd even showed up there with the cops the other day, claiming to be Narcisa's father. When she couldn't be found, the shotgun-toting thugs settled for whoever they could squeeze a few coins out of, terrorizing the whole befuddled crew till they'd taken in enough beer money to make the visit worthwhile.

Doc was working hard at it now, trying to make Narcisa's last remaining refuge uninhabitable for one and all. Under pressure of ongoing police harassment, sooner or later they'd have to rat her out to him.

Bastard! I wanted to skin him alive. With this new threat, Narcisa might go missing again, maybe for good . . . *Shit!* As long as I was around, I knew she'd be safe from his clutches.

Still, he was out there, lurking, hoping to catch her alone. My blood boiled as I stood there waiting. Now, I'd have to keep an eye on the place, just to make sure Doc was kept at bay.

66. THE GUITAR

"The privilege of absurdity; to which no living
creature is subject but man only."
—*Thomas Hobbes*

As Narcisa and I sat talking at a little hole-in-the-wall eatery in
Lapa, Her Majesty rattled off a new wish list, pestering me to buy
her a guitar.

"A guitar? Are you serious?" I raised a skeptical eyebrow.

As Narcisa swore that a musical instrument would be the start of
a whole new life for her, I wished I could explain that the road back
from addiction is a long, complicated, demanding trudge. But I knew
she didn't want to hear any of that boring recovery crap. Biting my
tongue, I sat back in my chair and let her ramble on about her sparkly
new musical pipe dream.

Narcisa was persistent. As always, she would end up getting her
way. Even knowing I was being played like a pawn shop banjo, I decided to buy her the guitar. Even knowing she'd never learn to play
it, that it would just end up lost, destroyed, sold for drugs, converted
to shit with her singular reverse Midas touch, I allowed myself to be
persuaded. Maybe I just wanted to show her I believed in her.

Narcisa was forever whining how nobody ever gave her any trust.
I didn't swallow it, of course, always remembering the Magic Gringo

who'd bet on her and lost to the Crack Monster. Still, I figured getting her a guitar would show her somebody still cared enough to try.

After lunch, I took her to one of the ancient, wood-paneled, turn-of-the-century music stores downtown. Stepping inside, I breathed in the hoary musk of generations of music, a magical aura of Pagode, Chorinho and Samba traditions. The place had the look and scent of a museum. Standing there in the cool afternoon shadows, I envisioned the passage of a hundred Carnavals, looking around as the wiry, smiling gray-haired mulatto behind the counter polished and gift-wrapped Narcisa's new guitar.

Outside, she shredded through the wrapping. Scraps of paper and cardboard went flying into the street like triumphant confetti. Extracting her precious instrument, grinning with pride, she strapped it across her back.

Ten minutes later, as we dodged through downtown traffic, Narcisa began slapping at my shoulder . . . *What now?* But I already knew.

Shaking my head, I groaned . . . *Up to the fucking favela to cop again!*

She assured me she just wanted to score some weed, to "take the edge off."

I stopped the bike and turned around to face her. "Ya think that's a good idea? Ya just told me you were gonna lay off that shit for a while . . ."

"*Relaxa, Cigano!* I telling you already, is only for get some *maconha* so I got de little something for e'smoke. Is de harmless weed only these time. No more crack."

Moments later, I was sitting on the bike by the entrance to the *boca*, watching Narcisa strutting down the narrow alley, her brand-new ego-trophy slung across her back, swaggering like a ghetto superstar.

On our way back down the hill, running low on gas, I cut the motor and coasted through the stillness of the early evening shadows. Narcisa sat behind me in silence, holding the guitar at her side. A soft wind blew through the strings, making a haunting little melody. She leaned close and whispered in my ear. "The *e'spirits* making these e'special *musica*, just for us, Cigano . . ."

A magical moment.

Back at my place, she plopped down on the sofa with her new prize.

After lighting a fat, stinky *basiado*, she began plucking away, tugging at the out-of-tune strings like an angry monkey, oblivious to the horrifying racket she was creating. Sixty seconds later, the guitar sat silent by her side as she concentrated on smoking her weed. Then, a few minutes later, she got up and propped the thing against the wall in a corner.

What the fuck? That's it? Really? Unbuttoning her shirt, she grinned and told me she'd give me the fuck of my life for a ride back up the hill.

So much for that big plan . . . What could I say? Strung out on Narcisa as bad as she was on crack, I stood and followed her perfect ass up to the bed.

The next day, as I sat watching her smoke herself stupid battling the demons of another mad crack attack, I glanced over at the guitar. From its lonesome corner, it seemed to be looking back at me. I shrugged and sighed.

That's where it would remain for the rest of the week, abandoned, forgotten and collecting dust, while Narcisa smoked herself to Alpha Centauri and back again; just another sad, mute little reminder of Hope's inevitable defeat at the hands of the relentless, bloodthirsty old Crack Monster.

Days later, sleepless and disoriented, I crawled off the infernal merry-go-round and up to the loft to sleep. Narcisa remained sitting on the sofa down below, smoking. Delirious with exhaustion, I conked out.

After an hour surfing the golden waves of slumber, I woke with a start. From below, a symphony of obnoxious, disturbing sounds assaulted my ears.

What the fuck? It sounds like a fucking catfight down there!

Narcisa, in a sudden outburst of crack-fueled inspiration, had decided to pick up her guitar again . . . *Arggghhh! Great!* I looked at my watch with shell-shocked, blurry eyes . . . *Perfect! Six in the fucking morning . . . Bitch!*

There were few things Narcisa could do to really piss me off anymore. I was so used to living in hell by then, I could have had a phone line installed in the Bottomless Pit. But prolonged enforced sleep deprivation is an insidious form of slow torture, proscribed even by the Geneva Convention. Its effects had frazzled my brain into a painful, throbbing mush, converting even my indestructible passion for Narcisa into a slow, seething, murderous hatred.

I climbed down from the loft, my fists curled into trembling cannonballs of vengeance. She dropped the guitar and threw me a look of such helpless innocence it stopped me in my tracks. Before I could say a word, Narcisa got busy, swearing not to wake me again, under any circumstances, if I would just give her some cash to go smoke somewhere else.

I wasn't buying it. I glared at her with cocked shotguns in my eyes.

Using all her paranormal powers of manipulation, she promised not to disturb me again. She swore. She cried. She pleaded and cajoled, staring at me with such an expression of heartbreaking sincerity that, reluctantly convinced, I handed her the cash.

At that ungodly hour, it seemed like money well spent.

As she got up to leave, I gave her one last cold, warning look.

She reassured me again with a warm, winning smile. "I *promise* it to you already, Cigano . . . *Juro!* By everything e'sacred!"

Without another word, I watched her snatch the guitar to take with her. As she headed for the door, she turned around and assured me she was just taking it to the park to "practice." I grinned and gave her a happy thumbs-up.

What else could I do? I was just glad to be seeing the last of her and her infernal Noise Machine—even knowing all she'd do was drag it around with her, a narcissistic little fashion prop. I pictured her down on the street with the guitar, banging it, bashing and scratching it, crawling in and out of the bushes to smoke as she envisioned herself a rock star on the stage of her own dementia. Still, I didn't care. If her grand musical delusions would afford her one little moment of pleasure, I was all for it. More important, I had her sacred vow that she wouldn't wake me again.

As I closed the door behind her, her final words rang in my ears like a celestial choir. "*I promise, Cigano, I no gonna wake you no more! Juro, cara! Por tudo que é sagrado! By everything e'sacred!*"

In that blissful state, hovering like a dizzy fruit fly, somewhere between denial, wishful thinking and total mental collapse, it never crossed my mind to question Narcisa's sacred oath.

As I dove back into my soft, sweet-smelling pillows, I was too burnt-out to consider that, for the single-eyed, obsessive old Crack Monster, there's nothing sacred in Heaven or on Earth.

I was a couple of hours into a deep, golden slumber when a series of short, insistent tapping noises woke me.

Tap tap tap tap tap tap.

What the fuck? It was the urgent sound of a fugitive, the desperate staccato flutter of a condemned soul seeking solace . . . *What now?*

Tap tap tap tap tap tap.

As it went on, I felt like I was being kicked in the head by Narcisa's big black boot.

Tap tap tap tap tap tap.

Again and again! Fuck!

Taptaptaptaptaptaptaptap!

Goddammit! Bitch! Shut the fuck up!

Wounded and disheveled, I scrambled down from the loft and yanked the door open.

As I stood glaring at Narcisa's pimply face, I wanted to clobber her. But something in her posture, her whole demeanor, stopped me cold. She stood before me in silence, radiating a slow aura of humility. Something I'd never imagined her capable of. It threw me off.

I stood frozen in the doorway, staring at her, paralyzed, disoriented, puzzled . . . *What's wrong with her? She looks totally cowed.*

Meek as a mouse, she slithered in past me. Then she stopped in the middle of the room and turned, groveling like an actor in a Greek tragedy, her head hung low in a dramatic posture of abject surrender.

It was a convincing show of contrition. But I was awake. I could feel the anger rising in my skull like a wave of bloody vomit.

Fuming, I snarled and raved. ***"What th' fuck is wrong with you!? Gimme yer word? Fucking liar!"*** I ranted on, working myself up into a frothing, mindless rage.

Prolonged sleep deprivation will do that to you.

Narcisa must have known it too. She scurried over to the corner, bent her knees and crouched down low, cowering, covering her face in shame.

That's when I noticed . . . *Wait! Where's her guitar? She came in empty-handed! Fuck! It's gone! Arrghhh! Shit! This oughta be good!*

She started mumbling, grumbling. "*Urucubaca! Aza-aar! Puta má sorte!* Bad luck, bad luck, bad luck, very bad luck . . ."

"What th' fuck are you babbling about, ya crazy little witch? And where's that fucking guitar, ehh?"

She whimpered and whined like a whipped puppy. "*A policia, Cigano! Maior azar!* They catch-ed me e'smoking in de *praça* . . ."

"What?"

"Yeh, mano! They e'sneak up from behind an' sock me on de head, an' then they take away all my drugs an' my pipe, an' they teef my *gui-tarr!* De *gui-tarr* you give to me, Cigano, de e'stupid police take it *awa-aay!* An' now they wan' de mo-ney for give it to me again!"

I stood staring at her in cynical disbelief.

"I am sorry, Cigano, so e'sorry! I am e'stupid e'stupid!"

Narcisa was pouring it on so thick, I knew it had to be a hustle . . . *It's a scam, another fucking lie!* Still, I was taken aback. I'd never seen her acting contrite like that, subdued and repentant. Submissive. It was phenomenal.

She's groveling! Apologizing! What the fuck? She even said "I'm sorry."

I didn't really care about some cheap guitar. But it was still kind of a shame, another little loss. I thought back to that magical "spirit music" when we were coasting down the hill.

Shit! Maybe she could've even learned to play it someday.

"My guitar-rrr!" She wailed on. **"They take it away my new guitaa-arrr!! Filhos de mil puta piranhas!! Son of a thousand bastard whoore!"**

Without another word, I handed her the cash.

Hanging her head low, Narcisa slunk back toward the door. I stood staring in disgust as she shuffled out into the blazing summer heat of another day of torment.

I knew the guitar would never be seen again, and the money would be smoked up in a matter of hours. I didn't care. As the door slammed behind her, I was focused on one thing only: going back to sleep.

"Good riddance, ya fuggin' freak-show! You can stick th' money, th' guitar and th' fucking cops up your ass . . ."

Muttering, I crawled up to the loft bed and kissed the pillow like an old lover.

67. THE SHADOW PEOPLE

"IMMORTAL BEINGS HAVE BEEN COMPARED TO STARS,
THESE ARE EXISTENCES THAT LINGER ON LONG
AFTER THE DEATH OF THE THING ITSELF."
—*Zeena Schreck*

After losing her guitar to the Crack Monster, Narcisa began talking about an optimistic new plan; a geographic escape this time. A change of scenery.

What she really needed now, she insisted, was to get away from it all and just go smoke her stash "somewhere else." Somewhere, anywhere off the beaten track; far from people and all the hassle and danger they represented.

She was still convinced that Doc was following her wherever she went. She may have been paranoid, but I knew the bastard really was stalking her. Even before Pluto clued me in on his lurkings, I'd heard the frightful tone of obsession in the old freak's voice when he'd called. I suspected he was up to more sinister doings than he let on. I could feel it in my bones. But, not wanting to add to Narcisa's angst, I dummied up.

Still, Narcisa sensed the need for a hideaway. God knows, she'd already smoked nearly everywhere in her relentless search for the Perfect High. From the bathrooms of fancy tourist restaurants in Copacabana, to the dingy crack hovels up in the favelas, surrounded by jittery, bug-eyed bandidos, she spent her life sucking on the blazing stem. I pictured her cowering in bushes all alone in the shadows of statues to dead war heroes on deserted military bases; in abandoned buildings, decrepit alleys, cheap flophouse rooms, park benches and jungle caves up in the hills; hiding in rocky seaside coves, crouched down under overturned fishing boats on the moonlit sand; in the cemetery late at night, surrounded by blazing Macumba candles and howling spirits of the dead. Ensconced in the shadows of her escalating madness, battling against the four dreaded enemy winds of hell, Narcisa had really tried it all, looked and searched everywhere, sought high and low, in her never-ending crusade; her Quest for the Perfect High.

All, alas, to no avail. She just couldn't get no satisfaction.

Everything had become a surefire buzzkill for poor Narcisa. To make matters worse for her, I'd finally banned her from smoking in my apartment. I didn't want her doing it around me anymore. I was in fear for my own sanity.

Seeing her in that state had become a painful reminder of the time I'd first been exposed to an otherworldly being. Some memories are best left undisturbed. I was just a child when I'd had that terrifying glimpse of spirit possession. The last time I'd seen Narcisa in the grips of the Crack Monster, it had all came rushing back—the dark memory of watching in horror, my soft young neck hairs standing on end, as a spirit took over an old woman's body.

It was at this low-rent, piss-reeking dive my mother used to drink at in the Rua do Catete. I'd watched, paralyzed with fear, as a chubby old Negress spat out a stream of ferocious African garble, then toppled from her seat, shaking, contorting like a decapitated chicken on the dirty marble floor. Something had looked right at me from her possessed bloodshot eyes that day; something inhuman that chilled my soul right down to its shivering, quivering core. That memory had haunted me the rest of my life.

Lately, I saw that same dark occult presence in Narcisa's eyes as she smoked. I could see her shape-shifting, morphing, mutating, being charged with a mute, frigid horror from seeing all sorts of ghastly invisible things. Things I couldn't perceive, but I knew were there; horrible, unspeakable visions from some hellish dimension, like the row of eyeballs she always talked about, watching her every move, peering down right into her soul from a crevice in my ceiling.

Then there was my statue of Ogum; the colorful painted plaster figurine of São Jorge: St. George, sitting on his shining white steed, spearing a lance into the dragon. The icon sat in a little shrine on my bookshelf; a symbol of my battles against temptation, my own daily victory over the Curse. It terrified Narcisa when she was high. Whatever infernal entities possessed her had a powerful aversion to my beloved spirit guide and protector.

The last time she'd been smoking in my place, she'd sat on the floor, glaring up at my Ogum with a tormented look of hate and fear, hissing like a vampire in the presence of the cross.

That had done it. Ever since that day, I'd told her to beat it when she was using; to go smoke that vile, demonic shit somewhere else.

Her mind unraveling, desperate for a new refuge, Narcisa decided to take the bus across town to the Parque Lage.

The stately old colonial park lies nestled in the heart of the Jardim Botanico, Rio's magnificent, rambling botanical gardens. Sitting among verdant acres of lush tropical jungle, the grounds stretch high into the hills beneath the right armpit of the giant white statue of Christ the Redeemer, Corcovado. With the *Cristo Redentor* towering above, its placid gardens and shady garden trails are home to a thriving *centro cultural*; a haven for local artists, poets, musicians, beatniks and bohemians.

Back when I'd first met Narcisa, she was always dragging me off to visit her favorite place. She'd spend whole days there at the Parque Lage, sitting by a stream, laughing and chatting with her friends.

Now it was just another place to smoke. All the poets, artists, musicians and seekers who had once inspired her hungry young mind there were nothing but another bother to her now. Boring, annoying talkers.

Poor Narcisa! Back when I'd first known her, she'd been so different *. . . What happened to her? She used to be so outgoing and alive . . .* She'd always adored hanging out with people, with strangers, friends, anyone, everyone. Narcisa would sit around for hours on end, debating about philosophy, politics, art and poetry, always on fire, exchanging radical ideas and learning new things, exploring and questioning, meeting new people, forever testing the limits in her marvelous, innocent quest for experience.

Back then, she'd been in love with life, fascinated with everything, like an excited kid with a sparkly new toy; outgoing and outspoken, always interacting with the world, shaking things up, seeking out wild new adventures. Now all she wanted was to hide away from human society; to be all alone with the Crack Monster.

Just before she left, concerned for her safety, I tried asking about her stalker. "Hey, Narcisa, have you still been seeing that old Doc guy following you around town?"

"Dickless? Hah! E'stupid old e'sheet! No way, *cara*! *Por que?*"

"Oh, nothing. I was just wondering, because, ya know, ya kept saying how you thought he was watching you all the time, I was just curious."

"*Menos*, Cigano! What de fock happen to you? You forgotted I am de crazy geer-ool, hein? Hah! Don' listen to de Narcisa talk!"

I bit my tongue. I wanted so badly to tell her what I knew, but I couldn't. Poor Narcisa already had enough trouble.

Getting off the bus by the entrance to the Botanical Gardens, Narcisa lit a cigarette, then trotted toward the gate. She didn't stop to smell the roses. She didn't stop for anything. Narcisa was on a mission for the Crack Monster.

She scurried past the regal old colonial mansion, with its tall marble columns. Ignoring the clusters of people she'd used to hang out with there, she moved ahead like a nervous shadow. Narcisa wan't interested in singing, laughing or playing chess with her friends anymore. Now Narcisa had no friends.

Keeping her head down, she trudged forward, deep into the bush, under the indifferent cement gaze of Christ the Redeemer. Finally, coming to a remote jungle cave, she crept inside and made her way deep into the musty darkness. Then she flicked her Bic and found a place to sit. But there was a problem.

Later that day, she told me all about it.

"Soon I go sit in there, Cigano, I get de pipe an' take one big *puxa*, an' then, *boo*! I look an' he sitting right there, watching me!"

"What? Who?" I wondered out loud, envisioning Doc.

She shrugged a casual grin. "*Um escorpião . . .*"

"There was a scorpion in there? So what'd ya do then?"

"*Nada*, bro. He just look me an' I look him, an' is all okey. We both sit an' look de other one, an' ever'thing cool, you know? I go an' blow some e'smoke for him too . . ."

I looked at her. "Ya got a fuckin' scorpion high?"

"I wan' e'study de reaction, you know, make de e'speriment, got it? But then ever'thing get worsted, Cigano! They all come like a big explosion, de *morcegos! Arrrggghhh!*"

"*Morcegos?* I was dumbfounded. "*Bats?* Really?"

"Yeh, mano! Hundreds of bat, Cigano! They all come fly out from back of de cave, squiking an' flipping de wing like de little *vampiro!* I e'say, '*Out! Get de fock out, go go!*' an' then I run out, go! *Afffff!*"

Narcisa hiked on, in search of a new spot. Coming to the end of the trail, she stopped and looked around . . . *Perfect, Max! Solitude!* She shimmied up into a tree and climbed all the way to the top. Then she loaded her pipe and fired up again.

"But is *ever'where* de e'same focking conspir'cy, Cigano!" Her frantic eyes grew wider. "*Fock!* No place I go any e'safety for me! I can' even e'smoke in peace way up high on de biggest tree! Even all de way out there, all de time some focker come to molest me!"

"Who th' fuck bothered ya up there?"

"De *macaco*, Cigano!"

My jaw dropped. "Monkeys?"

Her big brown eyes bugged out of her face, boring into me like a pair of giant screws, fastening my brain to that surreal moment. "Ya-ass! So so many de e'stupid monkey, Cigano! An' then they all go an' attack me!"

"Wha—how?"

"They all e'standing around in de trees, bro, an' they e'start e'scream at me, an' then they all go an' throw de tree branch an' de fruit, an' even de rock! *Fock!* These focking monkey very *agressivo*, more worst even than de human! *Porra!* I gotta get de fock out, so I climb down real fast go go! *Out!*"

I sat looking at her, unable to comment, afraid to laugh.

After an awkward little silence, tears welled up in her big tormented eyes. Then she spoke again, in a sad, throaty little whimper that broke my heart. "Is no place no good for Narcisa e'smoke no more! No any place, Cigano, got it? Ever'body bother me ever'where I go! These why I don' wan' e'stay live in these e'sheet world no more." She started sobbing.

I took her in my arms, like a frightened child, trying to soothe her. "It's okay now, baby, don't worry . . . *shhhhh*. Everything's gonna be okay."

*"Uuuaggghhhh! Is never gonna be okey, Cigano! Nunca!
What else more I can do now, hein, Cigano? What to do?"*

I didn't know what to say. But Narcisa was weeping, whining, waiting for an answer.

Confused, I stammered the first thing that came to mind. "Maybe
. . . maybe it's not just the people, or the places you go to . . . ya know?"

I could feel a darkness creeping over her. Narcisa stopped crying. I
felt her stiffen. But I'd already taken the leap. Now I had to fall.

I blurted it out. " . . . Maybe it's what you're *doing* that isn't working
for ya anymore . . . Did you ever stop to think of th—"

Narcisa pulled away fast, wiggling out of my arms like a snake. She
twisted around and sat across from me, hissing, staring at me as if
she'd just swallowed a cat turd. I was a bug. An asshole. An enemy. I'd
just said the stupidest, most offensive thing she'd ever heard.

*"Menos, Cigano. Meeeenos! Shut de fock up now, hein!
Talk less! De less you talk now de better, got it?"*

I got it. I shut the fuck up.

68. HELL'S BELLS

Days later, we were sitting on my sofa when Narcisa fixed me with a glazed look. In the odd little childlike voice of that creepy spirit entity, she drawled a weird question.

"Have an'body ever die for you, Cigano?"

Before I knew what was happening, she stood up, strode across the room and scrambled up onto the window ledge. She stood there on the windowsill, teetering five floors above the hard, cold pavement below.

Jesus! No!

She looked back over her shoulder at me with that glassy, faraway expression. Then, just as she turned to jump, I ran over and grabbed her by the waist. As I hauled her back inside, Narcisa let out an eerie, blood-chilling howl, like a wounded, tormented ghost.

After she'd calmed down, I asked her why she'd tried to kill herself. She just shrugged, as if she didn't remember a thing.

Things were getting bad. Worse than ever. Days blurred into nights in a vague, timeless limbo. I swore I could hear the unseen things howling, prowling around the periphery of my awareness. A dark presence of doom was looming over us. I could sense it everywhere. I prayed and prayed, as Narcisa slipped away, deeper into the bottomless pit.

One night, after another long, crazed, sleepless mission, she began glaring at me, cursing under her breath. I looked at her in wonder. Narcisa had become obsessed with the notion that I was a "clone," an impostor.

When I laughed and assured her I was the same person I'd always been, she ordered me to strip off all my clothes so she could examine my tattoos, one by one.

"You don' fool me!" She hissed like a viper, grabbing at a weathered old blue-green anchor tattoo on my chest and clawing at my skin till it bled. "These *tatuagem* no de e'same one was there before! *Good try!* What you *do* to him, hein? Where de Cigano?"

My mouth dropped open.

"Is no good you lying to me, cuz I know you de *clone*, so don' try even make no more trick on me, got it? Hah! May-be I crazy, but I no so e'stupid like you focking Shadow Peoples think!" She took my face roughly in her hands and peered into my mouth, inspecting my teeth like a horse, counting the gold ones, one by one, insisting they were "fakes."

Crying out in anguish at the evil spirits, the dreaded Shadow People, she lamented how they'd usurped her Cigano, her faithful caretaker, her friend, her man, leaving nothing but a soulless, robotic "clone" in his place. A spy. A conspirator. An enemy.

And so Narcisa rampaged through her life, a mad, solitary maze of progressive torment and impending doom; always looking for a new tree, another cave, a new refuge to hide from the Curse; going out day after day on her crazed, unholy crack missions, each time convinced it would work out better the next time. It never did. Narcisa was going down fast. I felt so powerless, all I could do was look up at my statue of Ogum and pray. Staring at the comforting, familiar image in silent supplication, tears welled up in my eyes as I recited the Lord's Prayer under my breath.

Pai Nosso . . .

Narcisa was my twin flame, and hers was burning out fast.

Que estás nos céus . . .

I lit another candle and set it carefully, lovingly at the base of the shrine, praying that my own flame would stay brightly lit.

Santificado seja Vosso nome . . .

Fighting to affirm my own unsteady faith, I prayed she might find the power to overcome the malevolent Curse of her warped, damaged mind.

Vem a nós o Vosso Reino!

I prayed for her to shed her weakness like a straitjacket and rise up from her crippled little empire of ashes, to be made full and healthy and whole again, flaming tall and strong, like a magnificent, triumphant phoenix.

Abrí os caminhos de luz . . . Por favor, Heavenly Father, keep me strong enough to reignite her dying little flickering spark . . . Help me light the way for her to Your loving care and protection, before it's too late.

But disbelief is more powerful than faith, because, unlike faith, it is reinforced by our cruelest, most primal animal instincts. And in that savage state, Narcisa hated all talk of God. Coming from a long line of Bible-thumping Pentecostal religious fanatics, unconsciously, she was plagued by the primitive, angry religion of her people; all their paranoid, unmentionable fears and greasy superstitions were bullwhipping her down the road to hell. Guilt. Shame. Original sin. Hellfire and eternal damnation. The works.

I'd always despised the so-called born-again Christians. To me, those sanctimonious, hypocritical fundamentalist churches were to faith what whorehouses were to love. Poor Narcisa. I felt so bad for her as I watched her trembling under the unforgiving glare of that cockeyed despot of a man-made, evangelical Christian God she both hated and feared.

"*Disastre, disastre, disastre, disastre . . .*" She began repeating the same word, "disaster," over and over under her breath, with a helpless expression of terrified, fervent anguish.

I struggled to hold my tongue. Finally, after ten minutes listening to her repeating that hellish mantra, over and over, I couldn't take it anymore.

"What fuckin' disaster?" I blurted. "What th' fuck are ya talkin' about? Yer whole fucking life's the disaster! Wake up, Narcisa! Yer sitting around smokin' crack all day long, fer fuck's sake, waiting for some big fire-and-brimstone doomsday shit! What th' fuck? Forget all that shit, man! The disaster's already happened! Don't ya get it? It's you! It's yer whole fuckin' world! It's the crack! Ya gotta stop smoking that shit!"

She sat there in silence, staring at me, too bugged-out to retort or retaliate. Taking advantage of the lull in her usual arrogance, I tried and tried to drive the point home.

"I can see it! The whole fuggin' world sees it, Narcisa! Only *you* can't see! You're the only one who can't see what's happening to ya, cuz that shit has made you blind! Why don't ya just admit yer beat? What th' fuck are ya waiting for? Just lemme take ya somewhere! Please, let's get you some help now, before it's too fuckin' late!"

I kept at it, trying to convince her to go into treatment.

I begged and pleaded. "C'mon, baby! Don't just sit there. *Por favor!* Say something. We gotta do something! You're dying here . . ."

Finally, she told me to shut the fuck up.

When I refused to let it go, she jumped up and ran out into the night, crying.

"Shit!" I groaned, stepping into my boots.

It wasn't safe for her to be on the street alone anymore. Anything could happen with that murderous old stalker creeping around the neighborhood. I knew I'd never forgive myself if the bastard caught up with Narcisa before I did.

With a weary sigh, I put on my jacket and picked up my keys.

69. CUPID GETS A GUN

"LOVE IS A TYRANT SPARING NONE."
—*Corneille*

I spotted her a couple of hours later, standing on the corner in front of the *paderia*. Looking around like a fugitive, babbling to herself, Narcisa was a scrawny, demented, homeless little shadow of herself.

As I sat observing her from a distance, it struck me again just how far gone she was. People were giving her a wide berth, some even crossing the street to get as far away from her as possible. Like animals, they could sense the shadow of Death on her. Narcisa had become a grim public warning; an urban ghost, haunting the streets, reminding passersby of their own fragile mortality.

After a while, she wandered into the store for a pack of cigarettes. I watched as she got in line at the cash register, pulling a ten-spot from her filthy, snot-encrusted jeans. As if sensing a phantom creeping up behind him, an elderly gentleman turned and glanced at her with a startled look, shoving his hand in his pocket, as if she'd managed to somehow extract his cash.

Narcisa picked up on it, like a dog sniffing fear. Glaring at the poor little fellow like a fiery-faced dragon, she started yelling, flecks of spittle flying, waving her crumpled banknote in his face. ***"Why de fock you looking me, hein? You think I teef it from you these focking money? Hah! E'stupid old e'sheet! I e'spending each*** *day more cash on de droga than you can earn in a whole focking month, got it?"*

He didn't get it. He just stared back in mute bewilderment. I cringed as pedestrians stopped in the doorway to marvel at her latest public outrage.

Shit! Narcisa was hurtling toward the bottom like a stone. Maybe it was a good thing, though, I mused sadly, a blessing in disguise that she was deteriorating so fast now. After all, for someone like her to want to stop what they're doing, there's no other way out but total, rock-bottom, ego-crushing defeat.

Narcisa was a slow-motion train wreck. It was just a matter of time.

After getting her home, another ugly catfight ensued. Objects were broken, clothes torn, tears shed and voices were raised to the heavens in a flying shit-storm of wailing frustration and rage. It all ended in the usual manner: an fiery explosion of desperate, sweaty, hungry sex.

Afterward, she sat beside me on the bed, smoking a cigarette, cool smoke rings hovering above her like tiny halos in the dim, sex-charged air.

"You know, Cigano, is too much *ironia* . . ." Her face glistened with an exquisite melancholy light. " . . . For de geer-ool is all like de big bad joke. She e'spend her whole life with de big dream de right man gonna come, you know?"

I nodded like a priest in the shadows of a confessional, waiting to hear all.

" . . . All de time she make so many big *plano* . . ." She took a deep drag off her cigarette. " . . . She make all kinda *sexo* with so many different mans. But really she only practice for when she gonna meet de one e'special one who all de time she dream about, de one she gonna love with de whole heart. An' all de time she e'stay dreaming, waiting, dream an' wait . . ."

Her deep, raw, childlike voice yanked a reluctant tear from my eye as she breathed out a bitter little smoky guffaw, folding her long, slender legs like the crosshairs of some ghetto Cupid's high-powered assault rifle, taking deadly aim at my heart.

Feeling my throat constrict, I ran my fingers along her firm white skin, cupping her velvet kneecap in my palm. As her hazy words fluttered in the dark like ethereal cobalt butterflies, I had a sudden, powerful feeling that I knew the rest, had already read the script.

" . . . An' then one day these person finally come into de girl life . . ." She fixed me with those intense laser-beam eyes, freezing my breath like an ice storm. " . . . An' then is all like de fairy tale! Everything perfect, just like all de time she dream about. Now she finally got it, de thing she always wan' so bad . . ."

As she talked on, the moment seemed to freeze and run back in time, like a recurring movie reel . . . *Déjà vu! Like a dream of another life.*

" . . . An' after all these time waiting, Cigano, now, just when she wanna do everything right, she gotta go an' do ever'thing *wrong!*"

Déjà vu! I know this . . . This has all happened before!

" . . . An' then you' find out de truth! An' de truth she *ugly*, Cigano! Because de real truth is you can never be happy, with *nobody!*"

I couldn't look away. A burning light shone in her eyes, dancing between the fibers of time and space. " . . . Because is inside of *you*," she whispered, "some-thing *terrível*, some dark *companheiro* who make it so you always gonna e'stay all alone! Inside, Cigano, got it? You always alone, even when you finally find de one e'special one, got it?"

I got it. I knew all about that dark companion. She was telling the story of my life. I never felt so close to Narcisa. We were birds of a feather. Birds with battered, broken wings. Homeless, hungry, lonely birds. Sad, angry birds. Birds without a flock, without a nest.

" . . . Because you never can be satisfy, Cigano. *Nunca!* When is cold an' raining, an' you homeless in de e'street, dreaming and wanting for de comfort an' de companion, then you find de e'special one who gonna give it to you . . ."

That's it! Somewhere in the back of my soul's infinite memory, I knew something important was being said. Narcisa was talking about me, about us, about the roots of the Curse itself. A weird electrical current seemed to crackle between her words as I listened, studying her face closely, intently, thirsty for any small clue to her terminal frenzy.

" . . . An' when finally you got it, all de thing you always wan', then, *porra*, you gotta go an' fock it all up. Destroy all, so you can go back to be all alone again! Because you wan' it only de freedom again now, got it? You wan' de freedom to go e'stay cold an' hungry, an' walk all alone on de e'street in de night, looking, wanting, all de time *wanting*, got it?"

I got it. I got it good. It was *me* she was talking about! My whole life! The long, restless, endless, hungry, directionless road to nowhere.

" . . . Because really, you only wanna *want*, got it? *No satisfaction! Nunca!* Is all just like de big game, Cigano, an' then soon you e'start to win, *boo!* Then you tire of playing. So you gotta go an' throw it away! Can' help it! Don' matter what is it, who is it, got it? Because no thing can satisfy nobody! That's why I am e'satisfy with nothing, bro, cuz I am really Nobody here, got it?"

Of course, I got it. I always had. Looking at Narcisa, she seemed so sad, so small, so agonizingly disappointed with herself, with her life, her unhappy stay on earth; so disillusioned by the cruel tricks her own weak humanity had played on her.

"*Princesa!*" I cried out. "You've done nothin' wrong! *Nada!*"

She folded her arms across her chest and shot me a skeptical look.

"Shit, man, it's just cuz yer too smart, too sensitive for this fucking world, too good! But that's why I love you, Narcisa, see?"

She kept staring at me, squinting, as if she was surprised that anyone who'd been tested and tormented, used and shit on and abused as I had could still love the tester, the abuser.

" . . . Lissen, baby, what would I want with a 'nice girl'? You're perfect for me, just the way you are. I just *get* you, Narcisa, and that's why I love you . . ."

Even as I said it, I could feel that deep déjà vu premonition again, as if I had just taken some sort of sacred vow, from which there would be no escape.

70. DEATH FROM ABOVE

"I'M GOING TO DIE," SHE SAID; THEN WAITED AND SAID, "I HATE IT."
—*Ernest Hemingway*

The next day, I was fast asleep when Narcisa tapped on the door. Without a word, I staggered over and let her in.

Breezing in past me, she halted in the middle of the room. She stood there like a statue, staring up at the ceiling fan with a dark look of panic, as if there were a giant guillotine blade there, teetering over her head.

"*Turn it out these e'sheet, Cigano!*" she hissed in a hoarse, trembling whisper. "*Now! Go go go! It gonna fly off an' cut us off de head, mano!*"

"Relax, Narcisa, it's just a fan. Can't come loose."

"*Do what I e'saying, Cigano! Por favor! I seen these thing happen one time! Is terrível, belief me! Go an' turn it out now, go go!*"

"What? Where'd ya see that shit?" I laughed.

"*No no no no no! Don' make no more question! They implant de e'secret microchip, for listening all de thing from my head, inside!*"

O-kay . . . Can't argue with that one . . . I went over and switched off the fan. It had been a long, blazing hot summer. Since before Carnaval, I'd been keeping that fan going day and night. It was running my electric bill to Alpha Centauri, but the little apartment was a Turkish bath without it. A week had passed since I'd seen the light of day. Giving in to her promise that it was "just this one time," I'd let up on the smoking ban. For the next several hours, I sat squirming in discomfort as she smoked and choked her brains out. Sweating in the dark, locked up in that stifling, airless little greenhouse with a babbling psychopath, finally, I couldn't take it anymore. I needed out.

"C'mon, baby!" I pleaded, mopping the sweat off my face and neck with a damp, clammy hand towel. "Let's just go for a little walk . . ."

She shot me a look as if I'd suggested we go scuba diving in the toilet.

Desperate for a break, I tried again. "Please, Narcisa. *Por favor!* We'll come right back, I promise. I just gotta go out and buy a pack of smokes."

After I agreed to buy her some more crack along the way, she nodded and rose to her feet as I breathed a deep sigh of relief.

Narcisa seemed to be moving in agonizing slow motion as we went down the stairs and crossed the street into the plaza. As we stepped into the park, all of a sudden she stopped, feet frozen in the dirt, glaring up into the muggy summer sky.

I turned around and watched her, confused . . . *What now?*

An anguished, distrustful expression crossed her face, like a storm cloud. Like a nervous dog on an invisible leash, she took a few more timid steps, then crouched down, like a soldier on a blazing battlefield. Then, without a word, she scurried off into the bushes like a lizard. I stood there, baffled, rubbing my chin, staring at the shrubbery, waiting for her to come out.

She didn't.

Shit! Now what? Nothing to do now, short of following Narcisa into the underbrush, I shuffled over and sat down on a bench. To kill the time, I started reading this old magazine she'd fished out of the garbage can in front of my building. As people strolled past, I plastered a stupid smile on my face and sat there. Time went by. I sat and I sat, waiting, acting casual; trying to breathe in any little meager scraps of everyday life, wanting desperately to appear normal. Stealing guilty little glances around, I leafed through the pages, struggling to look like a regular person, without a care in the world.

Yep! Just a regular, normal, everyday guy, that's me, just sitting here on a park bench, reading a magazine, waiting for my girlfriend to come slithering out of the fucking bushes! Shit!

After what seemed like a very long while, Narcisa emerged at last. Dried leaves and cobwebs clung to her hair. I stared at her and bit my lower lip to keep from laughing. She slid onto the bench beside me, looking around, peering up in the air with a frantic, paranoid expression. Curious, I glanced into the sky. Vultures were circling high above. Narcisa grabbed my arm and bored into my soul with those big, tragic doomsday eyes. "*Pronto!* These is it, Cigano!"

"What?"

"De *aviso*, de last final warning for me! Narcisa *finish* now!"

I stared back at her, saying nothing, waiting for her to go on.

"*Maior urucubaca, porra!* Lookit, mano, is de *urubu*. De buzzard! Lookit now! You see it, Cigano, hein? Is right up there, lookit!"

Still confused, I looked around.

Narcisa gestured skyward with her nose, afraid to point and draw attention to herself.

I looked up again. There they were, all right. Buzzards.

"Yeah?" I shrugged. "So?"

"Is very bad thing these big black bird, Cigano!" She winced. "Is de warning, de omen!"

"Huh? Howzat, baby?"

"These horrible creature, they know I gonna die soon, so they going round an' round up in de circle, waiting for de Narcisa heart e'stop so they can come down an' pick on my bone with de horrible long black beak an' claw! *Arrrggghhh!*"

I couldn't speak. I just sat looking at her in dumbfounded pity.

Suddenly, Narcisa grinned; a strange, tragic little smile, her face shining with a proud glow of serenity. Surrender. Total acceptance of her own imminent demise. Fearless and calm.

Then, with a sudden majestic gesture of defiance, she jumped up from the bench and raised her angelic white face skyward, shaking an angry fist with the middle finger extended at the circling birds, shouting into the air, in her beautiful, raw, savage growl.

"Foda-se! Vaza fora, seus filhos da puta, vaiii-iii! Go! Fock off! You don' gonna get on me yet! No way! You can ride round up there an' wait, got it? You no gonna suck on these bone! No before I suck up de last focking drop out from these e'stupid life! Got it?"

She fell silent. She just stood there, glaring up.

Finally, she spoke again, more softly this time. "Hah! *Now* you got it, e'stupid! Good!"

With a curt, businesslike nod, Narcisa spat on the ground and strode off, having made her point to the looming, indifferent heavens above.

"'*Bora, Cigano!*" she barked. "Let's go, mano, c'mon, go, go!"

Shaking my head, I got up and followed her out of the park.

What else could I do?

71. A TRIP TO THE COUNTRY

"HE THAT IS DISCONTENTED IN ONE PLACE WILL
SELDOM BE HAPPY IN ANOTHER."
—*Aesop*

No matter how desperate things ever got, Narcisa always maintained there was an easy way out. I'd been hearing about it for months now.

Salvation awaited, in one simple, optimistic magical formula:

A Trip to the Country.

That cheery little pipe dream was the foolproof solution to all her woes, she claimed. A lifelong marathon of trauma and self-destruction would be wiped clean forever by a quick, painless little change of scenery.

Craving relief from the escalating weirdness of our life in Rio, I was half inclined to believe her. There was just one small snag.

I hated the Great Outdoors.

Unlike many of my people, I despised the country. Most Brazilian Roma—restless, dirty-faced, nomadic gypsies—are well content to spend their lives roaming the rural backlands in caravans of broken-down cars and vans, even on horseback. Not me. In all my decades of travel, the countryside had always seemed little more than a boring, faceless backdrop; a means to an end. Something to endure on my way to the next city.

I'd grown up a city Rom, begging for change, hustling and scamming on the dirty, crowded, hungry streets and favelas of Rio. That familiar urban terrain had always been my jungle, my forest, my Happy Hunting Grounds. I could never stomach the country, with its endless, tedious acres of soulless, empty, vapid, melancholy nothingness. I dreaded those dreary, muddy vistas of drab little shacks where nobody's ever home; the crooked dirt roads that never go anywhere. No. The country had never been my kind of picnic.

Narcisa had been working on me over the weeks, though, expounding on the many wonders of the bucolic life, painting a joyful little picture of an idyllic rural paradise where we could live happily ever after.

The faster things deteriorated at home, the more her eager sales pitch began to appeal to me. She swore that if she could just get away from the cutthroat streets and favelas of Rio for a while, everything would be different. Well, what did I know? Hadn't I operated by the same basic formula over a lifetime of running away from people, places and things? My frantic gypsy geographic acrobatics had indeed enabled me to dodge my own drooling demons for quite some time. I'd lived on the road for decades. Until I'd come face-to-face with myself in prison, I, too, had always been a firm believer in quick geographical cures for deep existential maladies.

Some habits die harder than others. Love and hope can run roughshod over logic and reason. Narcisa had me just about sold on her grand road trip plan. All that was needed to seal the deal was one last boot to my head.

Soon enough, it came.

Narcisa had been pushing the outer limits of her body and mind to the snapping point for weeks; toasting her brains to ashes, teetering on the edge of complete physical and mental breakdown. By the end of her latest weeklong run, I could smell the stench of death on her.

At my wit's end, I begged her to give it a rest. *"Por favor, princesa!"* I stood over her as she sat on the sofa smoking rock after rock, her eyes popping out of her skull like alligator eggs. "Why don't ya just chill for a while? Give it a break, already, before ya kill yerself!"

She shot me a look of disdain. "I wish I can kill myself, Cigano! I just wanna finish an' go home to my own *planeta* , but is no possible! Only de good peoples can dead young here. So I never gonna dead, cuz my soul she completely corrupt! Hah! Nothing can kill me! *Nada!* I got de cockroach blood in my vein, bro! *Fock!*"

I rolled my eyes and groaned.

"Menos!" Shrugging me off, she fired up another huge rock. "Lissen, Cigano, e'soon we gonna go. I almost ready for get de fock out an' e'stop e'smoke these e'stupid e'sheet forever!"

I stared at her. "Are you serious, Narcisa?"

Her eyes lit up. "Just wait an' you gonna see it, mano! After tomorrow we gonna go away to de nature! Gonna visit de beautiful waterfall an' de jungle, an' every little thing gonna be beautiful! *Perfect, Max!* Only de tree an' all de little animal there, only eat an' e'sleep, simple like that, got it? So now just you leave me for have de fun some more, just a little more while, an' then I gonna be e'sick of these e'stupid *droga*. An' then we gonna go far far away from these e'sheet city!"

"You mean it!" I looked at her, incredulous. "Ya really wanna go . . . ?"

She fixed me with a look of such innocent sincerity, I was a Believer.

Then she closed the deal. "Is only these one thing I wan' in de life now, Cigano! I wan' it more than any other thing in de whole world!"

I was sold.

A few days later, the Big Day arrived at last.

Narcisa stumbled in more dead than alive. She informed me that we'd be leaving town right away, as soon as she "rested her eyes" for a few minutes. Then she dropped onto the sofa and passed out like a cadaver.

Aside from the nightmares, she didn't move for the next eighteen hours. I could only tell she was still alive because she kept talking in her sleep. Every few minutes, she would cry out, whimpering in child-like terror, her ghostly, emaciated carcass contorting in heartbreaking spasms of delirium. But for the most part, though, she lay still as a corpse. I even checked her pulse a few times, just in case, half fearing she'd given up the ghost and slipped away in her sleep, like a sneaky kid.

No such luck for her. Narcisa lived.

The next day, she rose up in a sputtering fury of jerky spastic move-ments, all pointy elbows and knees, sharp insults and fiery complaints. Pushing past me, she rummaged through my kitchen like a prison riot, banging drawers and slamming cupboards. Silverware clattered, skittering across the floor. Plates and glasses shattered as she ripped her way like a maddened baboon through another agonizing feeding frenzy.

"Go down-stair to de boteco an' get it for me de Coca Cola!" She shouted, shoveling dripping gobs of food into her face. *"Anda logo, cara, vaiii-iiii, porra! Go! Go . . . An' get me a pack of cigarette, de good one, you cheap gyp-say e'sheet! An' da morthes!"*

"Huh? Wha . . . ?" I stopped, my hand on the doorknob, a standing question mark, waiting for a translation.

Swallowing another mouthful with petulant determination, she scowled. *"De matches, you e'stupid e'sheet! Match-es! Match-es! You go deaf now, hein? Retard like e'stupid old man, hein? Porra! Retardado! Idiota! Lesado! Imbicil! Babaca!"* She went back to her chewing, glowering, rolling her eyes like lemons in a slot machine as I beat it out the door.

When I returned, she was lying faceup on the sofa, snoring. Her mouth hung open like a gaping grave, her dirty gray feet pointing toward the ceiling like a pair of lopsided tombstones. Pizza crust, candy wrappers, cigarette butts and ashes littered the floor.

I stood over her, holding the sweaty Coke bottle in my hand, like a wilted bouquet, a jilted, lovestruck farm boy, a survivor in a tornado's wake, shaking my head, surveying the devastation.

72. THE BIG DAY

"OUR GREATEST FOES, AND WHOM WE MUST
CHIEFLY COMBAT, ARE OURSELVES."
—*Cervantes*

Twenty-four hours later, Narcisa arose from the depths. Right away, the orders began flying across the room like squawking birds of prey, jolting me from a sound sleep.

"Food! Foo-ood! Comidaa-aah!!"

Groaning with fatigue, I scrambled to the refrigerator, desperate to get her fed and shut her up. She snatched the plates from my hands as fast as I could fill them, attacking the food like a starved wolverine on its hind legs. Then she scampered off with an overflowing plate.

When I emerged from the kitchen, Narcisa was sitting on the toilet with the bathroom door open, still eating, crapping her tortured guts out. Ignoring her gluttonous savagery, I went over and opened the long-shuttered window to a spectacular purple and red sunrise.

"Today's the big day, princesa!" I beamed through a fuzzy haze.

"Porra! Shut de fock up, e'stupid e'sheet! Close these focking door an' get de fock outa here, go! I trying to def'cate! Out! Go!"

I slunk off like a wounded mutt. I got busy clearing the sofa and floor, then went and hid out in the dark little kitchen, washing dishes.

Suddenly the infernal idiot chatter of the TV was hammering my ears. *What now?* I peered back into the room. Narcisa had pulled the shutters closed again. She was sitting in darkness before the giant glowing eyeball, like a glassy-eyed zombie, lost in a surreal hellscape of morning children's programming.

What the fuck is this shit? Animated teddy bears with screeching, ratlike voices, babbling weird nonsense talk. Retarded-looking idiots dressed as clowns, farmers, witches and goons, running around in circles, squeaking like deranged rodents and butchered pigs!

Fuck! What the hell is she watching in there? I stared at the screen, feeling mounting waves of disgust as a giant cockroach pranced into center stage. All the other repulsive creatures made a dancing ring around the wretched thing. They all began singing together, squealing with infuriating, high-pitched shrieks.

Fuck! I could feel a red cauldron of hate welling up in my gut. I grimaced at her through clenched teeth, producing a painful smile. "Baby, we should probably be leaving soon, no . . . ?"

She responded by hurling an overflowing ashtray at me, scattering cigarette butts and ashes all across the clean floor I'd just swept.

"Jesus, Narcisa! What th' fu—" I moved in front of the television.

"Menos!! Shut de fock up, Cigano, go! Moo-oove, e'stupid!" She screeched and cursed, as a glass whizzed past my head and shattered against the wall. **"I watching de—"**

That's it, goddammit! I jumped on her like a disturbed alligator and grabbed her by the throat. Hauling her up to her feet, I pinned her against the wall. Shocked, hateful eyes of outrage popped out of her pimply face as I banged her head against the hard plaster twice, **tok**, **tok**, screaming, raging, spitting. **"You have gone too fuggin' far this time, bitch!"**

It was on. Narcisa fought back like a savage beast. We struggled, knocking plates and furniture asunder. Finally, I got her pinned to the floor. Lowering my knees down onto her arms, I tightened my grip around her throat with both hands.

As her face turned red, she realized her best efforts to struggle free were no match for my sizzling rage. She gave up and stopped fighting.

I got over it fast, of course, like I always got over it. Sitting on top of her, looking down at her in that helpless state, I began to feel bad. I told her I'd let her up if she promised to calm down and quit breaking things. She nodded and I let her go.

But Narcisa wasn't finished. The guilt card came out right away. "You think I ever gonna go away together with *you* now, hein, Cigano? Why for, hein? So you can *beat* me in de country an' kill me an' left me there for de animal an' de ants to eat my carcass, hein?"

I wanted to crawl off and die as she ranted on, sobbing, working herself up into a high-pitched, hysterical, mindless new frenzy.

"No focking way I going anywhere with you, ever! Nunca! You a dangerous maniac, Cigano! I don' trust you no more! You are violent an' crazy an' bad! I shoulda listen to Doc! He tell me long time ago you a very bad man! A criminal! I never wan' see you again, got it?"

I got it. Narcisa was going stark-raving nuts again, foaming at the mouth in wild spasms of poisonous, uncontrollable fury.

She spun around the room like a frantic top, struggling into her filthy clothes, howling, hollering that the was leaving forever, that I'd never see her again.

Blah blah blah . . . I knew her blustery threats were pure pigshit. I'd heard it all before. And still, no matter how many times I lived through one of Narcisa's mad tirades, it always felt the same to me, that this crisis would be the last. As she raged on, I could feel the shadow of disaster approaching like an atomic fallout cloud. Reliving the horrors of my violent, unstable childhood again and again with Narcisa, I would soon come to a deep understanding that some hurts you simply never forget. It was the same feeling I'd always lived with as a little boy, watching my mother in a drunken rampage, raging, insulting, violent, insane. Each

time Narcisa threw a fit, I feared it would be the time where someone would really get hurt, or locked up, or killed, just like when I was
a helpless, frightened little kid; always waiting for that tragic, violent,
heartbreaking ending. Always fearing the worst. Danger was in the air.

Still spitting and cursing, Narcisa started for the door. I knew the
streets were a minefield of peril for her in that murderous, hysterical
state. Once again, I was filled with horror, fearing for her life.

Worried for her safety, with Doc out on the prowl, I jumped between her and the door.

Locking it fast, I pocketed the key. "Where th' fuck ya think you're
going, huh?" I stood there with my arms crossed, blocking her way.

"Moo-oove!" She pushed, prodding, bellowing, trying to get
around me.

"Calma!" I gave her a gentle shove backward. "You're not going
anywhere! Not like this, Narcisa. Not till ya chill th' fuck out! I'm not
letting ya go out there to run the streets like a mad cow! Are you out
of yer fuggin' mind? They'll murder ya this time!"

"Moo-oove! Open de focking door, e'stupid! I wanna go!"

"Go where? When th' fuck ya gonna go? Jesus! When are ya gonna
wise up, ya crazy bitch? I'm just trying to protect you here."

*"Protect me? By lock me inside these e'sheet place?! Hah!
You de crazy one! Complete insane! You wan' protect me,
hein? Who gonna protect me from YOU, hein!?"*

I didn't budge. Narcisa pulled out her next weapon. Blackmail.

"Ha-alp! HA-ALP!! I prison inside here! POLICIA!"

Oh shit! Noise! Neighbors! Police! Fuck!

I stood frozen in horror as she screeched on, her piercing wails
rattling the windows.

"SOCORRO!! HAA-AALP ME!! PLEE-EEZE!! POLICIA!!"

I could hear the neighbors banging on the walls as the nightmare
began again. Panicking, I grabbed her arms and shook her, desperate

to shut her up before an army of pissed-off residents broke my door down to murder us both. As usual, it was six in the morning.

She just yelled louder. ***"OH JE-SOOZ, HAA-AALP!! HA-AALP!! HA-AALP!! SAAM-BADY, POR FAVOR!! HE GAANNA KEE-EEL MEEE!!"***

Jesus! Shut up! Gotta shut this crazy cunt up!

I clamped my hand over her screeching blowhole and she bit me like a rabid dog, drawing blood from my fingers.

"Arrrggghhh! Bitch!" In a sudden knee-jerk reflex, my fist flew back and connected with her jaw. ***Pow!***

I guess I'd hoped to knock her out and stop the insane drama. But at the last second, I hesitated and pulled my punch to a weak, ineffective blow.

Instantly, I regretted it . . . *Oh shit! What have I done?*

Narcisa glowered at me with blazing eyes of hate. She charged past me and put her shoulder to the door, smashing the lock open. I heard the latch crack, and then she was out in the hallway, wailing her lungs raw.

"Arrrggghhh! You HIT me! Filho da puta-aa! You never gonna see me again, nu-unca! Never no more, sua merda! Filho da puta-aaaahhh!"

She ran off, howling like a flaming demon in hellfire, her angry curses echoing off my neighbors' doors all the way down the hall, stomping down the stairs like a herd of rhinos, shrieking all the way.

I listened in dread. Then she was gone.

My heart slunk like a whipped dog into its corner . . . *Shit shit shit!*

Consumed with remorse, I hurried down the stairway behind her, cursing myself with every step . . . *Shit shit shit shit shit shit shit!*

By the time I ran out into the street, she was gone . . . *Shit!*

I looked around in panic . . . *Where the fuck is she? Fuck!* I jumped on my motorcycle and rode up the block, going slow, looking left, looking right, looking, looking . . . *Shit! Shit! Shit! Where the fuck is this fucking head case?*

Finally, I caught up to her on the corner. She was standing in the middle of the busy sidewalk, crying, shouting, cursing, wailing.

I got off the bike and ran over. "*Stop* this shit, Narcisa!" I grabbed her by the arms and shook her. "Just shut th' fuck up, ya loony bitch!"

Emboldened by the presence of spectators, she spit a big green wad of crack-polluted phlegm right into my face.

Fu-uck! That did it.

I shook her till her eyes rattled, then brandished a big, angry, white-knuckled fist under her nose. ***"Narcisa, stop this fuckin' shit right now, motherfucker, or I swear to Christ, I will beat you till I'm fuckin' tired! And I don't give a shit who's watching!"*** I turned to the crowd of people and glowered. ***"Anybody got a fuckin' problem with that?"***

They shuffled away. It was just me and Narcisa.

I glared at her. "Let's go, you! C'mon! *'Bora!*"

Cowed, she crumbled at my feet, cowering, whimpering like a whipped mutt. ***"Okey, okey, Cigano! Plee-ease! Don' beat me no more! Por favor!"***

I could see she was working herself up into a state of blind hysteria again, blubbering, crying and hyperventilating in fast, spastic little pants, like a dog. Then, without warning, she pulled her pants down. Squatting on the sidewalk, she started peeing, a cowering puppy swatted with a newspaper.

Shit! Right then, I saw it all clearly: something I'd never fully gotten before . . . *That's it! There it is* . . . The shadow of all the terrors she'd provoked for herself over the years. Narcisa was reliving it all in a monstrous, self-perpetuating, endless nightmare loop of trauma; reviving all the injuries of her abused, mangled, mutilated inner child.

She never talked about it much, but I could see it all in that sad, doleful moment. All the beatings she had taken all her life had left Narcisa permanently shell-shocked, traumatized forever. And still, she was constantly asking for more. She'd been doing the same thing over and over for years, I realized, like some fucked-up, unconscious need to punish herself, to beat herself up for the crime of existing . . . *Shit! Poor baby! What a fucking mess!*

Finally, she began to run out of momentum. Seizing the moment, I apologized. I groveled and begged her forgiveness.

It worked. Narcisa relented . . . *Truce! Thank God!* We were both tired.

As we shuffled back into my building, past the disapproving stares of neighbors on the sidewalk, I didn't care. I was just relieved the latest battle was over.

Back upstairs, Narcisa's mood brightened. With a nervous little grin, she told me how, as she'd heard my motorcycle approaching, she'd run to a pay phone to call someone for help; but the number she dialed was mine. We both laughed as she recounted how the phone had rung and rung, unanswered, while I cruised up the street, looking for her.

I was still chuckling when I saw her expression shift.

Oh, shit! What now? Her grin faded as she explained that's when she'd pushed the panic button. She went on with a sheepish look, telling me she'd hung up, then made another call.

I looked at her in dread . . . *What now? Don't tell me this crazy freak show called the fucking cops on me! No! She wouldn't . . . Would she?*

Narcisa stared at the floor, mumbling that she'd rung Doc.

"What?"

I stared at her till she hung her head in shame. Then, with another little shit-eating grin, she stammered some sort of an apology.

"*Arggh*, whatever." I shrugged. "Forget it. It's done. Don't worry about it, baby . . ."

She grinned and got undressed, and we climbed up to bed. She was going to make it all up to me now, the only way she knew how. As Narcisa worked her magic, I put the whole affair out of my mind, like a bad dream.

An hour later, we were kicking back on the sofa, smoking cigarettes, talking about our upcoming trip, when a frantic knocking came at the door.

I got up, thinking it was the guy I'd called to fix the lock she'd broken. . . . *Wrong!*

Doc barged right in and pushed past me, stumbling across the room, huffing and puffing like a hyperactive clown. ***"Narcisa! Querida-ah!"*** He stood in front of her, whimpering like a cocker spaniel bitch reunited with its missing puppy. ***"My poor, daah-ling daughter! Thank heavens you're all right! Get your belongings, Narcisa! I'm taking you to a safe place, far away from this horrible, depraved monster!"***

I was too shocked to move. Before I could grab him by the throat and give him the bum's rush, Narcisa flew up in his face and ordered him out. Baffled and rebuked, the murdering little psycho slunk out the door, glaring at me with a chilling gray look of stifled rage. And then he was gone . . . *Slithered out of a beating again!*

Somehow, we wrangled each other through the rest of the morning.

The time had come at last. The road was calling.

Narcisa nodded at me and winked as I put on my jacket and stuffed a change of underwear and a toothbrush into my pocket.

73. ON THE ROAD

"Bizarre travel plans are dancing lessons from God."
—*Kurt Vonnegut*

Blasting through the raging downtown traffic, I grinned like a happy dog, luxuriating in the long-awaited magical moment unfolding. As we dodged through the mad, horn-blaring, bubbling stew of cars, trucks and buses, I pondered our upcoming adventure with growing excitement, Narcisa clinging to my back like a needy, greedy monkey, singing her crazy little alien anthem: *"Can you show me, where's de exit, to these e'sheet world? Cuz I tire tire tire of de human being . . ."*

Inhaling sputtering black gusts of diesel exhaust, we followed the endless toxic river of Avenida Brasil out into the dark, foul-smelling outskirts of the city. The apocalyptic outlying slums were a spinning, septic whirlwind of poverty and chaos, punctuated by the ever-present trudging legions of ragged, haggard street vendors, weaving in and out among the stalled vehicles like hungry dogs. I took it all in, like a dream . . .

Cars, trucks, buses, dogs, motorcycles, jeeps, vans, bicycles, an endless zombie procession of sweaty human traffic, staggering, standing in the road like sluggish statues of defeat, selling roasted peanuts, cheap paçoca candy and bottles of água mineral, ass-drip open-sewer ghetto-rat-shit tap water they put into old plastic bottles. Humanity. Shirtless sweating, rapacious rat hordes of hell, selling everything, bargaining, hawking, bartering, pawning, wagering their tired little lives, their souls, their asses, their dying, decaying grandmothers' pussy fart's straggling, haggling, whoring ghosts. Hopeless lost souls of hell, trudging through a decaying shitstream of traffic, wandering, somnambulant herds of the damned, peddling, touting, vending, begging, cheating, stealing, lying, living and dying, drowning in ass-reeking, undulating oceans of infected shit-brown mosquito dung ass-water, suffocating, miserable beggars of forgotten progress and boundless disorder, shuffling back and forth from car to car in a perpetual dead-end gridlock maze of lack and loss, strife, frustration and impotence, suppressed, drooling rage and seething, soul-stifling, lifelong destitution, disappointment and death. Interminable poverty-stricken thundering minions of hell, an overflowing stampede of rancid humanity, spilling like cockroaches from bottomless miles of putrid favela sewers, and the whole fucking earth is a vile, vacuous ghetto of the soul in this festering open wound on the face of our world, our reality, our godforsaken planet's living, breathing, choking, smoking, hopeless, hateful urban hellscape . . . Our City of God, Rio de Janeiro, in the Year of Our Lord, 2010 . . . Fuck! Can you show me, where's de exit, to these e'sheet world? Get me the fuck outa here!

Sweating, wincing, holding my breath, I gunned the motor harder, harder, traversing the sprawling tangle of blighted ghettos, till finally, the teeming, reeking industrial wastelands of the city faded into a fetid, septic mist behind us; and then, like magic, we were cruising along a long, empty stretch of road, breathing in a clean new scent of lush, tropical green humidity and fertile red earth, a slow-motion, freeze-frame slide show of the senses.

Surfing the shimmering black ribbon of highway into a warm southern wind, it was like an old movie I'd seen before, a long time ago. My heart rejoiced as we rolled along under expansive blue skies, past green hills and pastures of grazing cattle, a gigantic mountain range looming in the distance as we made our way toward the country village of Penedo.

Penedo. A couple of hours south of Rio, Narcisa's little hometown sat nestled in a fecund, fertile valley, surrounded by a towering mountain range and an infinite expanse of wild, untouched rain forests. I knew the place vaguely, having passed through it a few times, long ago in my travels; a breathtaking mountain paradise, where weekenders fleeing the choking metropolitan infernos of Rio and São Paulo flocked to bask in its pristine scenery and cool country climate.

Riding along, I conjured up utopian images of the crystalline waterfalls and fresh, oxygen-laden air ahead; an idyllic pastoral setting, where, Once Upon a Time, Narcisa had run free and unencumbered, an enchanted fairy-tale princess, bouncing through the magical woods of childhood, innocent, happy and free—before destiny gave her an angry shove down the road to hell.

Approaching the outskirts, just as we passed a palm-roofed roadside hut selling coconuts and bananas, Narcisa began slapping me on the back.

Over the roar of the motor, I could hear her shouting.

"Pare! Pare aqui!! E'stop here, Cigano. E'stop!"

Slowing the bike, I pulled over to the side of the highway. "Wassup, baby? Ya gotta pee?" I cut the motor and waited.

Still sitting behind me on the motorcycle, Narcisa lit a cigarette. After she'd taken a couple of pulls, I reached over, plucked it from her fingers and took a long, deep drag.

Bad move.

She freaked. *"Arrgghh! Filho da puta! These is my cigarette! Odio! Arrrgghhh! Fock you! I haa-aate you!"*

Fuck! I'd forgotten during our calm, scenic ride that Narcisa without her drugs would be as volatile as a truckload of traveling nitro . . . *Shit!* Before I knew what was happening, she'd exploded into a screeching, demonic fury. Leaping off the bike like a lightning bolt, red-faced, shouting, raving, she landed in the middle of the highway, right in front of an oncoming truck!

Oh fuck! No! Truck! Truck! Barreling down on her like a freight train! Shit! No time to think! Flash! Adrenaline! Panic! Grabbing her, yanking her out of the jaws of death as the truck flashes by, big horn booming like a bomb blast, and it's gone!

Gone! Sweet Jesus! Just one more second to death!

I winced as I watched the screaming behemoth speeding off in the distance. In a shuddering flash I pictured the horror of witnessing Narcisa's death . . . *Flattened! Roadkill! Narcisa! Bones and guts splattered across the highway in a bloody red mist! Jesus!*

Obrigado, Senhor! Thank you God! Thank you!

Did Narcisa thank me for salvaging her life again? Maybe, in her own strange way. As we stood by the side of the highway, she began pointing and waving at the ruins of an old shack, about a hundred meters back from the road.

I looked up into the dense jungle clearing. What was left of the dilapidated hovel was half consumed by overgrowth.

"Lookit, Cigano!" Her eyes filled with angry tears. "See de little *casinha* over there? Is de e'same wonderful home where I grow up with my beautiful mother! Nice place, hein? Hah! I wonder if it e'still got blood on de walls from when these e'stupid bitch get e'stab by her focking trick!"

I looked at her, not knowing what to say.

"Yeh, bro, I got it de very good memory of these focking place! Got it all, right inside here!" She dug her finger like a knife into the side of her head. "I only six year old when I gotta save these e'stupid witch life in there! Hah! I shoulda leave her to die! E'same place when I twelve year old I get rape by these ridiculous woman friend when she pass out drunk! *Puta babaca!* I cry an' cry, but she never come an' help me! Only me ever gotta give de help to her! Hah! Now you understand, Cigano? You happy now, hein?"

Standing by the side of the road, haunted by the phantoms of her savage past, Narcisa broke down and sobbed. I could feel the pain behind her tears. Unlike her usual bouts of maudlin self-pity, I knew she was crying for something wounded deep inside, mourning a brutalized, traumatized child.

Her sudden urgent impulse to stop at that particular place, and her subsequent dive into the road there, all began to make sense. In that moment, everything about Narcisa became clear to me: her hungry, hyperactive lust for life, and her bitter, cynical hatred of it; her nihilism and passion and fierce, furious intensity.

Standing beside her, I watched my little friend being mugged and raped again and again, dragged down into the dungeon, the angry torture chamber of her memory. Those deep, unconscious drives that push us all around like rag dolls had just pushed poor Narcisa right into the path of a speeding truck.

She was exhuming her childhood, crying for each dark, secret injury of the past. As the tears rolled down her face, I felt a powerful wave of love and compassion. Still, I knew there was nothing I could say or do that would ever make it better. I just stood there beside her, a silent witness to her suffering, thinking . . . *Maybe love really is the only hope of redemption for people like us . . . Maybe if I can just love her enough . . .* I hoped and prayed it was true—that maybe this fucked-up, blood-thirsty, painful love was a sort of spiritual surgery, a last little chance for redemption for us both. Maybe confronting our wounds together could help us mend our crippled souls somehow.

I tried to hug her and she let me, but only for a moment.

Then, as if suddenly reminded of her own hopelessness, she broke away and stormed off down the highway, shouting that she was through with me forever, that I should go back to Rio, that she was sick of me, that this would never work out.

I followed along in silence, letting her walk off her rage, but staying close behind her, just in case she got any ideas of jumping in front of another vehicle. She didn't, of course. I knew that hadn't been a conscious move. Narcisa was basically a coward, a runner, like me.

Still, I caught her by the wrist just as another big truck roared by.

"Sai fora, cara!" She yanked her arm away. *"Vaa-aaza, porra! Just go away, Cigano! Beat it! Go!"* She stomped off again, crying and howling like a wounded, tortured ghost as I hurried along behind her.

After a minute, she stopped and turned around to face me.

"Porra, Cigano! Mete o pé, vai! Just go an' leave me alone, go! I already e'say to you it won' never work, porra! I warn you long time ago when you first go with me!"

I could see the agony in her face, her flashing red eyes. Unable to speak, I just stood there facing her, feeling powerless and sad.

"Yeh, now you got it! Now you got it all de focking trouble that I am! Just go back now, Cigano, go! I am unlucky to you! I unlucky to every-body, okey? Got it now?"

I got it. Narcisa was drowning in a stinking, solitary cesspool of self-hate. And I knew I couldn't leave her there all alone. She turned and started walking away again. I kept pace as she stumbled down the highway, yelling over her shoulder.

"Get de fuck out, Cigano, vai, porra! Vaza! Beat it! Rala o peito, mermão, vá embora, vai! Go back to Rio an' leave me die here alone. Narcisa no you problema no more . . ."

That did it. I grabbed her by the shoulders and spun her around to face me. *"Lissen! I already told ya, Narcisa! It's too fuckin' late for that!"*

She looked at me and I looked back. Time stopped. If God is Love, I could see His face right there in the burning depths of her eyes.

I heard my own voice shouting, pleading. *"Years I've loved you, Narcisa! Since the first day we met! Since before I was born! I was born to love you, don't you get it? You ARE my fucking problem!"*

She crossed her arms like a pair of swords and glared.

"All right, goddammit!" I was crying now too. *"If ya really wanna die, Narcisa, it's okay with me! I will respect your decision, all right? What else can I do? But just know this: remember the time you asked me not to give up on you and I said I wouldn't? Well, that was a promise I made! Um compromisso! That means something! It's important, got it?"*

She kept looking at me, saying nothing. I knew Narcisa would rather have flaming bamboo shoots shoved under her eyeballs than ever admit it, but she got it.

She dried her eyes and told me to shut the fuck up.

I shut the fuck up.

She didn't say anything more as she followed me back to the bike. Without a word, she got on. She sat in silence for the rest of the ride.

I didn't know it then, but her desire to return to the place of her birth in an effort to get clean was significant in some deep, unconscious way; like a primal homing instinct; some sort of profound self-healing process struggling to emerge from the depths of her soul.

It was as if Narcisa, by intuition, was seeking a cure for the Curse by diving blindly into the festering, buried wounds that fed it; that dark, ugly corridor of memory roots, going all the way down to the core of the deadly soul sickness of her addiction.

Our Trip to the Country was destined to be a fumbling, half-hearted, weak attempt by Narcisa to meet the Curse head-on.

But it was an honest and valiant attempt, all the same. And I respected her all the more for the courage of her intention—even as I continued to despise the goddamned Curse she carried, with a hatred that was sublime.

74. TANGLED ROOTS

It was almost dusk when we pulled into Resende, the medium-sized neighboring city just before Penedo on the highway. Narcisa still had family and friends scattered around the area from the days of her youth. Even though she was only nineteen, that youth seemed a lifetime ago, long buried under furious years of ashes, road dust and ruin.

Our first stop was some guy's house, where she picked up an old bag of clothes she'd stashed there God knows how many months or years before.

As she fetched her stuff, I remembered her leaving a similar satchel with me, back before she'd disappeared to New York. It was still sitting in my closet. As I stood watching, Narcisa spilled the contents of her bag out onto the sidewalk, extracting a moth-eaten wool-lined sheepskin jacket for the cold mountain nights ahead.

Narcisa, like any good gypsy, had lived her whole life on the road. And, like me, she had all these little stashes of clothes and books and gewgaws stored all over the place. Watching her rummaging through her stuff, like an archeologist opening the Mummy's Tomb, I could relate. I still had things of my own stashed with people all over the world.

As we walked back to the bike, I noticed a ratty-looking hairball of an old, decrepit bum shuffling up the street toward us. In painful slow motion, he limped forward, staggering under the unbearable weight of the sky.

Thinking he was going to ask for change, I reached in my pocket for some coins. As he drew closer, though, I realized he was only in his early twenties, maybe even younger . . . *Woah! This poor guy's tore up from the fucking floor up . . . Musta been a rough night!*

As he made his excruciating approach, I winced. His was not an easy face to look upon. Sporting two black eyes, a crusty, freshly broken nose and other nasty contusions and abrasions, he was covered in dried blood and filth.

Suddenly Narcisa dropped her bag and strode right up to him.

With a split lip and bloody, broken brown teeth, her old friend contorted his mouth into a brave little smile, squinting into the sunlight. "Long time no see, Narcisa."

She frowned. "What de fock they do to you now, hein?"

"What I done to myself is more like it . . . You know, the usual shit."

She grinned, shaking her head. "Yeh, well, take care you-self, bro . . ."

"Yeah, you too, Narcisa . . ."

That was it. He shuffled off down the street.

She got back on the bike and we rode off.

Rolling on through town, Narcisa told me the guy was one of her original gang of teenage stoners, kids she'd grown up with running the streets there before she'd taken off to Rio.

"He look pretty fock up now, Cigano, but he one of de few most lucky one . . ." She let out a bitter little guffaw.

"Whaddya mean?" I grimaced. "Guy didn't look any too lucky to me."

"Yah, well he more luckier than most de peoples I know here, bro. He still alive. Hah! Ever'body else I know in these focking place dead or prison, Cigano. All de peoples I grow up with was de drugs addict, e'same like me."

"Everybody?"

Narcisa chuckled. "Ever focking body, brother! Hah! From de time we was just little childrens here, we all just wanna be high all de time. We use to wait de big truck come e'spray poison for de mosquito, an' we all go run behind for inhale de chemical an' get de buzz, ha ha!"

Riding along past all her familiar old haunts, Narcisa kept chattering in my ear, reminiscing out loud, with dark, humorous bravado. "Hah! First time I take de real drug, Cigano, I was only five year old!"

"Ya got loaded when you were five? How? On what?"

"*Poisé, mermão!* I chew up de whole bottle of de diazepam from my mother drawer. Hah! I get *so-oo* fock up, bro, they gotta take me to de hospital for get my stomach suck out. But I know from very first time I *like* it, got it? Hah!"

She giggled like a kid, reveling in the memories. "Lissen these! When I e'stone like that, a mosquito come an' sit on my hand, but I only look him, cuz I too fock up for even kill these little animal, got it? I sit an' watch he e'stick de little needle in de e'skin for drink my blood, an' then, *boo*! His little leg go all soft an' then he fall over an' dead, bro! *Fock!* Overdose! Hah! I e'say, *wooooo-woooo! Perfect, Max!* Hah! *Thank you come again! Next?*"

I laughed. Narcisa's cheerful mood was contagious. Things were hopeful. Confession being good for the soul, getting out of Rio seemed to be doing her much good already.

Slapping me on the back, she kept talking. "Lissen these e'sheet, Cigano! When I was twelve year old, I go e'smoke all de time in de favela over here with my friend, guy name Ricardo, sixteen-year-old boy, he always got it de best drug cuz he work for de local gang, got it? One time I gone up in de favela with him, an' then de other gang come in for invade de *boca*, e'same like de Rio, shooting guns, *bum bum bum! Fock!* One bullet pass right by my head, so close she lift my hair up an' I feel de hot on my ear, *wssshh*! My friend jump up in front of me to shoot, an' then *pim!* De whole top of he head come off! *Caralho!* I got de guy brain all on my face! *So-oo* much blood ever'where! *Porra!*"

I made the sign of the cross as Narcisa grew quiet.

We rode along in silence for a while, following a wide brown river.

"These always been my reality, hein, Cigano." She sighed as I maneuvered across a clattery old wooden bridge. "Ever'body I know here long time dead. All but me! An' I always e'stay thinking, 'Why only me, hein?'"

Why indeed? Again, I was reminded of my own twisted, bloody roots. Like Narcisa, I had a whole lot of friends on the other side.

Our next stop was her grandmother's place, on the outskirts of town.

A world of birds sang from a big, looming shade tree as I pulled up to a humble little one-story house on a sleepy backstreet. Narcisa hopped off the bike and marched right in, as if she were coming from around the corner, rather than years of mysterious absence.

Snatching a banana from a wicker basket on an ancient wooden table, she devoured it in two quick bites. I stood in the doorway, watching with amusement as she paced in hyperactive circles around the shadowy space, exchanging monosyllabic monkey grunts with a gray, faceless old woman.

It all seemed strange. I couldn't imagine Narcisa even having a grandmother—as if she'd just been hatched and slithered out from under a rock or something. The haggard-looking crow talked over her shoulder as she washed some dishes. Narcisa didn't bother introducing me, of course, as I lingered in the doorway, neither in nor out. The woman didn't even glance in my direction as I stood there like a statue, waiting for the awkward visit to end.

After a few minutes, Narcisa grinned and pulled me outside by the arm, and that was it . . . *Thank you come again! Next?* It was all a familiar fucked-up family routine.

Motoring through the neat little provincial city's center, she unloaded a rambling narrative into my ear. "I am *infamo* in these e'stupid town, Cigano. Notorious! That's me." Her hot breath on my neck gave me a quick chill. "Hah! I use to torment ever'body in these e'sheet place. Is only e'stupid clones peoples here, you know?"

Chattering on nonstop, Narcisa pointed the way along the rough cobblestones. ***"Hah! Well, now I am back!"*** She spun around behind me, hurling gleeful insults at some astonished pedestrians standing on a corner. ***"Got it, you e'stupid focking monkey-face clone peoples? Hah! Now you got it!"***

"God help th' poor bastards, baby!" I laughed, running my hand over her knee as we rolled along the quiet, tree-lined streets.

Narcisa was approaching her first full day of abstinence. I grinned with satisfaction. She was really doing it! A whole twenty-four hours off drugs! Fifteen minutes later, we were riding along the base of a towering granite mountain range, arriving at last in the quiet country village of Penedo.

We checked into a charming rustic chalet beside a babbling stream, then went for a stroll through the empty streets of the placid off-season resort. The night was cool and smelled of wet earth, pinecones, wood smoke and the vast, insect-twittering jungles beyond.

We went into a cozy wood-paneled inn, sat at a big wooden table and ordered some steaks. While we waited for the food, Narcisa led me across the street to a little Finnish *sorveteria*. Dessert always preceded a meal for Narcisa. Just because. We stuffed ourselves on ice cream; every sticky candy-coated gummy bear topping on hers.

Then we went back over to the restaurant for a real sit-down country dinner. There were candlelight and linen napkins, a crackling fireplace, the works. We sat talking in low, intimate tones, looking for all the world like a normal little honeymoon couple. And Narcisa was eating! It was astounding. She was even making plans.

Tomorrow, she declared, we'd go up the mountain to visit the magical waterfalls and all her special, sacred places; a mystical world where she'd spent an enchanted childhood surrounded by fairies and high spirits of the Intergalactic Ashtar Command, benevolent psychedelic visions and positive vibrations. That's how it had all been, she reminisced, back in the beginning, before all the violence and madness and chaos of the Curse.

As she chattered on, I smiled; Narcisa was coming home at last, to reclaim her innocence, her goodness, her youth. And she was sharing it all with me! Life was good!

Finishing our meal, we sat quietly, sharing a cigarette and coffee. After a while, she told me she wanted to score a dime bag of weed.

I gave her a look. "Are you serious?"

No big deal, she assured me, just a "little something to take the edge off," so she could get some rest. The way she put it, it sounded okay . . . *Sorta* . . . *Maybe not the best plan in the world, but whatever . . . Just to hear her talking of sleep . . . What harm can a few joints do?*

I fired up the bike and we rode off into the cool, crisp night air.

Passing through Resende again, she directed me along the placid, tree-lined streets of humble dwellings and little corner stores. As we came to the outskirts, the scenery began to change. The commerce became sparse, the streetlights disappeared, the houses thinned out, and then it was all dirt roads, crooked clotheslines and garbage-strewn, dusty, dark, winding ghetto paths. Everywhere I looked were decrepit, run-down hovels, muddy dead-end pathways and miserable dead-end lives. Favelas. We rode on, past block upon block of creeping, septic slums; a crazy quilt of sorrowful little tin-roofed shacks, constructed of wooden crates and discarded cardboard political posters, the smiling, well-groomed faces graffittied with mustaches, vampire teeth and devil horns.

As I slowed for a big pothole, a motorbike with two skinny teenage riders passed. The pilot flashed a casual thumbs-up. Narcisa returned the gesture. They seemed to know each other. As the bike sped ahead, I saw a small black Uzi dangling from the passenger's shirtless back.

We came to a little dirt clearing. She told me to stop and wait for her. Snatching the ten-spot from my hand before I could speak, she sprinted across the road and up a steep dirt path, disappearing into a cluster of shacks half hidden in a dense patch of banana plants.

With a weary sigh, I leaned back on the bike, my feet resting on the handlebars, waiting, watching a gang of tattered, barefoot Negro children playing soccer in the dust.

Everything smelled of shit and urine and rotting meat. Massive gray pigs foraged through piles of garbage, rolling around in the murky, mosquito-infested black mud. Another pack of kids was competing with the hogs, picking at the trash, looking for something to eat.

A swarm of buzzards circled above, waiting for something to die.

Exhausted, I leaned back on the seat and dozed off.

75. IN THE COUNTRY

A rooster crowed, snapping me out of a sweaty stupor. Time had passed. I sat up on the bike and looked around.

How long . . . ?

I checked my watch.

Forty-five minutes? What the fuck? Where is she?

Getting off the motorcycle, I stood there in the dirt, looking up and down the road. Skinny chickens scratched at the ground across the way.

Silence. No Narcisa.

She's taking a long fucking time for just going to score a little bag of weed . . . Wait a minute . . . No! How? Could she . . . ? No! Not here!

I spotted her creeping across the road with that jerky, spastic body language I knew so well.

Aw, shit! No! Really?

She shuffled up and stood before me in guilty silence, shifting from foot to foot, staring at the ground, confirming my worst fears.

Shit! Of course! She could find a crack spot on the fucking moon!

She stood there, tapping her foot, her eyes averted.

I looked at her and sighed . . . *Shit! Shit! Shit!*

Finally, she broke the silence. "I fock it all up again, Cigano . . ."

I just stared at her.

She shrugged, looking up at me with those big, tragic brown eyes. "Yeah? So what now?"

"You know . . ." she mumbled with another helpless little shrug.

I knew. I pleaded with her to reconsider. We'd planned this trip for so long, come all this way . . . *blah blah blah*.

Narcisa stood her ground, of course. I relented. Of course. I gave up and shut up. I reached in my pocket for the money. What else could I do? I told her she'd better not even *think* of smoking up in that fucking shack again.

She nodded with a shy little grin.

"I'm serious, Narcisa. If yer not back in five fuckin' minutes, I swear to Christ, I'm leaving yer pathetic crack-smoking ass down here and goin' back to Rio alone, and ya can go fuck yerself! Got it?"

She nodded again, without the grin this time. She got it. She gave me a quick, tight, shamefaced little hug, then snatched the money from my hand and sprinted away.

I stood in the dirt, shaking my head, frowning as she ran off like a happy kid on her way to an amusement park . . . *There she goes! Off to the Magical Kingdom of Psycho-land! Shit!*

I sat back down on the bike and waited, brooding, glancing at my watch. Four minutes and thirty-two pissed-off seconds later, I turned the key and fired up the engine.

Fuck this crazy bitch! I'm outa here!

Right then, Narcisa came charging across the road like a doe with its tail on fire.

"Go go go, Cigano, go go . . ."

She jumped on back and squeezed me tight as I tore rubber and dust out of there.

Fifteen minutes later, we were back in the chalet; our quaint little honeymoon hideaway with the babbling fucking brook.

Narcisa made a beeline for the bathroom and it was on. Again. All of it.

She crept back into the room, then got down on all fours and started crawling around on the floor like a mortally wounded anteater.

Great! Here we go again . . . Instant full-blown crack cocaine psychosis . . . Just like that, just like back in Rio! Shit! Goddammit!

I looked on in disgust as Narcisa smoked and her mind unraveled. I was growing dizzy just watching her . . . *Jesus! Hugging the walls . . . Peeping out under the door . . . Switching the lights on and off . . . The TV . . . On . . . Off . . . The water . . . On . . . Off . . . Bathroom door open . . . Closed . . . Open again . . . Toilet seat up . . . Down . . . Lights on . . . Lights off . . . Fuck! . . . Creeping, peeking, peering, crawling, bugging, tweaking, spun . . . Shit!*

So began our first night in the country.

After a few hours, of course, she needed to go back for more.

I tried to talk her out of it. "Baby! We came all the way out here for you to get *off* that shit, remember?" I put a gentle hand on her shoulder. "Just *think*, Narcisa. *Pense! Por favor!* There's still time to get off this hamster wheel, man!"

I might as well have been trying to convince her to put on a clown suit and eat a sack of raw potatoes. She just stood there, looking down, shaking her head back and forth like a stubborn old donkey.

She looked into my eyes, whining. "Is no good now, Cigano. I already e'start it! I gotta go all de way. Just one more time, *por favor*! No way I gonna e'stop now, *porra, cara* . . ."

I knew it was true. I conceded. I'd take her to cop again. There was just one little thing that had to be taken care of first.

She knew.

Stripping her jeans off and flinging them in the corner, she lay back on the bed. "Hurry up an' go fast now, Cigano, don' take too long, go!"

I worked it home . . . *Fuck! Sweet home!*

"Go, Cigano, go go! Finish fast, hurry, hurry up, *go, go* . . ."

"Shut th' fuck up, Narcisa! How'd ya like me to tell ya to hurry up while you're smoking yer fuckin' crack?"

"Menos, Cigano! Less talk! Go!"

"You got your drug and I got mine. Respect that! Got it?"

She got it. She lay back and took it like a pro till we were both soaked in sweat.

An hour later we were speeding through the night again.

And so it went. Our first couple of days in the country.

It was the sleep deprivation that got me at the end of day two, going into day three.

Blurry-eyed, I told her I'd had enough, that she was going to have to give it a break and let me get some rest.

She flipped. ***"Fock you! I gonna keep e'smoking an' you no gonna e'stop me!"***

"Maybe I can't stop ya, Narcisa, but I can stop buying it for you."

Her eyes blazed. ***"You think I depending on you for any focking thing, you e'stupid old e'sheet!? I depend only on these e'sheet, Cigano, got it?!"*** She grabbed her crotch in her fist, clutching her pussy like a bag of salami. ***"Hah! I gonna go to de highway an' take ten bucks from every truck driver who e'stop till I got de money for keep e'smoking, got it?"***

I got it. Emotional blackmail. I sat just there, rolling my eyes.

Not getting the reaction she wanted, Narcisa turned up the volume, stomping around the cabin like an enraged baby storm trooper.

"Hah! Pau no seu cu, seu otário velho! Fock you, Cigano! If I go out these focking door, you never gonna see me again, got it!? You decision, mano! An' don' take too long time to think, or I gonna decide it for you, e'stupid old e'sheet!! Ar-rrggghhh!"

Calling her bluff, I said nothing. Did nothing.

I sat back on the bed, trying to rest my eyes.

It didn't take long.

Narcisa shot across the room and lunged for my pants.

Fuck! She was halfway to the door with my wallet when I jumped up and grabbed her. Spinning her around, I snagged it back. In a burning white flash, she grabbed an empty Coke bottle from the dresser, smashed it on the floor and gouged the jagged, angry glass into her wrist, hard.

I watched, paralyzed in horror, as she dug into the wound, fishing for a vein to pluck out.

She cried, wailing like an anguished ghost as dark red blood ran down her fingers, splattering onto the floor . . . *Oh God! Blood! Blood! Jabbing! Stabbing! Sharp! Glass! Bloody! Deep! Cutting! Blood! No no no, God, no! Blood blood, oh God, no no no! Stop!*

That was it. She won. Right then. Checkmate.

I ran over and grabbed her . . . *God God God!*

I threw her down on the bed. . . . *Oh, God, God! Blood blood! Make it stop! Oh, God, help me please, help us, God!* Tearing off a strip of bedsheet with my teeth, I could taste the hot, metallic fire of Narcisa's blood in my mouth as I tied it tight around the deep, bleeding wound . . . *Blood blood, bubbling from her wrist like oil! Fuck! Please, God, por favor, help me, help me, help me stop all the blood, blood blood blood blood blood blood!*

In a flash, I was reliving my dark past, sobbing, weeping, blubbering, telling her everything would be all right . . . *Okay, it's okay, I'll get you more crack! I'll buy you all the fucking drugs you want! I'll do anything, whatever you want! Oh God, please, baby, please please please, por favor, no! Just don't hurt yourself anymore! Oh God, stop the blood, please, God! Don't cry, don't die, please, baby! I'll take care of you! Please, please, God, please don't bleed, don't die, don't die again, don't leave me all alone again, please. I love you, don't go, no no no! Stop the blood, please, God! Don't die now, please please!*

Tears clouded my vision, and there I was again, standing in shorts and high socks. Little Ignácio, frozen in the doorway after school, breathing hard, crying, looking down at his mother lying on the floor, blood seeping across the dirty white tiles, a creeping, hellish red nightmare shadow . . . *Blood blood blood* . . . So much blood, blood, blood, weeping from the obscene, gaping dark wounds on both her wrists, her throat cut open . . . *Naked and red and dead dead dead* . . . *Please, Momma, please wake up! No no no, don't die, don't leave me all alone! Por favor por favor please please please, don't go, no no no no no!*

After a dark, heart-pounding eternity, Narcisa calmed down and started breathing normally again. I lay down beside her, holding her to me tight, hugging her as she sobbed and blubbered and shook. I had never felt so powerless, so unable to help someone—not since that awful day when little Ignácio was five years old. And in that moment, like that lost, confused little boy, I felt love. Love and sadness. A great sad wave of hopelessness swallowed my heart like the cold, dark mountain fog outside. All I could do was lie there and cry with Narcisa, holding her close as she wept and sobbed and trembled like a kitten in the rain.

I told her that everything would be all right—even though I didn't believe it. I held her and told her I'd do whatever she wanted, that I would always take care of her and protect her from the Curse. I didn't know how, but I would, goddammit! Over and over, I promised her protection and care, love and understanding and compassion, again and again, hypnotizing myself, taking myself back and back and back, again and again, until I was that little five-year-old ghost, promising his momma he'd save her, again and again and again; the only thing in this fucked-up miserable hell-pit of a world that ever fucking mattered.

76. TEARS OF A CLOWN

"There is always some madness in love. But there
is also always some reason in madness."
—*Nietzsche*

Our next couple of days in the country were a strange, blurry montage of marginally functional weirdness. Somehow we made it. Before leaving to go back to Rio, Narcisa insisted on going up the mountain to visit her special waterfalls; the secret spot where she'd first become aware of the World Unknown. The place where she'd known her happiest years as an innocent country girl, talking to the spirits, all alone in the wild green woods of childhood.

She spent the day there hunched over in a dark grotto beside the beautiful crystalline cascade, smoking crack, while I slept fitfully on a shady rock nearby.

On the ride back to Rio, Narcisa cried in heartbreaking spasms of remorse, for having sullied even her magical, sacred places now with her sickness, her sadness, her madness, her addiction: her Curse. I could hear her muttering, moaning, insulting, berating and cursing herself, all the way home, repeating the same tragic little words, over and over, again and again, in a low, unhappy self-hating growl, a hellish mantra of self-made torture.

"Idiota! You so e'stupid e'stupid e'stupid! So disrespect! So e'stupid, so disrespect, so disrespect, so e'stupid e'stupid e'stupid! Idiota!"

I knew Narcisa was waging a sad, solitary battle back there, struggling with her mind, her memories and traumas and terrors; fighting with the nightmare of her past, the disease, the demons, the crack, in waves of foul, unending torment, shadowboxing with herself, under the looming shadows of the Curse.

I rode along in silence, brooding, saying nothing, but thinking much . . . *Poor thing! And me, what the fuck was I thinking coming down here? Why why why?*

Never again! Not if I live another hundred fucking years, never again will I ever go back to the fucking country! Never! I promise! I swear to Christ! A solemn fucking oath!

B ack at my place again, it was as if we'd never left Rio; as if the whole trip had been one big, long, nasty hallucination, a fleeting fever dream.

That's when Narcisa gave me the only real present she'd ever given me.

Her ring. Silver and amethyst. Purple.

Maybe she was grateful I'd stuck around to care for her after her botched suicide attempt. Maybe I was "proving" myself to her at last.

Smiling, she popped it off her finger and handed it to me. I held it in my palm like a precious icon. I didn't know what to say. I stared at her and blinked as grateful tears welled up in my eyes.

"My grandmother give me these *anel*, Cigano, an' now is for you. From de Narcisa."

Beaming, I slipped it onto my pinky finger.

A perfect fit . . . Treasure!

After that, we started getting along better. As the days went by, her mood began improving, if in a typically surreal manner.

A few nights later, Narcisa showed up at my door, soaking wet, dressed in an extraordinary outfit; an improvised rain suit, pieced together entirely from multicolored plastic bags. She told me she'd snatched the makings of her stylish new ensemble from the raging favela alleys during the previous night's flashing tropical downpour.

The next afternoon, we went for a walk up in the old hilltop neighborhood of Santa Teresa. Still wearing her weird costume, Narcisa looked like a cross between a visiting alien queen and some kind of mad-eyed gutter punk samurai.

To add to the overall surreal effect, she'd donned that bright red plastic clown nose again. She'd just confiscated it back from her Casa Verde crony, Pluto, as we passed him at a busy intersection, juggling bottles, bumming coins from a captive audience of weary motorists.

Skipping alongside the crooked old trolley tracks, Narcisa chattered away like a hyperactive monkey, telling me about her hair-raising ninja adventure during last night's booming thunderstorm. Breathlessly, she described how she'd cheated the Reaper once again, as a fallen power line struck by lightning buzzed at her feet, a deadly high-voltage sidewinder, spraying sizzling sparks, twisting and writhing all around her. As she jabbered on, I could picture her out there in the middle of the raging storm, cracked out of her skull in some dark ghetto alleyway, hopping around like a drug-maddened matador.

Suddenly she stopped and looked at me. Her eyes grew wide as doughnuts.

"These focking sabotage was because of de *Doc*, Cigano!"

"What?"

"*Poisé, mermão!* These focking guy he try an' kee-eel me again in de night, got it? Only reason he don' succeeding these time cuz de Narcisa too fast for him! Hah!"

I looked at her in shock. She was convinced the fallen power line had been part of Doc's evil plot to do her in by electrocution, just as he'd dispatched his mother.

As we walked on, I sighed and said nothing.

After stopping at a little corner *paderia* for a snack, we were standing out front, smoking cigarettes and watching the world go by, when Narcisa's eyes zeroed in on a pair of stocky, pink-skinned white girls, foreign tourists, about her age, trudging past with backpacks and cameras, speaking English.

Suddenly, she called out. *"Hey, you! Oi! E'stupid gee-rool! Lissen to me! It don' matter how much focking mo-ney you got! You e'still always gonna be FAT!"*

The gringas turned, took one look at Narcisa and scurried off. She left me standing there and followed behind them, hounding, badgering, bedeviling them, shouting and gesturing, like some kind of wild-eyed, clown-garbed fire-and-brimstone Pentecostal evangelist.

"Hah! You wanna run away from de truth, hein, e'stupid? Hah! Go ahead an' run! Go an' make it you big visit to de Dr. Pitangi for get de e'spensive lippy-suction operation with all you focking dollar an' deutchmark an' pounds e'sterling!! But even he can no save you from de bad genetica, unlucky cow! Mooo-ooo! Hah! You can go an' buy it all de Calvin Kleins an' de Dolce Gabbana, de Versace, de Chanel, de Louis Vuitton! But always, always you gonna be de fat-ass ugly e'sheet eater pig! Chicken head with two fat elephant bottom! You born to be fat, an' you gonna die fat, fat, FAA—AAT, GOT IT?!"

Cringing with embarrassment, I lunged along behind her as she raved on at the top of her lungs. People stopped on the sidewalk to gawk.

When I caught up to her and hustled her away, Narcisa was howling with glee. "Hah! I *ha-ate* it all de fat peoples, Cigano! E'special most I hate de fat rich ugly *gee-rool*! An' de e'stupid foreigner too! Hah! I never miss one little chance to insult these e'sheet-face e'stupid little cow peoples, got it?"

I got it. What could I say? That was Narcisa. And I loved her. The good and the bad; all the monumental extremes and insane, passionate contradictions of her. I loved her, and I loved it all. Only God knows why.

Maybe because nobody else could or would.

Back home, still half dressed in her Raggedy Ann clown getup, Narcisa tried to start a big fucking fight with me. Literally. It all started because I wasn't fucking her fast enough!

I'd been giving her the big daddy long-stroke for over an hour, hitting it slow and steady, enjoying every moment, each holy detail, fucking her like it was the fucking Fuck Olympics. Narcisa was still wearing her clown nose—which at that point I was just trying to ignore.

Suddenly, without warning, she looked up at me with those big, bulging lunatic eyes.

Then she said it: ***"BO-RING!!"***

What?!?

Shit! I kept going, stroking it faster, wanting to climax and get it over with.

That's just what she was after, apparently.

"Boring, Cigano! Puta merda, cara! You focking like de old mans! Hurry up an' finish these boring e'stupid e'sheet now, vai, anda logo, porra!"

That did the trick. Without a word, I finished up and pulled out . . .

And just when everything was going so good lately . . . Shit!

Ball-breaking bitch! Thank you come again! I didn't really take it to heart, though. I already knew I was the only man who'd ever given her any sort of pleasure. This was just her way of taking revenge on me for inflicting that humiliating indignity on her.

The more I came to understand the bizarre, fucked-up pathology that made Narcisa tick, the less her insults had the power to hurt me. Narcisa could be as brutal and mean-spirited in bed as she was uninhibited, authentic and passionate in every other area. But the good sex was only when she was high as a jumbo jet. Without drugs, Narcisa's libido was frigid as a Popsicle.

Either way, though, she always liked to hit below the belt.

"Bo-ring! Hurry up an' finish, you e'sheet!! Gimme my focking money now, go, or I gonna kee-eel you when you e'sleep, e'stupid dick, go go go!"

I just shook my head and laughed to keep from crying.

77. THE PARTY

"THE WORLD IS FULL OF PEOPLE THAT HAVE STOPPED LISTENING
TO THEMSELVES OR HAVE LISTENED ONLY TO THEIR NEIGHBORS TO
LEARN WHAT THEY OUGHT TO DO, HOW THEY OUGHT TO BEHAVE,
AND WHAT THE VALUES ARE THAT THEY SHOULD BE LIVING FOR."
—*Joseph Campbell*

A few weeks later, I got invited to a party; some kind of posh little art reception for a painter acquaintance from the Rio Claro, the funky local bohemian café up in Santa Teresa that had been my regular hangout over the years of Narcisa's absence.

Narcisa had left me high and dry again, after starting another big fight over nothing. I was alone on another tedious Saturday night, with nothing to do but worry and brood.

Hoping to get my mind off her, I decided to go check out the party. Anything seemed better than sitting at home alone, worrying.

Since getting tangled up with Narcisa, I'd pretty much dropped off the face of the planet. Some of my friends and acquaintances seemed kind of concerned lately—especially the ones who'd seen me with her over the months. With the exception of Luciana, nobody really got my involvement with Narcisa.

Random people would call from time to time, making all sorts of stupid, irritating little comments—as if they knew anything about my fucking life.

"What you doing with that crazy crack-smoking freak, Ignácio?"

"You a good looking guy, man, smart, fun. You could get any girl you want!"

"Haven't seen you around lately, Ignácio! Where you been?"

"What's up with you and that crazy whore?"

"Jailbait! Cuidado, amigo!"

"Don't tell me she's staying with you now!"

"Man, you supposed to be street smart, brother, you gotta know better!"

"What's up, Ignácio? You all right?"

I felt all right, given my surreal circumstances. But I didn't know how to explain it to anyone. Moreover, I couldn't be bothered. I hadn't seen any of those people in ages, anyway.

They'd been calling a lot over the last few weeks, trying to pry me loose from my only drug, Narcisa. Wanting to get them all off my back, once and for all, I decided to make an appearance.

It was a typical warm, lively late-summer weekend in Rio. Narcisa was off running the streets again, doing whatever a Whore of Babylon does on a Saturday night. I'd been trying to keep from thinking about her, but it wasn't working.

I needed to get out and do something, anything.

As soon as I arrived at the address on the invite, I could tell at once it was nothing like the Rio Claro. This was one of those pretentious, trendy art gallery/restaurant/bars; just the sort of tiresome little bourgeois scene I'd normally shun like a leper colony. Bored and antsy, though, with nowhere else to go, I decided to stick around.

I parked the bike and shuffled up to the door. I gave my name to a big lumbering suit-and-tie motherfucker, and a burgundy velvet rope was held open for me.

Squeezing past all the fancy, fabulous-looking Beautiful People lined up outside, I sized up the festive atmosphere. Right away, my dark mood got darker. Inching my way through the crowd, I felt hideously out of place. All alone in that fashionable, groovy art setting, I was a strange, awkward bird, flying into a strange nest.

I could hear Narcisa's voice echoing in my head . . .

"Bo-oring!"

I pretended to look at the uninspired, overpriced, derivative "art-work" for a few minutes, then moved on, muttering. *"What a load of bland, pretentious crap!"*

After nodding to a few faceless people I barely knew and didn't care to know any better, I made a beeline past the bar and found a corner. Getting my back up against a wall, I stood there, feeling like an outsider looking in; a spy in the world of those squeaky-clean, trendy art types. I sneered as they sang and danced and laughed, hooting and shouting at each other above the music, exchanging backslaps and kisses and warm, familiar embraces.

I stood there. And I stood there. And I stood there some more . . .

The night dragged on, the drinks went down, and their loud, obnoxious party chatter got louder. Pretty soon, they were all drunk as a roomful of soccer fans . . . *Aggghhh! Those fucking high-pitched idiot voices! Like a battalion of screeching, squeaky, retarded brats!*

Drunks! I hate fucking drunks! Crackheads are so much more interesting!

Feeling increasingly alienated and uncomfortable, suddenly, it hit me . . . *Shit! I might as well be sitting in a fucking cave all alone, like Narcisa . . . I am alone here! I got nothing in common with any of these shitheads! Nothing! People . . . Shit . . . Who needs 'em? Why the hell am I even here? This is their world, not mine . . . Bastards all know each other . . . Me, I fit in here like a turd in a fucking punchbowl!*

The party was a strange, foreign, baffling little ceremony, filled with weird, unfathomable, unspoken codes of conduct I knew I would never get. I could feel it in the air; this vague, confusing sense of unity, bonding all those stuffy upper-class art types together; a mysterious, alien Something I could never be a part of. It was a depressing reminder of the persistent sense of dark alienation I'd always felt deep in my heart, all my life.

For some reason, though, I couldn't bring myself to just walk out. I stood there, chain-smoking, sucking on a soda, feeling painfully sober, wondering if I would ever fit in anywhere; or if I was forever condemned to a bitter, angry, morbid existence on the margins of human society . . . *Where are my fucking people, my tribe? Gypsies? Family? Friends? Hah! They're all long dead and gone! Ghosts. So who do I belong to in this world anymore?*

Nobody.

That's when it hit me, like a cold blue flapping tuna fish slap in the face.

Nobody, that's it! That's Narcisa! She's Nobody, and I'm Nobody too!

All of a sudden I was seeing the world through the shattered kaleidoscope of Narcisa's eyes. And it all looked senseless to me; drab and lifeless. Stupid, annoying . . . *Bo-ring!*

I stood there like a statue of Scorn, watching, taking in all the ugly details.

All the women looked painfully old to me, nasty, creepy, evil and corrupt. Faces like rotten fruit, eyes as insipid and dull as donkeys' assholes.

Disgusted, I started muttering under my breath. "Jesus! It's like a fuggin' plastic surgery convention gone wrong! Look at that withered old hag laughing over there, braying like a fucking mule! Ugh! Had so many fucking facelifts she looks like a dying cocker spaniel with its ears pulled back . . . Shit! What the fuck am I doing in this shithole?"

Lurking in the shadows, moping and groaning like an angry ghost, I sank deeper into a dark, depressed, cynical funk. The people all seemed to be moving in painful slow motion, like bloated squid floating around in a big cloudy bowl.

Look at these idiots! The Elite, the Rich, the Beautiful People . . . Vampires! Wealthy, privileged friends and relatives of a handpicked little mob of corrupt, bloodsucking politicians! Liars! Cheaters! Thieves! Murderers! Oppressors! Pam-

pered, overfed, soulless clones! Ugghhh! Rich people! Catholics! Fat-ass, useless, overfed, bloody bloodsuckers! Reptiles! Parasites!

I could hear Narcisa's disembodied shouts echoing in my inner ear, growing louder and louder . . . *"Porra! Que merda, Cigano! They should all be feeded to de homeless bums in de Lapa! Ha! Burn them an' eat de focking flesh!"* Her words sizzled in my brain like the crackling of rancid meat on a rusty favela grill; the troubled, trembling cry of my own frazzled soul . . . **"Hah! You can go an' buy it all de Calvin Kleins an' de Dolce Gabbana, de Versace, de Chanel! But always, all de life you gonna be de fat-ass ugly e'sheet-eater pig!"**

I eyed a pair of chubby girls, about Narcisa's age, chattering away gaily.

Shit! Where are the whores in this place? There aren't any! Not a single one!

"You all gonna die fat, fat, FAA-AAT, got it? Chicken face with two fat-ass elephant botttom! Ugh! You all de whoore! De lost whoore! Hah!" Her thoughts were my own thoughts, exploding in my brain like grenades on a haunted battlefield. *"Bo-ring! You loose it all you e'special whore magic now, e'stupid geer-ool! You all been corrupted by de society an' de television an' de e'stupid focking Jees-ooz Church!"*

I watched those girls and compared them to Narcisa. They seemed less than human. Sleepwalkers. Zombies. Cardboard cutouts . . . *Those boring, innocent, unformed, expressionless baby-doll mouths . . . Cold, complacent and lifeless . . . Plastic dolls, with souls of plastic!*

I realized these were the clone people Narcisa always talked about . . . *Stupid, predictable, chubby-faced plastic cherubs . . . Decorations . . . Trophies . . . Secure . . . Contented . . . Dead!*

Standing there in my dark, leprous corner, I felt like an invisible predator, lurking, leering, slobbering at a herd of fuzzy pink polyester bunnies. I wanted to rape and plunder and smash them all. Punish them! Set them on fire and watch them burn and melt into grotesque, insane, agonized aberrations like Narcisa.

As I felt the shadow of my solitude envelop me like a comfortable, warm straitjacket, I knew I'd been kidding myself, shedding pity on my indignant little friend; seeing her as a mad, antisocial witch, a sick, misanthropic freak of nature.

What shit! She's no more of a freak than I am!

Suddenly I missed Narcisa. I missed her like I'd never missed her before.

"What de fock you waiting for, hein, Cigano? Get de fock out from these e'sheet place, bro! Out! Go go go! Mooo-ooove, e'stupid!"

I beat it out the door like the devil was chasing my ass with fire.

78. QUEEN OF THE NIGHT

"For him without concentration there is not peace. And
for the unpeaceful, how can there be happiness?"
—*The Bhagavadgita*

As I crossed the street, loud music whipping at my back, the party was well on its way to becoming one of those tiresome affairs where bottles crash and flabby, unloved women howl like dying poodles into the indifferent night. I looked back. The place still hadn't burst into flames. Yet. I sucked my teeth and spat on the sidewalk.

Too bad.

Just as I got to the bike, my cell phone began to vibrate, jumping like a silent firecracker in my pocket. I fished it out and looked at the trembling, blinking blue screen.

Pay phone . . . Collect call . . . Narcisa! Yes! Thank you, Jesus!

Twenty minutes later, I rolled up to the corner by the Casa Verde, and there she was. Narcisa, the Queen of the Night; the eternal dirty-faced, homeless waif. She was crouched down in an empty doorway under the looming, scraggly shadows of a giant, ancient mango tree. Beside her sat the little bag of clothes she'd taken with her after our latest fight. On her lap were all her notebooks—a mini-library of the damned, filled with her illegible crack scrawls.

Narcisa was still scribbling furiously into one of the ash-blackened journals as I pulled up. She looked so meek and harmless in the shady yellow streetlight glow. Some poor fool out walking might even have mistaken her for an innocent schoolgirl sitting there doing her homework, writing in a schoolbook while waiting for her daddy—unless he looked a little closer. Then God pity the unlucky bastard!

I parked the bike and got off.

Edging over, I noticed Narsisa seemed uneasy, shaken, frazzled, afraid.

Fuck! Her eyes are big as saucers . . . She's all freaked-out . . . What now?

As I stood looking down at her with eyes of love, her voice reached out of the darkness like a prayer. "You don' wanna fight with me no more, hein, Cigano?"

"Of course not, baby! But, hey, ya look all stressed-out. What's up?"

Looking up with eyes like glowing globes, she told me she'd just come down from the favela, where some horrible new drama had occurred.

I sat down beside her, getting ready for another of Narcisa's frantic day-in-the-life accounts from the trenches of her interminable battle with life.

"Today is a very *ba-ad* day, mano . . ." She began describing how, just as she'd started to smoke her stash in a dingy little shack full of jittery, coked-up, trigger-happy bandidos, a rival gang had come rolling into the *boca*, guns ablaze, automatic weapons crackling in the dull, businesslike language of murder; business as usual up in the favela, but bad timing again for poor, shell-shocked little Narcisa.

One of the dealers had been sitting beside her, holding an AK-47 in one hand and a crack pipe in the other. Caught off guard, the guy had taken a slug to his head, which exploded like a rotten watermelon right before Narcisa's bugged-out eyes. She babbled on, spitting her words like bullets, telling me how she'd scrambled for cover and somehow managed to get out of the slum-turned-slaughterhouse.

"I *know* these boy, Cigano!" Big tears clouded her eyes, running down her face like beads falling from a rosary. "He just a young boy, an' he always was nice to me. *Porra!* All de time he use to tell me be careful. *Para que!?* Why I wan' be careful for, hein? He all de time too much careful up there with his big gun, an' look him now! His brains is de dog food! *Fock!*"

She grew quiet, replaying on the tattered movie screen of her mind the massacre she'd just witnessed. Tears flowed. I sat there beside her, feeling sad. I hugged her and whispered in her ear, telling her everything would be all right.

"I am sorry, Cigano! I am de devil! I only make it de big e'sheet an' de bad luck for ever'body. *Porra!* I am very sick in de brain!"

Stroking her long brown hair, I kissed her on the cheek, breathing in a hit of her wild, sensuous animal musk. "*Tudo bem, princesa. Relaxa.* It's over now."

Finally, she calmed down. I took her by the hand and led her over to the motorcycle. She seemed completely drained, depleted, as if a tooth had been knocked out of her face by what she had just experienced.

I shook my head and sighed. I knew Narcisa would never regain whatever little scrap of innocence she'd just surrendered. The Crack Monster was robbing her of herself, piece by piece. Whatever would eventually be left of her was going to be someone else. Someone without hope.

We rode back to my place in silence.

Once again, I thanked God for bringing her back to me alive.

A few days later, searching for Narcisa, I parked in front of the Casa Verde. Taking a deep breath, I got off the bike and ventured inside the rancid old squat. As I came to the top of the dark, rotting wooden stairway by her cramped attic hideaway, out of the corner of my eye I noticed a little flash from the shadows. Something was moving behind a crumbling plaster pillar to my left. *What's that? Some-*

body wearing a shiny watch or something . . . It was hard to make out in the dark, but I sensed it wasn't the usual faceless, glue-addled squatter. Someone wearing a watch or a chain was lurking in the hallway, right across from Narcisa's cubbyhole.

I could feel gooseflesh crawling up my back as I pulled the big switchblade from my back pocket and opened it with a resounding **CLACKKK!**

"Get th' fuck out from there!" I growled. "Show yer fuckin' face while ya still got one! Don't make me come and slice you up, fucker!"

I saw him recoil like a furtive gray rat, then scurry off down the stairwell.

Doc!

79. LOBOTOMY

"I SAW AND I KNEW THE SOUL OF HIM, WHO
COWARDLY MADE THE GREAT REFUSAL."
—*Dante*

I followed the old stalker as he scrambled out onto the street. Hurrying behind, I caught up with him halfway down the block.

He stared at me in shock as I grabbed him by the throat and pinned him to a sooty brick wall, working the knife blade up under his Adam's Apple.

"I guess it's time to have a foot-to-ass talk with you, ya little shit!" I barked, spittle flying into his ruddy red face.

His beady black bughouse eyes darted around as he began to struggle.

I gave him a poke with the point of the knife, drawing a thin bead of blood from his neck. *"Keep still or yer dead meat, motherfucker! Got it?"*

He got it. He went limp.

Right away, he started talking, pleading, whining. "Please, Cigano! *Por favor*, allow me to explain! It's not like you imagine! *Por favor!*"

His breath stunk like a dead dog's asshole.

I let go and shoved him down into an empty doorway, pocketing the blade. *"This better be good, ya limp-dick little shit! Desenrrola! Spill it!"* I stood over him, glowering, but keeping my distance from that crooked cesspool mouth.

Doc's cheek began twitching, as if with a life of its own. His demented yellowed eyes moved around in frantic little stabs. Sick eyes. "I have things all arranged, Cigano!" His high-pitched, nasal whimper drilled into my ear like a giant housefly. "I'm on *your* side! *Escuta! Por favor!* Narcisa needs our help! I know people who can assist! The director of the state mental hospital is a personal acquaintance of mine. Dr. Monteiro. He has everything prepared. You must help us to save Narcisa! All we need to do is bring her in, and they'll perform all the necessary *procedementos . . .*"

"*Procedementos?*" I blurted out. "Whaddya babbling about, ya fuckin' screwball? *What* fucking procedures?"

Doc fixed me with those swirling nuthouse eyes. "I have done extensive research into cures for Narcisa's deplorable mental condition and, well, the best and most practical option is something known as electroshock therapy. It's proven extremely effective in treating all sorts of pathological disorders. Of course, it's no longer legally performed here in Brazil, technically, but with the right sort of contacts—"

I lost it.

"I hear them fuckin' electric shocks did wonders for yer mother, huh?"

His black reptilian eyes glazed over, measuring me for a coffin. If looks could kill, I would've been turned to dust on the spot. Then he snapped back into his habitual mask as the groveling, ass-kissing, harmless little do-gooder. "I don't know what in heaven's name you're referring to, *senhor . . .*"

"Ya know exactly what I'm talkin' about, ya bitch-face creep! Narcisa told me all about yer dirty past, ya murdering little psycho!"

"Our dear Narcisa certainly does possess a fanciful imagination at times!" He flashed a nasty yellow-toothed grin and cleared his throat, staring at me just long enough for me to see the full extent of his madness. " . . . But all that sort of antisocial behavior can finally be corrected now! I have it all worked out. They're prepared to admit her immediately, Cigano!"

My jaw dropped. I couldn't believe my ears.

Doc's eyes lit up like a pair of lynch mob torches as he prattled on. " . . . And then, if all should go well, Narcisa shall be cured! The chances are favorable for at least a partial recovery. And, if there aren't satisfactory results from the shock treatments, well, there are still other, more advanced options to pursue. I've already taken care of that detail as well. Her mother and I have been talking a great deal lately, and the woman is completely in favor of Narcisa being transferred to a private facility and receiving the operation . . ."

"Operation? What fuggin' operation?"

"*A lobotomia, Cigano!*"

I was too shocked to speak . . . *Lobotomia? A lobotomy? What the fuck?!*
I glared at the old demon in stunned disbelief.

His mouth moved, a squirming pit of filth. "All we need now is two thousand reais to pay for basic expenses. This sort of *procedemento* can't be done by legal means anymore, of course, but we can have it performed by a specialist in the Amazon, at a private facility just outside Manaus, where they have ways around certain silly bureaucratic formalities . . ."

I gawked at him . . . *Is this little psycho for real?*

As reading my thoughts, his tone changed to a melodramatic, confidential half whisper. "Actually, Cigano, I was planning on contacting you quite soon about all this, you know. After all, I'm well aware that you've been supporting Narcisa these last several months, and that's damned commendable of you, sir, I must say. You have saved her life, *senhor!* But she requires professional intervention now. Her life is totally without value the way she's living it! Surely, even someone like you can see that she must be saved, an—"

"Saved!? By you?! Ya murdering little woman-hating faggot! Sua merda! Get up, motherfucker! Stand up and get yer beating, ya sick little shit!"

Doc remained sitting.

Just as I was about to haul him up by his neck, he called out to a passing police wagon.

They stopped. A beefy Negro sergeant behind the wheel poked his head out the window. *"Qual foi?"* The cop eyed me with a disinterested glimmer of suspicion. "What's up? Ya got a problem over there?"

"Oh no, officer, there's no problem at all," Doc chirped as he stood up slowly, smoothing his rumpled shirt, like a sick pigeon preening. "My dear friend here and I were just having a little discussion about yesterday's *futbol* match. I was just wondering if you good fellows might be able to enlighten us as to the score . . ."

"Buy a fuckin' newspaper, *porra!*" The big thug spat out the window, then pulled over to the curb in front of the bar.

Doc continued eyeing them significantly as they got out, shouldering their heavy black AR-15s like prospectors' tools, and walked up to the counter for their weekly payoff from the drug-peddling barkeep.

"I'm sure you don't really want any unnecessary involvement with the *policia*, Ignácio. That is your name, *senhor*, isn't it? After all, you know as well as I do how the authorities frown on dirty gypsy predators with long criminal records who supply illicit drugs to poor, innocent young girls! *Pedofilo!*"

Looking at his dark, self-satisfied smirk, I knew this Doc was dangerous. And I realized he wasn't about to give up.

Jesus! Blackmail's his game now! Two thousand bucks. Enough cash to bribe some quack to perform an illegal lobotomy, if there even is still such a thing . . . Or maybe it's just a straight-up extortion . . . Either way, this evil little parasite is out to fuck us over good.

The next words he said clinched it.

"But there's no need to worry, my dear *amigo*. All of your shameful little peccadilloes are safe with me. Narcisa's mother need never know anything more about your perverted little relationship with her daughter. Heavens forbid! That woman is an absolute horror, believe me! And she could actually make some serious trouble for you. One of the members of her beloved church group is a federal court judge, you know . . ."

He paused, grinning with as many teeth as a horse. The insane look on his face sent a chill down to my gut as he sighed dramatically, then went on. " . . . But not to worry, dear Ignácio, you can just leave that illiterate peasant to me. And please, please, don't forget our little agreement. Two thousand reais, Ignácio. For Narcisa's cure. That's all we shall require for my daughter's care and treatment. Everything else will be taken care of, trust me."

"Trust you!?!" I shoved him back against the wall and grabbed him by the throat, choking him into bug-eyed silence. ***"Ya filthy little rat-fucking shit-eater! Listen to me real careful now, ya dirty cocksucker, cuz I'm not gonna tell ya again!"***

I could see his rodentlike eyes widen with mute terror as I tightened my grip on his windpipe, spitting the words into his face, one by one. ***"If I ever catch you within shouting distance of Narcisa again . . . I will cut yer fuckin' head off . . . and I will feed yer ugly, shit-eating face, piece by fuckin' piece,. to the stray dogs up on the morro . . . Got it!?"***

His eyes nodded in terror. He got it.

" . . . And that's not just a threat, ya little turd! It's a fuckin' promise!"

I let go and backhanded him once, fast and hard, across his ruddy cheek.

He yelped like a kicked poodle.

I turned and stomped back over to the Casa Verde, without looking back.

I didn't tell Narcisa about the incident. When we got back to my place, though, I informed the baffled-looking old *porteiro* that I would not, under any circumstances, be receiving visitors.

80. LOWER COMPANIONS

"We often give our enemies the means for our own destruction."
—*Aesop*

Later that night, Narcisa cried out in her sleep.

"Ai aii aiiiii aiiii Não-oo! Por que ele e eu não!? Why gotta be him? Ai aii! Is me who deserve to dead, no him! Aiii aiiii! God see all an' he gonna come an' get me! He gonna send de devil for punish an' torment me forever! Aii aii aii aiiiii! Não-oo!"

When she awakened with a blood-chilling scream, I asked her what she'd been dreaming about. She said she'd had a horrible nightmare. Then she began telling me another twisted, tragic story from her twisted, tragic past.

She was only eleven or twelve, she said. She and her friends had a revolver someone had stolen from the military base in Resende. Bored, stoned-out kids with a gun, someone suggested a game of Russian roulette. Seemed like a good idea.

Narcisa, always in a hurry to die, went first, of course. She didn't lose. She spun the chamber and passed the big, heavy pistol over to the next kid, her best friend.

Pow!

He lost.

As she told the story, I felt like crying. Narcisa played it off like it was no big deal. I was horrified . . . *What a cold-blooded little lizard!*

Then I realized she was just fronting again. Whenever Narcisa talked about her past, she tried to act all cool and collected, pretending it didn't faze her a bit. Nonetheless, little clues were always slipping out. I could tell when she cried out in her sleep, whimpering like a puppy in the rain. The memories were in there, a big festering open wound. Nameless fears and traumas brewed and bubbled below the surface, opening portals to hellish nightmare realms; the Dark Side, from whose angry depths hordes of restless, homeless spirits of the damned marched into her life and followed her around like an invisible mob of occult beggars.

The Shadow People. She'd been speaking about them a lot lately.

"Is like de big black *vulto*, Cigano! She very fast, all de time moving around de room! I can see it in de corner of my eye, an' then, *boo!* She just go disappear! *Boo!* Like that!" She snapped her fingers. "But I can feel these thing is there always, looking me, playing with me all de day! An' it make me to remember so many crazy thing I seen . . ."

"What kinda things?"

"Focked up thing, bro!" Her eyes grew wide. "Like de black magic womans in my town, sometimes they borned de clandestine baby in de home an' don' register it, you know, an' then they go kill de *neném* for give it to de devil!"

I was in shock. No wonder Narcisa was so disgusted with life. "That's fuckin' insane!" I stared at her in horror. "You seen people sacrificing babies? *Fala serio . . .*"

"*Juro, cara!* These why I e'say fock you to these e'sheet backward place an' I gone to de city for live with de punks. With them, de thing is different, got it? These punk anarchist peoples de most honest an' authentic peoples in de whole world!"

I thought of the befuddled stoners of the Casa Verde and rubbed my chin. "Howzat, baby? What makes ya think they're so special?"

"Is cuz all de time they rebel against de society an' question ev-er'thing, Cigano. De e'stupid Catholic an' Christian peoples, them de most ignorant liar of all! Hah! Fock, bro! I seen my own peoples do so much wrong thing."

"What things?"

"All kinda crazy e'sheets, Cigano. Like my daddy, he was de black magic man, you know, an' he use to take me to de Candomblé cere-mony, an' I seen all kinda black magic voodoo an' Quimbanda works when I just a little geer-ool . . ."

"Your father was into all that stuff? Seriously?"

"Yeh, well, they e'say he convert to de Je-sooz when he e'stay in de prison, but is all bool-e'sheets! Hah! I know better! Is just for get de e'special *privilégio* in there by pretend to be with de Je-sooz peoples. Is like a big focking mafia, these e'stupid Jes-ooz organization, got it?"

I got it. I knew what Narcisa was talking about. I'd seen those fun-damentalist preachers coming to the prison in Mexico, bribing, bul-lying and brainwashing inmates to get control of their minds. Those arrogant, self-righteous Bible-thumpers were always crowing about how some fairy-tale Jesus was the "only cure" for alcoholism and ad-diction. What shit!

The whole thing disgusted me. The same globally financed McChristian churches were operating all over Brazil now too, con-spiring with the most corrupt political forces in the country, like a plague of spiritual termites. For the church leaders, it was all about money, property, power and mass mind control. They even owned their own television networks, using their ill-gotten funds to spew out a hateful, twisted neo-Christian dogma, masking a dark, insidious hidden agenda. I'd seen Narcisa watching those obnoxious, suit-and-tie, pie-in-the-sky *pastores* on the TV. Their shameless double talk disgusted me. I despised how they weaved their underhanded, fear-based, moneygrubbing spell on the gullible masses.

As a traditional gypsy *drabarni*—a clairvoyant healer—my own Tia Silvia had been driven underground by those bigoted, sanctimonious assholes when I was a kid. In the ensuing years, the plague of so-called Christian churches had grown into a modern-day Inquisition, wreaking devastation on the spiritual life of the poorest, most vulnerable segments of Brazilian society. I knew exactly why Narcisa was so revolted by it, and wanted nothing to do with her own creepy Bible-thumping family background.

"Hah! More I think about about my focking family, bro, more I don' wanna come from de e'stupid peoples I come from! When I was a kid, Cigano, I become de *satanista*. All de kids in my village hang out in de *cemitério*, for e'smoke de *maconha* an' drink wine there, like de big cemetery gang. It was my favorite place, no e'stupid peoples for molest me in there. I never wanna go home no more, so I go e'sleep in de crypt together with de cadaver. Then I make de big pact with de devil an' do all de ritual for call up *Satanas*, using de thing I teef from de *tumba*. Hah! I use to have de big collection of stuff we take out from de people's grave!"

"Yeah?" I raised an eyebrow. "What kinda stuff?"

She guffawed. Coldly. Without mirth. "Hah! No so much de value thing, Cigano. You know, de cemetery worker, they already teef all that kinda e'sheet when de peoples go for bury, so I take it just de e'skull an' bone an' de teeth sometime, thing like that. I hide all de *bagulho* in de yard behind my mother house. Hah! I making all kinda *magia negra* in her home, doing de black magic right there, e'same time she go de e'stupid church for pray to de Jes-ooz! Hah!"

I shook my head. "Woah!"

"*Poisé, merão!* Sometime I even go trade de e'skull an' bone to de bandido for a big bag of *cocaina*. De drug gang use to like all these kinda sinister e'sheets, back in the time before de drug boss all join de focking Je-sooz church like all de other e'stupid peoples . . ." She flashed an evil grin, reminding me how, in a typically surreal move, the evangelical churches had managed to convert even the drug traffickers.

Narcisa took another big hit. Exhaling slowly, she set her pipe down and looked around. A guilty, worried look flashed in her eyes, as if someone might be listening.

Then, she started yelling at the accusers. ***"Malditos! Shut de fock up! I don' give a fock, porra! I didn't do nothing to you . . . Don' care if you de owner of de focking e'skull! You don' need it no more so fock off! You finish here, got it? Delete! Thank you come again! Doiii—iing!"***

As she ranted on, arguing with her invisible tormentors, I could feel a chill crawling up my spine, like Arctic Ocean water in a vein.

Narcisa was giving Doc just the ammunition he needed.

81. LUCKY CHARM

The next afternoon, as we rode through frantic downtown traffic, all of a sudden Narcisa stood up and leapt off the back of the bike, landing right in the middle of the street, like some crazy drunken kung fu ninja.

What the fuck? I pulled over to the curb and turned to look.

There she was, standing in the center of a rushing stampede of vehicles, red-faced, yelling, cursing, spittle popping from her pissed-off gullet.

Shit! What now?

She began scurrying around in frenzied circles, darting between the speeding cars and trucks like some kind of crazed matador, holding her hand up in a futile attempt to halt the unheeding flow of speeding metal. Then, as I looked on in horror, she got down on all fours and started scrambling around on the ground.

Furious, she glared up at me. ***"Porra! Sua merda! Don' just sit there, you e'sheet! Get off you e'stupid moto, porra!! Help me find it, go!!"***

"Find what, ya fuggin' freak show?" I called back, bewildered.

"Minha Mer-ka-baaa, porra!! My pen-dant, goddamn you! It fall off!"

Horns honked as cars screamed past her within a spider's ass crack. Shaking my head, I got off the bike and stood there, watching the show. Pedestrians stopped on the sidewalk to gawk. Somebody said something about the *"porra louca"* crazy girl, and asked me if I knew her. I just shrugged and looked on at Narcisa scampering around in the road, wild-eyed, looking for her lost charm. Her Merkaba.

Narcisa's cherished mystical icon was a small silver pendant; an unusual geometric form made of two interconnecting pyramids, resembling a three dimensional Star of David—a "tetrahedron." She didn't call it her lucky charm, but that was the gist of it. She'd picked it up on her ill-fated visit to the Holy Land, and she was obsessive about the thing. She never let it out of her sight.

Narcisa had always been obsessed with the secret sciences. I remembered the complex psychedelic forms she would draw in her notebooks when she was high; weird symmetrical renderings she referred to as "interdimensional portals." She insisted those singular designs held the power to connect her with Alpha Centauri. And she believed her Merkaba pendant to be a powerful occult talisman.

Fascinated by her confusing explanations, one day I'd researched the subject, leafing through old books in the musty secondhand bookstores on the Rua da Carioca. The Merkaba, it turned out, was indeed referred to as a "divine light vehicle," used by ascended masters to commune with higher astral planes. The odd geometrical form was said to represent the "spirit/body surrounded by counter-rotating fields of light"—spirals of energy, like the human DNA helix, which could transport a spirit-body from one dimension to another.

One book I read through explained that by holding the Merkaba's image in consciousness, one could activate a "nonvisible saucer-shaped energy field around the human body, anchored at the base of the spine." Once energized, this imaginary "flying saucer" was said to be a vehicle for astral projecting into higher realms. As I'd sat reading, I'd thought of Narcisa's little alien song. *"Can you show me where it is de exit to these e'sheet world?"*

For Narcisa, the Merkaba was a one-way ticket home to Alpha Centauri.

Watching her pawing at the ground looking for her pendant, I recalled her telling me how every time she'd taken the thing off, some terrible disaster had befallen her. Denial was her middle name. And now, once again, poor Narcisa was the hapless victim of a cruel, inauspicious jinx; an unjust twist of unkind Fate.

Ironically, I'd just warned her that it was hanging from its frayed string by just a thread. I tend to notice little things like that. She'd hissed at me and told me to go fuck myself and mind my own fucking business. Now, there she was, crawling around on all fours in the middle of traffic like a bug-eyed hedgehog. Taking her advice, I minded my own business, even as I ground my teeth, seething with that special brand of resentment reserved for the ungrateful.

Narcisa finally located it; but not before it had been run over several times.

She stormed over to where I was standing, waving her damaged charm in my face like a dead frog. ***"Pronto! See it now? Is ruin! You happy, hein?"***

I was almost curious. "Why should I be happy, Narcisa?" I eyed her coolly, smiling. "Here, lemme see that." I took it from her hand and twisted it back into shape.

It still looked a little crooked, but not too bad. I handed it back to her.

She threw it into my face. ***"I hate you!! You make these e'sheet happen by think an' talk about it! You manifest it!! Is all YOU fault!!"***

Fed up with her mad metaphysical tantrum, I got on the bike and started it. "You coming?" I smiled.

Narcisa snatched the damaged Merkaba up from the pavement. As she stood there, holding it in her hand, I felt kind of bad for her. But there was nothing I could do.

"You have destroy my Mer-ka-baaa! I hope you get ass cancer an' die!"

I spat on the ground and took one last look at her hateful face. Then, I gunned the throttle, pulled out into traffic and rode away.

As Narcisa's hysterical voice echoed in my ears, I found myself wondering for the umpteenth time . . . *When will this intolerable fucking insanity ever end?*

Weird occult forces were closing in all around us. I could feel it.

I knew we were in desperate need of help.

82. HELP FROM BEYOND

"Everyone needs help from everyone."
—*Bertold Brecht*

The ancient Negress was a striking figure.

Immaculate flowing white gowns. Long lace petticoats and skirts. Rows of heavy, colored crystal beads hanging across her bony chest. A spotless white cloth tied tight around her head. All the regalia of an elder spirit medium; a Mãe de Santo. A Mother of the Spirits. But it was her eyes that said it all. Those dark, glowing orbs had the glaze of the World Unknown.

Mãe Caridade—or Mother Charity—was a high Macumba priestess. A seasoned initiate of the time-honored Afro-Brazilian mystical arts of the Umbanda and Candomblé, the wise old shamanic healer was a living channel into a complex web of esoteric forces and occult powers of the spirit world.

I'd been invited to her *terreiro* by Luciana after calling the day before, lamenting about Narcisa's latest meltdowns. Narcisa had been on the warpath for weeks now; violent, unreasonable, irrational, bloodthirsty, insane. She'd been running in especially bad company over at the Casa Verde lately too. At my wit's end, fearing for both our lives, I told Luciana over the phone that I was losing my fucking mind. Things were getting worse by the day. I could feel the darkness closing in. And still, I couldn't give up on trying to help Narcisa.

In desperate need of spiritual orientation and guidance, I jumped at her invitation to go to the *gira* the following afternoon.

My old friend showed up at my door just before noon. She gave me a firm, warm hug, and we went downstairs for some sweet black coffee.

As I told her of my latest woes, Luciana reached across the wobbly wooden *boteco* table and took my hand. "Poor Ignácio." She smiled. "I know just how you feel, baby. Love's brutal when you got a broken picker. But what else can you do? You can't just run out on her now . . . You really care about this Narcisa, huh?"

I nodded.

Sunlight streamed through Luciana's jet-black hair. Her kind, loving smile was like a sunrise at the end of one of Narcisa's all-night horror missions.

"I really been wanting you to meet this Mãe de Santo, baby." She patted my hand. "I got a feeling she's gonna be able to give you some real help. God knows you deserve it, Ignácio, after all you've done for this poor girl."

"I just don't know what to do anymore, Lu." Tears welled up in my eyes.

Luciana kept smiling. "Everything's gonna be all right . . . You ready?"

" *'Bora então.*" I nodded. I blew my nose with a thin paper bar napkin, then we got on the bike for the long ride out to the remote Umbanda center.

An hour later, we were cruising down a winding two-lane high-way, way out on the outskirts of town. After passing through a tangled clump of septic-smelling rural favelas, we were deep in the country, surrounded by green hills and jungle. As Luciana pointed the way, I followed a steep, narrow dirt path up to the secluded hillside *sitio* where Mãe Caridade was holding session.

"You know how the *gira* works, right?" Luciana rubbed my shoulder as we approached the hidden outpost. "I know it's not your first time at a *terreiro*, but . . ."

"I guess it's been a while, huh, Lu?" I grinned.

I thought back to the different ceremonies I'd been to with my Tia Silvia as a kid and all the other *centros* I'd visited with Luciana. But that had all been a long time ago, back when Luciana and I were just Narcisa's age. Even then, we'd been seeking spiritual relief from the Curse. We'd never gotten far, though. Neither of us had been able or willing to face the true source of our mysterious "existential dilemmas"—our own ravenous drug consumption. Maybe things would turn out better this time, I mused, now that we were clean and sober.

"You still remember, right, Ignácio?" Luciana's voice drifted into my thoughts. "You know how when the drumming and singing stops and the spirits incorporate in the mediums? Just pray, and always remember that they come to help . . ."

I nodded and sighed. "God knows I could do with some help, Lu."

"Just tell them what's going on, if they ask. Sometimes, they already know why you're there. It's pretty incredible. They can give you real good insight, tell you all the kind of things you need to know about, especially coming through Caridade."

"Tell me about her, Lu."

"Caridade? She's the one who incorporates a Preta Velha, an ancient African entity called Vovó Catarina de Angola. This woman is the real thing! She was born in old Africa, in Angola, and was initiated into the Umbanda as a little girl. She's really old. Nobody really knows just how old she is, but they say she's over a hundred, and she's been helping people all her life. Caridade is pure love, Ignácio!

Closest thing I've ever seen to a real saint. She just lives to help others. You'll see . . . I'm so glad you're here, baby!" She gave my arm an affectionate squeeze. "God knows you can use more than just human help now."

Luciana would know. She'd been trying to clean up for decades before she finally got free from her lifelong cocaine addiction. Since then, through AA and her Umbanda practice, she had really changed. I was glad to be there with her; happy to be anywhere, as long as it was far from the Crack Monster and Narcisa's angry spirits. Riding up the winding dirt path through a little rural encampment of thatched-roof huts, I prayed to Pai Ogum to open my heart to whatever guidance I might receive from the spirits there.

As we passed a crude wooden gate and entered the *terreiro*, the ceremony had already begun. Drawing closer, I could hear the conga drums and moody, monotonous African chants of the *pontos*. I parked beside a simple rustic shack with wood smoke rising from a chimney. We were greeted by a young woman with rough indigenous features, dressed all in white. She smiled and pointed the way along a narrow dirt path.

We made our way downhill, into a shaded clearing, then sat on a rock beside a waterfall. We watched in silence as a dozen mediums, all dressed in the traditional white ceremonial garb of the Umbanda, danced on the packed dirt in swaying, trancelike circles. Long, heavy *guias* of colorful crystal beads swung from their necks like underwater plants as they swayed back and forth, flowing in and out of this and other dimensions, chanting and singing the traditional *curimbas* in a deep, hypnotic cadence. Other workers moved around the circle, spreading sage smoke and Palo Santo incense from earthen jars dangling on thick hemp ropes, while two white-haired Negroes beating on big wooden *tambores* led the *oração*.

To the right of the drums was a long wooden *congá*. Plates sat on straw mats on a rough wooden table under a thatched palm roof; exotic food offerings to the spirit guides. The *oferendas* were surrounded by dozens of colorful *imagens* of Catholic saints, devilish *exús*, angels and carved wooden statues of the various Orixáis. The altars were covered with long-stemmed white, red and yellow flowers.

Right away, my eyes fell on a large ancestral African wood carving of Ogum, the mythological Yoruba warrior god—my Orixá, or spirit-guide. Paí Ogum looked fierce and powerful, brandishing his pair of mighty swords.

I could smell a sickly-sweet odor from the open champagne bottles as a persistent cloud of mosquitoes hummed around my face. The bubbly liquid had been poured out into delicate crystal *taças* on another shrine, covered with dozens of blazing white candles. The ground was peppered with weird esoteric geometrical symbols scratched into the hard dirt in white chalk markings, closed off by a giant circle of protection.

A little silver bell was rung by one of the mediums. The drumming and chanting halted.

Silence.

An old woman, who appeared to be the chief shaman, began shaking and contorting as she was "mounted" by her Orixá and taken over by the entity. Fascinated, I watched as her whole physical countenance began to change, shape-shifting, transforming, morphing into the spirit of the Preta Velha: the Old Negress. The wise and venerable ancestral spirit of Vovó Catarina de Angola.

The spirit "riding" the woman's wiry frame was handed a clay pipe by one of the helpers. She lit it and puffed up a great cloud of smoke.

After walking around the terreiro, inspecting the other mediums, giving her blessings, she looked up with a fierce expression of unearthly authority. With a slow, steady eye, she peered into the crowd, looking around, checking out the assembled people, one by one. Then, her trance-glazed gaze fixed on me. Her lips were moving, saying something. I couldn't hear a sound as she pointed a thin, leathery finger, beckoning me to come.

Feeling a familiar otherworldly chill in my gut, I rose. Luciana put a reassuring hand on my shoulder and gave me a gentle shove forward.

83. MOTHER OF THE SPIRITS

I shuffled across the clearing and stepped into the circle. A cloud of mosquitos hovered around my face like they were about to inherit the earth. I could feel my sweat-soaked cotton shirt clinging to my back as a white-clad assistant led me over to a little wooden stool. I sat down before the wizened old Mãe de Santo.

She studied me with bright, glowing eyes. Then, she reached out and took my hand in a firm, cool grasp, addressing me with an archaic cackle. "I knows ya already, me son, hey?"

I had to ask her to repeat herself in order to understand her ancient Portuguese. She was speaking an obsolete dialect; from old Mother Africa, before the time of the slave trade and her ancestors' forced pilgrimage to the New World.

She stared into my eyes. "Ya done come here befo' to see I, hey, *meu filho*?"

I shook my head and told her it was my first visit to the *terreiro*.

She seemed to be contemplating my words as she took several deep pulls on her tobacco pipe. As we were enveloped in a cloud of gray smoke, I knew she was making contact, sending her intentions and prayers aloft to the spirits.

Spitting a gob of brown saliva into the dirt, she spoke again. "Yah! I knows ya, *filho!*" She held me with that haunting, ironclad stare. "Ya done come befo' I in de other times, yea, wee gypsy-mon!"

I looked down and shrugged, feeling goose bumps covering my arms and back, despite the oppressive country heat.

"Come fo'ward den, *queridinho*, come close an' mek fe' me embrace ya . . . Come up closer, de-ah one . . ." Whispering kindly, she reached out and pulled me to her with powerful arms, holding me in a long, hard embrace.

I could feel the magnetic charge of her love. It was like a jolt of electricity charging into me, shuttling me into another state of awareness. Tears filled my eyes, and I went limp.

She gave me a gentle shove back and looked deep into my soul. "*Filho de Ogum!*" She held me with her intense stare, addressing me with the formal title: "Son of Ogum."

I lowered my head again as Caridade spoke on, in a calm, forceful tone.

"Ya gal-frien', her got de good an' pow-ful guidin' spirit what mek de protection fe' she way in all she eart'ly roads. *O Santo Guerreiro, Ogum.* Same like ya self, hey, young warrior,"

"*Saravá, patacori, Ogunyé!*" I nodded a salutation to my beloved Orixá.

"Ya gal, dis one dem calls Narcis-sara, she got de big spirit troubles, ya seen'? *Um baito encosto. Um espirito obsessor.* Ya understan' ya granny, hey?"

I nodded as Caridade went on, talking about Narcisa's spiritual weight, the Curse. Sinking into the dark, swirling pools of the old woman's eyes, all of a sudden, I began feeling dizzy and nauseous. It was a sign, I knew, of an *egum*. The presence of a spirit; a ghost. My mouth went bone dry, and at once my mind's eye was seeing an image of Narcisa, sitting behind me on the motorcycle, slapping at my back, yelling . . . *"Pare aqui!! E'stop here, Cigano! E'stop e'stop!"*

It had been late. Well past midnight on a Monday, Day of the Dead for Rio's many practicing Macumbeiros. As Narcisa beat at my shoulder like some cocaine-maddened racehorse jockey, I'd slowed the bike. Before I could come to a full stop, she'd vaulted off the back and hit the ground running. I closed my eyes and pictured Narcisa sprinting back to the crossroads, pilfering the *oferendas*, grabbing a bottle of *cachaça* sitting at the curb.

I shook my head, remembering the look on her face that night; so pleased with herself and her cool nihilist punk irreverence, as she swaggered back over, munching on a fresh *acarajé* and swigging from the forbidden bottle.

"Epa! Olha o azar!" I'd shot her a warning look. *"I wouldn't be drinking that stuf—"*

"Menos, old Dona Maria! Meeenos! These e'stupid Macumbeiro e'sheets don' got no powers over me, porra! Hah! Shut de fock up!"

I'd only been half joking at the time. Half. Sitting before Mãe Caridade now, looking into those dark, wise African whirlpools, it didn't seem funny at all.

The Vovó spoke on in a grave, patient tone. "Ya try an' give de help fe' she, *filho*, cause ya de more stronger warrior den she are. Ya already been to de dark place befo' an' ya done fight many de hard battle fe' mek ya way inna de light."

"I try to help her, Mãe, I do! But she's so hardheaded, so stubborn!"

"Me knows all 'bout dat, *filho*. Me kin sees it all right he-ah." She grimaced, looking down at a glass of water by her feet.

Silence.

Finally, she looked up again, staring right through me with a knowing little smile. "Her t'ink she too much clever, *meu filho*, an' her s'pose she knowin' all 'bout de occult world. But her don' know nuttin' a'tall . . ."

She stopped and studied the water again.

Silence.

She nodded. "Ya gots fe' know dis one t'ing, *filho*. All a de gal stubborn way no only she 'lone self. Is no just she 'lone inna she body now, child, seen? Ya understan' what I sayin'?"

I could feel my face scrunching up as I tried to decipher her cryptic speech.

"Dis small ga-al, dis one ya call Narcis-sara, her so *innocente* dis po' wee t'ing, her don' even knows how much de trouble her put inna she self, ya seen?"

I nodded, watching that somber, dark leathery face.

Silence.

She sat there for a while, shaking her head, muttering, praying, as the coin of awareness began its slow descent into my gut. Then, it dropped with a sickening *clunk* as she spoke on in a confusing rush of archaic language.

From what I could make out, Narcisa had been some sort of sorceress in another life, with great psychic abilities she carried into this incarnation. But she'd used those powers to do harm. Her present suffering was a purification, the old woman explained, to pay off some dark karmic obligation. For me, it appeared to be a promise I'd made in another life to help her in her mission to do better in this one. My own karmic debt. It all made sense as I thought of the many odd déjà vu moments I'd felt around Narcisa.

After another long pause, as if listening to instructions, Caridade nodded. Then, she went on, confirming my worst fears. Narcisa had opened the gates to hell for herself. Her addiction resulted from her attempts to escape her mission, leaving herself wide open to occult spirit possession.

"Her got de hungry *obsessor* sittin' 'pon she heart now . . ." The old woman started coughing. "So much smoke all 'round dis po' child! *Urrffff* . . ." She grimaced, struggling to catch her breath. "Is de *vampiro* what attach to she. I feels it 'pon she chest right now, *filho*, suckin' de life out. An' she spirit body lookin' black, all cover wit' ashes, full a hole an' all cut up, like a wee bird what de cat got! Yah, her got de jealous spirit enemy all 'round she self."

"What kinda sprits?" I cocked my head.

"Some a dem de dead peoples what can't get free from de physical world. Other ones still livin' inna human form, *incarnados*. All a dem feedin' 'pon she life force . . . An' someone livin' close by she what gots de negative *carga* 'pon dem, fe' sho'!"

I watched her lips moving like the wings of a vulture flapping over a corpse. As goose bumps crept up my back, I thought of Doc and Narcisa's mother.

"What do you mean, Mãe?" I swallowed hard, dreading the answer.

"*Pois é, meu filho, são os vampiros espirituais!*" She nodded; Caridade repeated the frightful prognosis of psychic vampirism. Then she took another long draw on the pipe.

Silence.

A cloud of tobacco smoke surrounded us again as she spit in the dirt, then began to explain. "Some peoples livin' in de same body wit' a vampire spirit, seen? Dem *parasita* gon' stay 'pon dis po' ga-al till she body all use up. An' if her don' change up she way soon, den her gon' go down fe' join wit' dem low spirit in de dark region, soon as she go fe dead."

It was hard to make out her words. I scrunched up my nose. Confused, I blurted out. "But *why*, Mãe? Why would some invisible vampire spirit wanna attach itself to a person?"

I looked into those bottomless black eyes as the old Spirit Mother explained how Narcisa was surrounded by all sorts of troubled spirits, both living and dead; mad, demanding, hungry, ghostly parasites, using her to sustain their earthly vices.

"Dem needs she physical form for dem own *sustenencia, meu filho.*" She gave me another sad look. "Dem gots to have de vehicle fe' keep goin' he-ah. Dem be livin' through she, usin' she body, seen? If she no get spirit help now, dem gon' destroy she . . ."

84. VAMPIROS

"The general population can be open to spirit possession at times of extreme depression and other low vibrational energetic states. Drugs and heavy drinking can seriously open the door, too. So can having sex with a possessed person. The energetic connection creates a mutual field which the spirit entities can cross."
—*David Icke*

The old Spirit Mother's words were boring into my brain like spikes.

"What can I do, Mãe?" I cried out, pleading through a haze of tears. "I *wanna* help her, but I'm afraid one of us is gonna die if we keep on like this! What can I do?"

Caridade put those strong, bony hands on my shoulder and pulled me closer, closer, until I was looking so deep into her eyes I thought I'd be sucked away.

"Is true de danger fe ye-self 'long wit' she, *filho*. If ya stays on together wit' dis Narcis-sara, ya can come to harm too if ye no takes big care!"

"What about *her*, Mãe? What's gonna happen to Narcisa if I leave her?"

Silence. I watched her dark, leathery face.

Finally, she shook her head and went on with a sad gimace. "If ya no stay by dis one no mo', den her gon' be gone fe' sho', soon come . . . A'ready her almos' finish. *Meu Pai Oxalá!* Her try fe' fin' a way fo'

live de life he-ah together wit' ya, but her gettin' so tire out now . . .
'*Tadinha* . . . Her can' go on dis way much mo' . . ."

There it was. My worst fears confirmed. If I stayed on with Narcisa, my life was in danger. But if I left, she'd be finished—and soon.
I thought of the promise I'd made at the Love House; my decision to
never give up on her. I could feel myself making it again. I knew right
then that it was easier for me to care about Narcisa's well-being than
even my own life.

Caridade must have known it too. She stared at me with a look of
such deep, compassionate unconditional love, I began to sob.

"Ya done see too much pain an' sufferin' inna dis world, young
gypsy boy, hey?"

I nodded. She spoke the truth. Like Narcisa, I'd been born to lose.
What else was left but to live to win another battle, or die trying?
There was no turning back.

"Dis no de firs' time ya got de big haz-ard 'pon ye. Don' vex yeself.
Ya Vovó gon' be wit' ya all de time now, young *guerreiro*. *Salve Ogum!*
Saravá!"

"*Saravá Ogum!*" Bowing my head, I repeated the salutation.

Caridade lowered her face. She stayed silent for a long while. Praying. Listening. Conferring with the Unseen.

Finally, she looked up again, fixing me with those all-seeing eyes.
"Who dis woman frien' dis Narcis-sara goin' roun' wit'? De one dem
calls Francisca-ara. Who dat one, hey?"

Fuck! I knew exactly who Caridade was talking about. Recently,
Narcisa had teamed up with an older alcoholic lesbian named Francisca, a so-called poet from the Casa Verde. A violent-tempered,
man-hating prostitute, that wretched creature was an ugly reminder
of what Narcisa could become, if she didn't die or get help. Out of
nowhere, this Francisca was everywhere I looked. Whenever I tried to

see Narcisa lately, her new friend would appear like a shadow. Hovering, looming, drooling like a filmy-eyed old bulldog.

I frowned and looked at Caridade. "That one really hates me, Mãe."

The old woman stared into the glass at her feet as I spilled my guts about Narcisa's loathsome new companion. Francisca was a big fan of Baudelaire, I told her, a loud-mouthed advocate of the mythical wonders of the Grape. But that one was no Baudelaire; just a vile, gutter-dwelling bum, pickling her brains in a reeking red cascade of cheap *vinho tinto*, which had surely never seen a grape. To me, she was like an outward expression of Narcisa's inner soul-sickness. Another face of the hydra-headed Curse; an omen of impending doom.

"*Pois, é, meu filho.*" Caridade nodded, as if she already knew.

The two of them had been going out drinking every night lately, I lamented. This Francisca would swagger around like a demented land crab, reading out loud from a book of Baudelaire's poetry, professing to channel his spirit. To see it, you'd think that miserable whore had made a pact with the devil or something. She was a real nasty piece of work; a loser among losers, even among the wandering beggars of Lapa. She'd broken both her legs once, after jumping, drunk, from a trick's hotel window. The bones had never set right, so she limped around all crooked, shifting back and forth like a ghostly drunken mule's rear end.

Then one day, Narcisa had started coming around, raving about this fantastic new role model she'd met. I was horrified when I realized the great undiscovered genius she spoke of was the same clammy figure I'd been seeing for years, stumbling around the streets of Lapa in the foggy predawn hours, stooped over like a pigeon-toed phantom, cloaked in a shabby overcoat the color of a wet rat, wine bottles clinking in her pockets, snarling and cursing at passersby.

The whole thing disgusted me.

Caridade spat in the dirt. "Yah! Me no likes dat one deh! Her got de dark vampire spirit walkin' together wit' she all de time . . ." She paused again, then looked up at me with a wry face of concern. "An' who dat *other* one me keeps seein' he-ah, hey?"

"Other one?" I raised a slow, weary eyebrow.

"Yah, filho, some ol' gray face mon me seein' roun' ya Narcis-sara. All de time he be watchin' she from inna de shadow, hey? Like one ogly ol' rat-face . . ."

Doc! Shit! I knew from Narcisa's friends at the Casa Verde that Francisca was friendly with the old murderer. The puzzle pieces were moving into place.

"*Armadilha!*" Caridade winced. "Me seein' much betrayal from bot' a dem. Sneakin' backhand trickin'. Ya Narcis-sara, her gots ta beware dem peoples!"

The old lesbian was the one, she inferred, who had been feeding Narcisa to Doc, selling him information about all our comings and goings—details she must have picked up from Narcisa's innocent boasts. It all made sense. Narcisa never trusted anyone—but when she did, it was always the wrong one. Broken picker.

Caridade spoke on, making reference to Narcisa's mother and other things. It was all a big tangled web of treachery, deception and danger . . . *What a fucking mess! God help us!*

My head was reeling as the old woman rested a cool, gentle hand on my arm. "Don' ya be vex now, hey, young gypsy boy. Dem dark works don' got no kinda power! No power a'tall! Because ya carries de mos' high protection."

I could feel tears welling up in my eyes again as her smile warmed my soul.

"Only God love gots real power! Don' ya gots *no* doubt! *Salve Ogum!*"

Then, she stopped talking. Silence. An unseen portal closed. She shut her eyes. When she opened them again, they were changed. Sedate. Her whole presence seemed to have deflated. It was done. I sat looking at her, feeling dazed and drained.

Caridade nodded and smiled. "Have you understood what the Vovó told you?"

It was a tired, meek little voice—completely different in tone and inflection from the one who had just spoken with such unearthly power and authority. This timid, sad-faced old woman sitting before me now seemed even unsure of the things that had been channeled through her.

"Have you understood the messages?" she asked again with a tired look.

I nodded, pulling a handkerchief from my pocket and wiping away my tears.

She reached over and hugged me again, with a formal ceremonial kiss on either cheek. Without touching my face. Like a spirit.

Then, very slowly, she stood up and shuffled away.

85. CATCH 22

"AND AS HE, WHO WITH LABORING BREATH HAS ESCAPED FROM THE
DEEP TO THE SHORE, TURNS TO THE PERILOUS WATERS AND GAZES."
—*Dante*

Now I knew for sure. The Crack Monster was killing Narcisa, and driving her mad on her way out. Desperate, I prayed for a break. Something had to give.

They say to be careful what you pray for, 'cause you might just get it. I would soon come to understand exactly what that meant. After my visit to Caridade, I began to pray for Narcisa harder than ever. Then, one day, out of the blue, all my prayers were answered at once.

Narcisa decided to quit smoking crack. Just like that. Cold turkey.

But this kick was worse than ever before. After endless days and nights of fist-clenching, teeth-grinding abstinence, and all the nightmarish emotional turmoil and abuse that always went with it, I came home one afternoon to find her sitting on my sofa, talking on my phone, calm as a lizard basking in the sun. An unattended cigarette was burning a smoldering hole in the cushion. Speaking an odd language I didn't recognize at first, Narcisa was laughing, chattering away as if I weren't there. In a flash, I realized she was speaking some sort of broken Hebrew.

What the fuck? Jesus! It must be that John Gold, the gringo banker! Her husband! And she's having a grand old time talking long-distance to him in God-knows-where! Bitch!

I couldn't believe my ears. She was roping her victim in all over again, and doing it right under my nose this time! On my telephone! Running up a huge long-distance bill for me! *Bitch!*

I stood frozen at the door, listening in mute shock, watching the whole bad movie unfold as she yapped on, cool as a cat, cooing and waxing with amorous, cynical charm . . . *Laying another trap for the poor bastard!*

I stared at her, fists clenching, my heart pumping with betrayal . . . *Bitch! Blackhearted whore!* I wanted to yank the phone line out of the wall and strangle her with it. But I swallowed my rage like a bubbling black cancer. Seething, I watched her lips move, like a pair of vipers slithering across my heart, as she spun her poisonous web. As she switched from Hebrew to a mixture of Portuguese and English, I realized the shift was intentional . . . *Dirty bitch! She's doing this shit on purpose! She wants me to understand every word she's saying!*

Like a knife in my back, I got it all. No excruciating detail was spared; he'd send her a ticket to Paris, where he was going soon on business, and then they'd have some quality time together; a second honeymoon . . . *Vile, detestable whore! Gold-digging, backstabbing, bottom-feeding, bloodsucking vampire! Harpy! Succubus! Snake! Medusa! Witch! Monster!*

My guts were cold as the bottom of a grave by the time she said goodbye with a phony Judas kiss and hung up. As she looked up at me, I lowered my head, feeling bitter tears of frustration, betrayal, horror and loss rolling down my face.

"Why you make all these cry for, hein, Cigano?" Her cold eyes taunted me. "You look just like a little *gir-ool!* Hah! E'stupid old trick! You think these e'sheet life with you got any meaning for me? *Fala serio, porra!* You really think I gonna e'stay around here an' be you focking girlfriend, de cheap *whoo-ore* for you ugly old self after I e'stop e'smoke de crack, hein? Hah! Think again, e'stupid!"

Feeling lost, powerless, unable to speak, I was that little five-year-old ghost again, watching his mother in a spitting, hissing, violent, drunken rage, tearing up the house, the furniture, the world; tearing his soul to little scraps of treachery and terror and abandonment, again and again and again. I could hear a strange, childlike voice leaving my mouth; tiny, helpless little words, like albino moths fluttering up from an open casket.

"I know it's been rough sometimes, princesa, but . . . I love you . . ."

She threw her head back and howled. ***"Love? Hah! I never gonna love you, Cigano! Nunca! You don' mean nothing to me! I wanna young man what got a future, no some e'stupid old walrus like you! Fala serio! Hah! I love only my husband, e'stupid! An' now I am clean an' e'sober, I gonna get ever'thing back! Thank you come again! Next?"***

Her spiteful grin curled up into a cruel, self-satisfied sneer. *"Ahh! Two week in Paris, together with my young, handsome, rich husband! Hah! Is so-oo romantico de Narcisa life, hein?"*

I gawked at her, openmouthed; the way you look at some horrible tragedy unfolding, and wondered what could possess her to treat anyone so badly.

She cracked her bubble gum and studied me like a dying fly. "Why you make de long face like e'stupid old dog, hein? If you really love me, then you e'suppose to be happy for me. Now I gonna get it back, all de good life with my beautiful young husband. You e'suppose to e'say congratulation to me!"

Congratulations? I stood there, shaking my head.

She glared back, then started screaming. ***"But no! You no happy! You so falso, so hipocrita, you only wanna see me*** *fail, wanna see me die, e'same like all de other e'stupid clones peoples, cuz you all full up with de inveja!"*

Envy?!? That's it! Bitch!

I snapped. *"Inveja? Fala serio, porra! You gotta be fuckin' kidding! Envy YOU? Gimme a fuckin' break, ya pathetic whore! You ain't looking fer a husband, ya frigid little two-faced liar! Ya just want an easy full-time trick!"*

Smirking like an evil lizard, she started humming, trying to drown out my words like a belligerent little brat. *"La la, I can' hear nothing what you e'say, la la . . ."*

Red-faced, I cranked up the volume. *"Yeah? Well hear this, bitch! You got th' fuckin' balls to sit here and run yer foul trap about LOVE!? Eu hein! You're a snake, Narcisa, a fuckin' worm! Yer not even human anymore!"*

She jumped up from the sofa and began dancing, shaking her ass as she scampered around, ransacking my apartment, throwing her things into her knapsack, singing her wicked little song. *"Can you show me—de exit—to these e'sheet place—cuz I tire tire tire of Cigano—Tire tire of e'stupid monkey face you you you, la la la . . ."*

I watched in disgust as she packed. It was really over. This time she wouldn't be back. I knew it, and I was relieved; and I was devastated . . . *So this is it! Fuck! It's finally done.*

"Okey, Cigano!" She sashayed over and stood in front of me, zipping her bag shut. "Now I gonna go de Casa Verde an' e'stay there, together with my poet friend an' all de e'squatter peoples, de punk anarchist peoples, my peoples, my *familia*. I gonna wait there for my husband send me de tickets, an' then I gonna go away, fly fly away to Paris! *'I wanna fly away. I wanna get away, I wanna fly-yyy awa-ayy!'* Merci boucoup come again! Next? Hah!"

Speechless, I stood watching her, waiting for the torture to end.

It didn't. "*Eiii,* why you look so *sa-aad* for, Cigano, hein? You e'suppose to be *happy* now, *mané!*" She was snickering, gloating, digging the knife in deeper and deeper. "Now you got ever'thing back again, you nice clean *apartamento,* e'same de way was all de thing for you before de crazy who-ore come an' destroy you life, hein? Hah! Happy now?"

Bitch! I stared at her with poison pumping into my heart.

Her malevolent grin was a postcard from hell. "Okey, gotta go now! Bye-bye, Cigano. Hah! *Next? Thank you come again!*"

Then, Narcisa walked out; right out of my life. Again.

86. THE LAST STRAW

"THE ONLY VICTORY IN LOVE IS FLIGHT."
—*Napoleon*

Days dragged by with no word. I went and tried to see her at the Casa Verde. Every day, I would sit on the bike out front while her friend Pluto went inside, trying to persuade her to come out and talk to me alone, away from her stoned-out cronies and her hateful lesbian sidekick. But each time, Narcisa told him to tell me she was "busy."

Bitch! Busy doing what? Busy sniffing glue in the dark . . . Busy my dick!

The few times I did manage to catch her alone, away from her man-hating twin, Narcisa was always too fucked-up to make any sense. And when she wasn't whacked out of her skull on wine, paint thinner or glue, she was colder than ever, distant, sullen and indifferent; shut down.

Finally, one day she came out and invited me in—ostensibly to look at some of her new "artwork." Of course, it was just another emotional booby trap. As soon as we got inside, though, Narcisa turned on me like a viper, insulting me loudly, mercilessly, viciously, trying to humiliate me in front of her bull dyke guru and an audience of slack-jawed bottom-crawlers.

She aired out our dirtiest laundry, right in front of a room full of stoned-out, lice-infested bums. I looked around at all her "good friends" and my heart folded in half . . . *Drooling, incoherent, shit-babbling,*

garbage-picking, bottom-feeding losers . . . Lunatics . . . Goons . . . Nihilists . . .
Anarchists . . . Rats! All laughing at me like the cackling, heckling demons of hell!
This fucking does it! I'm finished!

Seething with hurt and humiliation, I turned and stomped out the
door. I rode straight home and packed. Then, I did what I do best.
I beat it. I took off running, leaving Rio and Narcisa behind—not
caring if I'd ever see her again.

For a moment, out on the highway, just before the final turnoff to
the long stretch of bridge connecting Rio to the highway north, I had
a sudden powerful urge to turn around. I could feel my little travel
valise strapped to the bike behind me, right where Narcisa used to sit.

Stop! Go back! Just turn around and go back to her! Go go go go go!

I slowed down and considered my options.

I could beg her . . . Bribe her . . . Threaten her . . . Kidnap her . . . Sedate
her . . . Kill her and have her stuffed . . . Whatever! Anything to get her back and
start over.

But I knew it was too late. There was no going back. Even if I stayed,
even if I could coax her into another temporary cease-fire, soon she'd be
stomping on my heart with her big dirty Nazi boots again, threatening
my life, using me as a doormat for the Crack Monster.

It never ends with this horrible, demented whore! Just keep going, man! Go!

I hit the throttle and picked up momentum again. Soon I was
riding through the countryside, speeding farther and farther away
from Rio.

At the end a long day's ride, I stopped. I parked and looked around,
and there I was: far from Narcisa, all alone in Vitória, Espírito Santo,
a medium-sized coastal city, a few hundred miles north of Rio. I
rented a room, just a block from the port, right in the middle of the
seedy old red-light zone, and just a quick ride to a beach.

A good enough place to lick my wounds in the quiet solitude of the
damned.

*J*ournal entry: July 2010—Vitória, Espírito Santo—Feels like I'm kicking heroin all over again here, sitting in this godforsaken hole on the forgotten edge of nowhere.

But this is worse than any heroin kick. Worse than anything! At least when you put the dope down, you can just walk away, and that's that. You never have to see the evil shit again.

Not this. This is like having a perpetual junk supply strapped to your nutsack, with a mainline straight to your heart, feeding you cruel, taunting little doses that are never enough, always whispering to you, calling you back, all day long, every day . . . "Come back, Cigano, I miss you, mano, come back, come back home now, come back come back, go go go go go . . ."

Even far away from her fiendish sphere now, I'm fucked beyond fucked! Because I finally know the whole ugly, devastating truth: that no psychic vampire or ghoul or hobgoblin or zombie or ghost could ever enter my experience, my life, my reality, my home, my mind, which I haven't invited in somehow, somewhere deep in the core of me. That's why Narcisa came creeping into my life like a phantom echo of recurring trouble and trauma, drama and doom. Because she really is Nobody. Nobody but the sum total of me! The sweaty, greasy, angry straitjacket of Self.

No way out! I can't even blame her for all this heartache. Because she is me and I am she, and that's all this crazy little spectacle ever was—just a dirty old broken mirror's reflection of my own deepest wounds. This screaming hissing snapping Snake Woman, this Medusa, this Monster, this Boogie Man, this Nobody, this Nothing is nothing but a physical out-picturing of my own inner landscape of troubles and traumas, memories and worries and wounds.

My memories. My mind. My own wounded, unhappy psychic perceptions.

That snarling, angry face staring back at me in the mirror is the face of the Curse! And if I ever want to change this fucked-up nightmare I've been living in all my life, I've got to find some way to alter my own reality as my mind sees it, really sees it, as I really perceive everything, right down to my deepest innermost being. Easier fucking said than done! No wonder Ogum is depicted as the warrior. This is a relentless, bloody battle, just like the one I lost to drugs.

Narcisa is just another drug now; my latest drug of choice. But was there ever really any choice? No. Never. Even now, after I've gotten away from the source and supply of the drug, the longing, the craving, the addiction itself lives on. Stronger than ever. I try and satisfy the compulsion with these small-town hookers. Pathetic! Trying to find comfort in sex, where there can be no love, only dependence. Addiction. Want.

*J**uly 18, 2010—Vitória—I'm a tired, lonesome old ghost again, staggering around, lost and haunted in the dirty gray fog of another dreary nightscape, another baffling maze of cold, lonely solitary shadows, limping along the rain-slick streets of another tired, faceless industrial port town, all alone again. Shit.*

So close to Rio, it feels like I'm a million miles away in this sleazy sexual exile from my bombed-out, ravaged little world back home. Seeking relief where there can be no relief, haunting the sleepy ruins of another heartless, homeless nowhere, trudging through this rusty old seaport, where the ships lay rotting at anchor, like dark, unfathomable shapes conjured from my own desolate memory banks.

I look up at the crumbling, weather-damaged buildings of sleeping souls as I pass in shadows, walking hand in hand with these little dockside whores, making our way to cheap hotel rooms by the port, little red-lit pinpoints of rented love and artificial warmth in a cold, dingy landscape of empty coastal winter. Why do they always have those irritating little red lights everywhere, even inside the rooms, I wonder? Just to remind you you're in a whorehouse? Just in case you forgot, maybe, as another strange chick starts to take off her clothes, pulling a rubber out of her purse and throwing it down on another anonymous bed?

Wandered into a half-dead boteco on a bleak, salty, damp corner, another sad little space of tired-looking sailors and aging hookers. I lingered at the bar awhile, just to pass the time, waiting to find another girl to pass the time with some more. Making love to pass the time; the time that makes the love pass. But there's no such luck. The love doesn't pass, and the time is what's eating me alive here.

Later, I'm plodding down the street with another one. We turn a corner, and there's this big black dog standing at the crossroads, like a spirit shadow of some misplaced Macumba statue. Weird. He's just standing there, looking around, as if debating which way to go next. A freight train blasts through the night, traveling fast between the dim warehouse alleys by the docks. The train passes and the dog takes off, trotting up the street at a steady, determined clip, like he's late to an appointment he just remembered or something.

The whore tugs at my sleeve, breaking the spell, and we enter a place of muted yellow light. We trudge down to the end of a long, dark corridor dotted with little red lightbulbs, all glowing like some eerie old funhouse Tunnel of Love. At a reception window of thick, blurry Plexiglas, a hard-faced little man with eyes like bullets demands ten bucks, then shoves a key through the slot, and it's on: another hour's worth of cheap fireworks for another fifty, until we're both worn-out, tired of grappling with each other on the sweaty black vinyl mattress.

Afterward, she gets up and starts getting dressed, while I stand in the bathroom, washing my dick off in the sink, glancing back over my shoulder, just to make sure she isn't rifling through my pants or something. But she's cool. Just another honest hardworking girl, peddling what the Good Lord gave her—not some crooked, crack-smoking, soul-sucking, merciless little bandida like Narcisa. We walk out together, and part ways on the corner with the usual quick, obligatory peck on the cheek, then off she goes, back into the whorehouse. I make my way down another clammy, deserted avenida of shadows and late-night silence, where people sleep in dark rooms all around me, dreaming of nothing. Nothing at all. Shit. What a fucking life!

87. PIGEONS, SHOES, LOVE, PAIN, SHIT

"MUCH OF YOUR PAIN IS SELF-CHOSEN. IT IS THE BITTER POTION
BY WHICH THE PHYSICIAN WITHIN YOU HEALS YOUR SICK SELF."
—*Khalil Gibran*

July 2010—Vitória. Sunrise over the dirty old docks. What a nasty fucking place to die, I'm thinking as I stumble along in the cool, salty morning mist. Dawn reveals a dank, defeated landscape, defined by creeping, sagging cargo trucks limping in and out of the banging, clanging industrial port. Their brakes hiss like a thousand poisonous snakes as a damp Atlantic winter wind follows me down the road, howling like a tubercular beggar's dying curse.

Ratty-looking pigeons patrol the birdshit-coated cobblestones in a stupid, fumbling, listless dance of aviary apathy, pecking at the ground for little crumbs of nothing. I kick out at them and they scatter off in a fluttering gray cloud of winged vermin, only to land a few steps down the cold, greasy sidewalk.

Pigeons . . . Narcisa always hated them. I remember when we were sitting one time at the fisherman's shack near the end of the beach in Copacabana. Some pigeons gathered at her feet, picking in the dirt. Narcisa stomped and kicked at them with her big black combat boot and I said, "Baby, don't hurt them. They're just little birds!"

She spat at those pigeons on the ground. "I hate de focking pombo, Cigano! These pigeon, he de most e'stupid of all de flying animal! So e'stupid he don' even know he got de wing for fly away from these e'sheet place! But he never wanna fly!

E'stupid ignorant pest! He just wanna walk around on de floor an' eat from de garbage, cuz he just like de focking beggar! E'stupid e'sheet! Hey you! Don' come around me, got it, e'stupid?!" And she spat at those trash-picking birds and kicked at them again, scattering them off into the dusty shadows of my soul's blighted memory. I'm looking at these pigeons now, picking at the road like a gang of miniature bums, and suddenly it hits me why she always hated them so.

Narcisa, in her perpetual existential discontent, despised those dirty scavenger birds for so starkly replicating her own ironclad mental matrix of self-imposed lack and limitation. She hated them for being a taunting little reflection of just how much she really hated herself for possessing that same slavish, garbage-picking mentality; the beggar's soul.

As long as I've known her, Narcisa has always lived her life driven by nameless fears and a tragic, unbreakable belief in her own worthlessness—shackled to her weaknesses, her crippled, unhappy self-image, condemning herself forever to life as a bum, a beggar, a delinquent, a thief, a liar, a cheat, a hustler, a loser, a whore; trapped by her own persistent blindness, that perverse inability to see the Goddess, the Princess, the magnificent winged Angel behind her poor, damaged, broken eyes; her goddamned fear of just spreading her wings and flying away from her crummy, stifling, sordid little earthbound existence of mental poverty.

Her world has always been a big, gaping deficit. That's why she always hated it when I called her my princess, my angel. Because inside, Narcisa saw herself as a pigeon; a lowly little earthbound rat, forever dragging the worthless burden of her dirty, broken wings through the squalid refuse of her own tainted self-conception.

Still, there was always that part of her that seemed to rise up and fly somehow. It would surface in the strangest places and times, reminding me that, no matter how close I ever got to knowing Narcisa, she would always be an enigma.

I've been thinking a lot lately about this one afternoon when I went looking for her at the Casa Verde. Narcisa was nowhere to be found, but when I climbed up into her cramped little attic cubbyhole, I came across a hastily scribbled note there, lying on the floor.

It read: "Thank you all for the courage to participate in my world, directly and indirectly, the permitted ones, and the invaders too."

The "invaders" she referred to were the Shadow People, those creepy, unseen spirit companions she spent her days and nights consorting with in solitary fits of delirium. Poor Narcisa! But even at the height of such soul-shattering paranoia, she'd still taken the trouble to thank them for their company! Maybe just that little drop of gratitude could save her from the solitary curse of her own self-centeredness—even if it was a wry sort of gratitude. Could someone really find thankfulness for something so disturbing, and even find a meaning for the disturbance, or just accept it as meaningless.

The cryptic message had been sitting up there amongst piles of other paper scraps, all scattered around the dark, moldy little space. There were many sketches of mysterious, intricate geometric patterns, all drawn in crazy psychedelic colors, all sizes and shapes. Looking around up there, I saw some other, larger designs she'd scrawled right onto the walls. Mandalas. They looked like multidimensional portals—as if she were trying to design some kind of doorway, through which to exit this world. Like the Merkaba pendant she always wore.

When I asked her later what it all meant, she told me the drawings were for "protection." She explained how she would sit up there in a position of a yogi, right in front of one of those weird Indian mandala things. She sketched it out for me in one of her notebooks, and those drawings I'd seen at the Casa Verde had looked just like it—flawlessly symmetrical, like a perfect image of some weird, complex digital imaging software impregnated into the wall.

How could it be possible? How long would it take her to measure and design something so exact like that, manually, while cracked out of her skull, sitting all alone in the dark, and with all the matching colors? It was a total mystery.

And then she told me about the lines, like rays of light, and about the occult energy they represented, and about the meaning of time and space, and all sorts of other wild esoteric shit. She was talking so fast, and seemed so sure of herself, like a scientist or something, she was confusing me with her mad paranormal visions. And still, I really believed everything she was saying—about the Shadow People conspiracy, especially. In that moment, it sounded like the most logical thing I'd ever heard, a very precise and intelligent explanation of the material world and the different dimensions and energetic planes. I remembered thinking she was mad, but it was a kind of singular, incomparable madness, a genius way beyond my comprehension.

Fuck! I can't stop thinking about her! I rode all the way up here just to get away from her, but there is no getting away! She's everywhere I look—even when I'm with these other girls. Especially with other girls. What a mess!

Earlier tonight, I almost fell asleep thinking of Narcisa while mechanically fucking this chubby-faced teenage whore in a dirty little room. I never even asked that one her name. She had a particularly anonymous quality, even for a rented cunt. I did tip her a fiver, though, with the standard friendly little kiss on the cheek as we said goodbye at dawn on a cordial, rain-slick neon street corner. What did it matter? I'd never see her again. Then, standing there at sunrise, I noticed it: one shiny black patent leather high-heel shoe, lying toppled sideways in the gutter, like a fallen drunk. Lost, crippled, thrown away, rejected and abandoned forever.

In a flash, the memories rose up to haunt me again; a hundred unwelcome mental images of all the girls and women I've loved and shared my life with and the gigantic collective shoe collection they all amassed over the years. And then, I thought of Narcisa's shoe closet back in the gringo's apartment in New York. Were all those shoes still there?

Where are they all now, all the girls, all the shoes?

I ambled away to the crooked music of night birds awakening the dawn. Then, off I went to find some breakfast and pass some more time, still thinking about Narcisa.

*J*uly 2010—Vitória—Life with Narcisa was always such excruciating, savage torture, it was inevitable we'd have to go our separate ways eventually—the only way to avoid some horrible tragedy. But as terrible as it ever was, this is worse. Because love is the worst drug of all. The most lethal. More than mere heartbreak or loneliness, this brutal self-imposed withdrawal from Narcisa feels *like dying! Narcisa's absence is a dark, bottomless pit of quicksand. I stumble around it all day long, then fall in again every night, sinking, drowning, suffocating, dying a thousand deaths, strung out on the potent, toxic chemistry still raging and rampaging between us like a crackling, blazing, devastating forest conflagration. Even from far away, I can still feel the heat, the stench of burning lives, the smell of ashes approaching. And it has already destroyed both of our lives, laid waste to those solitary survivor's worlds we each inhabited separately, before getting sucked like bugs around a garbage fire into the irresistible gravity of each other's dizzy orbit.*

Now, for the first time in my long, womanizing life, I want nothing to do with other girls. It's no use anymore. Shit! All the enticing little whores I used to love. She's killed them all off! Fuck-brained, ball-breaking bitch of a pissed-off, hissing Medusa! Burning all illusions, torching it all to ashes! Even the simple, innocent pleasure of easygoing casual sex with strangers has been ruined by her insane goddamn "metaphysical orgasms." That's what she called that shit!

Not that it's any consolation, but I know I've wrecked it all for her too. Because no matter how much she always bitched and lamented and whined, restless and dissatisfied, longing nostalgic for her old solitary hooker's life, complaining of being bored and underpaid since hooking her little red whore-wagon to my broke but enthusiastic dick—I know it's all been ruined for her too now. Because now she can't stand the idea of sex with other men anymore, either. At least that's what she told me once, in a rare moment of lucid sincerity.

Maybe I just spoiled it for her by loving her too much. Now she'll need to find another one like me. She will never find another man like me. They're all dead from self-inflicted gunshot wounds to the head. And I live on. Shit! I wanna die.

88. END OF THE LINE

"THE DEGREE AND KIND OF A MAN'S SEXUALITY REACH
UP INTO THE ULTIMATE PINNACLE OF HIS SPIRIT."
—*Nietzsche*

July 2010—Vitória. End of the line for my homeless, wandering, lonely dick and crippled heart, I march the bastard whorehouse alleys of the port again, looking for some body to grab hold of, a way to pretend for just another brief rented moment that I'm not all alone on this cold, spinning dust ball in space. Same shit. Another week gone by. The same late-night stench of stale piss and rotting garbage; same old drab rhythms of tired-out fuck music echoing from another grimy, low-rent whorehouse. Whatever hookers are left over like errant soldiers from the frantic weekend all look ruined and ugly and tired now. Dull, hungover and crabby, they lurk around the bar in dreary, defensive little fuck-clusters, like gangs of drooling, vacant-eyed war refugees.

After a few more listless turns around the stinking streets of this hammerhead zone of ruined desolation, I stumbled upon a fuzzy-faced little morena with a row of lopsided stars tattooed across a slouching brown shoulder.

"Quer fazer um sexo?" the disembodied female voice droned from the shadows as I passed the darkened doorway.

I stopped for a moment and glanced into a pair of listless bovine eyes, shaking my head.

"Nah . . . Not in this dump, darling."

I'd already been in that cut-rate hump-dungeon the night before, and I wasn't going back again—not for a round with this old bag of bones anyway.

No thanks! The place was nasty, and I do mean nasty. Pissy, humid, bunched-up bundles of newspaper rolled in a filthy, cum-encrusted gray sheet for a mattress, laid out on a narrow concrete slab in a doorless little cubicle, with shit- and blood-stained walls. Cold cement floor, slimy with snot and spit and jizz and God-knew-what-the-fuck-else, punctuated with sluglike used rubbers. Ugh! After stepping, barefooted, on one of the squishy scumbags in the dark, airless chamber, I'd wanted to cut my fucking foot off and leave it behind in there.

As I turned to walk on, the whore persisted with a winning smile, pointing to the corner.

"We could go to the hotel over there . . ."

I stopped and looked her up and down. What this hag lacked in charm and youth and looks, she was going to make up for now with a display of professional zeal. Probably because she knew with that infallible hooker radar that I could take it or leave it.

She gave me another cheery little grin. There was still a spark of life in the old sweetheart. I had to give her that.

"Dizaí . . ." I shrugged, without interest.

She kept smiling, trying her luck. "Cinquenta?"

I shook my head and started away again, mumbling. "Another time, gostosa . . ."

She called out behind me. "I could go for forty . . ."

I grinned and turned around. This one meant business. I kind of liked her attitude. Yeah, she was started to grow on me . . . like a staph infection.

" . . . If it's only for an hour . . ." she added quickly, saving face.

"Aw, why not?" I nodded.

Nothing else to do. I took her by the elbow and led her across the street—thinking of Narcisa the whole fucking time.

August 2010—*Vitória—Wandered back into the corner bar around two in the morning. Sat there till sunrise, surrounded by sad little street whores, nursing a lukewarm Guaraná soda. Feeling like a bug-eyed toxic frog croaking all alone* *in a shitty little mud puddle of lost memories and regrets, condemned to replay the same old movie again and again, I thought back to what Narcisa had told me in that weak, stoned-out burst of uncustomary openness: that after being with me, she would "rather die" than go back to turning tricks on the street.*

I remembered how I'd just laughed and told her, "Baby, people like us, we're so fucking rotten inside, even Jesus can't save our fucking souls. And the devil don't want us either. That's why we're stuck with each other now."

I hadn't bought what she said anyway. Not really. I just figured "Once a whore, always a whore" and shrugged it off at that. But now, looking back, I think the problem is that she really didn't want to be a whore anymore. At least not a common street hooker. I'd even fucked that up for her. Just like she's smashed it all to pieces for me. All my pretty little floozies, so careless and carefree, friendly and pretty and horny and fun. Ruined now. Dust. Ashes. Shit.

So here we are, stuck in another terrible, gut-wrenching dilemma. Love is shit. Even separated by all this time and space, it hasn't helped. Nothing helps. There's no relief anywhere. I am really, finally, totally, completely fucked! They used to be such great kissers, these simple country girls. Now I don't even give a shit. It's like kissing a cow. I loved them all listlessly these last few weeks here, fucking them without desire, unable to even come half the time, always thinking about Narcisa. Being with other girls after Narcisa is like doing some boring, slightly painful, tedious manual labor. Like eating dirt.

After a few more miserable little turns around the zona, I gave up and went up to bed. Alone. No fun. No relief. Nowhere to go. Nothing to do. Shit.

August 2010—Vitória—Another lonesome Sunday afternoon, sitting on a big granite rock by the sea, writing in a notebook, all alone. Isolated. Alienated. Bored.

Humanity looks as appealing to me as a bucket of worms.

I'm an outsider here. A weirdo. A freak. People come and go. Every once in a while, someone wanders up, looks over my shoulder and asks me what I'm writing. When I mumble "poetry," they just smile and drift off to go get a beer.

Why do they even ask, I wonder? Curious, I suppose. Whatever. I may as well be explaining quantum physics to a rock oyster. Nobody else reads or writes around here. Many can't, I guess, but even if they're not illiterate, that shit's just "school stuff" for people these days. It's not the way of the common man. Too busy watching the box, or slaving to pay the bills. The systematic dumbing down of the whole stinking planet.

Maybe I'd be better off on Alpha Centauri too.

A stout brown woman with a wide smile stands nearby, fanning fish on a grill with a frantic little scrap of cardboard. People crowd around her, hungry, thirsty, waiting to eat. Me? Shit. I've long lost any taste for food.

6:00 p.m.—Dusk falling over the beach. The last light of day reflected in tremendous pastel sunset over the dark, rolling waves. Oily black silhouette figures of the day's last late swimmers; fishermen casting their big white nets out over the water, contrasted by the huge dark mass of sea, waves, rolling in and out, in and out. First winking, blinking lights of night. Little fishing boats bobbing over the horizon, like tiny dots of fire twinkling in the distance.

Sitting by the water, I stare into the sky, listening to the sound of the rolling breakers, punctuated by the dreamy, birdlike screams of children at play; a constant background jingle-jangle song of voices and tinny amplified instruments reaching across the sand from little beachside botecos along the lazy Sunday avenida, all weaving their ineffable rhythms into the night's fading memory. Soon they'll all be at home, watching their televisions, or sleeping in their beds, while I sit awake and write, writing, writing, trying to write her off my mind.

Lord Jesus, when will this fucking torture ever end? I ask the sky as the first lonesome star appears beside a perfect, sharp, bright sliver of cold, cold moon rising up over the horizon.

Alpha Centauri? Whatever.

An enormous white ship of glittering, fiery lights emerges from behind the big rock at the end of the beach, reminding me of the night I first met Narcisa. Everything reminds me of Narcisa. There is nothing but Narcisa. Even the little waves breaking at my feet seem to whisper her name . . . **narcisa narcisa**

narcisa narcisa narcisa . . . *and I sit like a castaway, thinking nothing, thinking everything, watching, wanting, waiting to go back to Rio, back to her sleazy siren's call.*

A ugust 2010—Vitória. I give up! Can't take it anymore. After a whole month away from home, away from Narcisa, a peaceful month, peaceful like the grave, I'm dying inside, suffering from this long, ugly white waiting period of stifling, empty withdrawal. Abstinence. Suffering her absence. Hurting, obsessing, longing, jonesing, dying for a fix. Dying for Narcisa.

The last week passed slowly, agonizingly, like a bleeding kidney stone. My mind keeps playing cruel, merciless tricks on me, and I can't stop the nightly flood of images of her wandering the greasy old streets of Copacabana, looking for a new man to save her from herself.

Shit. I'm like a racehorse slobbering at the gate now, waiting for the race to start. The rabbit. The gunshot. To my heart. Sitting at a table in a shack across from the mechanic's garage, waiting while the guy changes the oil on my bike. Eating a plate of homemade moqueca de peixe. Fish and coconut milk stew; flavors charged with a nostalgic taste of cilantro, spices and the sea. Nutrition for the long ride back to Rio.

Chew. Swallow. Wait. Like a condemned man eating his final meal. Gotta scramble if I'm gonna make it back home by nightfall. Appetite's gone. I'm a soldier going back to the battlefield; adrenaline pumping through my heart like a shot of bitter poison. Push the plate away. Call for a cafezinho. Light another cigarette. My tenth one today, and I've only been up two hours. Shit. I wonder where she is now. What she's doing. Who she's with.

89. WINTER'S GRIP

"HE YET CRAVED THE DRINK THAT WOULD BRING
THE WHOLE RUIN DOWN UPON HIM AGAIN."
—*Charles Jackson*

I knew all along that Narcisa's big pipe-dream honeymoon trip to Paris would never happen; the gringo would surely come to his senses and pull the plug.

But I also knew that, soon enough, there'd be another gringo; another sucker, another fool. Another Savior. For Narcisa, there would always be another one to rescue her and abandon her, again and again, perpetuating the endless cycle of rescue and rejection, abandonment and dependence, trauma, drama and disappointment; terror, hatred, suffering, sorrow and loss.

There would always be someone to give her another little shove into the pit; another excuse to be bitter; to hate the human race and to feel sorry for herself. Another reason to hurt, and to inflict her pain on others. Another justification for Narcisa to take it all out on the next unlucky bastard who strayed too close.

But I always understood what motivated her, and that made it hurt a little less. Didn't it? Beyond my constant thoughts of her inevitable infidelity, though, I really missed her. I missed everything about her; her laughter, her fire, her sorrow, her joy. Her need. Her hanging on to me on the back of the bike—all of it, all of her.

The absence of Narcisa followed me like a crippled beggar's shadow, all along the long ride back to Rio, just as it followed me every day of my life; a deep and persistent melancholy longing. Nostalgia. *Saudade*. The unshakable ghost of her memory covered me like the chilling ocean mist as I rolled down that long, lonesome highway, limping home to Narcisa, jonesing for another dose, another fix; another hit of her sweet, crucial poison.

Back in Rio, a cold, drizzly Carioca winter had taken hold of the city.

The skies were the color of pigeon shit. A damp, foggy desolation hung over the streets Narcisa and I used to prowl together, like a foul, foreboding omen.

The winters in Rio always seemed to manifest this sordid, murky *other* climate. A dingy sort of spiritual mold, existing just below the surface of things, like a clammy phantom breath blowing in from places unseen on winter days, transcending all earthly measurements of temperature and climate. An indefinable shadow-presence; a persistent, oppressive otherworldly gloom, crawling across your skin like a dead man's hand.

I remembered the cold, humid winters of my youth, that dank, dreary, unwholesome, indefinable sheen in the air, where even the bright, cloudless sunlight seemed frozen in place, tainted with a vague, pallid aura of despair. Like a lens smeared with a greasy rag, its sickly haze permeates everything and everybody, troubling even the Cariocas' dreams with uneasy frights and cold sweats in the deathly pre-dawn winter stillness.

As I trudged the streets of the neighborhood, searching for Narcisa, I thought back to another somber winter's morning, decades before. It was in a darkened little flophouse room, where I lay holed up with some nameless whore, sleeping off another hangover. A phone had rung, and a shadowy voice stretching across the slippery reaches of time had informed me of my father's passing. I'd never even known the man, and I didn't know what it was supposed to mean to me. I didn't cry. I didn't care. It didn't matter. I didn't cry then, nor did I think about how that's where it all must have started for me—the very roots of my own impossible love for poor, tragic little birds with scorched, broken wings like Narcisa—with some nameless trick who they said was my father, some anonymous swinging dick who'd stumbled into the insane, unhappy vortex of my poor, deranged mother's raging soul sickness; the Curse.

I guess other people must feel compelled to cry when somebody tells them their father has died. Was I supposed to? No idea. I felt nothing. I just rolled over and hugged the whore's sleeping body, clinging for dear life to the only warmth I knew. Then, I went back to sleep. What else could be done?

The following day, though, I ascended the crooked cobblestone path up to the crumbling ancient colonial church of Gloria. And there in that shadowy sanctuary, I lit a lone candle. More as a matter of course than out of any real feeling, I prayed for my unknown father's soul.

Boa viagem . . . Safe travels to you, whoever you are . . . Were . . . Weren't . . . Whatever . . . Thank you come again!

Now, I remembered that long-gone foggy winter's day again, as I plodded along the slick gray streets, reliving its piercing silver needles of rain and winter cold. And now, I cried at last—for my father and for me and for my mother and for Narcisa, and for all the lost, homeless, hopeless Narcisas in the world; for all us poor, demented little monkeys scrambling around on this lonely old dustball in cold, futile circles of ashes and ruin, searching for the answer to another gloomy winter's riddle. Shit. All ashes and dust and shit.

At each desolate corner, I felt the ghosts of Narcisa and myself living out our daily battles of love and terror. The specific memories, the visual ones, filled my heart with a singular type of pain, sharper and quicker, stinging me in a deep, tender place inside, like damp, rusty little knifepoints. I looked for her at all her usual haunts. She was nowhere. But I could feel it, sense it already; like some ancient built-in antenna, telling me what I already knew, deep down in the cold, forlorn pit of me. If Narcisa was in Rio, I'd know it. I would feel it.

She was not. I knew. Narcisa was gone.

It would take a bit of detective work to find out about her, but I knew just where to go. All I had to do was bribe her stoned-out cronies at the Casa Verde for information.

The first thing I discovered there was that she'd been kicked out of the squat a few weeks before, right after I'd left town. That in itself was significant, since the place had always been a safe haven for the most unwelcome dregs; the lost, the damned, the crazed, the unloved, the unwashed and unwanted. They'd all been beaten and booted and kicked around and kicked out of everywhere all their lives, ever since being kicked out of the womb. In keeping with their general dislike of rules, the only sacred law of that marginal last gasp community was that nobody could ever be expelled from the Casa Verde.

But they'd had to make an exception to their sole, lonely little regulation, just for Narcisa. As I put the pieces together in my mind like a faded old jigsaw puzzle, I could hear her voice whispering in my inner ear, spurring me on.

"These why I get kick out, Cigano! Cuz I am Nobody here! Nobody, got it?"

I got it. Longtime Casa Verde residents would never forget the day she'd misplaced her Merkaba pendant in there. Up for a week, smoking crack all alone in the attic, Narcisa had stashed her charm in a crevice in the wall so the dreaded Shadow People wouldn't get it. But she'd hidden it so well in her crack-fueled paranoia, she'd forgotten where it was. Then she'd accused the others of stealing it. In a misguided attempt to enlist their communal sympathy, she'd gone on a rampage, breaking things, kicking at the squatters with her big steel-toed combat boots, threatening to kill them all like roaches if someone didn't come across. Not having the slightest idea what she was talking about, they'd all dummied up. In a typical rage, Narcisa stormed out, clamping a padlock she just happened to have in her jacket pocket onto the rusty chain on the front gate, locking all the befuddled stoners inside.

Surrendering to the memory, I could hear her voice again now, screeching like a buzz saw as I'd stood outside that day, watching in horrified silence.

"Now I gonna go an' get de gasolina an' we gonna find out who teef my focking Merkaba! An' if he don' give it back, I gonna burn down these focking e'sheet casa, an' all you teef motherfocker gonna burn up inside, got it?"

They'd gotten it. Narcisa had been banned for the first time then. The Casa Verde was still standing, of course. Luckily for the good folks there, Narcisa had soon gotten sidetracked by the Crack Monster, forgetting her homicidal arson mission.

Within days, she was back among them again, as if nothing had ever happened.

I shook my head, shrugging off the memory like a ghostly hand, as I wandered into the decrepit old hovel, seeking a clue to her present whereabouts.

With the exception of Pluto and his flaming homosexual pick-pocket sidekick, Zé—Narcisa's two closest cronies on the streets—the residents all hated and feared me as much as they did her; mostly because every time we fought, she would run right back there, telling them all sorts of delusional tales of brutality, violence and cruelty on my part. Nonetheless, it usually only took a bottle of cheap wine or the price of a can of shoemaker's glue for her "good friends" at the

Casa Verde to climb all over each other to rat her out to whoever wanted information. Including Doc.

Even given the usual incoherence of that spaced-out bunch, I began piecing together the beginnings of a story from their confusing, babbling accounts. Doc, I learned right away, had been involved somehow in Narcisa's latest disappearance from the ranks of the befuddled.

Shit! No!

I guess the look on my face inspired pity. Finally, Pluto pulled me aside and confirmed—over the drinks I bought him in the cheerless little *boteco* across the street—that she had indeed split town.

Narcisa was holed up in the country, he informed me with a downcast look, somewhere near her hometown in Penedo, living off a weekly allowance from Doc—with all the inherent tangled strings such an arrangement would attach to her shattered little soul, like an infestation of Casa Verde lice.

90. CRIME SCENES

"THERE ARE CHARACTERS WHICH ARE CONTINUALLY
CREATING COLLISIONS AND NODES FOR THEMSELVES IN DRAMAS
WHICH NOBODY IS PREPARED TO ACT WITH THEM."
—*George Eliot*

I listened with a mixture of fascination and dread as the two teenage barflies talked off the rounds of beer and *cachaça* I bought them. As the afternoon dragged on, I got the full lowdown on Narcisa's latest misadventure.

Shaking his big, sad woolly mammoth mulatto head, Pluto confirmed that the gringo had indeed backed out at the last minute. Predictably, their tearful Paris reunion had washed out. Suddenly stripped of her grandiose travel plans, and cut adrift from me now too, Narcisa soon left the Casa Verde to rampage the city streets like a headless goat from hell. But before that, Pluto said, she'd become further entangled with the creepy lesbian, Francisca.

"Fuck e'stupid shit-cow bee-eeches!" Zé chimed in with mincing effeminate contempt—ending any lingering illusions of Gay Unity at the Casa Verde.

Pluto's eyes swung on his pal, hovering there like a straight razor. Zé said no more. As I called for another round, Pluto picked up his story again. In another weak attempt to dodge the Crack Monster's insatiable demands, Narcisa had taken up wine-tasting with her soul-sucking sapphist soul mate.

Not a bright concept, I mused, given Narcisa's explosive temperament, emotional instability and unlucky genetic heritage . . . *Shit!* I grimaced at the image of her lurching around the greasy old streets of Lapa, drunk on cheap wine, with that foul creature in tow.

After getting thrown out of the squat one chilly evening for refusing to share their toxic red swill with the others, Narcisa and the dyke had kicked up a boisterous man-hating tandem tantrum. Then, off they went, Pluto said, as his partner Zé—who hated everybody, especially women—sneered into his beer.

Suddenly, the tipsy faggot began singing, with a sarcastic, rot-flecked, slobbery grin.

"Jus' de two of us . . ."

Pluto stopped again and glared, as if contemplating the most efficient way of decapitating his obnoxious pal. Finally, he sighed and continued. He'd taken them to a burned-out, abandoned house up in the cold, windy hills of Santa Teresa, he told me, where they'd all guzzled the bitter remains of the wine, sitting around in the dark.

I gave him a curious look. Was this little degenerate banging Narcisa now too?

As if sensing my misgivings, he explained that he'd only been trying to help. Feeling sorry for Narcisa, Pluto hadn't wanted to see her out on the street again, having to hit up Doc for cash. It made sense. Pluto was a loyal friend.

As he talked on, I called across the counter for the next round. Powering down another shot of *cachaça*, he described a damp, depressing scene that night. It had been dark and cold and raining hard, he said, and the roof had been leaking. Everything was damp and miserable. Then, out of nowhere, a drunken, belligerent Narcisa had started a big fight with Francisca and split.

I didn't bother asking what it was about. I knew Narcisa never needed a reason for a violent outburst. Any pretext was a good enough

motive to storm out into another cold, rainy night, all alone. As I pictured her out on the wet winter streets of Copacabana again, looking
for the action, a grim soundtrack echoed in my mind, like the voice
of a little lost ghost.

*"Game Over! Hah! Thank you come again! Next? An' then you just wan' it
de freedom to e'stay cold an' hungry again, an' walk all alone, walk, walk, walk
in de street, wanting, wanting . . . wanting to want, got it?"*

Pluto talked on, describing Narcisa's latest deadly downward
spiral. Loose on the the streets, all alone again, she went looking for
the action. Following her time-tested script, she soon found it. As my
drunken informants narrated a surreal voiceover, I watched the whole
sordid drama playing out in my head, like a movie:

*Opening scene: Narcisa back in Copacabana . . . She comes across a group of
gringos, sitting around a table at a beachside kiosk, drinking . . . Cameras rolling
. . . Action!*

*She goes up and speaks with them in her frantic, singsong broken English,
weaving a well-practiced spell, hamming it up for the camera, reeling 'em in.*

*Narcisa, sitting, drinking with the gringos . . . Vodka caipirinhas, one, two,
three, down the hatch . . . Fade to blackout . . .*

As the liquor-spawned demons flowed from their boozy wormholes
to dance like tipsy fireflies in her bad bad blood, Narcisa began a
crooked ballet of seduction for the gringo with the money. I could see
it all. Narcisa, back in Copacabana, working it hard again. Pouring it
on thick. Milking the image. Playing her role of the precocious, hard-
luck, homeless waif, down on her worn-out whorehouse heels . . . *Like
a fucking Dickens character . . . Oliver Twisted! Yeah, gringos are suckers for that
kinda shit . . . And Narcisa must have been putting on an Oscar-winning performance. Cuz now she was gonna get paid and get some good strong crack smoke into
her head, even if it killed her! Yeah, that's how Narcisa likes to talk . . . Death or
glory! No half measures for my bittersweet little pirate princess . . . Life or death!
Right now! Go go! The big trembling tightrope . . . A hush falls over the crowd . . .*

The drinks went down, and Narcisa got her good old ho-stroll mojo working again. As Pluto narrated, I could picture her out there, feet dancing on the street, her head unattached. Performing, posturing like Madonna, microphone in hand, strutting across the stage. Controlling the audience. Shouting. Gesturing. Seducing. Posing. Telling them all her best war stories. Weaving her mad, compelling mind-control spells. Reeling 'em in for the big, fat mother-lode-winning hand!

But there was a surprise guest appearance at her commend performance that night, when the gang of kids from the local ghetto crack den spotted her, sitting by the beach, speaking English with a bunch of tourists; fat, overfed, pink-skinned imported chickens. Ripe for the plucking. Easy prey for a pack of Copacabana *pivetes*. Narcisa was well acquainted, of course, with every tough little slum rat from all the nearby favelas. The skinny teenage thugs she smoked crack and weed with up in the hillside shantytowns were just part of the everyday scenery of her sordid little world. She knew them all by name, rank and police file.

They stood there in the shadows, grinning like a pack of threadbare jackals, checking out her action. Then the oldest one strode over. Greeting Narcisa with a casual fist bump, he whispered in her ear, instructing her to lure the gringo with the cash and big shiny watch around the corner. He and his partners would do the rest.

By all accounts, Narcisa had been drinking hard and heavy that night—something I knew from years of bitter experience she should never do. The last time I'd seen her drunk, she'd taken her clothes off and lay down butt-naked, right in the middle of the Avenida Atlantica, on a busy Saturday night, taunting passing motorists, daring them to run her over.

Somehow I'd managed to get her home intact that time.

But on this cold, rainy Copacabana evening, there would be no Cigano to get Narcisa home, or to watch her back in any way. In that truculent booze-addled state, high as a seven-foot-tall bullet-proof pimp, she told the cool little thugs to fuck off back to their dirty nigger hovels and find their own fucking pigeons. Narcisa had already marked her gringos, and wasn't in a sharing mood.

Sailing on a sea of gringo vodka and a bellyful of cheap squatter's wine, there would've been little thought of consequences for my swashbuckling little pirate. Pluto let out a sad guffaw as he went on with his tale. The gang of young predators had been so unnerved by her audacity, they just stared at Narcisa for a beat, trying to gauge what form of madness might have overtaken her. Mistaking their silence for weakness, she'd strung together one of her classic poetic litanies of guttersnipe insults and curses. I could almost hear her growling as she unleashed a torrential sewer spray of serpent-toothed verbal abuse on the adolescent toughs.

"Then she get her ass beat like a *real* man, hehehe!" Zé snickered.

It was on . . . *BAM! And she's down on the ground, getting kicked around like a stolen beach ball, in a hailstorm of blows to her body, face and head!*

"Aiiii!! Aiiii! Aiiii!"

With Narcisa's anguished howls echoing in my inner ear, I winced as Pluto went on with his tale. The gringos she'd defended had scurried off, he said, back to the safety of their luxury beachfront hotel, leaving poor Narcisa all alone to take a man-sized beat-down.

By another account I got later, though, it seemed the true story had been somewhat less altruistic on Narcisa's part; that she'd in fact been jumped that night by some neighborhood kids, for bullying an old lady selling beer and shots of *cachaça* from a Styrofoam cooler on the sidewalk in front of the Holiday Bar.

According to my other source—a local cabdriver close to the action on the Copacabana ho-stroll—the unfortunate vendor had committed the heinous crime of refusing to spot Narcisa free drinks when she couldn't pay for what she'd already consumed. Narcisa's septic sewer trap had flown open and exploded in the startled woman's face. After the indignant *camelô* shouted back in anger, a crowd had gathered. Insults flew, escalating into a shoving match, the cabbie told me. Then Narcisa head-butted the vendor's young helper in the face, breaking his nose. A small mob of local youths had then jumped in and beat her down like a mad dog.

Knowing Narcisa's dirty street fighting tactics, the cabdriver's version sounded more plausible than the heroic tales of derring-do she'd concocted to impress her Casa Verde cronies. Either way, it was just another day in the life for Narcisa. Whatever really happened that night, the point remained: she'd gotten shit-pants drunk, blacked out, then fucked with the wrong people again. She'd gotten herself stomped pretty bad this time too, it seemed. I was told she had needed dozens of stitches to the head, after my acquaintance drove her to the hospital, getting the windshield of his cab kicked out for his trouble by a hysterical, drunken Narcisa, howling, spitting and bleeding all over the seat.

To make matters worse, the police had been called to the emergency room, where she'd had to be restrained after breaking an expensive gringo X-ray machine. Narcisa fought back like a wildcat, cursing, spitting and biting. Then she'd gotten lumped up again, this time by the cops, after being carted off in a headlock. Narcisa's mother was contacted to bail her out, after even the jailers grew tired of her shit. As the woman reluctantly parted with her church money at the *delegacia*, there was yet another round of deranged public scandal and violence.

Once the dust cleared, Narcisa tucked her frayed, beaten tail between her legs and limped away from Rio. Back in her hometown, penniless, homeless and destitute, she'd caved in to desperation and called Doc. Taking advantage of my absence, the repugnant little creeper got his balls up and ran straight to the rescue, renting her a shack in the middle of nowhere, then following up with his ward on regular weekend visits.

With her Dickless Old Cushion now restored to his long-coveted station as Savior, Narcisa was hiding from the world now, somewhere at the edge of the jungle near Penedo.

According to Zé, who hated Doc with a vengeance, the old blood-sucker had finally succeeded in poisoning Narcisa against me for good. In shock, I looked at Pluto, who confirmed that Doc had indeed planted all sorts of cowardly seeds of distrust in Narcisa's mind, sup-posedly extracting a solemn promise that she was done with the Evil Gypsy forever.

Her friend shrugged with a deep, mournful sigh. Reaching across the counter, Pluto downed the last of his beer in one long, unhappy gulp. Looking up, he informed me that Narcisa had vowed to never set foot in Rio again.

91. INTO THE VOID

> "HEAVEN, TO KEEP ITS BEAUTY, CAST THEM OUT, BUT
> EVEN HELL ITSELF WOULD NOT RECEIVE THEM FOR FEAR
> THE WICKED THERE MIGHT GLORY OVER THEM."
> —*Dante*

My first night back, it rained until dawn.

All alone in the apartment, I crawled up to the loft and stared at my bed, unmade and still wrinkled with the body marks of Narcisa's last tortured sleep there.

Nothing had changed, but everything had changed. As I knelt on the mattress, the faint scent of her filled my senses with memories. The smell of her greasy, unwashed hair on the cold, abandoned pillows sent me crashing into a spell of restless discomfort. Shit. How could a physical space feel so empty and alone, yet so alive with someone's presence?

Uneasy in my skin, I climbed back down and lay on the sofa. I tried to sleep, but I couldn't stop my mind. I looked up at the ceiling, listening to the voices in my head. The stories I'd heard at the Casa Verde were echoing like a silent riot in my brain. I got up and paced the floor. Every chilly, desolate inch of the place was haunted by Narcisa's living ghost. Finally, exhausted, I sat down in the cool, empty porcelain bathtub and passed out.

Early the next morning, after only a couple of hours of fitful rest, I went out on a frenzied shopping spree. Tearing through the crowded pedestrian alleys of the Sahara, I purchased all sorts of little gifts. Then I loaded the bike with a bulging duffel bag.

This time I was on a mission. Barreling down the highway toward Narcisa, I could hear the phantom echo of her voice whistling in the wind . . . *"Is because inside of you some terrible thing make it so you always gotta e'stay all alone. Inside. You wan' only to want, Cigano! Cuz nothing can never e'satisfy Nobody, got it?"*

I got it. Again and again, I got it. Rolling along through the hot, sticky country air, I reflected on our times together, contemplating Narcisa, the riddle of her existence; digging in my memory like an archeologist, digging, dusting, excavating.

Right then, flying through time and space, it hit me like a stone.

Game over. Nobody. Nothing! Fuck! That's it! It's God she's been talking about! The Void. The Unnamable. The One. First Cause. Prime Creator. The Big Kahuna! That's why nothing satisfies! Because no fucking thing can ever fill the God-sized Hole!

And now, my frazzled little runaway chicken had finally come home to roost. To find herself. To find Nobody. To find Something. To find Nothing. To find God. Running, forever running, that blind, mindless idiot creed we both know so well. Addicts like us are so good at it, always running away from people, places and things, like some monstrous, self-defeating reverse homing instinct; as though maybe if we could just run long or far or fast enough, we might be able to outrun the plague of our existence, that endless loop of toxic, traumatic horror-show night-mare memories that rule over our lives and loves and destinies.

Yes, I mused, Narcisa had finally come full circle; running right back into the festering old rancid pains of her past. Into the wound.

And that's just how I found her that day. Wounded. Quiet. Sub-dued. Lost, humiliated, beaten; right back where she'd started out so long ago, living all alone in a miserable little dirt-gray shack on the outskirts of nowhere, at the edge of her long-abandoned hometown.

It was late afternoon when I pulled into Penedo. I stopped and fished the hastily scrawled scrap of paper from my pocket, squinting in the sun to decipher Pluto's garbled directions to the remote hamlet where Narcisa was holed up. I rode on out of town, past fences made of branches and flimsy rusted wire, then nothing but sprawling acres of empty, open land.

I traveled on for almost an hour without seeing a car. Startled by the noise of a motorcycle, flocks of giant condors took wing in feathery black explosions. There were threadbare horses and cows here and there, and the occasional scrawny feral dog. Other than that, nothing. With each passing kilometer, I was heading into a forgotten era, where gaunt-faced brown men in tattered straw hats, carrying long machetes, bounced alongside the muddy path on ragged donkeys with giant tragic eyes. Then, no sign of life for another hour.

Finally, I saw it. I brought the bike to a halt and parked beside a stagnant, mossy brown bog, trembling with mosquito larvae. I got off and stood there in the insect-humming stillness, staring at the decrepit gray wooden shack.

Like a phantom in a dream, Narcisa appeared at the door. I flashed a wide smile. She just stood looking back at me in silence, as the frozen, timeless moment registered in my brain like a faded old photograph.

Seeing her like that was a shock. She seemed to have aged several years. To add to the surreal effect, she'd bleached her hair. She must've done it before leaving Rio, along with the other Casa Verde denizens, in another desperate attempt to rid themselves of their ravenous plague of head lice. Narcisa's straw-white hair, combined with the ravages of malnutrition and crack addiction, had left my poor baby looking like an emaciated old sunken-eyed, demented drag queen's ghost.

I beamed at her with eyes of love. As she ushered me in without a word, I marveled at her situation. She seemed cowed and bowed and humiliated. I stood in the doorway, shifting from foot to foot as she turned her back and began organizing her few meager, crappy, burnt-out possessions. I couldn't believe my eyes. Narcisa, circling the bowl in some empty dirt-floored shack, going round and round in futile little circles in a cold, cruddy hovel in the middle of nowhere, licking her wounds in a stifling little empire of ruin.

Still, there was her invincible armor of pride—that unpardonable sin by which even the angels fall. I could see it in her shy little grin, as she turned and broke the silence at last, addressing me with a guarded drawl.

"*E aí, Cigano?* Whassup, bro?"

Narcisa's proud, defiant soul was still alive; flickering like a feeble old neon whorehouse sign, sputtering on bravely, even in the shadows of defeat.

It was a weird, awkward reunion, right from the start.

First off, she wasn't alone there. She had this creepy older sister hanging around. It was strange. She seemed like a prop. A buffer. Protection. As I beamed at her, Narcisa appeared unable to look me in the eye. There was none of her usual badass, blustery posturing; no frenetic, grandiose accounts bubbling forth from that shamefaced little grin to explain how she'd ended up in such a pitiful state.

Narcisa, for once, was oddly subdued.

To make things weirder yet, this sister—whom she'd rarely spoken of—was nothing like Narcisa. Pudgy and unattractive, drab, dull-looking, and seemingly devoid of any personality, she had a long, brutal scar running across a flat, expressionless face, like an extra cunt on a cow. A real dirt clod, the woman was dressed tastelessly, like one of Narcisa's "clone people," and wore the vapid, sedated glare of a chronic pill popper; someone unlucky, someone unloved. Saying nothing, she just kind of hovered there, like a fart in the gloomy air, plopped down on an uncomfortable-looking little cot, glaring at me in surly silence, sizing me up, as I unpacked the duffel bag full of gifts.

Narcisa herself remained strangely distant and aloof. I got the distinct impression she'd set it all up that way on purpose, even though there was no way she could have known I'd be coming. Still, it gave me the creeps. Especially the sister, just sitting there like a jealous old watchdog, not leaving. It was as though Narcisa was frightened to be alone with me now; as if I represented something in herself that she was struggling to deny.

After her initial chill, though, she appeared glad enough to see me, in a cool, distant sort of way. Still, I couldn't help wondering if that subdued sparkle in her eye was only twinkling because I'd brought that bulging bag of presents. As I unpacked it, slowly, Narcisa's old swagger sprung back to life—one gift at a time.

I was so glad to see her, I barely noticed all the lingering weirdness. At first. I hadn't even noticed him standing there when I first stepped in, but, besides the sister, there was this other ghoulish little fellow who just appeared out of nowhere. Like the somber sister, he too said nothing. He just stood there, lurking by the door, smoking a big, stinky *basiado* and staring at me in silence, like a resentful spider monkey.

I looked around and wondered . . . *Who the fuck are all these freaks? What kinda fucked-up Twilight Zone scene have I stumbled into here?*

But I knew. They were just part of the scenery. Wherever Narcisa went, she always gathered a following of zombielike hangers-on. Here they were again.

Narcisa didn't bother with any introductions, of course; and, given the collective creepiness of the moment, none were forthcoming. We all just stood around in a listless, insipid fog of greasy, oppressive alienation; everyone but the rude, stodgy sister, who kept her fat ass firmly planted on Narcisa's hard little cot—the only place to sit in the cramped, colorless space.

Time was frozen in a awkward gray silence of the tomb. Jealousy, confusion, envy and suspicion weighed heavy in the air, like cyanide gas seeping into an execution chamber.

Then, with a start, I picked up on something else. Something malevolent: I could sense another unhealthy, unseen presence, lurking in the shadows.

Doc! My gut went cold with a sudden, powerful flash of déjà vu as I heard the words of the old spirit medium, Caridade, echoing in my brain.

"She spirit infested, ya seen? Her got de jealous spirit enemy all 'round she. De vampiro inna human form, an' dem all gots de evil eye 'pon she, fe' true!"

I felt gooseflesh creeping up my back as I watched a small brown scorpion disappear behind a crevice in the wall, like an omen. Unseen phantoms were all around us in that place, whispering toxic, occult curses into the lifeless air. I knew Doc had been visiting her on weekends, bearing gifts, spreading lies about me to anyone who'd listen. He'd obviously gotten his hooks into Narcisa's ugly sister. That sort of explained her distrustful, sulky demeanor.

Finally, Narcisa started trying on all the new clothes I'd brought for her, posturing and strutting around her hovel like the Whore of Babylon on parade. Still, I could see that, deep inside, she was beaten. I stood watching her, musing sadly. All her big plans and dreams, everything shot to pieces. There she was, rotting away with the rest of the dead-end small-town drunks and druggies and end-of-the-line losers from her troubled, unhappy past.

I was so happy to see her, though, I just stood there, grinning like an idiot, hoping to lighten the tension somehow.

After a mute, throbbing eternity, the Creepy Sister and the Sulky Guy finally wandered off into the gathering night—without so much as a civil word being spoken. Like ghosts.

O nce Narcisa's gloomy visitors departed, her mood began to brighten.

I could see she was trying hard to pry the rusty fortress gates of her heart open again. Then, all of a sudden, the clouds parted and the sun shone through as she smirked at me with that old endearing, childlike grin.

"*Ei,* Cigano, you got my back, hein? Let's go for a ride, bro, go, go!"

She didn't have to ask twice. I practically flew out the door. I got on the bike and fired up the motor. As soon as she jumped on behind me, her long, elegant arms wrapping around me like old times, I knew it was still there . . . *Yes! We're still us!*

But as we rode away, I could also sense that other chilly Something, sitting between us like a phantom passenger. A vague shadow of fear. Trepidation. Suspicion.

I did my best to ignore it as I navigated the winding country roads. In silence, we rolled through a nearby village, then off into the sprawling jungles, where a deep country darkness enveloped us like a shroud.

Narcisa said nothing; and then there was nothing but the motorcycle's headlight on the dark path ahead. As the steady rumbling growl of the engine propelled us through the night, she held on tight, her long arms wrapped around me, like old times, and that was all that mattered.

We rode for a long while like that, rolling through the forest, deep into the long, moonless *madrugada.* The air was crisp and cold and smelled of pine trees and cedar smoke and Narcisa. Without a word, she steered me with her finger along the empty roads, finally pointing to a steep turnoff, snaking up into the dark, looming winter mountains.

We rode and rode forever, up a winding path, with a sheer granite wall on one side and a dark precipice on the other. I could feel my ears pop from the altitude as we came at last to a rustic village in the foggy heights.

Shaking with stinging cold, our bones rattling like icicles, we pulled into the sleeping hamlet at last, teeth chattering, numb with bitter fatigue. A few minutes later, we found a warm, furnished mountain cabin for rent.

I parked and we checked in for the night. Inside the chalet, Narcisa swallowed a handful of pills. Downers. Having been off crack for over a month now, that was her new, Doc-approved, legal kick. Then, she smoked some weed, hacking and coughing and choking like an old man in an iron lung after each greedy toke.

As the drugs eased the raging war in her head, she began dancing around in the sparkly new dress I'd brought her, pirouetting like a maddened epileptic white giraffe to whatever music replaced the Shadow People's angry nightmare soundtrack in her tortured inner ear.

Watching Narcisa dance again was like witnessing a lightning storm, a tornado; something elemental, dangerous, powerful, crucial and indescribably beautiful. I looked on, transfixed, as she glided across the rough wooden floor like a wild, swirling funnel cloud; a blue-veined, mad, translucent phantom.

Finally, I couldn't take it. "Baby, baby." I took her in my arms. "Get yer clothes off! I gotta be with you, inside you, right now, right now!"

"You gotta make it fast, Cigano! Hurry up, go, an don' take so long, go!"

She pulled her shorts off and lay back on the fluffy goose-down quilt, spreading her long white angel legs for me. After a month away, her warm, wet hole was a magical portal to home; and then I was right back where I'd started, back where I'd sworn to never go again, right back where I belonged, hugging her insides, eating her alive, lost and drunk, drowning in her smell; the dark, toxic magic of her presence.

Rocking back and forth on the storm currents of her sacred, over-powering, magical madness, climaxing fast and hard, I went limp all over, sinking deep down inside her, kissing her long and soft, our languid breaths mixing into a forbidden, stupefying, musky poison.

Then, we passed out.

The rest of the night was a tangled, soporific underwater orgy, a tender war of arms and legs and bellies and backs, unconscious caresses, hugs, snores, groans, farts and grunts. Holding each other close for warmth, we shifted around like restless sands on a desert of dreams.

I fucked her again while she slept; drinking in her hot, sedated, snoring breath, moving soft and slow as I worked it in and out, a stealthy safecracker in the house of Eros. Narcisa never stirred as I tunneled into her feverish, wet core and came again and again forever.

92. DIGGING

"If someone tells you who they are, believe them."
—*Maya Angelou*

The next day, we awakened in silence.

We dressed and made our way down a dirt path to the bike. Without a word, we took off along the winding mountain road.

The spectacular vistas looked new and different in the light of morning; uplifting and magnificent. A few minutes later, we stopped at a humble little roadside eatery, overlooking the vast jungles and valleys stretching below forever.

As we sat by the window, eating warm bread and jam and soft white goat cheese, smoking cigarettes and drinking sweet black coffee, Narcisa began telling me stories of her childhood; all sorts of funny little tales of growing up in the country; all the petty rivalries and fights she'd been in with other children, her dreams and hopes; the random injuries and battles of a feral child bouncing over these same rutted dirt paths in search of wings to fly off to faraway lands.

The burning morning sunlight seemed to glow behind her eyes as her brain exploded softly into the World Unknown. "First time I listen to de voices, Cigano, I was just a little girl."

"What voices, baby?"

"Just voices. I donno, mano, but always I use to feel it, like a *presence* of somebody, something invisible, e'standing close by, but I never know what was it, you know?" She shrugged. "Sometime I even can sorta see it, like de kinda shadow thing, moving, but I never know who is there. When I get more older, I e'start notice that any time I get upset an' go close by de *electrodomestico*, de radio or television, whatever, was all de time de big interference . . . An' whenever I think about something real hard, or maybe I wan' for some kinda thing to happen, it always just *happen*, you know?"

I was impressed. "Woah. That's some wild shit, Narcisa."

She studied her coffee. "No so much, bro. For me, always seem like normal thing. It never bother me . . . But some really e'strange kinda thing e'start happen . . ."

"What kinda things?"

"Like one time when I get real angry, I go an' e'stand by de TV an' *bum*, she just blow out, an' de e'smoke come out de top. No more picture! Finish! Fock!"

Narcisa went on to explain how she'd always had trouble because of her weird telepathic and telekinetic gifts, starting from early childhood. It got worse as she moved into adolescence. Being seen as "different," she was labeled as a freak in her backward, religious small-town community. Finding herself bullied by other kids, being avoided and hated on as a liar or a witch, or simply crazy, Narcisa began her retreat into her own little fantasy bubble.

Her eyes lit up. "Before I take de drugs, first time I get de buzz, I was just a little geer-ool, Cigano, maybe only three year old . . ."

"*Caralho!*" I looked at her, stunned. "Three years old? How?"

" . . . Yeh, mano. I use to take off de back from these radio my mother got, an' then I go an' stick my finger inside!"

I laughed. "What th' fuck did ya do that for, ya little maniac?"

She grinned. "For feel it de e'shock, Cigano! Was my very first time buzz. Hah!"

"You *liked* that shit?"

"No really." She giggled. "First time I do it, I e'say, *'Ai aiii, porra! I never gonna do that again.'* But next day come, e'same thing, I go an' look de radio an' I e'say myself, *'No no no, don' do it, Narcisa, don' do it . . .'* But I just gotta try again, one time more, you know, so I go an' put my finger again an' *bzzzzz! 'Ai ai aiii! Fock, never gonna do it again!'* Then next day come, I look de e'same e'stupid radio an' I thinking again, *'No no no, don' do it' don' do it . . .'* an' then I e'say, *'Fock it, gotta try again'* an' then, *bzzzzzz! Zow! 'Ai ai aiiiii!'* An' you know, I keep doing these e'same e'sheet for years, e'same focking thing! Hah!"

Narcisa fell silent. Then, finally, with a faraway look, she shrugged. "I only e'stop play with these e'stupid radio after I go take de real drugs, got it?"

I got it. She'd found a way to quiet the voices, to live in peace with her unwanted paranormal sensitivity. Narcisa was instinctively self-medicating.

After leaving home, she said, she'd visited spiritist centers and *terreiros*, consulting with different psychic mediums. She detailed how she'd finally blown her mind open like a mineshaft to hell, after taking her first drink of psychedelic tea, made from the sacred indigenous ayahuasca plant mixture, at the tender age of twelve. In the ensuing years, she'd met with all sorts of other mystics and UFO students, up in the mountains, before declaring it all a waste of time.

She told me how she'd stumbled through every occult sect and cult, one by one, burning bridges behind her as she went, leaving a trail of cynical disillusion in her wake.

Narcisa had always been studying the dynamic laws of the universe, it seemed, if only to better defy them. Even as a child, she'd already been staggering through the mystical psychic minefield she wandered in, lost, today.

For a curious little warrior spirit like Narcisa, always thirsty for new sensations and awareness, whatever desperate dirt path she stumbled onto would always turn out to be a high-tension tightrope walk into the light of knowledge.

As she talked on, I gazed at her with a new admiration.

Narcisa's whole life, as weird and contradictory as it appeared to me at times, was a long, painful, frenzied, hyperactive quest for Truth.

93. BATTLE SCARS

"O FOOLISH ANXIETY OF WRETCHED MAN, HOW INCONCLUSIVE ARE
THE ARGUMENTS WHICH MAKE THEE BEAT THY WINGS BELOW!"
—*Dante*

I leaned forward, listening to Narcisa, taking careful mental notes, like an archeologist dusting a patch of rock for some tiny clue to mysteries transcendent and sublime.

As we sat there overlooking the lands of her birth, she began relating the many sins of her forefathers. Desperate to escape the harsh realities of her violent, unhappy home, from an early age Narcisa had made books her only friends. But the drugs had eventually robbed her of the focus to continue her studies, cutting her off from that magical world of mysticism, philosophy and letters.

With a sad little shrug, she confessed she'd read her last complete book at the age of thirteen, Nietzsche's *Ecce Homo*, but she'd never read another one since.

"Hah! I take so many different kinda drug, Cigano, now I got only de two little brain cell left inside my head." She tapped at her forehead with a spoon. *"Anybody home, hein?* Hah! Only these little two all de time make de big war with de other one, got it?"

I got it. Like myself, it was a miracle Narcisa could even put two words together.

Shaking my head, I smiled sadly. "Jesus, baby! Didn't it ever occur to you ya mighta had a problem? Why didn't you ever try to quit?"

She shrugged. "Well, I try an' stop forever these one time, Cigano, but, I donno . . . I guess it was kinda e'stupid . . ."

With a sheepish grin, she told me of her one heroic attempt to reclaim her soul and get clean. When she was fifteen, she said, she'd fled back to Penedo, after many hard months in Rio. One drizzly gray morning, depressed and hungover, too proud to ask anyone for help, Narcisa trudged off into the jungle, all alone, shedding her shoes and clothing along the way.

As we sat smoking cigarettes and drinking coffee, she gestured at the imposing mountain range and vast tropical rain forests below, detailing three full moons she spent out there, all by herself, living like an animal, wandering the bush by day and sleeping at night, ingesting only berries, roots and herbs for sustenance.

Many of them, she said, were familiar psychedelic plants.

Narcisa's voice fell to a whisper. Her eyes flashed like colliding stars as she described her months in the wilderness. After nightfall, the crackling, twittering darkness would burst to life with ghostly sounds and weird, shadowy shapes of unseen creatures and alien spirits. Trees called out in dark, menacing tones, rustling their spindly limbs with eerie, malevolent intent.

Breathless, she spoke of the mysteries of the forest, lit only by piercing knife shafts of light, swirling with glittery, colorful insect mists. Boisterous toucans with gaudy, oversized beaks, and screeching monkeys skittering around overhead were her only company on that long, lonesome pilgrimage through the thick green tapestry.

I looked out at the distant waterfalls threading shimmering paths down a granite mountain, like crystalline tear-trails. "Fuck, baby! Nobody knew where you were all that time?"

She shook her head slowly. "*Ninguém!*"

Everyone had assumed she'd simply gone off into the bush to die, she snickered. The natives were shocked, then, when she appeared, months later, swaggering back into town, clothed only in foliage. Dirty, disheveled, savage-looking and scrawny as a lean, hungry young wolf, Narcisa was carrying only a thatched reed bag she'd constructed like an Indian, filled with magic mushrooms and other medicinal plants.

"Hah! De focking peoples all look me like I am de focking e'spaceman!"

After that, Narcisa became something of a local legend.

She stopped talking. As she sat staring out over the scenery, her long, contemplative hush was like an invisible gun taking steady aim at my heart.

Finally, she cocked her head and went on. Soon after her long, lion-hearted jungle walkabout, Narcisa put her thumb out on the highway again, and headed back to the dirty old killing grounds of Copacabana. There she would surrender, once and for all, to her addiction, and all that came with it; prostitution. Crime. Homelessness. Begging. Hustling. Stealing. Long, livid days and threadbare nights of filthy, tattered, shattered destitution in the chaotic, heartless urban jungles of Rio.

Anything would've been better for poor Narcisa, it seemed, than the frightful prospect of living a life without drugs. That had all been just before I'd met her. But even then, she already knew she was beat. And still she refused to quit.

I got it. Drugs were Narcisa's only hope for any small peace of mind, stolen in brief moments of stoned-out, incoherent relief.

Over the years, the seeds of madness grew and raged like a lightning-fueled forest fire. Narcisa grew increasingly violent and irritable, breaking things, starting streetfights with strangers and cutting on her own hated body, just to remind herself she was alive.

"I use to really like make de cuts on myself, Cigano!" She grinned, running the table knife longingly across her forearm. "But I never go too deep. I wan' only de pain for feel de control of it. Is really crazy de sensation, bro! Hah! But one day I go cut too deep, *oops*, an' I fock up a tendon or veins or whatever . . . Lookit, you see it here?" She pointed with pride to the jagged Frankenstein scar running down her left forearm like a fleshy malediction.

I winced. "That's some nasty *cicatríz*, baby. Looks like ya fucked yerself up good there."

Narcisa's eyes glowed like a world of mad fireflies. "Hah! I was e'staying with my husband, in de big hotel in Copacabana, an' after I cut it, I just wanna get more higher, cuz de pain in my hand get so bad, you know? But I gotta make de big e'scandal for these focking gringo buy me more drug, cuz he keep e'say, *'No more drug now for you,'* so then I go an' cut my wrist again, more deeper de next time, an' then I put de knife on my throat an' I e'say him I gonna finish myself if he don' buy me de focking drugs right now, got it?"

I got it. Blackmail. Emotional extortion. I shuddered as I recalled her suicide threat in the country with me. As I stared out over her childhood home, I replayed the stories she and Doc and others had told me of her people's brutal legacy. Knives, stabbings, cutting, blood, rape, betrayal. I thought of how it all played out in her life, again and again, in a noxious, repeating cycle of unfocused primal rage.

Narcisa's stories trailed off into the afternoon like a long, ghostly archeological expedition, unearthing more surreal clues to her being. She told me of her following years, scrambling around like a frantic, bug-eyed ferret in a burning maze, falling into all sorts of scenes and taking every possible combination of drugs. She did whatever she had to do to get them, of course—unwittingly following right in the footsteps of her hated whore mother.

With a mischievous grin, she recounted her exploits as a teenage prostitute. Schooled in the offbeat ho-stroll scams of the streetwise squatter chicks at the Casa Verde, she always demanded cash up front from the gringos she went with in Copacabana. Even as a seasoned "sex worker," Narcisa had never cared for either prospect: work, or sex. And she did whatever she could to dodge the dreaded moment with her unfortunate clients.

She described how, once inside a trick's hotel room, after getting paid, she would slowly, seductively begin to undress. Then, at the last minute, she'd reach into her panties, extracting a tampon soaked in red wine stashed in a plastic bag.

Before the gringo's mortified eyes, she'd fling the "bloody" cotton wad against the wall with a resounding *fwap*.

Laughing, I pictured a disgraceful red menstrual trail snaking down a spotless white hotel room wall, and a grossed-out, red-faced gringo scurrying to the door in horror, holding it open for Narcisa to depart. Untouched.

"Hah! *Perfect, Max! Thank you come again! Next?* These e'sheet always work, Cigano! An' they never even one time ask for de mo-ney back! Hah!"

As she chattered on, I was reminded of Narcisa's playful, innocent lust for fun and excitement; how her whole world had once been a big, wide road of daring adventures—until she'd stumbled into the nightmare realm of the Crack Monster, where the Curse had seized her soul like a red-eyed, screaming chimpanzee, sending her into a deadly tailspin and stopping her dead in her tracks.

After that, the best poor Narcisa could do as she ran around in futile little circles of ruin was to write down her thoughts, seeking mental refuge in crooked philosophical speculations and poetic pretzel logic, as she went progressively mad.

"De best philosophy for me is de Nietzsche, Cigano, got it?"

I got it. I remembered having read through her notebooks filled with confusing, contradictory quotes from the enigmatic German visionary scribbled into the margins. After she'd disappeared to New York, I'd sat up many a night, racking my brains to decipher her long, surreal poems. It seemed I'd always been seeking an answer to the riddle of Narcisa's mind. As the years crept by, my digging had trailed off in a sad little dead-end labyrinth; page upon page of tattered, ash-blackened, trembling, illegible nuthouse scrawls . . . *What a waste!*

Finally, she gave me another wry little grin. "So that's it, Cigano. That's me. *Thank you come again! Next?*" She winked with a shrug.

Then she fell quiet. Narcisa was finished talking.

I sighed and stood up, beaming at her with a deep admiration . . . *My brave little warrior* . . . Choking back a tear, I shuffled over and started the bike.

Narcisa got on and we rode off down the long, bumpy mountain road.

94. CHECKMATE

"MORALITY IS CONTRABAND IN WAR."
—*Gandhi*

By the time we arrived back at her shack, it was dark. Thankfully, none of her macabre associates were hanging around this time. But, as the night deepened, it got colder and damper in her crude little hideaway. The uncomfortable, dirt-floored hut seemed all the more sordid and desolate after spending the previous night in a clean, warm, well-appointed chalet.

Soon enough, Narcisa grew fidgety and grumpy. I watched as she puttered around in the dark, scrounging for weed scraps to roll a joint. I tried to make conversation, but her replies were curt, monosyllabic grunts. Narcisa was tongue-tied, frozen; as if she'd expended her lifetime supply of words up on the mountain.

I suggested we get on the bike and ride back to Rio. What did she have to lose? I couldn't see any reason for her to stay.

She hemmed and hawed and balked and stalled. It was weird. I knew Narcisa. Something was wrong. She was scared of something! But why?

Has that asshole Doc threatened her? What the fuck? Why doesn't she wanna leave?

I was puzzled; but, as usual, I said nothing. Standing by the only window, looking out, I watched a dark-skinned boy in a straw hat struggling with a donkey. The mule had stopped in the middle of the dark dirt path; no matter how hard the kid tugged at the lead, it refused to budge. I looked on as he cursed and kicked at the stubborn creature, trying to bend it to his will. No dice. The donkey wouldn't move. Finally, he threw his hands up and walked away. Then, slowly, at first, the donkey began to follow.

The little vignette reminded me of Narcisa and myself.

She was the donkey and I was the boy.

To pass the time, we sat down on the cold dirt floor and played a few monotonous games of chess on the little portable set I'd brought her.

I frowned as she won twice in a row. "How'd ya learn to play so good?"

"I teach it to my own e'self, Cigano. I play de game all my life."

I looked at her. "All yer life? *Como assim?*"

"From when I about two year old." She shrugged.

I raised a skeptical eyebrow.

"Whatever, bro! I donno exactly how many year old was it, okey? What is it matter, hein? Is irrelevant . . . But de *Xadrez*, she pretty e'simple, got it?"

I didn't get it. I told her I didn't see it as such a simple game.

"*E simples, sim!*" She insisted.

Then, with a confident smirk, she started to explain the game of chess for me—as only Narcisa could.

"Okey, so lookit, bro . . ." She held up the king, her mad eyes bugging out of her head like a pair of trembling dragon eggs about to hatch. "These one, he de most weakest one, got it? He only can take de one little step at a time, like de cripple man, de beggar, got it? De *rei*, he really de most retard one of all de army! Hah!"

She must have read the question marks in my eyes as she continued explaining the mysteries of chess.

" . . . But these king, Cigano, he also de most important soldier. Cuz he de onliest one who got any value, de lone one what really worth any e'sheet. But he no got just de human power. He represent de *real* Power, de complete Power!"

She stopped and looked at me, cutting down into my soul like a jeweler's torch with those big soulful, bulging bughouse eyes. "*Treasure!*" She breathed the word, revealing the Secrets of the Universe.

I shook my head and grinned, thinking of how everything really was like a big game of chess for Narcisa; her own life-sized struggle for Power and Treasure. Narcisa always had to win; and usually she did, being expert at all things involving conflict. Argument. Debate. Mind control. Scandal. Blackmail. Strategy. Revenge. Sabotage. War. She could never bear to lose a game or an argument, no matter how wrong she ever was. Logic and fair play were just boring, irrelevant trivia.

I recalled the way she'd always invent her own weird nonsense words to win at Scrabble. The one time I dared challenge the point, she'd ended the game by turning the table over in my face. I smiled, thinking of all the little letters flying through the air that day, like shrapnel in her endless battle with the world.

But Narcisa was more than just a sore loser. Her indomitable pride saw to it that she simply never conceded failure. That was her trick. No surrender. Ever. Even when she lost; especially when she lost. As I thought about it, I realized that Narcisa's inability to submit was the real reason she could never get free of her addictions. Because she appeared to be constitutionally unable, or just fiercely unwilling, to take the critical first step by admitting defeat and asking for help.

She'd been to the AA and NA meetings with me over the years, but even those fleeting moments of grouchy, halfhearted compliance had always turned out to be a far cry from any real surrender. Narcisa just couldn't let go of the delusion of her own supremacy as the omnipotent ruler of her fucked-up little universe.

"*Who cares to admit complete defeat?*" The AA twelve-step book begins, inviting hopeless drunks and addicts to look at the wreckage of their lives with unflinching self-honesty; never an easy task for an alcoholic or a drug fiend—even a weak, defeated one standing at death's door. But how could someone like Narcisa possibly admit defeat? It just wasn't in her nature.

How many times had she shuffled into those meetings with her head hung low in shame and remorse, vowing to never take another drink, another hit of weed, another step toward the Crack Monster? Only to find herself right back in its clutches again, because she'd gotten cocky and let her guard down after only a few days of grouchy, begrudging abstinence.

Narcisa seemed completely ignorant of the dangerous occult forces conspiring against her.

How could I help her? I couldn't, I realized. No one could, not unless something inside her changed.

How many well-intentioned fools like Doc and her estranged husband and her mother had already beaten their heads against the brick wall of Narcisa's ironclad resistance? They'd all tried to bend her to their wills with their half-assed schemes and shortcut "cures"—only to find themselves so frustrated, disappointed, injured and resentful, they'd eventually become as insane and irrational as her.

I could see the danger of falling into that sort of downward spiral of gnawing self-pity and self-righteous anger myself, but, somewhere deep inside, I truly abhorred the idea of trying to dominate another human being. That was probably the only thing that kept me from just tying Narcisa up and hauling her off to the loony bin myself. Mostly, though, I knew it wouldn't work; not for a real addict like Narcisa. She was too proud to change; too skilled at the age-old art of opposition.

As the evening deepened, she beat me again and again, game after game, smirking at her unchallenged superiority. Finally, she grew bored. We put the chessboard aside and sat there in the dull little hovel, looking at each other in stultifying, dumb-faced silence.

I could feel a familiar clammy tedium creeping in on us. Once again, I was in checkmate in Narcisa's big game. No move was safe. There was nothing more to do. Like that willful old donkey outside her window, Narcisa wouldn't budge. She wouldn't come back to Rio.

Never one to admit her fears and risk losing face on the battlefield of life, she couldn't verbalize her ambivalence, of course. But I could smell it crawling all over her. She was still licking her wounds from the horrific, demoralizing beating she'd taken in Copacabana.

And those painful memories, together with the doubts and suspicions Doc had planted in her mind, kept Narcisa's feet rooted to the dreary dirt floor of her shack, like a stone-faced monument to Defiance.

95. OPENING THE WOUND

"WE ARE HEALED OF A SUFFERING ONLY BY
EXPERIENCING IT TO THE FULL."
—*Marcel Proust*

As Narcisa sat there, scowling in silence, I could see the fear working at her like a lone termite, gnawing away in the back of her brain.

We sat and sat and sat on that cold dirt floor, till we were both bored to delirium.

Finally, restless and edgy, I stood up and smiled. "Lissen, Narcisa. If you're still all stressed-out about that shit that went down last time you were in Rio, I just wanna tell ya, I got yer back now, an—"

"Menos, Cigano! Just shut de fock up about these e'sheet! I don' wanna talk about these focking thing, got it? Menos!"

I got it. I bit my tongue. But I needed to convince her she'd be safe.

When I tried again, she averted her eyes, growling. *"Menoo-oos! No more you e'stupid talk, Cigano! I don' wanna listen all these kinda depressive e'sheet, got it?"*

I got it. I shut up.

Time crawled by like a cold, lonesome cockroach climbing the dirty wall of her shack. Narcisa sat there frowning, pouting in mute dissatisfaction, seething with disgusted, pent-up rage; and still she wouldn't give an inch.

I could feel it. I was being shut out again, maneuvered into check-mate; out the door, out of her confidence, out of her life again. I knew it so well: that cold, dark, clammy, empty feeling, freezing my guts, choking my heart.

My blood ran frigid and bleak and blank, and then I was back, standing in gloomy shadows of the past; a helpless little boy, silhou-etted beside a hazy image of little Narcisa, watching her mother being stabbed in a frenzy of bloody chaos. I could feel it all, the suffering of her whole life experience. Her world. Her disease. Her Curse. My Curse.

Pain enfolded my soul like the mouth of a giant, slobbering walrus as I slipped away, falling down into the wound; back, back in time, like little Narcisa. Little Ignácio, a tiny five-year-old ghost, standing in the foggy night. Smell of eucalyptus disinfectant and garbage and blood. Shaking in the winter cold, shivering in a pair of tissue-thin pajama pants, holding a dirty, ragged old teddy bear. Little Ignácio, paralyzed with fear, watching as the White Ambulance of Death screams off into the night, spinning colored lights flashing like a demon Christmas tree, disappearing into the distance . . . taking his momma away forever.

It was no use trying to pry anything out of Narcisa. I knew better than to talk anymore. There were no more words. As the night lin-gered outside like my dying mother's weak, final curse, I did what I'd learned to do long ago: I shut down. I shut down and shut the fuck up.

Shaking my head, drowning in a swirling mist of pain, resentment and gut-wrenching, recurring horrors, I sat back down and stared at the wall, watching the cold, lonely cockroach of time crawl by, saying nothing.

After a dark, heartless eternity, I heard a car approach . . . *What now?* Then a shout, a male voice in the darkness, calling out, calling her name.

"Oi, Narcisa! Sou eu! Monstro! Vem, vamo'nessa, gatinha! C'mon, let's go, kitty cat, we gonna go drink some wine, baby! Party! I got some good weed!"

Narcisa jumped up, grinning like a dog with two dicks.

"I gonna go with my friend now, Cigano!" She ran for the door, shouting to me over her shoulder. "Gotta go! Hah! *Thank you come again!"*

I sat there on the floor, reeling in shock, saying nothing, staring at her.

She turned around and faced me with her hands on her hips, glowering. "Lookit, if you wanna come an' party with us an' be e'social to my friend, you can come too. But I no gonna e'stay an' sit all de night here with you an' look you make de long face like e'stupid old monkey, got it?"

I got it. My stomach froze up and died as my eyes wandered over to her cot. The pack of condoms peeked out at me from under the thin mattress like a scorpion in its nest. Not my brand. I swallowed hard . . . *Shit!* She hadn't even cared enough to hide them.

I got up and followed her to the door. I stood looking at her. Incredulous. Wordless. Wounded. Shutting down again. But there was more. With Narcisa there was always more. More disappointment. More betrayal. More pain.

"Melhor é você voltar pro Rio já, Cigano! Vá embora! Anda logo, vai, vai!"

Each word struck me like a frozen fish hammer blow to my churning guts.

Just-you-go-back-de-Rio-now-Cigano-go-away-now-go-go!

Fuck! This isn't happening! If this coldhearted bitch says another fucking word, I swear I'll get out my knife and cut my fucking throat right here and now!

I didn't move.

Narcisa glared at me. Then she took an ice pick to my soul.

"Lissen, Cigano, I got a new life now in these place, okey?

Got de new boy friend, bro! What de fock I e'suppose to do when you go away an' leave me alone, hein? I no gonna e'stay all alone an' just wait for you come back!"

I will die! Freezing to death! Frozen arctic barren desolate Dead Sea Black Pit of Death! Cold! Her dirty black heart is cold as a prehistoric glacier!

"You no wanna take care of me no more, porra, so I come an' e'stay here! These my place now, my peoples, my life! Go back de Rio, mano, go! Vaza, vai!"

Cold as the fucking grave!

I ran out into the road behind her. Standing in the darkness. Smell of pine and eucalyptus and cold, desolate winter night. I could hear myself shouting, crying, screaming with all the hurt and rage and indignation of a throwaway child. A bastard child. An abandoned child.

"I only left cuz ya dumped me! Ya dodged me and insulted me and pushed me away and treated me like dirt, Narcisa, till I couldn't fuckin' take it anymore! You're th' one who ran out on me, just like you always done! And now yer doin' it again!"

I was that battered little orphan again, howling against the frozen, empty, uncaring, unblinking stars, spitting, crying, raving in pain, cursing, bellowing into the cold, merciless, meaningless darkness of the Wound.

" . . . And I still come back! Ride all th' way down here with a bag of presents, just to see you and bring ya home! Well fuck you, Narcisa! Santa Claus is dead! Finished! G'wan, go out and play with yer new victim now, ya bloodsuckin' whore! This time I'm done with yer shit for good! Finished, got it!?!"

She shouted back, spitting flaming daggers of venom. *"Hah! You wanna see me, Cigano? So now you seen me! What? You think you the boss of me cuz you gimme some cheap fock-*

ing presente? Well, I don' wan' nothing of you! Nada! Now I gonna go out with my real boyfriend, de one who e'stay with me here an' now, got it?"

I got it. Like a knife in my heart. I could feel my soul going cold and numb. Dying. Shutting down as Narcisa dug the blade in deeper.

"Why you make all these drama, like de little gee-rool, hein? Vaza fora, porra! Beat it, Cigano! Just get de fock out, go! Maybe I see you around some time, hein? Bye bye, Cigano, thank you come again, bye bye, bye bye bye!"

Still shouting, she jumped into the car and it sped off down the road.

I stood there, seething in mute anger and dread, watching the flickering red smear of taillights disappear into the night like the White Ambulance of Death.

Everything went quiet. Silent and cold as a cheap, concrete tombstone.

I stood in the dark, empty road for an eternity. My blood froze, then boiled again with anger and hate and despair, my heart sinking into a foul, bloody swamp of shit. And then there was nothing. Nothing but little Ignácio, standing all alone in the dark again, surrounded by silence and whispering echoes and ghosts.

Feeling numb, I got on the bike and rode off into the night, alone.

Running for my life again. Shutting down. Brokenhearted. Again.

96. SISTER MORPHINE

"LIFE IS A PROGRESS FROM WANT TO WANT."
—*Samuel Johnson*

As I sped down the dark, lonesome highway, frenzied thoughts raced around and around in my head, like swarms of angry hornets.

Going back to Rio! Just like that! Twenty-four hours was all it took for it all to turn to shit this time! Why? I never felt so close to her as I did today up on the mountain . . . She opened her heart to me, like she never did before. Because she missed me! I know she did. She missed me, as much as I missed her. I could feel it. It was real! So what just happened? Suddenly, she turns on me like a rattlesnake!

Why? She took me to the top of the mountain and told me her secrets, opened up to me! And then she dashes me into the pit! What does she want, anyway?

Insects fluttered in my headlights like a biblical plague. I rode on through the night, barreling away from Narcisa like a homeless robot on automatic pilot, lost in a nightmare stew of dismal feelings and reflections. Questions.

I looked to the road for answers . . . *What the fuck does she want?*

The road looked back in silence.

No answers. Riding along, I could feel tears running from my eyes and across my face, drying in the foul, answerless wind of the long, empty, silent road.

Back in Rio again, I tried to resume my old life. Life before Narcisa.

There was no old life. No more life. No more colors in the sights, no music in the sounds, no passion in the girls I brought home every night and fucked robotically, monotonously, mechanically, just going through the motions; warm, nameless, anonymous bodies I tried to console myself with, and invariably failed.

My friends tried to cheer me up, telling me she was an evil bitch, a hopeless crack whore, a lowlife criminal scumball, that she wasn't worthy of my concern, that I was better off without her. They invited me to party after stupid, boring, tedious party, introducing me to all kinds of faceless little chicks.

They meant well. But everything looked useless and ugly, stifling and dead.

It was no use anymore, and I knew it. The accumulated weight of the month I'd spent away from Narcisa's savage spell had drained me of all power to resist her silent siren calls. I could hear her whispering to me all the time now, even in my sleep, with that voice that wasn't a voice, but a living, breathing presence.

"You don' wanna get involve with me, Cigano. If you go down these road together with me now, you can never go back! Never never never, got it? Come back an' get me now, Cigano, come back come back come back go go go!"

I was at a fork in the road. Waking up alone on that haunted sofa, shaking in cold sweats in the dismal winter shadows, crying, moaning, worrying, obsessing, thinking about Narcisa, I knew I was caught in a trap. And I knew she knew it too.

Bitch! She knew! Deep inside her dark, deadly core of harm and hurt and suffering and abandonment and betrayal, the miserable little bitch knew! And when I went to get her, she knew she really had me! Like a cat you've left alone for too long, she snubbed me as punishment for ever trying to get away from her in the first place.

As the days passed like a long, dreary funeral procession, I knew that, deep in the heart of me, I had to have Narcisa back, at any cost.

Whatever ideas I'd ever had about pride, integrity, self-respect, dignity, recovery, sanity, boundaries—all that shit—I knew they were going right down the toilet now, one by one.

One good flush from Narcisa always did it.

I didn't care.

Just before dawn, I strode into the all-night pharmacy in Copacabana, where I used to know a guy. Roberto was another Brazilian Rom, an old-time Carioca gypsy who'd been working there since I was a kid. We'd done some "business" back in the day. Roberto was still doing business there.

I shuffled up to the counter. "*Sar san tu!*" I smiled, greeting him in the broken Romani of my youth.

Roberto recognized me right away. "*Ignácio! Mixztô, prala!*" He graced me with that crooked gold-toothed grin I used to know so well.

A warm Roma hug and a rough-bearded kiss on either cheek. After catching up a bit, I told him what I wanted. Not that I needed to. He nodded and winked.

He stepped into the back for a minute, then came out, still grinning.

I took the bottle of liquid morphine and stuffed it in my pocket.

I went home and sat on the sofa.

The little brown bottle sat on the shelf, looking at me. I looked back at it.

Then, out of the darkness, Sister Morphine started to speak.

"You know, Ignácio, what you're doing is all fucked-up! Feeding the sick young girl *morfena* now? End justifies the means? Really? Where does it end? When she's dead? What are you gonna say then? You did the best you could? Ha! You really believe that shit? What do you think your fucking AA program has to say about all your self-serving bullshit?"

My mouth fell open. I sat there, squinting at the bottle in horror.

"What? Don't you even know you're full of shit anymore, Ignácio? Are you really that delusional now? You aren't helping her! You're just strung out on that fine young pussy, and now you wanna control her—just like you wanted to control 'em all! Cuz you couldn't control your momma, right, little boy? What a joke! If she wasn't a slave to the crack, she'd never have nothing to do with a washed-up old whore-chasing loser like you, Ignácio. Ya know that, right?"

I stared at the bottle.

"Maybe you better just use me for yourself now, eh?"

I stood up. "Lissen! *Por favor!* It's just . . . I *need* her! You don't get it! She's my soul-mate. Look, I just need you this once, to help me bring her back. It's important this time! I'm not trying to hurt her, see? If it wasn't me, it'd just be someone else, someone worse. I wanna help her so we can be together, don't you get it? I just gotta get her to come back to Rio somehow, that's all . . ."

I bargained with Sister Morphine, pleaded with her, reasoned with her.

"I don't wanna listen to your tired old junkie horseshit, Ignácio! I've heard all your limp-ass excuses a thousand times before!"

And indeed she had.

"But this time it's different, I swear . . ."

Sister Morphine cackled like the very voice of spite. "You swear? Ha! Hahaha! Don't make me laugh! Your word means nothing! You're a sick, cowardly little loser, Ignácio! And you always were, all your miserable life! Hah! Born to lose, that's you! So don't kid yourself, Ci-ga-no-oo! You're no better than Doc or any of the rest of them stupid *gadji* bloodsuckers, and you know it! You're dead inside! Dirty. Tainted. *Mahrime!* You don't know what love is! Never have!

That little piranha really got your number, boy! Takes one to know one, eh? Hah! You're just using her anyway, the way you always used everybody! You're a taker, Ignácio, not a giver, remember? Once a taker, always a taker!"

Her words cut into my soul like an evil surgeon's scalpel, again and again. And still I listened on, powerless to make it stop.

"Just forget about the little whore! She's got nothing to take. She's finished, dying, washed-up. And she'll never give a shit about you! Whore's just a fucking whore, remember? You might as well just pop this bottle open and drink it down right now to kill the pain. Then you'll feel good. Isn't that all you ever wanted out of life? To feel good? Don't you want to feel good right now? Huh, Ignácio?"

Tired of listening to the morphine, I cursed it, screaming in outraged disgust. ***"Ya don't know shit about what I want, ya backstabbing, lying old bitch! I've changed! This is my fuckin' life now! My soul! You got nothing I want! Nada! Go fuck yerself two times! Once for me, and once more for Narcisa!"***

The bottle stopped talking. It sat there on the shelf. Looking at me.

I heard a rooster crow off in the distance as I passed out.

When I woke up around noon, the morphine was still there, looking at me in silence. I threw a change of underwear and a toothbrush into a plastic bag, stuffed the bottle in my jacket pocket and bolted out the door.

Flying through the countryside, my thoughts were on Narcisa. I'd seen it all that last time: how she'd managed to draw every lowlife, small-town drunk and drugged-out creep in Penedo right to herself, like magnetic shavings in some cheap, sordid little puzzle game. I'd lost a week's sleep back in Rio, thinking how it was just a matter of time now before she got herself into some tragic, subhuman shit-water jam down there; the kind of jam you don't get out of.

If I didn't get her out of there now, away from Doc's greasy clutches, I'd never be able to live with myself and all the nagging what-ifs in the wake of whatever horrible calamity would befall her next. I knew I'd always blame myself for not going back. And there was still a chance; still hope for Narcisa. After all, she was still alive. And she was still my cross to bear. Like it or not, Narcisa was my Twin Flame. I knew it, and now I had to act.

I thought of her ending up drunk and destitute, pregnant from some blacked-out, passed-out, stoned-out hillbilly gang rape, spending the rest of her life raising chickens, or locked up in some backwoods nuthouse with weekly visits from Doc and her mother. It was slow, insidious torture . . . *Arrggghhh! I can't fucking take it! My brain's gonna explode! Narcisa! No-oo! Hold on, baby, I'm coming!*

Halfway there, I was hit with another wave of nervous anxiety. My stomach freezing and churning, flipping and sinking, I pulled into a truck stop to call her. I needed to hear her voice. But I knew I was mostly calling to avoid catching her by surprise and walking into something I didn't want to see.

I fished out the scrap of paper and dialed the *merceria* down the road from her shack. As I stood there, waiting for them to send a boy on a mule to tell her there was a call, I swallowed hard, again and again. I knew I'd called her bluff by splitting last time. Narcisa surely missed me as much as I missed her.

I stood by the highway, chain-smoking, waiting, feeling the sweat creeping down my back as the big trucks barreled by on their way to São Paulo. São Paulo. Thinking of that endless, heartless urban sprawl to the south, I saw Narcisa; my poor, lost little friend wandering the cold, soot-blackened alleys of Crakolândia, like a sick, lost zombie ghost, crazed and crying, frightened, demented and dying.

It was too much to bear. I had saved her life. There was no turning back. I was responsible for Narcisa now. Standing there with the heavy plastic receiver pressed to my ear, waiting, I knew I had to finish what I'd started.

Finally, her voice came on the line. My mouth went dry. My heart did a little fluttering death dance as I stammered that I was on my way.

"*Porra!* Why it take you so long, hein, Cigano? I think you gone away again forever! All these days I waiting for you come back, bro! I am sick of these e'stupid e'sheet place! My bag all pack up. I wanna get de fock outa here fast! Out! Right now! Come now, Cigano, go, go!"

Looking up at the dark thunder clouds rumbling across the mountain range like shadows of giant, roving black cats, I told her I was a couple of hours away still, if it didn't start pouring and slow me down.

"*Duas horas? Porra!* Is too long time! Hurry now, hurry, go fast now, *anda logo, cara, vaa-aaiií,* go go go!"

I told her to wait for me at the *merceria*. I was clear about that. No way, I said, would I ever go back to that miserable little hell-pit she'd been staying in.

I hung up. I got on the bike and gunned it through a booming, apocalyptic lightning storm, till I thought the whole fucking world would explode.

When I arrived, sopping wet, an hour and a half later, Narcisa was sitting in the dirt by the *mercado*, eyes closed, sunning herself with her back against a tree.

As I pulled up, I noticed she didn't have her ever-present purple knapsack with her, or anything else . . . *What the fuck? Where's all her stuff?*

I got off the bike and strode over. She didn't get up to greet me.

"What's up, Narcisa? Ya just gonna sit there?"

Silence. I tried again. Nothing.

Offering my hand, I heard my voice, a lost, dry-mouthed little croak. "Ya gonna get up? Where's all yer stuff, baby?"

Silence . . . *Aw, shit! Now what?*

I tried again. "Hey. Are we gonna get going now, or what . . . ?"

Finally, without taking my hand, Narcisa started to rise, moving in agonizing slow motion. Saying nothing, she glared at me defiantly, defensively, as she stood with her back to the tree, her arms folded across her chest like a pair of shotguns.

Scowling, she spoke at last. "We gonna go, ok-ey, but only to de waterfall. That de most far I gonna go with you . . ."

I felt my stomach going cold . . . *What? And I just rode all the way from Rio to get her! What the fuck?* I stood looking at her like an injured dog.

"Lissen me, Cigano!" She began opening the chess game, setting up the pieces. "I am in a very bad humor, okey? I didn't get no focking *droga* these whole focking day, an' I no gonna just jump up an' run off with you to somewhere!" She was shaking her head back and forth like a stubborn, superstitious old donkey. "No way I gonna go nowhere now, no way, no without I got it first some drugs, *porra*!"

I gawked at her. "Can't ya just wait till we get to Rio?"

"Rio? An' what de fock gonna happen if I go away from here, hein? What if you wanna take me somewhere bad, for do some kinda bad thing to me, hein?"

I stood staring at her in shock. "Bad thing . . . ?"

She glowered back at me. "I don' trust you no more, Cigano."

What?!? She doesn't trust ME!?!

Stung by her words, I spit on the ground. "Well, fuck! That must be what a guilty conscience looks like, huh Narcisa?"

Silence.

I stood there, bewildered, looking at her, thinking, my heart plummeting south like a dropped bucket of shit. It was Doc! Desperately afraid of losing her to me again, he must have been back there since I left, poisoning her mind.

I seethed inwardly. A painful silence reigned. Narcisa didn't move.

Finally, sick of waiting, I got back on the bike and started the motor.

I was about to ride off when she began inching toward me, just like that willful old donkey. Without a word, she got on.

As we took off, she sat in silence, stiff as a mannequin, arms hanging limp at her side, like a distant stranger. Baggage. Off we went, up to the fucking waterfalls.

Ten long, depressing minutes later, I parked under a giant purple jacaranda tree and followed her down the little dirt path. I could hear and smell the mist of raging water as we hiked toward the falls. Flying insects hummed and buzzed around my face. When we got to the pond by the rushing cascade, Narcisa stopped.

I looked at her. Crowned like a queen by a misty little rainbow glimmering in the sunlight behind her, she turned around slowly, hands on her hips. She stood eyeing me with a pouting look of regal challenge.

There was a truculent tone in her voice as she held out her hand, palm up.

"Give it to me, these *morfina* you e'say you got, Cigano, go."

I hesitated.

Her fingers quivered with impatience. "Give it to me these e'sheet now, go! Gimme de focking *bagulho*, an' then go sit over there an' leave me de fock alone."

She pointed a stern finger at a big rock by the stream.

A dragonfly hovered over the water, skittering wildly across the surface, all hyperactive and frantic and jittery. It reminded me of Narcisa when she was high. I smiled, feeling that familiar old wave of fond tolerance.

I reached in my jacket and pulled out the little brown bottle.

Narcisa reached out and I dropped it into her hand. The fingers stopped quivering. She twisted the cap off and sniffed it with a suspicious little grimace.

Watching her, I remembered how Narcisa had always been so entranced by all my junkie war stories—all the gruesome tales of failure and humiliation in the grips of my heroin addiction; miserable accounts I'd only shared in a well-meaning attempt to inspire her to get clean. But, no matter how ugly a picture I ever painted, it was still attractive to her. Every dark, deadly detail.

It made sense. Having taken every other drug known to man, and delved into every demented perversion of the human spirit, of course Narcisa would need to add opiates to her curriculum vitae.

I'd always refused to get it for her. I'd never been able to stoop so low. Until now.

I thought again of my predawn crisis of conscience with the morphine bottle, even as I rationalized my actions with a flurry of new excuses.

Well, at least it's not as quick a death as crack . . . Maybe it'll even slow her down . . . If I could survive it, so can she . . . If I don't give it to her, somebody else will.

My addiction was progressing, right along with hers. There was no going back. I knew I'd do whatever the Crack Monster and the Pussy Monster wanted.

I watched her as she examined the bottle, like a caveman with a handgun.

Then, finally, she shuffled away, shouting back over her shoulder. **"Okey, now don' make no more talk in my ear, hein? I don' wanna hear one more focking thing from you e'stupid mouth, Cigano, got it?"**

I got it. I looked on in silence as Narcisa went and sat on a rock downstream.

After a distrustful little pause, she shouted over to me again. *"An' you better no give it to me some kinda poison, hein!"*

Shaking my head, I walked over to another rock and sat down, thinking . . . *So she does have a conscience . . . She knows she did me dirt last time I was down here.*

From a distance, I watched as Narcisa uncapped the bottle and upended it, pouring the bitter elixir down her bottomless gullet. She sat there for a while, just staring off into space. Finally, she lay back on the rock and stretched out like a long albino lizard basking in the sun, waiting for the long-anticipated opiate kick.

After a few minutes she felt it.

I guessed it must've done the trick as she sat up again, looking relaxed. She flashed me her crooked grin—the sneaky kid I loved and waited on hand and foot.

Slowly, she rose, and that delinquent shit-eating smirk approached. She took me by the hand, like a dog tied to a leash, waiting for its master.

I wagged my tail and followed her up the little dirt path.

"Okey, Cigano! *Boa, mermão!*" She was slurring her words as we got to the bike. "Is pretty good, these e'sheet! I like de buzz. You got some more, hein?"

Before I could reply, she tugged at my arm.

"Eii, lissen, bro, now I gonna trust you again! Let's go now. *'Bora, Cigano!* We gonna go for another ride together now, go, go, go!"

"Where to this time, princesa?" I asked, hoping she'd say Rio.

"Resende, Cigano! *'Bora! Go, go, go!*"

Resende. I knew just what that meant.

97. BACK IN THE SADDLE

"Every man has inside himself a parasitic being
who is acting not at all to his advantage."
—*William S. Burroughs*

Resende, the next town over on the highway, was more like a miniature metropolis, with plenty of crack cocaine for sale in the surrounding ghettos.

We tore through the city center, then out into the familiar favelas.

I handed over the cash, and Narcisa stocked up on the rock.

I didn't care anymore. If she smoked us both into a smoldering pile of ashes, no problem—as long as we were together.

If she was telling the truth, she'd been off the stuff for more than a month now, appeasing the Curse with whatever booze, weed, pills, coke, and other random shit she could get her hands on.

Narcisa was well overdue for a rendezvous with the Crack Monster.

Drugs in hand, we checked into a roadside motel. She turned the lights down low, and it was on again. We dove right back into our old routine of marathon sex for marathon drugs . . . *More more more! Go go go* . . . Old-time rock-and-roll music blasted from the bedside radio, as Narcisa danced her way back into my heart.

Soon enough, the old crack psychosis kicked in again too, sending her straight into the good old, familiar, jittery panic attacks. Everything was just like before as she skittered around the room in jerky, paranoid little circles.

"Lookit, Cigano!" She gestured, whispering, pointing, wide-eyed, to her shadow creeping across the wall. "I got de *two* shadow now, no only one like de normal peoples! One of them no from me! Is come from *them*, de Shadow Peoples! *Olha!* See it there!"

I sucked my teeth and sighed. Narcisa was literally scared of her own fucking shadow now . . . *Shit!* Why even bother pointing out that there were two light fixtures causing the double reflection? What would be the point? She was already gone.

It was amazing how fast the stuff converted her into a state of bug-eyed terror. Perversely, it was thrilling to me, watching her bugging out under its lash. Seeing that wild, untamable, hyperactive woman-child rendered instantly helpless, frozen in fear, was an unquenchable source of lust for my own dark compulsions.

Yes, we'd both gotten sicker over time.

As soon as the pounding fright of her last hit died down enough for me to approach without giving her a heart attack, I grabbed her and held her fast, pulling her panties down under her skimpy denim miniskirt. Narcisa went limp and stood frozen, wheezing and panting, like an undernourished greyhound run half to death. I could feel her heartbeat fluttering like a captive bird in her scrawny rib cage as I backed her against the wall and worked it into her slobbering wet cunt. Drooling like a hungry jackal, I put her down onto the bed and fucked her like an animal. I climaxed with a piercing scream from deep inside, then I started to go at it again right away. Narcisa clawed at me like a drowning cat as I rocked her back and forth on the sweaty sheet till I came again, screaming like a drooling demon in hell.

Finally, I went limp in her arms, sweating, panting, exhausted.

Narcisa didn't stay still for long. She spent the rest of the night up, smoking and pacing the room, while I fell in and out of a troubled, uneasy sleep.

The nightmares were cinematic, frightful, unforgettable:

Walking down the stairway by the Love House in the still of night, from the corner of my eye, something indistinct, rustling in the shadows, moving in weird freeze-frame slow motion, like a silent movie. Something spooky. Sinister. Surreal.

I turn a corner and I see her. Narcisa, wearing her purple bomber jacket. She's hunched over something, crouched down like a big glowing silent predator . . . A panther, a vampire, a giant bat, some terrible, malevolent being. And she's feeding on something, someone, perched atop an immobile human body.

Everything is bathed in a eerie golden light. Moving closer, I see a familiar leathery face. It's Mãe Caridade! The old woman is lying on her back, immobile. Narcisa is inhaling, consuming, feeding, sucking the life force from her chest.

I run over, yelling. "Baby, baby, princesa, what are you doing? Stop it! Get up! Leave her alone! Para, porra! Stop! She's helping us!"

Narcisa turns and looks at me. But it's not Narcisa. It's my mother! Then, it's not my mother anymore. She's morphed back into Narcisa again. As I look on, she shape-shifts anew, this time into a gray-faced, snarling Medusa, all covered in ashes.

The snakes are hissing in her hair. The hideous hell-creature begins to laugh, cackling and howling, a mad, furious, demonic phantom laughter.

I feel myself going numb, paralyzed. I can't breathe . . . Can't move . . . I cannot scream . . . I am turning to stone, disintegrating into dust and ashes at her feet, as her frightful howls echo and fade to nothing in my crumbling, cold, dead ears of stone.

Awakened with a start, I bolted up on the bed, looking around in panic.

Dazed, disoriented, my eyes fixed on Narcisa. She stood by the window, playing with the latch, the curtains, glancing around like a scared animal, her face frozen in a gray mask of terror.

The Shadow People were closing in on her.

I went over, took her by the hand and led her back to the bed. Putting her down on the hard, round vinyl mattress, I fucked her again till I climaxed long and hard, screaming; howling like a deranged ghost. ***"Fuck, fuck, fuck, fuck fuck!"***

Without a word, she got up and went back to smoking the rest of her stash.

I lay back on the bed, thinking . . . *For a streetwise old malandro, I'm getting pretty good at ignoring all the warning signs* . . . Then I passed out again.

By morning, Narcisa was out of drugs.

She looked at me and I knew.

It was time to take her back to Rio.

98. THE THING THAT WOULDN'T DIE

"PHYSICAL DEPENDENCE IS THE SIMPLE CELLULAR
ADAPTATION OF THE BODY. IN CONTRAST, ADDICTION IS A
COMPLEX, LIFELONG DISEASE OF THE ENTIRE SELF."
—*Robert L. Dupont, M.D.*

I've always said you can tell how good a chick fucks by the way she sits on the back of a motorcycle. But, in all my decades of riding up and down the four corners of hell with all kinds of chicks, there'd never been a perfect fit like Narcisa.

The ride home with her was three hours of heaven . . . *Triumph! Ecstasy! Victory!* As we sailed down the road, she wasn't just holding on to me, but making love to me, hugging my soul with her entire being, her unquenchable, bottomless Need; embracing me right down to my cells, like a mother holding a fetus in the timeless, warm opiate stupor of the womb. And I never wanted her to let go again. I could have kept on riding forever like that, with Narcisa clutching me like a baby monkey clinging to its mother's back. I didn't want to stop; not for food or gas or a piss; not for anything, ever again. All I wanted was to keep riding with her forever, together; until the engine exploded, till the wheels fell off, anything to keep that mad, obsessive, crucial momentum going; reveling in our boundless, unstoppable need as we sped on through time and space together, going, going, going down the long, euphoric highway to nowhere . . . *Motion, speed, movement, go go go!*

Like magic, we rolled into Rio, blasting through the old frenetic downtown traffic, Narcisa clinging to my back, like a hungry crustacean of Need and Doom and Want and Salvation, as we dodged between cars on the long, breathtaking overpass, seeing all the familiar sights of this Rio de Janeiro we both lived in and created and hated and loved together.

My soul soared like a drunken white seagull as we flew past the antique Victorian concrete wedding cake ferryboat terminal of the old Praça XV, and the little Santos Dumont Airport, cruising into the green, green Aterro do Flamengo, Sugarloaf Mountain looming monolithic and spectacular across Botafogo Bay.

We turned off by the staid old whitewashed Hotel Gloria, into the neighborhood, and then we were winding along those old, familiar *ruas* we knew and lived and loved and hated; streets we patrolled together forever. Drowning in a spicy stew of memories, we sped on through the crumbling cobblestone alleys of Lapa, past the Love House. And then I could see my building up ahead, and I knew we were really, finally home . . . *Together! Twin Flames of Hunger . . . Boundless addiction to Love* . . . And, like Narcisa, I only wanted to want anymore; to live and die in that perpetual state of endless longing, addiction, need and desire.

I fully, finally knew at last that I would go to any lengths to keep it alive; to make it my mission, my purpose, my meaning, my passion, my obsession, my life.

My blessing. My Curse.

The days blurred into weeks in a fuzzy replay of everything we'd lived together before; all those excruciating months we'd somehow survived, then tried, both really, really tried so very, very hard to escape and put behind us forever.

Now, I knew, there was no escape. Our toxic, tainted love had become the Thing That Wouldn't Die. And I knew it wouldn't die. Ever. Even if it killed us both to survive.

Narcisa swore that this time it would all be different; and this time I really, truly believed her. I wanted and needed to believe. I really did. And she really meant well this time, I knew. She really, really did! This time, she swore she was going to "moderate." And I was going to help her by telling her when it was getting out of hand.

That was our new Best-Laid Plan of action.

And we really believed it.

Such was the degree of our self-deception.

Within days, Narcisa was worse than ever; smoking all day and all night, out of control, plummeting south of insanity, south of hell, running on a doomed, demented hamster wheel of progressive, escalating madness.

As the days flickered by in a surreal, timeless sleepless blur, I watched in horror, feeling powerless as a squirrel in a raging tornado, as the red spiders of delirium crawled across her brain, dragging her down, down, down into the filthy little hole where they fought and fucked without respite.

It was all just as Mãe Caridade had warned. As Narcisa raged and rampaged through her life, teetering on the edge of collapse, I could almost see the otherworld beings dancing in her body. She'd finally been reduced to a teetering, dilapidated, rusty vehicle for tortured spirits of the damned; a living, breathing, walking, talking portal to the Dark Side. A haunted zombie ghost.

And still, she wouldn't sleep. She didn't dare! Terrified to even sit down anymore, Narcisa lived in constant fear of passing out and being carried off to those wretched, demonic regions she struggled so valiantly to avoid—even as she cranked open the gates of hell anew, again and again, smoking more and more crack in a futile quest for release from the never-ending cycle of torment.

Then, one day, after weeks without sleep or food, sucking on the crack pipe day and night, Narcisa finally toppled over and crashed.

And still there was no rest. Even her dreams were visited by unspeakable tortures. She cried out and whimpered, tossing around on my sofa, a doomed, desperate, frightened little refugee, struggling with angry mobs of parasitic spirits.

Over the next few weeks, though, I began to notice a subtle shift. Even as her madness progressed, she seemed to be trying to open up to me; a quiet little cry for help. Narcisa was suddenly groping for a deeper connection of some sort. Out of nowhere, she began confiding in me like never before; sharing her most intimate fears, memories, hopes and dreams; exposing a whole new vulnerability, a humanity I'd rarely seen in her.

One day, on my birthday, after sitting up smoking for hours, scribbling furiously into one of her journals, she looked up and handed me the notebook.

"*Feliz aniversario, Cigano.*" She grinned with a calm expression of pride, before going belly-up on the sofa.

Staring at the unexpected gift in my hands, I was astonished; amazed she'd even remembered it was my birthday. And she'd actually taken the time to write something, just for me. It was phenomenal!

As she snored the day away, I sat down beside her and opened the book.

For Cigano. Happy birthday from N.

Stairs, high and Low. What height! What depth!

I've been up and down so many stairs. So many times. Often getting right to the last step at the top. Dizzy, unbalanced, I fell.

I'VE BEEN PUSHED DOWN STAIRS, AS WELL, HITTING MY HEAD, STEP BY STEP, HURTING MY BODY ON THE WAY DOWN. I'VE PUSHED SOMEONE ELSE, AND THEY GOT HURT TOO. I'VE SLIPPED BY ACCIDENT. I'VE BEEN CARRIED IN ARMS AND AWAKENED DOWNSTAIRS AGAIN.

STAIRS. UGLY, OLD, BROKEN, MADE OF WOOD, OF METAL, OF CONCRETE. IMMENSE STAIRCASES THAT LEFT ME BREATHLESS! THE SPIRALS, THE SIMPLE, THE STRAIGHT, THE PORTABLE STAIRS. LADDERS. STAIRS OF MOSAIC TILES, WITH CRACKS IN BETWEEN. EVEN FIRE ESCAPES.

I'VE WALKED, I'VE RUN, I'VE SLID DOWN BANISTERS. AND RIGHT NOW, I'M JUST CRAWLING UP AGAIN, ONE LITTLE STEP AT A TIME, SO I WILL NOT DROWN IN A FLOOD.

I'M HOPING THAT, ONCE THE WATER SUBSIDES, I MIGHT GO DOWN AGAIN. BUT I HAVE THE IMPRESSION IT WILL COME UP HIGHER STILL, SO YES, I WILL JUST STAY RIGHT HERE.

I DON'T WANT TO GET PUSHED, OR PUSH ANYBODY ELSE ANYMORE. EVERY TIME I GOT TO THE TOP, I ALWAYS HAD TO COME BACK DOWN AGAIN, FOR SOME REASON I DO NOT RECOGNIZE. GO UP AND GO DOWN, UP AND DOWN, AND STILL ASK WHY.

I ONCE WENT UP A BEAUTIFUL STAIRWAY, AND WITH COMPANY, BUT I FELL AGAIN!

ANOTHER TIME, I WENT UP A HORRIBLE, SHAKY OLD STAIRCASE, WITH SOMEONE VERY SLOW. AND ANOTHER TIME, WITH SOMEONE VERY QUICK.

NOW, THE ONLY THING I AM SURE OF IS THAT I WILL BE STAYING. STAYING. SITTING RIGHT HERE ON THIS SAME LITTLE STEP.

BUT IT'S NOT SO BAD HERE.

I CAN ALWAYS SHARE IT WITH SOMEONE WHO WANTS TO SIT HERE TOO.

I DON'T KNOW IF I CAN OR IF I SHOULD STAY. THESE ARE NOT MY STAIRS, OR EVEN MY STEP. BUT I WILL NOT GET OUT. NOBODY GETS ME OUT OF HERE! I WILL NOT RISE AND FALL AGAIN. NOT GOING TO DROWN ON PURPOSE EITHER. NOT THAT I HAVEN'T TRIED.

MAYBE I'LL TRY TO SWIM AGAINST THE CURRENT.

MAYBE I'LL GET TO ANOTHER SET OF STAIRS. BUT NOT JUST NOW. MAYBE I'LL WAIT FOR COMPANY, TO TRY TO CLIMB TOGETHER, AND FALL TOGETHER, OR THROW EACH OTHER DOWN.

THERE WAS A TIME WHEN I WAS UP THERE, AND I MADE FUN OF SOMEONE WHO WAS DOWN HERE. THERE WAS ANOTHER TIME THAT WHEN I WAS DOWN HERE, AND SOMEONE UP THERE MADE FUN OF ME. THERE WAS A TIME THAT I MADE SOMEONE COME ALL THE WAY DOWN TO GET ME, SO WE COULD GO BACK UP TOGETHER. BUT THEN I COULDN'T LEAVE.

MAYBE I'LL JUST MOVE OVER TO THE NEXT STEP, TO HAVE MORE TIME TO DECIDE IF I WILL GO UP OR STAY AND DROWN. PERHAPS THE WATER WILL RISE, FORCING ME TO GO UP.

BUT EVEN SO, ALL THE STEPS IN THE WORLD ARE NEVER ENOUGH TO ESCAPE.

IF I COULD, I WOULD BE IN BED SOMEWHERE, TOGETHER WITH SOMEBODY, CUDDLING IN OUR SLEEP, MAYBE EVEN JOINED IN THE VERY SAME DREAM. I WILL NOT FORCE ANYONE TO CLIMB OR FALL ANYMORE, BUT NOBODY WILL FORCE ME TO CLIMB OR FALL ANYMORE EITHER!

PERHAPS DEATH! PERHAPS LONELINESS! PERHAPS SORROW! MAYBE JUST FLOW . . .

AND HERE I AM NOW, STILL SITTING ON THE VERY SAME STEP. THE CURRENT IS GETTING STRONGER, COMING CLOSER. MAYBE I SHOULD JUST LET IT TAKE ME. MAYBE I'LL EVEN FIND SOMEONE DOWN AT THE VERY BOTTOM. WE'LL KISS. WE WILL BE NEITHER FAST NOR SLOW.

Tears ran down my face as I closed the book and kissed it. I knew that writing that poem and giving it to me was a huge leap of trust for Narcisa; a gigantic risk for anyone as injured and traumatized as she. And I appreciated it. Like a pirate burying hidden treasure, I tucked the notebook under my mattress, where it would be safe from the Crack Monster.

In the days to come, I tried to let her know I wouldn't betray her fragile little spark of confidence. Even as darkness crept in all around,

I could sense a tenuous new bond of complicity and mutual respect growing between us, like age-old adversaries bowing to each other before a battle to the death.

There was something new happening, something different, beyond the raw, passionate sex and tangled network of compulsions that bound us together like prisoners. As the days shuddered into weeks, we grew all over each other again, like a fungus. And, at last, she just surrendered to it, accepting my gestures of love and kindness. She began to treat me like a friend, a confidant, a partner—more than just a necessary evil, a trick, a sucker, a vic. She showed her new affection in all sorts of small ways—like taking my hand as we walked in the street. That was new. Before, she'd always just ran ahead, without concern for where I ended up.

Suddenly, we were struggling to be a couple; a partnership. I knew how important a connection like that was for an addict like Narcisa, for anyone who'd ventured so far into the solitary wastelands of addiction it seemed there was no way back. Could it be she was finally trying to bond with someone? Up till now, Narcisa's relationships had always been geared at dominating others, or depending on them like a spoiled, needy brat. Never before had she expressed the slightest desire to interact with anyone on a give-and-take basis. Now that changed. She started daydreaming out loud, fantasizing about our future—a future that seemed dim and unattainable, given her diminishing capacity to function; and yet there was an *intent* behind her childish pipe dreams now, a sudden desire to love and be loved by another. That alone was a miracle. She even startled me one afternoon when she started musing about what we'd name our child. At first, I almost choked . . . *What? No! That day the rubber broke! Please, God, don't let her be pregnant! Not now!* Then I remembered she was just high. Still, it was significant. And uncommon.

A few hours later, she surprised me again with yet another gift. A scrap of cardboard with a quote in Latin she said was from Nietzsche: **_INCRESCUNT ANIMI, VIRESCIT VULNERE VIRTUS._** To my amazement, she had drawn it out in an intricate style, nothing like her usual scribbled, illegible crack scrawls.

It was obvious she'd taken time and care to craft the thing. When she handed it to me, I told her it was beautiful. She grinned with pride and told me to keep it in my wallet, next to the photo I kept of her there. I was dumbfounded. Before, she'd always made fun of me for carrying that picture of her. Now even that had changed.

When I asked her what the mysterious little saying meant, she stared right down into my soul with those big, bulging brown eyes.

"It e'say something like these, Cigano: 'De e'spirits increase, an' de vigor grow from a wound.'"

Turning the card over in my hand, I pondered its meaning. . . . *The Spirits increase. Vigor grows from a wound . . .* Scratching my head, I could feel that odd sense of déjà vu again. Then I remembered a similar phrase I'd heard before, somewhere.

God enters through the wound.

"Whaddya think it means, Narcisa?" I looked at her, perplexed and fascinated. "I mean, what's its significance to you?"

She looked at me, rolling her mad eyes like a pair of loaded dice.

"Hah! These from de Nietzsche, Cigano! You so focking e'smart, bro, you figure it out for you own self . . ."

99. SHE WHO TRAVERSES THE SKY

Mateus Segatto was an interesting cat. An old friend who, like myself, had been to hell and back, courtesy of the Curse. Like me, he'd been a hopeless alcoholic and hope-to-die dope fiend. As outcast delinquent kids growing up on the mean old streets of Rio during the military dictatorship of the seventies, we used to call him "Sorrisol"—or "Smiley." That fond nickname had stuck, and eventually blossomed into headlines and nationwide infamy for Mateus.

He'd sure had his fifteen minutes of fame in the late 1980s—followed by a long stay in federal prison for bank robbery. Dubbed "the Smiling Bandit" in the press, Mateus had been a notorious hard-core career criminal, who lost his touch and ended up a loser—all as a consequence of liquor and drugs. After serving over a decade in one of Brazil's hardest penitentiaries, my old friend was now a free man again.

A Buddhist, clean and sober for many years now, Mateus was a very different human being today from the crazed, violent-tempered young thug I'd once run the streets with. He'd done it all, and fucked it all up good—the way only addicts can fuck it all up.

Now Mateus was doing much better.

A few weeks after our return to Rio, late one foggy evening, Narcisa disappeared again. After a long, sleepless, worried night, by sunup I still hadn't heard from her. By noon I was famished, anxious, angry, lonely and exhausted.

I had to get out. I rode over to the Rio Claro. I hadn't eaten any real food in weeks—at best a quick snack, standing at the crowded *paderia* counter, Narcisa, tugging at my arm. *Hurry, Cigano, go go go!* I was craving a real sit-down lunch.

Riding up the hill to Santa Teresa, I wondered if Mateus might be around, since he lived next door to the place. It had been months since I'd last seen him.

As I stepped into the shady little café, I spotted him right away, ensconced at his regular corner table. Mateus had a face like Louis Armstrong's voice. Unforgettable. Looking up, my old friend beamed at me like the sun.

"Ah haah! Faa-aala, Ignácio! Como vai, meu velho companheiro?"

It was turning out to be a pretty rough day for me: sleepless, stressed-out, ragged and worried sick over Narcisa. It must have showed.

I knew that when Mateus asked how you were doing, he meant it. And he was the one guy who could relate to my situation. Right before his imprisonment, Mateus had been shacked up in Copacabana with this coke-crazy whore. His affair with that vile live-in succubus had almost taken him out for good. Mateus had been there. I recalled how I'd always marveled that a street-wise *malandro* like him could have ended up pussy-whipped by some saggy-ass, low-rent street rat like that. Their brutal alliance had rattled on for ages, till he'd ended up in prison and lost everything—including her. Today his gruesome, troubled past was just part of his long, colorful life story; a survivor's tale.

I strode up and greeted my old comrade with a bear hug. He gestured to a chair. I sat down and we talked, catching up, exchanging local news.

Finally, I began spilling my guts about Narcisa.

Mateus got it. Sitting at his table, eating shiny green Portuguese olives and soft white Minas cheese, smoking and drinking strong black coffee, we bantered on, joking and laughing like the kids we'd once been together, back in another life.

After a while, he stopped talking and gave me a funny look.

"What's up, mano?" I looked at him, puzzled.

He studied me long and hard. Then he began explaining that my Narcisa was a spiritual archetype—a sort of angelic entity; not just some random whore; not even a *person*, he implied. Not in the conventional sense.

I could tell Mateus was serious. There was something in his manner that rang true, like the way Caridade had explained things.

What Mateus told me that day would give me pause for contemplation—especially when I thought of that dreamy little card from Narcisa in my wallet . . . *The Spirits increase. Vigor grows through a wound.* As he talked on, I pulled it out and handed it to him. He sat staring at it for a long time, turning it over and over in his hand, as if judging its spiritual weight and value.

Then, with a wide grin, my friend started to tell me about the Dakini.

"She *dance*, manu! Like a crazy sky dancer! De Dakini, she like a personification of de *energia vital*, a pow'ful female energy form, see? She look pretty terrible, but only if ya don' know all de good thing she bring. De Dakini only come round when de warrior ready. You won't even see her come till ya *preparado*, spiritually, to learn all de thing she can show ya about you own true inside self."

He fell silent again, studying Narcisa's little card. Then he handed it back and stared me with those bright black eyes of humor and compassion.

"Ya always been a lucky bastard, Ignácio!" He chuckled, shaking his head. "Ya always fell right on ya feet, like a cat. And no matter how far down the toilet ya gone, ya could climb right back out again, and den you use ya experience to help de other peoples. That's a callin', manu! A gift. *Papo serio!* Most people never find dey gift. But ya found yours. Ya just like dem old-time samurai, bro." He stopped and looked at me. "Ya know what dat word *samurai* mean?"

I shook my head.

"Means *servidor!* 'Him dat Serve.' Dat's you, brother! How else you coulda survive all dem hard years? Ya know ya shoulda been dead long time ago, manu, same like me. When I got outa de jail an' I heard from Luciana how ya got off drugs, *porra*, dat was de big inspiration to keep stayin' clean myself. And now ya helpin' dis girl too, same way . . ."

That threw me off. "Nobody can help her, man! Fuck! I've tried everything, brother, but she's so fucking broken! All I can do is pray . . ."

He nodded. "Can't nobody make nobody else wanna change, but I know ya never give up ya faith, *guerreiro*. So ya helpin' her spirit like dat. And she for sure helping you! Yeh, ya really meet de match for ya self dis time, bro! *Parabens!*"

Still feeling a little sorry for myself, I looked at Mateus and grimaced . . . *Parabens? Congratulations? What the fuck?*

He laughed. "Lemme tell ya something, Ignácio. I been knowing ya since we was kids, so lissen careful, *mermão*. When ya was just a little boy, somebody told ya to go to hell . . . '*Vá pro inferno, meu filho!*' Ya know what I mean?"

I nodded. Mateus had known my people. He knew the hell I'd grown up in.

" . . . Ya had a tough life as a kid, same like me. I remember when ya momma die and ya end up livin' in de street all alone . . . '*Go to hell!*' Dat was de instruction ya got from ya mother, manu . . . And ya musta really took dat shit literal!"

We both laughed. A deep, warm survivors' laughter. It felt good. Solid.

" . . . So den ya gone out and made a holy fucking mess of ya life. Just like ya peoples taught ya, see? Same like me, ya gone right to hell, and ya stayed on livin' there for years. Ya spend so much time in de hell, manu, ya settle down in there. Hah! Maybe ya get to feelin' comfortable livin' in hell. But for years now, ya been doin' good and lookin' for ya way out. So dis what I sayin' here. Dat's how ya got a beautiful Dakini come to show ya de exit . . ."

I rubbed my chin, nodding, thinking of Narcisa's portentous little song. "*Can you show me—de exit to these e'sheet world . . .*"

Mateus bent forward and stared at me hard with those dark, piercing eyes and whispered. "Sometime ya think ya girl is de devil. But she really an *anjo!*"

"Some fucking angel!" I guffawed, sucking my teeth. "*Ninguém merece!*"

Mateus poked his big, stubby armed-robber's trigger finger in my chest and howled with laughter. "Hah! What ya thinking I mean when I say *anjo*, Ignácio, huh? I'm not talkin' 'bout some kinda little pink-face baby cherub doll like ya seen on de church wall, fucker! Not for you! Hehehe! Dis Dakini, she like de extermination angel, bro, hahahaha!" He fell back in his chair, cackling like a mad monk.

I stared at him, impressed by his sincerity. His enthusiasm was infectious.

"So a Dakini's kinda like a blessing in disguise, huh?" I grinned.

Mateus nodded with that enigmatic Buddhist smile. "*Sem duvida, mermão!* Check it out!" He started waving his hands in the air like a pair of dancers. "She look like a fierce demon-monster, but I tell ya, she only come for de good!"

I listened as he explained that Buddhists in deep meditation can hear the bones of her victims rattling and clattering as the Dakini makes her approach, heralding transcendence over Maya, the Big Illusion of Ego: Fear, Want, Greed. Selfishness, Anger; all the hydra-headed attachments and addictions of the Curse.

I left my encounter with Mateus with a renewed sense of faith. As the long, weary days flashed by like a surreal, sinister slideshow, more and more I found myself contemplating the apocalyptic, sacred form of the Dakini. At times I swore I could see her moving behind Narcisa's mad, frenetic dancing shadow.

Soon there came a sudden and frightening resurgence in Narcisa's savage mood swings. Things were getting scary again. Out of nowhere, she'd turn on me and strike like a swift, shiny Black Mambo, drawing blood as she moved in for the kill.

I knew it was inevitable. The closer Narcisa came to trusting me and allowing me in, putting her secrets into my fumbling hands like precious jewels, the more violently she had to flip whenever she turned again. And now her hateful outbursts were escalating from the usual angry, childish temper tantrums into true demonic fits of destruction; growing more insane and brutal in direct proportion with our growing intimacy. It was like some greedy toll or tax, a spiteful vengeance being exacted by her unseen oppressors for the ground they'd lost by her letting someone else in. Me. Now they were demanding their pound of flesh. Retribution.

As the days rattled forward like a hell-bound train, I could feel the presence of those malevolent, shadowy forces of opposition increasing all around us; rapacious, angry spirit enemies, multiplying in strength and numbers. It was a persistent reminder of Caridade's grim admonishment that my life was in danger.

By choosing to stay with Narcisa, I'd made some horrendous pact with dark, unseen forces; and the closer I came to hauling her out of the pit, the more deadly the battle became. As I relived the traumas and dramas of my ultraviolent childhood, a day at a time with Narcisa, I kept picturing the crazed, bloodthirsty Dakini.

I'd been thinking about my mother a lot, as if she was standing somewhere nearby, whispering, warning me from some weird, long-forgotten dream zone . . . "*Cuidado, Ignácio! Take caution, meu filho!*" With each passing day, I could sense the same madness that had killed her reverberating from the humid shadows of the past and jolting through Narcisa, like some ugly, ferocious, unseen electrical current.

I'd been thinking of old Doc lately too; his freaky claim that Narcisa was possessed by the spirit of the alcoholic mother he'd murdered in a bathtub. I began to fear he'd end up killing Narcisa too, if he ever caught up with her. I could feel him watching, lurking in the darkness, stalking, closing in on us, in some awful mission of twisted karma and occult retribution. At times it seemed I was watching the whole mad spectacle of our lives from a distance, like some creepy old black-and-white horror movie I'd seen before. My waking hours became a twisted maze of ceaseless déjà vu. Dark things were hovering in the air, like pieces in a big, ugly jigsaw puzzle, as I thought about my poor, mad mother and the deadly, predatory Curse that had ruled her life, then taken it, once and for all, in a hideous final act of barbaric self-destruction.

The tragic slow dance of suicide is a solitary, narcissistic, self-centered process. But I knew that the mere absence of a will to live is never enough to kill anyone. To end one's own life requires a serious conscious effort. I couldn't stop thinking about the events leading up to my mother's death. As Narcisa slipped deeper into madness,

I found myself reliving the fear and insecurity, confusion and outrage; all the bitter, stinging frustration of a lonely, frightened little boy
caught in the eye of a rampaging nightmare of hurt and violence.

Narcisa took to walking the streets wearing this old motorcycle
helmet she'd pinched from my closet—as if somewhere at the back of
her mind she too could hear the harsh, pounding echoes of impending danger; the nagging memory of her near-fatal head-bashing.

One morning, after being up smoking for a week, she gave me a
tragic look of despair.

"You know I already dead, Cigano. *Defunta* . . ." Her eyes glistened,
filling up with tears. "De girl you see now, she only de *fantasma*, a
ghost who pretend de Narcisa e'still alive. But today I know de truth,
Cigano. Now I really know!"

She hung her poor, sick, tormented head and wept.

I held her and cried into her musky hair, which reminded me of the
cool winter smell of my mother's embrace. But, as usual, I said nothing. There was nothing to say that would ever make it better.

Like Narcisa, I too had long ago learned the rules of the game.
Back when I was just a little kid, I'd been taught to mind my own
business, and to keep my fucking mouth shut.

100. THE LONGEST DAY

"THEY HAD ALL TURNED ASIDE, AND GONE OUT INTO THE WILDERNESS,
TO FALL DOWN BEFORE IDOLS OF GOLD AND SILVER, AND WOOD
AND STONE, FALSE GODS THAT COULD NOT HEAL THEM."
—*James Baldwin*

After another long, chaotic mission, Narcisa crashed. This time, she stayed in a deep, comatose slumber for three whole days and nights; locked away in my dark apartment, sheltered from the blistering, blazing world of trouble outside, snoring, coughing and wheezing, hibernating like a sick baby bear.

When she finally crawled out of her moldy grotto of tortured dreams, she woke up shouting her lungs out, booting me out of a sound sleep. ***"Food! Foo-ood! Hungry, Cigano!"***

"Huh, wha—" My eyes popped open to a smell of burning rubber. It might have been my brain melting. I looked around, bewildered.

Narcisa was trying to repair her broken flip-flops with a cigarette lighter. She looked up, howling like a mad, red-eyed coyote. ***"Foo-ood!! Hungry! Naa-oow! Go-oo!!"***

I groaned, shrugging off a heavy blanket of fatigue.

Without another word, Narcisa tore right out the door. *Fuck!* I struggled into my boots and ran out behind her, wiping sleep from my eyes. Hot on her frantic, speeding feet as she hit the sidewalk, I stumbled along in blurry-eyed misery, feeling like a helpless spectator to impending doom, as some awful inner compass seemed to guide her footsteps, a block at a time, steering her into the throbbing, meat-grinding monkey-pit of humanity she hated.

And so it began: The Day That Wouldn't End.

After a long, torturous hour, trudging the sweaty, tumultuous downtown streets behind her, I sat brooding at a tiny corner table in a bustling self-service cafeteria, feeling a vague sense of guilt for the terrible calamity of Narcisa being there. Cringing with embarrassment, I watched, horrified, as she pushed and shoved and prodded her way through the packed food lines, poking old grandmas in the kidneys with her tray, her famished, reddened eyes blazing, stabbing, jabbing, spitting, hissing, insulting, yelling, foaming at the mouth.

"Fock! Moo-oove it, go go go, you e'stupid focking slow old cow peoples!! Hungry! Fome! Arggghhh! Move moo-oove, porr-rraaa!! Go go go go go!"

Still chewing the last greedy mouthful of her meal, food scraps clinging to her face like shrapnel, she pulled me out the door, and into a throbbing, horn-blaring intersection. I felt like a fight dog going into the pit, running behind her as she hurtled through the frenetic asphalt labyrinth. The world was a sweltering monkey-muddle of anguish and stress, swarming with crazed, heat-maddened, rat-eyed commuters and nervous downtown shoppers, all jostling around in a boiling nightmare stew of high-tension, frenzied urban angst; a terrible slow-motion massacre. All that mad, hyperactive activity was like some kind of new drug for Narcisa . . . *Shit!* I groaned as she elbowed her way through the crowds with a hate that was bright and splendid in its pristine, savage purity, bumping against people, shouting and cursing, *"Move! Moo-oove, e'stupid."* Flailing away like a trapped wildebeest in that clamoring sea of living, breathing human meat, she was pushing and shoving in a mad, manic rush to get somewhere, anywhere, nowhere, everywhere at once.

"Hurry! Beep beep! Moo-oove, e'stupid! Fo-ock!"

As she dragged me along behind her like a crippled appendage, another furious feeding frenzy began. Shopping. The force of her bottomless Need was unstoppable. Her anguished, whining demands raged in my ears like a blaring emergency siren.

"Buy me these, Cigano, an' let's get that, an' I wan' some of those! Ooh aaahh, such a pretty jacket! Buy it! Give it to me! Now! Go go! I need new shoes! Gimme more money, Cigano, go, go! Gimme gimme gimme, go go go!"

Powerless, I watched as Narcisa tore through shops, touching, sampling, pinching, feeling, fondling, smelling, molesting, trying on and discarding item after useless, overpriced item . . . *Fuck! Shit! Jesus, help me!* It was like witnessing some horrible, senseless slaughter. I was ready to go home and sleep forever. I wanted to keel over and die, to lie down in my grave for relief. And still we marched on, through those hot, humid, greasy streets of Need.

It was remarkable, seeing Narcisa drawn like a frantic summer insect to the very material objects she'd always claimed to despise. As loudly as my rebellious little anarchist always railed against the whole concept of consumerism, I could see she was equally seduced by it too. It was the pure, unencumbered heart and soul of Addiction; that perverse need in her, questing for eternal happiness in all the expensive, trendy gadgets and gimmicks and fancy, rhinestone-encrusted Gucci poodle-turd-holsters, beckoning from the glittering shop windows.

Poor Narcisa just couldn't hide an inconvenient and persistent longing for all the luxury trinkets and vacuous status symbols of the wealthy—those evildoing, idle-rich wannabe-gringo *parasitas* she'd always said should be ground into hamburgers and fed to the poor.

Her brain was a nervous buzzing hornet's nest of agonizing, stinging contradictions as the day dragged on like a stumbling, drunken wretch. Watching her coveting everything she saw, I flashed back to when I'd found her again, after her long, mysterious disappearance.

There she'd stood that cold, lonesome, windy night, hungry and destitute, strung out, crazed and abandoned, crying, shivering all alone in the rain. At first I'd thought it odd to see Narcisa in such a sordid state. Where was the old prideful princess then? The one who'd always deemed herself so superior to the lowly station of a common street hooker?

How the Mighty I Am had fallen! All the way down from the exclusive top-shelf call-girl joints at the other end of the beach, toppled from her Made in America Plastic Fantastic Magical Gringo Honeymoon American Dream Love Boat Cruise, down, down the wobbly ladder of her own bright-eyed consumer dreams, to that decrepit state of pitiful, dirt-poor demoralization; filthy, homeless, clad in burnt-out, torn-up, tragic tatters. But still clutching an equally filthy, battered Louis Vuitton bag to her breast; a depressing little relic that looked like it had been excavated from King Tut's fucking tomb, along with its unlucky owner.

Where were all her Louis Vuitton consumer dreams then?

Having squandered away all my cash on her every frivolous whim, by noon I was broke again, unable to buy her any more clothes and shoes and spangles and gimcracks and whim-whams and baubles, bangles and beads . . . *Thank God, it's over at last!* I breathed a deep sigh of relief at the prospect of finally going home to rest.

But here would be no rest. Now she insisted we go straight to the big fancy Rio Sul shopping mall near Copacabana next . . . *Go, go, hurry, hurry, Cigano, go go go!* My nerves were shot. Seeing double with fatigue, I tried to explain I was broke. I pleaded, reminding her I'd already bought her a hundred useless trinkets.

No dice. Narcisa didn't care. She wanted to go to the mall.

I fretted over my latest dilemma as we sped across town, zigzagging though deadly bumper-to-bumper traffic, risking life and limb as she babbled on in my ear, telling me to hurry . . . *Fuck! Where am I gonna get any cash? I haven't been out to hustle in eons! I can't! Narcisa needs me all the time now! And I have agreed to this madness! Begged for it! Shit! I needed her more than I needed money, more than my sanity! Now I have no sanity! Now I have no money! Oh God! Oh fuck! What a shit-fest!*

With a sinking dread, I spied the gigantic glittering mall, looming dead ahead. As we drew closer, I shuddered, brooding . . . *Fuck! The way things are going, I'm gonna end up homeless. A beggar. A bum, eating out of garbage cans in Lapa with crippled, mangy dogs . . . My left eye will be infested with little green bugs, eating their way into my brain . . . Narcisa has run off with another rich gringo . . . to Paris . . . Staying at the Ritz, with her new husband . . . Another crackhead . . . A rich one, with a platinum credit card! Shit! A famous rock star, with a bigger dick than mine . . . Mick Jagger. Johnny Depp. Paris Hilton. Louis Vuitton!*

Fuck! I wanna die! I'm never gonna make it!

Drowning in a rancid whirlpool of morbid reverie, I parked the bike by the entrance to the monolithic shopping complex, then we staggered toward the tall sliding glass doors of the big air-conditioned consumer dungeon.

As we stepped inside, Narcisa stabbed me in the arm with her finger.

"Wha—?" I stopped and looked at her. "Whassup?"

She fixed me with those big intense Alpha Centauri eyeballs. "Lissen, Cigano! We gonna make it de democratical operation now, got it?"

"Huh?" I stood staring at her, straining my failing brain, trying to get it.

"Come now, go, go, let's go, c'mon, mano, these way, go go go!" Narcisa grabbed my arm and pulled me away from the door. "Lookit!" She pointed to a bench. "You gonna e'stay sit down here outside, an' you can do whatever you wan', okey? Go e'smoke a cigarette, read you book for a few minute, got it?"

"Where're you going . . . ?"

"I gonna go inside an' look all de thing for few minute. When I finish, you gonna buy me a little *presente*, an' then we gonna go some other place, got it?"

I got it . . . *More fucking shopping . . . And me flat broke! Shit!*

I plopped down onto the bench and sat there, smoking, worrying, wondering how to get some cash. After a while, I got up and wandered through the parking lot.

I spotted a shiny new car with a fat leather purse sitting on the seat. *Bingo!*

I was quick. I was slick. And, then, like a ghost, I was back at my post by the door, sitting on the bench, smoking, looking around, waiting for Narcisa.

Feeling better with a pocketful of money, I relaxed and started to scribble into my little notepad. I wrote on, glancing at my watch from time to time.

An hour . . . Two . . . Down to my last fucking smoke . . . Fuck!

Finally, restless and bored, I got up and ventured into the mall, looking around, upstairs and downstairs, this way and that, calling out her name.

Then, I saw it. A flash of silver light streaking by, tearing down an aisle like a rocket ship to Alpha Centauri, as Narcisa flew past me with an empty shopping cart.

"Oiii, Cigano! Look look, lookit these crazy thing, go go!"

I looked. There she was, stopped in the middle of the aisle, holding some bizarre-looking kitchen utensil she'd already forgotten about.

She gazed at me with those intense, sweating eyes that were the whole universe in a glance. "De art exist so de truth don' destroy us, got it, Cigano? That's Nietzsche! *Thank you come again!* Hah! Now I gotta go an' deficate! *Next?*"

She turned and wandered off again, talking to herself. As I listened to the words, my jaw dropped. She appeared to be reciting poetry. In French!

"Le Poète est semblable au prince des nuées. Qui hante la tempête et se rit de l'archer; Exilé sur le sol au milieu des huées, Ses ailes de géant l'empêchent de marcher . . . **Arrrggghhh! Gotta go! Tenho que defecar, porra! Where de fock de toilette on these e'sheet place, hein? I gonna e'sheet on de focking floor here! Puta que o pareu! Ninguém merece! Afffffff!"**

I stood there, scratching my head as Narcisa staggered away, talking to herself, reciting strange, anguished words, looking for a toilet. My eyes trailed her down the aisle as a pair of concerned-looking security guards followed in her wake, their walkie-talkies crackling like a soundtrack of imminent doom.

Fuck it! Nothing I can do . . . I better just beat it.

I slunk back outside and sat down on the bench again, hoping no one had seen me breaking into that car, praying Narcisa would be all right in there. Watching the door, I lit my last cigarette, crumpled up the pack and tossed it into the gutter.

Finally, she emerged, wearing a shiny new green silk shirt she'd boosted right under the guards' noses. Relieved, I smiled. Grinning like a cat, she jumped up in my lap and just sat there, just breathing, saying nothing; a rare interlude in the long, dizzy day. I was happy, grateful for the peaceful silence of the moment.

As she finished smoking my cigarette down to the filter, a beautiful teenage girl with flaming red hair came over and asked her for a light.

Narcisa's eyes brightened. I was reminded how she was always a sucker for the pretty girls. Before becoming a full-time Crack Monster, she'd used to have such a great knack for reeling in cute young girls like herself.

Smiling, Narcisa lit the girl's cigarette, looking her up and down.

I recalled the fun times we used to have together, twin predators out on the prowl. Now it was all just another tired old pipe dream for poor, lonesome Narcisa, long dried up and burnt to ashes. The pretty redhead smiled back, then wandered away.

But Narcisa was happy, her insatiable ego sated for the moment.

"You see it, how de pretty geer-ool come talk to *me*, Cigano?"

I looked at and nodded. "Uh huh . . ."

Narcisa's face seemed to shift in and out of focus as she gushed. "*Yeaa-aas!* She ask to *me* for give it to her de fire! '*C'mon baby, light my fire!*' Hah! *Perfect, Max!* Hah! So many other peoples in these e'stupid place, an' de most pretty gee-rool with de red hair like fire, she wanna talk to only de Narcisa, got it, Cigano?"

I got it. I nodded again, smiling absently, the way you smile at a slightly retarded child who's doing really well.

"Someday, Cigano, after I quit e'smoke these e'stupid e'sheet, we gonna make de big party, you an' me an' all de pretty young gee-rool! We gonna have a big house with a e'swimming pool, an' I gonna invite them all come over an' make de crazy *orgía*, ever'day!"

She gave me a quick hug, pushing me away at the same time. "Okey, Cigano! *Chega! 'Bora daqui!* Enough these focking place now. *Bo-oring!* Come on, bro, go, we gotta go, *'bora, mermão, go, go go go!*"

I stood up. We strolled over to where the bike was parked. Narcisa hopped on the back and I gunned the throttle, easing out into the road.

For the first time that day, I was feeling good. As we sped off into the mad rush of afternoon traffic, Narcisa hugged me hard, holding me tight, bathing my soul like the sun.

An hour later, after a quick fuck-stop at home, we were back on the street again. There was no stopping Narcisa now. She had to keep going, no matter what.

I stumbled along behind her, sweating, frazzled, incoherent. My mouth tasted like a sick Chihuahua had crapped in it before crawling off to die; my dick was numb from our endless fucking. I was her slave. Now, she insisted, we had to go back downtown, to buy her all sorts of crucial, critical art supplies she swore she absolutely needed and must have right away, right now, *go go go go go!*

Ten minutes later, we were weaving through the teeming anthill pedestrian alleys of the Sahara, a neuron-shattering battlefield of crowded little discount stores.

Narcisa vaulted off the back of the bike, before I could stop, landing cockeyed and demented on the sidewalk, knocking an old woman right to the ground.

Looking over, I heard her cry out, *"Aiiii, desculpe! Sorry! You okey, lady?"*

Before the astonished pedestrian could catch her breath, Narcisa was gone like a streak, a blazing silver phantom, flashing off into the thundering herds of glassy-eyed, zombie shoppers.

101. OUR LADY OF ASHES

With a weary groan, I parked the bike, then plodded along behind
her.

By the time I caught up, she'd already barged into a store and
pitched a flaming red-eyed tantrum. As I approached, she was standing in the doorway, yelling at the startled salespeople.

***"Morons! Idiots! Incompetents! Troglodytes! Neander-
thals! Midgets! Monkeys! Mummies! Slaves! Clones! Too
e'stupid to know you alive!"***

"Narcisa! Baby, baby, whoa, *calma*, take it easy! You'll bust a fuckin'
vein, man! Easy now, princesa, easy, *easy*, c'mon, let's go now . . ."
Slowly, gently, I eased her away and down the busy sidewalk.

On or off crack, it didn't matter anymore. Narcisa was the same
hyperactive, jittery, frustrated mess. She had the attention span of a
housefly, a small tropical fish. It was phenomenal. As she ranted and
raved and pouted and screeched, I regarded her in wonder . . . *Jesus!
She's like a hysterical, pissed-off three-year-old!*

Heads turned on the street to gawk at the petulant brat in a grown
woman's body. Once again Narcisa was the center of attention. All

eyes were upon her. In my half-delirious, sleep-deprived state, I could only giggle like an idiot, laughing to keep from crying.

Fuck! I oughta take this pissy little freak of nature to join the fucking circus!

All of a sudden, I could see it all clearly . . . *That's it! Hope for the future! Narcisa would make a fantastic sideshow attraction!*

Lay-deees and Gentlemen!! Step Right Up and See Her Majesty the Overgrown Baby!! O Circo Cigano Voador Intergalatico Transdimencional Ignácio V. Lobos Proudly Presents: Her Highness, Our Lady of the Ashes, Goddess of Transcendent and Savage Grace!! All the Way Live from Alpha Centauri, Faster than the Speed of Light!! This Day Only, Right Now, Go Go, the Amazing One-of-a-Kind Two-Headed, Bug-Eyed Freak of Nature, Narcisa, the Infantile, Ranting, Raging Crack Monster!! The Red-Hot Flaming Whore of Babylon!! The Genuine One and Only Princess Nobody, Sovereign Ruler of Nothing!! All the Way to Nowhere from Nowhere!! Today Only, Folks, Go Go Go!! Step Right Up and See Her Turn Purple, the Mystical Color of Transformation and Redemption!! Choking Her Black Heart Out on Crack Fumes as She Complains and Pisses and Moans and Pushes and Shoves and Smokes Herself into an Early Grave, a One-Way Trip to the Lower Regions of Hell, or a White Light Spiritual Awakening Through Great and Terrible Torment and Suffering!! That's Nietzche, Got It? Watch Her as She Spins Out of Control in a Death-Defying High-Wire Tightrope Walk Between Hell and Salvation!! That's Right! Senhores and Senhoras, Ladies and Gentlemen, Boys and Gee-rools, Step Right Up and See the Focking Show!! Meet Her in Person, the Inimitable, Untamable One and Only Dakini!! Exterminating Angel of Myth and Legend, the Goddess Kali, Medusa, the

***Snake Lady, the Serpent Girl, Our Lady of Red-Hot Smolder-
ing Ashes, Creator of Confusion and Trouble, Chaos and De-
struction!! Step Right Up into Her Mad Realm of Ashes and
Ruin and Dust!! Come and Meet the Devil's Handmaiden
Herself!! Go Go Go!! Thank You Come Again, Come Again,
Come Again, Come Again, Come Again!!***

Hallucinating again! Jesus! Fuck! My mind was plummeting fast, circling the bowl with Narcisa's in a churning, burning, psychedelic
nightmare stew, as we struggled and stumbled and lumbered and la-
bored through that agonizing, endless mission. Like a pair of wobbly
drunks making their crooked way along, we staggered around in a
buzzing forest of insane, impetuous whims and demands as she tore
through more store aisles, pestering, prodding, nagging, shouting out
new and outrageous orders and demands.

**"Get me these! Go go! Don't forget those ones too! Go,
porra! Go! Go!"**

As I stood in line at a cash register, waiting to pay for another
shopping basket full of useless crap, she stomped around in feverish
little circles of infantile fury, coming back again and again to tug at
my arm, pleading, whining, crying.

**"Let's go!! Come on!! Hurry up, go, Cigano! I don' wanna
e'stay in here an' look it all de e'stupid ugly fat old retard
cow peoples! Go! Moo-oove, e'stupid!!"**

Narcisa didn't give a shit who she embarrassed or offended. And,
strangely enough, nobody but me even seemed to even notice her at
all. As we walked away, I thought again of the Dakini. It was uncanny, the phenomena of Narcisa's presence; it was as if people weren't
able to see her. Maybe she really *was* a ghost, I mused, some sort of
weird, shape-shifting figment of my own deranged imagination. A
prolonged, interactive hallucination.

Finally, we made it back to the bike and took off. As we motored through Cinelândia, the Times Square of Rio, she started slapping at my back again.

Shit! What now? Groaning, I slowed down as she leapt off the bike and ran off. I pulled over to the curb and watched as she tore off down the street like an angry wasp, dashing through the crowd, pushing, shoving, bouncing against pedestrians; tripping, stumbling, slipping and sliding out of her broken flip-flops, stubbing her toes on rocks in the sidewalk, cursing, howling, screeching at hordes of unseen ghosts.

Shaking my head, I looked on as she stopped to confer with some ratty Casa Verde panhandlers sitting on the sidewalk like a pack of mangy dogs. It was a painful sight. Narcisa's world on those dirty downtown streets had always been an interminable, pain-oozing rocky road of trouble. And she was an underworld legend, known to every shit-licking, piss-guzzling, drugged-out, dog-fucking loser, hustler and bum in town. Wherever she went, the subhuman scum of the greasy old streets would cluster around her, like barnacles clinging to the hull of a sinking pirate ship. Whenever she went out in public, there were always a dozen filthy, glassy-eyed derelicts orbiting around her. And wherever we went together, I always felt like a harried schoolteacher with a busload of retards at the zoo . . . *Nar-cisa! Please take your hand out of the alligator pond, sweetie! That's a good girl . . .*

Finally growing bored with running amok like a pit bull in a chicken coop, Narcisa stumbled over to where I sat waiting on the bike. Leaning back with my feet up on the handlebars, I was trying to write in my journal, to keep from passing out and falling off.

She kicked off her ash-gray flip-flops, then plopped down on the dirty sidewalk at my feet, like a wild little flea-bitten mutt, growling and mumbling to herself, chewing on a candy bar she'd pinched from a careless street vendor. I waited for her to get up so we could leave, but she just sat there on the ground, grumbling, watching the world's feet tramping by. When attractive young girls passed, she looked up and whistled, yelling out lewd invitations and catcalls, like a beer-drunk construction worker.

And she never took that old helmet off . . . *Shit!* She'd spray-painted it pink somehow, but the black still showed through, giving it the look of a giant shaved rat clinging to her head; and she'd been wearing it all day long lately, every day for the last week. It was depressing, but it seemed oddly significant somehow . . . *Whatever, who knows? Might even come in handy for the next time she loses her fucking mind, her brain pounding like an angry midget locked in a closet, telling her to mouth off to the wrong people and catch another good and proper head-bashing! Yeah, she's all ready for her big one-way trip to Alpha Centauri now, space helmet and all . . . Countdown, ready for blast-off, three-two-one, go go go!*

I sat there, brooding, watching her and praying.

Jesus! God help us! God? Where the fuck are you, Lord? Oh, God, please help me! Please! I am so fucking tired . . . Okay, listen, God, I solemnly swear that if you will just help me get through the rest of this horrible day, I promise I promise, I promise, I fucking promise you, Dear Lord, that I will never, ever take Narcisa anywhere again! Ever! I swear! Amen.

102. PANDORA'S NARCISSISTIC BOX

A few days later, Narcisa arose from the Great Crash with another Grand Plan. She shook me from my first sound sleep in days, announcing that she had decided to "be good" now and stay off the crack. Forever.

"Never again, Cigano! I finish with these e'stupid drug now, forever."

They say Denial isn't a river in Egypt. Beaming at her through blurry vision, I jumped right out of bed to offer my encouragement. But Narcisa's bright-eyed morning pledge would turn out to be a far cry from what I'd hoped. After walking out, bored, halfway through the NA meeting I dragged her to, she climbed right back on the good old Marijuana Maintenance Wagon. She spent the rest of the day sitting on my sofa, watching cartoons, hacking and sputtering like a broken vacuum cleaner, choking and smoking and stuffing her face.

Whenever I tried to talk to her, she turned up the TV and tuned me out. Once again, Narcisa was lost in a sullen, smoky weed-cloud of junk food and junk TV, only breaking her tedious vow of silence to bark out orders for more food and Coca-Cola.

As the hours oozed by, her vacuous weirdness was wearing my

nerves to a sizzling frazzle. But on some other deep, primal level, she seemed to realize she needed some sort of spiritual help. She began reading Holy Scriptures from an ash-blackened old Bible she'd pinched from another crackhead at the Casa Verde.

"De Spirit of de Je-sooz he e'speakit to me, and de God Word it is in mine mouth!" she croaked as she stuffed her face with another handful of potato chips.

What? Fuck! Gluttonous little freak-demon!

I stared at her in horror as she munched and crunched, while preaching away, reciting an incoherent litany of hell-and-damnation gospel-spew.

Shit! Narcisa had finally reverted to her fundamentalist Christian roots. Hours rumbled by as she battered my sleepy ears with a wearisome garble of weird, incomprehensible petitions to Jehovah, praying for some Santa Claus Jesus to parachute down from the sky and save her lazy, self-centered ass as she sat parroting Scriptures, begging a Big Pimp Sugar Daddy Lord to send her Magic Gringo with a plane ticket to rescue her from the rescuer I'd become, but was not good enough to be anymore, because now I *existed*, God forbid! *Gotta go! Thank you come again! Next?*

Finally bored with preaching, she slunk over my laptop on the table. I watched from the corner of my eye, cringing inside, as she started to open all her old, unread emails. After a year spent crawling the gutters, missing in action, now Narcisa was going to renew her erstwhile whorehouse contacts . . . *Great!*

I could feel the ugly green demon of jealousy tugging at my guts as her face glowed in the reflection of the computer screen, like some creepy monster movie vampire.

A few minutes later, she grew impatient. Back to the sofa. Then, with the TV blaring, Narcisa passed out, wearing two pairs of pants as a makeshift chastity belt. With her grimy combat boots propped up on my pillow and the dirty pink motorcycle helmet still fastened to her head, she snored the rest of the day away.

Her emails sat open on the table, calling out to me like a glowing white loony ward. Like a man in a trance, I went over and stared at the screen.

Powerless to resist, I sat. My finger hesitated over the cursor.

Then I did it. I opened up Pandora's Inbox and dove into a stinking nightmare swamp of outdated whore-correspondence, a grim archeological dig into a burnt-out, ruined netherworld of hooker-hustle. The Whore of Babylon's mad realm.

My stomach froze as I dug like a soot-faced miner, burrowing down, down, deeper and deeper into that dark, uncharted tunnel; into the site, the tomb, the wound, into the land of a thousand johns, a thousand tricks, a thousand vics, a thousand tricks and a thousand swinging dicks. Unable to stop, I read on, one email at a time.

Hey little cutie, it's me, Fabio, remember? You came over to my place over Carnaval, and we partied and you spent the night, and I really want to see you again. Here's my number. Call me . . . **Arrrggghhhhh! Delete!**

Then, I hit pay dirt. An unread email from the estranged husband.

It was months old, asking if she was dead or alive, wanting to know where to send the divorce papers. I kept reading, digging down, down, into the wreckage of ashes and ghosts and demons, raping my mind, skull-fucking my bloody eyes out!

As I read the next one, my soul froze . . . *What the fuck?* Narcisa had been working on some other guy, some random gringo sex tourist, right before I took her in . . . *Look at this one! It's from the same day I found her in Copacabana!*

I kept reading, dusting off the pieces, digging deeper. And it hurt. A smarmy spasm of jealousy reared its ancient reptilian head in my heart like the Loch Ness Monster, bubbling up from a stinking, maudlin swamp of dark, unhappy emotions. But I couldn't stop digging. Down, down, down, down I went, like a diligent archeologist, an impartial scientist, a suicide kamikaze pilot to hell.

With a gut-chilling wave of disgust, I stared at the gringo's words ... *"When you kissed me that night on the beach"* ... *Arrggghh!* **What?** *When she **kissed** him?*

What the fuck? This guy says he'd "never been kissed with such passion ..." A gringo! Some shit-eating, pink-faced little foreign clerk! A goddamn fuck tourist! Some anonymous trick! Bitch! She never kissed me! But she was kissing some faceless, nameless gringo shit-fuck with "passion"?!?

Miserable, poisonous cow! Dirty, backstabbing whore!

I wondered if I would ever recover from loving Narcisa.

I wanted to scream. I wanted to gouge my eyes out with a fucking spoon. I didn't. I just sat there, reading the rest of the email. And the one after that. And the one after that . . .

103. THE DEVIL'S KISS

"THERE'S A BAD ODOR ABOUT A MAN WHO'S BEEN BETRAYED."
—*Maureen Howard*

As Narcisa snored the hours away, I went through the rest of her emails.

There were dozens of them, but I kept going back to that one stinging nightmare message, reeking of the tomb of ancient rejection and betrayal.

A gringo, another sucker, another trick, another savior, another hustle, another clit-twiddling wanker—another man! Some random ass-faced foreigner, Austrian, German, Swiss, whatever . . . Another White Knight from some nice, clean, logical, safe, milk-fed, well-governed, prosperous little European shithole, with photo attachments of the stupid mamaluke standing in the snow . . . Fucking pine trees jutting out of the white powder like demon fingers reaching up from hell . . . Grinning like a fat, overfed Cheshire cat in his well-bred, well-adjusted, wealthy little gringo Winter Wonderland, like fucking Santa Claus. Arrogant little beer-swilling piss-monkey, standing there in his pretty, pastel-colored, sporty gringo ski clothes, skiing the Swiss Alps or the Matterhorn or Mount fucking Everest!

Go shit up a fucking pine tree, ya goofy little ass-clown!

As I read on, picturing Narcisa and this gringo together, all of a sudden, I started laughing; the bitter death-grin cackle of a murdered little ghost.

Fuck! Some shit-brained gringo trick! Bitch! Fucking whore was hijacking another dumb bastard all along, and right under my clueless fucking nose! An-

other Magic Gringo to swoop down and rescue her and carry her off to his neat, civilized, law-abiding Swiss Army Knife-chocolate-factory-clockwork-yodeling Nazi-world of fairy tale dreams and twinkling Disneyland Happy Endings! Knockwurst-chomping Master Race prick, all dressed up in his fancy, state-of-the-art, hi-tech German ski gear!

Looking at the gringo's pictures, I conjured an image of Narcisa out on the slopes, skiing in designer black leather German underwear, flying through the snowy pines at supersonic silver speed, a crack pipe dangling from her breathless blue lips and a Bible tucked under her arm, shouting, screaming, raving.

"Sinners! Sinners! Arrrggghhh! You all going to hell! Go go! Moooove, e'stupid!"

Hallucinating from sleep deprivation, the day was a long waking nightmare of betrayal. I kept going back to that email, again and again, seething at the realization that she'd spent her last days before me hustling, in the long whore tradition of her mother's godforsaken race of whores, trying to reel in some other poor fool, just like her mother's grandmother's whoring mother's man-murdering whore-ghost before her, and on down the line of snatch-peddling strumpets and floozies and good-time girls and backstabbing, blackhearted, sidewalk-slithering trollops, all the way back to when they were all whore cavewomen, bartering their beet-red whore-monkey asses for bunches of green bananas.

Suddenly, I heard a faint sound of dry, bloody bones, echoing in my ear.

The Dakini was coming!

I could hear her approaching, dancing into the long, dark hazy night of my soul, hypnotizing me, holding me riveted to the screen, getting closer and closer, rattling down the lonely road to nowhere, whirling and gyrating her wild, feverish Whore of Babylon Dakini dance, grabbing me, dragging me down, down, down, into the pulsing depths of a wound that never closes, never heals, never mends, never ends . . .

Hey little cutie, it's Fabio, remember me? You came over to my place during Carnaval and we partied and you spent the night. I really want to see you again. Here's my number. Call me . . . The Spirits increase . . . Vigor grows through a wound . . . You don' wanna get involve with me, Cigano. If you go down these road together with me now, you can never go back . . . I no gonna e'stay all alone an' wait for you come back . . . The spirits increase . . . I must say, I really miss being kissed kissed kissed by a girl, kissed kissed kissed by a girl with so much passion, so much passion, so much passion, passion, passion . . . I hope you're well, little sweetie, little sweetie. Take care of yourself. Love, Hanz.

Take care of yourself. **What?** *Take care of* **yourself***? Why? How? Fuck! That would defeat the whole fucking purpose of being Narcisa, of being the Whore of Babylon, this heartless, merciless, stone-faced bitch of a pagan idol that I have worshipped and given my stinking, defeated lifeblood to feed and be fed to forever.*

I looked up from the computer, to Narcisa's crashed-out carcass littering my sofa, and the spirits increased, bringing me back to the beginning, back to when I'd first met her; back to when she was still the Charming Waif, the Beguiling Hostage-Taker, the enticing little Acid Queen, before her mask melted away to expose the stone-cold heart of an unsmiling succubus, a false idol to love that wasn't love at all, but its psychotic, two-headed twin of domination and grabby, crabby, clinging dependency, that frigid, murderous, malevolent bitch of Addiction, drawing me closer and closer, till I'd put my throbbing, raw, bleeding red heart into her filthy, crack-blackened crab claw, again and again, until she really, finally had me. And then, she yanked open the gates of hell, releasing the demons, the spirits, the spooks and hobgoblins and ghouls to extract their fiendish retribution. Because that one who'd first drawn me in, the Smiling One, the Dancing One, the Homeless Waif with a Cosmic Fishbowl and a Need I thought I could fill with my tainted, crippled love, now she was gone! Now only

Medusa remained, snarling, spitting, snakes hissing, spewing ashes from her tangled, lethal dreadlocks of hell-bent doom and eternal bondage of self-obsession and want . . . *I must say, Narcisa, I really miss being kissed by a girl with so much passion passion passion. The girls here are all so cold. I hope you're well. Take care of yourself, little sweetie. Love, Hanz. Love, Hanz. Love, Hanz. Hanz. Hanz* . . . This Hanz's words were stuck in my brain like a sticky strand of half-chewed bubble gum. As I sat reading the gringo's email again and again, sinking deeper into that festering swamp of jealousy and betrayal and regret, I remembered a night in Copacabana, when some little whore had stuck her bubble gum in my hair while sitting behind me on the bike. Another girl on the ho-stroll had told me the only way to get rid of it was to cut out the gummy strands of hair, and that was what I'd done, with her help . . . *What was her name, anyway? I screwed her twice and gave her a nice tip . . . She was a good egg, that one.*

I read the email again . . . *I really miss being kissed by a girl with so much passion . . . Love, Hanz* . . . Hanz. Shit! Another poor, clueless bastard she tried to run off with, because, like me, Narcisa always tried to run from the pain of her existence; even if she couldn't run because the pain was inside her, tattooed onto every rancid, corrupt cell of her being, the indelible portrait of an abandoned child; and if she couldn't run to drugs or to Jesus or Ashtar or Mickey Mouse, Narcisa always ran to people. She could jump right into your soul and suck it dry as the desert sands of Alpha Centauri, trying to dodge the pain of being in her own inconvenient, miserable, tortured, passionate beggar's psyche.

Passion passion passion passion . . . I couldn't get the gringo's haunting, taunting words out of my head. Kissed with passion? Was this fucker talking about the same Narcisa I knew? She never kissed me! Not since the first week we were together, back when she was still roping me in, fattening me up for this hellish slaughter; but after that, it was months before she ever let me kiss her again, always turning her face away, clamping her lips shut like a clam, like I was trying to shove a fucking poison dart into her mouth or something. Shit.

Only months later, after I'd marched through the gauntlet of clamoring demons in the torture chambers of a screaming medieval hell to get her back, after I'd proved myself a hundred times as a worthwhile hostage, an asset, a sucker, a chump, a doormat, a worthy adversary, only then had she finally kissed me again.

Ah, but when she did, it was as addictive as everything else about her, nibbling away at her soul in passionate little bites as I fucked her and we disintegrated into a lingering humid mist of lust; running my tongue long and slow across her teeth, her crazy pink gums and lips, drinking in her essence like a mad, sex-crazed vampire, inhaling her insane, fevered breath like a crackhead sucking in the lethal smoke.

Suddenly, I got it . . . *Jesus fuck! That's it! Kissed with passion! Fuck!*

Maybe that tight-ass, beer-swilling Nazi Aryan fuckwit Hanz didn't know it, but I knew what all that so-called passion was! I knew its smell and its taste and its effect, like I know the smell of boiling heroin in a bent, blackened spoon as I hold a trembling match under it, preparing the next crucial fix to jam into a screaming, yearning, hungry black-and-blue vein.

It's the passion of Desperation!

Only another addict could ever be attracted to that shit. For guys like Hanz, when it's time to go back home to Austria or Germany or Bulgaria or wherever, back to Stuttgart, back to Gringolândia, back to Lipshitz, back to the bank, it's just time to go, and that's that. Not for an addict like me. For me, that mirror-image desperation kiss was the Kiss of Death. The Devil's Kiss. And it's addictive as crack or heroin or chocolate or hang gliding. Doesn't matter what it is. It's all addictive! It's the bloody, screaming, monkey-ass-banging human condition! Peanut butter milk shakes, miniature golf, television, computer games, work, sleep, sports, whatever. Anything, everything! Because the addiction isn't in the substance, whatever it is. It's in the mind. And that's why Narcisa was so hard for me to ever put down. Because you can put down the crack, the booze, the milk shake, the girl, the boy, the billy goat, the vibrating dildo, the heroin, the fucking church bingo, whatever. You can put it all down, again and again and again, but you can never shut down the mind, even after the brain is dead, blown to wiggling, tormented, quivering smithereens! Because the mind lives on forever. You can kill the body, but the mind will never stop chattering away in the depths of your being, like some insane, blazing, black-hearted ringtailed monkey sitting in a screaming, bleeding tree whose poisonous roots reach all the way down to hell! That's why people like Narcisa and I just keep running and running and running, jumping into other people's souls, seeking relief where there can be no relief. Unsettled, restless and discontent, looking for that glow-in-the-dark Day-Glo plastic Jesus to save us. People like us just keep running and running, trying to outrun the eternal plague of ourselves.

The Curse.

And Narcisa would truly prefer to rule in hell than serve in heaven. She even told me that once, when I tried to tell her I couldn't be with her twenty-four eye-bleeding hours a day, seven fucking days a week, that it just wasn't possible, that I had to work at some point, get some sleep, go to the bathroom, whatever, that if I didn't break away from our endless loop of sex and drugs and addiction to tend to some stupid mundane concerns, like paying a light bill or hustling up a little money, getting some food, going to the dentist, soon we'd both be out in the street, eating shit, picking through the garbage, sleeping under a fucking bridge.

That's when she'd said it:

"I prefer go an' live under de bridge together with somebody than e'stay all alone. If you don' gonna take care of me, then I gonna get somebody else, got it?"

I got it. Now, I really, finally got it. Some body. Any old warm body would do. Not anyone in particular. Just whoever! Whatever. Any old human body . . . *Bitch!*

I got up and crept over to where Narcisa lay snoring on my sofa. I stood over her, looking down at her sleeping form, contemplating smothering her with the pillow and putting us both out of our misery for good.

Something stopped me.

Shutting down, exhausted, I limped back over and closed the glowing computer screen. Then I climbed up to bed and fell into a deep, dreamless sleep.

104. MOMENT OF TRUTH

"BECAUSE LOVE HAS BEEN SO PERVERTED, IT HAS IN MANY
CASES COME TO INVOLVE A MEASURE OF HATRED."
—*Germaine Greer*

Narcisa's latest clean-and-sober kick didn't survive the week, of course.

But she did. We did. And then, there we were again; right back where we'd started—two enemy prisoners-of-war, trudging through the muddy, bloody old trenches, lost on a raging battlefield of love and terror. It was as if we were bound to each other, handcuffed together in an angry rolling short-circuit flaming death-machine hamster-wheel ride through hell; living it all out again and again, day by day, hour by hour, in an exploding nightmare minefield of recurring troubles; struggling, fighting, pushing, pulling, shoving, hating, waiting for the inevitable bitter end, which never seemed to come.

But it would all be coming to a head soon, I knew. I could feel it. My heart bled and hurt, like a crown of thorns was squeezing the life from it, puncturing it, bleeding it like a leaky rubber on the devil's throbbing, blinking red cock, as we battled through the days, struggling to get away from the madness of each other, away from ourselves; away from the stinking, bottomless pit of agony, rejection, betrayal, abandonment and suffering; away from our own unhappy karma and hellish addiction to each other. We split up again and again, sometimes half a dozen times in a day. But we couldn't get away.

Then, one dreary, rainy gray afternoon, it happened. I made the Big Decision.

I decided to leave Narcisa for good; to get out of town and stay away this time; just get on a big long-distance bus and go somewhere, anywhere, far, far away this time.

I'd been thinking of leaving for weeks already, formulating and sculpting the vague, fuzzy notion into a picture in the back of my brain. It had been sitting there, festering, growing like a poisonous seed of silent treachery planted deep in the foul-smelling, blood-soaked soil of hurt and abuse. Then, all of a sudden, *boom*, it all just snapped into focus.

We'd been sitting around the apartment during a momentary lull in the war. Things were even going fairly well, for once. I'd just unveiled my new tattoo for Narcisa: her name—**NARCISA**—emblazoned over my heart; an optimistic tribute to my princess; an inflamed, bloody symbol of my undying love and devotion.

Having learned to draw tattoos pretty well in prison, I'd finally worked up the elaborate design she'd been nagging me about for months—a purple butterfly for her forearm. The new tattoos would be our own indelible little rites of passage. I'd just told her I'd take her to the tattoo place downtown, where I knew a guy.

Out of nowhere, it came: the Backlash. She jumped up and started storming around the room, all agitated and crazy-eyed, shouting at me.

"Que tatuagem, hein? What focking tattoo, porra? Hah! Idiota! Otário! Babaca! Don' you know it, Cigano? I never gonna love you! Don' wan' no focking tattoo from some e'stupid old sucker! Nunca! I only been using you all these time, e'stupid old trick! Soon I get better, I gonna go back with my husband again—only man I ever gonna love, got it?"

She stomped out the door, slamming it. The walls shook like a bomb blast.

I got it. That was it: the official Beginning of the End.

I don't know why it all fell into place so effortlessly that day. Her latest tantrum wasn't any worse than the other thousand times she'd shit all over me, but somehow, that was it.

The End.

After she left, I picked up the phone and dialed.

Doc answered after the second ring. *"Pronto . . ."*

"You win, fucker!"

"Ehhh? Cigano . . . ? Is that you? What on earth are you talking about, man? Is Narcisa all right?"

"She's all yours now, shit-for-brains!"

Silence.

"I'm leaving town, ya little turd. I'm finished, got it? You and that miserable whore deserve each other. Good luck, and good fuckin' riddance, Dickless!"

Silence.

I hung up. It was done.

After that, as the days oozed by, the more abuse Narcisa heaped on me, the more I looked forward to the day I'd put the whole nasty nightmare behind me for good. I'd made the call to Doc, I realized, to cement my decision. Now there was no turning back. My traveling bag was packed, waiting in the closet, ready to go. Everything was ready.

I still hadn't told Narcisa. I thought it would be best to wait till the last minute. Now I was just biding my time. But, even as she taunted me, mocking me, pushing all of my buttons at once, I took little comfort in knowing I'd soon have the last laugh. Somehow, I just couldn't bring myself to hate her.

Still, my mind was set; I knew some terrible new trouble was coming. It was too late for Narcisa. I would have to get away now, before it was too late for me.

And, like the last time I'd tried to leave her, I knew it would hurt. I didn't want to leave. But I knew I would have to.

Now I was just waiting for a sign, an omen; waiting for the Dakini to show up with all guns blazing and make the next move; waiting for that bloodthirsty exterminating angel to give me the one final push I couldn't possibly ignore.

Soon enough, it came.

105. THUNDER AND LIGHTNING

It started at the end of another mad, manic four-day crack run. There was a frigid wind blowing in over the bay, a prelude to another angry winter storm rumbling up the coast from Antarctica; one of those dark, evil-smelling nights that get down into your bones and make your insides shiver like a dying chicken; the kind of night where every drunken *festa* ends in a gunfight. A night where meek little office workers murder their families and just keep drinking.

Anything could happen. Madness was in the air.

Narcisa had been up on her feet, dancing for hours on end, naked, like a ragged white ghost raised from its tomb; twisting, turning, gyrating, she was a frantic electric tigress in heat, weaving her savage, backbreaking sex-magic spell of horny Dakini lust and passion around my eyes, my soul, my groin.

Safe at home, sheltered from the impending storm, seduced into a glassy-eyed stupor, I'd given in to her relentless manipulations and bought her a good, solid supply of the deadly yellow rock. I'd had my way with her sinewy, crack-ravaged carcass, again and again, and it was good; as good as it had ever been. There was no stopping. It just went on and on and on.

Each time I climaxed, she jumped right up and slithered back into that frenzied, seductive, serpentine rite that grabbed me again; and then I was hard again, ready to go at it again, one more time. *Go go go!* I'd throw her back down on the sofa and feast on her like a starved wolverine, feeding on her twisted carnal energy, her essence, her body and spaced-out alien soul.

But I wasn't smoking crack to stay awake. Finally, I came crashing back to earth. She'd been promising for hours that we'd go to sleep at the end of that tireless marathon run, so I'd kept going somehow, knowing there'd soon be an end to it all, then rest for my weary soul. But the minute her stash ran out, she changed her mind.

Pushing away the sandwich I made her, she told me we had to go get more.

I looked at her in shock . . . *Oh, God, no! No more, please . . . I can't go on anymore! No fucking way!* I was done. Burnt. Destroyed.

Narcisa stood her ground. She didn't need any rest, she insisted, just more crack . . . *More more more, go go go!* I shook my head and told her she could go on with her mission for as long as she wanted—but without me.

"I gotta get some fucking sleep now, Narcisa, I'm gonna keel over and die!"

"You gotta take me up there, Cigano! I too tire to wa-alk!"

"Of course yer tired. Ya been up fer four fuckin' days now! *Por favor!* Ya promised we were gonna crash when you were done with this last batch . . ."

"Just one more time, Cigano, go! Take me an' we gonna go again, go go!"

"I *can't*, Narcisa! I'm fried. A big storm's comin'. It's cold and raining out there, and I'm not smoking that shit to stay up fer days like you. I gotta get some sleep."

She stared at me. I could see her face darkening.

Then she snapped. *"E'sleep!!"* She vomited the word like a burning radioactive Gila monster, hateful, bloody claws snatching at the air in front of my face. *"Fock you e'stupid e'sleep!! Hah! Why you don' just go an' fock you focking mattress, hein? Seu veado! Faggot! All de time you only wanna e'sleep like e'stupid old womans! E'sleep sleep sleep like old bitch, cuz you don' got de dick to be a man, hein!?"*

I recoiled in horror. But the Crack Monster was just getting warmed up.

"Hah! You wanna go e'sleep now, hein? Good! Bravo!! Okey, so now you can go an' kiss you focking pillow an' fock de pillow an' de mattress an' e'sleep together with you e'stupid focking pillows, Cigano, got it? Cuz I am e'sick of you an' all you e'stupid old lady bool-e'sheet! Hah! You can go fock you e'self now!!"

Raving on, she started getting dressed, struggling into her denim miniskirt and a sparkly see-through blouse I'd bought her. My heart sank like a fish turd to the bottom of the sea.

"Whaddya doin', Narcisa? Where ya goin'?"

"Gonna go to Copacabana an' find de REAL man, de young gringo who got plenty mo-ney an' don' jus' wanna e'sleep all de time! Hah! I need a REAL man who like de young girl an' gonna make me e'satisfy, got it? Now you can go an' get all you focking e'sleep, old lady, old bitch, an' you can dream about de Narcisa getting de REAL fock with de REAL man, de YOUNG man, HANDSOME man, no UGLY an' OLD an' e'sleepy an' e'stupid like you! E'sweet dream, old lady!"

As Narcisa raged on, I wanted to choke her. I wanted to kick her in the teeth, in the cunt; anything to shut her up. I wished she was dead, that she'd never been born. That I'd never been born.

I took a long, deep breath. Lowering my head, I sat down on the sofa and closed my eyes, breathing in and out, praying, saying nothing. Exhausted, I could feel myself shutting down, going numb again, as I sat there in the silence of the tomb, waiting, waiting, slipping in and out of consciousness, waiting for her to finish her mad tirade and storm out the door.

106. SOUND AND FURY

"TROUBLE AND SUFFERING ARE OFTEN EXTREMELY USEFUL,
BECAUSE MANY PEOPLE WILL NOT BOTHER TO LEARN THE
TRUTH UNTIL DRIVEN TO DO SO BY SORROW OR FAILURE.
SORROW THEN BECOMES RELATIVELY A GOOD THING."
—*Emmet Fox*

I was already half asleep as she clomped across the room and stood over me, jabbing her crack-blackened finger into the tender wound of my fresh tattoo.

"Eiiií!! Wake up, e'stupid!"

My eyes shot open as a bolt of searing red pain screamed up from my chest to the top of my skull. *"Arrgghhh!"* I jumped up.

Narcisa stood there before me, facing me down, pointing the blazing twin shotgun barrels of her eyes right in my face, wailing like an ambulance siren.

"You think you gonna sit down an' go e'sleep now, hein? Hah! Não!! No focking way, e'stupid! First you gonna gimme some focking mo-ney!!"

I winced in pain. Blood was running down my chest, staining my shirt where she'd punctured the thin tattoo scab. I could feel my hands balling up into angry fists as she cackled on like a bloodthirsty bird of prey.

"Hah! Why you wanna go make my name tattoo on you, hein!? Fala serio! You try make de joke, e'stupid clown!?

No funny!! I wan' you take off these e'stupid tatuagem now, go!! If you don' take these e'sheet off, I gonna cut it out, got it!?"

Hollering, she reached over and started tearing through the clutter on my table, piled with pens and paper and books and writing and drawings.

Watch it! She's looking for something sharp! Fuck! My scissors! Stop her!

Wide awake now, stomach churning, I followed her like a shadow, ready to disarm her if she tried something crazy.

In a flash, she snatched up the butterfly I'd drawn for her, her voice booming like thunder. **"Hah!! I clean my ass with you focking e'stupid picture! I don' wan' these focking e'sheet!!"** Before I could stop her, she balled it up, ripped it to shreds and threw it into the air like a swarm of murdered moths.

I watched in disgust as she turned to the dresser and began rummaging through the drawers, strewing my clothes all across the floor. **"Where my focking blue-jeans jacket, hein, e'stupid trick!?"**

I bent down to pick it up from the scattered mess. "Right here," I growled through clenched teeth. With a sigh, I handed it over.

I'd always loved that jacket . . . *Shit!* I sat back down and closed my eyes again, holding my head in my hands, praying for her to finish and go.

When I looked up again, she was trampling across my clean underwear with her filthy black boots. Then she stomped into the bathroom, grabbing the bar of soap from the sink, slipping it into her pocket, along with my toothbrush and toothpaste.

"What th' fuck ya think yer doin', Narcisa?"

"I am leaving you, Cigano! I gonna go away now forever!! Very far away, so I never gotta see you ugly e'stupid monkey clown face again no more, never!"

She stormed past me again and snatched up my cigarettes, cramming the pack into her bulging jacket pocket. I stood watching, waiting, praying for her to finish her demented scavenging spree and leave . . . *Please! Just get the fuck outa here already, you freak!*

As I continued trying to ignore her, Narcisa scurried around the apartment like a crazed looter, bellowing, cursing.

She turned and glared at me. ***"You got any mo-ney for me, old lady?"***

I rolled my eyes, saying nothing.

She reached over the coffee table for the ring I'd taken off the night before. Snatching it up like a lizard eating a fly, she slipped it onto her finger.

No-oo! The only fucking thing this selfish little creep ever gave me!

I shot up from the sofa. "Hey, that's mine! Gimme that, ya cunt!"

She stood facing me, her mad, bulging eyes blazing like a tiger.

"You don' do nothing to earn it, so is no belong to you! You wanna buy it from me now, hein? Other way you gotta kill me to get it back! You gonna kill me, now Cigano, hein? G'wan, do it! Go! Kee-eel me now! Go ahead! Do it! Go!"

In that moment, I hated Narcisa. She actually wanted to die at my hands. I could see it in the hollow, dark pits of her eyes. She was a soulless monster of limitless destruction, lower than a cockroach, a rat; she didn't even care about her own fucking existence anymore, other than as a cheap bargaining chip in her sick, narcissistic little mind games . . . *Miserable whore!*

Those malevolent orbs were glowing with hatred and spite, taunting, challenging me to end her unhappy life with such poisonous dementia, it disgusted me to the core. I couldn't stand it. I looked away. Backing down. Shutting Narcisa out. Shutting down again.

Then she grabbed my wallet off the dresser.

That's it! I flew across the room and snatched it out of her hand.

She tried to punch me in the face. I ducked. With a flashing surge of adrenaline, I grabbed her by the throat and slammed her up against the wall, hard.

"That's it, bitch! Now yer gonna leave, got it, Narcisa!? Get th' fuck outa my fuggin' house, ya miserable little shit!"

She fought back, struggling, shouting. As her face went red, she ratcheted her voice up an octave. *"Lemme go-oo!! Leggo-oo!! Me larga, seu covarde!! Coward!!"*

Her words were a noose closing around my neck. I tightened my grip on her windpipe, choking her, pinning her to the wall as she screeched on.

"Socorro!! Haaaalp!! Some-bady haa-aalp me!! He kee-eelling me!!"

Jesus! Neighbors! They're gonna call the fucking cops! Panic stabbed at my guts, like when the UP elevator you're in suddenly starts going down—only worse. A million times worse. This elevator was going all the way down to hell . . . *Gotta shut her up!*

Still holding her against the wall with one hand, I clamped my other hand over her mouth. She started biting and scratching me with her filthy, ashy fingernails, those septic, savage crack-claws grabbing at my face like a pair of maddened tarantulas. Then she snatched my glasses off. Everything went fuzzy.

In a burst of wild emotion, I was that feral little gutter urchin again, struggling in a life-or-death street fight. Half blind, I grappled with her, trying to get my glasses back. She kicked me in the shin with her steel-toed boot, then stomped down on my bare foot, hard.

I howled in pain. *"Arrgghhh! Filha da puta!"*

Before I could stop her, she threw my glasses to the ground and stomped on them, grinding them into fragments, all the while wiggling like a wild albino boa constrictor, trying to get free. I struggled to restrain her. She fought back with wild animal force, screeching like an air-raid siren. *"Socoro!! Haaalp!! Por favor!! Haa-aalp!! Some-bady haa-aalp me-ee!!"* As we battled on, knocking things asunder, she made a sudden grab for my balls. I pivoted sideways. Clutching a big handful of her hair, I started banging her head against the wall, *thump thump thump!*

As if from very far away, I could hear my own disembodied voice shouting, *"Shaddup shaddup shaddup!!"* as I pounded her head on the hard plaster, *thump thump thump*, in rhythm with the angry sounds flying from my mouth like missiles.

"Shaddup shaddup shaddup shaddup shaddup!!" Thump thump thump thump thump! "Shaddup shaddup shaddup shaddup shaddup!!"

In a blur, Narcisa's hand vanished behind her back, then came up flashing silver with the big butcher's knife from my kitchen. With a hot wave of horror, I realized she must have tucked it into her belt line when I wasn't looking. Before I could react, the slashing cold metal sliced into my face, and there was blood pouring from the wound. I could taste the sweet, warm liquid flowing into my mouth. I let go of her throat, grabbed her forearm with both hands and slammed it down against my knee, hard. The blade went skittering across the floor. Then, in a burst of wild animal strength, Narcisa broke free! Quick as a flashing white rattlesnake, she lunged after the knife.

No! Grab her! Don't let her get it, man! Get her! Stop her! Quick!

I ran up beside her and yanked her by the arm. As she bent down, going for the knife, I spun her around and brought my knee up to her face. *Splaafftt!*

Narcisa reeled back, stunned. I saw blood on her mouth. Her blood. *Good!* I grabbed her and turned her around again, fast, pinning both arms behind her back . . . *Got ya now! Bitch!* Breathing hard, I held them in place, tight.

Dazed, she quit struggling. She was beaten, at last.

You lose, bitch!

But this was the game where everybody loses. Nobody wins. That's why Narcisa had won. Because she was Nobody, and now she had won for good, by losing. Because now she'd gotten just what she wanted; another brutish, bloody, violent drama. Another excuse to hate and feel sorry for herself.

Blood dripping from my face, breathing hard, holding her arms behind her, I kneed her in the back, then marched her toward the door.

"This has been a long time coming, ya miserable, degenerate little shit!"

Even shouting at the top of my lungs my voice sounded very far off, as if broadcasting from a distant radio somewhere.

"Yer outa here fer good now, bitch! And don't you ever come back!"

Cursing, I edged her out into the hallway . . . *Almost out now . . . Almost out. . .*

Suddenly, in another wild surge of demonic strength, she wiggled free. Before I could grab her, she flashed past me at the speed of light, the speed of rage, the speed of a furious, homicidal, raging Crack Monster.

Fuck! No! Get her! Stop her!

It was too late! Back inside, she reached up onto my little altar on the shelf, snatching my hand-painted plaster statue of São Jorge . . . *Ogum! No!* She grasped it in her dirty black crack-claw.

No! My Ogum! Oh God! No! São Jorge! Pai Ogum!

She stood there, glaring at me, snarling, baring her yellow teeth like a mad, rabid hyena, holding it in her angry fist, my faithful icon of peace and protection and faith and love and hope and power and comfort through all the months and years and lifetimes of pain and torment and torture and terror of Narcisa.

No-ooo!

I looked on in frozen dread as she dashed it to the ground.

Craauuu!

Paralyzed with horror, I watched in surreal slow motion as she brought her big black Nazi boot down, down, again and again, stomping at the broken pieces of my Ogum, my hope, my faith, smashing and grinding it into a pile of colorful dust.

Snapping out of it, I grabbed her and shoved her out the door again, hard. I slammed it behind her, then opened it a crack and slammed it again. And again! Again!

Boom! Boom! *Again! Again! Slamming it!* ***Boom! Boom! Boom!*** *Slamming, slamming, slamming the door behind this evil, horrible, dirty, depraved, crack-smoking hell-monster forever! Forever!*

Breathing hard, I went over to the empty altar. Blood dripped to the floor as I looked down at my proud, beautiful statue of Ogum, lying in a bloody pile of plaster rubble. A flash flood of memories tore through my head; all the times I'd stared up at that image, praying . . . *Pai Ogum, guerreiro invencível na fé em Deus, protect her from the Curse, meu Pai amado! Protect her from herself and from all things seen and unseen! Ó, meu Pai Ogum, please keep her safe another day!*

I could hear her shouts booming in the hallway. Narcisa was still out there, spewing a pestilent stream of vile, demonic curses. Then she started kicking at the door so hard I thought it would fly off its hinges.

Boom! Boom! Boom!

I kept quiet, not moving.

Boom!

I felt a mad, violent surge of temptation to pull the door open.

God help me! I'm gonna drag this fucking miserable cunt back in here and tear her to pieces with my bare hands!

Boom!

But something stopped me; as it had always stopped me.

No! Just wait . . . Don't give in to her now!

Boom!

Bitch! I'm gonna open that door and rip your fuckin' lungs out!

No! Just wait! It'll be over soon . . . Just wait her out!

Boom!

I stood with my hand on the doorknob, battling myself, trembling with rage . . . *Bitch! I'll fuckin' murder ya! No! Don't do it . . . Stay cool, man . . . Don't do it! Just wait! She'll get tired soon and leave . . . She will . . . Soon you'll be done with her shit forever! Just wait!*

I held my breath and waited.

Finally, I heard her raving curses fading into the distance as she huffed and puffed away, clomping off down the stairwell.

Silence.

I cracked open the door, half expecting to see Narcisa still standing there, those horrible blood-red eyes blazing like a horror movie werewolf.

I looked out. The hallway was empty, quiet. The way it should be. The way it was before Narcisa . . . *She's gone! Yes! Gone! Thank God!*

I closed the door again and double-locked it, then staggered into the bathroom, dripping blood across the floor. I got a towel and pressed it over the deep, painful gash in my face. I held it there, hard, applying steady pressure. Then I went over to the window and opened it. I squinted out, without my glasses, my eyes searching, slowly adapting to the blurry night outside.

A cold wind gust blew into the room, and I let it blow. A picture clattered off the wall. Loose pages of writing flew from the table, circling the floor like confused phantoms. Windows must always be kept shut when a *sudeste* is blowing into Rio.

I didn't care. The apartment was a deserted, haunted museum now, a graveyard, a tomb. Narcisa was gone forever. It was over. Nothing mattered.

As I stood looking out, the frigid wind slapping at my face died down. Then, the only sound was the twitter of bugs in the quiet plaza below. I listened to the sticky, sinister hissing of the crickets and *cigarras* from the unseen world of nocturnal insects down there, all quietly eating each other alive in their invisible battles of life and death. A damp wind rustled the leaves of the coconut palms in the dark plaza, swirling dust and paper scraps around in little circles. And then there was nothing but the persistant hum of the great urban beast.

Suddenly exhausted, I closed the window and turned around, surveying the wreckage of my home. Angry ghosts of recent violence reverberated in the stillness. I bent down and kneeled on the cold, dirty wooden floor, praying, picking up bits of my faith's broken, bloody rubble.

As I rose to my feet again, I could feel a sudden pounding headache coming on.

I scrunched up my eyes, trying to quiet the faint echoes of rabid shouts and rattling, dancing bones in the dark, haunted chambers of my inner ear. Rattling, clattering, mad, destructive Dakini bones . . . *Getting louder, louder, louder . . . Pain!*

107. THE POSSUM

"WE ARE SO CAPTIVATED BY AND ENTANGLED IN OUR SUBJECTIVE
CONSCIOUSNESS THAT WE HAVE FORGOTTEN THE AGE-OLD FACT
THAT GOD SPEAKS CHIEFLY THROUGH DREAMS AND VISIONS."
—*Carl Jung*

Outside, the wind boomed and rattled at my shutters. The storm was picking up again. I could hear garbage cans banging together down on the street. A loose power line thumped against the side of the building with a dull, eerie sound, like someone kicking a corpse. Exhausted, I limped over to the sofa.

There was a bitter, rancid taste of adrenaline and blood in my mouth. Wincing from the sharp, throbbing pain where Narcisa had brought her size-forty steel-toed Gestapo boot down on my bare foot, crushing fragile bones and tendons, I could still hear the echo of her bottomless spite, those agonizing parting words spitting through my brain like bullets in a favela shootout.

"I never gonna love you! Nunca! You gonna e'stay all alone forever!"

In their wake, a familiar phrase washed over my burning thoughts, like a soft ocean wave . . . *Antes só que mal acompanhado . . . Foda-se! Fuck her! Better off all alone than in bad company . . .* I knew Narcisa was the worst of all the bad company I'd ever kept. And still, I felt a sick, hopeless wave of regret. But what else could I do? I'd had it up to my neck with her shit; enough to last me a lifetime.

Shaking my head, I opened the closet and took out my worn leather travel bag. I was fucked if I stayed now, and fucked if I left. Either way, I was truly and finally, totally, fatally fucked. Because this time, little Ignácio had hitched his little red wagon to a blazing comet from Alpha Centauri; to a mad, screaming Dakini in a howling, haunted house of mirrors. Mirrors. Because she was me, from start to finish. The Alpha and the Omega. The Dakini in the mirror.

I stared at the wall. I glanced at my watch. Time to get going. I still had to bring my bike up the hill to store with Mateus before catching a bus to the station.

Suddenly, it was all too much to think about. Maybe the wind was doing something to my mind. It was rattling at my window like a battalion of angry ghosts. I felt a weird dizziness overcoming my thoughts. As my vision grew fuzzy, I fell back onto the sofa.

Slipping away into an fitful, delirious stupor, a whirlpool of words bubbled up from a bottomless wound and swirled around and around in my head, like an alphabet soup of falling stars . . . *Drifting out to sea . . . Princesa, tigresa, eyes of fire, smoke, thunder, brimstone, sulfur, all elements of your perpetual elemental being. Love. Hell. Abandoned houses and empty castle corridors we've walked together forever, broken. And I saw that essence of harm in your eyes and I held it, held your heart in my rough, greasy beggar's hand for a moment as I held you in my arms, my love, and you cried out in nightmare slumbers, from nether realms where demons rule and shout from bottomless black wormholes, down, down in the underworld ether, running amok between our hot breath where I got all tangled up and didn't know anymore who was me and who was you, and I cried and cried while I fucked you alive, princesa. I cried for your loss and I cried for your hurt, crying for the poor, stupid, impotent words that could never heal, never mend or amend the filthy black cancer of your earthly experience, my love.*

I am sorry, so sorry, amor, but I must leave you to die all alone now . . . Slipping, I'm slipping down . . . I'm falling, love . . . I'm so sorry for the famished poverty of these words, bright crippled birds without wings, without mercy, nothing but snails and slugs in cruel disguise. And at last I couldn't save you from their cold and savage embrace. I could not bring you to a light to shine between those sleazy ghosts and show you the way home . . . I'm sorry . . . I'm falling away now, amor, falling down down down into delirium opiate nightmare slumber again, paralyzed, powerless, going down again . . . Going down down down down . . .

Narcisa is asleep. Sleeping in a big, luxurious parlor of an ancient Spanish castle where I've brought her to live, safe and secure, happily ever after . . . My princess.

Late at night, she wanders into my chambers, holding a big floppy-eared, shaggy stuffed animal. Trembling, afraid, she's crying like a little girl. Tears run down her face as she tells me of a plague of possums in her room. Poor Narcisa.

"It's nothing, princesa!" I laugh. "Don't worry. They're just harmless little creatures. Here, come, baby, I'll show you."

Then, we're back in her chamber. There's a small gray possum sitting in the middle of the room, on the shiny white marble floor, hissing at us, bearing its hundreds of flashing little yellow teeth, like sharp, pointy knife blades.

I reach down and pick it up by the back of its furry neck, like a kitten.

Suddenly, it twists around and sinks its fangs deep into the flesh of my arm, like syringes full of heroin! I try to subdue it, but it struggles and fights! It is powerful! I wrestle the tiny devil, but there's no subduing the beast. I slow down as I feel a familiar, bittersweet dope rush. I can taste it way in the back my nose, my palate, going numb and warm as Narcisa looks on with a smug "told you so" smirk.

I make a decision. I must kill the possum. I bend over and lay it down on the ground, holding it in place with my hand as I put my boot heel to its head, applying firm, steady pressure with the weight of my body . . . More . . . Some more . . . There! I hear a sickening **pop** *as its skull cracks open like a walnut. The possum stops moving, stops struggling, stops. It is still.*

I turn around and go back to Narcisa.

Eyes wide, she screams! "Cigano! Cuidado! Take care! She no dead!"

Narcisa is standing before me, face frozen in fear, pointing to the bloody gray furball lying on the floor behind me. I turn around, ever so slowly, feeling sluggish. Tired. Stoned. Lazy.

Slowly, the possum begins moving again. It is stunned. Weak. Then, it turns its head.

It's alive! I run over, wrap a towel around it and pick it up.

"What you gonna do, hein, Cigano?"

"I'll take it out and throw it into the highway. A truck will run it over."

"No-oo! She gonna come back an' get us, Cigano! You gotta kee-eel it!"

"But I already did, princesa! It's half dead now, dying . . ."

"Never mind, Cigano! De other half gonna come back an' get us!" Her big, pleading eyes bore down into my soul. "Is gonna come back . . . Is gonna!"

The limp, bloody little bundle I'm holding starts to move, slowly, weakly. Then, all of a sudden, it begins thrashing around in my hands, and it's free! Quick as a bird, it shoots out of the towel and jumps onto me, snapping those awful little dagger-point flashing fangs at my face, tearing into my arm again, drawing blood!

Arrrggghhh!! Blood! So much blood! Startled, I drop it, feeling sickeningly sober and aware. As it falls, it latches on to my crotch! Pain! Pain! Its jaws clench on to my balls, like an insane, ravenous, snapping hell-lobster!

Slowly, carefully, I pry the thing loose. The possum is weak again. I drop it to the floor. It crawls off under the sofa to hide. It is dying, mortally wounded.

In that surreal dream state, where impressions are instantly translated into an odd, subliminal reality, I immediately know it isn't a possum. Not at all! It's the essence of pure, undiluted Darkness. An energy that can't be killed or stopped. Addiction. Pure Evil. The Curse.

I fish it out from under the sofa with my foot and punt it across the floor, like a ball. Slowly, cautiously, I kick it out the door, then I turn back into the room.

Wait! This isn't the same place we were just in. This is the door of my apartment—the place I just threw Narcisa out of in another weird dream. What's going on? I feel disoriented again. Stoned . . . Don't know where I am or what I'm doing here . . . I look around and realize Narcisa is gone. Where is she?

I go out the door and wander the empty castle corridors, searching for Narcisa. She is nowhere in sight. I call out to her, my voice echoing from the cold, high walls of the big, empty marble palace . . . Princesa! Princee-eee-saaa! Princee-eee-saaa! Princee-eee-saaa! Finally, I plod back into her chamber, calling out to her again and again . . . Princ-eessss—aaa!

Nothing. Tall, cool, shiny stone walls. Echoes.

No answer . . . Princ-eessss—aaa! Only echoes. Hollow. Empty. Dark. Alone.

I shuffle out onto the balcony and stand there, looking down.

I see her! Narcisa is in the plaza down below, laid out on a park bench, like a bum, huddled under a gray blanket of cold, damp newspapers.

I turn and run down the stairs. So many stairs. They seem to never end.

I can hear her voice reciting sad, familiar words.

"I've been up enough and fell enough. Go up and go down, up and down, and still ask, why?" Her words echo in my ears like a condemned man's final plea, as I run and run forever, down, down, down an interminable, empty white marble stairway. I can hear frantic piano music rattling, clattering like wild Dakini bones of confusion, and then I'm down there, beside her. Standing over Narcisa.

Looking down at her face, I feel sad. Disappointed. Powerless. Lost.

I reach out and touch her arm. Her flesh is cold and gray as the clammy, damp newspapers covering her like a shroud. "Por que, princesa? Why do you come here to die alone in the park like a beggar when I've given you a beautiful castle to come and live in? Por favor, princesa, please! Please come back home!"

She looks up at me with those big, sad, ironic eyes. "Here is de most comfortable place for me to die, Cigano . . ."

"Por favor, princesa! No! Come home, please!" I start to cry.

She pushes my hand away. "Just go now an' leave me e'stay here alone, go!"

I feel so sad and powerless to do anything for her.

She shakes her head and turns away.

Devastated, crushed, I turn and limp off into the night, alone.

108. INTO THE STARS

"THE WOUND IS THE PLACE WHERE THE LIGHT ENTERS YOU."
—*Rumi*

I woke up covered in sweat and dried blood. My whole face was hot, throbbing in pain.

Everything hurt. Nothing was right. Just like kicking heroin.

Not knowing if it was day or night, I squinted at my watch.

Two hours had passed.

I stayed like that, lying in the dark for a long time; thinking, remembering the haunting details of that weird, melancholy dream, afraid to go back to sleep.

Then, in that odd half-waking state, laying in the shadows of my haunted room, out of the darkness, I saw the face of my mother. My beautiful mother. My insane, demented, violent, unstable, unstoppable, suicidal mother.

Surrendering to the vision, I called her hazy image up from the dim, angry, forbidden back rooms of my being.

Closing my eyes, I could make out her face clearly.

She looked just like Narcisa.

My mother, Dolores, the Spanish word for "Pain," was only twenty years old when she'd murdered herself and left me an orphan.

Dead at Narcisa's age, the poor, deranged creature had gone through her short, savage stay on earth dragging the name of Pain behind her like a death sentence. And pain would be her final legacy to me; with all her sensual, passionate, mad Romani fire and laughter and gaiety; her joy and hope and childish, optimistic lust for life; and her dark, unnamable agony and confusion; that obscene, insatiable hunger for death.

The Curse.

I called to memory the way I'd found her that stinking, cold, humid winter day. Her naked white body sprawled crazily across the dirty yellow linoleum, like a broken doll, lying dead on the floor, covered in the expired blood of her sad, chaotic little life. Everything splattered with that dark, oily blood. Blood. Blood, so much fucking blood, weeping from both her cold, dead bluish wrists. The flesh of her throat ripped open like a gaping black pit of bottomless horror. Her body lying there, immobile, like a thrown-out, deflated balloon, dull and tinted with pinkish red flecks of blood. Her skin cold and gray as a bundle of wet newspaper.

Blood everywhere.

So much blood! Bad blood. Sad blood. Alcoholic blood. *Mahrime* blood. Cursed blood. Tainted, poisonous, angry, irritable, broken, tragic blood.

My blood.

How deeply ingrained that kind of psychic scar tissue really is; how persistently it runs right down to the very core and essence and lifeblood of who we are and always will be, people like Narcisa and me.

And how perfectly appropriate, I thought.

The Spirits increase. Vigor grows through a Wound.

I could feel it as I lay there in the dark; the healing grace of Redemption, entering my life through an old, cold, festering, long-forgotten wound.

I could hear my mother's voice again now, echoing, whispering to me in the cold winter wind whistling outside my window.

"Lembre bem disso, meu filho, meu filho, meu filho . . . Remember the lessons well, my son, my son, my son . . ."

I remembered how, when I'd finally come around on that big old, cosmic karmic wheel of fortune, in answer to whatever stifled, choking, crack-croaking, terrified desperation prayers Narcisa had already long forgotten, she had wanted to kill me; to destroy me for the crime of existing; for the crime of loving her.

But there was an even more heinous offense I'd committed against my poor Narcisa: the crime of making her feel and care for another human being. And for that unpardonable transgression, I had to be sentenced to Death; had to be destroyed. Because, for some strange and terrible reason, out of all the men Narcisa had ever run to and run with, seeking relief from the unrelievable, seeking a way out of the fierce, brutal bondage of herself, I was the one who had gotten to her. And somewhere, deep in the heart of her, she knew it, and she kept coming back for more; just as I kept coming back and letting her in again and again and again. For, rather than being another blind-eyed John, another Trick, another Vic, another escape hatch, another way out of herself, somehow, by the Grace of God, or the Curse of the Devil, I had seen through her steel-plated mask. And so, I'd unwittingly become the way back; back into the primal core of her own hellish, festering wounds, her pain, her soul; just as she had been for me.

Because I was her and she was me. The Dakini in the mirror.

Twin Flames. Nowhere to run. *O lungo drom.* All roads lead to the light. Even the road to hell. The road we both knew so very, very well.

I rose up on the sofa. I was shivering all over. It might have been the cold wind blowing through my window, but I didn't think so.

Sitting there, looking around the empty apartment, covered in goose bumps, all of a sudden, I got it; just how profoundly the pain and fear and hurt and confusion of the past are permanently embedded into the deepest roots of our being, like the sharp yellow teeth of that squirming, unstoppable, feral creature snapping at my poor, beleaguered balls.

Some pains you never get free from.

Right there, in my trembling room, lying on that haunted sofa, in the silence of the night, shaking in cold sweats and blood and pain, it reached out of the murky gloom and grabbed me, holding me there, immobile: The Truth. The Law. The key to the Curse: for however so long as I lived in the shadow of those dark, uncharted fears and traumas, those memories of harms and hurts of the past, for just that long, my past would be my future, and there would always be another Narcisa. Another Dakini. Another lesson. Another Dolores. Another series of Pains.

Growing pains.

The pain would never end.

Some pains you don't get over. Some pains simply become an integral part of who you are. The best you can do is learn to live with them and survive.

Because you can run and run and run, little Ignácio, but you can never ever hide . . . Forget it . . . Just open up the wound and look inside, again and again, until you are healed at last, reborn and renewed in a vital, cleansing baptism of pain.

INCRESCUNT ANIMI, VIRESCIT VULNERE VIRTUS

The Spirits increase. Vigor grows through a Wound.

Winds of change, blowing and echoing through the windows of my mind.

"Learn this lesson well, little Ignácio, my son . . . my son . . . my son . . ."

And at last, I knew I wouldn't go looking for her again.

Not this time.

This time, Narcisa was gone forever.

I lay back on the sofa, staring at my worn old traveling bag sitting packed on the table, ready to go.

As the wind howled away outside my window, I thought of the long road ahead. *O lungo drom.* My only home.

Finally, I fell asleep.

I dreamt of my bittersweet Dakini, Narcisa, traveling home at last, back to Alpha Centauri, flying through the stars at the speed of light, light, light!

After that, I did not dream again.

ACKNOWLEDGMENTS

First, I must give major thanks to my dear brother-by-another-mother, Johnny Depp, for his invaluable encouragement and support. From the day he first read the original Heartworm Press edition of *Narcisa* and told me of his wish to republish the book under his new imprint with HarperCollins, the spark of hope he lit in my heart was often the only light guiding me through the daunting process of bringing this new, revised work to completion. Over the years, he has selflessly shared his home, heart and patronage with a struggling writer. Johnny is a modern-day Medici, an old-school benefactor to the underground, the underdog and the dispossessed. For those angelic, soulful qualities, and for his loyal friendship, vision, generosity, love and undying belief in my humble efforts, I am eternally in his debt.

I also need to give special thanks to the great American indie publishing house, Heartworm Press, and its visionary founder, Wesley Eisold. Along with Max G. Morton and Anthony Smyrski, their collective foresight and courage were responsible for the original U.S. edition of this book. A big hug to punk rock kingpin Howie Pyro for playing matchmaker between Heartworm and a fledgling early draft of *Narcisa*.

Another deep tip of the Cigano hat goes out to the great American writer, my dear friend Dan Fante. His support and example have been a constant inspiration.

My fair colleague, Lydia Lunch, and her brother-in-arms, the superlative English author Chris Campion, are also at the top of my gratitude list for their invaluable encouragement and assistance, and for putting me together with a real literary agent who cares, the persistent and attentive Anthony Mattero of Foundry Media. Especially, I wish to bestow loving kudos upon my dear friend and longtime editor, Alessandra De Benedetti—to whom this book is dedicated—for her unrelenting loyalty, patience and indispensable input and advice through the long, challenging marathon of *Narcisa*.

Special posthumous thanks also to the iconic American authors Charles Bukowski and Hubert Selby Jr., who both took time from their brilliant careers to share generous wisdom and advice with an unknown writer. They are both unforgettable examples of how this whole deal works.

Last, but certainly not least, an expression of eternal gratitude to my muse and longtime partner in crime, the inimitable Brazilian poet Talita Cassanelli—to whom this book is also lovingly dedicated.

There are many other good people, entities, and institutions to whom I owe a deep debt of thanks as well, for their help, inspiration, and guidance. Many of them, like Alessandra and Talita, have been with me constantly throughout the process of bringing this book to life. Other supporters came along later in the game, kindly offering advice and moral sustenance. Others have simply lent a quick suggestion or a kind word along the way. Still others, whose names and contributions have been misplaced in the anonymous mist of my own forgetfulness, will nonetheless linger forever, deep in my heart of gratitude.

Principally, I would also like to thank:

Michael Signorelli and Barry Harbaugh of HarperCollins, Christi Dembrowski of Infinitum Nihil, Oscar van Gelderen, Vera Perrone, Mayra Dias Gomes, Robert Crumb, Billy Shire, Carlo McCormick, Tonico Monteiro de Carvalho, Iggy Pop, Jim Jarmusch, Herbert Reichert, Joe Coleman, Matthew Bishop, Jerry Stahl, Luiz Segatto, Joe Ryan, Pat MacEnulty, Michelle Delio, Marc Gerald, David Alan Harvey, Miguel Filipowich, Tony Smallwood, Stacey Richman, Denis Fahey, Kenneth Shiffrin, Ratso Sloman, John Bloodclot, Sami Yaffa, Debbie Harry, Eugene Hutz, Lawrence G. Smith, Wes Guptil, Justin and Brigitte Smith, Dan Depp, Paulo Lins, Steve Bonge, Anisa Claire, Chris Davis, Leon Ichaso, Daniela Austin, Kembra Pfahler, Ida Maria, Hannah Alazhar, Victoria Talbot, Pavlo Pushkar, Jerome Ali, Richard O'Connell, Noah Levine, Amy Fields, Narcissa Jones, Walter Gregory, Dra. Lais de Siqueira Bertoche, Cândido Netto, Genevieve Altamira, John Freund, Julia Cameron, Tony Fried, Yvonne Westbrook, Peter Kuhn, Ariel Electron, Alex Orbison, Johnny Carco, Bara Byrns, Christine Natanael, Rama Devi, Michelle Cushing, Leslie Westbrook, Cheyenne Crowe, Lisa Douglas, Jason Black, Johnny Brenner, Pascal Perich, Faustine Ferrer, Dayane Fox, Captain Kirk McFadden, Chris Lohnes, Robert Williams, Nick Wong, John Jardine, Elizabeth Kelsch Lloyd, Daniel Vandenberg, Lizzy Cline, Jesse Quinones, Mattew Perez, Deborah Sogatz, Duda Dalm, Tom Nolan, Jesse Craft, Alcoholics Anonymous, Narcóticos Anônimos Grupo Posto Nove, Bob Anderson and Primetime Recovery, Al-Anon Family Groups, Adult Children of Alcoholics, the Augustine Fellowship, Familia Vacite and União Cigana do Brasil, Vovó Catarina de Angola, Mãe Iansá, Santa Sara, Seu Tranca-rua das Almas, Paí Ogum, Salete Andrade, Georg Schmitt, Phillip Hutson, Heather Watson, Alfred Rinaldi, Mary Haswell, Jane Gang, Asia Argento, Matthew Perez, Steve Kane, Lou Perdomo, Justin Wade, and Kyle Overacker.

ABOUT THE AUTHOR

Described by rock icon Iggy Pop as "the great nightmare anti-hero of the new age," Jonathan Shaw is a world-traveling outlaw artist, novelist, anti–folk hero, and whorehouse philosopher, writing in the tradition of Celine, Bukowski, Henry Miller, and the Beats. Widely known as a legendary tattoo master and notorious creator of underground art styles, since his disappearance from the skin trade Shaw has gone on to redefine himself as a groundbreaking avant-garde literary figure.

A child of the fifties, Jonathan grew up the unlikely spawn of a brief, violent, and unhappy marriage between American jazz legend Artie Shaw and Hollywood starlet Doris Dowling—best known for her supporting role in the Oscar-winning Billy Wilder classic *The Lost Weekend*. His surreal literary worldview was shaped during the tumultuous Vietnam era, then sharpened like a straight razor by massive teenage LSD consumption and close personal interactions with some of the weirdest minds of a very weird time in America.

After running with the likes of Frank Zappa, Jim Morrison, the Manson Family, and Charles Bukowski, the aspiring young writer fell prey to heroin addiction and was swept away in a degenerate wave of juvenile delinquency, self-destruction, and moral degradation. Fleeing for his life, he left 1970s Hollywood behind to travel the world by thumb and tramp freighter. In his early twenties, he ended up in Rio de Janeiro, Brazil, where he resides to this day.

Many years clean and sober, the heavily tattooed author was recently referred to by Marilyn Manson as "a decorated veteran of the drug war." Long retired from the tattoo industry he once set the standards for, Jonathan Shaw writes full-time today, while living to test the limits of his reality. Traveling the South American backlands by motorcycle, he draws inspiration from a wide range of underworld situations and acquaintances, including gypsies, witch doctors, outlaw artists, drug addicts, criminals, and whores.

He is the author of two popular books from the innovative American publisher Heartworm Press. Foreign language translations of Shaw's off-beat subterranean classic are published in Spain, Holland, France, and other European countries, as well as in Latin America. Other new works, including a book of short stories and his epic, multigenerational autobiographical novel *Scab Vendor: Confessions of a Tattoo Artist,* are also slated for publication.

With a fan base that includes fellow authors Lydia Lunch, Jerry Stahl, Dan Fante, the late Charles Bukowski, and Hubert Selby Jr., as well as cultural icons like Johnny Depp, Jim Jarmusch, and Iggy Pop, new releases of Shaw's dark cult-masterpieces are long-anticipated events.

A half-breed Romani gypsy, the road is in his blood. When not traveling the world, Jonathan resides mostly in Rio de Janeiro, between frequent visits to other home bases in New York City and Southern California. He has one adult son living in Buenos Aires, also an accomplished artist. He enjoys the company of his loved ones and cats, as well as an extended tribe of old and new friends, fans, well-wishers, and partners in crime, all over the world.

His motto: "Comforting the disturbed and disturbing the comfortable—since 1953."

He enjoys reading, bodysurfing, independent films, beans and rice, birds, kittens, motorcycles, and psychotic crack whores.

His favorite color is black.